1973

Carol Marie Werner
March 14, 1960

A *Bess Streeter Aldrich* TREASURY

A Bess Streeter Aldrich TREASURY

with an introduction by

ROBERT STREETER ALDRICH

APPLETON-CENTURY-CROFTS, Inc.
New York

579–1

Library of Congress Card Number: 59–12539

PRINTED IN THE UNITED STATES OF AMERICA

Contents

Introduction

Novels

Short Stories

Introduction

Home to the Aldrich family was the little village of Elmwood, Nebraska, twenty-three miles east of the state capital, Lincoln. Here my mother lived as a country lawyer-banker's wife and widow, wrote her books and stories, and raised her daughter and three sons.

Elmwood is rather a pretty little town set in the midst of gently rolling farm land—a town of tall, stately elm trees and comfortable, unstylish homes. It was, in our growing-up years, a town where the fire bell clanging in the middle of the night brought everyone out to follow the volunteer brigade; a town of school picnics and "kensingtons" and church suppers, with everybody bringing a covered dish; a town where, as Mother wrote, "you have to hear the band practicing in the G.A.R. Hall every Monday night, whether you want to or not," and where the band thumped and tooted along Main Street on Memorial Day and the colored bunting decorating us kids' bicycle wheels made us feel extra patriotic.

In short, it was any little town typically Midwestern. But when one has said that, he has not expressed much more than could any bored traveler dashing through on the highway in an automobile. As Mother so often remarked in her stories, a home, to those who live there, is quite a different thing from what it is to the merely observing eye. "You cannot break the radii which stretch out from the center of a good home. They are the most flexible things in the world. They reach out into every port where a child has sailed, into every country where a child has strayed—these radii of love. They pull at the hearts of the children until sometime, somewhere, they draw the wanderers all back into the family circle."

So with us. With the passing years and our removal to other places the little town remains for all of us something close to the heart, etched in with our memories of Mother herself.

Mother was born Bess Genevra Streeter in Cedar Falls, Iowa, February 17, 1881, the child of parents already middle-aged. James and Mary Streeter had come with their respective families from Illinois into Blackhawk County, Iowa, in the early eighteen-fifties. Being born late into a family including numerous uncles and aunts who well remembered the pioneering days gave Mother her first insights into that earlier time. This circumstance took a great deal of explaining to those who thought that she herself had come west in a covered wagon.

Bess Streeter started writing in childhood, turning out poetry and stories. At seventeen, when she graduated from high school, she got five dollars from the Baltimore *News* for "a love story" and spent the money on a chiffon parasol.

But teaching claimed her. She went through Iowa State Teachers College in her home town and taught there six years. She taught for a year each at Boone, Iowa, and Salt Lake City, Utah, and for three years in Marshalltown, Iowa. It was at Marshalltown that romance came in the person of Charles S. Aldrich—"Cap," as Mother called him, for he had been a young captain in Cuba in 1898—who shared meals at a boarding house frequented by young-lady teachers. After their marriage—and after the birth of a daughter, Mary Eleanor—the young couple moved in 1909 from Iowa to Nebraska, where "Cap" and his brother-in-law purchased a small bank at Elmwood, and where James, Charles, and I, arriving in that order, were born.

Even with marriage, a daughter, and the move to Nebraska the "writing bug" stayed with Mother. In 1911 a $175 prize in a *Ladies Home Journal* contest seemed a turning point; "Look again," said Grandma Streeter when Mother announced the news, "it must mean $1.75." In later years Mother laughed at her own blithe attitude then: writing seemed so easy, you wrote and got a check. But her sales were small and scattered until in 1918 John Siddall of the *American Magazine* bought *"Mother's Dash for Liberty,"* the first of the Mother Mason stories. A letter to Siddall from an American soldier in Germany told how the stories had reminded men of home. The editor asked Mother for more, and another series of stories, involving the Cutters, followed.

Still, writing was a hobby, though one seriously undertaken, until a dark shadow fell over the happy, innocent world of our home in Elmwood.

Papa—that was always our name for him—died suddenly one May Sunday in 1925 while attending services in the little church which he had helped to build. A kindly, tolerant man, he had been especially proud of Mother for her writing. I recall sitting on the arm of his chair while he read aloud from *Mother Mason:* he had said, half jokingly, that she might become the family breadwinner, and in the bitter blow of her loss Mother was faced with turning what had been a hobby into a career.

The Rim of the Prairie, her first book written after Papa's death, got its title from the phrase he used to describe the rise of land east of Mother's study window. She looked that way for courage, faith. "I will lift up mine eyes unto the hills . . ."—this was her favorite Psalm.

Her home was a big two-story house of brick and stucco, surrounded by a spacious lawn bordered with tall elm trees, and she gave it the name "The Elms." In that room called the study we children might play while Mother worked. There was no shutting us out; the writing had to be combined with the tasks of a mother. It was only natural then that her stories were woven of her own family life, small town troubles, the growing pains of her four children. And, of course, her own particular philosophy.

But her small town people knew her best not as an author, but as neighbor and friend. There was always a sympathetic interest in people, a sense of humor, something stimulating that would cause someone to remark: "I always get a lift from talking with your mother." Indefinable, this quality, yet so real to those who knew her—a kind of spark that went equally into her writing and her associations.

Three books had been published when Mother embarked on *A Lantern in Her Hand*. Many things went into the writing of it, but one was a conviction derived from her memories of her Iowa people that it was false to depict the prairie woman only as gaunt, beaten, driven mad with despair. There might be truth in the stereotype, but not the whole truth: Mother was too well aware of the faith, courage, and humor of her own forebears. Although she wanted a tale that faced up to the harsh truths of that early day, she felt that quite as important were those intangibles of spirit which had made her own mother say to her when she was old: "Don't feel sorry for us, we had the best time in the world!"

Mother did not have to research the spiritual side of her heroine, Abby Deal, but for the historical accuracy, the "little" (but vital) facts, she did not rely on invention. She spent many months reading, interviewing old settlers, gathering and sorting material. It was a point of pride with her that the remaining old-timers could find no serious fault with her facts (and the memories of old folks can be remarkably sharp), but could honestly say: "Yes, that's just how it was."

A Lantern in Her Hand was first published in 1928. Not long after came *Miss Bishop*, Mother's tribute to the schoolteacher, which had its origin in a news item sent by a friend informing her that the first old building at Iowa State Teachers College was being torn down. However, that was but the germ of the story. Always, with Mother, a great deal of thought and planning went into each novel, although always she drew upon actual historical backgrounds. *Miss Bishop* was made into the motion picture "Cheers for Miss Bishop" starring Martha Scott.

From the nineteen-twenties, of course, the trend of fiction was bent in a wholly different direction from that of *A Lantern in Her Hand* and *Miss Bishop*. Mother was well aware of this (we *did* hear about the great world in our little town), but she was too independent to worry about it. As she remarked of the former novel, much later: "*Lantern* seemed destined to be lost in the wave of the popular type of the times. That it has made new friends each year since that day might be a bit of a lesson for young writers: Regardless of the popular trend of the times, write the thing which lies closest to your heart."

Mother's travels took her to Hollywood and to the East, but her home in Nebraska remained at the center of her affections. With her children grown, she built a beautiful new house in Lincoln, moving there from Elmwood in 1948 to live next door to her married daughter, and there she spent her last years. But the little town nearby was not forgotten and old friends remained close. To her children—Mary, wife of a Lincoln businessman; James, an artist; Charles, an engineer; and Robert, a newspaperman and writer—she was always alert, warmly interested in their problems, and inspiring.

Shortly after World War II a letter from Admiral Chester W. Nimitz told Mother of the inspiration her books had given men who read them during dark times, reminding them of home and the things they were fighting to preserve. So it had been with her stories at the time of the first World War. And thousands of letters over the years came from people, young and old, who had found a new freshening of the spirit in her writings. "The radii which stretch out from the center of a good home" had reached beyond the little Nebraska town to touch the hearts and minds of readers in many far-off places.

—Robert Streeter Aldrich

A
Bess Streeter Aldrich
TREASURY

A Lantern in Her Hand

INTRODUCTION

CEDARTOWN sits beside a great highway which was once a buffalo trail. If you start in one direction on the highway—and travel far enough—you will come to the effete east. If you start in the opposite direction—and travel a few hundred miles farther—you will come to the distinctive west. Cedartown is neither effete nor distinctive, nor is it even particularly pleasing to the passing tourist. It is beautiful only in the eyes of those who live here and in the memories of the Nebraska-born whose dwelling in far places has given them moments of homesickness for the low rolling hills, the swell and dip of the ripening wheat, the fields of sinuously waving corn and the elusively fragrant odor of alfalfa.

There are weeks when drifting snow and sullen sleet hold the Cedartown community in their bitter grasp. There are times when hot winds come out of the southwest and parch it with their feverish breath. There are periods of monotonous drouth and periods of dreary rain; but between these onslaughts there are days so perfect, so filled with clover odors and the rich, pungent smell of newly turned loam, so sumac-laden and apple-burdened, that to the prairie-born there are no others as lovely by mountain or lake or sea.

The paved streets of Cedartown lie primly parallel over the obliterated tracks of the buffalo. The substantial buildings of Cedartown stand smartly over the dead ashes of Indian campfires. There are very few people left now in the community who have seen the transition,—who have witnessed the westward trek of the last buffalo, the flicker of the last burnt-out ember.

Old Abbie Deal was one of these.

Just outside the corporate limits of Cedartown stands the old Deal home. It was once a farm-house, but the acreage around it has been sold, and Cedartown has grown out to meet it, so that a newcomer could not know where the town ceased and the country began.

The house stands well back from the road in a big yard with a long double row of cedars connecting the formal parlor entrance and the small front gate. However, in the days when the Deals lived there, scarcely any one used the little gate, or walked up the grassy path between the cedars. All comers chose to enter by the wide carriage-gate standing hospitably open and beckoning a welcome to the lane road which runs past a row of Lombardy poplars to the sitting-room porch.

The house itself is without distinction. There were no architects in the community when the first of its rooms were built. "We'll have the living-room there and the kitchen here," one told old Asy Drumm. And old Asy, with few comments and much tobacco-chewing, placed the living-room there and the kitchen here. The result was weather-proof, sturdy and artless. When the country was new, homes, like dresses, were constructed more for wearing qualities than beauty.

Twice, onto the first wing-and-ell, old Asy, a little more glum and tobacco-stained, added a room, until the house had attained its present form. That form, now, is not unlike an aeroplane which has settled down between the cedars at the front and the cottonwood wind-break in the rear. The parlor, protruding toward the road, might contain the engine. The sitting-room to the left and a bedroom to the right seem the wings, while the dining-room, kitchen, and a summer kitchen beyond, trail out like the long tail of the thing. If one's imagination is keen he can even fancy that the fan-shaped colored-glass window in the parlor may some day begin to whirl, propeller-like, and the whole house rise up over the cedars.

The interior of the house, during Abbie Deal's lifetime, was a combination of old-fashioned things which she had accumulated through the years, and modern new ones which the grown children had given her. A dull-finished, beautifully-proportioned radio cabinet stood opposite a home-made, rudely painted what-not. A kitchen table, with a little declivity in one corner, in which old Doc Matthews had rolled pills in Civil War times, stood near a white enameled case which was the last word in refrigeration. A little crude oil-painting of a prairie sunset, which Abbie Deal had done in the 'seventies, hung across the room from a really exquisite study of the same subject, which a daughter, Mrs. Frederick Hamilton Baker, had done forty years later.

Abbie Deal kept everything that had ever come into the house. Every nail, every button, every string, was carefully hoarded. "This would make a strong bottom for one of the kitchen chairs some day," old Abbie Deal would say, when in truth the bottom of the chair was as strong as its legs. Or, "Save those stubs of candles from the Christmas tree. I can melt them and run them into one big one." The characteristic was a hang-over from the lean and frugal days when the country was new, when every tiny thing had its use. As a consequence, there was in the house the flotsam of all the years.

One of the daughters, Mrs. Harrison Scannell Rhodes, on her annual visit out from Chicago, protested once: "Mother, if the house only represented some one *period!* But it's such a jumbled combination of things. They're not antique. They're just *old*."

"And why should it?" Old lady Deal flared up a little. "*I'm* no one period. I've lived with spinning-wheels and telephones . . . with tallow-dips and electric lights. *I'm* not antique. I'm just *old*. It represents *me*, doesn't it?"

You will infer from the retort that old Abbie Deal was a strong personality. And you will be quite right. The fact that she lived there in the old home until her eightieth year, over the protests of children and grandchildren, attested to that. At the time she was seventy, they began trying to pry her away from "The Cedars." They talked over various plans for her—that she should go to Omaha to live with Mack,—to Lincoln to live with Margaret,—that she should have rooms at John's right there in Cedartown,—that Grace should give up her teaching in Wesleyan University temporarily and stay at home. When they had quite definitely decided on the Lincoln home with Margaret, old Abbie Deal spoke. "I will do nothing of the kind," she said with finality. "I am going to stay right here. And kindly let me alone. Because a woman is old, has she no rights?"

After that they did not press the matter. They "let her alone," but they drove in frequently, for only the Chicago daughter lived far away. Sometimes, on Sundays, the lane road contained a half dozen high-powered cars parked there through the dinner hour and the afternoon. But not one son or daughter could ever become reconciled to the idea of driving away and leaving her there.

"When I think of fire . . ." one of them would say.

"Or of her getting sick in the night . . ."

"Or falling . . and no one to help her . . ."

"Or any one of a dozen things . . ."

"Yes . . . something will happen to Mother some day."

And they were quite right. Something happened to Mother. Last July on a late afternoon, while suppers cooked and children of the north end of town played "Run, Sheep, Run," in her yard, old lady Deal died.

A neighbor woman found her lying across the foot of the bed, fully dressed, while the slice of meat which she had been cooking, burned to a crisp.

Of the five middle-aged children, seven grandchildren and three great-grandchildren, not one was with her. They all came hastily in response to the messages. Within two hours' time, a shining limousine, two big sedans, and a roadster all stood in the lane road. For the first time, when the cars turned into the driveway by the Lombardy poplars, no little old white-haired woman with bright brown eyes, had come hurrying out to give cheery greeting. That queer, solemn hush of death hung over the whole place. It was in the quivering droop of the cottonwoods,—in the deepening of the prairie twilight,—in the silence of the star-filled summer sky.

They all gathered in the parlor with its modern radio and its old-fashioned what-not, its elaborate new floor-lamp and its crude oil-painting. All of the children and several of the grandchildren were there. Mackenzie Deal, the Omaha banker, was there. John Deal, the Cedartown attorney and state legislator, was there. Mrs. Harrison Scannell Rhodes of Chicago, who had been visiting in Omaha, was there. Mrs. Frederick Hamilton Baker, of Lincoln, and Miss Grace Deal, of Wesleyan University, were there. They were people of poise, men and women not given to hysterical demonstration, but at the first gathering they all broke down. For a brief quarter of an hour there in the old parlor with its familiar objects, they let their grief have sway. For a little while there in the farm-home of their youth, they were but children whose mother had left them lonely when night was coming on.

When they had pulled themselves together, their greatest grief seemed to be that she died alone. In deepest remorse they blamed themselves. Standing there together in common sorrow, they said the same things over and over to each other:

"Didn't she seem as well as ever to you last week?"

"I'll never forgive myself that I played bridge all afternoon."

"Do you suppose she suffered much?"

"Or called for us?"

"Isn't it *dreadful?* Poor Mother! So many of us . . . and not one of us here just when she needed us . . . and after all she's done for us."

Only one,—Laura Deal,—a twelve-year-old granddaughter, turned away from the window where she had been looking down the long double row of cedars, and said in a clear, steady voice: "I don't think it was so dreadful. I think it was kind of nice. Maybe she didn't miss you." She looked slowly around the circle of her elders. "When you stop to think about it, maybe she didn't miss you *at all.* One time Grandma told me she was the very happiest when she was living over all her memories. Maybe . . ." She hesitated, a little shy at expressing the thought in her heart, "Maybe she was doing that . . . *then.*"

This is the story of the old lady who died while the meat burned and the children played "Run, Sheep, Run," across her yard.

CHAPTER I

☙ ABBIE MACKENZIE was old Abbie Deal's maiden name. And because the first eight years of her life were interesting only to her family, we shall skip over them as lightly as Abbie herself used to skip a hoop on the high, crack-filled sidewalks in the little village of Chicago, which stood at the side of a lake where the bulrushes grew.

We find her then, at eight, in the year 1854, camping at night on the edge of some timberland just off the beaten trail between Dubuque and the new home in Blackhawk County, Iowa, to which the little family was bound.

Abbie and a big sister of fifteen, Isabelle, were curled up together under two old patchwork quilts in one of the wagons. Another sister, Mary, and a little brother, Basil, were in the other wagon with their mother. Sixteen-year-old James and eleven-year-old Dennie, the men of the party, were sleeping near the oxen, so that the warmth of the animals' bodies would keep them warm.

Because she had propped up a small section of the wagon's canvas cover, Abbie could see out into the night. The darkness was a heavy, animate thing. It hung thickly about the wagon, vaguely weird, remotely fearsome. It seemed to see and hear and feel. It looked at Abbie with its stars, heard her whispered words with its tree-leaves, felt of her warm little body with its cool breeze fingers. Something about the queer closeness of it almost frightened her. Something about the hushed silence of it made her think of her father who had died two years before. She summoned a picture of him into her mind, now,—recalling the paleness of his long, thin face, the neatness of his neckcloth, the gentle courtesy of his manner. Thinking of him so, she punched Isabelle with an active elbow. "Belle, tell me about Father and Mother."

The big girl was a little impatient. "I've told you everything I remember."

"Tell it again."

"I should think you'd get tired of hearing the same thing."

"Oh, I *never* do."

"Well . . . Father were what they call an aristocrat. He lived in Aberdeen, Scotland, and his folks, the Mackenzies, had a town house and two country houses. He belonged to the landed gentry."

"What's landed gentry?"

"It means he were a gentleman and didn't have to work."

"Will James and Dennie be gentlemen?"

"Of course not. We lost all our money."

"Tell how we lost it." Abbie settled herself with complacence. There was an element of satisfaction in having had such a foreign substance at one time, even if it was long before her birth.

"Well . . . Father were a young man and never had to do nothing but enjoy hisself, and he were out one day following the hare and hounds . . ."

"Tell about that."

"That's hunting . . . a pack of hounds after a rabbit . . . and he got away from the rest of them and were lost."

"The rabbit?"

"No, dunce-cap, . . . you know I mean father. And he come to a peasant's cottage."

"What's peasant?"

"Awful poor people that have to work. But don't stop me every minute. I always forget where I were. Well . . . and he wanted a drink. And a sixteen-year-old peasant girl come out of the house. They were Irish, but I guess they were working for some folks in Scotland. Anyway it were Mother and she got a drink for him . . . were pulling up the rope and he took the rope and pulled it up hisself. Just think! A *gentleman* . . . and Mother were sixteen . . . just *one* year older than me. Abbie, do you suppose there'll be an aristocratic landed gentleman out in Blackhawk County where we're going?"

"No . . . I don't think so. Go on."

"Well, Mother were pretty . . . Irish girls about *always* are . . . and there were a rosebush and Father asked her for a rose and she pulled one for him. Abbie, don't you tell anybody, but I've got a little rosebush done up in a wet rag in the wagon and I'm going to plant it out in Blackhawk County."

"Ho! Ho! It takes years and years for a rosebush to grow big enough to have flowers to pull off for a-*ris* . . . for a-*rist* . . . for gentlemen. Go on."

"Anyway, Father took his rose and went away and the next day he come back."

"Were he lost again?"

"No, dunce-cap! He come back to see Mother a-purpose. And he come other days, even after that, and they would walk over the heather hills together."

"What's feather hills?"

"Not feather! *Heather!* . . . a little kind of weedy grass. And all the neighbors shook their heads and said they'd seen *that* thing happen before from the gentry . . . and . . ." Isabelle whispered solemnly, "*no good ever come of it*."

"What did they say that for?"

"I can't tell you now. You wouldn't understand. When you're as old as me, you will. But just the same, Father *did* marry her and took her to Aberdeen to the big Mackenzie house. Mother wore her best dress and her best headshawl, but even then, all fixed up that nice way, the Mackenzies didn't like her. Father's mother were Isabelle Anders-Mackenzie and she were awful proud and I hate her for not liking Mother. I hate her so bad that I'm sorry I'm named for her. If Mother would let me, I'd change it to Rosamond. I read about a Rosamond and she . . ."

"Go on about her . . . not *you*."

"Well . . . she were ashamed of Mother, but she had to take her in because she were Father's wife, and she dressed her up grand and tried to make her different. But when Mother would go back to see her folks, she'd put on her peasant dress and wear her shawl on her head and slip away. And Sundays when the Mackenzies would go to the kirk . . ."

"What's kirk?"

"Church. Where were I? Oh . . . the aristocrats set down below and the peasants all set up in the loft . . ."

"Like a hay loft?"

"No. Stop interrupting, or I won't tell you one thing more. And Mother wouldn't leave her folks, the O'Conners, so Father went and set with them and the Mackenzies were just *sick* with shame. Then Grandfather Mackenzie died, and a long time afterward . . . after Janet and James and Mary and Dennie and I were all born, Grandmother Isabelle Anders-Mackenzie . . ."

"I just *admire* to hear that name . . ."

"There you go again. Now I'm through telling it."

"Please . . . I won't stop you again."

"Well. . . . Grandmother died, too. Then Father come to America on a sailing vessel, just for a pleasure trip, and he were gone so long and folks thought he weren't coming back at all . . . and Mother cried something terrible . . . and Father had signed a note for a man . . ."

"What's signed a . . . ? Oh, . . . go on."

"And it made him lose all his money. Men come and put cards up on the house and stables while he were gone and the signs said there were going to be a roup there."

"What's . . . ? Go on."

"A roup's an auction sale. There were fifteen saddle-horses in the stables, but after the roup cards went up Mother were not allowed to touch one on account of the law, and so her and James and Janet walked twenty-seven miles to have her father and mother come and bid in some of her things. She's got 'em yet in that little wooden chest with calf-skin all over it. It's in the other wagon and I know just what's in it because I saw 'em. There's a white silk shawl with big solid roses in the corners . . . all *four* corners . . . and a jeweled fan . . . and a breast-pin with lavender sets and a string of pearls. There are just as many things as there are girls in our family and Mother says each girl are to have one for a keepsake. I know which one I want . . . the silk shawl. I tried it on once when Mother were gone and I looked a lot like the painting of Isabelle Anders-Mackenzie that hung up on the landing of the stairway in the great hall. Course, you understand, Abbie, I never said I hated her *looks* . . ."

"Which one is Mother going to give me?"

"I don't know. She aren't going to give 'em to us until our wedding days. Of course, Janet didn't get hers on *her* wedding day because she got married out here in Blackhawk County before we come, but Mother'll give it to her to-morrow when we get there."

"Go on . . . you're forgetting the end of the story."

"Oh, well, you know it anyway. When Father got back to Liverpool he heard all about the money and the property being lost, and the things being sold, and he never even went to Aberdeen but sent for Mother and all five of us children to come to Liverpool and we all crossed the ocean. I were seven and I can remember just as well . . . and when we got to New York, you were born."

Abbie breathed a sigh of relief. It was a welcome respite after a narrow escape. With every telling of the story, almost it seemed for a time that she was not to be born.

"Now tell about the painting of Isabelle Anders-Mackenzie that hung on the landing of the stairway in the great hall." Abbie rolled the magic words from her lips in delicious anticipation. This was the part she liked the best of all.

"Well . . . it were beauteous. It were in a great heavy gold frame . . . and as big as life. I can remember it just as well. In the picture she were young, you know . . ."

"And beautiful . . ." prompted Abbie.

"And beautiful. She had reddish-brown hair like yours . . . and she were standing by a kind-of . . . a table-thing, and she had on a velvet dress that swept down and around her . . . and she had a hat in her hand with a plume . . ."

"A flowing white plume . . ." corrected Abbie.

"A flowing white plume," repeated the more matter-of-fact Isabelle. "And she had pretty hands and long slender fingers that tapered at the ends."

Abbie held her hands up to the opening of the canvas on the wagon and peered at them in the moonlight. The fingers were long and slender and they tapered at the ends. She sighed with satisfaction, and slipped them under the old patched quilt.

"And nobody knows what become of the picture?" It was half statement, half question, as though from the vast fund of information which Isabelle possessed, she might, some day, suddenly remember what had become of the picture.

"No. It were sold at the roup. I don't know who got it."

Abbie sighed again, but not with satisfaction. Of all the beautiful things that were sold, she felt that she could have missed seeing any of them with better grace than the portrait. In her immature way, she resented the sale more than any other thing,—the passing of the lovely lady into other hands. Jewels, money, furniture,—they seemed lifeless, inanimate things beside the picture of the woman who was flesh of her flesh. It ought to have been saved. It was their own grandmother who stood there forever inside the heavy gold frame, in the dark velvet dress that swept around her,—and with the flowing white plume—and the long slender fingers that tapered at the ends.

"Well, I wish we had it here with us, Belle. We could have it all wrapped up in quilts in the wagon . . . and then some day out in Blackhawk County when we get rich, we could build us a grand house with a wide curving stairway and hang the picture on the landing . . . and everybody that come . . ."

"Abbie! Belle!" A voice came suddenly from the other wagon. "Sure 'n' you're the talkers. Settle yoursel's now. We want to get a good early start by sunup."

Abbie started. From a dreamy journey into the fields of romance she had been drawn back to the prosaic world of reality by her mother's voice. She could not quite reconcile good fat Mother with the romantic figure of the pretty girl at the well, picking a rose for an aristocratic gentleman. But then, Mother was almost an old woman, now,—thirty-seven.

Abbie turned to the opening in the canvas cover and looked out again at the night. Yellow-white, the moon rose higher over the dark clumps of trees. A thousand stars, looking down, paled at its rising. An owl gave its mournful call. The smell of burning maple boughs came from the fire. A wolf howled in the distance so that James got up and took out the other gun from the wagon. There was a constant tick-tacking in the timber,—all the little night creatures at their work. It was queer how it all hurt you,—how the odor of the night, the silver sheen of the moon, the moist feeling of the dew, the whispering of the night breeze, how, somewhere down in your throat it hurt you. It was sad, too, that this evening would never come again. The night winds were blowing it away. You could not stop the winds and you could not stop Time. It went on and on,—and on. To-morrow night would come and the moon would look down on this same spot,—the trees and the grass, the wagon-tracks and the dead campfire. But she would not be here. Her heart swelled with an emotion which she could not name. Tears came to her eyes. The telling of the story always brought that same feeling.

"Isabelle Anders-Mackenzie," she said it over until it took upon itself the cadence of a melody, the rhythm of a poem. "I shall be like her," she thought. "I have hair like her now and hands like her. I shall be lovely. And I shall do wonderful things . . . sing before big audiences and paint pictures inside of gold frames and write things in a book." She wondered how you got things put in a book. There were some books in one of the wooden chests over in the other wagon. A man with a long name that began *S-h-a-k-e-s* . . . had made some of them. They had been Father's. Mother didn't read them. She didn't read anything but her Bible. Even that was hard for her, so that she read the same verses over and over. Yes, she would be like Father and Isabelle Anders-Mackenzie, not like Mother's family with their cottage on the side of the hill and their dark shawls over their heads. She would be rich and lovely . . . with a velvet dress and a long sweeping plume . . . under the moon . . . and the night wind, . . . that felt of your body with its long . . . slender fingers . . . that tapered at the ends . . .

Abbie Mackenzie slept,—little Abbie Mackenzie, with the mixture of the two strains of blood,—with the stout body of the O'Conners and the slender hands of the Mackenzies,—with the O'Conner sturdiness and the Mackenzie refinement. And she is to need them both,—the physical attributes of the peasant and the mental ones of the aristocrat,—the warm heart of the Irish and the steadfastness of the Scotch. Yes, Abbie Mackenzie is to need them both in the eighty years she is to live,—courage and love,—a song upon her lips and a lantern in her hand.

CHAPTER II

THE sun, shining through the propped-up canvas of the wagon, wakened Abbie. Wide-eyed, she looked out through the aperture upon the same setting of the night before. But now it was changed. The child lived a life in each of two distinct worlds and it is not possible to say which one she most enjoyed. One of them was made of moonbeams and star-dust, of night winds and cloud fancies, of aristocratic gentlemen and lovely ladies. The other was the equally pleasant one of boiled potatoes and salt pork, of games with Basil and Mary, of riding a-top old Buck or picking wild flowers at the edge of the timber.

Just now the prosaic world of everyday seemed the more attractive of the two. James had replenished the night fire and Mother was cooking breakfast, with the odor of frying pork and corn-cakes strong on the air. The team of horses and the oxen were eating close by, the horses guzzling their grain noisily, the oxen chewing slowly and stolidly.

Maggie O'Conner Mackenzie was a heavy, dumpy woman, her body the shape of a pudding-bag tied in the middle. One shawl was wrapped around the shapeless figure and a smaller one, over her head, was knotted under her fat chin. Strands of heavy black hair showed around the edges of the head-shawl, and the face enclosed in its folds was round and smooth, fat and placid. Only her dark Irish eyes, the color of the blue-black waters at Kilkee, and a dimple in the middle of her rolling chin, gave a touch of reality to the old romance of the peasant girl.

This was the last day of the journey which had been of three weeks' duration. (Six decades later James Mackenzie was to make the journey back with a grandson in one day.)

Breakfast over, the little cavalcade set out with much noisy chatter,—reminders not to forget this or that.

"Did ye put out the last o' the fire, Dennie?"

"Fasten that buckle on Whitey's bridle, Belle."

The mother drove the horse team,—James, the oxen. Walking along beside the latter, James' boyish "Gee" or "Haw" or "Whoa How" rang out with valiant attempts to make the notes stentorian. Buck was a red and white animal, Boy a brindle. As they walked, they swung their huge heads rhythmically from side to side, the brass buttons a-top their horns shining in the morning sun. Almost at the first rod's length of the journey little Basil had to stop the procession to change from one wagon to the other. Belle rode on the seat with her mother, but, because it was early and cool, Abbie, Mary and Dennie walked behind, darting off the trail to gather Mayflowers or wild Bouncing-Bets. Sometimes they jumped over the young rosin-weeds and wild blue phlox and occasionally they caught on the back of the wagon, clutching onto the household goods and swinging their feet off the ground for a few moments.

About nine, they forded a stream. The oxen ahead crossed slowly, lumberingly, with many stops in that foolish, stolid way they had. When they were across, Mother Mackenzie drove her team into the creek bed. As the horses were going up the bank, one of them stumbled, crowding against its mate. There was a creaking, and backing, a shouting and a tipping. One sack of flour began falling slowly, and then another and another. Eight sacks of flour, pushing against each other, slipped slowly into the water like fat, clumsy, old men, reluctant to wet their feet.

Maggie Mackenzie was out and managing her horses by way of their bridles, while James, running back from his own wagon, assisted in bringing order out of the catastrophe. Then some one called excitedly, "Look out for the bedding," and two great pillows started floating down stream with majestic motion, as though the geese from which their contents had been plucked, were suddenly coming to life.

"Och!" And "Och!" The mother wrung her hands in distress. Eight sacks of flour and two pillows were a fortune.

Abbie and Dennie and little Basil, their laughter high with excitement, all ran along the side of the creek bed after the pillows. In the meantime, James and Belle were wading into the stream and pulling out the sacks. To the mother the disaster seemed more than she could bear. "Och! If I ever get there," said Maggie O'Conner Mackenzie, "sure 'n' I'll never l'ave the spot." Sure, and she never did. Many years later she died a quarter of a mile from the place where she first stepped out of the wagon.

When the last sack was retrieved, the entire family, with much dire foreboding, crowded around James, who was opening a sack to see how the contents fared. It was as though the whole of life's future hung on the outcome. To their extreme relief the wet flour had formed but a thin paste, which, with a few moments drying in the sun, now high and hot, would form a crust and keep the precious contents unharmed.

In spite of the delay the family reached the settlement on the Cedar River by the middle of the afternoon and stopped near the log cabin of Tom Graves, the man whom the older sister Janet had come out to marry. Janet, herself, hearing the creaking of the wagons, came hurrying down the grassy trail to meet them, a three-weeks-old baby in her arms. The baby was something by way of surprise to the entire group of relatives, his arrival having taken place after the family had started westward.

Maggie O'Conner Mackenzie, with much clucking and chirping and adjustment of clothing, welcomed her first grandchild.

"Sure 'n' he's the big one. How did ye get along? Is he good? Did ye have a doctor or a neighbor woman?"

Janet answered them all even while her mother was still talking. Oh, yes, there was a doctor,—Doc Matthews over at town. Cedar Falls was quite a place. It had a sawmill and a hotel and a store, a dozen log cabins, and a few frames ones. The school-house had the only tower bell in the state. For pay Tom was to haul in a load of wood for the doctor's office stove,—he had a two-roomed house, part log and part frame.

The oxen behind them slathered and snorted. There was the smell in the air of newly-cut chips. The woods back of the cabin looked thick and impenetrable beyond the short arrows of the sun. And then Tom Graves, himself, came out of the timber, his ax, the insignia of the fight, on his shoulder.

"Here is my mother, Tom, and this is Belle and that one is Mary. And that boy is James and this one Dennie and here's little Basil. And over there with the reddish-brown hair is Abbie,—we almost forgot her."

So much was to be said, and all at once. "We've got a house all ready for you, Mother. It was Grandpa Deal's sheep shed. The Deals have been here for three years, but they've moved down farther on the prairie now in a fine big log house, and you can have this until you get your own cabin done. We've cleaned it all out for you and hung a thick quilt over the opening, and if it storms you can come in with us."

And so Maggie O'Conner Mackenzie, who had lived in the great Aberdeen town house and on the two Scotch country estates, was to make her bed now in a sheep shed.

Every one turned in to help with the settling. From the wagons they took out the walnut bedsteads and the bedding and the highboy. They brought in the heavy, cumbersome guns and the powder-horn and the splint-bottom chairs. Maggie Mackenzie brought in her flat-iron into which one put glowing hickory embers through an iron door, and she hung up the iron tallow-lamp with a home-spun wick hanging over the side like a tongue hanging grotesquely from the side of a mouth. If she could have foreseen that two granddaughters, Mrs. Harrison Scannell Rhodes and Mrs. Frederick Hamilton Baker, were going to stage a polite but intensive campaign over which one could have the old tallow-lamp in her sun parlor, a half century later, she would have shaken her fat sides with laughter.

Everything was out of the wagon now,—everything but one. Abbie, standing in the grassy trail in front of the old sheep shed, was watching for it. On tiptoe there in her ankle-length starched dress, her red-brown hair wound around her head and tucked into a snood, she was the picture of watchful waiting. She might have been carved in marble as "Expectancy."

"Let me! Let me!" she called, when her mother was bringing out the calf-skin-covered box from under the wagon seat.

"If ye'll carry it carefu'."

No need to caution Abbie to be careful. In a warm feeling of pleasure over the temporary possession, she clasped her arms around its hairy sides and the "M.OC." initials formed by nail-heads.

Inside the box lay all the accouterments of another life. In its skin-covered depths was all the equipment of an entirely different world. They were symbols of things in life to come. They represented the future in which she would some day live. She got down on her knees on the dirt floor, with its earthy odor, and pushed the little chest into the far, dark corner under her mother's bed. Lovingly and lingeringly she relinquished her hold upon it. For a few moments she saw herself in that future, her red-brown hair in curls, over her shoulders a white silk shawl with roses in the corners, its folds held together with a lavender breastpin. There was a string of pearls around her neck, and she was waving a jeweled fan with long, white fingers that tapered at the ends. There was soft music playing. She came out on a high stage ready to sing. Lovely ladies and courtly men were clapping their hands. Some of them stood up. She smiled at them and waved her jeweled fan. . . .

"Abbie . . . Abbie . . . where are you?" Quite suddenly, the gorgeous trappings fell away. She was back in the everyday world, hearing loud voices calling her.

"Abbie! . . ." The voices were raised high in fright. She scrambled out backward from under the bed.

"Abbie . . . Abbie . . ." Dennis and Mary were running toward her, their faces white with fear. "The Indians are coming. A man here on horseback says the Indians are coming down the river."

Abbie scrambled back under the bed and brought out the hairy chest in her arms. Not to any wild and heathenish Indian was Abbie Mackenzie intending to relinquish the only tangible tie that bound her to the lovely lady.

CHAPTER III

IN THE midst of the hurry and confusion and fright, Abbie gathered that they were all to get back into the wagons and "go down to Grandpa Deal's," wherever that was.

Everything that could be handled easily was thrown into the wagons. Janet rolled a fresh batch of bread and raised doughnuts into a homespun tablecloth. Tom tied old Whitey to the back of his wagon and put her new calf in the end of the box so she could see her offspring and not bellow for it. Abbie clutched the hairy chest in protecting arms. The cavalcade started lumberingly down the river road. Through the dark timber they drove, over spongy moist leaves, past thickets of sumac and hazel-brush, their hearts pounding in alarm, their bodies tense with fear, every tree the potential hiding place of an Indian.

Out of the cool river road and onto the hot, flat prairie they came as suddenly as one opens a door upon a bright, heated room. For two miles they drove over the faintly marked prairie trail, coming then to another wooded section and to the largest house in the community,—a big log structure which looked palatial to Abbie's eyes after Tom Graves' one-roomed cabin and the sheep shed.

Other horse and ox teams were hitched to the straw-roofed log stable. Other families were scurrying into the house with smoked hams and batches of bread and valued possessions in their arms. Not far from the back door of the big log house, Abbie, still grasping the hairy chest, stopped to watch a boy of twelve or thirteen caressing the sleek, quivering head of a young deer, tied to a tree by a strap around its neck.

A small, severe-looking woman in a black calico dress, with a black netting cap tied under her sharply pointed chin, was scolding nervously. "No, Willie, you can't. I won't have it. It's bad enough to have the whole kit 'n' bilin' in the country comin' 'n' trackin' up,—all the rag-shag 'n' bob-tails bringin' their stuff."

"But, Mother," the boy plead, "I'll keep her by herself. I'll get her up the loft stairs."

"No,—you sha'n't, Willie Deal."

And then a big, powerful man came out,—a man with only one arm, his left sleeve pinned to the side of his coat. He had a shock of wiry black hair, and an equally wiry beard which gave him an unkempt look. But his eyes were blue and twinkling and kind,—they held the calmness of blue ice, but not its coldness.

He put his one hand on the boy's dark head, now, and said quietly, "You'd best let her go, son. She'll take care of herself,—and it's only fair to give her her freedom."

Without a word the boy cut the strap at the fawn's throat, and even while he was unloosing the piece around her neck, she darted from him lightly, gracefully, into the hazel-brush.

Inside the big log house where all seemed confusion, Abbie, after a time, sought out the dark-haired boy.

"Do you think you'll ever get her back?" she asked shyly.

"Get what?"

"Your little deer."

"Naw, . . . never." The boy turned his head away.

Abbie's heart seemed bursting with sorrow for him. There was that word again,—*never*. It was the saddest word! It made her throat hurt. Willie Deal would never, never have his little deer again.

With his head still averted, the boy said tensely, "I found her . . . 'n' raised her . . . myself."

Abbie put her hand out gently and touched the boy's arm.

"I'm sorry." Her voice held deep sympathy.

"Aw . . ." He threw up his fine dark head. "I didn't care."

But Abbie knew it was not so. Abbie knew that he cared.

It seems precarious business to take time to describe Grandpa and Grandma Deal, when a band of disgruntled Indians is reported on its way down the Shell Rock, but, pending its arrival, one ought to know a little of Gideon Deal and his wife. They were not yet out of their forties. Indeed, their youngest daughter, Regina, was only nine, but through older offspring scattered about the community, several grandchildren had been presented to them, and so, to differentiate them from other and younger Deals, the titles "Grandpa" and "Grandma" had been bestowed early upon them.

To the other settlers Grandpa Deal seemed as substantial as the native hickory timber in whose clearing he had built his house. He was both freighter and farmer. Two of the grown sons worked his place, while he himself drove the six-ox-team over the long trail to Dubuque and back, with freight for the whole community. For this,—and for his reputation as a wit,—he was known far and wide. To fully appreciate his wit, one must have taken Grandma Deal into account, for she was the background against which his droll sayings stood forth. The little wiry woman, fretful, energetic and humorless, was intolerant of wasting time in fun-making. Grandpa Deal, kind, easy-going and jolly, was always picking up every little saying of his partner's to bandy it about with sly drollness. There was never any loud laughter on his part, just a twinkle in the sharp blue eyes appreciative of his outlook on life. Grandma Deal spent her time hustling about, darting in and out, scolding at Grandpa, finding fault with the children, the well-sweep, the weather, everything that came under her eagle eye or into her busy brain.

Just now, however, Grandma was not scolding. Grandpa was not joking. The news of impending disaster had brought them to a common ground of fear. Most of the other families of the community had gathered now in the larger and stronger Deal home in response to the rumor of the Indian uprising. Already the men were stationing guns near windows and barring and barricading doors. Several women were running bullets in the little salamander stove, a queer affair whose short legs in front and long legs in the back, gave it the appearance of an inverted giraffe. One woman was hysterical; another a little out of her mind from fear, kept wanting to go back out doors where there was air.

All night they waited for whatever Fate had in store for them. In the morning, a man rode up on horseback, a young boy, about Willie Deal's age, behind him in the saddle. It was Doc Matthews, who had come to bring word that the hostile band of Indians had gone north.

Immediately there was the confusion of getting ready to leave. Grandpa Deal told those who lived farthest away to stay and make a visit for the day. Abbie could hear Grandma Deal sputtering about her husband's freehanded hospitality.

The boy who came with Doc Matthews was his son Ed. He had been east all year to a boys' boarding school. He was dressed in a nice suit and a flat white collar and a little round hat.

He stood and looked at Willie Deal in his homespun suit. Willie Deal stood and looked at Eddie Matthews from the Philadelphia boarding-school. Their contempt seemed mutual.

The Indian scare, then, had gone into nothing. The wagons went lumbering back across the prairie and through the damp, dark river road where the hazel-brush and sumac knotted together under the native oaks and hickories.

All summer long, the Mackenzies lived in the sheep shed, while their own log house was being built. James and Tom Graves were building it, and Dennie was helping, battening the inside with long split saplings and filling the chinks with mud.

All summer long, Abbie went happily in and out of the sheep shed with the patchwork quilt in front for the door. There were so many lovely things to do that one did not know how to find time for them all. There were flowers in the deep, dark recesses of the Big Woods,—wild honeysuckles and Bouncing-Bets and tall ferns that one could pretend were long, sweeping, white plumes.

Sometimes Abbie would take one of the longest of the ferns and, with a slender twig, pin it on a wild grapevine leaf or a plantain for a hat. Then she would drape one of her mother's dark shawls around her sturdy little body, and standing on a grassy hillock in the clearing, pretend she was Isabelle Anders-Mackenzie, the lovely lady.

And then she had a whole set of dishes hidden in the hollow of an oak at the edge of the timberland. James had made them for her from acorns, removing the nut and whittling little handles for the cups. And she had a child for which she must care constantly. It was an elongated-shaped stone with a small round formation on the end for its head. She put little Basil's outgrown dress on it and a knitted bonnet. She liked the feeling of the stone against her breast. It seemed heavy and like a real baby. Sometimes in carrying it about, her heart would swell in potential mother love for it. But sometimes there was no need to pretend about a baby, for there was Janet's real, live one to hold and rock. Janet had a low, wooden trundle-bed for him that pushed under the big bed. It was rough on the outside and the ends were made from the sawed round disks of a tree.

One afternoon, Willie Deal came up to the Big Woods with his shaggy-haired father to see Tom Graves. Willie Deal had remembered Abbie and brought her a plant in a clay jar he had made. The plant was a green, lacy, fern-like thing, and there were three little, round, scarlet balls on it.

"Whatever are they?" Abbie wanted to know.

"They're love apples," Willie told her. "But don't you ever dare put one up to your mouth. They're tremendous poisonous."

Abbie promised that she never, never would so much as touch the poison. For how could Willie Deal and Abbie Mackenzie in the 'fifties know anything about vitamine-filled tomatoes?

And then, in the fall, Janet's baby was not quite well. No one seemed to know what the matter could be. Maggie O'Conner Mackenzie doctored him with castor oil and peppermint. Grandma Deal sent word by Tom Graves to give him sassafras tea and tie a little bag of asafetida around his neck. When he seemed no better, Janet, pale and worried, said maybe they ought to send for Dr. Matthews. Abbie was frightened beyond measure when she heard that, for she well knew that a doctor was the last resort for saving one who was sick. Tom went out immediately to saddle a horse and go for the doctor. Janet told Abbie to hold the baby while she went out to the lean-to kitchen for warm water. Mother Mackenzie had gone over to her own home for flannel cloths.

And then, Abbie was calling them and crying all in the same breath, "Janet, . . . Mother, . . . come quick . . . oh, come . . ."

Janet was in the room like a flash, a wild bittern at the call of its young. Abbie could scarcely talk for crying: "I was just holding him as steady. He acted queer, . . . and threw up his arms. He got kind of bluish. What ought I to 've done?"

Doctor Matthews came with Tom. He said, yes, the baby was dead. Janet was wild with grief. Sitting on the edge of the bed, she rocked the little cold form back and forth in her arms and would not let them take him from her. Rachel, who lives again in every grieving mother, was crying for her child and would not be comforted.

Over in their own cabin, Abbie sobbed aloud on the bed. Suddenly she sat up, "I hate God," she said. Maggie Mackenzie hushed her quickly and told her it was tremendous wicked to say that.

"But he made death. I hate death. I *hate* it."

"The poor colleen," her mother said to Belle. "She's smart like the Mackenzies, . . . but faith . . . an' she has the Irish heart."

CHAPTER IV

☙§ BY THE time Abbie was eleven, she was doing more work. Life was not all play now. One of her tasks was to thread the wicks into candle molds, for her slim fingers were more agile than her mother's short, thick ones. She had to poke the long wick-string through all of the six molds, and carefully loop the tops over a stick to keep them from slipping. Her mother would then pour the hot tallow into the molds and set it away to harden. Abbie was always anxious to see the finished product slip out. She would watch her mother plunge the molds into hot water to loosen the hard grease, and then, "Let me, . . . let me," she would call, and sometimes Maggie Mackenzie would let her carefully work the shining cream-colored candles out of their containers.

There were a dozen other tasks for her to perform,—drive the cows to drink, gather eggs from the chickens' stolen nests among the sheds and stacks, and the daily one of going to school.

But even work could take upon itself a mask of fun. One could pretend, when threading the wicks into candle molds, that one was stringing pearls accidentally broken at the ball,—that the long walk through the hazel-brush to the schoolhouse was between rows of admiring spectators who, instead of a mere rustling in the wind, were whispering, "There she goes,—there goes Abbie Mackenzie, the singer."

For Abbie was always singing from the elevation of her grassy knoll in the clearing. It made her happy to walk up the little incline, turn and bow to an unseen audience, throw up her head and let forth her emotions in song. Her heart would swell in a feeling of oneness with Nature and the Creator of it, and there would come to her a great longing for things she did not quite know or understand.

The log school-house sat in a clearing of timber just out of the river's high-water line. The hazel-brush and sumac tangled together under its windows and there were butternut and black walnut trees behind it. The desks were rough shelves against the walls on three sides of the room, and in front of them were three long benches of equal height, so that a strapping six-foot boy or a tiny six-year-old girl could, with economy, use the same seats.

While studying, the children sat with their backs toward the teacher, but when it was recitation time they had to put their legs up over the benches and turn to face him. Abbie always crawled over slowly, holding modestly on to her dress and three petticoats. But Regina Deal would flip over daringly in a whirlwind of skirts and pantalets. The cloaks and bonnets were hung on nails on the one side of the room which contained no desk-shelf. The water-pail and dipper were on a bench by the door, which made a sloppily wet corner, excepting on those winter days when the dipper froze in the pail. The room was heated by a stove in the center, and one unhappily roasted or froze in proportion to his proximity to the stove.

Sometimes the contents of the dinner buckets were also frozen and one had to thaw them out before eating. On fall days, a few of the more adventuresome of the squirrels and chipmunks whisked in and out of the window-opening in the logs, purloining the crumbs for waiting families.

In the spring, when the maple sap ran, every one crossed the river in flat-bottomed boats and helped in the little sugar camp. Louise and Regina Deal showed Abbie and Mary Mackenzie how to make maple eggs. They took tiny pieces of shell off the small ends of eggs, carefully removed the raw contents, ran the maple sap into the hollow molds, and after it had hardened, picked off the shells,—and behold, there was a platter of candy ready for the winter parties.

The fall in which Abbie was eleven, the entiie crowd of young people on the north side of the river was invited to the Mackenzies'. Already there was a social distinction being drawn between the north, or country side, and the south, or town side, of the river. The party was for Belle, who was soon to be married. Belle had planted her rosebush by the log cabin, but the chickens had pecked at it, and the pigs had rooted under it, and no aristocratic gentleman had come by,—only a plain farmer boy who had hired out to Tom Graves.

The young folks came in lumber wagons along the river road under the full moon. The few pieces of furniture were set out of doors to make room for the party, and there were tallow candles lighted and placed high up on shelves. In an iron kettle there was taffy cooking to be pulled later, and platters of pop-corn balls and dishes of maple drops, into which hickory nuts, butternuts, hazelnuts or walnuts had been stirred.

The crowd played dancing games to their own singing and hand-clapping:

"I won't have none of your weevily wheat,
I won't have none of your barley,
I won't have none but the best of wheat,
To make a cake for Charley."

When the fun was at its height, a horse and rider drew up at the door, and some one called out, "Hey there, . . . you." The young folks, upon going out to see who it was, found Ed Matthews there with a deer carcass, which he had been pulling behind him with a rope. Ed, who was sixteen now, was dressed in "city" hunter togs, a leather-looking coat and pants and a cap with a long bill in front. His boots were almost hip-high and fitted snugly to his legs.

When they were crowding around to look at the deer, Abbie first saw the strap drawn taut on its neck. Immediately, she was looking up into the face of Will Deal,—a darkened, flashing face. The young folks all discussed the queer fact of the strap being on the deer's neck. But Will Deal said nothing. And Abbie, sensing that Will did not want to tell about it, said nothing.

Regina and Louise and Mary Mackenzie all invited Ed Matthews in to the party. He accepted, and immediately became the center of the games and dancing. But for some reason the party was not so pleasant. For some reason, Ed Matthews, in his city hunter togs, had spoiled the party.

When the horses were hitched to the wagons and the young folks were all leaving, Abbie touched Will Deal on the arm.

"It was your little deer, wasn't it?"

"I 'spose so."

Something intuitive made Abbie say, "I'm sorry *he* was the one who shot it."

Will's face flashed darkly, "Aw, shucks! . . . I don't care."

But Abbie knew that it was not so. Abbie knew that Will Deal cared.

Two years later, Grandpa Deal was sent by the county to the General Assembly. Word trickled back to the settlement that he was well liked by his constituents, and that he was called "Old Blackhawk" and "the wag of the House."

Will Deal, eighteen now, had done the freighting from Dubuque all fall during his father's absence, but when spring came, an older brother assumed the business while Will took over the farm work. Once when Abbie came by, he stopped the team and sat on the plow-handle and called out to her to come and hear a letter from his father. It began, "Dear Friend," and ended, "This from your affectionate father." It said that he hoped Will could comfortably till the fields, that there was some talk of dividing two of the counties, that board was tremendous high,—three dollars a week,—that his sister, Harriett, had left on the stage, that the Pikes Peakers were beginning to run, and that he looked for quite a rush this spring for the gold regions. Abbie felt quite proud of the fact that a young man like Will Deal would read his letters to a thirteen-year-old girl.

It was only a few weeks later, that an old Springfield friend of Grandpa Deal's was nominated for the presidency of the United States. When Grandpa Deal came home, he said that if you'd known Abe Lincoln as well as he had, you'd never in the world think that he'd have been picked for the nomination, but just the same there was hoss sense inside his long hide.

All summer long one heard political talk here and there,—about slavery and secessionists and the outcome of the fall election. Men would stop in wagons on the river road and talk so long that their teams would amble a short way into the woods, cropping at the juicy ferns. Grandma Deal scolded all summer about it. Abbie heard her say that she kept dinner hot so many times for Grandpa, who was talking to groups around the store over in town or on the schoolhouse steps, that she had a notion to quit cooking for him altogether.

All winter the talk grew thicker and more heated. While Abbie did not fully understand it all, she knew in February, when the Southern Confederacy had been established, that things were at some sort of a crisis. But from hearing Grandpa Deal talk, she felt confident that when Abe Lincoln would take his seat in March, everything was going to be all right. And Grandpa Deal was to have plenty of time to talk, for his old job of freighting from Dubuque was to be taken from him. Slowly, but surely, the construction of the Dubuque and Sioux City road was being carried westward.

Abraham Lincoln took his seat in March, but everything was not going to be all right. Twenty-seven days later the first iron horse from Dubuque shrieked its triumphant way across the Deal farm, and on into Cedar Falls, and the old-time freighter's task was finished. The train's arrival was timely for the community, inasmuch as events were to follow which would suspend construction and cause Cedar Falls to remain the western terminus of the road for four years.

Abbie had now passed her fourteenth birthday. On an April afternoon, with the river high and clods of snow still at the roots of trees, she went into the timber to look for anemones and Dutchmen's breeches, for dog-toothed violets and the first signs of Mayflower buds. Coming out on her own particular grassy knoll in the clearing, she went up to the hillock, in one of those moments of desire to let out her feelings in song. To the squirrels she may have seemed an ordinary girl clothed in a green-checked gingham dress, with reddish-brown curls twisted up into a snood, but the squirrels were not seeing correctly. For Abbie knew that she had a dark velvet dress that swept around her feet, a string of pearls on her neck, and in her hand a hat with a sweeping plume. She was holding it carelessly at her side with her long, slender fingers that tapered at the ends.

At the top of the knoll she turned. A sea of white faces looked up at her. To the casual observer it might have seemed a mass of wild plum-blossoms. Even before she sang, the audience applauded vociferously and a few people stood up. An onlooker, who was not magic-eyed, might have thought the wind merely blew the blossoms. Abbie bowed, smiled, —waited for her accompaniment to begin. She fingered her pearls, and smiled at the girl at the reed-organ. All at once she realized that the girl at the organ was a talented orphan whom she had been befriending. It made her feel happy, light-hearted. She threw back her head and began singing:

"Oh! the Lady of the Lea,
Fair and young and gay was she,
Beautiful exceedingly,
The Lady of the Lea."

The song embodied for her all the enchantment of the Arabian Nights. It opened a door to a magic castle. It smelled of perfume and spices. It stood for wonderful things in life to come.

"Many a wooer sought her hand,
For she had gold and she had land."

Her voice rose melodiously high and sweet and true.

"Everything at her command,
The Lady of the Lea."

Her heart seemed bursting with love of the trees, the sky, the melody.

"Oh, the Lady of the Lea,
Fair and young and gay was she,"

There seemed a gleam ahead of her,—a light that beckoned,—a little will-o'-the-wisp out there beyond the settlement in the Big Woods. It was something no one knew about,—Mother nor Mary nor Belle. Only for her it shone,—for her, and other lovely ladies.

"Fanciful exceedingly,
The Lady of the Lea."

When the song had died away and Abbie was bowing to the invisible audience, she heard it, "Abbie, . . . oh, Abbie . . . hoo-hoo!" Mary's voice was calling and crying in the distance. She slipped out of the clearing, climbed the stake-and-rider fence, and saw Mary coming,—calling and crying and coming toward her. "Abbie, they've just got word out from Dubuque that Fort Sumter was fired on."

Abbie clutched her. "What, . . . what does *that* mean, Mary?"

"It means, . . ." Mary's voice whispered it hoarsely, "Grandpa Deal says it means *war*."

CHAPTER V

☙ YES, it meant war, with James leaving at the first call, and Belle's young husband enlisting without her knowing his intentions. Abbie thought she could not stand it to see them go. It seemed that life was doing something to her which she could not countenance. She had a queer sensation of wind blowing past her,—of wind that she could not stop. She stood in front of the Seth Thomas clock on the shelf in her mother's cabin and watched the hands moving above the little brown church painted on the glass of the door. *Oh, stop Time for a few minutes until we can do something about the war.*

But the winds blew past, and the clock hands went around, and James and Belle's husband and several of the neighbor boys had gone to war.

And by 1862, when Lincoln's call for additional volunteers came, Dennie, who was nineteen now, went into the Cedar Falls Reserves, a group of one hundred stalwart fellows. And Abbie again went all through the torn emotions of parting with Dennie and hating war.

And then she learned that there was one thing worse than going to war. And that was not going to war. Will Deal told her so. To be twenty-one and able-bodied, and see the Reserves entrain and not go! He was ashamed, and miserable. But his father, with his one arm, and in the Assembly as he was,—and no one to farm,—and Regina and Louise and his mother all depending on him,—he could not go. It seemed queer that of all the people in the community, Abbie Mackenzie, who was only sixteen, should be the one in whom Will Deal confided. And because Will Deal had done this, Abbie told him some things she had never told a soul,—that some day she was going to be a big person. She could feel it in her,—that she was going to do great things, sing before vast audiences, and paint lovely pictures in frames and write things in a book.

"You know, Will, I don't want people to laugh at me,—and I don't believe you would. But sometimes it all comes over me, that I can do these big things. It's ahead of me, . . . kind-of like a light in the woods that shines and stays far away. And when I read verses, . . . or hear music, . . . or sing, . . . it beckons me on, . . . and my throat hurts with wanting to do something great."

Will did not laugh at her, but instead, looked at her queerly for a moment, noticing for the first time that her skin was as creamy-white as the May-flowers that grew in the Big Woods, that her lips were of deep red tints and her eyes of deep brown ones, and that her mop of curly hair held them both,—the reds and the browns.

And then, the next year, Ed Matthews, who had been east to college, was drafted. And Doc Matthews called Will out of the field where he was cutting wheat with a cradle, and told him he would give him five hundred dollars to go in Ed's place.

Will walked to the house, laid the sack of gold pieces in his mother's lap and said, "I'm going, Mother. There's the money to hire the work done."

He left from the new Dubuque and Sioux City station two miles from his father's place. Grandpa Deal was there, sick at heart, joking the boys. Grandma Deal, in her black cap tied under her wrinkled face, was there, scolding that Will was going, that the coach would be crowded,—scolding and sputtering in her little nagging way. Why didn't they stand back? Why didn't they go to-morrow? What made every one so noisy? Maggie O'Conner Mackenzie, in her white cap tied under her plump, placid face, was there. And Abbie Mackenzie, in a sprigged delaine over hoop skirts, and with a little pancake flowered hat tipped over her forehead, was there. *Oh, God, stop the wind blowing by,—the wind that blows Time away. Stop the clock hands until I can think whether* Will *Deal ought to go to war.*

And then, something happened. The train was ready to start. There were good-bys and noise and tears and confusion. Will Deal shook his father's one hand, and kissed his mother's little wrinkled cheeks and Regina and Louise,—and started to shake hands with Abbie Mackenzie, but suddenly kissed her instead. And if battles have been lost and kingdoms have fallen over less, who is there to blame Abbie Mackenzie, that her own little kingdom was in a state of revolution when she left the station and drove home in the lumber-wagon across the prairie and over the damp, dark river road?

In the fall of '64, when she was seventeen, Abbie herself was teaching the home school,—in a new white schoolhouse with green blinds, but standing in the same spot where the hazel-brush grew in tangled masses down toward the river bank. There was only one big boy in school that autumn, a harmless unfortunate, whom Grandpa Deal termed a "three-quarters wit." The others were "with Sherman." And Sherman was before Atlanta.

Abbie's thoughts seemed always with them, those boys in shabby blue: James and Dennie and all the old neighborhood schoolmates. Through the monotonously droning reading of the McGuffey readers, the ciphering and the cramped copybook work, she thought of them. "God bring them all safe home. Please bring them home, God, . . . James and Dennie and Will Deal." There were other friends and schoolmates, but no one so big and fine and clean as Will Deal, and so understanding. Whenever she craved understanding, she always thought of Will Deal, who did not laugh at her fancies, but gave her sympathy instead.

Ed Matthews, who had paid his way out of the draft, came home that fall for a few days. Ed was going to be a doctor like his father. Several times he had stopped his horse at the schoolhouse door and, with the reins over his arm, talked to Abbie. She was a little proud of the attention. It was rather complimentary to be singled out from all the the girls in the neighborhood for attention from Ed. She could not quite make up her mind whether she really liked Ed or not. Will Deal didn't like him,—had never liked him. But Will was prejudiced. And it was nice to see a young man dress as Ed did. In his riding outfit he certainly looked tony. There were some rumors around about Ed,—something about his drinking at times, and riding at dusk down a by-road which decent people avoided,—but no one had verified them, so far as Abbie knew, and, anyway, people were probably jealous of him and his opportunities.

In that week of October on a Friday afternoon, when the hazel-brush was as brown-burnished as Abbie's hair, and the Big Woods a mass of scarlet and bronze and crimson, she closed the schoolhouse and left for home.

In the distance she could see the new, stylish, high-top buggy of Doctor Matthews going down the lane road where the honey-locusts, yellow now, bordered the north side of the Deal place. She was thinking that she could have ridden home with the doctor if she had been out a little earlier. Not that she cared, for it was pleasant walking. Who could believe that the guns of the war were booming in the South this Indian summer day? When nearly home she paused, turned abruptly, and climbing the stake-and-rider fence, walked through the oaks into the clearing where the October sun flecked down through leaf shadows. Not for several years had she visited the old grassy knoll between the huge trees. She went up to the top of the knoll now and faced an invisible audience in that old intangible dream which she always had with her. Half amused at her own childishness, half earnest in her actions, there in the seclusion of the woods, she unloosed from its binding ribbons the reddish-brown mass of her hair. She unbuttoned the top buttons of her lavender-sprigged delaine dress and pulled it down over the creamy whiteness of her shoulders, tucking in the edges to hold it. Then, with her reddish-bronze hair, with its overtones of gold, framing the Mayflower petals of her skin, and with her warm brown eyes half closed, Abbie Mackenzie threw back her head and sang:

"Oh, the Lady of the Lea,
Fair and young and gay was she,
Beautiful exceedingly,
The Lady of the Lea."

The notes rose like the nuptial flight of birds, notes of desire and a longing for their fulfillment.

"To her bower at last there came,
A youthful knight of noble name,
Hand and heart in hope to claim
And in love fell she."

They throbbed with the joy of life and the pathos of it, with the beauty of peace and the sadness of war.

"Still she put his suit aside,
So he left her in her pride,
And broken-hearted drooped and died,
The Lady—"

A twig snapped and the note snapped with it. Frightened, Abbie whirled to the sound. Ed Matthews stood near her, his blond face aflame. Abbie gave a startled cry, and in fright and embarrassment, clutched the neck of her gown. But Ed Matthews had her in his arms, was kissing her full red lips and the creamy Mayflower petals of her neck, burying his flushed face in the red-bronze of her hair.

"Abbie, . . . Abbie, . . . you coquette! . . . You're wonderful, . . . gorgeous. I love you. I never knew . . . I want you. . . . You're going with me. . . . You'll marry me. . . . I'll take you east . . . to New York. . . . Your voice . . . I didn't realize . . . You can have the best teachers . . . I have to go back to-morrow . . . Abbie . . . you *coquette* . . . ! And we have to-night left . . . to-night is ours . . ."

Swept away on the tide of Ed's passionate words, she seemed to be without thought or comprehension. When she could speak, she found herself saying almost without her own volition, "Don't, Ed, don't *touch* me. You've no right. *You've no right.*" She was trying to button the high neck of her dress, pushing Ed's protesting hand away, twisting up the red-brown curls of her hair. Ed's laughter disconcerted and frightened her. He seemed so very sure of himself,—and of her.

It was sundown when they reached the Mackenzie cabin. For a long time they stood in front of it, talking. Ed's flushed face bent to Abbie's.

"I *think* so, Ed, . . . but I'm not sure. It's sudden and, . . . when you come in the spring I'll know my own mind."

"You're playing with me. You *are* a coquette."

"No, Ed, . . . I'm *really* uncertain."

"Uncertain about marrying me?" Ed's opinion of himself was not what one would term feeble. "Uncertain about going to New York, . . . with *that* voice? . . ."

"Oh, Ed, *if* I went, . . ." Abbie was suddenly childish, wistful, "would I be a lovely lady?"

Ed Matthews' banter and his high-handedness were stilled, his passion and his ardor quieted. He bent and kissed Abbie's pretty tapering hand. "You would be a lovely lady," he said gently.

When he had gone, Mary and Mother Mackenzie drew Abbie in to tell them what it was all about.

Importuned to secrecy, Mary was excited beyond the completion of sentences. "Abbie . . . *you* . . . Doctor Ed Matthews . . . to go to New York . . . your voice . . . teachers in New York . . . it might be in the opera . . ."

Mother Mackenzie asked gravely, "Do you *love* him, acushla?"

Abbie turned burning cheeks to her Irish mother and clutched her plump shoulders "I don't know. Tell me, mother, what *is* love?"

"That," said Maggie O'Conner Mackenzie, "I canna tell ye. An' no one can tell ye. Sure, an' I mind an' I knew it though, mysel'. I look for you to know it, yoursel', Abbie."

Abbie went up to her loft room. She wanted to be alone. Love? Was this love? To be able to go to New York and study? Her voice . . . a new world . . . the world of courtly men and lovely ladies . . . of silken shawls . . . of strings of pearls . . . of flowing plumes. But that world also held Ed Matthews with his eyes that were not quite steady, with his disconcerting laugh and the vague, unproven rumors. But he loved her, that was certain. Or . . . was it so certain? His kisses . . . Abbie's face burned with the memory. She thought of Will Deal and the day he had left for war two years before. Will had kissed her, too—

Quite suddenly she wished she could talk the whole thing over with

Will Deal. Will would help her know her own mind,—help her understand what love was. Of all the people she knew in the whole world, Will was the most understanding. He was so steady,—so dependable. "Oh God, bring Will Deal safe home soon to help me know."

CHAPTER VI

☙ AND then the presidential campaign of '64 was on in full swing. Over in town there were parades and banners and torchlights and much bombastic oratory. General Sherman was close upon Atlanta and Grandpa Deal was close upon General Sherman. For he had been delegated by Governor Kirkwood to go to the first division of General Logan's Fifteenth Army Corps to bring the vote of the Iowa contingent back to the state. Many weeks elapsed before his return. Atlanta fell. All communication to the north was severed, for General Sherman had started on his wearisome march to the sea. And with the tramping columns rode Grandpa Deal on a horse whose mane was as black as Grandpa Deal's own bushy head. A veritable old man of the sea he looked upon his return, grotesque appearing, with the bag of ballots swung over his shoulder by a strap, a faded carpet-bag in his one hand,—in the bag the government's pay to many of the Iowa boys.

Abbie was "boarding around," and was at the Deal house for the week when Grandpa came. He told his experiences to the family in high glee, his ice-blue eyes twinkling behind the bushy brows. "I'd al'a's throw the old bag down," he would relate with silent chuckles, " 'n' give it a kick for extra measure, so's nobody'd allow the' was any value to it,—'n' all the time the' was two thousand four hundred and twenty-two dollars in its old insides."

"Did you," Abbie moistened dry red lips, "did you—happen to see Will?"

The chuckles died. Yes, he had seen Will, had in fact kept as close to Company B, 31st Iowa Regiment as he consistently could. He had tried to make Will ride the horse a few times when he was exhausted. He had sat around the campfire with him a few nights, when the boys sang and joked and told stories to keep up their spirits. "Was the awfulest dense pitch-pine smoke from them campfires ye'd ever see. Boys used to kinda apologize to me about 'em, bein' as how I was a sort o' guest on the march. But I'd al'a's tell 'em black smoke didn't interfere much with my complexion."

In a few minutes he said soberly: "Will's been caught stealin'."

"Stealing?" A sharp pang of apprehension went through Abbie. She and Grandma Deal turned to each other in mutual fright.

"Yes, sir, . . . stealin'." Grandpa Deal's forehead was puckered in agony.

"My boy stole?" Grándma's little worried face took on an added anxiety.

" 'Twas at Savannah. Provisions was one ear of corn to the man. There was transports layin' right out there in sight off the coast with food on for our boys. Couldn't get in 'til fortifications fell. 'N' then my boy . . ." His voice shook in mock sorrow. "My boy went to the corral," the eyes began to twinkle, " 'n' stole two ears of corn from some army mules 'n' boiled the corn for supper."

Grandma was provoked. "You ain't got no call to be scarin' me that way," she sputtered. "You ain't got no call to spend your life jokin'."

"Oh, come, now, Ma. Better to laugh than to cry. Will maybe'll be remorse-stricken all the days o' his life,—to hear the brayin' in his conscience of them poor, helpless, skinny, mouse-colored government mules."

When Abbie was starting for school, Grandpa casually followed her out. "Had a good visit with Will." He cocked one eye up at the well-sweep.

"Did you?"

"Yep. He wanted to know how all the Iowa folks was."

"Did he?"

"Yep. More specifically, he wanted to know how all the Blackhawk folks was."

"Did he?"

"Yep. Collectively, he wanted to know how all the folks in our community was."

"Did he?"

"Yep. Individually, he wanted to know how *you* was."

"Oh, . . . did he?"

"Yep. He says to me," . . . Grandpa carelessly picked up a handful of snow and threw it at a rooster. "If I can rec'lect his words exact, they was, 'How's my Abbie-girl'?"

Abbie walked over the crusted snow in a maze of conflicting emotions,—behind the hard little stays of her waist a burning letter from

Ed Matthews and plans for her future,—in her heart, the memory of Will Deal's one kiss, more poignant than either.

A new minister and his wife came to the growing town that fall and made a round of calls among the country folk. They were Vermont people. The Reverend Ezra Whitman was dignified, pompous, a little pedantic. Mrs. Whitman was refined, soft-spoken, a graduate of a girls' seminary. She took a great interest in Abbie, so that the young teacher began going into town to see her. She found that Mrs. Whitman was something of an artist. The little new frame house in which the couple lived held several oil paintings that seemed the acme of art to Abbie, and there was always an unfinished canvas on an easel. The paints fascinated the girl. She longed to get her hands on them. Something in her eyes must have flashed its unspoken message, for one day Mrs. Whitman asked her if she would like to try her hand with the brush. It thrilled her beyond words. Crudely enough, but with some intuitive knowledge, she did a little clump of trees on a piece of waste canvas.

"I'll never be satisfied until I can do it well," she said. From that time on, at Mrs. Whitman's invitation, she began painting with her, riding over to town when she could, tramping the two and one-half miles through slush or mud when there was no other way to go.

"It's your voice, though, that shows the greater promise," Mrs. Whitman told her. "I wish I could help you with that, too. Mr. Whitman's sister will know what to tell you when she comes. She teaches voice in my old seminary."

And when the sister came, and heard Abbie, she was enthusiastic. "It's good," she told them all. "It's more than good. It's splendid. You can do really big things with it. You must try sometime to come East for lessons."

But Abbie was too bashful to tell her that already she had an opportunity to go to New York to study. Her praise had its influence in Abbie's decision. If her voice was really as good as Mrs. Whitman thought—— And so, on the day in April that Lee surrendered, Abbie Mackenzie surrendered, too. She wrote the letter to Ed Matthews that she would marry him. When she had sent it over to town to be mailed she went to her old grassy knoll in the clearing to sing. But she did not seem to sing well. Something seemed lacking. The melody sounded flat, unlovely, like a song from which the soul had fled.

In the weeks that followed, Abbie felt restless, nervous and a little sad. She told herself that it was on account of Lincoln's assassination.

And indeed, some of it was, for the whole settlement mourned. But not all of her mood was due to the President's tragic death.

On a day in May, with the honey-locusts all in bloom, she stood at the door of the schoolhouse, and watched the train from the east shriek its way across Grandpa Deal's newly planted corn-fields. She washed her blackboard, set her desk to rights, locked the schoolhouse, and started home. And, quite suddenly, she saw some one coming down the lane. Abbie stood still, her heart pounding tumultuously with the uncertainty of the figure's identity. The world was a lovely painting of sunshine, blue skies, honey-locusts, bees on the blossoms,—a palpitating, throbbing world of spring.

Will Deal in his blue soldier's suit was coming toward her. She could not take her eyes from his face. He was smiling, questioningly, a little quizzically, and with something that was infinitely more tender. He slipped the knapsack from his back and held out his arms. Swiftly, lightly, Abbie went to him.

"Oh, Will, don't let me, . . . don't let me do it," Abbie began sobbing a little wildly, almost hysterically. For two years Abbie Mackenzie had not shed a tear and now she was crying wildly in Will Deal's arms. Will held her close, smoothed her hair back from her creamy-white forehead.

"Do what, Abbie-girl?" He was all gentleness, all desirous of understanding.

"Marry Ed Matthews."

Will caught her fiercely, held her closer, kissed her red lips, laid his face to her cheek that was like Mayflower petals. And Abbie thought of ships that come home to the harbor.

"I should say I won't. He could buy me in the draft . . . but he can't buy my Abbie."

"I was afraid all the time, Will."

Will held her close,—smoothed her red-brown hair.

"Afraid of what, Abbie-girl?"

"I don't know. Just afraid."

"You're not afraid with me?"

"Not with you, Will. Why is that?"

"Because I love you and you love me."

"Yes, that's it . . . and I'm not afraid."

"Of life with me, Abbie-girl?"

"Not of anything, Will, with you."

"And you'll always love me?"

"Always, Will, . . . in this life and the next."

The afternoon sun rays lengthened across the fields. The honey-locusts dropped in the lane. The bees made noisy forages into the hearts of the blossoms. Will and Abbie lingered, all the melody of life a-tune, all the heaven that they desired, there in the lane under the honey-locusts.

CHAPTER VII

THEY were married on a winter's day of 1865, when Abbie was not quite nineteen and Will was twenty-three. The day was mild, even warm, a phenomenon for that time of year. "A weather-breeder," every one called it. A few men shed their coats and worked in their shirtsleeves during the middle of the day, so that they might tell of it in years to come.

Maggie Mackenzie and Abbie and Mary set the furniture out of the log house, so there would be room for the guests. Janet's two children were designated as a committee to keep the chickens off the various pieces, but so excited were the youngsters over the elaborate culinary preparations, that during a period of the abandonment of their posts, an old hen flew up on top of the high boy and laid an egg in the work-basket.

Abbie had made two new dresses from cloth sent out from Chicago. One was a wine-colored merino, the other a brown alpaca, both made fashionably full over hoop-skirts, with panniers at the side. A new little hat, the shape of a butter-bowl, with ribbon bows on it, added much to her pride.

Toward evening of the great day, Abbie was all of a-flutter because there were so many things to do. There was still water to be heated in a boiler on the stove and the wash-tub to be brought in for her bath. She had to skim a pan of milk, so that she could make the skin of her face and hands soft with cream. And she nearly forgot the flour she was to brown in the oven with which to powder her body. Basil, fifteen now, helped take the hot water on its perilous journey up the loft ladder with the saplings nailed across for steps, and lifted up the wooden tub on his strong young shoulder.

In spite of the unusually warm day, it was a little chilly for one's ablutions in the loft room, but Abbie was young and vigorous and used to it. She put on her muslin chemise and pantalets and her tight little stays, holding her breath until she could lace them so that her two hands could almost span her waist. Into her bosom she slipped a little netting sack of dried rose petals, which smelled faintly and tantalizingly of bygone Junes. Then over her head she dropped and fastened the long collapsible hoop-skirt, with its nineteen bands of white covered wires. There were three white muslin petticoats, starched almost to chinaware stiffness and ruffled to the knees. Abbie and her mother had hemmed seventy-two yards of ruffles by hand. Grandma Deal had one of the Howe stitching machines, but not all families could afford one. Then, at last, she put on her wine-colored merino with its countless rows of flutings of the same material and side panniers.

She was patting her hair into place and pulling out the long shoulder curl, when her mother came puffingly, slowly, up the loft ladder. Mother was getting old now. She was forty-seven,—heavy and placid. Her fat round face in its white cap with strings tied under her two chins, appeared in the loft opening. Abbie went over to her and took her hand, so that she would not fall. She saw that her mother had the calf-skin covered box in her hand.

It was several moments before Maggie Mackenzie could talk, puffingly, after the climb. "Abbie, I want ye to have the pearls. I'm savin' the fan for Mary. Janet has the breast-pin, you know, and Belle the shawl. Belle always stuck 'n' hung fer the shawl. And the pearls are fer you. Ye'll ne'er starve as long as ye have 'em." She opened the little hairy-skinned chest and took out a small velvet box and from it the pearls themselves. She twined them through her short stubby fingers, their creamy shimmer incongruous in the plump peasant hand. "They were Basil's fine mother's. After she died, . . . Basil gave 'em to me in the days of wealth. Sure, but it wasn't the wealth that brought us happiness. Many's the time I've hated it . . . longin' for a little house somewhere, . . . out of the wind 'n' rain, . . . 'n' not many things at all, at all. . . ."

There were tears in Abbie's brown eyes when she took them. She held their creamy luster in the palm of her firm young hand. Into her mind came that old admiration for Isabelle Anders-Mackenzie. The touch of the jewels seemed to bring her near, to call up the vision of the lovely lady who was wearing them in the wide gold frame,—the lovely lady with the sweeping velvet and the long flowing plume and the fingers that tapered at the ends. Some day she was going to be like her. Some day she, too, would be lovely and gracious and wealthy. All of life was before her. All the future was hers. And that future now held Will, with his steady gray eyes,—Will Deal who was like a quiet harbor. Song, soft and meltingly tender came to her lips:

"Oh, the Lady of the Lea,
Fair and young and gay was she,"

She held the pearls up to the wine-colored merino and looked in the small oblong glass.

"Beautiful exceedingly,
The Lady of the Lea."

Then she turned to her mother. Her face was flushed, tender. "Thank you, Mother, . . . so much, . . . I'll keep them always. But with the dark dress and the high neck, . . . I'll just not wear them to-night. After awhile when Will and I are wealthy, I'll wear them. And maybe we'll have, . . ." Some reticences existing at the time, the blood swept Abbie's face, ". . . maybe we'll have a daughter some day and *she* can wear them on her wedding night, . . . in white satin . . . and all the things that go with it . . ."

Abbie swept across the dingy loft room, her hoops swinging in wiry bounces. She knelt down by her mother's chair, her skirts forming a huge circular mound, and laid her head against the older woman's. "And besides, Mother, *you* understand, don't you . . . when you follow your heart you don't need *pearls* to make you happy?"

It was time now. Abbie went down the ladder with the saplings nailed across for steps. She had to go backward so that her hoops could navigate the descension with some degree of modesty. The fiddlers were playing, "The Girl I Left Behind Me." Will, looking big and fine and handsome, was there in the black suit Grandma Deal had made him. Grandpa Deal, with his one arm and the kindly twinkle in his ice-blue eyes, was there,—joking. Grandma Deal, in a black cap with black strings tied under the face that was covered with the faint tracing of hosts of wrinkles, was there. She was nervous, fretful, scolding. Why didn't the men stand back? Why didn't they shut that door? Where was that preacher keeping himself? A thousand mental worries like a thousand gnats irritating the peace of her mind. Whole families had come in wagons. Regina Deal and her beau and Dr. and Mrs. Matthews were the only ones who had come in high-top buggies. When the doctor and his wife came in, there was a little buzz of excitement, some whispering that they wondered whether or not it was true that young Dr. Ed had wanted Abbie.

A solemn hush fell on the company.

"Inasmuch as we are gathered here together in the sight of the Lord." Suddenly, Abbie wanted to halt the ceremony. There seemed nothing in her mind but that odd thought of a wind rushing by, a wind she could not stop,—Time, going by,—Time which she could not stay. Stop Time for a minute, until she could think what queer thing was happening to her.

"Do you take this woman, . . . sickness, . . . health, . . . 'til death, . . ." What a queer thing to talk about now,—death,—when it was life that was before them ". . . this man . . . lawfully wedded husband . . . ?"

"I do." *But, oh Will . . . Will . . . who are you? Do I know you?*

And then, quite suddenly, Abbie Mackenzie was Abbie Deal. The fiddlers played "Money Musk," and "Turkey in the Straw." The company danced,—square dances of intricate design. Grandpa Deal wanted to take a partner, but Grandma Deal said no, it was foolish for an old man, fifty-five. But Maggie O'Conner Mackenzie danced, alone, lightly and puffingly, in the middle of the floor, to:

> *"Oh the days of the Kerry dancing,*
> *Oh the days when my heart was young."*

There were biscuits and chickens and cakes and cider to be eaten from tables formed by putting long boards over saw-horses. And then, more dancing.

Will Deal's dark serious face bent low above Abbie's creamy-petaled, flushed one. A long row of love-apples stood in the window.

CHAPTER VIII

WILL and Abbie drove to Grandpa Deal's in a two-wheeled cart behind an old white mare. So slowly did they drive that several passed them on the river road,—Grandpa and Grandma Deal and Louise in a lumber-wagon with a fine big team, and Regina Deal and her beau in the new high-top buggy. Grandpa laughed and called out some saucy jokes, but Grandma told him to hush his foolishness and 'tend to his driving.

Will and Abbie had the front bedroom of the big five-roomed log-house for their own. In the weeks that followed, Will went about the regular farm work for his father, and Abbie put her young shoulder to the wheel of the housework. For Will's sake she tried to meet his mother's petty nagging with forbearance. But it wore on her like the constant dripping of water on a stone. Grandma Deal was a chronic grumbler and a born pessimist. She saw bad signs in Nature's most ordinary activities. If a dog ate grass, if a bird flew through the house, if the moon rose from a cloud, the direst things were about to happen. And life meant nothing to her, apparently, but work. The first break of day and the last ray of sunlight saw her at the hard tasks of the housework. And when all other duties seemed done, she immediately brought out a box of intricate quilt blocks, The Rose of Sharon and The Star of Bethlehem, The Rising Sun or the Log Cabin. For Grandpa Deal, Abbie had nothing but love. His Yankee drollness could always bring a bubbling laugh to her lips and his stump of an arm gave her added tenderness toward him. Looking at the two, she used to wonder how he could keep so cheerful. He never crossed Grandma, never argued with her in any way but jovially, never lost his temper. "Now, Mother," he would say, "can't you see the funny side of that?"

"No, I can't," she would retort, "and neither could you if you'd stop your foolish jokin' and keep your mind on your work."

It never went into a quarrel. When it approached one, Grandpa would go whistling out to the barn to work. Yes, Abbie loved Will's father better than his mother. In the same way did she enjoy and dislike Louise and Regina. Louise was energetic, pleasant, peace-loving. Regina was selfish, a mischief-maker and a shirk. The young farmer with whom Regina was now keeping company had come first to see Louise. Although Abbie knew little of the circumstances, she felt quite definitely sure that Regina had maneuvered the transposition with adroitness.

All spring, Abbie, fearful that the family might think she was not doing her part, took more than her share of the household duties. She helped boil the maple sap down into sugar, swept and dusted, baked and cooked, and took over the entire care of the chickens. Louise worked with her faithfully, but Regina slipped out from under the tasks with all the agility of an eel.

And then Abbie was not well, . . .

"She's not doing her share," Abbie overheard Grandma's sputtering. "I told you it was too good to be true. I said all the time it wouldn't last."

"Now, Mother," Grandpa's voice came gently, patiently, "I think I know what's the matter. You wouldn't want her to overdo."

"Overdo, nothing. I brought eight babies into the world. And I ain't ever seen the time anybody cared if *I* was overdoin'."

"Now, Mother, I wouldn't say that. It was hard, but you was healthy and I always got help for you."

"Yes, a passel o' neighbor girls that wasn't worth their weight in salt. Now, I s'pose it'll fall on me to take care o' Abbie. Noboby cares if I die or not."

Abbie heard Grandpa go whistling down to the barn. Then she threw herself on the bed and cried tears of sensitiveness and discontent.

More and more she wanted her own home. If it were no better than the old sheep shed that she lived in one summer when she was a little girl, at least it would be their own. Will was good to her,—so kind and understanding, but he did not seem to sense how much she wanted a home of her own.

Abbie's baby was born in January of 1867. Roads were drifted and Doc Matthews, in a coonskin cap with the tail down his back, came on a horse, his saddle-bags full of quinine and calomel.

Nature had to take its course without much aid from its handmaid, Science—and Nature took a fiendish course with Abbie. Two days and a night she wrestled with Nature, as Jacob wrestled with the angel. And then she had a son. Lying there after her ordeal, with the baby on her arm, she knew the age-old surge of mother-love. All her old love of life seemed to concentrate on one thing,—the little soft, helpless bundle. The world of romance, of courtly men and lovely ladies was a world of unreality,—and only Will and the little son were worth her thoughts.

Mackenzie Deal, they named him, but it was too big a mouthful for so small a bit of humanity, and it was not long until every one had shortened it to Mack. Will was inordinately proud of him. Grandpa Deal and Louise came in several times a day to see him, but Regina was not overly interested. Grandma Deal sputtered about the care of him. Why didn't Abbie keep more shawls around him? Why did she let the sun shine across the bed that way? Why did she ask the doctor all those questions when he didn't know as much about babies as a mother?

When Abbie was up, life grew richer, more full. Her voice took on a mellowness. With the baby in the high-backed wooden rocker, she crooned old lullabies which Maggie O'Conner had brought from the whins of Bally-poreen.

As little Mack grew that year and crept and then stood on fat wobbling legs by the chairs, Abbie's desire for a home of her own reached gigantic proportions.

"You know, Will," she brought up the subject in the spring, a little shyly, half hesitatingly, "I wish we could have a home of our own. Your folks . . ." She dropped her eyes that Will might not see the telltale evasion in them,—"are good to me, but I'd so like my own little house. It needn't be half as big . . . or nice . . ."

To Abbie's surprise Will turned on her in a sort of suppressed fury. "I don't like it either, you needn't think. I'm thinking every day what to do. What am I here? A hired man for Father. I'll never get anywhere. And now we've got the baby . . . I'm glad you've been the one to bring it up. It decides me. We're going out to Nebraska to start for ourselves."

"*Nebraska?*" It had the sound of South Africa.

"Yes, . . . there are too many settlers here. And as long as I'm anywhere around here I'd always have to work for Father. It ain't right, I tell you. And another thing, Abbie, our boy sha'n't be tied down. He can do what he wants. And we're going to Nebraska,—you and I and little Mack."

"Oh, no, Will, not out there. Anywhere around here, but not to that far-off place. Why, Will, . . . my mother . . . my brothers and sisters . . . your folks . . . they're *all* around here . . ."

"You can come back to visit them, I promise you that, Abbie, whenever you want to. It's a wonderful opportunity. It's the poor man's country. We can get railroad land dirt cheap . . . or lease school lands near the river or even push on farther west and homestead."

"It's dangerous, Will. There are Indians."

"Well, so are there Indians here. A whole camp of 'em over by Fisher's Lake."

"But they're peaceable, . . . and those out there . . . Oh, Will . . ."

"It's been fourteen years since the government made the treaty with the Indians out there . . . fourteen years ago, they gave up their title to all that land out there bordering on the Missouri. I guess when it's been that long settling, we'll find it in pretty good shape. . . ." Will was talking definitely, stubbornly, as though the question were settled. Abbie was so frightened at the turn the argument was taking that she studiously kept her voice calm.

"The baby, Will, . . . we have to think of him. There won't be good schools . . . or doctors . . ."

"It *is* of him I'm thinking . . . the big future for him out in the newer country. He'll be a farmer. All the Deals have always been for the land. . . ."

Fathers have always thought it,—that their sons belong only to them. Small wonder that Will Deal made the mistake of forgetting something, forgetting that the baby was also a Mackenzie, that his mother held her head as Isabelle Anders-Mackenzie had helds hers in the wide gold frame,—that her hair had the gold-brown tints of the lovely lady,—that her long slender fingers tapered at the ends.

"But, Will . . ." Never had Abbie so thoroughly felt that queer sensation of being swept along by the wind which she could not stop,—of Time, which she could not stay. "Will . . . my voice . . . Mrs. Whitman . . . Every one thinks I ought to do something with it. And my painting, Will . . . to go away out there . . ."

"Oh, we'll find you good teachers out there. No, Abbie, I've been thinking it over a long time and it's my chance. We're going in the summer. I'll be getting everything ready. The army money will buy the wagon and oxen and the land, . . . and I'll make up my mind soon about it, . . . whether to buy near the river, or homestead farther out."

So Will had said he was going West. The era of this freedom had not dawned. Abbie Deal's man had said he was going to Nebraska, and Abbie had to go too. It was as simple as that, then.

They began preparations, with Abbie still protesting that Nebraska was too far away and too uncivilized.

"It's been a state since March of last year," Will gave equal arguments in its favor. "They've got the site all chosen for the new capital. It's named Lincoln. Queer when you stop to think about it that an old friend of Father's should ever get big enough to be president and have a town named after him,—ain't it?"

But Abbie was not thinking of the recently martyred President. "Yes, but they say the place they've chosen is away out on the prairie with just two or three log houses." She was not so willing to believe the best of the infant state as was Will.

He sought out all the good news he could find to cheer her. Once he brought an Omaha newspaper. "Talk about a new country, . . ." he was enthusiastic. "Everything's as citified as can be in Omaha, . . . and we won't be so far from there. The paper says it has fifteen thousand inhabitants, . . . a regular city. How's this for you, eleven churches and five schools, and five banks. It says, 'Dealers in gold dust, bullion, coin and exchange.' And the Union Pacific's got an overland mail route clear to Laramie, with two trains every day."

"Yes, and you read on a little farther. You're leaving out some things. I saw that paper myself, Will Deal."

Will laughed. "Oh, five breweries and sixty saloons, . . . that ain't so bad. And besides there's a hoop factory."

"Well, I don't care about that. They might even go out of style some day, although Regina thinks they never will. I wouldn't care if they did. Even if they do make you look stylish, they're not comfortable."

And all the time Abbie was getting together her little possessions, and Will was preparing the outfit. He had intended to make a new ox-yoke, had in fact already cut the maple, and some pliable hickory for the bows, when Mother Mackenzie gave him the sturdy yoke that she had used fourteen years before on the trip out from Illinois. He painted the names of his ox team, "Red" and "Baldy," on it and in the center, "Nebraska, 1868."

After some correspondence with an old army friend, Will bought his land, "sight unseen." He was pleased with his purchase. It was railroad land and he paid two dollars an acre for it. Some people from Michigan by the name of Lutz were getting two quarter-sections near him.

"It's only thirty-five miles from Nebraska City and about ten miles from Weeping Water. The county seat, Plattsmouth, has a hotel and some houses and a grist mill . . . It only takes a couple of hours to grind a sack of corn."

"Yes, providing you've got the *corn*." Abbie could not yet enter heartily into the plans.

"Oh, we'll have the corn all right. They say the soil is the finest and blackest you ever saw."

And then, before they were ready, Abbie knew that she was to be a mother again.

On a morning in July they started. Red and Baldy, in front of Grandpa Deal's, stood hitched to the prairie-schooner in their stupid, stolid way. All the possessions were in the wagon, covered now with its new white canvas. Every one was there to see them off. Mother

Mackenzie, with her pudding-bag-shaped body and her blue-black Irish eyes and her white cap, brought the calf-skin-covered box and the Seth Thomas clock with the little brown church painted on the glass.

"You take the chest, Abbie . . . I want ye to have it. You can keep the pearls in it. And the clock, too, . . . it seems like it's yours. I mind how ye was al'a's sayin' no one could stop Time."

The Reverend and Mrs. Whitman came. Mrs. Whitman had a box of paints and some canvas for Abbie. "Keep on with your little painting talent, Abbie," she told her.

"Yes," the Reverend Whitman said, a little pompously, "and with your music. We can do with our lives whatever we will, you know."

"Yes, I know," agreed Abbie.

Grandma Deal, in her black cap, was sputtering because she had not had time to put her bread in loaves. Why didn't they tie the chicken-coop on better? Why hadn't they started the day before? The weather looked as though it might storm. What did they bother with a dog for? There, a bird flew in front of the oxen,—that was a bad sign.

Doctor Matthews stopped in his new top-buggy.

Grandpa Deal's ice-blue eyes were clouded with sadness. "Good luck to you, my boy. And Abbie, a real daughter couldn't have been kinder."

Abbie's heart was in her throat. Oh, stop the wind rushing by. Stop Time for a few minutes, until she could think whether this move was the thing to do. Life was not right. It was not meant that you should leave your own this way. It was not meant that weeks and weeks of travel should separate you from your folks. The baby, little Mack, would forget Mother Mackenzie and kind old Grandpa Deal. And the next baby would never know them.

Only one thing gave her strength for the parting. Only one thing gave her courage to make the long journey to the raw new state. Her love for Will. Abbie's love for her husband had retained its sweetness and its ardor. And in her heart she knew that as much as she cared for her people,—as dear as were her mother and sisters and the old settlement to her,—they did not outweigh her love for him. If being with Will meant making a new home in a far, unsettled country, why, then, she chose to journey bravely to the far, unsettled country.

Abbie threw up her head fearlessly. "Well, we're ready."

"Good-by . . ."

"Take good care of little Mack."

"Oh, Abbie, Abbie . . ."

"Mother . . . good-by . . ."

"Janet, dear, . . . Mary . . . Belle . . . Louise . . . Thank you all for all you did . . . Good-by . . . Yes, we'll write as soon as . . . Kiss Grandma, Mack-baby . . ."

Will was boyishly gay. For the first time he felt free from "the folks,"—his own master.

"Well, here we go." He cracked the long black snaky-looking whip. "We'll come back rich." He laughed in excitement.

The wagon lurched,—steadied, moved on.

"Good-by . . . good-by . . . good-by . . ."

Hands were in the air,—a sunbonnet waved,—an apron was thrown over some one's head. There was sobbing. Abbie's hand was on her hard, dry throat. It felt as though it must burst. Stop the wind. Stop Time for a minute. The wagon lurched ahead.

Far back in the road Abbie could still see the little group, painted flatly against the white of the fence and the green of the honey-locusts.

Will's eyes, full of the light of hope and courage, looked to the west. But Abbie's, tear-misted, clung to the east.

CHAPTER IX

☙ IT WAS three weeks later, on a hot morning, that Will and Abbie and the other two families, whose land was to join theirs, broke camp, twenty miles out of Plattsmouth, where they had crossed the Platte on the ferry. The journey over western Iowa had been one endless lurching through acres of dry grass and sunflowers, thickets of sumac, wild plum and Indian currant. And now, save for the little clump of natural growth near the wagons, there was still not a tree in sight, not a shrub nor bush, a human being nor any living thing,—nothing but the coarse prairie grass.

The heads of the two Lutz families were brothers, Oscar and Henry. Oscar had a wife and three small children, Henry, a young bride and her little six-year-old orphaned nephew. Grandpa Lutz, a mild-mannered, gentle old man, had also come into the new country with his sons. They had traveled from Michigan, the two younger men by wagons, several weeks prior to the others. The women, children and the old gentleman had gone by train to Quincy, Illinois, where they had taken a river steamer to Hannibal, Missouri, crossing the Missouri to St. Joseph and taking a boat up the Missouri to Plattsmouth. There the men, having preceded the party, had waited a week for the boat to appear.

"I'd go down every day and kick the post the boat was goin' to tie up to," Oscar Lutz was telling Will.

Will laughed. "What for?"

"Oh, I don't know. Had to take all the delay out on somethin' or somebody, so I kicked the post instead o' Henry, here."

Sarah, the bride, was a pretty girl. Her hair was crow-black, her cheeks pink as prairie roses, her little black beady eyes had merry wrinkles of laughter around them. Life seemed a joke to her. This forenoon she had decorated the wagon with Indian paint brush, which burned like flames of fire against the dingy white of the canvas cover.

Abbie, in her illness from heat and fatigue and pregnancy, could only sit and wonder how young Sarah Lutz could be so happy and active. Nothing seemed to worry or frighten her. Apparently she had not even been disturbed by the story of the graves at Eight-Mile Grove,—the seven graves under the little clump of trees fenced around with slabs which the blacksmith there had told them were brought from the saw-mill at Rock Bluff. They had asked him innocently enough who was buried there. Abbie almost shivered now at the thought of his answer.

"Claim jumpers 'n horse thieves 'n sich," he had said indifferently. And, shifting his tobacco, had added definitely, "Hung. Vigilance committee." And more grimly specific, "To that there tree."

"Hung?" Some one had repeated in the silence that followed.

"Yep. Hang 'em in summer," he had explained cheerfully, " 'n' poke 'em under the ice in winter."

Abbie shuddered again at the memory of the grim voice.

The journey on from camp was across the vast prairie itself. As the morning passed, the heat rolled over Abbie in waves like the rippling of the grass. She looked out from the canvas to see Will plodding along, his shoulders drooping. He had not called back any gay cheery thing all forenoon. The grass out there,—would it never cease to wave? There were four rhythmic beats like music, but music which irritated rather than soothed one: *Blow . . . wave . . . ripple . . . dip.* It beat upon her brain, so that she turned wearily away from the sight. And then, as one fascinated by something distasteful, she looked again. Yes, it never ceased from those four beats: *Blow, . . . wave, . . . ripple, . . . dip, . . . blow . . . wave . . . ripple . . . dip . . .*

Little Mack was sleeping, and Abbie dropped over beside him. She closed her eyes and kept her mind on the lane beside Grandpa Deal's with the honey-locusts and the maples, on the black walnut grove back of his house and the hazel-nut thickets around the schoolhouse. How cool and pleasant the schoolhouse looked with the green shutters against the white siding! How good it would seem to draw water from Grandpa Deal's well. In fancy she pulled up the bucket with the windlass and put her face into its cold, dark depths.

She slept,—and sleeping, walked in the cool of the maples and oaks in the Big Woods, picked anemones and creamy white Mayflowers. She dropped down in a bed of cool ferns behind Janet Graves' house in the timber. Suddenly, the wagon creaked and lurched and she opened her eyes. Hurriedly sitting up, only half cognizant of where she was, she looked out through the canvas. The sun shone hot on the flat prairie. *Blow, . . . wave, . . . ripple, . . . dip. . . .* An intense nausea seized her,—the *mal de mer* of the prairie-schooner passenger lurching over the hot, dry inland sea.

Later in the forenoon they sighted a fringe of trees against the unclouded sky. It seemed an oasis,—or was it a mirage to vanish when they should come to it?

"The Weeping Water," Henry Lutz called back. And they knew they were getting near to the new home.

They crossed the shallow, winding stream not far from a stone mill. A man with milk-pails in his hands paused to watch the cavalcade. Will, walking by his ox team, was wet to the boot-tops.

The man grinned and called out jovially: "You've got your baptism of the new country now. You're branded. You'll never go back."

"I don't want to go back," Will called out with equal jocosity. Abbie in the wagon almost moaned from nausea, heat and homesickness.

On the other side of the stream there stood a team of oxen hitched to a covered wagon so odd-looking, that even Abbie sat up in interest. The wagon-box was a rowboat painted a gaudy blue, the bow curving toward the stolid oxen's buttocks, the stern forming the base of the rear canvas doorway. A man with his wife and two babies waited for the others to come up. Gus Reinmueller, he said his name was, and jerking an indifferent thumb toward his wife, he gave a laconic, "My voman, Christine."

Christine seemed as stolid as the oxen, her face as patiently expressionless. One could not have told whether she was old or young. Her colorless hair was braided in small braids and wound flat from ear to ear, looking like a small oval-shaped rug pinned on the back of her head.

This was the third family, then, to be going up into the same section with the Deals. And together, after a lunch, the wagons journeyed on to the west. In a long, straggling line they journeyed stolidly and silently toward the sun. Of them all, only Sarah Lutz sometimes called out a cheery comment. Abbie lay on the wagon bottom, so ill with nausea and heat, that it seemed she could never again take any interest in life.

Toward evening another long fringe of trees penciled itself against the dipping sun.

"Stove Creek," Henry Lutz called back. And they knew they were at their destination.

There were old buffalo wallows along the creek banks, shallow declivities, where the huge beasts had rolled and stamped out the mud. The sight of buffalo chips, too, reminded them that the time was not long past since the shaggy fellows had ambled leisurely along the creek bed. They crossed the creek, which was little more than a ravine now, with its few inches of water. And then Henry Lutz, who was in the lead, stopped.

"Well, here we are," he called when Will and Abbie had caught up with him. "This is yours." He had a rude paper plan in his hand. "Mine lies over there to the west. Oscar's is to the north of mine, and Reinmueller's,—" Gus and Christine had come up in the ridiculous boat wagon. "Reinmueller's is exactly south of Deal's."

Abbie crawled out of the wagon-box. She was stiff and ill and her head ached from the blinding sunlight. Sarah Lutz, with her round rosy cheeks and her beady black eyes, was out of her wagon, too, and over to Abbie's.

"Well, you're home." She was chuckling in her merry way. "This is where you live,—and my good gracious,—you've got callers." She shook hands with Abbie in mock formality. "May I come in and sit a while? Yes, thank you, I'll take the rocking-chair, Mrs. Deal. Yes, thanks, I'll have a cup of tea."

It made Abbie laugh a little, too, the nonsense of it at such a time. And then, "Boo!" Abbie squealed and jumped and ran for the wagon. A little dark, lizard-shaped thing had darted close to her feet with the speed of lightning.

"They're just swifts," Will told her, "as harmless as mice."

"Yes, and just as horrid," Abbie called back.

They camped in a group for the night. It made quite a party: Will, Abbie and little Mack, the Oscar Lutzes with their three children, Henry and Sarah Lutz with Grandpa Lutz and little Dan, the orphaned nephew, Gus and Christine Reinmueller and their two babies.

The wagons formed a circle, with a single campfire in the center. The sun slipped down behind the rim of the world. One of the men found a spring in the creek bed and brought water. The others fed the horses and led them down to drink. The women folks got supper and washed the plates and cups at the side of the creek bed. The children were put to sleep in the wagons and the older people gathered around the fire. The stars came out, pale yellow flowers in the sky's own prairie.

A coyote howled. Another answered. It made Abbie think of a night on the journey from Illinois when she was eight, and yet this was different. Then, they had been close to the woods,—the sheltering woods. They had heard all the little night creatures at work, all the tiny rustlings of the timber. But this, paradoxically, was a silent noise. There was complete silence,—save for those distant coyotes. Silence,—save for a faint sound of shivering grass. Silence, so deep, that it roared in its vast vacuum. Silence,—grass,—stars. The group around the fire seemed suddenly too small to be alone in the still vastness, too inadequate and helpless.

What if—? Even as her fear formed itself into thought, she saw through the shadows a figure—and another—and others steal with panther-like tread between the wagons and the creek bed.

CHAPTER X

ABBIE could frame no words. She could only reach forth her hand and touch Will's arm, a nightmare of fear upon her. Will and the other men of the party were also looking toward the shadowy figures in the dark.

"They're friendly," Will whispered, "there's nothing to be afraid of."

Friendly? Were they friendly?

All night the Indians camped near the creek bed a little to the north. Abbie, with Mack upon her arm, did not close her eyes. Only a year and a half before, the Fort Phil Kearney massacre had occurred. Only two months before, Red Cloud had sent word that he would not sign the great Fort Laramie treaty. They were so much nearer hostile Indians here than back home. You couldn't tell from what tribe these were. You couldn't tell in the dark how many there were. All night Abbie lay in an agony of fear, her body tense, her little son at her breast.

In the morning, fears were dissipated. If there had been any evil from them it would have been during the night. They proved to be a small group of Pawnees, with their squaws and papooses. They had dozens of skinned chickens across their ponies, the flies thick upon them.

One of Henry Lutz's horses was missing from the bunch which had been staked together. After a half-concealed conference among the men folks, it was deemed wiser to accept the loss and not question the matter. One of the braves evidently had ridden away on it. The Indians ate, broke camp, came over to the settlers and examined their outfits. A brave pointed to Oscar Lutz's wife, who was not exactly dainty in size, and shrugged massive shoulders jovially, at which the other bucks showed symptoms of ingrowing mirth. They took their time to peer into all the wagons. One man picked up a little bright-colored shoulder shawl of Sarah Lutz's and coolly transferred it to the shoulders of his squaw. The others gave a few grunts of satisfaction, fell into a long straggling line and started toward the northwest, the red and black of the appropriated shawl growing fainter in the distance.

Abbie wondered if she ever again would pass through such a fearsome night.

As Henry Lutz had said, the Reinmueller place was south of the Deal acreage and his own joined it at the west. Abbie was glad to find that Sarah Lutz was the one who was to live nearer to her. She had taken a great fancy to the bride with the round rosy face, the jet black hair and the little beady black eyes that seemed always twinkling. For Christine Reinmueller she held no great liking. Christine was uncouth, not quite clean, her little tight braids wound flat from ear to ear, greasy looking.

The wagons were now each driven onto the families' respective holdings, forming little homes on wheels until the rude houses would be finished.

As far as eye could see, the land lay in long rolling swells, unlike the monotonous flatness which characterized part of the state farther to the west of which they had heard.

There was nothing to be seen in any direction but the prairie grass and the few native trees which traced the vagrant wanderings of Stove

Creek. The undulating land covered with prairie grass, the straggling line of trees along the creek bed and the cloudless sky composed the entire picture,—these, and the Deal, Reinmueller and Lutz covered wagons,—little toys in the vastness of the lonely prairie.

Gus and Christine Reinmueller set about at once making a dug-out at the end of a ravine near the creek bed. They dug into the low hillside, set sturdy tree trunks a short way from the opening and covered the top with poles cut from the branches of trees, across which they packed a solid roofing of sod. Into this, with only the hard dirt floor, and the one opening, they moved their few possessions and their two baby boys. To Abbie it seemed that they were burrowing in like moles. But Gus was too anxious to get to work on the land to put much time on living quarters.

The Lutz family began a frame house at once, Henry and his brother both working on Henry's, so that when it was finished, the two families could live in it while Oscar's was being built. They took turns making the long trips to Nebraska City for material. The foundation of the house was merely rocks under the four corners, which, free for the picking up, were hauled from Weeping Water. The house itself was a two-roomed affair, with rough boards nailed up and down on the studding, and battened with narrow strips, but without plastering, so that for the first winter, Henry would nail burlap sacking all over the interior.

Will started a sod house. He did not feel that he could yet build as good a frame as he wanted, and every one said soddies were warm in winter and cool in summer. He cut strips of sod three feet long and laid them up as a mason would lay so many huge bricks, leaving places for the windows which Henry Lutz agreed to haul out from Nebraska City with whatever other lumber Will needed. The inside dimensions of the house were thirty by eighteen, so that when the partition was run through, the general living-room was eighteen by twenty and the bedroom eighteen by ten.

Abbie's physical ill-feelings and homesickness had been with her thus far through the making of the house. The sight of the prairie grass blowing and dipping in the wind under the cloudless sky still gave her a sensation of dizziness and nausea. The water from the spring at the edge of Stove Creek had a peculiar taste, so that she longed for the old well-water back home. She longed also for a sight of her mother's placid face under its white cap, and for a talk with Belle or Mary or Janet. In her low state of mind she felt uncertainty concerning their prospects, strange forebodings for the future, a torment that she was to die at childbirth and leave Will and little Mack.

But on an afternoon when Will was putting on the sod roofing, something lifted from Abbie's heart. Perhaps it was only because she was physically better that the deep depression seemed lightened, the intense homesickness for old scenes lessened. She put Mack to sleep in the wagon and walked farther up the long rolling land.

A sense of lightness, such as she had not known for weeks, was upon her. A revival of hope and courage possessed her. This was their own land. They, who had never owned a foot of ground, were now the sole owners of one hundred and sixty acres. Rich soil, too, Will said,—black and rich. A farm of their own upon which to make a home,—a home for Mack,—and one other! She wondered, as all mothers have wondered, which the new baby would be. And could not quite determine, as all mothers have been not quite able to determine, which she rather it would be. A boy would be the nicer for one reason,—he could be a chum for Mack. But a little girl,—down in her heart she hoped it would be a little girl. She remembered what she had said to her mother in the old cabin loft, back home. "Some day we may have a little girl. We will be rich then and she can wear the pearls." Well, maybe the baby would be a girl,—here was the good black soil upon which to get rich,—and over in the wagon were the pearls. She and Will were young. Life was all before them. With neighbors not far away, it was not going to be so lonely. Sarah Lutz—already she loved Sarah. And Christine Reinmueller,—even though Christine was so "Dutchy," she was kind hearted. Their own land, two babies, youth, neighbors! No, life here was not going to be so bad.

She raised her head to the cloudless September sky.

"Oh, the Lady of the Lea,
Fair and young and gay was she,"

Her voice rose clear, full-throated, mature.

"Dreamed of visions longingly,
The Lady of the Lea."

Yes, she and Will would soon be wealthy. Will had said so. Youth, babies, friends, wealth! She put the joy of it into melody:

"When she held in bower or hall
Banquet high or festival,
On every side her glance would fall . . ."

A crow, flying above her, wheeled and dipped down toward her, "Caw! Caw!" it threw down at her saucily. Abbie broke off singing.

"Were you jeering at me?" she called after the vagrant wanderer.

"Caw! caw!" it threw back raucously.

Maybe it was a sign. Maybe it was a *bad* sign. Grandma Deal would have said it was. Then she threw back her head and laughed. Oh, well, she was young. Her voice wouldn't run away and leave her. In a little while she could get to a teacher somewhere,—over the prairie to Nebraska City or back to Plattsmouth, or perhaps even up to Omaha some day.

As she started back to the prairie schooner, with the song unfinished, a long, slimy, gruesome Thing slipped, belly-flat, through the grass. Abbie shuddered and scrambled into the sheltering wagon.

The rough edges of the black sod of the house were now treated to a thick coat of mud plaster and a board floor laid. The low partition, over which she could hang clothes, and the crude board door, Abbie papered with hoop-skirted feminine paragons of style out of Godey's *Ladies' Book*, from which vantage point they looked down upon the humble interior with supercilious pride.

This, then, was the house into which Abbie moved from the prairie schooner,—Abbie, the granddaughter of Isabelle Anders-Mackenzie with her town house and her two country estates, her silk shawl, her pearls and her jeweled fan, her reddish-brown hair and her long slender fingers that tapered at the ends. But with the same pride that had rearranged the sumptuous furnishings in the ancestral home across the sea, Abbie now hung curtains at the windows, tacked burlap gunny-sacking on the floor, put down the small braided rag rugs, and made up the two clean beds. Under one of these she put the calf-skin-covered chest which held the pearls and the paints, and in the deep window-seat formed by the width of the sod strips, she set the Seth Thomas clock with the little brown church painted on the glass. There was one "boughten" cupboard for the dishes and Will made another one of store boxes to hold Abbie's books,—the Shakespeare plays and the Bible, the McGuffey readers, and a few other textbooks.

There was a four-holed stove whose long pipe protruded through the sod roof, three chairs, and a table with a declivity in one corner of it in which Doc Matthews had always rolled pills. A couch, which might also serve as an extra bed, was made of the same type of sod strips which had been used in the house, and covered with a feather bed and "The Rose of Sharon," one of Grandma Deal's quilts of intricate design. The rooms were both furnished now. The little soddie was not much of a house, but it was that other thing,—that intangible thing of the spirit called home.

As soon as his work on the house was finished, Will started on a shed for the stock. And in the mild October weather before the frosts had come, he broke sod on one portion of the land, so that it would be ready for slightly easier plowing in the spring.

With November the mild weather ceased. The winds, that seemed never still, blew harder from the open country to the north and west. Dried tumbleweeds, round in shape and as large as bushel baskets, rolled over the prairie with the winds, like great platoons of charging cavalry. Abbie, standing sometimes at the little soddie window, would watch the ceaseless riding of the brown-coated swashbucklers, the unending onslaught of Nature's artillerymen. On and on they came,—mounted rifles, dragoons, hussars,—columns, companies, regiments, brigades. They swept by, to disappear in the distance, only to be followed by reserves from farther out on the prairie.

It gave her a sense of fear,—fear that the unseen force which sent the slender-stemmed, globular-shaped weeds on their endless journey, might suddenly send her, too, on the hard ride.

When Will took the long drive to Nebraska City for supplies, her desolation seemed complete. She would catch up little Mack, who was a year and a half now and toddling everywhere, and hold him to her with a prayer for safety from all the unknown terrors,—Indians, winds, prairie fires, storms, her own hour of travail.

Will brought back corn meal and one precious sack of white flour for which he had paid ten dollars. So sparing was Abbie in its use, that it was nearly spring when the last bit was baked and the sack made into an apron for herself.

It was in the middle of the first night in March that Abbie knew her hour had come. The March winds, like so many wild March hares, were running past the little soddie. Will dressed hurriedly, replenished the fire, and with a word of encouragement, was gone into the night. Abbie, bolting the door behind him, knew the greatest fear of all for prairie women,—to be alone on the desert of grass with the pangs of childbirth upon her. "Oh, God, bring Will and the doctor safe home." The winds blew. Little Mack slept. Abbie's body was wracked. "Oh, God, send some one."

And then some one pounded on the door: "*Ein! . . . Las mich ein . . .* Christine." Abbie opened the door, and Christine Reinmueller came in, her fat face red from the cold wind, her little tight greasy braids flattened from ear to ear. She looked beautiful to Abbie.

It was hours before Will came with the doctor from Weeping Water. And then Abbie had her little girl,—the little daughter who was to wear pearls and all the lovely things that should go with them. Will brought Mack in and showed him the new sister, and Mack promptly welcomed her by poking a fat forefinger into her eye and mouth to see if she really worked.

They named her Margaret,—for both grandmothers. "It will please them both," Abbie fibbed politely. Almost she could hear Grandma Deal saying: "What did they do that fool thing for?"

Mackenzie Deal and Margaret Deal! A son and a daughter! Such a big family! She and Will laughed together in their relief and happiness.

And now, Abbie's love was divided between two babies. No, that is not true. There is no division nor subtraction in the heart-arithmetic of a good mother. There are only addition and multiplication.

March was cold, windy, snow-filled,—the land a desolate waste. Grayish-white snow over the low rolling hills,—a grayish-white sky like the pale reflection of those rolling hills in an opaque glass! And into the gray vastness of the sky, three little thin lines of smoke from the stove-pipes through the roofs of a dugout, a chink-battened frame and a soddie,—incense ascending to the God of Homes!

And then, the miracle! Spring came over the prairie,—not softly, shyly, but in great magic strides. It was in the flush of green on the elders and willows by Stove Creek. It was in the wind,—in the smell of loam and grasses, in the tantalizing odor of wild plums budding and wild violets flowering. Nature, the alchemist, took them all, the faint odors of the loam and the grasses, the willow buds and the little wild flowers, and mixing them in her mortar, threw them over the prairie on the wings of the wind.

Will could scarcely wait to begin spring plowing. Only then would it seem that the work on the place was really under way. He saw the frost ooze out of the broken sod and the heavy rolling clouds lose their frozen firmness. Twice he made an attempt to start the hand-plow and found the ground not ready. And then on a morning, with the prairie-lark calling to him, he started. Abbie took the baby in her arms and went out, with Mack toddling by her side. Gyp, the young dog of nondescript breeding which they had brought with them, ran frantically about, chasing some little flying thing. Abbie constantly darted a look near Mack, never allowing him more than a few feet from her, the fear of the deadly rattle-snake always with her.

Usually undemonstrative, Will slipped an arm around Abbie. Serious and reticent, he seldom voiced his deepest feelings. But now he spoke them:

"It'll be a pull, Abbie-girl, but some day you'll see I was right. The furrows will go everywhere up and down these rolling hills. Bigger plows than mine will roll them back. There'll maybe be a town here," he pointed to the limitless horizon, "and a village there. Omaha will be a big center. The little capital village of Lincoln will grow. It's bound to come. Not to-day,—nor to-morrow, but some other day and some other to-morrow. You'll live to see a fine capitol building and schools and stores and churches and nice homes."

Prophetic words! A town lies here and a village there. Huge tractors turn a half dozen furrows in one trip across the fields. Omaha and Lincoln are great centers for commercial, industrial and educational interests. Where once the Indian pitched his tepee for a restless day, there are groupings of schools and churches and stores and homes. And Abbie Deal lived to see the beginnings of the tall majestic tower of the most beautiful capitol of them all lift its white shaft to the sky,—a capitol unashamed of its native products, into whose marble artistry have gone the buffalo and the corn and the goldenrod.

Will stood a moment, a little abashed at his emotion, so that immediately he said lightly, "Well, here goes."

The first loam turned back, clean-cut with the sharp knife of the plowshare, mellow, black as a crow's wing. A fringe of coarse grass held fast to the heavy soil, as though the two could not be parted after all these wild, free centuries together,—the grass maiden clinging to the breast of her prairie lover.

Abbie turned abruptly and went into the house with the babies. Inside she cried a little into the long roller towel,—she did not know just why. Then she pulled herself together. "This will never do. There's no time for idle tears. If I am to do my share in all that Will thinks he sees,

I must get a good dinner for him." The man at the plow, the woman at the stove,—it was symbolic.

That spring the new life began in earnest. To Abbie, the future gleamed with bright prospects. New settlers were coming in every day,—already the precinct had thirteen families. In such a little while the community would be well settled. In such a short time they would all be rich. And so Abbie Deal went happily about her work, one baby in her arms and the other at her skirts, courage her lode-star and love her guide,—a song upon her lips and a lantern in her hand.

CHAPTER XI

❧ THAT summer was a summer of hard work and high hopes. Everything was to be done. Will, in his keen desire for results, worked early and late. He broke out more raw prairie and planted it, cut and hauled wood from the creek, chopped it in stove length, cared for his stock, and did the work of two men. He dropped into bed when he could not see to do anything more and was up before the sun rose over the fringe of elms and elders and willows on Stove Creek.

And Abbie? Abbie took care of little two-year-old Mack and the new baby, Margaret, washed with little water, ironed with cumbersome flat-irons next to a cook stove that was a fiery furnace, cooked from a meager store of supplies, made soap out of doors, standing over the hot contents of a huge iron kettle, sewed and mended, tried vainly to keep the house clean, and took sole care of the chickens, which, like their owners, boasted a sod residence. The tapering Mackenzie fingers were never idle.

Will had many long trips to make, and Abbie, bundling up the two babies and taking along supplies for them, went with him. They drove the long way to Nebraska City to get cottonwood seedlings from the sand-bars there, as the little young trees growing in the pliable soil could be pulled out with one twist. They left feed and water for the chickens, but took the cow with them, tying her to the wagon. Abbie put in her churn with some cream in it, and the lurching motion of the wagon furnished them with butter, which was passable, although decidedly not as good as when cooled in the spring water. Will took his double-barreled shotgun along and killed prairie chickens on the way, which Abbie, as she sat in the back of the wagon, picked to cook for supper.

"It's a good thing we're not trying to run away from the law," she called out to Will, "for we could be traced clear across the prairie by a trail of chicken feathers."

Whenever they came to the homesteads of settlers they tried to move straight with the surveyed sections, but over railroad and school lands they drove to their destination through the trackless prairie grass as straight, if not as swiftly, as the crow flew.

Both the cottonwood and the willows would grow also from cuttings, so that on their return Will brought up a huge cottonwood branch from the creek and Abbie cut the whole thing into slips for Will to set out to the north of the sod house for a potential wind break. From their own creek bed they obtained willow whips and these were planted near the chicken house. Every one was planning for future shade.

To the north and west of them, Oliver Johnson, a young bachelor and a Dartmouth graduate, put out a timber claim. By planting and caring for ten acres of trees for eight years he would be able to obtain a good one hundred and sixty acres from the government.

In every activity on the place Will took pains to plan right. "We have to think what we're doing and lay it out just as we want it in the future," he told Abbie. "We'll be able to build a good frame house one of these days and we want the whole place planned so we'll not need to make changes."

Abbie pondered a great deal over the arrangement. "Right over there, Will, the new house ought to be . . . on that rise of ground. Then some day there'll be a road. I can kind-of see now how it will be. A nice house up there on the rise and the road running east and west past the house, then a lane road turning in from the main one. And fences. . . . Oh, I think, Will, when we get fences, I'll like it better. It seems so sort of heathenish to come across the country any way. There ought to be nice straight roads everywhere and fences to show where our land begins and ends. And a picket fence around the house yard . . . a nice fence, painted white . . . with red hollyhocks and blue larkspur along by it, against the white pickets."

Will laughed. "You're quite a dreamer, Abbie-girl."

Abbie did not laugh. She was suddenly sober. "You have to, Will." She said it a little vehemently. "You *have* to dream things out. It keeps a kind of an ideal before you. You see it first in your mind and then you set about to try to make it like the ideal. If you want a garden,—why, I guess you've got to *dream* a garden." Then she looked out at the small plot of vegetables, and laughed,—not quite joyfully, a little ruefully. They looked so wilted and so lackadaisical, so uninterested in life, those potatoes and turnips and beans.

All this time they had used the spring at the edge of the creek, and now Will was digging the well. Henry Lutz came over to operate the windlass that raised the buckets which Will filled with dirt. In return for the work, Will was to assist Henry in the same way as soon as his own well would be finished. On one of the days of the well-digging Henry brought word that the Burlington road had sent its first train across the Missouri at Plattsmouth. It made the men feel good. Things were coming along fine, they told each other.

On a later afternoon Henry could not come, and Abbie, as anxious as Will that the work should go forward, pitted her own young strength against the weight of the dirt-filled buckets. All afternoon, her face purple with heat and exertion, she worked under the sun's fire and in the wind's hot breath, only leaving her post to nurse the baby at her heated breast.

When it seemed that she could not stand it longer, that through the perspiration of her eyes she saw only a tortuous shimmering heat over the land, Will signaled to be pulled up.

Slowly, painfully, exerting every ounce of strength she possessed, Abbie wound the rope of the windlass. Suddenly, treacherously, the handle slipped from her perspiring hands and struck her head with black and blinding force. When she came slowly back from the dark spaces of some vacuous cavern, she could hear Mack's wailing cry of, "Muvver . . . Muvver," as he bent over her and pulled at her fluttering eyelids,—could hear Will's faint and frantic call, "Abbie . . . Abbie . . . where are you?"

She sat up and tried to recall just what had happened, suddenly remembering that Will must have been dropped back into the well with terrific force. He might be badly hurt. It gave her strength. She was up and calling to him. No, he was not hurt, was shaken up a little, but nothing to worry about.

And then Abbie must go for help to get Will out. Over and over she cautioned little Mack to stay away, up by the house, explained repeatedly how he must not go near the big hole. Then, bruised and bleeding at the forehead, she went across the hot prairie to get Gus, the fear of the horrible rattle-snake present with every grass-hidden step. There was no one home at the Reinmuellers'. Repeated callings brought no one from the dug-out or rude sheds. Back to the Henry Lutz place she sped, where she found Henry and Sarah, who immediately hitched the team, brought her back in the wagon, and rescued Will.

Indians came through the community every little while in their straggling, single-file way of traveling. They were said to be friendly, but the settlers could not trust them. Nothing ever filled Abbie with so much fear as the sight of two or three unidentified figures appearing upon the horizon. And in August, when news filtered into the community that a band of ten government surveyors had been massacred by a band of Sioux under Pawnee Killer out in the Republican Valley, she felt that only a word from Will would be needed to abandon everything and go back home.

Only a few days later four of the fear-inspiring creatures stopped at the house and signified they wanted eatables. They ate greedily of the pork and beans Abbie set before them and when they seemed satisfied, coolly turned the remaining food into their dirty blankets, and went on over the prairie in their straggling single-file way, the poles of their tepees dragging from the scrawny ponies' sides.

It was late that same month that Henry Lutz came tearing up to the Deal soddie on a horse.

"Something has happened to little Dan," he called without dismounting. "We don't know what. Go over and stay with Sarah, will you, while I ride for Doc Keeney?"

Will hitched the horses hurriedly and Abbie got in with Mack and the baby, Margaret. When they started away they saw Christine coming, so they drove back and waited for her.

Sarah Lutz was frantic, her round rosy face drawn with fright. They had been pulling their cabbages from the weed-bend of the creek to make kraut, she said. Dan helped a little, but about four he said his leg hurt. "We told him to rest . . . thought he was just tired. He complained more about it after we got to the house . . . and when we looked at it . . ." Sarah covered her blanched face with her hands. "It's swollen . . . twice as big . . . and it's . . . Oh, God, Abbie, it's black."

Doctor Keeney came. He went into the little bedroom and when he came out, his tired face above the grizzled beard was drawn and his eyes grief-filled.

"It's . . ." he threw out his hands in a gesture of despair, "snake-bite. I'll do what I can . . . but . . . it's too late. . . ." He had whispered it, but the words rang through the room . . . tolled through the house. Little Dan, with his sunny ways, to be a victim of the Menace!

They all waited there in the night,—waited for death to find little Dan on the wild barren prairie. Such a little boy for death to find in the vastness of the new country! But it found him. Riding over the prairie with the wind that was never still, the white horseman found him.

Will made the pine box down at the barn, and Abbie and Christine lined it with Sarah's best quilt. Sarah, grief-stricken, would let no one else wash and dress him. Henry rode to Plattsmouth for a missionary minister. Other settlers came long distances to the Lutz house in their wagons. Their sympathy was deep and sincere. And it took concrete form. They brought wild-grape jelly and corn biscuits, baked prairie chickens and a roast of pork.

They buried the little boy on a knoll of the Lutz land. The settlers with bared heads stood around the deep yawning hole in the ground. Abbie, her throat too stiff and tense to follow the melody correctly, sang an old hymn. The minister talked of a God who made all things work together for food. Abbie thought she could not stand it! Death! How she hated it and feared it!

There was not a tree near. The August sun blazed down on the rolling hill. The hot wind from the southwest blew over it. The blackbirds and crows flew and wheeled low above it. The coarse prairie grass bent before the wind, *Blow . . . wave, . . . ripple, . . . dip. . . . Blow, . . . wave, . . . ripple, . . . dip. . . .*

CHAPTER XII

THERE was very little crop that fall. The settlers learned that sod-corn never amounts to much. What few ears formed, Will fed on the stalk.

"I don't care. I'm not disappointed," he said, "I knew it would take a year to get a start."

But Abbie knew it was not so. Abbie knew that Will cared.

The stubble and roots, rotting all winter in the newly broken fields, fertilized the ground, and so it was with high hopes that Will went into the field the first spring of the 'seventies.

Abbie's summer was one of fighting sickness, in addition to her many tasks. Both children had the measles and the whooping cough later, as did the Reinmuellers' three and Sarah Lutz's new baby daughter, Emma. The mothers doctored them as well as they could with simple remedies, catnip tea and Indian herbs, hanging over their beds, watching anxiously for every change. When her children came out from under the cloud of illness, Abbie felt that it was like coming out of a dark cavern into the sunshine. Once more she sang at her tasks.

The crop of 1870 was only fair. So much hard work for so little results! Nothing but the cottonwoods seemed to thrive luxuriantly. Already after their second summer, some of those which they had brought from the sand-bars were as tall as Will. Their little shimmering, dancing leaves were a solace to Abbie. They seemed courageous and cheerful, undaunted by the hot sun, undisturbed by cold rains, unafraid of the rushing winds.

Will had set out an orchard now. Oscar and Henry Lutz had sent east to their brother for nursery stock, and the Reinmuellers and Deals ordered fruit trees, too. The spindling whips of apples and cherries with their names still tied upon them, looked a rather hopeless lot rambling row upon row over the raw prairie.

There was always so much to be done. One never could satisfy the demands of Work, that taskmaster which drove every one in the new country before the lash.

Sometimes Abbie would stand at the door of the soddie and look across the unshaded prairie where the sunflowers added their brilliant yellow to the blinding yellow of the sun, and standing so for a few moments, she would think of the lovely lady with the bronze tints in her reddish hair. She had wanted to be like her. But how could one be a lovely lady when there was not always enough water to keep immaculately clean?

Will was her strength and her courage. In one of her hours of depression she had only to confide her mood to him, to have it lifted by his optimism.

"Everything is going to be all right," he would assure her. "Think of the Burlington road reaching Lincoln last week. Think of it! Building right up,—everything is."

"Yes, but Will,—there are so many things we need. And I want, . . . Oh, Will . . . I want an organ so *bad*. I'll be twenty-four this fall . . . and my music . . ."

"My, you're getting old," he would joke her "Most an old woman, ain't you?" And then more seriously, "Maybe you can have your organ next year, Abbie-girl. We'll have good crops next year."

But next year, 1871, the crop, like the others, was only half a crop. Will was right about the land. The soil itself was rich enough. But the rains held off. Day after day the clouds, as white and dry and puffy as milk-weed seeds, scudded high with the winds.

In that fourth fall, on a mild September day, the air was hazy and they could detect the telltale, far-off odor of smoke. Not a man left his home. Will, the Lutz brothers, Gus Reinmueller,—all were out for hours plowing wide strips around their places. They knew there were only three things that would stop a prairie fire in its mad, wild flight, and even those were ineffective at times,—wide strips of upturned loam upon which there was nothing for the fire to feed, creeks that were wide enough to prevent the flames from leaping them, or a back-fire,—the burning of a wide strip of prairie grass by the settlers themselves, so that when the flames arrived they found themselves beaten by their own kind.

It was close to three in the afternoon when they saw it roll in from the northwest, the black of the smoke, and the low running scarlet of the fire.

Stove Creek, the best friend in the world to the four families that day, lay between them and the hideous advancing Thing. The men, Will and Gus Reinmueller, Henry and Oscar Lutz, all scattered along the creek bed, ready to pounce upon any flying embers that might cross the deadline. All afternoon the women carried wet gunnysacks back and forth. They could see the little house where Oliver Johnson "bached it," standing in the way of the angry flames. Oliver, himself, came across the creek over to the Deal side, riding one horse and leading the other, a big wash boiler in front of him. He had been away, he said, and arrived home only in time to grab a boiler, thrust his Sunday suit, some money, a tin-type of his girl into it, and leave. Even as they talked, they saw the little house catch fire and almost immediately a great bunch of geese feathers flying up into the air, like a puff of white smoke.

"There goes my mother's feather bed," was Oliver's laconic remark, as he fell into the work of wetting the gunnysacks along with the others.

When the last of the jaws of flame ceased reaching for their prey, the land across the creek was a desolate black waste, the trees on the north bank charred and gone. One more enemy was temporarily vanquished. But it had left its mark on the land and the fear of it branded forever in the minds of the settlers.

The next spring, the State Board of Agriculture, through a resolution offered by J. Sterling Morton, a Nebraska City man, set aside the tenth of April, as a special day on which the settlers should plant trees. They called it Arbor Day. Although Will had set out a great many trees previously, he spent the day adding to his own windbreaks and hauling cottonwood saplings for Henry Lutz who was sick at the time.

When Henry was up again, he built an addition of two rooms on to his house and opened a store in one of them, the stock consisting of six brooms, ten bolts of cloth, a dozen bottles of patent medicine and a few staple groceries. His first customer was Christine Rinemueller who bought brown denim for her baby's dress. She put one corner of the goods between her teeth and pulled on it. "Everyt'ing . . . *sie reis* . . . rip." She jerked the cloth to test its strength. "You t'ink dis *sie reis* . . . rip . . . nein?"

A few rods to the east of the Lutz combination store and house, Oscar Lutz built a blacksmith shop and hired a blacksmith-preacher to do the work. For six days Sam Mowery labored at the anvil and on the seventh day the Reverend Samuel Mowery preached three miles away in the schoolhouse known by the appropriate appellation of Sodom College. A store and a blacksmith shop! People began saying, "Over to the Stove Creek store," and then, "Over to Stove Creek."

Mail was brought now by a man on horseback, en route from Weeping Water to Ashland. Twice a week he would stop with the little packet at the Lutz store, as Henry had been made postmaster.

They began to talk about getting a doctor to come in. Will heard of a young Dr. Hornby, who had just arrived at Nebraska City after graduating from Rush. He rode on horseback to interview him, and the young fellow returned on his own horse behind Will, his mutton-chop whiskers blowing back against his pink-cheeked boyish face, his medicine-case and a valise tied on the saddle.

A store, a post office, a blacksmith shop, a preacher, a doctor,—and all in two buildings. The town had begun.

It was Sarah Lutz and Abbie Deal who began talking about the crudeness of the "Stove Creek" title. They were both setting out little cedar trees, Sarah in a clump behind the store, Abbie in a row in front of the soddie.

"Cedar City, Abbie," Sarah said suddenly.

"Or Cedartown," Abbie added.

"Yes, I believe I like that best . . . all in one word."

Cedartown! A store and a blacksmith shop! But the Deals and the Lutzes, the Reverend Samuel Mowery and his wife and Dr. Hornby would all correct any passerby who asked innocently if this was Stove Creek.

"Cedartown," they would say impressively. And so, Minerva-like, Cedartown had sprung forth from the brow of the prairie.

The crop of that year, 1872, was as poor as that of the previous summer. In September, Abbie's third child was born. Sarah was there helping, now, and Christine was at home with her own new baby. The child was a son, healthy, loud-voiced, hungry. Abbie and Will joked a little over the size of their family and they argued some over the newcomer's name. Will wanted to call him John.

"It doesn't sound just right," Abbie protested. "John Deal. It's too short . . . like 'Tick-tack' . . . or 'Pot-luck.' "

"Oh, I don't care," Will gave in readily enough. "I just liked it. It sounds solid and substantial as though he might amount to something."

Abbie pulled the little soft sleeping form into the hollow of her arm. "I *know* he'll amount to something."

After that she could not get the thought of the "John" out of her mind. "John Deal," she said it over several times. "Will's right. It just fits him. Some day people will say, 'Go and ask John Deal. He's a smart man. He can advise you.' " She lay and smiled at the vision. If the faith of all the mothers could blossom to its full fruition, there would be no unsuccessful men in the land.

Mack was nearly six now and Margaret four, so that when Abbie was up again, and strong enough, she began to teach them their letters. Will painted a board with black paint and brought some soft chalk-like deposit from the Platte with which they could print. The oldest Reinmueller and Lutz children had started to school at Sodom College, but Abbie would not let Mack go so far. So to her other labors she now added teaching.

All winter during the deep snows when they were shut in, she gave the children lessons to do, hearing them recite in their queer little ways, while she was mending or mixing bread or ironing. It was tiresome, shut in the small soddie, and spring was a welcome guest. On Easter morning, accompanied by the faithful dog, who would kill a snake whenever he found one, Abbie took Mack and Margaret and little John down to the creek bank for flowers. Will had made a wagon in which to pull John, the wheels of round disks cut from a young cottonwood, and now at seven months, the baby lay in it and blinked solemn eyes at the April sky. It was an advanced spring and they found blue and yellow violets, Dutchmen's breeches, ferns, and the tiny red buds of the hawthorn.

"Smell!" said Abbie, "smell the springtime on the prairie." And Mack and Margaret stood and sniffed miniature olfactory organs.

"What makes it smell sweet?" they wanted to know.

"Because everything,—every little wild plum-blossom, every little tiny crocus and anemone and violet and every tree-bud and grass-blade is working to help make the prairie nice," Abbie told them. [And who is there to say this was not a beginners' class in philosophy?]

The day was hot, with a strong wind from the south, so that they did not stay long at the creek bed. On the way back to the house it clouded, and by the time they had reached it, the drops were falling. In the night the rain changed to snow and when the family awoke in the early morning, the storm was shrieking around the soddie with cyclonic fury. Great wet clumps of snow were being hurled against the small half-windows and snow had been driven through the cracks of the door. The wind and the snow, whirling together in their wild Bacchanalia, seemed laughing drunkenly at the tiny pigmy inmates of the tiny prairie house.

Will started to open the door to go to his stock and could scarcely shut it again against the storm's rage. In the brief interval of its half opening, huge chunks of soft snow, with a rush and roar of wind had been blown the length of the room. With the life of the stock depending upon him, he made another attempt to leave the house in the afternoon. He succeeded in getting to the barn, but came back discouraged, for the snow had blown through every crack and crevice.

By the third day of this holocaust of Nature's, the storm abated. Will found some of the chickens dead, and his horses and three cows had stamped so much snow under their feet that their backs were nearly to the top of the shed. There were dead prairie chickens everywhere, and the trees along the creek bank where the little family had so recently picked violets, were packed so solid as to make a snow wall.

The snows melted and the creek rose. The flowers bloomed again and summer was upon the land.

But if the previous years had been hard, that one seemed to reach the lowest point of the settlers' existence. The panic of 1873 was upon the state. The bottom of the market dropped out and prices were so low that it did not even pay to haul the scanty crop to market. When eggs were five cents a dozen and butter eight cents a pound, cattle and hogs two cents, wheat fifty cents a bushel, and corn eight, of what use to haul them all thirty or forty miles? Of what use to haul a load of corn a day's journey and bring back a load of coal which cost much more than the corn? So Will and Abbie, along with the neighbors, began burning the corn for fuel. It made a fire of intensity, a fire that crackled and held its heat as well as any coal. Sometimes, too, they used hard twisted hay. When winter came on, Will took Abbie's washboiler and removing the two front lids of the cook stove, turned the boiler upside down over the open holes, forming a sort of drum that seemed to heat the room a little better.

The crop of 1874 was the sixth crop and it seemed to give a little more promise than the previous ones. By the twentieth of July, Will had laid by all his corn. Most of his small grain was in the shocks, but one oat field of a few acres was still uncut. Standing there under the July sun, its ripened surface seemed to reflect back the yellow rays. In the afternoon Abbie went out to pick a mess of beans. The garden had come to be Abbie's care. Aside from the potato crop, to which Will attended, she looked after the entire garden. It was quite generally so,—the men bending all their energies to bigger things, the corn and wheat and the stock, with the chickens and the gardens falling to the lot of the wives. Some of the women went into the fields. Christine Reinmueller was out beside Gus many days. Will drew the line at that. "When you have to do that, we'll quit," he said.

Abbie, in her starched sunbonnet, began picking beans for supper. She could see Will and Henry Lutz working together, shocking the last of Henry's oats. To-morrow the two would work together on Will's last stand. It was nice for the men to be so neighborly.

It seemed hazy in the west. By the time she had finished the long rows, a big panful of the yellow pods in her arms, Will had come home from the Lutzes'. In the welcome shade of the house Abbie took off her bonnet, wiped her flushed, perspiring face and waited for Will to come up.

"My . . . it's a scorcher." She looked hot and tired.

In a moment of tenderness, more to be desired because of its rarity, Will picked up Abbie's hands. The slender nails were stubbed and broken,—the grime of the garden was on her tapering fingers. He lifted her hand suddenly and kissed the hollow of it. As his lips touched the calloused palms, his eyes filled with rare tears. He uttered a short swift oath, "I wish you didn't have to, Abbie-girl. It's tough for you.

Some day . . . in a few years . . . we'll pull out. Weather conditions may change . . . the land will be high. . . . You can have better things . . . and your organ. That singing and painting of yours . . . maybe we can get to a teacher then. . . ."

It affected Abbie as it always did. In a moment like that it seemed the end and aim of everything . . . the family. All her dreams for herself were as nothing. In her own moment of emotion she returned, "We'll make it, Will . . . don't worry!"

For a moment they stood together looking out over the raw rolling acreage. Even as they looked, the sun darkened and the day took on a grayness. They looked for the storm, and heard it as soon as they saw it,—a great black cloud roar out of the west, with a million little hissing vibrations. Their eyes on the sky, neither moved. Then there was a cessation of the roaring, a soft thud of dropping things, and the cloud of a billion wings lay on the fields.

"Grasshoppers," they said simultaneously, incredulously.

The grasshoppers swarmed over the young waist-high corn and the pasture and the garden. By evening the long rows of sweet corn had been eaten to the plowed ground. The tender vines of the tomatoes were stripped down to the stalk. The buds of the fruit trees were gone. Part of the garden was a memory. The chickens had feasted themselves to the bursting point. Gus Reinmueller, driving up to the door, could hardly control his raring horses, so irritated were they by the bouncing, thumping pests. The farm was a squirming, greenish-gray mass of them.

All evening Will sat by the stove with his head in his hands. It was the first time he had visibly lost his grit. Abbie went over to him and ran her hand through his hair. She tried to think of something to console him. "Don't, Will. . . . There's one thing we can do. There's the string of pearls. We can always fall back on it. There must be jewelry stores in Omaha that would take it and pay well. You take the team and make the drive. . . . You can do it in three days, . . . and I'll look after things here. When Mother gave the pearls to me, she said, 'You'll ne'er starve with them' . . . and we won't, Will. We'll sell them for the children's sake."

Will threw her hands away from his hair roughly and stood up. "Hell . . . no!" He yelled it at her. "I've taken your music away from you and your painting and your teaching and some of your health. But, *by God,* . . . I won't take your mother's present to you."

He slammed the rough soddie door and went out to the barn.

CHAPTER XIII

☙ BY THE next night the stalks of field corn were skeletons, a few delicate veins of leaves left, like so many white bones bleaching on the desert of the fields. At the end of three days the oat field was stripped almost as bare as the day the plow had finished its work. The young orchard was a graveyard of hopes. Some of the small grain previously harvested had been saved, and luckily, one digging of early potatoes was in the hole in the ground in which Will always kept them. But everything else went through the crunching incisors of the horde. It was as though the little grayish-green fiends became a composite whole,—one colossal insect into whose grinding maw went all the green of the fields and the gardens, all the leaves and tender twigs of the young fruit trees, all the dreams and the hopes of the settlers.

The pests were everywhere. With nightmarish persistence, they appeared in everything. As tightly as Will kept the well covered, he drew them up in the bucket, so that he began going back to the old spring for water. Abbie caught them eating the curtains of the little half-windows and sent them to a fiery death. She was forced to dry the weekly wash around the cook stove, her one attempt to hang it in the sun ending speedily with a dozen perforations in the first billowing garment.

The garden was a total loss. They had tried to save some of the beans by putting gunny-sacks over them and weighting them down with stones from the creek bed. The grasshoppers, after eating the beans, had begun on the gunny-sacks.

"Will they eat the stones, too, Mother?" Mack wanted to know. And they could not laugh at him.

Abbie wrote a letter to her sister Mary, telling of this last hard piece of luck. Even letters were expensive luxuries so that one was made to do for the entire group of relatives back in eastern Iowa. She gave the letter to Will, who said that he would ride over to the little post office in the Lutz store as soon as he had finished caring for the stock. In an hour Will came in holding the letter by a corner. The edges of the envelope had been eaten all the way around with little neat flutings so that the two sides fell apart and the letter fluttered to the floor. The pocket of his old denim coat, where the letter had lain, was flapping down, cut on two sides by the same diabolical jaws.

What could you do? You could not fight them. You could not kill them. They were an army with an uncanny and unnatural power. Abbie looked out upon the devastation of the fields and the garden upon which they both had worked so hard. The hot wind blew over the ruins with Mephistophelean laughter. She looked up at the cloudless blue,—huge, cruel, sardonic.

"God, . . . *you* ought to help," she cried aloud. "We can't do it alone. *You* ought to help!"

All through August, Abbie went about in a dull, stupid way, depressed by the last hard luck that had descended upon them and the knowledge that her fourth child was coming. She was nervous,—cross to Will and to the children. Sometimes, in a temper, she jerked one of her little tots by the arm or spanked one angrily,—figuratively standing off and looking at her own actions in contempt. She seemed doing things she did not want to do, seeing a nervous, cross woman, who was not herself, allow her love for husband and babies to begin slipping. The song in Abbie's throat was stilled that summer and not even an echo of the melody lingered on. For the first time she was sorry about her condition, sorry and bitter. One more mouth to feed, she said to herself acridly,—she, who was a born mother. And then, in a sudden revulsion of feeling at her disloyalty to motherhood, she thought, "Oh, I don't want to feel that way about a child. I ought *not* to say that . . . I won't . . . I *never* will again."

In the letter which came in time from her sister Mary, was the comforting word, "Well, Abbie, you ought to have married Dr. Ed Matthews. His wife was here visiting this summer and she had fine clothes,—a purple silk dress and a little lavender velvet bonnet with pansies on and the widest satin strings, and lavender silk mitts. She has a Paisley shawl, too, and a big cameo breast-pin."

Abbie let the letter fall into her lap and sat thinking of Ed Matthews in New York. Occasionally some one had written an item about him. "Ed Matthews and his bride came to visit. She is an eastern girl, and tremendous stylish." And later: "They say Ed is in a New York hospital where they have as many as fifty beds."

And now sitting there with the hot wind blowing over the stripped fields, Abbie's thoughts went back to the knoll near the Big Woods. "You're wonderful, Abbie! You're gorgeous! You coquette! I'll take you with me. You can study all you want . . . with the best teachers. . . ."

If she had known—if she could have foreseen—the drouth and the grasshoppers,—the blizzards and the winds that were never still—the hard work,—and the privations,—the song that might never be sung,—the four babies in eight years. "No. . . . No!" She pulled herself out of the dream. "No. . . . No! Don't let me think it. Don't let me *think* of thinking it. It's wicked. There's nobody but Will. It's just the crop failures and the terrible hard luck that made me think it. Those things have nothing to do with love." But even as she said it, Abbie knew that it was not true. Abbie knew that unless you are very strong, those things have something to do with love.

In an overwhelming return of affection for the children, she picked little John up and covered him with kisses, her tears on his cheeks. She drew Margaret to her and cuddled her, too. Margaret's little hand had a dingy rag around it to cover a cut, and in an ecstasy of mother-emotion, Abbie kissed the little hand, kissed the plump baby neck between the soft brown ringlets and the colorless calico dress. She went to the door and called, "Mack, come in."

"What do you want, Mother?"

"Nothing, Mack, . . . nothing but to kiss you, darling. Oh, little son, I love you so. Kiss Mother, Mack."

Mack, who was seven now and a little superior to the demonstration of women folks, stood the ordeal with fortitude and then pulled quickly away. "I'm helping Father sort things, . . . all the nails for him, . . . the little ones, . . . and the horseshoe ones, . . . and . . ."

"That's it. That's a good boy. *Always* help Father, Mack. He's the *best* father in the world. You'll never forget it, will you, darling?"

She did not want Will to know what Mary had written, so she read the letter aloud to him, blithely skipping the tart reference to Ed Matthews.

During that summer the whole family went in the wagon along the creek to scour the thickets for wild grapes and wild plums. Abbie rode three miles on horseback to a Mrs. Tomlinson's to get some late pieplant which had miraculously escaped the scourge of the robber insects. And when Will came in one day with two huge beets which he had found when taking down a pile of boards, Abbie sent word to Henry Lutz's to come over and the two families feasted on potatoes, corn bread and sliced boiled beets.

Every one was in want. In the early fall people began going past the house. "Going home," they all reported. Many times parties of them stayed all night. They had their own quilts and would arrange their beds on the main-room floor. They were beaten, they said. One could stand a few disappointments and failures, but when everything turned against one, there was no use trying to fight.

"The land hasn't turned against us," Will would argue stubbornly. "It's the finest, blackest loam on the face of the earth. The folks that will just stick it out. . . . You'll see the climate change, . . . more rains and not so much wind . . . when the trees grow. We've got to keep at the trees. Some day this is going to be the richest state in the union . . . the most productive. I'll bet anything next year . . ."

Always "next year"! It was a mirage, thought Abbie, an apparition that vanished when one came to it. Six times now they had said, "Next year, the crops will be fine."

And so she could not throw off the blue mood that had descended upon her, a horde of worries that had come upon her even as the horde of grasshoppers had come upon the land. The thought that there was nothing to do with; that they could scarcely keep body and soul together; that she probably would never be able now to do anything with her voice; that another child was coming,—they all harassed and tormented her. All fall there was in her mind a tired disinterest over things. In spite of what he said, that surface courage which he pretended had returned to him, Abbie detected that Will, too, was morose. To her keen eye he seemed dull and stoical, underneath an assumption of cheerfulness.

Before cold weather, the old grasshoppers were gone, but first they had taken infinite pains to leave a reminder of themselves in the newly broken prairie everywhere,—holes the size of lead pencils in which they laid one to two dozen eggs in a sack. In a six-inch square of ground, Will testing their number, found a double handful of the next year's hatching. There seemed not even a hope for the following crop.

It was in November that the barrel and box came from the folks back home. Will drove up to the soddie with rattling announcement of their arrival. A letter from Grandpa Deal had been the forerunner of the donations and already Abbie knew that an old brass horn of Dennie's was among the things for Mack. She determined to slip it out without his knowledge and put it away for Christmas. They all gathered around the barrel while Will pried open the top, Mack and Margaret dancing about it an ecstasy of excitement. The first thing to be taken out was an envelope marked "For Abbie," in Grandpa Deal's handwriting. In it was twenty dollars. Abbie cried a little, tears of love and homesickness, happiness and relief, and put it away with secret thoughts of the desired organ. She sensed that Grandpa had slipped it in with his one hand the last thing, so Grandma would not see it.

There were flower seeds and sugar and beans, seed-corn and dried apples in the barrel. Mother Mackenzie had tied and sent two thick comforts. Regina Deal sent an old soiled white silk bonnet with a bead ornament and a cluster of three little pink feathers on it,—"tips," Abbie told the children they were,—and a pair of dirty white "stays" and some old white hoop-skirts. Abbie laughed until she cried at the sight of them.

"Maybe I could put the hoops over some stakes next summer and keep the setting hens in them," she suggested. She put them on over her work dress, the hoops and the stays both, and perched the dirty bonnet on her red-brown hair, dancing about in them, the three noble tips nodding with uncertain dignity as though, like their former owner, they had no sense of humor. She pushed Will and Mack and Margaret into position for a square dance and showed the children how to "whirl your partner" and "alamand left." The four of them pranced around in the impromptu dance, the children in their patched dingy clothing, Will in his denim work things, and Abbie in the foolish soiled cast-offs which Regina had sent with so little thought. The two older children laughed and clapped their hands and shouted that they had never had so much fun in their lives, and little John toddled in and out and between them in an ecstasy of bubbling spirits.

It broke something in Abbie, some tight-bound band around her heart and throat, which had not been loosed for months. She hid the old brass horn of Dennie's in the bedroom. She put away the precious dried apples and pop-corn, the seed-corn and the big solid Greenings from the orchard behind Grandpa Deal's house. She hugged the huge warm quilts as though they were the fat pudding-bag body of Maggie Mackenzie. The bad luck was temporary. They were young and well. The children were all healthy youngsters. Why, how wicked she had been! She was only twenty-seven. She mustn't let her voice rust the way she had done this summer. In another year or so she could have an organ and maybe even get to a music teacher. She mustn't let youth slip away and her voice go with it. She was ashamed of herself that she had not sung for months.

"Oh! the Lady of the Lea,
Fair and young and gay was she."

Her voice rose full-throated, mellowed now with tribulations and sympathy. The children clapped their hands that Mother was singing.

"Beautiful exceedingly,
The Lady of the Lea."

She replenished the fire of twisted hay and corn-cobs in the stove with the four holes and the iron hearth in front. She cooked cornmeal mush for supper and set the table. Several times she sang the same verses over.

"Many a wooer sought her hand,
For she had gold and she had land,"

The teakettle sang and the children chattered happily at the window. She lighted the coal-oil lamp with the red flannel in the bowl and washed her hands in the tin basin. The prairie twilight came on. The winds died down.

"Everything at her command,
The Lady of the Lea."

Will came in from doing the chores.

"It's the nicest time of day . . . isn't it, Will . . . the red fire of the corn . . . and the steaming teakettle . . . supper ready . . . and the children all alive and well . . . and you and I together?"

Will put his arm around her for a brief, rare moment.

"It's the nicest time of day, Abbie-girl."

CHAPTER XIV

YES, the coming of the barrel seemed to put something back into Abbie which had been gone temporarily,—laughter and hope, courage and faith. She began planning right away for Christmas. Mack was nearly eight, Margaret six and little John two. They were going to have the finest Christmas they had ever known. To Abbie's pleasure, Will entered into the preparations, too. He was as glad to see Abbie come to life as she was to see him throw off a little of his moroseness.

She told Gus and Christine Reinmueller their plans.

"*Ach!*" Christine snorted. "So? *Gans närrich* . . . voolish."

"A hell of a Christmas we'll have," was Gus's equally enthusiastic response.

But Abbie found sympathy in Sarah Lutz,—Sarah, with her little black beady eyes and her cheerful, energetic way.

"You know, Sarah, I think every mother owes it to her children to give them happy times at Christmas. They'll remember them all their lives. I even think it will make better men and women of them."

"I think so, too, Abbie. We're going to have a cedar tree hauled up from the Platte. Henry can you get you one, too."

All day long Abbie worked at the tasks that demanded attention, washing, ironing, patching, mending, baking, churning, caring for the chickens,—all with meager equipment or no equipment at all. Two wooden tubs, three heavy, clumsy flat-irons, a churn with wooden dasher, scissors, needles and thread, and a baking board with a few heavy dishes and utensils. But from them, clean clothes, sweet butter, neatly made-over suits and dresses and food that was palatable. The tapering Mackenzie fingers were calloused and burned and pricked. As tired as all these tasks left her, she would get the children to bed early and then bring out the Christmas things and begin working on them.

She got out the precious paints Mrs. Whitman had given her and worked on a picture for Will when he was away. It was a scene of the prairie with a clump of cottonwoods in the foreground. She tried to get the afterglow of the sunset but even though she worked faithfully, she could not get it. "If I only had some one to help a little," she would say. "Some day I want to take some painting lessons again. If I could just make a picture as I want to,—it would satisfy something in me."

From the barn she got clean husks and made a family of dolls for Margaret. She made the bodies, heads and limbs from the husks and braided the corn-silk for hair. A man, a lady and a baby, she made, and dressed them in corn-husk clothes. Will built a small bedstead for them. Out of one of the coats in the barrel she made Mack a new suit and concocted a bonnet for Margaret out of the old one Regina had sent, trimming it with a little wisp of the pink tips. With her paints, she marked off a checkerboard for Mack, and Will whittled checkers from the circumference of some small cottonwood branches. She cut a pattern and made a calico dog for little John, stuffing it with corn-husks, and covering it with knotted ends of carpet rags to give it a woolly appearance. She ironed out brown wrapping paper, tied the pieces with yarn and drew waggish-looking cows and horses on it for him, too.

Margaret laboriously hemmed a handkerchief for her father and Mack made him a box for his newspapers. There was a State Journal now, and as scarce as money was, Will had subscribed. "We can't drop out of touch with other parts of the country," he had said. "And we must know what the rest of the settlers are doing."

The children could talk of nothing but the approach of the wonderful day. The word "he" had only one meaning in their vocabulary,—a portly gentleman with a white beard and a sack on his back.

"Are you sure he'll come this year, Mother? Heinie Reinmueller said he wouldn't. He said his mother said so."

"Of *course* he'll come," Abbie assured the three. "Because Father and I are making things, too, to help him when he comes."

With Scotch-Irish cleverness, she could think of a dozen things to do with her meager supplies to add to the festivities. She ran tallow in tiny molds for the candles. She made a little batch of molasses candy and baked cookies in star and diamond shapes. She boiled eggs and painted faces on them and made little calico bonnets for them.

Christine was contemptuous toward the unnecessary festivities.

"For dot . . . no time I haf. You learn 'em vork . . . cows milk 'n' pigs svill . . . 'n' dey for foolishness no time haf."

"Oh, don't let us ever get like Reinmuellers," Abbie said. "We're poor. If we were any poorer we might as well lie down and give up. But we can fight to keep civilized . . . can fight to keep something before us besides the work."

On the day before Christmas the snow lay deep on the prairie and the children's greatest anxiety was whether "he" would find the little house which was half buried. Margaret, with the characteristic ingenuity of the female of the species, suggested tying a piece of bright cloth where "he" would notice it. And Mack, with the characteristic daring of the less deadly of the same, got on top of the low house via a crusty snow bank and tied one of little John's red flannel shirts to the stove-pipe.

At lamp-lighting, they all hung up their stockings, even Will and Abbie. The children were beside themselves with excitement. By their parents' stockings they put the little presents they had made for them. They danced and skipped and sang. They cupped their eyes with their hands, pressing their faces to the little half-window and looking out into the night. The gleam of the stars was reflected in the snow, and the silence of the sky was the silence of the prairie.

"I see the Star."

"So do I. Right up there."

"It looks like it was over a stable."

"Yes, sir. It looks like it was over a manger-stable."

"Now it looks like it's stopping over us."

"Yes, sir, it looks like it's stopping right over *our* house."

Wide-eyed, they went to bed. The three faces in a row on the pillows, with the patchwork quilts tucked under the chins, were flushed with anticipation.

"Always keep the Christmas spirit going," Abbie told them. "Promise me, that when you get big and have homes of your own, you'll keep the Christmas spirit in your homes."

"We will," they promised in glib and solemn accord.

When at last they slept, Will brought in the little cedar tree. The morning found it trimmed with popcorn and tallow candles. And a marvelous flock of butterflies had settled upon it. Their bodies were of dried apples dipped in sugar and their antennæ were pink and feathery, looking surprisingly as though they had once adorned Regina Deal's bonnet. Will had made and painted Abbie a corner what-not with four shelves, secreting it in the stable behind some straw bedding. And he had constructed a monstrous hobby-horse for the children, the body and head of cottonwood chunks, real horse's hair for mane and tail, reins and a bit in the steed's cut-out mouth. The wooden horse of Troy never looked so huge. And then the old brass horn was unwrapped.

"I'm so excited," Mack said, in solemn ecstasy. "I'm so excited . . . my legs itch."

Historians say, "The winter of 'seventy-four to 'seventy-five was a time of deep depression." But historians do not take little children into consideration. Deep depression? To three children on the prairie it was a time of glamour. There was not much to eat in the cupboard. There was little or no money in the father's flat old pocketbook. The presents were pitifully homely and meager. And all in a tiny house,—a mere shell of a house, on a new raw acreage of the wild, bleak prairie. How could a little rude cabin hold so much white magic? How could a little sod house know such enchantment? And how could a little hut like that eventually give to the midwest so many influential men and women? How, indeed? Unless, . . . unless, perchance, the star *did* stop over the house?

CHAPTER XV

THERE was a great deal of suffering among the settlers. It was extremely cold. The government issued flour and beans and some army clothes left over from war days. A supply came to the Lutz store and Will took advantage of the offer of the flour, but only after some protest of pride.

"I don't want to, Abbie,—like beggars."

"Will Deal,—from your government, after you fought to keep it going!"

In the Lutz store, one day later, Abbie met Mrs. Tomlinson from Poor Man's Hollow. She had on one of the blue army coats and a pair of men's coarse army shoes.

Word came from back home that Grandpa Deal was very sick,—the disease which had caused his arm's amputation, had broken out again.

A few weeks later in the winter, Grandpa Lutz, Henry's and Oscar's old father, died. Homesick for the neat Michigan farm and a sight of lake water, uncomplaining, gently, he died. And once more the settlers stood around an irregular hole in the ground on the Lutz knoll of land where little Dan lay.

With scarcely a fortnight's passing, a letter came from Louise Deal telling of Grandpa Deal's death, too. In a winter of intense cold, little to eat, a dubious outlook for the future, and the worry of Abbie's pregnancy, the news of kind Grandpa Deal's death seemed too much to bear.

"I sat by his bed and Ma was mending stockings over by the window where the light was," Louise wrote. Yes, Grandma Deal would not want to be wasting any of the daylight, thought Abbie, as she read with tear-dimmed eyes. "He said, 'Sis!' . . . you know he sometimes called me that . . . 'Sis, how do you reckon it'll be, all gold and wings and harps and pearly gates? No meadows and lane roads and maple sap running and honey-locusts and young corn growing . . . and no jokes?' I told him I didn't know, and then in a little while he nodded his head over to where Ma was sitting and said, 'Sis, it'll be mighty lonesome sittin' around waitin' for her.' And when I looked at him again he was dead."

Abbie could not see the rest of the letter for the tears. She had loved Will's old father.

The winter seemed nothing but snow and cold, trouble and misery.

Only the children were happy. Too young to sense the desperate straits of the family, they played joyfully through the winter and worked cheerfully at the little tasks assigned them.

It was cold and rainy through March and part of April. And then spring came. Spring on the prairie, with the teal flying out of the coarse grass, with the willow and the cottonwood and the elders over by Stove Creek bursting into green joyousness, with sweet-William and blue phlox, mousetail and wild indigo nosing up through the sod, with the odor of loam and sub-soil coming over the low rolling hills on the wings of every breeze, with the white clouds scudding low with the wind, and with hope, which springs eternal.

To Abbie the winter had seemed one nightmare of trouble and one endless toot on an old cornet. Out of the hoarse and heterogeneous collection of sounds, Mack had evolved the faint semblance of two tunes. But the noisy affair had its advantage, for when he began herding hogs on the prairie, its guttural sounds assured her that he was all right.

It was hard for Abbie to put in the garden. Nature did not mean to have a woman bend to severe tasks at such a time. Mack and Margaret did a great deal of it under her supervision. Mack, with his eight years, could hoe the rows, and Margaret, with her six, could drop and cover the seeds. Even little John, who was nearly three, wanted to "d'op 'em in," but as he had a wild and superior disregard for keeping various seeds separate, he was persuaded to make mud pies at the edge of the patch.

The Lutz store distributed government seeds and Will went hopefully to his spring planting. But first he tried hard to get rid of the young grasshoppers on his wheat acreage by laying long rows of straw across the fields into which the infant grasshoppers crawled for warmth. He then set fire to the straw and destroyed a portion in that way. With the other men of the neighborhood, he disposed of a countless number of the pests to the government for two dollars a bushel. Never was money more thankfully received.

The small grain came up with much promise. More grasshoppers hatched, small as little gray-green flies, and promptly ate it up.

In spite of the desperately hard times, Henry Lutz seemed able to buy another eighty. He paid one thousand dollars for the eighth-section, a nice acreage lying south of the young Cedartown. Incidentally, his heirs sold it many years later for twenty thousand dollars.

All the neighbors now joined the Grange, a union of farmers, which some fondly thought would better conditions. It met in the schoolhouse, where there was a great deal of talk without much result, and where the women formed an auxiliary. Because of her condition, Abbie did not join, but she helped Sarah Lutz sew the regalia,—red calico robes, a cross between a cardinal's vestments and a Mother-Hubbard, which were to be tied with white sashes. Sarah told Abbie confidentially that she was *Pomona*, and young Mrs. Oliver Johnson was *Minerva* and that Christine had been *Scylla*, but when they assigned her the name she thought they said "Silly," and had straightway announced that even if she couldn't understand English very well, she knew when she was called names, and departed in high dudgeon.

In May, two young men stopped at the house just before dusk. They were driving six hundred sheep from the Ozark Mountains through to Cozad, which lay beyond the hundredth meridian on the edge of the country known as the Great American desert.

They were fine, upstanding fellows in their early twenties, the nephew of the editor of the Boston *Transcript*, and a chum. The uncle had just died the previous December and left the nephew five hundred dollars. With an equal amount of money the friend had joined him and formed a partnership. Besides the sheep, their chattels seemed to consist of a wagon, three small horses, a coffee-pot and a skillet.

They made camp for the night a little to the north and east of the Deal place, taking from the wagon a collapsible corral consisting of yards and yards of muslin, one end of which they tied to the wagon wheel and then used stakes driven into the ground for temporary fence-posts around which to wrap the muslin.

After the children were in bed, the young fellows came to the house and talked with Will, but Abbie stayed in the bedroom. The next morning they went on to add their fine young courage and energy to the building of the state.

Only a few mornings later, Abbie sent Margaret out with the old dog to call Will in from the field, and told Mack to take John up to Reinmuellers. When Will came hurriedly in, he unhitched, threw a saddle on old Bird and rode over after Dr. Hornby. Sarah Lutz came riding out with the doctor in his cart and Christine came down, too. The baby was born in the afternoon.

Abbie, relaxing, was filled with that age-old gratitude that her ordeal was over. Peace enveloped her,—peace and relative ease. Her fourth child! How queer! Well, she would love it and care for it tenderly.

Looking out in the other room she could see Will and the doctor, Christine and Sarah all close together. They were whispering. It seemed silent out there,—too silent,—a whispering silence. A great fright seized her, so that she raised herself up and called sharply, "Will!"

Will turned and came quickly into the bedroom.

"What's the matter, Will? I can tell there's something the matter."

Will took Abbie's hand. "It was a little son, Abbie."

"'*Was*,' Will? Not . . . not . . . ?"

"He didn't live, Abbie-girl."

"Oh . . . no . . . no!" She broke into wild sobbing. "Oh, God, not that. He's all right, Will. Go see if he isn't all right. My babies are always all right."

But when Will did not go and only tried to quiet her, she had to believe it. She was inconsolable. "Will, it was because I didn't want him at first."

And when he tried to reason with her, she would not listen. "I know better than any one. I'm punished. I didn't tell anybody. But I was bitter. And now I've lost my baby." In her whole life Abbie Deal never cried so wildly.

Sarah Lutz dressed him,—Sarah, with her black beady eyes softened with tears. And then she brought him in,—a beautifully formed child with a face like a tiny white rose. Abbie wanted him beside her, wanted to hold him.

"My baby . . . he's so cold, Will. I never had a cold baby. I want him to be warm." She did not talk rationally. "I hate death and I'm afraid of it. But I *did* want him, Will. After a while I wanted him. It was just at first." Rachel, who lives again in every grieving mother, was crying for her child and would not be comforted. And when she had worn out her hysteria and quieted, she said she wanted him to have a name. "Basil, Will,—after my father." Sarah came in and smoothed her hair, talked to her gently, and said they were going to take him over and put him by Dennie and Grandpa Lutz.

"*Ach!*" Christine came in and clucked her sympathy. "A boy, too! With the land he should help."

Abbie turned her face to the wall. Christine had no finer feelings. She lay and thought of her sister Janet and her dead baby. She could hear the faint pound, pound, of a hammer out at the barn. Every hammer stroke hit her heart. They were going to take the baby over to the Lutz burial knoll. There was no one there but Dannie and Grandpa Lutz.

Dannie . . . Grandpa Lutz . . . and now little Basil Deal . . . three to make a cemetery. In a new country you had to make homes and roads and wells and schools . . . and you had to make a cemetery. You couldn't get around it . . . you had to make a cemetery, too.

She lay there and thought of the knoll and the prairie grass and the low picket fence against which the tumbleweeds piled . . . where the blackbirds wheeled and the sun beat down and the wind blew. She hated the barrenness of it. If she could put him in a shady place it wouldn't be quite so hard. But to put him in the sun and the coarse grass and the wind! She and Sarah would go over and plant some trees some day. She heard the rattle of the lumber-wagon and raised herself up to look through the little half-window set in the sod. She could see Will and Sarah in the wagon. Will was driving, and Sarah had a little wooden box across her lap. When the big lumber-wagon rattled away from the house, Abbie lay back on her pillow. For a long time she could hear the sound of the lumber-wagon rattling over the prairie.

CHAPTER XVI

☙§ It was several weeks before Abbie could get around again to do all her work. Christine or Sarah came over and helped a little each day. Service finds its greatest opportunity and its least begrudged hours of labor among neighbors in a new community through which lines have not been drawn and into which class has not yet come.

Abbie could not get over the loss of her little son. Always she saw him in shadowy outline among the others. All her life she was to say, "Now he would be seven," "To-day he would be twelve," "He could have voted to-day for the first time." Yes, Abbie Deal was a born mother,—one of those women who love the touch of baby flesh, who cuddle little children to them, who, when their own babies have grown, catch up some other woman's child to fondle.

On the day in June in which Abbie did her first full day's work, the grasshoppers lifted their wings and flew to other fields,—as complete and unified a departure as their coming had been.

There was no small grain that summer, but a half-hearted corn crop seemed on the way. Settlers by the score were returning east. Scarcely a day passed which did not see some forlorn group go by the house. Many of the covered wagons carried statements painted on their wagons, which would have been humorous if they had not been so tragic. "Going back to Pa and Ma," was one. Another held a huge caricature of a grasshopper strangling a man with its forelegs and antennæ, and the laconic words, "He wins."

Abbie, standing at the door and watching one of these bedraggled-looking outfits pass, said bitterly to Will, "When do you think our time is coming? Look at the clouds, Will. Even the clouds seem always going east."

Will did not answer. He turned on his heel and went down to the straw-covered dug-out which served as a barn. Watching him go, in his faded blue shirt and overalls with their many patchings, and his dingy old hat, Abbie called to her mind the fine figure he had made in his wedding suit,—fine enough to draw the attention of any exacting young woman. Ten years ago! And the minister at home had said you could do anything with your life. But that was not so. Life did things to you. Ten years! Small wonder that love would break under circumstances like these. Standing there in the soddie door, she seemed two personalities. One argued bitterly that it was impossible for love to keep going when there was no hope for the future, suggested that there was no use trying to keep it going. The other said sternly that marriage was not the fulfillment of a passion,—marriage was the fulfillment of love. And love was sometimes pleasure and sometimes duty.

"You traitor," she said suddenly to herself, "You Judas! As though hard luck could kill my love for Will! Will's not to blame. It's a fine love that a little bad luck can smother! It can't touch it . . . it can't. Love is the light that you see by. It's all in the world we've got to light our way, and it takes both of us to keep it bright. And I'm not doing my share . . . I'm not. I'm glum and sad and discouraged. And I'm not going to be any more. There are only two things that can help us,—and that's our courage and our love. From this very minute on I'm going to try to cheer Will up more. I'm through being down-hearted."

She turned to the children. They were all around the table looking at a little picture Margaret had drawn. Margaret was always drawing. Abbie ran to them, closed warm maternal arms around all three, and bumped them together in a return of girlish spirits, so that they laughed at her unusual playfulness, their faces sparkling because Mother was full of fun. How readily they responded to all her moods. And how careful she must be with those childish impressions.

"You shall wear them, Margaret," she kissed her little daughter, "you shall wear them yet."

"Wear what, Mother?"

"The pearls."

"What are pearls, Mother?"

"Wait . . . I'll show you."

She got it from under the bed,—the old calf-skin box, and the children gathered close with excited anticipation. She took the pearls out and ran them through her fingers.

"Oh, Mother . . . the pretty beads!" Margaret's gray eyes glowed.

"Shucks, I'd rather have a watch," from the masculine Mack. Little John was not even interested.

Abbie laughed and held them up, their creamy luster inappropriate against her work-worn hand. She put them around Margaret's little sunburned neck, and they hung down over the dingy gray calico dress with incongruous comparison.

"You shall wear them, darling. Some day you shall. We're going to make it come true. We've *got* to make it come true." She caught Margaret to her. "It takes faith and courage and love and prayer and work and a little singing to keep up your spirits, but we're going to do it."

In September, Mack and Margaret started to school to a little new one-roomed frame building which some one already had christened the Woodpecker School. Little Emma Lutz started, too, and two more of the Reinmueller boys,—Christine's idea being that it would be a good thing for them to know how to write their names, at least, and figure up bushels. On good days the children trudged the long grassy way, and on bad days, Will stopped his work long enough to take them in the wagon. Abbie shed copious tears the first morning they started, and then laughed at her own inconsistency.

"I wanted them to have a school closer than Sodom to go to, and then I cry when they do have," she said to Will. But Will said he knew how she felt. Will was always so understanding, Abbie thought gratefully.

That winter of '76 and '77 was another one of great hardship, but like many things in life, it had its pleasant side. A reading circle was formed and met at Woodpecker School every Friday night. Its members wore ribbon badges upon which Sarah Lutz and Abbie had printed the mysterious letters "S.C.L.R.C.," which, when the mystery was eliminated, were discovered to stand for the title of Stove Creek Precinct Literary Reading Circle. The membership was divided, like all Gaul, into three parts, and if there were not Belgians, Helvetians and Germans who fought and bled, at least, the "Reds," the "Blues," and the "Yellows" met in forensic frays. On one Friday night the "Reds" performed, the next two Fridays the "Blues" and "Yellows" respectively, and on the fourth Friday night a big contest was staged, in which the star members of the various colors mingled in one grand rainbow spectrum, with people imported from outside the precinct sitting in judgment upon the efforts. That winter the schooner *Hesperus* was wrecked, little Paul Dombey died, Hamlet met his father's ghost and the Raven quothed more times than there were meetings,—new "pieces" being at a premium, as they were.

Whole families came, ensconced on straw in the bottom of wagon-boxes which had been put upon bob-sleds. Every one brought heated soap-stones or hot flat-irons, as more than one load came from twenty miles away. The Henry Lutzes brought their reed-organ in the sleigh each time, so there was always music. Abbie was put on for a group of songs whenever the "Blues" performed, and always led the chorus singing. "Three Blind Mice" and "Scotland's Burning" were the favorite rounds. As for the favorite choruses, while great partiality was shown toward "Juanita," "Annie Laurie" and "Revive Us Again," for sheer volume there was nothing like "Pull For the Shore" to open the throttle. Young blades who could not carry a tune were filled with an irresistible impulse to sing whenever the life-line was brought out, and when the sailors began to make more rapid progress toward the lighthouse, they would grab oars, as it were, open their mouths and bellow like young steers.

In September of 1877, Abbie gave birth to a girl. The high bleating cries of the child were music to the mother who could never erase from her mind the misery of that whispering silence of two years before. They named the little girl Isabelle. "Maybe *she'll* be the lovely lady," Abbie thought as she ran her fingers through the tiny moist ringlets of reddish-brown hair.

The first Sunday Abbie could get out, Will hitched up the horses to the lumber-wagon, and they drove to the dedication of the new frame church near the Lutz store. Henry Lutz had donated the land, and a dollar collected here and another one there, had bought the lumber which was hauled from Nebraska City. All the men of the community for miles around had given their time for the labor, and now a little unpainted church stood at the four corners.

It had been nine years now since the Deal and Lutz and Reinmueller wagons had first crawled across the prairie. A few fences had appeared, and the old buffalo trail had begun to take upon itself the semblance of a roadway. Tracks were plainly visible, worn by the feet of a thousand oxen and horses and the wide iron rims of the dingy prairie schooners. Between the trails the grass still flaunted, and the graceful goldenrod nodded its plumed head, as a queen bows when her subjects pass by. Sweet William and blue phlox, mouse-tail and wild indigo crowded the grass of the roadway, and when the tiny primrose was gone, yellow and white mustard elbowed their way in to take the place.

The cottonwoods had shot up with unbelievable growth. The leaves, with their peculiar double motion, seemed always twinkling, always dancing. The silhouettes of the grayish-green clumps against the prairie sky were Abbie's poetry and her paintings, her sermons and her songs.

Cedartown now had its church and its school, its store and blacksmith shop, and six houses assembled in the same vicinity. And it had its cemetery, for Henry Lutz had given the community the knoll where Dannie lay. There were seven mounds inside the picket fence where herding stock could not trample. Yes, in a new country you have to make a cemetery.

Crops were no better. They were put in each year with hope, and they came up with promise. But the dry, fluffy clouds scudded high across the blue sky without moisture, or the hot winds blew, and the settlers would harvest a scant half-crop. In some way, Will and Abbie held body and soul together. In some way, the children seemed to get enough to eat and to thrive and grow.

In the fall of '79 a man with a violin case stopped at the house and asked if he could have supper. He had been drinking, and Will, contrary to his usual hospitable manner, talked with him for some time before he decided to invite him to stay.

After the meal the guest took out the violin and played for the family. The music seemed to steady him, for when he drew the bow across the strings all the wild sweet bird songs of the forest came from them. To Abbie, with her deep-worn love of music, if was enchantment.

"Can you, . . ." she asked, when he had finished, "can you play a song called 'The Lady of the Lea' . . . ?"

For answer, he drew the bow again and the melody came lightly, delicately, hauntingly. Abbie had not sung it for four or five years, but now she threw back her head and took the air to the violin's accompaniment.

"Oh, the Lady of the Lea,
Fair and young and gay was she,
Beautiful exceedingly,
The Lady of the Lea."

In the sod house with its cook-stove and the turned-over boiler and the burning twisted hay, with its crude what-not and its sod bed, its store-box book-shelves and its burlap floor covering, she put into her voice all the longing of her heart, all the vague hopes for the best that life could give her children.

"For she had gold and she had land,
Everything at her command,
The Lady of the Lea."

It was as though, through sheer force of will, she was trying to make all the desires for her children's future come true,—all her dreams for them turn to realities.

"Dreaming visions longingly,
The Lady of the Lea."

"You have a good voice," the stranger said soberly. "You ought to do something with it."

"There are lots of things one *ought* to do," Abbie replied,—and looked over at Will to see whether he had detected the bitterness which she had not been able to keep out of her reply.

The man put his violin carefully, tenderly, into the case. "It's a Stradivarius," he said. "A man in Omaha offered me six hundred dollars for it."

Will looked up in surprise. "Offered you six hundred dollars . . . for a fiddle?" It seemed a fortune. "And you mean you wouldn't sell it?"

"No," said the man simply. "I couldn't. Thank you very much for the supper." And he went, a little unsteadily, out of the door.

Abbie walked over to the small-paned half-window set in the sod, and looked out at the gray twilight coming across the prairie. The winds that were never still blew past the house in their unending flight.

How queer people were. All the folks in the new country were hoarding things, hanging on to old heirlooms. They became their symbols of refinement and culture. Sarah Lutz had a painting that drew your eyes to it the minute you opened the door. Oscar Lutz's wife had a pink quilted bedspread that she kept rolled up in newspapers. Even Christine Reinmueller had a bright blue vase with magenta-colored roses on it, standing up on top of the cupboard. They stood for something besides the land and the corn and the cattle. They must hang onto them, never lose them out of their lives, for if lost, everything was lost. She must hang onto the pearls and everything they stood for; Sarah must keep her painting; Martha Lutz, her bedspread; Christine, her blue vase. Else what was there in the future for the children?

"No," said Abbie aloud at the soddie window. "No, he couldn't sell it."

For some time she stood there, watching the half-intoxicated man go east across the prairie.

CHAPTER XVII

☙§ THE snow began in October that year and did not leave until the last of March. Wherever there were fences, the drifts piled high and obliterated them, so that one would not have known any had been built,—Nature's little joke, as though she were laughing at the settlers for their pains.

The children's attendance at school was broken constantly by severe snowstorms, so that Abbie again did much of the teaching herself. She often searched her mind for new ideas, trying to think what more she could do for the children. Time was slipping away and conditions were no better. Even if she must face the hard fact that she could never do anything more for herself, the children must have some of the best things of life. Will was working day and night, making an old man of himself before his time. *She* must do more for the children some way. She must not let them grow up without a taste for good things. They ought to know more about music and have more reading material, and because they were not getting them, in some way she must instill in them a *desire* to have them. They must never be satisfied with things as they were. Even if she and Will were to live in a soddie all their lives, cut off from those things, the children must want to have them. If the desire were deep enough, they would find a way to seek them out as they grew older.

She began getting down the Shakespeare plays for a while each evening, and requiring Mack and Margaret to learn a passage or two. Over and over she made them repeat:

> *"The quality of mercy is not strained*
> *It droppeth as the gentle rain from heaven*
> *Upon the place beneath."*

Or, perhaps:

> *"There's a divinity that shapes our ends,*
> *Rough-hew them how we will."*

Mack protested. "Aw, shucks, I don't see any sense to them."

"It's for your own good, Mack," she would say. "Some day when you're older, the meaning will all come to you. And you'll be glad you've learned so much of them."

But Mack was more interested in his old brass horn. There was a six-piece band over at Cedartown now, and that spring one often heard the far-away blare of the three brass instruments, the toot of the fife and the rumble of the two snare drums. The organization was preparing for the first Fourth of July celebration in the community and patriotic airs were as much in evidence as the spring winds. Mack, herding hogs, would sit at the western border of his father's land and windily blow out the same tune which the band was practicing. As he was usually two notes behind the others, his part in the proceedings sounded like an echo. It began to bother the legitimate performers, so that, more from sheer self-defense than enthusiastic desire, they invited him to join them. Mack's round freckled face beamed at the invitation as one receiving a congressional medal.

All masculine hands donated work that spring toward the building of a small frame G.A.R. hall. It was completed in time for the Fourth of July celebration and dedicated with much oratory and a baked bean supper. Sarah and Martha Lutz and Abbie had sewed yards and yards of unbleached muslin together to form the top of a bowery, over which were placed branches cut from the trees at the creek-bend and under which all the residenters within a twenty-mile radius danced.

By 1880 the Deal land was all fenced. The fence was a symbol,—

man's challenge to the raw west. Every fence post was a sign post. More plainly than flaunting boards, they said, "We have enclosed a portion of the old prairie. We hold between our wooden bodies the emblem of the progressive pioneer,—barbed wire. We are the dividing line. We keep the wild out and the domesticated within." The road, too, which followed the old buffalo trail had been surveyed and straightened. Man's system had improved upon the sinuously winding vagaries of the old buffalo, and the road, although still grass-grown, ran straight west past the house. The development of the road is the evolution of the various stages of civilization.

But though man could fence the prairie and direct the way of the road, he could not control the storm. "This far shalt thou go and no farther," the God of the settlers seemed to say. Snows, droughts, blizzards, dust storms, rains, hot winds and the little pigmy people,—He held them all in the hollow of His hand.

On the seventeenth of April, the Deal family drove in the lumber wagon across the prairie to attend the funeral service for a distant neighbor. The day was warm and windy and disagreeable. Little miniature whirlwinds of dust spiraled themselves ahead of the team and the dry particles of dirt blew back in their faces. As they rode, the wind grew in volume and the dust clouds thickened with the rising of the wind. Before the fury of its force great sheets of top-soil from the newly plowed fields were lifted into the air and thrown with violence over the land. When the family reached the schoolhouse, they found their neighbors sitting there with dirt-blackened faces, almost unrecognizable. The room was dense with dust-clouds, the little building shivering in the onslaught of dirt. At one blast of wind more severe than others, the minister paused in the midst of the funeral eulogy and said, "There are times when it is wiser to think of the living than to honor our loved dead. I think it wiser that we disperse at once and drive to the cemetery."

Will and Aibbe thought they could not get home through the terrific storm. It was like swimming the waves of a dirty sea. Abbie held Isabelle closely, and Mack and Margaret kept John's hands in their own. In fear of colliding with some one, Will did not drive the horses off a walk. Slowly they crawled over the prairie, through the dense dust clouds, with only occasional moments of the lifting of the dirt, in which Will, watching for the road, would guide the blinded team back into the trail. The storm was like a blizzard in its fury,—a black blizzard, with grit and dust for snow, and with field dirt for the drifts through which they drove.

Eyes and ears were full of the gritty earth particles, and at times it seemed that they would suffocate. Then Will would stop the team for a rest, before plunging again into the black whirlpool of dust.

At home again, Abbie thought she could not endure the sight that met her eyes. Over the burlap floor-covering lay a soft inch-thick carpet of dirt. Over the curtains and the beds lay the same grimy substance. It floated on the waterpail and in the milk in the cupboard. There was nothing in the house in condition to eat and nothing that could be worn without washing. And so, once more, the young pioneer mother bent to the task of fighting the elements, to help make a home on the prairie.

Surprisingly, that year, crops were good. There was an indication of better times to come. Prices went up. Will and Abbie began talking and planning about the new house. No, that is not quite true,—*Abbie* began talking and planning about the new house. It is the woman's prerogative. Mack was thirteen now, Margaret eleven, John eight, and Isabelle three. They were getting too old to be packed in like little chickens in a coop, Abbie said. Every moment that was free from the ever-present hard work, she sat with pencil and paper and drew plans for a house.

"Even if it's just a few rooms at first," she would say to Will, "they'll be nice, and we'll plan it so they can be added to as times goes on. Can you think of anything grander, Will, than a sitting-room, all with clean, new, white plaster, and a kitchen that's built to be *handy*, and two upstairs bedrooms for the older children?"

"I'd like to do it for you, Abbie-girl. Maybe we can, if I do a lot of the work myself."

That summer they stopped at the J. Sterling Morton's as they had often done, on their way to Nebraska City, and the visit inspired them both to greater activity in making a better home. The Morton house seemed the last word in grandeur with its bay windows and real shingled roof, its fancy wall-paper and figured carpet, its tidies on the backs of all the chairs and splashers behind the wash-bowl and pitchers.

That fall and early winter, remarkable weather prevailed. It was unusually warm. Migrating songsters stayed on,—the robins and the bluebirds, the phœbes and the red birds. Even an occasional meadow-lark gave its June call in that wonderful Indian summer. There was in the air that haze which is found nowhere but in the midwest, and at no time but late fall when winter loiters on its way,—that glamorous haze which is not air, nor sunshine, nor smoke, but a little of all three,—air from over the wild, free prairies, smoke from a thousand burning weed-bends and brush fires, and sunshine filtered through the sifting, shifting smoke and air. There was bronze on the clumps of oaks along Stove Creek, red on the maples, yellow on the cottonwoods, green in the late pastures, white clouds dipping low, and over all, that haze, which is not smoke, nor air, nor sunshine, but a little of all three.

In the last half of December the spell broke. The winds blew over the prairie. Tumble-weeds from far out on the open, rushing headlong before their terrific onslaught, piled up against the fences and the little buildings. The leaves on the clumps of trees by the creek blew into nowhere. The pickets around the little cemetery caught and held a brown drift of leaves and tumble-weeds. The birds scurried before the wind. The snows came.

By Christmas the snow was fifteen inches deep on the level, and crusted over,—a delicate shimmering steel, which held up men and the lighter animals on its surface. Will could not get to town with his team, but would walk over to the store with a sack on his back. Snow-drifts were ten and fifteen feet deep. Days were bright, sunshiny and zero at noontime. Nights were clear, white-lighted, and twenty-two below.

All winter the deep snows held. On ranches farther west thousands of cattle died. The spring found many of the ranchers ruined. The snows melted and the streams ran high. Stove Creek came half way up the pasture, and departing, left behind the slag of the creek-bed.

When the weather settled, the Deals started the new house. And Abbie Deal thought heaven could not hold more joy than the planning of those five rooms. Will hauled stone from Louisville and pine and cottonwood lumber from Nebraska City. And one day when there was a sick cow and he could not leave, Abbie went alone for the lumber. Old Asy Drumm came with his hammer and his saw and his plug of tobacco, and watching him labor, one would have thought there was some invisible mechancial connection between his jaws and the other tools, so harmoniously did they work.

"We'll have the sitting-room there and the kitchen here," Abbie told Asy. And old Asy, with few comments but much tobacco chewing, placed the sitting-room there and the kitchen here. The result was weatherproof and sturdy, but only in the light of later years was it proven artless. Only to other than the eyes of Abbie Deal did it ever appear devoid of artistry. To Abbie it was always a thing of architectural beauty, for it was conceived from love and desire in the days of her youth.

There were three rooms downstairs,—a sitting-room, a kitchen, and a bedroom for Will, Abbie and little Isabelle. Up the uncarpeted pine stairs was a room for Margaret, and one for Mack and John.

"I've planned it so we can build on a room later right to the front," Abbie would say. "Then, some day we can cut double doors from the sitting-room into a new parlor."

The cedar trees, which Abbie had set out years before, had not lived through the droughts. So now, they put out a new group, nine on each side of a potential path leading up to the front of the house. Lombardy poplars in a long row were set at right angles to the main road, following the track to the barn which Will's wagon had worn in the thirteen years. "It'll make a nice shady lane road," Abbie would plan, "and some day we'll have the white picket-fence." Yes, the real home was beginning to shape itself.

In the middle of the summer they moved into the half-finished house. They scarcely knew what to do with all the space. They could not quite get used to the fact that the family of six could spread itself out all over five rooms. After the old two-roomed soddie, the simple, plain house seemed a palace. It represented a big move forward. They were about to see daylight. After thirteen years they were actually beginning to witness results. Trees were commencing to give shade. Orchards were beginning to bear. Better crops were being harvested and higher prices given. To Abbie it seemed that for the first time they were really going to live.

The Deal family was representative of other families, its condition indicative of state conditions. The western half of the state began to be settled. The old range cattle ranches were practically finished. The "grain farmer" was moving in. Wagons again passed the Deal home, going west this time. Prairie schooners once more crawled over the old buffalo trail, pushing on now to the grassy valleys which lay between the sand hills or to the fertile plains beyond.

CHAPTER XVIII

THERE were good crops again the next year. No longer did the dry, fluffy clouds scud high across the blue. They gathered and fell in a benediction of rains. And there were no hot winds.

It put courage and high hopes into every one. A great relief was in Abbie's mind. There seemed something to live for, something ahead for the family, at last.

Abbie had her house-yard fence now, so that the chickens could not molest her flowers. Sea-blue larkspur and blood-red hollyhocks flaunted their colors against the dazzling white of the pickets. Flowers in the yard! No one but a rancher's wife, who had lived in a soddie and up to whose door had come the pigs and the calves and the chickens, could realize what it meant to have a fenced house-yard with flowers.

Life was crowded with hard work for Abbie, but it was also full of compensations. There were the children, well, capable, bright.

Mack at fifteen was big, overgrown, with a round, freckled face that reminded Abbie somehow of her mother's fat, placid one. Mack made friends everywhere. He seemed to have that knack of fitting in with every one. "It may stand him in good stead some time," Abbie would say to Will. He lived the life of the typical farm boy who had to work by the side of his father. With two old coats, a cap, a muffler and overalls tucked into knee boots, he froze in the winter hauling wood or caring for the stock. With a hickory shirt, home-made pants, galluses and a flappy straw hat, he roasted in the summer at the plowing or haying.

Margaret, thirteen, was always drawing. Her sleek dark braids and gray eyes were bent above paper and pencil whenever she had leisure time. The cottonwoods and the cedars, a bit of path between the elderberry bushes, a spray of graceful goldenrod,—she was always trying to get these down on paper.

John, ten now, gave evidence of being a replica of his father, quiet, serious, uncomplaining, reminding Abbie of Will when he was a boy. Isabelle gave promise of becoming the family beauty, for although only seven, she was attractive with her reddish-brown curls, her brown eyes and her fair skin,—and always singing at her play in a clear childish voice. "My little 'lovely lady,'" Abbie used to say to herself. "How glad I am I named her Isabelle."

It had been thirteen years since Abbie and Will had followed the trail behind old Red and Baldy, and Abbie had not been back home.

"You can come back to visit whenever you want to, I promise you that, Abbie," Will had said. And she had not gone back once. But she did not blame Will. He had been helpless to keep that promise. And now this summer he said that she must go. All the plans were made, with a new brown cashmere dress in the process of construction.

Abbie sang at her work, that after all these years she was to go back home and see her mother and Belle, Janet and Mary and the boys.

And then, Mack did not feel well. Dr. Hornby came and after some time decided it was to be a run of fever,—typhoid. Abbie put away the unfinished dress and hung over Mack's bed for weeks. He pulled through, but by the time he was strong enough to be up, the fall had come and the rains, so that the roads to Lincoln and Nebraska City were impassable, and Abbie's plan for a trip back home had gone into nothing.

It was only a few weeks later that Will came in from putting up the team after a trip to Weeping Water and said: "Abbie, you can get out your old paints. There's a woman in Weeping Water just come from some place back east and they say she's a real artist. They say she'll take some pupils and I told 'em my wife was always wanting to try her hand . . ."

Abbie was already on her way to the calf-skin box under the bed, with Margaret close behind her. When she had come out with the chest and opened it, Margaret was still at her elbow, her gray eyes wide with anticipation.

"Oh, Mother,—I didn't know you had any paints now. You just said you *used* to . . . Oh, Mother, *why* did you never tell me?"

"Why did you want to know?"

The young girl's eyes were bright gray lights. "Oh, Mother . . . I want to use them . . . I want to go and see that woman . . . Oh, Mother . . . *something* in me . . ."

Will was cross. "That'll do, Margaret. You don't understand. Before you were born, when your mother came out here, she wanted to . . ."

"Will," said Abbie sternly, "hush! Of *course* you may try them, Margaret. And we'll take you over to Weeping Water some time to see the artist."

When Abbie left the room, Margaret did not even look up. She was sorting the tubes in the little box, touching them lovingly as one would touch jewels.

When Mack was seventeen, he went to Omaha with his father and came back changed. He was through with farm life and he didn't care who knew it. Will said he'd better settle down and get to work and Mack said no, he wanted to get a job in Omaha. Will said it was a boy's fool notion and Mack said it was nothing of the kind, that he was almost eighteen and he knew what he wanted. Never did Abbie feel so helpless to handle a situation, so uncertain what to say or do.

"He doesn't want to sweat," Will told her with sarcasm. "He wants to wear a white collar."

"What do you want to do up there?" Abbie was trying to keep the conversation peaceful.

"Oh, I don't know just *what.* Get in somewhere and work up."

"Get in *somewhere* . . . but *where* . . . and what?" Will had no patience with the wild scheme.

"Anything that's where there's business and a big town . . . anything but the farm."

And Will had said that the Deals had always been for the land.

Abbie stood between them for days. "Oh, Will, don't you see? The farm is distasteful to Mack."

"A farm has been good enough for smarter men than Mack."

"We don't all want to do the same thing, and Will, you said you couldn't do anything just working for your father. You've always been so understanding. Then try to understand Mack."

Abbie talked and prayed. "Oh, God, it's such little things we need help in,—such every day affairs." She saw Will's disappointment and she saw Mack's ambitions. Torn between the two, she could only smooth matters over for both.

"Let him go, then," Will said suddenly, as one who could no longer hold to his point. "But I wish to God, Margaret and Isabelle had been boys. Maybe we could get something done around here then." He slammed the kitchen door and went down to the barn. Abbie, fighting back the tears, told herself that he didn't mean it. Will loved his girls,—and he didn't mean it.

By fall Mack had a job in an Omaha bank. Henry Lutz knew one of the officers well, and it was through him that Mack landed the work which consisted in part of sweeping and dusting, but which "beat plowing corn all to pieces," according to the wielder of the broom and duster.

Abbie had thought she could not stand it to see Mack leave home. All day long she had sewed shirts and mended socks for him,—and all night she had stared into the dark with the worry of her boy going to the city. But with the arrival of his letters, some of her anxiety vanished. When at Christmas time he came home to spend the day, he was full of "bank talk." One would have gathered from his conversation that he was at least on the board of directors.

In the spring of '85, the day which had been set aside by the various governors for planting trees was legalized as a holiday,—and J. Sterling Morton had given Arbor Day to Nebraska, which, in turn, was eventually to give it to the other states. That summer Abbie again planned the delayed trip back home. Before she was ready word was noised about that an academy was to open in Weeping Water in the fall. It was to have a full three-year academic course preparing students for college, with special attention to the languages.

"For what anybody two vays vant to talk . . . ?" Christine asked.

"I felt like telling her no one could object if *she* would stick to one way," Abbie told Will. Christine's language was no better than when she had first arrived in the prairie schooner. Quite often she used both the German and the English words in the same sentence.

Emma Lutz, Margaret's chum, and a year younger, was going to the academy. Henry and Sarah drove over to Weeping Water in their high-topped buggy with the natural-colored maple wheels and a red tassel on the whip, to get a place for Emma to board.

Abbie could think of nothing else when she heard it. An academy! Margaret ought to go,—Margaret, at sixteen, with her braids of soft dark hair, her big gray eyes, her gentle manner, and her love of painting. She ought to have more schooling, to meet more young people. Several times that summer Emil Reinmueller had come over to take her to neighborhood socials. It worried Abbie a little. Emil was nineteen, a blond young giant, stolid, crude, virile. What if . . . ? "Thou art mated to a clown and the grossness of his nature will have weight to drag thee down," Abbie had read from Tennyson's *Locksley Hall*. Emil was no mate for Margaret with her love of the niceties of life. What could a mother do? What had *her* mother done? Nothing. "I married the man I wanted," Abbie thought. What if Margaret, with her high ideals and her painting talent—what if she should suddenly turn and say, "Mother, I'm going to marry Emil." What could one do? The worry of it was constantly with Abbie.

She began trying to plan how she could send Margaret to the academy with little expense. The money for the trip back home would pay the first tuition. Will did not like the idea. "You've planned this trip for years. You ought not to give it up for her. And she's just where she can really help you, now, at home." He argued, "You've got yourself to think about."

"Oh, no, I haven't," Abbie said quickly, "I've got the *children* to think about."

He gave in, a little grudgingly. If Abbie thought she could manage— And Abbie knew she *must* manage.

She took the team and drove the ten miles to Weeping Water. When she came back, she had a place in the minister's family for Margaret to work for her board, and a dress pattern of red and gray plaid for best. It was all they could afford now, but on the way home Abbie mentally made over Margaret's old dress and one of her own, trimmed a hat, and relined a winter coat.

In the last half of the summer they tied two quilts, as Margaret had to furnish her own bedding. They made over the clothes in accordance with Abbie's previous brain convolutions, mended cotton stockings, ironed out hair ribbons, made a work-apron out of flour-sacking, and packed and repacked the small trunk. Abbie could not think how the home would be without Margaret. Quiet, gentle, fun-loving, ready to help, Margaret had always been at her right hand.

Will was to take Margaret and Emma in the lumber-wagon, so the trunks could go with them. Emma had several new dresses and a dolman,—the latest thing in wraps. It was made of black watered silk, waist length in the back and to the bottom of the skirt in front, with cape-like appendages for sleeves, and rows of braid, cord, beads and buttons rambling nonchalantly all over the whole structure. Added to this grandeur was a new gold watch on a long chain which went twice around her neck and eventually came to rest in a pocket sewed on her bosom, the pocket constructed of lace so that the gold of the watch would shine through. Henry Lutz was very proud of his purchase. "There's a whole horse around Emma's neck," he would announce with complacence. It sounded rather startling at first hearing, until one realized he meant no acrobatic feat, but that the price of a horse had gone into the chain.

Will went over to town after Emma and her trunk first, and then the two came back to the farm for Margaret, who had been ready for an hour.

"You're sure you'll get along, Mother?"

"Why, of course I'll get along." Abbie was outwardly calm and confident, while all the time there was that queer sensation of a wind rushing by,—a wind she could not stop,—Time going by which she could not stay. Oh, stop the clock hands! Stop Time for a minute until she could think whether it was right for Margaret to go away and leave her.

"Good-by, dear!" Oh, stop the clock hands!

Will was calling. "Trunk's in. All ready in there?" Stop Time for a while,—until she could think—!

"Oh, Mother, do you think I *ought* to go?"

"Of *course* you ought to go." Head up, Abbie was smiling.

"Good-by, then . . . !"

They were down the lane road now, past the Lombardy poplars. Now they had turned east onto the main road. Margaret was dividing her handkerchief between her eyes and waving. Abbie waved and smiled,—waved and smiled,—as long as they were in sight. Then she turned and ran blindly into her bedroom and shut the door. And, whether she has driven away in a lumber-wagon or a limousine, the mother whose daughter has left her for the first time, will understand why Abbie Deal ran blindly into her bedroom and shut the door.

CHAPTER XIX

§ THAT fall, Dr. Hornby, Henry Lutz and Will Deal went up to Omaha to interview the powers that were, in regard to the railroad coming through Cedartown instead of farther to the north as the plans seemed to be. Later the Superintendent came down and was driven through the farming section by Henry Lutz. In consequence, Cedartown drew the branch line, and with many an expression of high glee, figuratively made faces at the Weeping Water delegation which had worked against the southern route.

Margaret's school year was a wonderful experience. There were thirty tuition pupils, about half from the town of Weeping Water and half from farm homes. The minister, in whose family Margaret stayed, had a nephew who was studying to be a doctor, and who had come to visit his uncle. "His name is Fred Baker and I wish you could know him, Mother," Margaret reported. "You never in your *life* saw such a fine young man."

Abbie wondered.

In July of '86, the railroad was finished through to Lincoln. And now, Cedartown would no longer sit out on the prairie by herself. No longer would twenty-three miles of snow drifts or deep ruts of mud lie between her and the capital city. Cedartown residents held their heads a little higher, spoke largely of "train-time" and "making connections for Omaha." Already the stones were in place for the foundation of the station. A train each way every day, mail in a sack being thrown carelessly out of a baggage-car instead of from a pony's back, a telegraph machine clicking noisily in a three-roomed station. What more metropolitan atmosphere could one desire?

The day that the first train came through was a gala one. Word has been wafted about by some occult means that any one who wanted to do so could ride to the end of the line free of charge. The entire Cedartown population, including two puppies and a cat, was on hand to pile hilariously into the box-cars and ride to the end of the road. Old Asy Drumm took his hammer and his saw and his tobacco, and drove over to the track with the Deals, as he had just finished building another room to the rear of the house. Upon their return from the free railroad trip, Abbie and Margaret began painting the pine woodwork in the new kitchen. Margaret, since her year in the academy, was a little fussy about the way things looked.

Abbie's plans for going back home that summer had gone into nothing on account of the new kitchen and the fact that she realized more and more that, because Isabelle was the musical one of the family, she must have an organ.

The Lutzes were getting Emma a fine new piano, so Will bought their second-hand reed-organ. On Isabelle's ninth birthday he brought it home in the lumber-wagon. Isabelle was beside herself with excitement. Her little legs pumped furiously up and down to get air into the creature's cloth lungs and her little, slender, tapering fingers ran nimbly over the keys.

Abbie, herself, sat down and tried to pick out a few chords of an old song, but her fingers were stiff and clumsy.

"By George, you're the one that ought to take lessons," Will said suddenly, "the way you always wanted . . ."

"No . . ." Abbie got up from the whirling carpet-covered stool. "No." Her lips trembled a little so that she did not look up. "At forty it's too late."

In the spring of '87 the community was presented with the first issue of the Cedartown *Headlight*, a small sheet with growing pains. It contained a great many items pertaining to "the growth of our fair city." It said that Mr. William Deal arrived in front of the editorial office in a fine new green lumber-wagon with red wheels, that on April fools' day a cow of Mr. Oscar Lutz's presented him with twin calves, that a box social was held in the G.A.R. hall, at which a good time was had by all. One gathered from an editorial that subscriptions could be paid with cobs, butchered beef and money, but that the greatest of these was money.

Crops continued to be good. Abbie thought that this coming summer of '87 would prove to be the one in which she could go back home. And then, before she was ready, she knew she was to be a mother. With Isabelle, her youngest child, nearly ten, Abbie thought she could not face motherhood again,—not at forty-one.

"That means I won't go back to the academy, Mother," Margaret told her. But Abbie said she would manage, that she *had* to manage somehow, for Margaret must finish.

In the fall, with Will protesting a little, Margaret and John both went to Weeping Water to school. And in November, Maggie O'Connor Mackenzie died, without having seen Abbie in twenty years. Bitterness came over Abbie with her grief. Why should life on the prairie have demanded so much of her? Why should twenty years have been so hard, so barren? By her condition, both her grief and her bitterness were accentuated.

At Christmas time, which was cold with deep snow, Margaret and John came home,—Margaret with her gray eyes luminous, her cheeks flushed with prairie-rose tints. She could not wait to tell her mother shyly that the young Fred Baker, who was a nephew of the minister, had been there again. He had only two more years in medical school and then he would be *Doctor* Fred Baker. He wanted her to write to him. And she liked him,—oh, *how* she liked him.

And Abbie wondered.

John, serious, quiet, "liked his work all right." Of all the children, John was the hardest to understand. One almost had to read his mind to get anything out of him. Mack, too, was home for the day. He had graduated from the broom-and-dust-cloth and was on the books all the time. His round face, from which the freckles had miraculously disappeared, had taken on a more alert look, his round china-blue eyes a keener expression.

Isabelle played and sang for them, "Way Down Upon the Swanee River," and "Bonny Charlie's Now Awa'," her childish voice soaring forth lustily, her slim little legs pumping vigorously.

Abbie was thankful the children were all doing so well.

Christmas over, Mack left for Omaha, and after New Year, Margaret and John went back to the academy. Elsa Reinmueller came over three mornings in the week to help.

On the afternoon of the twelfth of January, Abbie put her shawl over her shoulders and walked down the road to Reinmuellers'. The day was like a spring one,—a soft, mild, spring day.

"It's probably the last time I can go to any of the neighbor's," she had said to Will, "and it will do Christine good to think I made the effort to come over once more to see her."

The sun was warm. There was moisture on the sides of the cedars and cottonwoods. Hens scratched in the damp, steaming ground on the south side of the straw stacks, their liege lords crowing ecstatically over their activities.

Abbie walked cumbersomely, heavy with child. It was hard for her at forty-one to get about. The old buffalo trail of twenty years before, with its faintly outlined tracks, was a well-defined road now, running on to the big town of Lincoln, as straight as the crow, except for one short deviation, where it formed a letter S over the new Missouri Pacific railroad.

As she neared the Reinmueller house, Gus drove out of the yard with two of the younger boys on their way to town.

Abbie drew her shawl closer around her and called pleasantly, "Spring is here."

"Ya," shouted Gus. "She's come, all right. Weather-breeder, that's what she is. Ya . . . look at that." Pigeons had settled down before his horses' hoofs, to rise with a whirr of wings and settle again. What did Gus mean? Was it a bad sign? Grandma Deal would have said it was.

How queer that Gus used so much better English than Christine, Abbie was thinking. It seemed that Christine didn't even try to talk right.

She found Christine alone in the square, box-like house which had replaced the dug-out. The girls had gone over to Lutz's store, Christine said. Rosie was going to work at Dr. Hornby's.

The two women talked for some time about trivial neighborhood things, beyond which they had little in common. Neighborliness, caused by the proximity of their houses and the fact that they had come into the new country at the same time, held them together. Christine was paradoxically rough and kind, penurious and unselfish. After a time,

Abbie rose laboriously and said she must go. At the door she and Christine stood for a few minutes in parting. The northern sky was the color of dark gray ashes. It was very quiet,—the hushed quiet of a waiting storm god who gloats a little over the peace of Nature before he assaults. Suddenly Abbie felt half frightened and did not know why.

The great gray clouds were now coming in from the northwest, rolling low over the land like billows of thick smoke from a thousand factories of the storm gods located somewhere beyond on the prairie. A single snarling blast came out of the clouds and needles of snow struck Abbie in the face.

Even while she hurried out of the yard, the wind was whipping her shawl about her and a great smother of snow was engulfing her.

"Come back, you," Christine was at Abbie's side.

"No, Christine, I must get home." She had to say it close to Christine's ear in the roaring of the storm.

Christine ran her arm through Abbie's, "With you I go." Abbie made a single feeble protest and then clung to Christine.

In the welter of snow they reached the far side of the road opposite the Reinmuellers', and Christine with her left arm hooked through Abbie's, ran her right hand along the top of the wire fence for guidance. The wind lashed them until they cowered from it. The snow, in great swirling masses, drove its stinging clods into their eyes and nostrils. Irregular drifts formed at their feet in a moment's time. When there came one terrific blast of wind more infuriated than others, Christine clung harder to the wire, the ugly barbs digging the flesh until the blood came. And then the composition of the snow seemed to change. It was no longer even slightly pliable, but a cruel, hard, dry substance which cut at them like bullets and nails and knives.

Abbie's strength in her present physical condition was going. She stopped and moaned at the necessity of pushing her cumbersome self into the jaws of the storm. Christine, with her more wiry robustness, half dragged the lagging body.

Suddenly, the barbedwire gave place to picket and Christine knew that the Deals' yard-fence was reached.

"Now, not so far," she shouted into Abbie's ear. They wallowed, slackened, stopped altogether, crouched before the fury, and then gathered themselves together and plunged on again. Abbie, with her waning strength, had ceased to think, except to obey Christine.

And then the pickets ended abruptly in a post, with space beyond, and Christine realized that it was the open lane-gate and that she had unknowingly passed the small front gate.

"Vait," she shouted. But she had no reason to encourage Abbie in waiting. For Abbie had sunk into the icy bed of a huge drift with the pangs of childbirth upon her.

CHAPTER XX

AND now Christine had to pull Abbie out of the drift and put forth all her effort to get the suffering woman to retrace her steps to the little front gate. She did not dare turn into the wide open gateway and run the risk of losing her bearings in the uncharted wilderness of the lane road.

In the added fear of her childbirth warnings, Abbie clung to Christine with all her strength. "Oh, . . . Christine . . . I can't go any farther . . ." The storm god took the words and threw them back into her face.

"Come . . . you!" Christine hurled savagely into Abbie's ear. "Of your man t'ink. Of your *kinder* t'ink. You're *verrückt* . . . crazy!"

Christine kept her freezing right arm through Abbie's, and plunging slowly ahead, grasped every picket with her left. Pausing, cowering, plunging, pulling Abbie's half-prostrate body, she came to the welcome cross-pieces of the small gate. "By de cedars ve tell," she called in Abbie's ear. They turned blindly, for all directions seemed lost in the mad whirl of snow, crawled through the gateway, and grasped the first cedar. "How many?" Christine was calling.

"Nine," Abbie moaned. She held onto the last far-reaching branch of the first cedar while Christine felt for the second.

"*Zwei!*"

Pushing on, cowering before the white smother, they crawled. The storm tore Abbie's shawl from her and the frozen icicles of her wet hair beat her face like tiny razor blades.

"*Drei.*"

As she felt Christine pulling her forward, the hideous agonizing childbirth pains shook her freezing body again and she sank in a wildly whirling drift.

"*Du narr!*" Christine snarled at her ear. "Come . . . *du narr* . . . fool!"

She set her teeth and plunged ahead while the icy needles drew something moist and trickling from her face.

"*Vier.*"

And now her breath was going. One could not struggle on when there was no air to breathe. Christine was pulling her. Because she had no breath, Christine was pulling her.

"*Fünf.*"

Abbie sank to her knees in pain. Christine jerked at her fiercely. "Get you up." In her ear Christine was yelling. "You die . . . you like dat dyin' maybe . . . nein? Your baby . . . you keel heem . . . you like dat keelin' your baby maybe?" No, she must not kill her baby, so she must do as Christine said. But it was so painful——

"*Sechs.*"

Abbie began to be too numb to feel the cold. What was the use of obeying Christine? Christine had no right to boss so.

"*Sieben.*"

The white suffocating smother was turning dark. There seemed no use fighting the hideous black thing that was closing her breath.

"*Acht!*"

Christine was pushing and dragging her. She ought to help Christine push and drag . . .

"*Nein!*"

Together they plunged to the wall of the house. By the loyal cedars they had found their way. In a war of snow, when the whole world was fighting it in mortal combat, only the cedars seemed not to have lost their heads. Only Abbie's cedars and Christine seemed faithful to her. Abbie knew that Christine was dragging her now into the warm shelter of the house. She heard Christine say something about: "Heis vater, qvick!" and then she tumbled into a sea of suffering to which there seemed no shore and in which time was not measured. It was hard to breathe. Sometimes she saw faces dimly which came and went. Sometimes she vaguely heard whisperings. Sometimes she smelled steamy woolens and moist hot flannels. Most of the time she was sinking under cold smothering water. Only one thing brought her back,—a light,—a lantern shining down into the icy waters. It shone to light the way back up for her. Each time she sank, she kept her eyes on the light and said, "Will . . . Mack . . . Margaret . . . John . . . Isabelle . . ." And the saying of the names bore her back to the surface and the light.

And then, in some queer intuitive way, she knew her life was going out with the tide. The light grew fainter and farther away.

She did not care especially, except for one thing. The light! She ought not lose sight of its faint gleam. Some tiny spark of memory kept reminding her that she must never take her eyes away from the far-off glow of the lantern. So that, sinking, she kept pulling herself feebly back toward its faint gleam with "Will . . . Mack . . . Margaret . . . John . . . Isabelle." She told the words over as a nun touches her beads.

Her mind was not lucid enough to understand that through constant utterance, she was trying to pray that she might come back to her responsibility,—that she had so much to do yet for the family,—that they could not get along without her. Over and over, she said them, "Will . . . Mack . . . Margaret . . . John . . . Isabelle." Each name a bead—each bead a prayer. And when her mind cleared a little, and she heard a strange new wail, she remembered a new responsibility and said them over again, "Will . . . Mack . . . Margaret . . . John . . . Isabelle . . . *the baby*." Each name a bead,—each bead a prayer. Fighting the icy waters feebly, with only the thought of the light to keep them from closing over her, she came back at times to the consciousness of the homely red face of Christine by her bed, nodding, jerking up, nodding——

And when the light grew clearer and more steady and the cold water seemed gone, Will told her that the baby was a girl.

"We'll name her Grace," Abbie said feebly, "Grace of God. She'll be a comfort. She'll stay with us longer . . . maybe . . . than a boy. Where's Christine, Will?"

Christine Reinmueller came in to stand by the bed, her short shapeless body in a blue calico dress, her greasy little tight braids of hair wound flat from ear to ear, her fat red face scarred with scratches.

Abbie reached up and pulled her down. Arms close around her, she kissed her rough cheek. "Christine . . . my friend . . . my friend for all my life."

Christine writhed in embarrassment, "*Ach! Du sans garrich* . . . voolish." She pulled away. "*Es ist nix* . . . nossing."

It seemed odd to Abbie to have a baby again after ten years. Sometimes she said she was afraid she had forgotten how to care for one. But when she grew strong, it all came back to her. The Abbie Deals do not forget.

Margaret graduated from the academy in the spring of that year. Fred Baker, the minister's nephew, who was to be a full-fledged doctor in one more year, arrived in time for the graduating exercises, and brought her a stereoscope with views of "Niagara Falls," "Hudson Bay by Moonlight," "The Wedding Party," and several others with subtle suggestions of a romantic nature. Margaret rode home in the lumber-wagon with the stereoscopic views in her lap and her head somewhere beyond the prairie clouds.

John went back to the academy in the fall, but Margaret was at home with Abbie for the year. And that year was to seem very short to Abbie, for Margaret was getting ready to marry the embryonic doctor. And as all the estate, real or personal, which the two owned, consisted of the stereoscope and the twelve picturesquely romantic views, the year was crowded with the making of quilts, the hemming of sheets, and the sewing of carpet-rags.

The next spring, Abbie's dream of a parlor came into the world of reality. They built it on the south side of the old part, protruding toward the road. They wanted it done before Margaret's wedding, and the wedding was already set for June. Old Asy Drumm, a little more stooped and silent and tobacco-stained, finished the last door-latch and the last piece of mop-board several weeks before the momentous occasion. John and Will painted the pine exterior and Abbie and Margaret varnished the pine interior. There were two modish details about that parlor of which Abbie was inordinately proud,—the fan-shaped colored-glass window toward the road and the double doors that slipped mysteriously into the wall when pushed backward. To be sure, in looking through the fan-shaped glass one saw a bilious green sky, sickly yellow cedars, a wavering blue picket fence and a nightmarish red lawn, but this was a mere bagatelle beside the touch of distinction it gave. Also the doors, after mysteriously disappearing into the walls, could not always be coaxed readily out of their hiding places, so that the women folk would have to call "John . . ." or "Father . . . come help us, will you?" Abbie was proud of them, though, and all her life made loyal excuses for "the doors sticking just a little to-day."

Abbie and Margaret rode up to Lincoln on the branch line, with its small engine, its one coach and baggage car, and bought a red and green sale carpet for the new parlor, Nottingham curtains, an oak patent-swinging rocker, and a marble-topped stand with a blue plush album. It seemed too much grandeur at one time for a single family to acquire. Abbie's rather critical conscience reminded her constantly that Rome was at the height of its glory just before the fall. She sewed the strips of carpet together and then the united family put it down over a layer of newspapers and fresh oat straw. Will, Abbie and John crawled along one side of the room on their hands and knees, pulling and stretching and tacking, while Margaret kept the straw pushed down as level as she could, so the result would not be Rocky-Mountain-like, and Isabelle kept little Grace, a year and a half old now, from putting the tacks into her mouth. When these two stupendous tasks were accomplished, and the carpet was taut and springy over its oat field, they put up the curtains, moved in the organ and the what-not, Abbie's old painting of the prairie, the new chair and the stand, the blue plush album and the stereopticon views, which, luckily, were to remain in the parlor through the wedding. Surveying the finished product, Abbie wondered if any of the Astors or Vanderbilts about whom she had read, ever had anything quite so stylish.

And then Margaret's dress was to be made and all the wedding to be planned. Margaret said she had her heart set on a navy blue silk with white ruching and—

Her mother stopped her. "Don't you . . ." Abbie was wistful. "Don't you wish we could afford a white satin dress and white slippers and a veil?"

"No, Mother . . . the navy blue silk is just what I want. As long as Fred and I are going right to the rooms over the drug store, I want my clothes to be suitable and I might never have use for a white satin again. Besides, now that I'm going to live in Lincoln, I want to save every penny toward painting supplies. I'm never happier than when I'm opening up the paint-box and getting at the oil and brushes. You know, Mother, my housework won't be much . . . just think . . . those few tiny rooms to keep and not any of the work there is here on the farm . . . and I'm going into my painting for all it's worth. I can't explain it to you, Mother, but there's something in me . . . that if I could just get down on canvas the way the cottonwoods look against the sky, or the way the prairie looks at sunset with the pink light . . ." she broke off. "Oh, I suppose you think I'm daffy . . . you wouldn't understand."

Abbie, at the east kitchen window, looked over the low rolling hills where the last of the May sunshine lay in yellow-pink pools on the prairie. Her lips trembled a little. "Yes, I would," she said simply. "I'd understand."

And then, quite suddenly, it was the night of the wedding. The moon slipped up from a fleecy cloud-bed and with silvery congratulations swung low over the farmhouse behind the cedars. The whole countryside was there. In a community where there have been few lines drawn, one does not begin to draw them at wedding times. The lane road held all manner of vehicles,—lumber-wagons, buggies, phaetons, carts, surreys, hayracks. The Lutzes were all there and all of the Reinmuellers but Emil, who sat on a milk stool in the barn at home all evening and sulked. Sarah Lutz looked stylish in her tight-fitting black dress of stiff silk, with jet earrings against her rosy cheeks. Christine had a new blue calico gathered on full at the waistline.

Mack surprised them all by driving up the lane road in a shining black buggy with canary yellow wheels, yellow lines over the horse's black back, and a yellow whip. He drove over to the Lutz's and came back with Emma Lutz, who was trying her best not to look important.

The presents were all in the sitting-room, the small things on tables. There were two red plush chairs, a stylish castor, a green glass pitcher with frosted glasses, three lamps with snow scenes on the globes, several hand-made splashers and tidies, and enough cold meat and pickle forks to supply a garrison of soldiers with fighting equipment. Gus and Christine, out of deference to the literary tastes of the family, had bought a huge volume, their decision over the purchase having been based upon weight rather than content, and which now, upon inspection, proved to be *Twenty Lessons in Etiquette.*

Some time before the ceremony Abbie climbed the uncarpeted pine stairs with the little calf-skin-covered chest under her arm. Just as her mother had climbed the sapling ladder in the old log cabin, she was thinking. Wasn't life queer? Such a little while ago, it seemed. Where had the time gone? Blown away by the winds you could not stop,—ticked off by the clock hands you could not stay.

Margaret was nearly dressed. Her blue silk, with its fifteen yards of goods, was looped back modishly over a bustle, the train dragging behind her with stylish abandon. Abbie sat down on the edge of her daughter's bed, the chest in her lap. "You know, Margaret, it was always a kind-of dream of mine that by the time you were married, we'd be well enough off to do a lot of things for you. I always saw you in my mind dressed in white with a veil and slippers,—not just that I wanted you dressed that one way,—but I mean as a sort of symbol,—that we'd be able to do all the things for you that should rightfully go with the pearls. But," Abbie's voice broke a little and she stopped to steady it, "things don't always turn out just as we dream,—and we're not able to do much for you. But anyway, you shall wear the pearls to-night if you want to."

Margaret, holding up her long dress, crossed the rag-carpeted floor in little swift happy steps, and threw young arms around her mother.

"*I* know all you've done for me, Mother." She took Abbie's rough hands in her own firm ones and held them to her lips. "And it's *everything*,—just *everything* that you could do. Never as long as I live can I ever repay it." There were tears in the young girl's eyes and to keep them back, she said lightly, "No, thanks, Mother, dear. I'm all right with my lovely blue silk and the white silk ruching at my neck. Keep them for Isabelle or baby Grace. You and father will be well-fixed in a few years. The land will be higher. You're having good crops now and by the time Isabelle is married, your dream can come true. And besides, Mother, dear," she put her young cheek against Abbie's, "*you know* that when you marry the man you love, you don't need jewels to make you happy."

Yes, yes,—how the words came back, borne on the breeze of memories! How swiftly the clock hands had gone around! Abbie could not speak. She must shed no tears on her little girl's wedding day. So, she only patted her and kissed her, smiling at her through a thousand unshed tears. And you, who have seen your mother smile when you left her,—or have smiled at your daughter's leaving,—know it is the most courageous smile of all.

And then it was time to go downstairs. Margaret and young Doctor Fred Baker came down the enclosed pine stairway and across the parlor, Margaret's silk dress dragging stylishly over the red and green spirals of the sale carpet. Isabelle pedaled and played the wedding march, lustily, the sound of the wind pumping into the reeds rather prominent above the melody.

A solemn hush fell on the friends gathered from all the farms and the little village. Abbie stood by Will, who was holding Grace in his arms. John was at her other side. Mack sauntered over and stood by Emma Lutz. Isabelle stopped playing and the voice of the preacher came hurtling against the silence:

"Inasmuch as we are gathered together—"

Abbie thought she could not stand it. She must call out in one great scream that she could not let her little girl go away from her.

"For better or for worse." *Oh, God don't let Margaret have to go through all the hardships I did.*

"Until death do you part." There, they were speaking of death again. Why did they always talk about death when there was only life before them?

"Do you take this man...."

And now Abbie was going to break down and cry. She threw up her head. No, not a tear, not a single tear! If she started, she would turn into a Niobe to weep herself to death.

And then, quite suddenly, Margaret Deal was Mrs. Fred Baker.

After that, with Isabelle pumping away faithfully, if windily, on the "Blue Danube Waltz," and "By the Blue Alsatian Mountains," some of the young folks danced on the new sale carpet, with the straw underneath working itself up into little hummocks.

There were biscuits and pressed chickens, cakes and lemonade out on the side porch. Christine Reinmueller and Sarah Lutz took turns in shaking the fly-brush with its long paper streamers over the tables, so that no unusual number of flies would light on the food. Every one had a grand and glorious time. There was only one queer thing about the whole affair,—a new dish among the refreshments which no one in the community had served before. Men folks going home, asked their wives why in Sam Hill the potatoes were all cold, and their wives said to hush and not show their ignorance, that it was something new called "potato salad" and it was *supposed* to be cold. At which, most of the men laughed long and raucously and said by golly, for their part, they'd take theirs hot-fried or baked in the skins.

And back on the porch of the farmhouse behind the cedars, Abbie Deal stood and watched her married daughter drive away under the starlit summer sky. Then she turned and went into the kitchen and wound the old Seth Thomas clock with the little brown church painted on the glass.

CHAPTER XXI

AFTER Margaret's marriage, life seemed to move along in a monotonous regularity that summer. Letters came from her twice a week and they were full of enthusiasm and plans. It was nice to have her so happily married, Abbie thought. Mack did not write so often. When he did, the letter was brief and businesslike. He had received a raise in wages. The president, himself, commended him about something. Omaha was growing. You would be surprised to see how large it was getting. One gathered the impression from Mack that he was joint-owner in all the enterprises. Well, it was a good trait, Abbie thought. Loyalty! It was nice for a boy to feel so much a part of a town.

John was helping his father with the farm work,—a silent boy. Abbie, looking at him curiously at times, wondered if she would ever understand him. Isabelle, at twelve, was practicing several hours a day, with no coaxing, "General Grant's Grand March" and "Dance of the Flowers." Sometimes, in her interest over it, she would forget time altogether, and Abbie would scold, "Come, Isabelle, too much of that at once isn't good for you." Little Grace at eighteen months was toddling everywhere and into everything. It seemed to Abbie that she pulled her out of one thing, only to turn and see her getting into something else. She loved her deeply. "Whatever would we have done without her?" she would say to Will.

There had been days of ordinary happenings in the summer of '89 until the heat of August hung over the land like a blanket.

Abbie had learned to know the prairie in all its moods,—and the mood of August was a lazy, somnolent one. There was a noticeable decrease in the songs of birds, for molting time had begun, although one could hear the cardinal's "what cheer" and the pee-wee calling his own name with plaintive patience all through the day and even after sunset and twilight. Elderberry bushes massed along Stove Creek, had exchanged their lacy headgear for black bonnets of ripe fruit. Along the grassy roadway, one's skirts touched Queen Anne's lace, field mustard and yarrow. Wild morning-glories tangled through the grass, and metallic beetles of iridescent red and green climbed the sticky stems of milkweeds. The yellow of sunflowers, the white of boneset and the azure blue of chicory stood in friendly groups on all sides, and everywhere there were plumes of goldenrod, like plumes from the hats of lovely ladies. Spiders, the highwaymen of all the insects, spread their webs in the pastures to hold up their victims. A covey of baby quail, nearly full-grown, could be flushed almost any time a horse and rider crossed a field, and down by the creek bed the mink and muskrat families had begun breaking home ties, with the brown sons and daughters hunting for themselves.

On one of these August afternoons, with the sun hot, and the hollyhocks blood-red against Abbie's white pickets, with the sound of crooning hens outside the windows and a settled air of languor over the whole farm, Abbie heard a sound of snorting horses, and looked out of the east kitchen window to see John's team charging down the field, the knives of the mower close upon their heels, and John not in sight.

With a horrible sensation of fright, so nightmarish that she seemed not able to pull her wooden limbs along, she ran out. John was lying against the barbed wire of the fence, white as the pickets of the garden gate, a sickening stream of scarlet trickling from his foot. Ill at the sight, Abbie ran to a small new plum tree and broke off its top. She pulled up the lower barbed wire of the fence and crawled through, snatching off her apron, and binding it above the ankle, with the plum stick knotted in between. John's eyes opened, and clung in fright to his mother.

"Mother, do something for me," he moaned in the old, little-boy way.

Abbie heard some one, who seemed not herself, saying, in a steady cool voice, "Yes, John, trust Mother."

The horses, frothing, now, at the bits and flanks, were standing against the fence at the far side of the field, trying to reach green corn-ears over the wire. Across the haystubble Abbie ran to them. On the way she kept saying, "Oh, God . . . one more thing . . . help me through this *one* more thing." With frantic movements, she unhitched and led the team back into the yard and hitched them to the lumber-wagon. She seemed to have acquired Amazonian strength. Isabelle, who had run out, was crying in silent fright. "Bring pillows from the beds," Abbie called. Back into the field she drove in the wagon. Fearful to leave the horses, which had not yet settled down to their usual docility, she tied them to the fence post.

"Mother . . . do something."

"Yes, John,—trust Mother."

Together, Abbie and Isabelle, pulling and lifting, got the suffering boy into the wagon with his head on a pillow. Already the apron was scarlet. Abbie jerked off the wagonseat, piling the other pillows on it, and propped up the mangled foot. She jumped out, untied the team, and climbed back over the wheel into the wagon-box.

"Look after the baby," she called to Isabelle, and started the horses out of the field on a gallop. Against the dashboard she stood and clung to the lines which almost cut her as they sawed through her hands. The wagon bounced and careened and rocked. The pins came from Abbie's hair, and the red-brown mass, faded now, and with a few graying streaks, fell over her shoulders.

In Cedartown, people ran out of their homes and looked after her. As she reached Dr. Hornby's, she had to use all her strength to get the team stopped. Men, running out from the little stores, came to help, catching the horses by the bits and tying them to one of the long row of hitching posts. Dr. Hornby and Henry Lutz and Asy Drumm carried the boy into the one-story office.

"Stay by me, Mother."

"Yes, John, I won't leave you."

Abbie held the boy's hand, her thick hair still tumbled over her shoulders while Dr. Hornby cut and cleansed and tied. When the last neat bandage was fastened, Abbie Deal slipped to the floor in a crumpled heap.

John's life was saved only by a few moments,—only by the time gained through Abbie's wild drive into town. For weeks, his foot propped in its one position, he suffered all the agonies of a cut and tortured tendon of Achilles. And always he was to carry a horny scar.

It was the nearest that death had come to the family since Abbie's long illness. Will and Abbie, sitting on the side porch, on a warm August evening, talked of it in low tones.

"Death . . . Will," Abbie said. "How the fear of it always hangs over me. If John had died . . ."

"Death," Will repeated it. "Death . . ." He looked beyond the Lombardy poplars, stared for a moment up into the deepening prairie twilight. "I wonder why we fear it?" He spoke as though to himself. "The naturalness of it! Wild geese flying over . . . cattle coming home . . . birds to their nests . . . leaves to the winter mold . . . the last sleep. How natural they all are, and yet of them all, we fear only the sleep. When my time comes I wish my family and friends could think of it that way . . . without tears."

"Oh, Will, don't talk so. If you should be taken away from me, I couldn't stand it."

"Oh, yes, you could, Abbie-girl. You could stand it. It's the people who have loved and then lost their love . . . who have failed each other in some way, who couldn't stand it. With you and me . . . all we've been through together and all we've meant to each other . . . with us, it couldn't be so terrible. Nothing could take away the past from us. You are so much a part of me, that if you were taken away, I think it would seem that you just went on with me. And I'm sure if I were the one taken I would go on with you, remembering all you had been to me."

So seldom did Will speak that which was in his heart. And now he had spoken. Abbie sat and looked out into the star-filled sky. There were the summer night odors,—clover hay and ripening apples and sweet alyssum. There were the summer night sounds,—cicada and frogs and a crooning bird. There were the summer night movements,—the trembling of the leaves on the poplars, a night hawk dipping low, a bit of lacy cloud slipping across the moon. For a moment, Abbie Deal seemed greater than herself, larger than humanity. For a brief time, a sense of deep wisdom was within her, a flood of infinite strength and peace enveloped her.

I would go on with you . . . remembering . . .

All fall and early winter John, suffering, blue, discouraged, was kept in with his bad foot. It had been a terrible cut, but it was healing; and he was not going to be crippled, thanks to the ministrations of a country doctor with few instruments and meager equipment, but with a sound surgical knowledge. Young Dr. Frederick Baker commended the older doctor's care of the case with the cheerful condescension of the recent graduate.

By studying at home and taking his tests, John was able to graduate with his class at the academy. Still favoring his foot a little, he went into the field with his father.

That summer of '90 was the summer of the great drought. Day after day, Will came into the kitchen with the pails of morning milk to say, "Another scorcher. Not a cloud in the sky."

The hot belching winds blew in from the southwest. The grass in the pastures knotted and scorched on its roots. The brittle leaves of weeds rattled, like so many tiny castanets, whenever the chickens walked through them. Blackberries hardened on the bushes and fell to the ground. Raspberries were purple warts. Peaches dried in the forming.

The small grain amounted to very little. The corn began to curl and brown and bake on its roots. Crops were stillborn in the womb of Nature.

Reports from other parts of the country were the same. The state seemed to have slipped backward into its beginnings, to be going through the same hard period experienced in the 'seventies. Rumor came from the northern border that the Indians were dancing the ghost dance. Abbie commenced to wish the family had not been so extravagant,—buying the organ and the carpet, and building on the room. That joke of hers about the fall of Rome was beginning to seem ill-timed.

But the bad summer seemed not to bother the children. Grace was two and a half now, "a smart little tike," every one said. Margaret came home sometimes, but her young doctor husband was too fearful of missing a case in the growing town of Lincoln to leave often. Margaret was as happy as Abbie had ever wished her to be. She was busy, too, with her painting, reveling in the time and opportunity to work with it. She brought sketches out to show Abbie and the two spent long moments talking them over.

Mack had good reports to make. Whenever he came for an occasional Sunday in his friendly, breezy way, Abbie always felt a renewal of pride in his virile young manhood, a feeling of elation over his unceasing energy.

"People like Mack," she would say to Will, "but what's better, they have confidence in him."

John was Will's standby in the farm work. Quiet, serious, seldom speaking his mind, he seemed to Abbie more and more like Will.

Isabelle was talking and thinking "music" all day. She was taking lessons now from a woman in Cedartown. Abbie always drove with her over to town on Saturday afternoons. While Isabelle took her lesson, Abbie traded out the butter and eggs she had brought to the Lutz store.

On one late Saturday afternoon in October, as Abbie was taking Isabelle over to town for her music lesson, she met Dr. Fred and Margaret riding out home with Oscar Lutz. They had come on the late afternoon train to surprise the home folks.

A warm feeling of happiness was with Abbie when she drove the old white mare back toward the lane road by the Lombardy poplars. Mack was coming the next day, too. Never did life seem so complete as when the children were all at home. Home was the hub of the wheel. Always she and Will would live there, and always, no matter where the children's activities led them, they would come home to father and mother in the white farmhouse behind the cedars. She was thinking this in a general way, and that she would have chicken and hot biscuits for Sunday dinner, when she turned into the lane road by the poplars.

Every one was out by the windmill,—John, Margaret, Dr. Fred Baker, Grace, Oscar Lutz, Gus Reinmueller. They were standing in a group,—a quiet, silent group,—only standing and doing nothing. Something smote Abbie like a chilling hand, clutching at her heart and throat. There was complete silence in the crowd,—a whispering silence,—the same hushed silence of the time when the baby was born dead. They all turned when she came up the lane road,—turned toward her, but did not move,—looked at her,—and were silent. Abbie got out of the buggy with wooden movements and went over to the group. Dr. Fred Baker was kneeling on the grass. By his side Will lay at the foot of the windmill, staring beyond the Lombardy poplars.

Abbie knelt down by him, too. But he did not look at her. He only lay and looked beyond the Lombardy poplars,—stared up into the deepening prairie twilight.

Oscar Lutz's voice, hoarse and far away, said: "Is he . . . ?"

Dr. Fred's, low and far away, also, said: "Yes . . . gone." He turned his head away and slipped a hand gently over Will's eyelids.

Gus Reinmueller gave a sob. Oscar Lutz said. "There was a *man* . . ." The children,—John, Margaret, Isabelle, little Grace,—all began to cry wildly.

Abbie Deal dragged her eyes away from Will and looked across the prairie as toward Golgotha. No one moved. There was no sound but the children crying.

The cows were coming up to the pasture gate. The leaves of the Lombardys floated onto the lane road. A bird flew into the cedars. A long wedge-shaped line of wild geese flew low. Will lay sleeping.

Suddenly, Abbie Deal seemed greater than herself, larger than humanity. A sense of deep wisdom was within her, a flood of infinite strength enveloped her. She rose and threw up her head. "Hush!" she said quietly to the children. Almost sternly she said it: "Hush! Not a child of Will Deal's is to shed a tear."

CHAPTER XXII

IT IS the prerogative of the dramatist to lower the curtain upon a scene and raise it upon a later one,—of the story-teller to close one chapter and begin another when time has passed. Real life is not so. There is no kind interval of time as the settings of the various experiences shift,—no heart-easing period of days between the chapters of life.

Life is Time's galley-slave, forever shackled to its relentless master. If its hardest blow be dealt at three o'clock, then four o'clock must be met and five and six,—the first dark, agonizing night and the first pale, torturing dawn.

And so it is unreal, even cowardly, to leave Abbie Deal wrestling with her deepest emotions,—living two lives; one within herself, wracked and tortured,—the other, an outward one which met all the old duties and trivial obligations with composure,—leave her in the garden of her Gethsemane, to meet her many months later. Only the children had kept her going. Only her motherhood, whose first characteristic was love and whose second was duty, had kept her hands busy and her head unbowed. These,—and one other thing which she could not explain: the unseen presence of Will himself. She told no one,—made no attempt to discuss the experience with any other. But much of the time Will did not seem to be away. Whether the phenomenon were of the spirit world with the metaphysical involved, a touch of the supernatural which no man understands, or only a comforting memory, she did not know. She accepted the solace in blind faith and with soul-filled gratitude.

Through what agency came the consolation she could not say, but she felt able to keep in touch with him. There was nothing of the weird about it,—no foolish incantations to the dead. He just seemed with her. It grew in time to give her a slight sense of peace. It took from the separation the raw, tearing hurt. They had been so close, so companionable, that she seemed always to know what he would have said or done under any conditions. She grew to imagine she was talking to him,—telling him the small inconsequential affairs of the household, just as she had always done. And he seemed to answer.

"We had the Lutzes out for supper, Will."

That was pleasant, Abbie.

She knew that she made her own answers, but paradoxically, they seemed not to be. She had known Will's opinions so thoroughly that, almost without her volition, the answers sprang to her mind.

"The Reinmuellers were quarreling to-day, Will. You know, Will, sometimes I think you and I are nearer even now than Gus and Christine."

That's true, Abbie.

"I shall never tell any one," she said to herself. "I know just how they would feel. They would look at me queerly and think I was 'touched.' You do talk to me, Will, don't you?"

Why, of course, Abbie-girl.

And so, like an unseen presence, it came to give her a sense of comfort, until the day on which there would come a reaction, and she would plunge into a dark state of depression during which she would turn upon herself with accusations of a childish belief in her own fragile imagination. And then, in time,—something would quiet her again. Something,—she did not know what,—the wind in the Lombardy poplars,—the spirit of the deepening prairie twilight,—the stillness of the star-filled summer night,—or the memory of a voice saying, "I would go on with you . . . remembering . . ."

The greatest antidote in the world for grief is work, and the necessity of work. And Abbie had more to do than she had ever done in her busy life.

John was the one upon whom she most depended. All the winter, after his father's death, he had looked after the stock and all spring he had worked faithfully putting in the new crop. Many times one of the Reinmuellers had helped out, but John had shouldered the greater share of the field work. His presence was the only solution now to the problem of making a living on the place. He was only eighteen, but in the years to come, if he wanted to marry, Abbie told herself that he could have a small house built near by,—or perhaps it would be better the other way around,—she and Isabelle and Grace could live in the small cottage and let John have the bigger house. John was so much like his father, quiet, faithful, uncomplaining. He had none of Mack's friendliness toward every one, but a reserve which was close to dignity. Every night, all winter, after the chores were done, he had cleaned up and with no explanation, mounted the enclosed stairs to his own room. What did he do there, Abbie wondered, as she built up the fire, so that the room above, heated by a "drum" on the stovepipe, would be warm enough.

It was when she was cleaning the room in the spring that she found the Blackstone tucked away between a home-made book-shelf and the wall.

"John," Abbie said to him, "something is on your mind. What is it? Won't you tell Mother?"

She had to work to get it out of him. And then, like one whose resistance had snapped, he turned on her, "It's working on this darned farm all my life. I hate it, I tell you." He had the fury of a reserved person who stores up his grievances until one exploding moment. It reminded Abbie of the few outbursts of Will during their years together.

Abbie put her hand on the back of a chair to steady herself. "What do you want to do?"

"Study law." And Will had said that the Deals were always for the land. "I think of it all day and then dream it. And I'm going to, some day."

That was like Will, too, Abbie thought,—to think a thing over for a long time and then come to an irrevocable decision.

"But I know what you'll say to that." He spoke almost sullenly.

It hurt Abbie so, to have him turn on her that way.

"I'm not unsympathetic, John. We'll have to plan some way it can be done if you feel that way."

"Yes, and have you mad and disappointed about it." Why, oh why, did children say things to hurt one?

"No, I'll not be mad," she controlled her trembling lips, "and I'm not disappointed. I'm proud of your desire, John. For just a few minutes I was . . . was confused."

"Then promise me you'll sell the place and take the two girls and move into town."

"No, John," Abbie said with dignity. "I'll not sell. Land is low, . . . and last year's crops so poor . . . No, it's my place and I'm going to stay on it. We'll manage, somehow."

"Then that settles it. I'll stay too."

For long weeks Abbie labored with him. He was such a good boy, so clean and energetic, and so stubborn. Then, when Abbie had argued over and over again how she could manage by renting part of the acreage to Oscar Lutz on shares, and hiring Pete Reinmueller for the part of the work she could not do herself, John went away to the University in the fall, with his one suit, a few dollars in his pocket, and the promise of two jobs,—caring for a professor's fires and a doctor's horses.

Isabelle entered Weeping Water Academy that fall, doing part-time work in the minister's family for her board. And not once did either she or John ever realize how many times their mother put on an old coat and felt hat of their father's and went out to some of the heavy work herself. Isabelle began immediately to make splendid progress in music under a good teacher from the East. "It's her voice, though, that's going to count," the instructor said. "We must watch it and guard it."

In the summer, almost the first minute that John came home, he put on his old clothes and went out to the field to work. But his course was to be long and Isabelle's must contain all the music she could get, so Abbie began figuring in what ways she could help the two more. After several weeks of thinking it over and consulting the boys, she took Oscar Lutz's offer for eighty acres or half the farm. Oscar paid her one thousand dollars in cash and gave his note for the other three thousand.

"It's not good business to sell for that," Abbie said. "I think land's going to be higher some day, but it's now that the children need a little help. I can get along. With the chickens and eggs and butter and my pension money, I can keep things going."

The crops were poor again, the drought of the year before almost repeated. In spite of the general depression Henry and Sarah Lutz went away on a trip back to the World's Fair at Chicago. Henry had many irons in the fire, a blacksmith shop, his store, the farms. He and Oscar seemed to get along. They always "came out of the big end of the horn," people said. Sarah looked dressy when she started away. She had a flaring black skirt and white shirt-waist and a stiff black hat which she told Abbie was a genuine Knox sailor.

"So's mine," said Abbie, good-naturedly. She took off her own shabby old hat and twirled it on her hand. "*Hard knocks*."

When Sarah came back, she had some little garnet earrings and a half-dozen spoons with the Fair buildings engraved on them and pictures of the Infanta Eulalie from Spain and Mrs. Potter Palmer.

In September, Abbie left Grace, nearly five now, with Sarah and went up to Lincoln to be with Margaret. She drove the team and took along the feed for it to save the two-dollar train fare that would pay for four music lessons for Isabelle.

She got up at three and had started at four. Hours later, at Stevens Creek bridge, she rested the team under some cottonwoods and ate breakfast out of a shoe box. It showered during the last three miles and the wheels threw mud and the buggy almost mired.

The Bakers had moved into a house with a yard and a stable. Dr. Baker's practice was picking up, although fees were hard to collect. The hard times permeated into all businesses.

Abbie walked the floor in an agony of sympathy for Margaret. "I went through this six times," she thought, "but this is harder than any of them." Sometimes she slipped into the bedroom. "Mother's here, Margaret," she said, cheerfully, "keep up your courage."

And then the Bakers had a son,—Fred, Jr., they called him.

At home again, Abbie found everything all right. Christine had milked the two cows and had taken care of the pigs and chickens. The farm activities, thanks to the Reinmuellers, had gone right on. Only the clock had stopped.

Abbie wound the works behind the door with the little brown church painted on the glass. She stood for a few minutes and looked at the homely painted face of the old Seth Thomas time-piece and listened to its sturdy faithful ticking. "A grandmother!" she said to it. "I'm a grandmother. And it's not quite believable."

"You—can't—stop—time—you—can't—stop—time—you—can't—"

"Yes, you're right," Abbie admitted. "We won't argue it." She put the key behind the little brown church painted on the glass and shut the front.

"Well, Will," she said to that comrade who was only spirit and memory, "you have a grandson."

I'm pretty proud of that, Abbie.

And then, the next spring, the whole community knew that Mack was going to marry Emma Lutz,—Emma, with her mother's beady black eyes and her rosy cheeks and a merry come-hither in her eyes. And apparently the whole community was pleased, for good-natured Emma Lutz was the village belle.

Mack was twenty-five, and having been promoted to a window in the Omaha bank with the mystic word, "Teller" on it, he was by way of being something of a capitalist in the eyes of his old neighbors.

They were married at the Lutz house over in Cedartown on an October evening of 1893. The Lutzes had a new house with a squatty cupola on the southwest corner that looked like a shingled bee-hive. The ceilings were high and there were wooden rosettes over all the doors and windows and some new-fashioned spindles on the stairway, through which little Grace fed wedding-cake to the monkeys, actively impersonated by the Oscar Lutz grandchildren. Mack and Emma left for Omaha at once, where Mack had rented a little cottage on Dodge Street.

Abbie was forty-six now. The gray streaks in the red-brown hair were prominent. There was a noticeable slumping of the lithe shoulders, a thickening of hips. The peasant body of the O'Conners was coming into its own. In all these years Abbie Deal had not done anything with her voice, and she had not painted. But as every good mother lives again in her children, her personal disappointments were assuaged by Isabelle giving great promise in her music, and Margaret improving in every canvas she did. So Abbie felt that the children were doing the things she had so deeply wanted to do. She realized that the time was long past for her to build any more hopes on developing either of those two talents for herself, but she still cherished a secret ambition to write something.

"If I could just get down life as I have seen it," she would think, ". . . and people as I have known them. . . . Old Grandpa Deal with his shaggy head and the twinkle in his eyes, and his wit and his patience with Grandma . . . the story of my mother with her head-shawl and her Irish eyes, pulling a rose for my father . . . Isabelle Anders-Mackenzie, trying to make a lady of her little Irish peasant daughter-in-law . . . the journey out from Illinois with the stolid old oxen and the smell of the burning maple boughs in one's nostrils . . . the first lonely nights of camping in Nebraska with the silence of the stars and the sky and the shivering of the prairie grass." It was something she could do. She vaguely sensed her power to construct the scenes in writing, knew that she possessed the emotions which one must feel before he can transfer those feelings to another.

It gave her a delightful sense of anticipation on this October day. With the half-crop husked and in the crib, she could begin to write down some of the things she desired. It gave her a feeling of buoyancy that all her hard work could not down,—a renewal of youthful desires. By careful management she could plan her time, so that there would be moments each day in which she could forget everything else and carry out this dream that was as old as herself. If the results seemed clever—the thought gave her a warm sensation of pleasure—she would show them to the children. And then,—if they were good enough,—there were several ladies' magazines now, which printed such things. How proud the older children would be of her,—Mack and Margaret, John and Isabelle.

"Do you think I could, Will?"

I'm sure you could, Abbie-girl. Yes, that was the answer Will would have made. Always kind, always encouraging, he would have said just that.

In the sheer pleasure which the vision gave her, she pulled little Grace up to her and hugged her. "Maybe Mother can find time now to do something she's always wanted to, darling."

Grace, looking over her mother's shoulder, pulled away.

"Look, Mother,—who's that coming?"

Gus Reinmueller was driving away from the front gate, and a tiny little figure in black, with huge old-fashioned bonnet, was hobbling up the path between the cedars, half-carrying and half-dragging an old black valise.

Amazed, and uncertain who her visitor might be, Abbie went out to meet her. It was Grandma,—Grandma Deal,—eighty years old, with a thousand wrinkles in her little shriveled brown face.

"Why, Grandma Deal!"

"Well, Abbie, I've come to live with you. I'd rather live with you than any of my own blood. It won't be long, though. I shan't last long. Why didn't I die when Pa did? What makes old folks hang on when they ain't no good any more to their relatives? What makes my daughters so hard to get along with?"

Abbie could scarcely believe it,—that Grandma Deal had packed up and come alone out to her. What could she do with her? How could she take care of her? In kaleidoscopic fashion her thoughts tumbled about. Why, it was all she could do to help Isabelle at the Academy, to give John assistance sometimes, look after the house and farmwork, and take care of little Grace. And this last plan,—this new thing of writing she was just planning to do. Why, it would take time to do it! How could she add Grandma Deal to her burdens?

Grandma stood in the pathway, the old valise by her side.

"Maybe you don't want me?" her voice rose thin and querulous. "Maybe you're like all the rest of 'em. Maybe I'd better go back. I won't go back to Regina's though, that's sure."

"Oh, Will, how can I ever take care of her, too?"

She's my mother, Abbie-girl.

Abbie put warm, tender arms around the little old black figure.

"Why, Grandma, how can you think it? You're Will's own mother. Of course I'll take care of you."

Grandma Deal pulled away and looked around her. "Whatever did you set out them cottonwoods for? I can't bear that white fuzz blowin' around. What did you face the house south for?" A thousand wrinkles in her little thin, brown face, a thousand worries under the old, rusty, black bonnet.

One arm around the bent, wiry figure, the black valise in the other hand, Abbie piloted the arrival into the sitting-room, where Grace was crying silently for fear of the queer little old woman.

"Why, Grace, this is your own Grandma,—Father's mother, and she's come to live with us. We'll give you our bedroom, Grandma, and Grace and I'll go upstairs to sleep.".

"What you goin' to put me in a bedroom on the east side for? Sun's hot there in summer and east winds blow on it in the winter."

"Well, you try it a while, Grandma, and we'll change the bed if you're not comfortable. Now, you rest and I'll go out and get supper." Oh, where would she get the strength to be patient with Grandma?

Out in the kitchen, she stepped to the side porch and looked up at the sky beyond the Lombardy poplars. How could she do any more than she was doing now? Where did a person get help for all the trials of life? Why must she always be doing something for some one else? Why had Will been taken away? How could she assume this added burden without him?

Whether it was of the spirit world, a touch of the supernatural, the wind in the Lombardys, or only a memory,—she did not know. But quite distinctly she heard it:

I would go on with you . . . remembering. . . .

CHAPTER XXIII

☙§ Grandma Deal lived with Abbie for two years, the last thirteen months of which she was bedridden, and during which she was consistent in only one thing,—regularly spending a portion of each day in wishing she had not come. Abbie washed for her and ironed for her and cooked as well as she could with a frugal larder, to satisfy her childish cravings. Sometimes she picked up the frail little body and carried her to a couch near the window. And in the two years, she did not leave Grandma with any one else a half-dozen times. Margaret and Mack and John all scolded about it. "It seems as though Mother *always* has some big extra job on her hands," they would tell each other. Regina, fat and easy-going, came out once to help with the care, but the arrangement was not a particularly happy one, inasmuch as Abbie had two to wait on then, rather than one.

Strangely enough, of the whole family, Grandma took the greatest liking to the one who did the least for her,—Isabelle. Dreamy-eyed, thinking of nothing but music, Isabelle seldom did anything for Grandma but sing for her. Home from the academy that summer, the girl was expressing her desire constantly for a piano instead of the old reed organ.

"What you alwa's wishin' for a pianny for when you know you can't have it?" Grandma wanted to know.

"I might just as well have some fun wishing for it," she announced pleasantly,—Isabelle was always pleasant,—"when I know it's as far away as the moon." And she sat down at the old reed organ and played a windy accompaniment to her thrush-like singing of "Home to Our Mountains."

Grandma lifted her little wizened face from the clean white pillow.

"Come here," she said suddenly. "Bring me the black bag out o' my valise, and mind you don't look in it, either."

When Isabelle had brought the bag, Grandma took out a smaller pouch, and with Isabelle's eyes almost starting from her head, counted out fifteen great gold double-eagles.

"There's your pianny," Grandma said tartly. "Gold . . . all of 'em . . . and minted in the 'fifties. I'm savin' ten of 'em to bury me. You tell your Ma. Tell her when I die . . . I want her to take the money out o' this bag and buy herself a railroad ticket and go along home with me. I ain't goin' to have no mistake made. Like's not if she wa'n't along they'd send me on to Chillicothe or Kalamazoo."

"Oh, Grandma . . ." Isabelle could not yet comprehend the gift of gold that had come from the Aladdin lamp of the little black bag. "How can I *thank* . . . oh, Grandma . . . I *never* can thank . . ."

Quite suddenly, Grandma broke into a dry old sobbing. "Don't thank *me* . . ." Her voice cracked weirly. "Thank your dead father. 'Twas his draft money. I'd never touch it." Her quavering old voice was torn into hoarse shreds, "Thirty years I kep' it . . . come in the house 'n' put it in my lap . . . said, 'Mother, there's your money' . . . blood money . . . I alwa's said 'twas. . . ."

Isabelle was frightened and ran out for her mother.

When Fritz Reinmueller and John, Oscar and Henry Lutz unloaded the wonderful shining affair at the parlor door, Isabelle would not have exchanged places with the first lady of the land. Grandma greeted the purchase with "What'd you get that color for? Why didn't you get a plush stool? What're you settin' it in *that* corner for?"

On a morning in July, Grandma's restless spirit took its grumbling flight, sputtering a little at the Lord for the time spent upon her demise. Abbie took a piece of Will's gold draft money, and with Grace, accompanied all that was mortal of Grandma back to the old home. "Poor Grandma," thought Abbie on the train, "I wonder if she's finding fault with the way the angel's wings are put on and the direction the River of Life flows."

It had been twenty-eight years since Abbie had traveled the miles toward the setting sun behind old Red and Baldy. After the services for Grandma, she stayed a week, finding a thousand changes. But the greatest change of all she found in herself. She did not like the old places as well as she had always dreamed. Houses were too thick. Trees were too close and shady. The air was too humid. She felt hemmed in. "I would want to see out more," she thought to herself, ". . . to far horizons. I belong to the prairie. That's home now."

She visited her mother's grave and Grandpa Deal's and the tiny one of Janet's baby with the wild honeysuckle tangled over it. Her mother lay under a tall pine on which the dried cones rustled all the afternoon in the summer breezes. Abbie sat and thought about her,—the little peasant girl whose life had changed because a young hunter rode by. She thought of the trail of graves across the country. Her father was buried in New York State, a little brother in Illinois, her mother in Iowa, her husband in Nebraska. A trail of graves marked the westward trek of her family.

When she got back to town they asked her to guess whoever she supposed could be there. "Dr. Ed Matthews' wife from New York City," they told her.

Abbie could not think that it would be so hard to meet any one. Surely, at forty-seven one did not care about things like that.

The woman was slender, wasp-waisted, beautifully dressed, her huge leg-o'-mutton sleeves the height of style. She had on a whole garnet set, a pin, earbobs and bracelet.

"They tell me you are one of Doctor's old sweethearts." She smiled at Abbie with her graying hair and her sunburned skin and her work-worn hands. Abbie's heart was pounding ridiculously. Certainly at forty-seven one ought to have more poise than that. She leaned over Grace and fixed her sash. When she raised her face it was composed. She smiled back, "Oh, he used to come past the schoolhouse sometimes where I taught . . . and stop to talk."

When Abbie came back, she stopped in Lincoln a day to visit Margaret. Fred, Jr. was two years old now, and sitting up to the table on Gus's and Christine's wedding gift of *Twenty Lessons in Etiquette*, but as far as Abbie could see, the association was a lost cause, for Fred, Jr.'s table activities were of such an adventurous type that an onlooker might gather he was sitting on *The Life and Voyages of Columbus*.

Abbie arrived at the farm to face the utter ruin of her corn crop. During that week of July in which she had been back to the old home, the hot winds had blown out of the southwest with their scorching, blighting breath, and the young, shoulder-high stalks were so many blistered pieces of pulp.

She had been home two days when Henry Lutz drove out to tell her that Sarah was not well enough to go to Omaha to be with Emma during confinement and to ask her to go in Sarah's place. The hot winds had wearied Sarah, Henry said,—just tired her out.

For a few brief moments Abbie felt a fierce resentment that Sarah was always so well taken care of. Wasn't it hot for her too? Just back from burying Grandma, after caring for her two years, with the chickens and the house and everything to see to,—wasn't *she* weary, too? Oh, why could she never live any life of her own? For a few minutes resentful thoughts tumbled about in her mind, and then she said cheerfully, "Why, yes, tell Sarah I'll go."

Mack and Emma had a sturdy little son, now, too,—Stanley, they called him.

"Another grandson, Will," Abbie said at home again.

We're both pleased, Abbie.

That fall Abbie put in her first small sowing of winter wheat, the new experiment about which some of the farmers were talking. In November, with a light dash of snow on it, the small rectangle of vivid green stood out on the landscape like a bit of spring which had lost its reckoning of time. The crop in its experimental stage did well enough so that she added to her list a small sowing of the other new one, alfalfa, the tiny bluish-purple flowers later sending out a haunting fragrance that vied with the sweet fresh odor of the red clover.

But in general, it was a hard row that Abbie was having to hoe. Under the best of circumstances, with plenty of man-power on the farm, the owners were having a series of hard years. For a woman to face the problems seemed next to impossible. She rented parts of the eighty to Oscar Lutz and Gus Reinmueller for a share in the grain. But one year of drought followed another, so that a share in a poor crop was sometimes next to nothing. Pete and Heinie Reinmueller worked for her at times on shares. If they butchered they took their pay in meat, if they cut down trees they took it in wood. The chickens, the horses and the two cows she cared for herself, and except at farrowing time, the pigs. She made butter and sold it to town customers, and she traded eggs and chickens for staples at the Lutz store. Aside from a cloak which Mack gave her one Christmas and a dress from Margaret, Abbie Deal had nothing new in the way of clothes for years. Every stitch, every penny, every thought was for the schooling of the children. "If you can help any one, help John and Isabelle get through school," she would say to Mack and Margaret. And those who think she was not cheerful through it all, do not know the Abbie Deals of the old pioneer stock.

She made light of her hard times. "I've worn the same black hat for so many years," she would say, "it's like an old friend. The jet ornament on it has gone the whole rounds. It's been sewed on the front and on both sides and on the back. And now next year, I'm going to try it sort of northeast between the front and side."

The Lutz families and the Reinmuellers had gone away beyond their original ownership of land. Henry and Oscar Lutz had bought several eighties from families who had given up and returned East. Gus Reinmueller owned six eighties now, instead of the two of the earlier days. He and Christine seemed to have a perfect obsession for adding acres to their possession. Everything went into more land,—nothing into the house or for the children. The Henry Lutz family was now the "best fixed" one in Cedartown. Henry had done well in the store, had bought and sold land by that sharp businesslike bargaining which brought him always the better of the trade. Unlike the Reinmuellers, the Lutz family was the first to get new things and conveniences. Sarah Lutz, with her little black beady eyes and her still rosy cheeks, was always well dressed, always merry, always hospitable in the new house with the fancy wooden rosettes and the stylish cupola.

The year that John finished his law course found an opportunity presenting itself to locate in Iowa with a friend. He took the Iowa bar examination and was in the firm by mid-summer. It seemed queer to Abbie that John should go back to her old state to live.

That same June, Isabelle finished the Academy, the star pupil in piano and voice. Abbie in her turned and made-over dress, sitting in the audience of the church where the exercises were held, cried a little behind her program, and there are those who will understand the nature of her tears.

That was the same summer too, that Mack and Emma turned into the lane on a tandem bicycle one afternoon. Abbie could not believe her eyes,—that Emma, the mother of a year-old boy, would pedal from Omaha on one of the mannish-looking things. Emma was gay and unconcerned about little Stanley. She had left him with "the girl." He was as "fine as a fiddle" and the girl knew "just what to do with him." Yes, Emma was going to be as carefree and irresponsible a person as Sarah, her mother. Dressy, too, like her mother. She had on a dark green wool skirt, tight-fitting over the hips and bell-shaped at the bottom. Her white waist had sleeves the size of smoked hams. She wore a green necktie, and on top of her huge head of black hair was perched a little creased felt hat with a green quill at one side,—an "Alpine hat," she told Abbie. How could a young mother take her duties so lightly, thought Abbie.

In the fall, Isabelle, dreamy-eyed with musical plans, went up to Lincoln to live with Margaret and attend the University. Abbie sometimes opened the sliding double doors and went into the parlor where the piano stood, silent now, and ran her long slender fingers, stiff and knotted with outdoor work, over the keyboard. Sometimes she sighed a little for a lost dream, but more often she thought only of her pride in Isabelle.

Grace, at eight was in the Cedartown school, quick, keen-eyed,—"smart as a whip," people said. For two years, Abbie had hitched up on bad days and taken her in to school, but now a second building had gone up in the north end of town, and Grace was no farther away from it than many of the town children. It lightened Abbie's work materially when Grace could skip off to school by herself down the lane road under the poplars.

It was not until early winter again, with its half-crop of husking out of the way, that Abbie turned to that old desire of hers, that girlish ambition to write some of the things she had heard and seen and lived.

In that saving, frugal way, born of necessity, she ironed out dark brown wrapping paper, which she had saved for years, and cut it into sheets. At forty-nine Abbie was finding her first opportunity to take time from duties which had always confronted her, to carry out this old ambition. For several afternoons she wrote of the things she had been wanting forever to get down on paper. The things she had wanted to say did not come as readily as she had always anticipated. The task was a little more labored than she had thought. When she had finished several of the brown papers, she put them away carefully in her bureau drawer.

Duties descended upon her again before she had a chance to read over what she had written—those urgent duties which seemed always to confront her. Isabelle came home for vacation, burning incense before Euterpe's shrine. Even as a freshman, she had been chosen one of the new members in a musical organization, and what was of more practical benefit, had been asked to sing in one of the church choirs. Isabelle's fresh mellow voice was the open sesame to meeting many new friends and experiences.

Christmas came and went with every one, but John, home. On

one of the short January days with the snow thick on the Lombardy poplars, Abbie, with almost a girlish enthusiasm, took out of the drawer the story she had written in the fall. She read it through and then, amazed and chagrined, she read it a second time. It was flat, insipid. None of the things which she had been thinking as she wrote, was there. The statements were dull and lifeless. Grace, at nine, might almost have written them. What was the matter? She, who had so loved life, and so deeply lived it, could she not of all people get down on paper that which she had lived and loved? Apparently not.

How did they do it, she wondered? How did those writers you loved make you live in their stories? How did their people move across the pages like flesh and blood friends? How could they bring tears to your eyes and laughter to your lips? How could the winds sweep through their books so that you heard its endless rushing? How could the prairie grass blow for them so that you saw it wave and ripple? How could the Mayflowers and the honey-locusts drip their fragrance for them, so that you smelled it across the years? She did not know.

For some time she sat in stunned disappointment and looked at the snow thick on the cedars, and the gray bowl of a sky turned over the world. All her life she had dreamed of constructing something. She had told herself that if only she could find time, she would write of life as it was. And she had found time. But she could not write of life as it was. She had tried to tell of the journey over the uncharted sea of grass, of the nights under the star-filled sky, and the winds that were never still. But the words she had set down had not told it. Only the memory of it remained in her heart, like a song that would never be sung. She thought of her younger days,—the gleam which seemed always ahead,—of the vague allure which accomplishing something in the arts had always held for her. And now she was nearly fifty and she was not to know the fruition of any of those hopes.

"Oh, Will, I am so disappointed," she said to that invisible comrade who was only spirit and memory. "I can only *feel* those things,—not do them."

Isn't motherhood, itself, an accomplishment?

She knew that she made her own answer, and yet it gave her a sense of satisfaction and peace. Will might have said it. It sounded like him.

"But I've made so many mistakes. . . . Will. . . . even in that."

You are a good mother, Abbie-girl.

Yes, it gave her a sense of peace and comfort.

CHAPTER XXIV

IT SEEMED to Abbie that the years began to move more quickly now. The leaves of the almanac over the wooden kitchen sink were turned with almost unbelievable rapidity. Abbie never tore them out and never destroyed one of these outlived chronicles of time.

"Don't you ever burn up any of the old things that have accumulated?" Isabelle asked when she was home from the University.

"Oh, no," Abbie said hastily.

"Why not?"

"Oh . . . I don't know. Some one might need them sometime. I've always found a use for everything." And so every button, every string, every paper sack was carefully hoarded.

Isabelle was in the second semester of her sophomore year. She had only two dresses,—her brown school dress and her tan Sunday one, but she had a knack of wearing them well. It was the Era of Throttled Throats. Isabelle would pin a long ribbon at the front of her neck, wrap it tightly several times around that maltreated part of her anatomy and tie it in a huge bow under her ear.

"It's a wonder it doesn't shut off your epiglottis or whatever it is you sing with," Abbie said in disgust.

Isabelle was attractive with her reddish-brown hair and eyes and her mellow voice,—attractive apparently to Harrison Rhodes, a young man who sang in the same choir with her. When he had been out to the farm and sung "Whispering Hope," with Isabelle, looking down at her while she played the accompaniment, Abbie thought that all who ran could read, and the language of the message was in that Esperanto, the universal language of romance.

"But then I'm sort of romantic, Will, and maybe I just imagine it."

I thought so, too, Abbie.

In June of that year a national political convention named a Nebraska man for its presidential candidate. He was defeated in November, but Abbie said, "At least they know now there are some states west of the Mississippi."

Letters came from John regularly and Abbie thought to herself, with no small amount of glee, that John was far more communicative through the medium of pen and paper than when he was with her. His firm was "getting along pretty well," although he himself was not doing much more than the collections and looking up references. He would be glad when he had a real case. Later he had joined the local unit of National Guards. They met and drilled right along. Rather foolish, maybe, when there was no likelihood of war, but it was good for them, as they were mostly fellows in offices. His foot bothered him yet sometimes,—a little stiff after he had drilled.

Peace had been over the land for thirty years,—and then suddenly there was no peace. Spanish-American controversies, which had been piling up like so many logs on a pyre, were touched off by a match of news which flashed across the land. The *Maine* had been sunk in Havana's harbor. And in the wing-and-ell farmhouse behind the cedars, Abbie Deal was reading a letter from John:

"And so we arrived here in camp Des Moines, Tuesday. It was the most impressive and magnificent sight I ever saw yesterday morning when we left. The G.A.R. and band and drum corps escorted us to the depot, and thousands of people on every side waved flags and cheered and cried as we marched along. At the station friends were bidding good-bys, and mothers, sisters and sweethearts were weeping and saying their farewells. . . . We arrived in Des Moines and our regiment was quartered in the speed stables. . . . We have ten box stalls to each company. . . . I didn't come home first for I didn't want to say good-by to you. I know how you will feel, Mother. But if you saw a bully licking a little youngster, you would think I was cowardly, if I didn't jump in and . . ."

Yes, yes, how the words came back! A boy she knew long ago had said that same thing.

War! War again! How terrible! O God, stop war!

"Our John's going to war, Will!" Abbie's stiff lips could hardly frame the words.

I would have wanted him to do his duty.

And then Abbie could think of almost nothing but her boy; could do almost nothing but fix things to send him,—cookies, a cake, a needlebook, a Testament. Always the Abbie Deals must be doing something for their children.

The letters came frequently. John was willing enough now to pour out his thoughts to his mother.

"Our regiments commence where the numbers of the regiments of the Civil War ceased,—that is, the First National Guard (the regiment our company belongs to) is now the Forty-Ninth."

Why, how terrible! Abbie looked up from her letter. How terrible that the numbers should go right on. Would they always go on? Mack's little boy, Stanley,—little Fred Baker, Jr.—four and six now,— In twenty or thirty years— The idea was unthinkable. O God, don't let the numbers of the regiments go right on!

"We found that we all had to submit to another physical examination by a regular army physician. This was bad news for me and I feared it on account of the scar on my ankle. A number were rejected and I was one. . . ." Abbie's heart gave a bound of relief. John's near-tragedy, then, had been a blessing in disguise . . . "but another examination before a board of regimental surgeons passed me. . . ."

And so there was no relief and no blessing,—nothing but war.

There were other boys of the neighborhood going, too, Fritz Reinmueller for one. "*Ach!* Wid plantin' time come," Christine said in her half-English. "Such a *schlechte zeit* . . . bad time."

How queer Christine was,—to think always of the land and the crops and the money.

It had been in April that John's first letter had come from the box-stall in the Des Moines speed stable.

On a warm night in May, Isabelle came walking up the lane road under the poplars. Abbie had not expected her home and she ran to the sitting-room door with cheery words of greeting. On the porch steps Isabelle stood and looked at her mother with wide tragic eyes. Did nothing,—said nothing,—but stood and looked with wide tragic eyes.

"Isabelle!" Abbie's heart was pounding tumultuously. "What is it?"

"I'm married." The girl's voice was dull, without expression.

"Married?" Abbie repeated in a voice equally as dull, and with equal lack of expression.

Isabelle put out her hand. There was a wide gold band on her slender finger.

"Last night. And he's gone."

"You mean you're married to . . . to? . . ."

"He's gone," she repeated dully. There was only one man in the world, so why name him?

"You married Harrison Rhodes . . . before he left?"

"For San Francisco."

Abbie pulled Isabelle into the house and with shaking hands took off the girl's hat.

"They'll be sent to the Philippines," Isabelle said in that same expressionless way. Abbie was trembling in every limb. She had read about such things happening to other mothers. And now it was happening to her. She could not think it,—that her own little Isabelle Deal had married in that hasty manner. Why, she wasn't even Isabelle Deal,—she was Isabelle Rhodes. Everything seemed tumbling about Abbie's head,—all her plans for her musical girl. Why, Isabelle was only finishing her sophomore year. And then, suddenly, Abbie thought of the pearls lying in their velvet box in the old calf-skin-covered chest, waiting for Isabelle to be a bride. For a moment, a great disappointment overtopped all her other emotions. Oh, why had Isabelle done this hasty thing?

"Oh, Isabelle . . . without a wedding! I've always wanted every one of my girls to have a wedding at home."

"Oh, what difference is a *wedding?*" And Isabelle began to cry, great wrenching sobs that shook her.

Abbie put comforting arms around her. "There . . . there . . . dearie. That's right . . . after all . . . what difference *is* a wedding?"

"He cared for nothing in the world but me and music," Isabelle said in her bitterness, "but he went to war."

Abbie held her close, rocked her as if she were a child.

"Yes, yes, Isabelle. They care for nothing in the world but women and their work . . . and they go to war."

Isabelle would not go back to school for the remaining few weeks of the year. She would only sit at home and wait dully. And now Abbie had the new experience of attempting to keep another person courageous. It was more trying than to keep up her own spirits. Why must she always be strong for other people? How Isabelle sapped at her strength! She seemed to have no stamina. Sometimes Abbie thought the girl was selfish in it, and then she would say. "But I'm her *mother*. I'm the *one* for her to take her troubles to." Abbie had John to think about also. She felt a little jealous that Isabelle was thinking of Harrison all the time, when John was in the same danger.

By the middle of June, John, the lawyer, was sweltering at drill in Camp Libre in Florida; and Harrison, who cared for nothing in the world but Isabelle and music, was sweltering before Fort Malati, doing outpost duty.

They came home in the summer of '99. Harrison, who had been in much action, came home fairly well; John, who had done only camp and guard duty, came pale, emaciated and weak from typhoid contracted in Cuba. Harrison and Isabelle made plans to move immediately to Chicago. Abbie thought she could not stand it,—to have Isabelle live so far away. Why did children do that? It made her envy Christine, whose children were all settling down on the various eighties that Gus had bought,—Heinie here, Emil there, even Fritz, just home from the Philippines, had married and started into the field.

Isabelle took the piano. "I hate to, Mother, with Grace eleven now. It seems selfish."

"No, you take it," Abbie told her. "Grace can't bear to practice. She just reads and reads. My,—how different you children all are."

And then it came about that Chicago seemed not far, almost neighborly, in comparison with John's new location. After recuperating at home that summer, John left for Seattle and Nome. Abbie was stunned. Nome,—in Alaska,—from which there could be no return in the fall after the ice had frozen, from which there could come no word until late spring when the ice had gone out. In his characteristic way, John had told his plan casually only a few days before he left. There was a future in Alaska. It was the place for young fellows. Fortunes awaited their picking up. He would open a law office in Nome and keep his eyes open for anything presenting itself on the side. He was using his army money for the purpose. How queer, thought Abbie,—just as Will had taken his army money for the long-ago trip into Nebraska. Soldiers of fortune, both.

Calm and dry-eyed, Abbie told her son good-by. But all winter, day and night, her thoughts were with him. Every night when she was ready for bed she would look over the snow-covered prairie to the northwest, toward the land to which no word could go,—toward the land from which no word could come.

It was June before the first of the winter letters came. There were many. John had written her often. Many nights, then, as she had stood looking across the snow-wrapped prairie, John had been writing to her. After all, no distance could sever the tie that bound them,—nothing come between her and her silent boy. The letters were of an intense interest to home-keeping Abbie,—descriptive of the gold rush. Most important of all, John had been appointed U. S. Commissioner and was going up above the Arctic Circle.

In the late fall of that year, when Mack's and Emma's boy, Stanley, was six, a second son was born to them. They named him Donald. And he immediately upset Abbie's plans for Christmas by acquiring colic to such a noisy degree that the Mackenzie Deal family decided to stay in Omaha behind closed doors with their vociferous offspring.

The annual Deal reunion did not prove so complete a success as usual with John and Mack's family all absent. Abbie went through all the preparations for the event, as she always did,—the pop-corn balls and the taffy candy, the tree and the little hidden packages, but it was never the same for her when one child was missing. This was the fourth Christmas John had been away from them. More than ever, Abbie's thoughts were with John in that far-off land of the midnight sun, now that he was so much farther away than Nome.

What was there about John that seemed always to bring her thoughts of anxiety, Abbie wondered? From the time he was small, it seemed that she had always thought and prayed more about John than any of the others. His silence, his independence, his way of doing things without telling her, worried her. And now in Alaska, above the Arctic Circle, with no means of communication until the ice floe should go out, —what was he doing? What were his experiences? His pastimes? His temptations? What sort of women was he meeting? Abbie would stop in her work and utter a prayer for him,—and, sent as it were from the bow of a mother's watchful care, bound by the cord of a mother's love, the little winged arrow on its flight must have reached Some one,—Somewhere.

The Dr. Fred Bakers were out at Christmas. Grace, twelve, and Fred Jr., eight, were the only children at the Christmas reunion that year.

Isabelle and Harrison, though, came from Chicago, enthusiastic over their music. They were both studying and practicing hours every day, and singing in a suburban church choir. They each had a few music pupils. Isabelle looked stylish in her brown silk shirtwaist and wide brown serge skirt with fifteen gores, stiffened with buckram.

The two stayed a day after the Fred Bakers had gone.

"Don't you get tired of all the extra noise and work, Mother?" Isabelle wanted to know when they were alone.

"Oh, my! No, dear," Abbie returned. "When you have children, Isabelle, you'll understand what I mean."

"I might as well tell you now, Mother,—we're not having children."

"Not . . . *what,* Isabelle?"

"I'd really rather be honest with you than hear you talk that way. We're not having a family."

"Why, Isabelle, you talk as though . . . as though . . ."

"But I mean it. We're really not well enough off. You know, yourself, Mother, that Harrison and I will never be rich and what's more, neither one of us really cares. Mack has a good business head on him and is well on the way now to being well-to-do. Doctor and Margaret seem to have the ability to lay up treasures where moth can corrupt. No telling what John will do. He may be a big attorney some day. We don't know Grace's future when she's only twelve. But all Harrison and I care for is our art. Music is our very life. Knowing that we're going to be so devoted to it and perhaps never be well enough off, we're just not having children."

"But, Isabelle, if people waited to be rich to have children. If *we!* . . . Oh, Isabelle! . . . You'd make me laugh if I didn't feel so like crying. 'Can't afford it?' How can you afford to *miss* it . . . little children . . . their soft warm bodies and their little clinging hands . . . their cunning ways . . . miss *motherhood?*"

"Of course, I might have known you wouldn't like it . . . but I want to devote all of my time to my voice. To have children you ought to have plenty of time and money for their development."

Abbie Deal looked out of the window, down through the long row of cedars. "To have plenty of time and money for their development." Instead of the cedars, heavy with snow, she was looking into a sod-house where a little painted blackboard stood against the mud-plastered walls, seeing one shelf of books and a slate and some ironed pieces of brown wrapping-paper. The mother there was hearing reading lessons while she kneaded bread, was teaching songs while she scrubbed, was giving out spelling words while she mended, was instilling into childish minds, ideals of honesty and clean living with every humble task.

For a long time Abbie Deal sat and looked out at the cedars bending under the snow, like so many mothers bending under their burdens. But she did not answer Isabelle. Maybe there was no answer. Perhaps there was no argument. She did not know.

CHAPTER XXV

JOHN's letters came again in the late spring, in them an echo of the breeze that blows over the Kotzebue Sound. "For Christmas dinner we had fish balls and egg sauce, baked white-fish, ptarmigan pot-roast, mashed potatoes, baked dressing, ice cream from condensed milk, and coffee. After the white people ate, the Eskimos took turn and made a thorough clean-up. When one of them found something that struck his palate, he proceeded to devour the entire contents of the dish. Eighty white people ate and twenty-five Eskimos. The miners came dressed in their parkas and mukluks. . . .

"Thermometer has been down to 38 degrees all day, 46 below in the night. This morning about eleven the ice began moving on the Keewalik and kept coming all day. There is an ice jam at the bluffs below town, and a number of cabins are in danger of being carried away. . . .

"Strike on Kugruh has been confirmed,—the whole river and benches have been staked."

Abbie, with the letters in her lap, would look out over the familiar fields, green in their spring wheat and their parallel rows of young corn, and wonder how a child of the prairie could have gone so far away.

And now Nature began to seem less parsimonious with her rains. No longer was the sky a dry blue bowl turned over the dry brown earth. Heavy with moisture, the clouds gathered and fell in a blessing of light showers or heavy, soaking rains. Out of Nature's benediction grew fine crops, better times, high land prices.

A union of farmers to market their own crops was being formed in many localities. Abbie took two shares of stock in the Cedartown Elevator. "It's the beginning of something pretty big, I believe," she told Mack.

In the fall, Henry Lutz died. And over in the house with the cupola and the wooden rosettes and the fancy grill-work, Sarah Lutz clung to Abbie constantly, so there was one more duty at hand for her. After her father's death, Emma came into the possession of a large amount of land. Selling here, buying there with good business judgment, and aided by the upward swing of prices, Mack, who was now assistant cashier of the bank, placed the Mackenzie Deal family on the best of financial footing.

One more year went by with John proving his ownership of the title "Judge Deal" in the land of the dog-team, and then he came back. In that characteristic way of suddenly doing something with no preliminary talk, he opened a law office in Cedartown. To Abbie, it seemed unbelievable and far too good to be true, that the wanderer of the family should settle down closer to her than any of the others.

Margaret was painting many canvases every year now. Pencil and drawing-book with her, she often came out home to wander for hours in the vicinity, sketching the cottonwoods or the maples or a rolling bit of pasture land. "When the day comes, Mother," she would say, "that I can get the light that lies over the prairie at evening, to suit me, I believe I'll be satisfied."

Isabelle, in Chicago for three years, was forging ahead in her career, singing at some of the select musical affairs. Abbie's natural garment of modesty showed large perforations in it, when it came to anything concerning her children's accomplishments. More than once she hitched up the old white mare and drove into the *Headlight* office to proffer some item about one of her offspring's achievements.

"The Deals all seem to do things," Abbie heard a visitor to the community say to Oscar Lutz once. The two men were sitting on a bench under her kitchen window, before one of the many neighborhood suppers. Abbie, paring potatoes, could hear every word of Oscar's reply.

"The children do. Will, himself, was a good man but not much of a manager. Was always planning some wild scheme for the whole community. You can't get anywhere if you spread your plans all out over the whole country. At all the school meetings he talked about the day when the country school would be graded like the town. Talked about the day when the roads would be fixed. Had some fool plan about hauling little stones from the quarry at Louisville . . . loads of little stones and gravel and running a roller over 'em. Heard him say once right after a long drought that Nebraska was the best state in the Union . . . had the best soil . . . that the day would come that the climate conditions would change and it would be the most productive of them all. Talked about trees . . . trees . . . trees. Was as loony as old J. Sterling Morton himself about setting out timber. Would go after saplings and cuttings and help haul 'em in for the careless ones if they'd set 'em out. No, he wasn't lazy . . . lord, no. . . . Just plannin' fer the whole kit 'n' bilin' of 'em instead of himself. Carried the whole precinct on his shoulders. Didn't leave Abbie anything very much besides this one half-section, but the five children and the good name o' Deal."

Abbie, bending over the potatoes, with the neighbor women bustling around her, said softly to one they could not see, "Will, I'm glad,—glad that you left me the children and the good name of Deal."

John was not much more than settled in his new Cedartown office when his thirtieth birthday arrived, via the 1902 calendar. Thirty having been the meridian between youth and old bachelorhood in Abbie's young day, she concluded quite definitely that he was never going to marry. And as has happened since the time Naomi's sons appeared before her with Ruth and Orpha, Abbie was suddenly astounded by John writing her, while on a business trip, that he was bringing home a bride. She was Eloise Wentworth, a teacher he had met in Iowa, and they would arrive on the four o'clock, Saturday.

Abbie sat with the letter in her lap, the world tumbling grotesquely about her. This bolt from the blue, so characteristic of John, was hard to realize. A peculiar form of jealousy tore at her. "I'll bet she did the courting herself," Abbie said grimly, and was too wrought up to laugh at herself. Why hadn't he picked out some one she knew? Emma Lutz, Dr. Fred Baker, Harrison Rhodes,—she had met and known them all before they came into the family. Why had he done this, anyway? Did he know the girl well? What was she like? Of all the children, John was the one who had to be handled with gloves. Would she know how to get along with him? Why hadn't he married one of the home girls? Why hadn't he ever mentioned the girl? All at once Abbie began to laugh aloud, almost hysterically. "I'm talking for all the world like Grandma," she said. "Oh, I mustn't let myself get like Grandma Deal."

She never dreaded anything so much in her life as the prospects of that meeting on Saturday. It took all of her will-power to get herself in hand to welcome them. She was glad that Grace was home with her. Grace was fourteen now and in the Cedartown High School. No longer did children of the community have to go from home and board at the old Weeping Water Academy, for the Cedartown High School was now accredited to the University. Grace was a nice girl and a good student,—efficient, neat, a little prim. Looking at her sometimes, critically, Abbie wondered why a keen sense of humor had been omitted from Grace's makeup. She laughed at a joke when it was in a column duly labeled as one, and warranted to tickle the risibilities. But humor, that vague, elusive thing which had pulled Abbie through many a monotonous day and over many a harsh experience, seemed a missing ingredient.

The two, Abbie and Grace, met the newly-married couple with the surrey. Abbie was fifty-five now, her once glorious reddish-brown hair colorless where it was not gray, her shoulders drooping, her body rather shapeless.

Eloise was pleasant,—a nice looking young woman with firm lips. She had on an Alice-blue skirt made the new way with all the gathers in the back, and dragging a little on the station platform. A tight silk waist of the same shade with a cream-colored lace fichu, and a blue hat fitting firmly to her coils of light hair in the back but protruding fashionably to the front far over the large roll of a high pompadour, completed her most up-to-date costume. She met Abbie half-way with cordiality. She fitted herself into the family, firmly, as though she had arrived with the preconceived idea that she was going to make the most of John's mother. Grace took a liking to her immediately. The two discussed school affairs earnestly, with Grace hanging on her new sister's every firm word. Abbie, cleaning up the table and listening to them, said to herself, "For all the world, I believe she and Grace are two of a kind."

"Mother," Eloise said firmly, after supper when John had gone over to the office, "I'm going to call you 'Mother' right on the start and then it won't be hard."

"I hope," said Abbie gently, "it won't be hard to call me 'Mother.' "

"Oh, no," Eloise said firmly. "I'm not going to *let* it be hard. That's why I'm beginning at once. Mother, John's and my marriage is to be different from other marriages."

"How, Eloise?"

"Because I'm going at it in a businesslike, systematic way."

"Yes," said Abbie, "that's a good way."

"I'm going to make our home a well-organized place of rest and peace for John."

"That will be nice."

"You see mistakes on all sides and *I'm* not going to make any."

"No," said Abbie, "of course you won't."

"I've been reading everything on the subject and I *know* that I'm well prepared."

"Yes," said Abbie meekly, "I think you are."

"She has everything, Will," Abbie said to the spirit who was comrade and confidante, "education, looks, high ideals, efficiency,—everything but a sense of humor. And oh, Will, *how* John will miss it."

He admires her, Abbie.

"And loves her, Will, and love covers many things."

The next year Abbie sold the rest of the acreage to Gus Reinmueller, retaining the five acres which contained the house and out-buildings, the orchard and one pasture. Gus paid twelve thousand dollars for it, giving four thousand in cash and an interest-bearing note. "Now we can plan for Grace to go to the University," Abbie said. "Grace wants to be a teacher and now I can help her."

Now that the land was sold, Abbie did not have to think of the responsibility of the crops, but her hands were still busy with chickens, and pigs and the cow. She drove a sorrel mare now back and forth, attending everything that went on in Cedartown, which she felt would benefit her mentally, and she did not miss a church service or Ladies' Aid. One of the attractions that summer, which she and Grace patronized, was an entertainment in the opera house, purporting to be a sort of magic-lantern show in which the people in the picture would move about as they were thrown on the sheet.

"It may be true," Abbie admitted, but added with frank suspicion that there was probably a catch in it somewhere.

The program opened with a piece by the Cedartown orchestra. Probably the Boston Symphony could have done as well, but old Charlie Beadle, who was leader and drummer, would not have admitted it. A male quartet next sang, "Out on the Deep When the Sun Is Low." One gathered the rather disquieting impression from their forlorn and hopeless tones that there was small prospect of ever seeing the center of the solar system again. Miss Happy Joy Hansen then spoke "The Raggedy Man, He Works for Paw," with so much childish lisping and so much coy twisting of an imaginary apron, that one never in the world could have guessed her age, unless he had known, as all Cedartown did, that, neither happily nor joyously, would she ever, ever again see thirty-two.

And then, the picture. The male quartet, having apparently recovered from the sad effects of the setting sun, launched forth into a spirited presentation of: "When Kate and I Were Coming Through the Rye." A field of grain was plainly visible on the cloth, and, incredulous as it seemed, it waved and jerked and twitched. Kate came into sight, and, unbelievable as it was, Kate also waved and jerked and twitched. A young man close behind her, with every indication of St. Vitus' Dance, also waved and jerked and twitched. But they moved. The advertisement had not lied. Across the sheet the people moved. "Dear, dear," Abbie said on the way home. "What next can they do? There's just nothing now left to be invented, Grace."

Late that fall, Abbie helped organize a Woman's Club. "I don't know that we will do a great deal of good, but we won't do any harm, and much of life is an experiment, anyway."

Christine was disgusted when Abbie told her. "A club! *Ach!* for what? To hit mit?"

On the very day in which Abbie drove home with the office of second vice president of the Cedartown Woman's Club upon her shoulders, a touch of the old raw prairie days presented itself like a bit of the past. She met Oscar Lutz with a wild deer which he had shot and killed in the timber a mile east of Stove Creek,—a young buck that, quivering and at bay, seemed the last survivor of his comrades that had once roamed the east-Nebraska country.

Grace graduated from High School when Abbie was fifty-eight. She gave the valedictory for her class, an earnest if youthful dissertation on "Heaven Is Not Reached by a Single Bound."

The Sunday after the exercises, all of the children, but Isabelle, were home for dinner. At the table Mack said: "Mother, you ought to offer the place for sale right away to get a buyer by fall. It will make some farmer who wants to retire, a mighty good place,—a nice little five-acre tract with the orchard and a pasture and all."

"I would have before this," Abbie admitted, "but I haven't been real sure in my mind that I'd leave at all."

They all voiced the same sentiment, "Oh, yes, Mother, you ought to move to Lincoln with Grace."

"There's no real use for your staying."

"With Grace gone, just think how lonesome you'll be."

Dr. Baker and Margaret were willing to have Grace and her mother live with them just as Isabelle had done for those two years. The Bakers had been married fifteen years now. Dr. Baker's firm was a leading one, Dr. Baker himself prominent in his profession. They had a nice comfortable home. Lincoln was a city.

"Oh, no, I wouldn't want to do that," Abbie said. "Not *both* of us. That would be one too many, anyway. If I go, Grace and I will have a little place of our own."

That set them off on another tangent. There were nice cottages going up everywhere, several attractive ones of the new type called bungalows.

Before they left, they went over all the arguments for selling. "The place is too big for you, Mother. What do you need of a yard this size? Or a house with this many rooms? Or a barn?" Their talk was sensible. All the arguments seemed on their side. "And above all the reasons, is the one that it's going to be lonesome for you here." They were unanimous in that opinion of their mother's coming loneliness.

Abbie thought about it a great deal that summer before it was time for Grace to go. At times she decided that she was foolish to stay in the old place. The children were right. It was only old-fashioned, narrow people who never made a change. She believed she would go up to Lincoln and look at cottages. In the city there would be a larger life for her, new contacts, opportunities to see and hear better things. Just as she had half reconciled herself to the plan, she would walk down the path between the cedars, which she and Will had set out, look at her hollyhocks and delphinium, blood-red and sea-blue against the white pickets, stand for a time and gaze over toward the heavy fringe of willows and oaks and elms along Stove Creek. Everything looked familiar,—friendly. There would never be another real home for her. Home was something besides so much lumber and plaster. You built your thoughts into the frame work. You planted a little of your heart with the trees and the shrubbery.

It was the only old home the children had ever known. There ought to be a home for children to come to,—and *their* children,—a central place, to which they could always bring their joys and sorrows,—an old familiar place for them to return to on Sundays and Christmases. An old home ought always to stand like a mother with open arms. It ought to be here waiting for the children to come to it,—like homing pigeons.

On the next Sunday Abbie was ready with her decision. "No, I've decided. I'm going to stay here. This is my home."

They went over all the arguments again. "The place is too big for you, Mother. What do you need of a house this size? Or a barn? And above all, with Grace gone, it will be too lonely for you here. . . ."

Abbie looked beyond the poplars, stared for a moment beyond the Lombardy poplars into the deepening prairie twilight.

"No," she said quietly, "you wouldn't understand. It won't be lonely here."

CHAPTER XXVI

❧ THAT fall after Grace went away to school, John's and Eloise's first child was born.

"You'll want me to come, won't you?" Abbie had asked Eloise with her usual desire to be helpful.

"Oh, no," Eloise had said hastily,—a little too hastily. "John wants me to have a *trained* nurse,—the very best."

Little hurts! Little pleasures! How they made up the whole of Abbie Deal's life.

Eloise named the boy Wentworth, and proceeded to bring him up by the ritual of a red volume in which she held implicit and humorless faith.

"It would make a dog laugh, Will," Abbie said at home to that invisible comrade who was only spirit and memory. "He was crying and she ran and got the little red book and looked up something in the index. I went over and picked him up and it was nothing but a safety-pin sticking him."

That was the fall, too, in which Cedartown was astonished and entertained by the spectacle of Mack Deal and Emma with the two boys coming to town in one of the new automobiles. The noisy approach was borne in upon the ears of the residenters some time before the machine's actual appearance, so that a welcoming committee, in the form of a large delegation of the citizens, was on hand to greet the proud owners.

Mack and the ten-year-old Stanley were on the front seat. Mack at the wheel, eyes bulging and elbows out at right angles, looked neither to the right nor the left as he piloted the popping, sputtering land craft through the choppy seas of a rough road. Emma, in the back seat with the four-year-old Donald, was in a state of perpetual motion, caused by dividing her frantic clutches between her youthful offspring and her large flapping hat, wound round with many yards of veiling. Through town and to his mother's house, Mack and his new possession were followed by a cavalcade of interested, not to say envious spectators. The crowd surrounded him when he pulled up in front of the small gate, Mack having decided that he would not try to navigate the lane road, with the eventual possibility of his inability to turn around or back out.

The machine, as red as Oscar Lutz's thrasher, was almost immodest in the exposure of its many complicated internal workings. There were wicker baskets along the side, which Mack explained to inquirers were for picnic lunches. There were a hundred other questions he was required to answer. Yes, he had bought the windshield and the lights extra. Thought he might just as well get everything while he was about it. Only thing he hadn't bought was a top. They cost a lot more and anyway it was so much harder to run the things with one on. You could get them put on later any time you wanted to. Yes, he had come the forty-six miles in three and one-half hours. At which almost incredible statement, there was a shaking of heads and murmured, "Gosh, . . . almost fifteen miles an hour."

All of the boys and most of the men in Cedartown visited the exhibit during the day, and a large aggregation was on hand to see the departure at four in the afternoon, the time Mack had set for leaving, so that they could get back to Omaha before they would have to light the carbon lamps in front.

The next year Abbie had five grandchildren, instead of four, for Mack and Emma were the parents of a girl, whom they called Katherine. There was considerable rejoicing in all branches of the family, for this was the first girl among the five small cousins.

Emma was back at her social activities soon after the baby's advent, much to Abbie's uneasiness. "Emma certainly takes her duties lightly," Abbie would say to Margaret, who was her confidant in all the daughter-in-law gossip. "She and Eloise ought to be shaken up in a hat. Emma is too easy about it all for any use, and Eloise makes such hard work of it, that it's painful to see her."

Near the close of her University course, Grace came home one Friday evening, ate supper with her mother and wiped the dishes for her, remarking quite casually, "Mother, Wilber Johnson, the engineering student I told you about, asked me to marry him."

Abbie, who was cutting bacon in readiness for breakfast, nearly cut a finger in her surprise and excitement.

"Why, Grace . . . and you've kept it from Mother two hours . . . you rascal! Well, he's a nice boy, I'm sure. I knew his father and mother years ago and better people never lived. She came as a bride to the half-section across the creek from us . . . where Fritz Reinmueller lives now. She could hardly help but have a fine son. Well . . . well . . . *my baby!* I can't *think*, Grace, that you're twenty and old enough to know your own mind. How soon the years go by. . . . It's the right way, though, and the natural one. . . . I'll be glad to see you. . . ."

"Goodness, Mother, stop and listen. . . . I'm not going to marry him."

"You're not?"

"Why, of course not. I didn't say so. I just said he asked me to. I wouldn't *think* of it."

"Then you don't love him?"

"Of course not."

"That *is* a joke on me . . . going on that way. He's such a nice boy and his folks are so nice and well fixed. I guess I never gave it a thought but that you meant you wanted to marry him."

"Well, I don't. I don't feel a bit like it."

"That's all right, dearie. I know just how you feel. He isn't the one, is he? But you just wait. There will be some one,—and then you can wear the pearls I've been keeping all this time for one of my girls to wear. I'm glad you know your own mind. Lots of girls don't. They just marry the first man that asks them. But you're a strong character, Grace, and I'm glad of it. One of these days the right one will come along. I've got a little poem in my scrap book that says:

"Asleep, awake, by night or day,
The friends I seek are seeking me;
No wind can drive my bark astray,
Nor change the tide of destiny.
The stars come nightly to the skies.
The tidal wave unto the sea,
Nor time, nor space, nor deep nor high
Can keep my own away from me.

You just think of it that way and one of these days you'll meet the right man."

Grace seemed a little impatient. "Oh, Mother, I don't know that I want to."

"Want to what, Grace?"

"*Ever* marry."

"Oh, yes, you do. Just now after this little affair you don't think so. But you will, Grace, you just wait."

In 1909 Grace graduated from the University with Phi Beta Kappa honors, secured a good high school position farther out in the state, and was not home until the annual Christmas reunion. When she came home she seemed to have developed a maternal attitude toward her mother which was paradoxically pleasing and irritating to Abbie. She was pleased that Grace was thoughtful and considerate of her, irritated that she began to think of her as old.

"Mother, you ought to take a nap every afternoon," Grace would say didactically. To which Abbie would retort, "I'm not exactly feeble yet, Grace." Or, "Mother, there's a splendid new book on avoiding old age. You ought to read it."

"I'm only sixty-two, Grace, and I don't see any signs of senility. You can't avoid old age, but you don't need to think about it."

A week after she came home at the close of her spring term, Grace went away to summer school. There was not a lazy bone in Grace's body, Abbie often said. She was energetic, efficient. Sometimes, watching her or thinking about her in the way Abbie was always watching or thinking about the children, she wondered if Grace was not just a bit hard, just a trifle unsympathetic. She seemed to have no patience with inefficiency, no time for any one who was not succeeding.

Abbie was ashamed of herself that she did not get more comfort and companionship out of Grace. She loved her with her whole being, but they seemed to antagonize each other at times. She sometimes admitted reluctantly to herself that Grace was not the daughter which she had dreamed she would be,—a daughter to sit and talk, a companion with whom to hold long discussions. She was too energetic to sit quietly anywhere, and whenever the two held any discussions they usually ended in Abbie having her feelings hurt.

Grace was always impatient with the old order of things, always so sure of herself, so certain that one could accomplish in this world whatever task he set himself to do. Her conversation was always dotted with the words "progress," "efficiency," "ideals." She spoke of everything in generalities: Citizenship, economics, causes, rights. Abbie was all for the individual. "Yes, but old Mrs. Newsome, Grace. How about *her*?" She could not think of people in masses. A great sympathy would surge up in her heart for the one whom life had used harshly. But when she would express herself, she would be met with a flood of information from Grace, a flat statement of statistics, before which she would be compelled to retire ignominiously.

"Why, I'm glad she's that way," Abbie would say to herself. "She's smart, Grace is. And she's only twenty-two. When you get older, you get more sympathetic with the underdog. When you grow out of your youthful years you have more charity for folks who haven't succeeded." It was so characteristic of Abbie,—charity,—charity that vaunteth not itself and is kind,—that she could not see how others could ever leave it out of their make-up.

In the last of the summer Grace was home again, having made several credits toward her master's degree. She was energetic even in the heat, ready to help with the work, full of plans for improving the house. "Dear, dear," Abbie said to herself, "Grace is so energetic, she is like the wind,—so active that she's tiresome."

It was during these weeks of activity that Grace decided to have an afternoon party for her mother,—some friends out from Cedartown and two or three from Lincoln,—women whom Abbie had met and enjoyed at Margaret's and at Sarah Lutz's. Abbie was pleased with the idea. It was kind of Grace to do this for her. "I suppose I would never get around to do it," Abbie admitted to herself. "That's one thing about Grace, she does get things accomplished."

Abbie made out her list, and Grace looked it over preparatory to inviting the guests.

"Mother, you're not going to have Christine Reinmueller?"

"Oh, yes, I am, Grace." Abbie was sure of herself.

"Not with those Lincoln women. I wouldn't care if it were just the Cedartown people. But not with those Lincoln women and especially not with Mrs. Wentworth. Whatever would *she* think of Christine?"

"I'm sure, Grace, I can't help *what* Eloise's mother would think of her!"

"I don't see how you can be so friendly with Christine, anyway. She's so Dutchy and so narrow and so ignorant."

Abbie Deal set her mouth to keep it from trembling. Loyalty . . . it was the very fiber of her. In that swift flight of memory with which the human mind can make a non-stop journey across the years, she heard: "Hold-tight. Get the ground up. You die already yet. *Du narr!* Ya . . . you like dat dyin' . . . maybe." She opened her eyes to the odor of steam, onions, hot water, flannels, to the sight of the homely red face of Christine by her bed, nodding,—jerking up,—nodding—

"Why, Grace!" Because she was so thoroughly agitated she said it mildly. "Why, Grace, she saved our lives . . . yours and mine. . . ."

"I realize it, Mother. I've heard all that a hundred times. But, heavens . . . is the debt never paid?"

To keep herself cool and poised and her lips from trembling, Abbie rose and started into the next room. In the doorway she turned.

"Never!" said Abbie Deal. "Never!"

CHAPTER XXVII

THE same summer that Sarah Lutz went abroad with Emma, Abbie spent her spare time building the seat under the cedars. This was her sixty-sixth summer. She had almost finished her sawing and pounding on a warm August afternoon, when she looked up to see Sarah driving into the lane road in her electric car.

Abbie's gray hair was stringing over her face,—perspiration on her forehead.

Sarah piloted the car, which she had dubbed Napoleon, up to the Lombardys' where Napoleon, with his usual caution, refused to climb a little rise in the ground. Sarah looked "dressy." She had on a lavender summer silk, little amethysts in her ears.

"Well, Sarah . . . you've been to London. And what did you do there?"

"Abbie, I frightened a little mouse under the chair." Sarah kissed Abbie, held her close for a moment. What good old friends they were! And how they understood each other.

"Abbie Deal, whatever are you doing?"

"Sarah Lutz, I do hate to start anything I can't finish, but if old Asy Drumm was alive I'd have him here on the dog trot."

"But what *is* it?"

"It's a seat."

"For what?"

"To sit on. I suppose you've grown so high-faluting in your travel, Sarah, that you think a seat ought to be a Louis-something *objet d'art*, as the magazines say. Well, it isn't. It's to sit on. I've been on the go for sixty-six years and now I'm going to sit down a little, and I can't think of a place I'd rather sit than here where I can look off to the fertile fields that have come out of the old rolling prairie."

"It *is* pleasant, Abbie. There's something about it, . . . after all my trip . . . the wide stretches of view . . . the way the rolling land meets the blue sky. . . . Well, it calls you back . . . the prairie does, just as the sea calls the fisher folk."

And then Christine Reinmueller turned into the driveway, trudging along in the inevitable blue calico, gathered full at the waist, her little greasy braids of hair plaited flat from ear to ear. Because she had looked so old when she was still young, Christine seemed to have changed less than the others. There was something ageless about her. As she had had no youth, she now had no age.

"Well, girls, here we all are."

For a long time the three "girls" sat under the trees and visited,—Abbie Deal and Sarah Lutz and Christine Reinmueller,—Abbie, the motherly home woman,—Sarah, who loved dress and travel,—Christine, with no thought but the accumulation of the land. Three varying personalities they were,—held together by a strange tie of memory,—friends, because on a long-ago hot summer day, three covered wagons in a long straggling line lurched over the prairie together.

When John's and Eloise's son Wentworth was nine, they welcomed a daughter, whom they named Laura, and whom Eloise proceeded to bring up by the ritual of a blue book, child training fads having changed, and the old red book of Wentworth's baby days having become a back number.

Abbie had six grandchildren now. Mack's son, Stanley and Donald, were twenty and fourteen. Stanley, having graduated from an Omaha High School, was East, at Dartmouth, and Mack and Emma were talking of sending Donald to a select school for boys. "He needs culture and poise," Emma explained to Abbie.

"Dear, dear," said Abbie, "culture and poise! At his age, his father needed clothing and provender."

Emma laughed. That was one thing about Emma,—she was like Sarah, her mother, good-natured, ready to laugh at herself as readily as at another. Abbie felt as close to her as to her own girls.

Katherine, Mack's little daughter was eight,—an active child, always on tiptoe like some gay sprite, too full of the joy of living to settle down.

Fred Baker, Jr., was twenty-two, already taking a medical course, with that characteristic following of his father which a doctor's son seems so often to possess.

As for Abbie's sons, themselves, they progressed. Mack, who had been in the bank twenty-seven years, was now a heavy stock-holder. John did law work for half the county.

The old Weeping Water Academy, closed now in 1915, its usefulness over. High Schools, accredited to the University, were accessible to every boy and girl. The state owned nearly two million acres of school land, which, under the law, could not be sold. And it held first place in literacy.

The summer Abbie was seventy was the one in which the children planned an intensive campaign against her staying longer in the old home.

"We've just got to take things in our own hands," they told each other. "Mother's fairly well, but no woman of seventy ought to live alone like this on the edge of town."

"Why hadn't she?" Abbie Deal asked. "What's the difference . . . the *edge* of town or the *middle* of town?"

They talked it over,—she might have a room at John's in Cedartown. Then she would not be so far from old friends. "If she lives with me," Eloise informed them firmly, "I shall take it upon myself to see that she gets the right balance in her meals, and the right number of hours of sleep. I've always thought Mother Deal ate more protein and less carbohydrates than she should, and she gets up too early for a woman of her age."

"So I'm to be brought up according to a *green* book, I expect," Abbie Deal said grimly to herself.

"I think my home is the natural place," Margaret told them. "I'm the oldest daughter and Mother is as interested in my oil work as I am."

"We've got such a lot of room," Mack put in. "I don't know what a person wants so much for, anyway. But now that we've got it, I wish Mother would come with us and help fill it up. What do you say, Em?"

Good-natured Emma was willing, although she reserved certain secret doubts over the compatibility of Mother Deal and eleven-year-old Katherine.

Isabelle's Chicago apartment was permanently out of the competition. But there remained one other plan. Grace could give up her work and come home.

"I'll be willing to, Mother, if you just *won't* consent to leaving. I'd come right in and take charge of everything." Grace's sense of organization, like a pointer, was already scenting out a dozen little hidden plans. And her forty-horse-power energy was already tiring Abbie. "I'd turn the parlor into a room for Mother and take her bedroom for mine. Then I'd be down here close to her. I'd get a tea-cart in case she needed a meal in her room. . . ."

"And you could wheel the chickens in, on the wheelbarrow, for me to feed," Abbie retorted. Now she ought not to have said that, she was thinking. Why, she ought to be thankful they were so kind. How many mothers could have that number of good homes at their disposal? But she did resent being planned about and talked over. After all they were her children. In spite of their years, she was still their mother. She had never let them run over her and she wasn't going to now. When they had quite definitely decided on Margaret's home for her, she spoke up:

"I'll do nothing of the kind. I'll stay right here. And kindly let me alone. Because a woman is getting old, has she no rights?"

Eloise was almost openly relieved. Emma knew in her heart that the possibility of certain dramatic situations between the rather high-strung Katherine and her grandmother were now permanently avoided. Grace admitted to herself that it would have been more of a sacrifice for her to give up her work than the others could dream; and Margaret, with a slight sinking sensation, pondered for a moment over the mental picture of the marble-topped stand, the blue plush album and the patent swinging-rocker, rubbing elbows with the furnishings of her artistic house.

So they "let her alone." But from that time on they said among themselves that mother was childish, that you had to overlook an elderly woman's vagaries, and that they must drive in more frequently to watch her so that no harm would come to her.

When Wentworth was thirteen, and Laura four, John's and Eloise's third child was born. It was a boy and they named him Millard. John telephoned the news to his mother, who was now seventy-one. Abbie hung up the receiver, put on her hat,—a new one since the demise of the rusty black with the itinerant ornament,—and walked over to Cedartown. She could not wait longer to see the baby. She had borne six children, herself, and this was her seventh grandchild, but she experienced that same excited interest over its advent she had known at all of those other times. The first thing she saw when she entered the house was a new book on child rearing lying on the table,—a *brown* book.

"Mother, you shouldn't have done this," John was half-provoked. "I would have come out to get you."

"I am a little tired, I'll admit, but as long as I've got two good . . . well, we used to say limbs . . . but they're legs now, so I'll says 'legs,' . . . I'm not going to lose the use of them if I can help it."

She held the baby (to Eloise's discomfiture, for it said not to do so on page nineteen), turned it to the light . . . said she saw a little of Eloise about its mouth, John in the shape of its head, something of Laura, and even, by some wild stretch of imagination, a look of its great-grandfather Deal around the eyes.

Eloise, weak and nervous, was complaining about her help. The maid was cleaning and cooking all right but she did not know how to handle Laura.

Immediately Abbie was offering: "Let me take Laura home, Eloise. I'd like to so well. I'll take good care of her for a week or so . . . as long as you'll let her stay."

Eloise was a little dubious about the proposition and took no pains to hide it. "What do you think, John?"

"I'm wondering if Mother ought to. She's seventy-one, Eloise."

"Oh, it's not of your mother I'm thinking." No, it would not be of her mother-in-law that Eloise would be thinking.

"Well, you folks decide." Abbie slipped out into the other room. But Eloise was one of those quaint souls who think that because a woman is old she is also deaf, and her voice carried very clearly to Abbie:

"It's Laura, herself, I'm thinking about. You know, yourself, John, that your mother is terribly old-fashioned. And I don't know just whether to . . . well, *trust* Laura with her that long. She thinks every one ought to drink sassafras tea in the spring. She would still use goose-grease on a child's neck for colds and wrap a flannel around it."

Abbie heard John's low chuckle.

"And do you know what I heard her say?" She was earnest and serious. "She actually said, John, that a *red* flannel was better."

John laughed aloud. "Oh, Eloise, you never did quite understand Mother. That was a joke."

"Well, I must say I can't always tell when she's joking, then."

But, between the devil, rather mildly represented by the maid, and the deep sea, quite definitely represented by her mother-in-law's out-of-date notions about children, Eloise chose what seemed the lesser of the two evils, and packed Laura home with her grandmother.

Abbie and the maid and John picked out the things which the triumvirate thought Laura would need during the stay, materially assisted by the traveler, herself, who put in a few choice articles in the way of a one-eyed doll, some red beads in a bottle and a tooth of her dog which had been presented to her by the veterinarian and which had escaped the sanitary eye of her mother.

John drove out home with them, let them out under the Lombardy poplars, and took the little bag up to the screened-in porch. And if Eloise could have known the supreme faith and confidence with which her husband was looking upon the situation she would have been attacked by the little green god of jealousy.

Abbie led Laura by the hand up the steps of the porch. It was not possible to say which was looking forward to the visit the more,—the guest or hostess. For Abbie, with Laura's little warm hand in hers, was happy almost to the point of excitement. No, Abbie Deal would never get over being a mother.

"We'll gather the eggs first," Abbie's voice held all the notes of interest which an anticipated journey might have brought forth. "And feed the chickens and then we'll have a little supper."

"What will we have, Grandma?"

"Oh, we'll have . . . we'll have . . . What would you like . . . nice fresh eggs boiled in Grandma's new little kettle . . . or some creamed toast . . . or baked potatoes. . . . ?"

"Mother doesn't let me eat potatoes at night."

"Oh, I see. That's all right. We'll do as Mother wishes."

"What are you smiling at, Grandma?"

"I guess I was just smiling to think how nice it is that you have so many things to choose from for your meals. You see when my children were little, it was so hard to get enough food for them, that *anything* agreed with them."

They gathered the eggs. ". . . in the very same egg pail your papa used to gather them," Abbie told Laura. And the child gazed with awe at the antique which had been saved from an age that seemed as remote to her as the one in which Noah's ark figured. They fed and watered the chickens. ". . . and see, . . . every time they take a drink they look up and thank God for it," said Abbie Deal, with a fine disregard for natural science and a sublime faith in her fowls' morale. They ate supper. ". . . and now, you'll wipe the dishes when Grandma washes them, . . ." with Laura excited beyond measure at the unusual confidence placed upon her close associations with chinaware.

Afterwards they went out on the porch and Abbie held the little girl on her lap. She cuddled her up and put her wrinkled cheek against the child's firm one. Oh, why didn't mothers do it more when they had the chance? What were clubs and social affairs and freedom by comparison? And what *was* freedom?

"Tell a story now, Grandma."

"A fairy one or a real one?"

"A real one about when you were little."

"Well, when I was a little girl . . ." Laura wiggled with contentment. "When I was a little girl I had a doll and you never could guess what it was made out of."

"No . . . what was it made out of, Grandma?"

"A stone . . . and it had a little round stone head. . . ."

Yes, Abbie Deal was contented,—as contented as countless mothers, in a rather topsy-turvy world, are still contented.

CHAPTER XXVIII

AND now war again,—war, spreading its fear and heartaches like the circling ripples of a wave to the most remote farms beyond the tiniest village. And in the old farmhouse behind the cedars Abbie had said good-by to young Dr. Fred Baker and Stanley Deal, her two oldest grandsons, looking big and fine in their khaki.

"You know, Grandma, from the time Germany ran over little Belgium, . . ."

"You wouldn't want us to stand by and let a bully . . ."

Yes, yes, the words came back,—the same words,—the same spirit. How the clock hands went around.

She saw them drive down the lane road, saw them turn at the big gate, through which they had so often come to play, and wave their khaki hats gayly. The wind was blowing from the east and the cedars bent before it,—blowing from the east like the breath of the war god. And Fred and Stanley were waving their hats gayly back to her, while the cedars bent and the wind blew from the east. They were like her own boys marching off to war. Children of her children, she loved them as she had loved their parents. Did a woman never get over loving? Deep love brought relatively deep heartaches. Why could not a woman of her age, whose family was raised, relinquish the hold upon her emotions? Why could she not have a peaceful old age, wherein there entered neither great affection nor its comrade, great sorrow? She had seen old women who seemed not to care as she was caring, whose emotions seemed to have died with their youth. Could she not be one of them? For a long time she stood in the window and looked at the cedars twisting before the east wind, like so many helpless women writhing under the call from the east.

All during those following strenuous months she felt almost as though the very outcome of the struggle depended upon her individual efforts. So she knit at home and at the G.A.R. hall, bought a liberty bond whenever she could, and conserving everything, ate frugally. And prayed,—prayed that right would prevail.

Fate willed that Fred Baker, Jr., and Stanley Deal should come back to their people from overseas. Young Dr. Fred went into partnership with his father, immediately; and Stanley, after a three-months' period of recuperation, took back his old job in the bank.

Grace was teaching now in Wesleyan University. Life was still real and life was still earnest to Grace, splitting an infinitive one of its cardinal sins.

At thirty she received her second proposal of marriage from one of the younger college professors,—and refused him. Abbie was deeply concerned about it.

"Are you certain, Grace, you don't love him?"

"Quite certain, Mother." Grace was airily sure of herself.

"But Grace, . . . you're thirty . . . even if you don't look it."

"Yes, I'm thirty, Mother. And thank you for the implied compliment."

"Of course . . . if you don't love him. . . . But he is such a *nice* man . . . and your being thirty. . . ." Abbie's voice trailed off uncertainly.

Grace laughed. "Can't you conceive of a woman being happy, Mother, without a man at her heels?"

"But, Grace, it's so natural, . . . so . . . normal."

"Well, that sort of thing doesn't appeal to *me*."

" 'That sort of thing!' Why, Grace, it's the finest thing in the world when it's the right man."

Grace was impatient. "See here, Mother, I have my life all mapped out, and a man doesn't figure in it. I want to be free and independent. I want to do more research work in the East. And I'm perfectly satisfied with my lot. I have at present one hundred and twenty students in my classes, a large number of whom are fitting themselves to be teachers. If two-thirds of them go out to teach, that will be eighty new instructors. They, in time, will teach an average of forty students each and the result is, I have directly and indirectly influenced three thousand two hundred students."

"Goodness sakes, Grace," Abbie said in exasperation, "you sound like government statistics."

And so Grace was not to be married and the pearls would still lie in the velvet box waiting for a Mackenzie bride.

But if there were no romance in the world for Grace, the little winged god was not without its victims in the Deal clan, for Stanley Deal and Dr. Fred Baker, Jr., were both married the same year, Stanley to an Omaha girl,—"popular in the younger set," as the papers unanimously agreed, and young Dr. Fred to a red-headed nurse with whom he had worked during the days in camp before going overseas.

The year that John was elected to the legislature, Mack was made a vice-president of his bank. John was forty-eight, tall, straight, his black hair showing two silver patches above the ear, his whole physique always reminding Abbie of his father.

Mack was fifty-three, and a bird's-eye view of him standing east and west, if the spectator chanced to be looking north, would resemble nothing in the world so much as one of the portly pigeons around his mother's old hay loft. He wore horn-rimmed glasses, went in for golf and Rotary and the Commercial Club, freely paid his church and associated charity subscriptions, thought a great deal of his first wife, who was also his last, and altogether was so decent and clean and so respected in the rather nervous business world, that he would have made an ideal target for the shots of any of the most weightily important and wordily devastating of the critics of our social structure.

Abbie took Lincoln, Omaha and Chicago papers, and with the same scissors that had cut out their homemade clothes, carefully cut out every item concerning her now rather well-known children. Sometimes she would run across one which gave her a few moments of almost wicked glee. One such was:

"Perhaps more through the influence of Mackenzie Deal than any other single person, this series of Shakespearean plays is being brought to Omaha, . . ."

For a few moments Abbie saw, in retrospect, a freckle-faced boy in a sod-house, hunching over a thick volume of plays and saying, "Aw, what's the sense in this?"

"Dear, dear," she said to herself, " 'There *is* a divinity which shapes our ends, rough hew them how we will.' "

After a year, Dr. Fred Baker, Jr., and his wife were parents of a sturdy son. Dr. Fred, Sr., and Margaret were grandparents. Abbie was a great-grandmother. Where had the time gone? Blown by the winds she could not stop,—ticked off by the clock hands she could not stay.

Tourists were flocking back now into war-torn Europe and one spring Grace began making plans to go abroad in the summer. She was thirty-three now. "Only four years younger than my mother was when we made the journey from Illinois," Abbie thought. "And Mother looked old enough to be her mother, if not her grandmother." What was the secret of it, she wondered.

One Friday night with the April buds bursting into pink froth on the peach trees, and the April moon caught in the top of a Lombardy poplar, Grace arrived home unexpectedly.

"Well . . . well . . . it's my baby." Abbie was as delighted as she was surprised. Life was full of nice things.

Grace, too, was happy to see her mother. "And why do you think I came?" She was sparkling, vivacious.

"You've got a beau," Abbie guessed right away. "You're not . . . oh, Grace, . . . you're not going to be married?"

"Oh, Mother." Grace laughed light-heartedly. "You're incorrigibly romantic, aren't you? Heavens, no! How you would enjoy tying me down for life. No . . . it's something about you."

"About me?"

"Yes." She seemed fairly exuding mystery and excitement.

"I never could guess, Grace."

"You're going abroad with me."

"Oh, no." Abbie was incredulous. "I don't think I could, Grace. You don't think I could, do you?"

"I certainly do. You know, Mother, I got to thinking about it in school and you are going, too. We'll take it very slowly. You're pretty well, you know, for a woman of your age. It just came to me as suddenly as a flash, . . . why couldn't Mother go, too? I didn't write it because I was too anxious to talk it over with you. You will have to decide right away on account of reservations."

"My! My! Grace." Abbie could not quite face the reality of the plan.

"Listen, Mother. How would you like to see the 'green coast of Ireland'?"

"My! . . . My! . . ." In moments of great emotion Abbie's words were few.

"And London Tower?"

Quite suddenly, to Abbie Deal, from somewhere out of the past there came a haunting melody. Its lilting notes wove in and out of the magical things Grace was saying. She could not quite catch its refrain, and the words, too, evaded her. In and out of her mind it danced with elfish glee, a little half-memory. Something about "having gold and having land."

"And go to Scotland and look up the old Mackenzie estate?"

"My! . . . My! . . ." That old refrain,—what was it? It seemed to come to her out of the night.

"And Stratford-on-Avon with Ann Hathaway's cottage? . . ."

"My! . . . My! . . ." Little half-memory, singing tantalizingly near her,—something that was "dreaming visions longingly." It flickered ahead of her, a will-o'-the-wisp from out of the past, beckoning her to come and do this thing. She could not place it, could not catch it. Whether song or poem, story or scene, she was not sure. She only knew it was something that was mostly joyous, but a little sad.

Bewildered, incredulous, undecided, she went to bed.

"Will, what do you think?"

I think it would be fine.

All night she turned and tossed with the excitement and the responsibility of the decision. Once she got up and rubbed liniment on her knees. Toward morning she slept, but fitfully.

When she made her kitchen fire and cooked breakfast, all the high enthusiasm of the evening before had vanished. She hated to meet Grace and break the news, dreaded to see the eager interest fade from her face.

As soon as Grace came down the old enclosed stairway, Abbie told her. "Grace, I can't go."

"Why, Mother! I thought last night you would."

"No, I can't, Grace. But you don't know how I appreciate your thinking of it, and wanting me. Don't I realize how much easier it would be for you to get around without me? Well, that makes me appreciate it all the more. It's one of the nicest, if not the very nicest thing you ever did for me,—to come home to talk it over. But I can't go."

"I think you're making a mistake, Mother. I'm quite sure you could get through the trip all right."

"No, Grace. I'm more disappointed than you can ever realize. I'm so disappointed that I almost wish you hadn't put it into my head. Isn't that childish? Last night I couldn't sleep for thinking about it. I was that excited . . . but when I woke up this morning from a little nap I had, I knew I couldn't go. I have pains in my knees sometimes until the tears come. And my spells of asthma are coming a little closer. I'm tied to a whole row of little bottles on the top pantry shelf. You wouldn't want me to have a spell of asthma in front of the Louvre or have to sit down on the Bridge of Sighs because I was all out of breath. It wouldn't be appropriate somehow. All the time my heart tells me to go, my mind says not. Desire says one thing and good sense another."

"I thought you would love it so."

"Oh, Grace, I would . . . when I was younger, *how* I would! Things just don't connect sometimes. When I was young I had no means or time, and now I have the means and time, I have no youth."

"Well, I don't want to be responsible about urging you against your judgment, of course. But I'm certainly sorry. I said to myself, 'I'll get half of my enjoyment from seeing Mother's enthusiasm.' "

"Thank you, dearie, for the thought, but I'll stay home and read about the trip. You write me from all the places you stop. And I'll just stay in my chair and travel with you. And if *anybody* could take a trip that way I know I can, for I've always thrilled over reading travels."

Grace was loath to accept the decision. "As I said, I'm sorry. You owe it to yourself, if you possibly can go. Your life has been so narrow, Mother . . . just here, all the time. You ought to get out now and see things."

Unwittingly, as so often she did, Grace had hurt her Mother's feelings. For a moment Abbie nursed her little hurt, and then she said quietly, "You know, Grace, it's queer, but I don't *feel* narrow. I *feel* broad. How can I explain it to you, so you would understand? I've seen everything . . . and I've hardly been away from this yard. I've seen cathedrals in the snow on the Lombardy poplars. I've seen the sun set behind the Alps over there when the clouds have been piled up on the edge of the prairie. I've seen the ocean billows in the rise and the fall of the prairie grass. I've seen history in the making . . . three ugly wars flare up and die down. I've sent a lover and two brothers to one, a son and son-in-law to another, and two grandsons to the other. I've seen the feeble beginnings of a raw state and the civilization that developed there, and I've been part of the beginning and part of the growth. I've married . . . and borne children and looked into the face of death. Is childbirth narrow, Grace? Or marriage? Or death? When you've experienced all those things, Grace, the spirit has traveled although the body has been confined. I think travel is a rare privilege and I'm glad you can have it. But not every one who stays at home is narrow and not every one who travels is broad. I think if you can understand humanity . . . can sympathize with every creature . . . can put yourself into the personality of every one . . . you're not narrow . . . you're broad."

Rather strangely, Grace was neither antagonistic nor argumentative. "You know, Mother . . . there's something to that thought. And another thing, Mother,—do you know, there's something about you at times that is sort of majestic and poetical. I believe if you had ever done anything with it, you might have written."

"No, . . ." Abbie Deal said wistfully, "no . . . I was only meant to appreciate it,—not do it."

At the close of the day Abbie went contentedly to bed. Her head was heavy. Her limbs ached. It seemed a little hard to breathe. But a warm feeling of comfort was upon her that she was to stay in the quiet backwater of her own home.

"I'm not going, Will."

That's too bad, Abbie. It would have been wonderful.

"I know it would have, Will. But you understand how it is."

I understand, Abbie-girl.

"I knew you would. Whenever I tell you things, Will, I always know you'll understand."

CHAPTER XXIX

☙ AT SEVENTY-EIGHT, Abbie had shriveled as the hazel-nuts near the old Iowa schoolhouse shrivel when the frost comes on. Her O'Conner body was shaped like her mother's had been,—a pudding-bag tied in the middle. Her shoulders were rounded. Her hair was drawn back into a small white knot at the nape of her neck. The girls were always trying to fix her up. They brought her dresses and shoes and gloves. But the feet that had carried her through nearly eight decades of activities had not kept their neat shape. The long Mackenzie fingers were as gnarled as they were tapered. Two of them twisted together grotesquely.

"Let me be," she said. "You can't make me over now . . . it's too late. I'll just keep on using plenty of soap and water. I like to see you girls look so nice. But there are too many things to do, to fuss with myself so much."

That summer the old settlers held a big picnic down on the Chautauqua grounds near Stove Creek. It was a gala occasion. Youth must be served,—but not on the day of an old settlers' reunion. Every one knew every one else. On all sides one heard the same type of comment: "Well . . . well . . . if it ain't Mamie Balderman. I'd never have known you. Heavier, ain't you?"

"That's Anne Jorden. I declare I believe she's carrying the same brown parasol."

"Yes, that parasol's as old as the schoolhouse."

"Your daughter, Lizzie? No . . . not *grand*daughter . . . you don't mean it? Why, it seems only a few years ago I was at your wedding."

Most of the old folks, who were there, had come into the country as young married people. Some of them were bent and gnarled and weather-beaten. Others looked sturdy and clear-eyed. Many of the babies who had been wrapped in old shawls in covered wagons or born later in the soddies were there,—now farmers and attorneys, doctors, preachers and bankers. By some peculiar thrust of Fate, that wag who plays jokes on us all, it seemed that those who had been poorest in the early days, were now the wealthiest,—those who had been of least importance, now the most prominent. Some call it the law of compensation,—others, luck. It is, of course, neither one.

Standing about in twos or knots, they were all talking in reminiscent mood. One heard snatches of life stories on all sides,—a whole drama in every detached phrase:

"Yes, sir, when I got into Omaha, . . . I had ten cents. Two men had just been drowned in the old Missouri, and I made the coffins, . . . got ten dollars for them."

"When the Mormon train went by, women and children were pulling carts. A child was crying . . . its foot painin' from a loose laced shoe. Ma said she used to have a kind of nightmare afterwards . . . 'n' in her sleep she would always be tryin' to find that child cryin' . . . in a long train of ox-carts that kept goin' by 'n' goin' by."

"Shucks, we made *our* syrup by boilin' down watermelon juice. . . . *Sure*, it took an awful lot!"

"Yes, Uncle Zim's gone. He and Aunt Mandy used to say if they ever saved a thousand dollars, they'd take it and get back East as fast as they could go. Finally they made it, but thought it would be lots nicer to have two thousand, so they saved and accumulated and then set the amount to four thousand. Never went back at all. Died four years ago, a few months apart. Left several large farms and bank stock besides ten thousand dollars to each of their seven grandchildren."

All of the groups were not of a peaceful character. Some were having heated arguments over the trivial details of episodes a half century forgotten.

"No . . . you're wrong, Sam, . . . it was eighteen seventy-one."

"No, . . . Joe, 'seventy-two. I remember because it was the year the pie-plant froze."

Or, "I remember you coming just as well that day because I saw your wagons . . ."

"I don't know why you say 'wagons,' Celia. There was no plural number, when all we had was a bed and two chairs and a bob-tailed cow."

And then it was time for the speech of the day. The young county attorney made it, from the airy heights of the band stand, at his side a glass of water on Abbie Deal's marble-topped table.

It was a good speech. It flapped its wings and soared over the oaks and elms, and eventually came home to roost with: "You . . . *you* were the intrepid people! You, my friends, were the sturdy ones. Your days have been magnificent poems of labor. Your years have been as heroic stories as the sagas. Your lives have been dauntless, courageous, sweeping epics."

" 'Sweeping' is the word, Sarah!" Abbie said when the applause had faded away into the grove. "I wish I had a dollar for every broom I've worn out."

Sarah Lutz's little black eyes twinkled.

"How about it, Abbie, do you feel like a poem?"

"No, Sarah, I was always too busy filling up the youngsters and getting the patches on the overalls to notice that I was part of an epic."

It was after the speech that Abbie first saw Oscar Lutz, who, at eighty-four, a little bent but as hardy as any old hickory, had come from California to be present at the reunion. Of the four old neighbors, Will Deal, Henry and Oscar Lutz and Gus Reinmueller, Oscar was now the only one living. He was well-to-do with his bonds and mortgages, his land and his California home.

"How are you, Oscar?"

"How are you, Abbie? It's mighty nice to be back . . . mighty nice."

"We're glad to have you, Oscar . . ."

"Went down to Plattsmouth yestidy and found the post where the boats tied up fifty-eight years ago."

"My! My! Oscar! Is the post still there?"

"Still there, Abbie. Gettin' old like us . . . a little rotten . . . but still there . . . and a good mile and a quarter away from water. River bed's changed that much."

"I can scarcely believe it."

"Everything changes, Abbie . . . folks and rivers. I kicked the old post when I found it."

"What for, Oscar?"

"Don't know, exactly, Abbie. Kind of a ceremony, I guess." He had a far-away look in his eyes. "Remember how I told you I kicked it when Henry and I was waitin' for the boat to come bringin' Martha 'n' Sarah 'n' Grandpa?"

"Yes, I remember, Oscar, . . . you said you was so impatient waitin' for Martha you had to take it out on some thing."

"Well. . . ." He was silent so long that Abbie thought he had finished with the subject. ". . . Martha's been gone twenty-two years . . ." The old man fussed with his watch. "Twenty-two years! Went down to Plattsmouth yestidy 'n' kicked the post again . . . like I was waitin' for somethin' . . . a boat to come in . . . or somethin'. . . . Foolish, wasn't it? Kind of a ceremony, I guess."

After the old settlers' reunion, Abbie spent a few days with Margaret Baker in Lincoln. John Deal took his mother up in the big sedan. On the same road that Abbie had driven her team over thirty years before, stopping at Stevens Creek to eat her lunch, John took his mother now over the hard packed gravel in forty minutes. He growled a good deal at the county commissioners over a mile stretch in which he had to slow down a little.

The Bakers had one of the lovely new homes of the city, artistic in every point, from the dwarf evergreens in front to the Russian olives in the rear of the garden. Margaret had overseen every detail to the last door knob. Dr. Baker was a specialist now. "*Which* side of the heart is your particular line?" Abbie asked him in mock seriousness. "Dear, dear, you doctors have got our anatomy so divided up and pigeon-holed that nobody knows where to go if he just happens to feel bad all over. You're not as smart as our old Dr. Hornby. When he first came to Nebraska, he practiced medicine and surgery, fitted glasses and pulled teeth, was a notary public and sold sewing-machines."

Margaret Deal Baker was fifty-four now, gray-haired, calm-eyed, level-headed, one of the substantial women of the city, her name a part of every artistic and civic endeavor. " 'Poise' is Aunt Margaret's middle name," Katherine Deal, who was sixteen and given to expressing herself freely, would say. Democratic to the finger-tips, Margaret Baker, with her lovely home and her prominent position, refused to forget her humble beginnings. "When I was a girl . . ." she would say, and go off into a hearty peal of laughter over the memory of some funny episode out on the prairie when the state was new.

"Yes, I go to the beauty parlor every week," she would say frankly to a group of well-groomed women. "I have a shampoo and hot-oil massage and wave. And when I was a girl, I was thankful to wash my hair myself once in a while with water from a rain-barrel with drowned gnats in it."

Grace, lacking humor, was sometimes disturbed by her sister's attitude. "There's no use *parading* the fact that you once lived on beans and cornmeal," she would say.

"But plenty of use in parading the fact that it was your ancestor who hung the light in old North tower," Margaret would get back, with her mother's twinkle in her gray eyes. The Revolutionary ancestors on her father's side were a source of great pride and solace to Grace Deal.

"At least Aunt Grace believes in the D.A.R. part of the Darwin theory," was another of Katherine Deal's airy quips.

On this visit of Abbie's to Margaret, she found the latter just finishing a canvas with final loving touches.

"What do you think, Mother?" Margaret, in her studio smock, stood back to watch her mother's face.

Abbie came a step nearer to get the best vision. For some time she stood and looked at the unframed scene standing on the easel. When she turned, her wrinkled face was aglow. "You've got it, Margaret. It's there at last, . . . the light lying in little pools on the prairie. You've caught it . . . just as you said you wanted to."

"Yes, I believe I've caught it. But think, Mother, I've been trying for thirty years to get it as I wanted it. What was the matter with me before?"

"I don't know, dear. I guess it's always that way. There's no short-cut to anything. The Master demands full time of us before we are paid."

For some reason little Laura Deal continued to be Abbie's favorite grandchild. The little girl answered Abbie's deep love for her with an affection equally sincere,—or perhaps, it was the other way. Perhaps the fact that Laura held such admiration for her grandmother enkindled its answer in Abbie's heart. From the time Laura was five she had brought her grandmother little stories of her own composition. Abbie had them all in safe keeping, just as she had everything else which had ever come into her possession.

One of the first of these literary achievements, laboriously printed, was:

"A man once on a time had a poket-buk ful of munny he lost the munny and too this day he has to worck."

"Laura has the right idea," Abbie told the relatives in high glee. "She has the whole philosophy of life summed up in a short story. She'll be a writer some day."

At eight, she had brought her grandmother more lengthy compositions, running largely to an atmosphere of delectable foods, and over which the whole clan surreptitiously laughed: " 'Oh, no,' said the young lady, as she nibbled daintily at a piece of chocolate pie with whipped cream on it and a cherry on top of that and a nut on top of that."

At eleven, Laura had discovered what romance meant, and her writing leaned conspicuously toward that direction. Abbie was sitting on a bench under the cedars on a mild spring afternoon when Laura came out of the house bearing the inevitable pencil and notebook.

"Listen here, Grandma. Here's my new one. It's called 'My Dream of Imagination.':

"*I was once a princess, a captive in castle grim*
And a dragon wanted to drag me to come and live with him.

Now I had violet eyes and long yellow gleaming hair
And people said I was beautiful with my pure white skin so fair."

Abbie listened with undiminished interest to the twenty-six verses of dramatic, not to say gory, suspense, through:

" '*Twas a terrible sight to see prince after prince fall dead*
But the dragon only laughed with glee and said he'd have me to wed,"

to the happy ending of:

"I gazed out of my turret,—it was my wedding day
When suddenly I saw some one riding who was not far away

I watched the shine of his armour glitter in the sun's bright ray

Then nimbly and quickly I saw him dismount. He had stopped to pray.

Then slowly arising I saw him make the sign of the cross
While grasping his sword in his right hand, he mounted upon his hoss.

"You know, Grandma, that worries me, to have to say 'hoss.' It isn't just right but neither is 'horse' with 'cross'."

And so they discussed it seriously, Abbie who knew that one may laugh *with* a child but not *at* him, and Laura, who knew that Grandma was one unfailing source of sympathy and understanding in a world which was beginning to be critical.

"Now, tell me about when you were young, Grandma . . . some of the things you've never told me."

"Well, there is something I never told one of my children . . . but now I'll tell it to you. Before I married your grandfather, another young man wanted to marry me. He was quite the catch of the community."

"Why didn't you, Grandma . . . why didn't you marry him?"

"I had a very pretty voice and he wanted me to marry him and go to New York to study music while he took some medical work. I was anxious to cultivate my voice and the whole thing was a very wonderful opportunity for me so I very nearly married the young man. But something happened that made me realize it was just the thought of the New York opportunity that was influencing my decision, rather than love for the young man himself."

"What happened, Grandma?"

"I saw Will Deal coming down the lane."

"Just coming down the lane, Grandma? Was that all?"

"Just coming down the lane."

"What became of the young man, Grandma?"

"He became a big New York surgeon . . . so . . . if I had married him . . . my life would have been very different. I guess women have done that from time immemorial. A young man walks down a lane . . . and a whole life changes."

"And you had to tell the other young man you wouldn't marry him, Grandma?"

"Yes, . . . I told him."

"Was he sad?"

"A little sad . . . and a little angry . . . and terribly surprised."

"Why was he so surprised, Grandma?"

Abbie Deal smiled reminiscently. "I think it had never occurred to him that any girl would refuse him."

"And what did he say?"

Abbie Deal pondered a moment. "That I cannot tell you."

"Because it was too romantic, Grandma?"

"No . . ." said Abbie Deal. And by this, quite suddenly she knew that she was an old woman. "No . . . because I have forgotten."

CHAPTER XXX

You will remember that Basil Mackenzie, an aristocratic young Scotchman, of Aberdeen, riding to the hares and hounds, wooed and won Maggie O'Conner from the whins and silver hazels of Ballyporeen. But what you do not know is that several generations later, the good Saints, up in high heaven's court, gave that couple three chances each to mold the life of a descendant . . . a baby girl . . . just born upon earth. Basil Mackenzie first crowned her with hair like the mist around the mountains of Glencoe when the sun shines through,—and immediately Maggie O'Conner gave her eyes the color of the blue-black waters at Kilkee. Then the man, remembering sensibly that the outward appearance is not all, endowed her with a keen Scotch mind,—but the woman smiled and slipped an Irish heart into her. For a long time Basil pondered cannily, wondering how he might use his last chance and finally gave her the sturdiest of Scotch chins,—but Maggie O'Conner laughed and pressed a roguish V-shaped cleft into the center of it.

Practical folks there are, who will not believe this; but here, nineteen years later, was Katherine Deal with her misty Glencoe hair and her blue-black Kilkenny eyes and her gay great-granny's dimple in the middle of her daur great-grandfather's chin. Sure, and what more proof could a-body be needin'? Here she was,—Katherine, the only daughter of Mackenzie Deal,—this warm summer afternoon, stretched out in her Grandmother Deal's hammock on the screened-in sitting-room porch of the farmhouse, her slim lithe body in its blue and white sport suit curved comfortably in the hammock's old meshes, one slim silken foot rhythmically tapping the floor.

"As free and irresponsible as any colt in a pasture," old Abbie Deal thought, as she look out at her granddaughter, "and just about as untamed too."

Across the lane road, under the Lombardys, Abbie could see the latest model of sport roadster, blue and white, a special order of Mack's. Whether Katherine's dress had been ordered to match the car, or the car to match the dress, Abbie did not know.

Old Abbie Deal and her granddaughter did not have a great many interests in common. They did not seem able to get along comfortably for any length of time. Katherine had not the slightest atom of her cousin Laura's interest in either the grandmother's opinions or reminiscences. With her usual blunt frankness, she had more than once announced before a group of the relatives, including the object of her remarks: "Granny Deal. . . ." (Incidentally, she was the only one of the seven grandchildren who called her "Granny.") "Granny Deal and I don't hit it off any too well." She said it with the air of one who modestly announces an accomplishment.

But for some reason, she had driven in alone from Omaha several times recently. The dashing new roadster had bitten off the graveled miles between Omaha and Cedartown frequently this summer of Abbie Deal's seventy-ninth year. Rather strangely, for her usual active self, the girl seemed to like to sit quietly under the cedars or swing idly in the hammock on the screen porch. This afternoon she had a book into which she occasionally dived, and as often dropped back in her lap.

Abbie pulled her chintz-covered rocker up closer to the screen door.

"What are you reading, Kathie?" she called.

"Michael Arlen . . . nothing but. He's delicious. Everything he says sounds silky. Listen to this, Granny:

'. . . love is like a hammer . . .'

'Oh, not a hammer!'

'A hammer, darling. It beats and beats inside him and presently it doesn't beat so regularly, and presently it doesn't beat at all. . . .'

"Doesn't that just melt in your mouth?"

"The words are very clever. But not all clever words are true."

"You said a bookful, Granny. And inversely most things that are true are not clever."

She seemed to have everything, thought old Abbie Deal, studying her attractive granddaughter. She had the Irish wit of the O'Conners, the Scotch canniness of the Mackenzies, the German self-interest of the Lutzes, the Yankee determination of the Deals. She carried everything before her. People did whatever she wished. She breezed in and out of every setting with self-assurance. She dominated every situation with poise. She told her parents what she thought of them and handed out indiscriminate advice to any of her relatives. And through it all she looked as lovely as a picture.

And now, Abbie, thinking of what the girl had just read to her, returned thoughtfully, "You can't describe love, Kathie and you can't define it. Only it goes with you all your life. I think that love is more like a light that you carry. At first childish happiness keeps it lighted and after that romance. Then motherhood lights it and then duty . . . and maybe after that sorrow. You wouldn't think that sorrow could be a light would you, dearie? But it can. And then after that, service lights it. Yes. . . . I think that is what love is to a woman . . . a lantern in her hand."

"Prosaic. . . . Granny, prosaic and uninteresting, albeit the romance chapter has possibilities. I choose to think of Mike's variety that 'beats and beats.' It's more thrilling."

"You'll see, Kathie, when it comes."

"Heavens,—the little grandmother speaks in the future tense,—and to me, Katherine Elaine Deal, wot has had several distinct and separate love affairs."

"Oh, Kathie, how can you speak so? . . . I doubt if one of those 'affairs,' as you call them, was love."

"Oh, but they *were*, *cher ami* . . . or *cher amie* . . . whichever you are. They were deep, thrilling, luscious love affairs while they lasted. *While* they lasted . . . !" She went off into a little rippling laugh.

Abbie Deal did not argue. She did not answer. She only sat and looked out at her granddaughter, flippant, sophisticated, wise, irresponsible, lovely. Because she had a deep-rooted clannish love for all her own people, Abbie Deal loved the girl,—but she did not understand her. They lived in two worlds. No, Granny Deal and Katherine did not hit it off any too well.

It was only a week later that Sarah Lutz came out to spend a few days with Abbie. Her seventy-seven years sat lightly upon Sarah. Her white hair, dressed rather elaborately, held a gayly colored, green jeweled comb in its coils and she had little emerald earrings in her small colorless ears. The natural pink in her cheeks of the early days had been replaced by natural pink from a box, and her small merry eyes behind their shell-rimmed glasses were still bright and twinkling. Her dress was of modern cut, and her dainty high-heeled slippers, by the side of Abbie's broad and altogether serviceable kids, looked, as they walked through the yard, like gay little yachts towing broad barges into harbor.

The two had just reached the sitting-room when they both jumped at the sharp sound of an auto-horn and looked out to see Katherine in the brilliant roadster turning into the lane road under the Lombardys.

"Honk . . . honk . . . the lark at heaven's gate sings," she called out breezily and slipped out of the car to run up to the house, her lithe young body aglow with health and energy.

"No?" she said in mock agitation at the sight of both grandmothers. "Not *two* old noble ancestors?" Katherine's reverence for old age was on a precise equality with her general timidity.

She gave them each a hasty peck and took immediate possession of the conversation. "I haven't seen very much of you lately, Sarah. But Abbie, here, . . . I have been cultivating her acquaintance this summer with malice. And the queer part, Sarah,—is that the little old dear doesn't have the slightest idea why I have been dropping in so solicitously."

Sarah laughed good naturedly, and Abbie asked, "Then it wasn't just because you wanted to see me, Kathie?"

"Oh, no," she admitted blithely, "it's all on account of Jimmie."

"Jimmie?"

"Jimmie Buchanan."

"Oh, . . ." Abbie remembered. "The young man in John's law office."

" 'The very same,' quoth the maiden, 'as a tear stood in her eye.' I've had a crush on him ever since I first saw him striding along with his little old textbooks across the campus. But I never dated him then. I suppose you can guess why?"

"No." Abbie Deal and Sarah Lutz gave up immediately, for the answers to Katherine's conundrums were usually as unique as they were varied.

"Because," Katherine said, mysteriously, "he was a barb."

"No," said Abbie. "Not that bad?" Abbie might not be conversant with half of Katherine's modern vernacular, but she did know that a barb was a non-fraternity man.

"Now . . . Granny . . . you're turning on the sarcasm. Don't you make merry with me. Yes, my loves, a barb, . . . *never* went into a frat." It was as though she spoke of Lucifer's fall or Napoleon's exile. "He probably washed his own shirts on Saturdays and ate at hamburger joints . . . and here I'm crazy about him. But he won't have me. I've done everything but fling myself on the cement walk in front of Uncle John's office and yell until he comes out and picks me up. Mother is getting a little discouraged about marrying me to the Prince of Wales. But she is still counting on some one of the Vanderastors . . . and here I am just foolish about Jimmie Buchanan and ready to throw myself at his re-soled Oxfords. He'll be Governor some day or Secretary of the Exterior. But in the meantime, he'll marry some neat little Jane that'll economize and have twins . . ."

"Kathie!" It was both grandmothers, simultaneously.

"Oh . . . very well . . . one at a time if you prefer," she went on unblushingly.

"He's a nice boy," Abbie Deal broke in to avert other verbal catastrophes. "John speaks so highly of him. I'll invite him out some night to supper when you're here."

"Oh, you needn't bother. I have already. It's tonight." She smiled at them cheerfully. "I'm going in to get him at six. You'll fix a nice little dinner, won't you, Granny?"

Abbie Deal sat down weakly. Flesh of her flesh was saying that. Blood of her blood was taking the initiative in a love affair. "Oh, Kathie . . . girls are so queer nowdays. They do such *forward* things. It would have been nicer for me to."

"Girls now-days," said Miss Deal, "do things immediately . . . right off the bat . . . snap . . . just like that."

"So I see," said Abbie Deal dryly.

"Now, here's the idea," Kathie went on, unperturbed. "You two old baby-dolls get up a nice little dinner while I go after Jimmie. Then I'll come home with him and put on a fetching pink apron and set the table and bring in the provender . . . and Jimmie will begin to think *I'm* the neat little Jane." She smiled at them with gay nonchalance. She patted them both. She kissed them each a time or two. And they gave in.

"She's yours, Sarah, as much as she's mine," Abbie said, when they were starting the meal, "and I, for one, am ashamed of her."

"Oh, . . . she's all right, Abbie. She's just outspoken."

"At nineteen, Sarah, I was married, and had Katherine's father, and had washed and ironed and sewed and made soap and woven rag carpet . . . and . . ."

"Yes . . . but, Abbie, you just couldn't do anything else. I can think of a dozen things that Kathie could do right now if she set her mind to it."

They prepared the dinner . . . the two old belles of another generation.

A little after six, Katherine dashed into the lane road at a speed which jangled the nerves of a flock of stolid Plymouth Rock hens, and set the brakes a few inches from a gander that stuck out his neck and expressed disapproval of the blue and white monstrosity.

"Honk honk, yourself," Katherine called out to the offended dignitary, and then came into the house with a nice-looking, clean-cut young fellow. She came triumphantly. "Well . . . here's Jimmie. It took handcuffs and an anesthetic to get him but I did the deed. Jimmie, you know Grandmother Deal, . . . but I want to present you to Grandmother Lutz. Grandma . . . Jimmie Buchanan . . . the conquered. Well," she waved an airy hand at the two old ladies, "how do you like 'em, Jimmie? I could love either . . . 'were t'other dear charmer away.' "

Abbie Deal was embarrassed beyond measure. She was used to the girl's wild talk before her own people, but she did not dream Kathie would keep it up when the young man came. Abbie looked at him. He was not disgusted. He was looking at Katherine with approbation and liking . . . even admiration. He *liked* her flippant talk. The young man, himself, *liked* it. Well, she gave up. She washed her hands of the present generation. They were away beyond her.

Katherine put on a rose-pink apron which she had brought with evident forethought, and winked openly at her respective progenitors as she carried in the food.

They ate the palatable if simple dinner together,—this rather incongruous little group, after which Katherine said demurely, "Now, Jimmie and I'll wash the dishes, won't we, Jimmie?" Which was something of an astonishing innovation in itself, as, heretofore, dish-washing had not been one of Katherine's favorite indoor sports.

A half-hour later, Abbie and Sarah went into the kitchen, just as

Katherine was hanging up her dishpan. "Everything all right, Granny?" she wanted to know.

"Why, I think so, Katherine. It looks very nice."

"Neat little Jane, am I not?" She grinned brazenly at Abbie Deal, who immediately reddened for her.

"Well, Sarah," said Abbie when they were alone, "my mother blushed and gave my father a rose by a well on the Scottish moors. I cried on Will's shoulder in an old honey-locust lane. Mack courted Emma after church and singing-school. And Kathie . . . Kathie goes out and gets her man."

Sarah Lutz laughed. "After all, Abbie, there's something honest about it and frank and aboveboard."

Abbie put the butter-crock back into the big white refrigerator. "Sarah," she said, "it may be honest and it may be frank and it may be aboveboard,—but it's not *subtle* and it's not *romantic* and it's not *artistic*."

Sarah Lutz's bright black eyes twinkled behind her shell-rimmed glasses. "If you're not all wet, old lady," she said solemnly, . . . "*you've said a mouthful.*"

CHAPTER XXXI

§ Abbie made her usual extensive preparations for Christmas that year. The daughters and daughters-in-law said a great deal against her using up so much energy. "But you might as well talk to the wind," Grace wrote to Isabelle. "There's something stubborn about Mother. She is bound to go through with all that mince-meat, doughnut, pop-corn-ball ordeal even if she's sick in bed afterward. Margaret wants us to come there to save her all that work, and Emma and Eloise have both offered their homes, too, but she won't listen. 'No,' she says, 'as long as I'm here, the Christmas gathering is here.' I've tried to tell her over and over that conditions have changed, that we don't live out on an isolated prairie any more; that she doesn't make one thing that she couldn't buy, but she just won't catch up with the times. 'They're not so full of the Christmas spirit when you don't fix them yourself,' she says. Isn't that the last word in old-fashioned ideas?"

So the clan came once more to the old farmhouse behind the cedars. Grace was the first to arrive in her own roadster, coming over the graveled highway from Wesleyan University. The others arrived at various times before Christmas eve. Mack and Emma, Donald and Katherine came. Only Stanley was missing from the Mack Deal family. Having married, Stanley had discovered that a wife's people must also be reckoned with. Margaret and Dr. Fred Baker, Dr. Fred, Jr., and his wife and two little boys came. Isabelle and Harrison Rhodes got in from Chicago on the afternoon train, the road boasting a flyer now instead of the old baggage-and-day affair of the time when the children were small. John and Eloise, Wentworth and Laura and Millard, who was eight now, all came over from their home on the other side of Cedartown in time for the evening meal. Every car was loaded to the doors with packages.

Abbie had an oyster supper. That, too, was a hang-over from the days when sea food was scarce and expensive. No matter that the bivalves were on every menu placed before the various members of the Deal family these days, Abbie continued to have an oyster supper each Christmas eve,—bowls of crackers alternating down the long table with celery, standing upright in vase-looking dishes, like so many bouquets from the greenhouse.

Jimmie Buchanan came over later in the evening and brought Katherine a gift. Jimmie was rather astounded at the sight of so many relatives.

"Every one has to be here," Katherine told him. "In all the wedding ceremonies, whenever a Deal is married, the question is asked, 'Do you solemnly promise to spend all your Christmases at Granny Deal's, forsaking all others as long as you shall live?' And if you can't promise,—out you go before you're in."

Abbie Deal was embarrassed beyond words. To speak so to a young man with whom you were keeping company!

Katherine went on, "No, sir,—it wouldn't be Christmas without the wax flowers in the parlor and the patent rocking-chair and the painting of the purple cow and the *whutnut*. Grandma makes us all animal cookies yet. Can you beat it? When I was big enough to read love stories by the dozens, she gave me 'The Frog That Would A-Wooing Go,'—not but that it had its romantic appeal, too. We always stay two nights and we have to have beds everywhere. Granny puts us in corners, on couches, sinks, bath-tubs, ironing-boards . . . and not one of us would miss it. Donald passed up a dance at the Fontanelle for it. You can't tell the reason, but the minute you see those old cedar trees and come up the lane under the Bombarded poplars with snow on 'em, you're just little and crazy over Christmas."

There were some very lovely presents that next morning,—the radio in its dull-finished cabinet for Abbie, jewelry, a fur, expensive toys and books,—an old musty smelling one for Emma, who had gone in for first and rare editions. Margaret gave her mother the painting of the prairie with the sunshine lying in little yellow-pink pools between the low rolling hills. "For I think you made me love it, Mother, when I was a little girl. I learned to see it through your eyes," she told her.

In the afternoon, Mackenzie Deal, the Omaha banker, in an overcoat and old muffler that had been his father's, spent a large share of his time out in the barn cracking walnuts on a cottonwood chunk. John Deal, the state legislator, went up into the hay-loft and potted a few pigeons with an old half-rusty rifle. Isabelle Deal Rhodes, the well-known Chicago singer, called her husband to help her get the old reed-organ out of the storehouse. She dusted it, and then, amid a great deal of hilarity, pumped out, "By the Blue Alsatian Mountains." One of the keys gave forth no sound at all, so that whenever she came to it the young folks all shouted the missing note.

By evening the younger members of the group had gone,—Fred Jr. and his family back to Lincoln, Donald and Wentworth to Omaha, while Katherine was off somewhere with Jimmie Buchanan. But the others, in the early dusk of the Christmas twilight, gathered in the parlor with the homely coal-burner and the lovely floor lamp, with Abbie's crude painting of the prairie and Margaret's exquisite one, with the what-not and the blue plush album and the tidy on the back of the patent-rocker.

"There was one Christmas we had, Mother," Mack said, "that I always remember more than the others. I can see the things yet,—my old brass cornet, a big wooden horse made out of logs, a tree that looked . . . well, I've never seen a tree since look so grand. Where in Sam Hill did you raise all the things in those days?"

"I think I know which one you mean," Abbie was reminiscent. "It was the year after the grasshoppers. Well, my son, your father and I made all of those things out of sticks and rags and patches and love."

It brought on a flood of reminiscences.

"Remember, Mack, the Sunday afternoon we were herding hogs on the prairie and that Jake Smith that kept the store at Unadilla, came along with his girl in a spring wagon, and threw a whole handful of stick candy out in the grass for us?" Mrs. Frederick Hamilton Baker, well-known artist and club woman of Lincoln, was speaking.

"Do I? I can see them yet, red and white striped,—and looking as big as barber-poles to me. I wondered how any one in the world could be that rich and lavish," Mackenzie Deal, a vice-president of one of the Omaha banks, was answering.

"And do you remember, John, how scared you were . . . the time we chased the calf and you grabbed it by the tail when it ran by you and the tail was frozen and came off in your hands?"

When they had all laughed at the recollection, Isabelle put in, "But I'll bet he wasn't as scared as I was once, . . . the time a man came to the door and told Father he was drawn on the jury. You all stood around looking solemn, and I took a run for Mother's old wardrobe and hid in behind the clothes and cried."

"Why . . . what did you think?" They were all asking.

"Well, I knew 'jury' had something to do with law and jails and penitentiaries. And I had heard of 'hung,' 'quartered' and '*drawn*' so the inference was that Father was going to be hung in the penitentiary."

"I remember once when I wasn't scared but *mad*." It was Grace's contribution. "It was when Aunt Regina came to help Mother take care of Grandma. I was modestly effacing myself under the dining-room table and she scooped me out with a sprightly, 'So this is little Grace.' Then she took me on her lap and put her arms around me and pressed me to her bosom and apparently forgot me, while she and mother verbally married off and buried all the relatives over my head."

"Why didn't you have the gumption to get down?"

"Too bashful, I suppose. That's where your ancient theories of child training come in. No modern child would stand it. But I just sat on while my legs went to sleep and my brain atrophied. I used to think I sat there a month. But I know now it couldn't have been more than a week."

"That's as bad as I was." It was John. "Remember that preacher that used to stop at our house, the one with the beard that looked as though it was made out of yellow rope?"

"Who could forget it? He tied it up like a horse's tail when he ate." They were all answering at once.

"The first time he stopped, he said to Mack, 'What's your name, son?' Mack said, 'Mackenzie.' 'And what's yours, little man?' he said to me. I was so scared I said 'Mackenzie,' too. Can you beat it? I'll bet there isn't a kid living to-day as bashful as that."

"Do you remember," it was Isabelle, "the old milk-wagon, John, you rigged up to peddle your milk in? I can smell the inside of it yet, the damp, sweetish odor of warm milk. Remember how you used to ring an old cow-bell and the women would come out with their pans and pitchers, and have their aprons twisted up over their heads? Think of the evil-looking germs that must have perched on the rims of those pitchers when the dust swirled around!"

And so they went on, recalling their childhood days,—days of sunburn and days of chilblains, of made-over clothes and corn-bread meals, of trudging behind plows or picking up potatoes, of work that was interwoven with fun, because youth was youth. Prairie children never forget.

Far into the evening they sat around the old coal burner, talking and laughing, with tears not far behind the laughter,—the state legislator and the banker, the artist, the singer, and the college teacher. And in their midst, rocking and smiling, sat the little old lady who had brought them up with a song upon her lips and a lantern in her hand.

CHAPTER XXXII

THE Mackenzie Deals were leaving the morning after Christmas.

"Can't you and Katherine stay longer?" Abbie asked Emma, a little wistfully.

"No, Granny," Katherine assumed the responsibility for the decision. "I've had a grand time, but now I must go, for I have a date tonight,—and a blind one at that, . . . a Minnesota U. man."

" 'A blind date.' For goodness' sake, Katherine, what is that?"

"Blind, Grandmother mine, means 'not seeing.' A date is a man with whom to while away a boresome hour or two. There, you have it . . . a man that you have never seen with whom to while away an hour or two."

"Kathie . . . you mean you've never been introduced to him?"

"Not only never introduced to him . . . but have never set limpid violet eyes upon him."

"Kathie . . . how horrible! Why, it makes me think of veiled people in heathenish countries."

"Quite so, and a merry little gamble it is. But see the thrill of it! Is he going to be dark, light, short, tall, a keen looker, or a crock . . . interesting or a prune? Will he glide up in a high-powered machine or rattle up in an egg-beater?"

"Kathie!"

"If Jimmie were going to be there I wouldn't have made the date. But Jimmie's not going to be there . . . and a poor girl has to have somebody to love her."

"Kathie," Abbie looked at her granddaughter as at some queer museum specimen, "do you know, you just make me wonder whatever your great-great-grandmother would have thought of you. Isabelle Anders-Mackenzie, her name was. She was gentle and refined,—very lovely and very aristocratic. She lived on the beautiful Mackenzie estates . . ."

"Stop . . . stop right there!" Katherine sat up, alert as a young deer with uplifted head. "For heaven's sake, why has no one ever told me that before? Why, our sorority is just *keen* about family. That's our *line*. I've been sort of uncertain about the past . . . a little shy in mentioning some of our aunty-cedents and uncle-cedents . . . not ashamed of anybody, y'unn'erstan', but just supposing they were all this same kind, . . . out-of-the-soil-up-to-God."

"Kathie!"

"And all the time I had this keen ancestor. Now, say it again, and very slowly . . . 'Katherine, your great-great-grandmother was Isabelle Anders-Mackenzie, a beautiful, aristocratic snob. She *was* an awful snob, wasn't she, Granny?"

"Kathie!"

"Think how my marriage could read: 'The marriage of Miss Katherine Elaine Deal to Mr. James Worden Buchanan . . .' I haven't said anything about this yet to Jimmie, but as the Chinaman says, 'Can happen,' and there's nothing like taking time by the fetlock. Picture this in bold bad type in the Sunday edition: 'Miss Deal is a direct descendant of the Anders-Mackenzies of Aberdeen, Scotland, Knights of the Garters' . . ."

Abbie Deal's old eyes twinkled. "But don't forget the other side of the house, too, Kathie. There were knights of the suspenders, too. Don't forget old Grandmother Bridget O'Conner, Kathie. She was an Irish peasant woman and she lived in a shack at the side of a hill on the edge of the moors. The chickens and the pigs ran in and out of the thatch-covered hut. She couldn't read a word and she couldn't write her name, and she smoked a black pipe. But if it wasn't for the sturdy plebeian blood of her daughter, Maggie (my mother, Kathie) you wouldn't be here."

Katherine waved it aside. "We'll pass lightly over the O'Conners. It's the Mackenzies that intrigue me. What more do you know about them?"

Abbie Deal told all that she could remember hearing from her sister Belle,—the story of the lovely lady,—of her reddish-brown hair and tapering fingers, and of the picture that hung on the landing of the stairway in the great hall.

"That settles it," Katherine arose. "I'm going right up to Jimmie and bring matters to a climax, by revealing to him just who I am. Right into the office I go and say, 'Jimmie, here comes the Lady Katherine Elaine Anders-Mackenzie Deal, great-great-granddaughter of Isabelle Anders-Mackenzie, who had flowing white fingers and a long reddish-brown nose that tapered at the end."

When the door had closed behind her, Abbie sighed and said, "Whatever are you going to do with her, Emma?"

"Oh, she's all right, Mother." Emma was always like Sarah, her mother, good-natured, easy-going. "She's just breezy. She tells me everything." Mrs. Mackenzie Deal temporarily disregarded the recollection of some of the things Katherine had told her.

When they had all gone, Abbie took a great deal of comfort with her new radio. The dull-finished, beautifully-polished cabinet put a new interest in life for her. At first in the wonderment of the thing, she rubbed the Aladdin lamp all day long. Sermons, jazz bands, market reports, monologues, she listened to them all with equal interest and amazement. A sermon from Denver, a talk on fruit tree culture from Lincoln, a dance orchestra from Omaha, interested her with equal intensity. Preaching and pruning and prancing, they were all the same to her. And when "The Ring of the Piper's Tune" came in, she shut her eyes and saw her Irish mother lift her skirts and do the Kerry dance as lightly as a thistledown.

"My, I wish you could hear the music, Will."

I've heard wondrous music, Abbie.

"There's nothing more now, Will, that can be invented."

There are things undreamed of, Abbie-girl.

And then Abbie had a letter from Isabelle. She was to sing from a Chicago station on February third.

"Find the station beforehand, Mother," Isabelle wrote, "so you'll not have any trouble that night or lose time trying to locate it while the program is on."

On the night of the third, Abbie sat up later than was her custom, so that she could hear Isabelle. Even then she experienced a little trouble in getting the station. "I suppose nothing's just perfect," she thought. "We always have to have some little grief to make us . . ." Suddenly she had them. But the program had begun. Isabelle's voice came forth in an aria as plainly as though she were in the room. When she had finished, the announcer spoke. "Mrs. Rhodes will sing her second number especially for her mother, listening in at Cedartown, Nebraska."

The piano, with violin accompaniment, played a few notes and then Isabelle's voice came again, full and clear:

"Oh, the Lady of the Lea
Fair and young and gay was she
Beautiful exceedingly
The Lady of the Lea."

And then it came to Abbie Deal. That was it,—the little half-memory! That was the old strain that had haunted her and which she could not quite remember.

"Many a wooer sought her hand
For she had gold and she had land . . ."

That was the forgotten melody,—the song of her youth.

"Everything at her command
The Lady of the Lea."

She was young again, singing on a grassy knoll, with the future all before her, with the years of her life still unlived.

"Oh, the Lady of the Lea
Fair and young and gay was she . . ."

Where had they gone, those years? Blown away by the winds you could not stop,—ticked off by the clock hands you could not stay.

"Dreaming visions longingly
The Lady of the Lea."

Isabelle finished the last verse of the song. Abbie turned off the radio, performed all the little nightly duties about the house, and undressed for bed. When she had turned out the lights, she stood for a few minutes at the bedroom window looking out at the night. It was moonlight and cloudless and very still. The trees stood etched in black against the white of the snow, their shadows as real as their substance. For some time Abbie looked out at the cedars standing silently there in the snow and the moonlight, like old women listening for something,—perhaps the strains of a song of their youth, and the dreams of desire.

CHAPTER XXXIII

IN THE spring, Katherine's affair with Jimmie Buchanan culminated in an engagement, duly announced on the part of Mr. and Mrs. Mackenzie Deal, by way of an elaborate luncheon and the Sunday papers,—the wedding to take place in the early fall. The immediate effect upon Abbie was to have her begin a quilt for the bride-to-be, on Monday morning, as soon as the chickens were fed and the dishes washed. For some time she pondered whether to do "The Basket of Flowers" pattern, "The Rising Sun," or "The Rose of Sharon," eventually deciding on the rose pattern, done in pink and white. Grace came home to find her in a puddle of pink and white blocks, her blue-veined fingers trembling a little over the stitches.

Grace scolded. "Mother, whatever are you doing that for? You can walk into any department store now and buy these very same old-fashioned patterns."

"They cost an awful lot."

"Maybe they *are* expensive. All nice hand work is. But *think* of the labor! Please, Mother . . . I'll be glad to get it for you . . . any pattern you say . . . if you'll just put the thought about doing it yourself out of your mind."

"No . . . it's more like a real gift if you do it yourself."

"But, Mother, Katherine wouldn't *care*. And there'll be *thousands* of stitches in it."

"And a thousand thoughts of love caught in the stitches, Grace."

No, you could not do much with old Abbie Deal when she had made up her mind.

Sometimes when she had sewed all afternoon she would walk over to Christine's "to get the cricks out of her back." On a cool April evening she found Christine sitting up close to her cook-stove cutting up potatoes for the morrow's planting. She wore the inevitable faded blue calico dress gathered full at her portly waist line. Her little greasy braids, neither white nor gray, nor yet any particular color, were wound flat from ear to ear.

"Oh . . . So it's you. Come in. Shall I make a light?" Christine wanted to know. And then added, with characteristic frugality, "If we sit up close the stove by, we not have to make it. Ya?"

Abbie looked around for Anna, Christine's granddaughter, who had been living with her for several years. "Where's Anna, Christine?"

"Huh!" Christine was evidently disgruntled about something. "Anna, she's gone to Omaha up."

"Omaha?"

"Ya. To vork . . . until she some money earn." She was excited. Her broken words came tumbling over each other. "I give Anna land all the same to her . . . eighty acres. Eighty acres to every child I give, I tell you. I give Anna the land from her dead mother. What keep I? Three eighties. Ya! Out of all that eleven eighties, for myself three I keep. Maybe I starve. Maybe I go the county house by. How they like their old mother go the poorhouse by? Anna care nothing. She come by me and say, 'Grandmudder . . . I haf it . . . the land . . . but I haf taxes to pay. Can I haf money the taxes to pay?' How you like? Huh? The land I gif her . . . do you hear . . . Abbie Deal? Eighty acres I gif her and she come already yet and say, 'For taxes no money I haf.' I say, 'Better you get and money earn for taxes then. Nein?' "

"Oh, and she's gone?"

"Ya, she's vent."

"But, Christine, Omaha is such a city. Don't you know about her . . . where she first went?"

"Oh, I guess herself she take care. She svill pigs and corn shuck. You learn 'em svill and shuck, and demselves they take care."

"Christine, why don't you sell some of your land and use the money for yourself? The three eighties you kept for yourself are worth a lot of money now. Sell one of the eighties and have more comforts and conveniences."

"Ya . . . and go the poorhouse by. How long I know I live? Only eighty-two I am. A man I know a hundred-and-four was when he die.

Maybe like dat I live. Maybe twenty year I live yet already. I guess dey not all my land get. Ya . . . when I die, over it quick dey fight. Not while here I stay."

Abbie Deal sighed. Well, she thought, one gets out of life largely what one puts in. Christine had put all her time and thought on the land and for reward she had . . . land.

As soon as the Cedartown school was out that summer, Laura came over to spend a few days with her grandmother. Abbie still found pleasant companionship in this particular grandchild, an understanding and sympathy deeper than the usual twelve-year-old girl possessed. The two seemed to hold a oneness of thought, a kinship of mind as well as of body. With none of Katherine's sophistication, the child yet seemed mature.

On this visit she would help her grandmother with the morning's work and then fly to the pencil and tablet which she kept hidden under the bench by the long double row of cedars. It was on a late June morning that the two were seated there under the big trees which, toy-size, the Deals had planted a half-century before. Laura took out her portfolio from the box under the bench, with, "Listen, Grandma . . . listen to this that I wrote this morning. It's about you and Grandfather Deal:

"I know not if 'twas beating rain,
That lightly tapped the window pane,
Or if the dying embers flare
Shone softly on my old arm chair.

"But in the scent of dusky gloom,
That stole within my chamber room,
It seemed that from the shadowy wall
I dreamed I heard you softly call.

"Maybe it was only the book I'd read,
But I heard your voice,—you, who are dead.
You called me by a name most dear
And then I knew that you were near."

There were tears in Abbie Deal's eyes. "Why, Laura,—you didn't do that yourself?"

"Yes, I did."

"But how could you . . . a little girl like you . . . how *could* you have the feeling?"

"Well, I don't know . . . I can't quite tell you. But I get to thinking about a thing and it almost hurts me . . . kind-of in my throat or somewhere . . . and then when I work away and get it all written down, I feel sort of happy afterward. I don't suppose you'd understand it."

"Oh, yes, I would," said old Abbie Deal. "I'd understand."

"I like to read my things to you, Grandma."

"And I like to have you, Laura. They seem splendid to me. I suppose they are not what critics call technically correct, but that can come with the years. It's the feeling you show."

For a long time they sat there in the morning sunshine under the cedars that had grown old. The flyer went through town, it's thick black smoke writing spiral-shaped figures across the blue slate of the sky. To the east, the wide rolling prairie held on its breast the young corn and wheat and the grass of the pastures. The Reinmueller boys, grandsons of Christine, were plowing corn, with a new type cultivator. To the south and west, Cedartown with its comfortable homes and its paved streets overhung with elms and maples, sat astride the great highway that was once a buffalo trail. To the north, behind the curving arch of a wide graveled driveway lay the silent city of the dead,—on a knoll in the center, the monuments of the Deal and Lutz families.

"What are you thinking about, Grandma?"

"That your life is like a field-glass, Laura. When you look into the one end, the landscape is dwarfed and far away,—when you look into the other, it looms large as though it were near at hand. Things that happened seventy years ago seem like yesterday. But, when I was a girl, eighty years seemed too remote to contemplate. And now, it has passed. The story is written."

"You sound as though you were sorry about something, Grandma."

"I didn't mean to, but I was thinking that when I was a little girl, my sister Belle used to tell me about our grandmother . . . that would be your great-great-grandmother. Her name was Isabelle Anders-Mackenzie. She was wealthy and beautiful and accomplished for her time. I used to think I would grow up to look just like her. I pictured her as an ideal and I would say to her in my mind, 'You'll be proud some day of the things I am going to accomplish.' All my girlhood I always planned to do something big . . . something constructive. It's queer what ambitious dreams a girl has when she is young. I thought I would sing before big audiences or paint lovely pictures or write a splendid book. I always had that feeling in me of wanting to do something worth while. And just think,

Laura . . . now I am eighty and I have not painted nor written nor sung."

"But you've done lots of things, Grandma. You've baked bread . . . and pieced quilts . . . and taken care of your children."

Old Abbie Deal patted the young girl's hand. "Well . . . well . . . out of the mouths of babes. That's just it, Laura, I've *only* baked bread and pieced quilts and taken care of children. But some women have to, don't they? . . . But I've dreamed dreams, Laura. All the time I was cooking and patching and washing, I dreamed dreams. And I think I dreamed them into the children . . . and the children are carrying them out . . . doing all the things I wanted to and couldn't. Margaret has painted for me and Isabelle has sung for me. Grace has taught for me . . . and you, Laura . . . you'll write my book for me I think. You'll have a fine education and you will probably travel. But I don't believe you can write a story because you have a fine education and have traveled. I think you must first have a seeing eye and an understanding heart and the knack of expressing what you see and feel. And you have them. So I think you, too, are going to do one of the things I wanted to do and never did."

Abbie Deal thoroughly enjoyed talking to this grandchild. Any of the rest of the family would have been a little impatient with an old woman's musings. The others were always so alert, so active, so poised for flight. Of them all, only little Laura Deal wanted to sit and talk and dream. She told her that now.

"You are a great comfort to me, Laura. You are something like me . . . a part of me. We think alike . . . you and I. Between you and me, I think my reminiscences bore the others. Well, well . . . old people used to bore me when I was young."

"They don't bore *me*, Grandma. They interest me."

Abbie smiled across at her. No longer could she look down upon Laura. The twelve-year-old girl was larger than her little grandmother.

"And we old pioneers dreamed other things, too, Laura. We dreamed dreams into the country. We dreamed the towns and cities, the homes and the factories, the churches and the schools. We dreamed the huge new capitol. When you walk under its wonderful tower, you say to yourself, 'My Grandfather and Grandmother Deal dreamed all this . . . they, and a thousand other young couples dreamed it all in the early days . . . and the architect had the imagination to catch the dream and materialize it. It is their vision solidified. They were like the foundation stones under the capitol . . . not decorative, but strong. They were not well-educated. They were not sophisticated. They were not cultured. But they had innate refinement and courage. And they could see visions and dream dreams."

"How does it feel to be old, Grandma?"

Abbie laughed. "Laura, it doesn't *feel* at all. People don't understand about old age. I am an old woman . . . but *I* haven't changed. I'm still Abbie Deal. They think we're different . . . we old ones. The real Abbie Deal still has many of the old visions and longings. I'm fairly contented here in the old home. . . . There was a time when I thought I never could be . . . but . . . some way . . . we get adjusted. I've never grown tired of life as some old people do. I'm only tired of the aches and the pains and the inability to make my body do what I want it to do. I would like to live a long time yet . . . to see what can still be invented . . . to read the new things that will be written . . . to hear the new songs that will be sung . . . to see heavy foliage on all the new shrubbery . . . to see all the babies grow into men and women. But there comes an end . . ."

"Don't talk that way, Grandma. It makes me feel like crying."

"Why, it ought not, Laura . . . not when Grandma has happy memories to live over."

"What memories do you have, Grandma?"

"I have many . . . my little girlhood days when Chicago was a village . . . the three weeks' journey from Illinois into Iowa . . . the fun in the Big Woods behind my sister Janet's house. I can shut my eyes and smell the dampness and the Mayflowers there. The old log school and then the new white one with green shutters . . . my wedding . . . the trip from Iowa into Nebraska. . . . There are many memories. But I'll tell you the one I like to think of best of all. It's just a homely everyday thing, but to me it is the happiest of them all. It is evening time here in the old house and the supper is cooking and the table is set for the whole family. It hurts a mother, Laura, when the plates begin to be taken away one by one. First there are seven and then six and then five . . . and on down to a single plate. So I like to think of the table set for the whole family at supper time. The robins are singing in the cottonwoods and the late afternoon sun is shining across the floor. Will, your grandfather, is coming in to supper . . . and the children are all playing out in the yard. I can hear their voices and happy laughter. There isn't much to that memory is there? Out of a lifetime of experiences you would hardly expect that to be the one I would choose as the happiest, would you? But it is. The supper cooking . . . the table set for the whole family . . . the afternoon sun across the floor . . . the robins singing in the cottonwoods . . . the children's merry voices . . . Will coming in . . . eventide."

"I think it's a nice memory, Grandma, but something about the way you say it makes me sad."

"But it's not sad, Laura. My memories are not sad. They're pleasant. I'm happy when I'm living them over. You'll find out when you get old, Laura, that some of the realities seem dreams . . . but the dreams, Laura, . . . the dreams are all real."

CHAPTER XXXIV

THAT summer,—the one in which Abbie Deal was eighty,—was the summer of the Great Harvest.

Nebraska was favored of the gods. Ceres' throne was in Nebraska. It was as though she chose the state from all others upon which to lavish her goods,—as though the bulk of her fortune had been given to a favorite child. From the old Missouri to the foot of the sand-hills,—from the Kansas border to the land of the Dakotas, the wheat fields, like the sun's reflection, lay ripe under the July sky. In every direction one saw a thrasher belching out its yellow breath of wheat straw.

The fields were springs from which never-ending brooklets of yellow wheat, pouring into the thrashers, rolled forth in golden streams to form a mighty river of grain.

The barley, rye and oats yield was also heavy. The beet sugar output was to be of gigantic proportions. A bumper corn crop loomed in promise for the fall,—three hundred million bushels were being predicted. Those who juggled with figures said that it would bring four hundred million dollars. The combined sum of all the grain figures was almost beyond comprehension. Poor conditions in many of the neighboring states, and a shortage in production in the east and south, added to the fancy that Nebraska seemed to hold the gifts of the gods in her lap that summer.

The crop moved to market in an unprecedented volume. The various transportation systems had prepared for their part in this great procession of the grains. Tens of thousands of workers had bent their backs to the task. Tens of thousands of freight cars had been assembled at various points, awaiting the signal to move. And the grain came in,—and the cars moved. To the east and to the west they moved for weeks, carrying new life blood to the nation.

It filled old Abbie Deal with an overwhelming pride. "Do you know, John," she said to her attorney son, "it makes me happy . . . proud and happy. When I think of all those early lean years . . . the droughts . . . the grasshoppers . . . the crop failures . . . and then this! 'Poor Nebraska' people said. They looked down on us . . . as though we were a lot of destitute relations. They sent us old clothes and seeds and dried apples. And to think we're sending grain in great trainloads."

"Mother," John chuckled, "to hear you, anybody would think you owned the state."

"I do, John. She's mine in spirit. I feel as though she had been on trial before a world court and the trial dragged out over many years. We, who loved her, had faith to believe she would come through unscathed. And in these later years she's acquitted . . . and vindicated. And to think she's one of the wealthiest states in the union . . . the only one, I guess, with no bonded indebtedness! I wish your father might have lived to see it. He was so loyal . . . and so faithful . . . and so hopeful. He didn't live to see all his hopes fulfilled . . . but he did his part in making them materialize. They were prophets, John . . . prophets in a strange country . . . those hardy young men who ferried across the Missouri and forded the Platte and the Weeping Water and the other streams. What a legacy they've left you all,—farms and cities . . . cattle on a thousand hills, . . . manufactories, . . . great educational institutions . . ."

"Mother, that sounds quite oratorical. You can put all that into a speech up at Lincoln on the twenty-ninth. That's what I came over to see you about. They told me in Lincoln to-day that they wanted you to come up and speak at the unveiling of the Donovan Marker. That's the sixtieth anniversary, you know, of choosing the site of Lincoln for the capital. They want those present who were here then."

"Oh, but I wasn't here, John. That was almost a whole year before we came. I've only been here fifty-nine years."

"Fifty-nine years is quite a while, Mother, and you're getting to be one of the few left, who came that long ago. They want you to make a little talk."

"But what can you say in a few words, John, that will cover fifty-nine years? I guess 'Behold what God hath wrought,' is the most condensed statement I can think of."

And then it turned out that there were to be two big events for

Abbie Deal in July. Katherine's wedding, which was to have been in the fall, was suddenly set for the twentieth. John was sending Jimmie Buchanan east on business, and in spite of the off-season time of year, the wedding was to take place so that Katherine could go with him. Already Katherine was being dined and fêted and showered by the friends who were still in town. Sarah Lutz was in California and was not coming back. "So *you* must be careful and not get sick, Granny," Katherine told her, "or we wouldn't have either of you at the big doings." She and her mother had driven down one afternoon to see Abbie. They brought her a lavender silk dress and a real lace cape-collar which Emma had bought in Vienna.

"You must be all dolled up, Granny," Katherine told her. "You must be massaged and manicured and you ought to have a permanent. I believe you would take a lovely one." She bent low over her grandmother's head and examined a strand of snow-white hair. "It looks as though it might have had a bit of natural curl in it once."

Oh, why couldn't they know? Why did an old woman seem always to have been old? Abbie was back on the knoll near the Big Woods, singing . . . her head thrown back . . . her thick hair curling and rippling over her creamy white shoulders. Why couldn't they understand that once she had kept tryst with Youth? Why didn't they realize that some day, they, too, must hold rendezvous with Age?

"Yes," said old Abbie Deal, simply, "it used to be quite curly."

It was just before they left, that Abbie said, "I have two presents for you, Kathie."

"Two, Granny? How lovely! Why two?"

"Well, one I am making myself so that you will always have something of Grandma's hand work. The other . . . the other, Kathie, is an heirloom, a string of little pearls. I want you not to plan for anything else for your neck. They're beautiful. Even you, with all your nice things, will be proud to own them."

"Fine . . . Granny! Fine!" Even so, it was said half carelessly. Things had come so easily to Kathie.

In the next two weeks, Abbie worked hard to finish the pink and white quilt with its rose-shaped blocks rambling up the borders. On the nineteenth, Grace came from summer school where she was teaching, and left immediately for Omaha in her roadster, as she had some shopping to do before the wedding. Early on the morning of the twentieth, Christine Reinmueller came over to receive her instructions from Abbie for caring for the place. The chickens were to be fed. Abbie gave minute directions for the ceremony,—the laying hens in the chicken-yard, whole corn out of one box,—the fries so-and-so out of a certain can. If it looked like rain, Christine was to turn the water-spout into the cistern. But if it rained too long, it ought to be turned out before it started to run over. And Christine was to pick the sweet-peas and nasturtiums.

John and Eloise Deal, with Wentworth and Laura and Millard, came for Abbie in the big sedan. Abbie had on her black silk with white collar and cuffs, and a new hat with a noble-appearing pom-pon on one side, which the milliner had told her looked "chic." Above Abbie's old wrinkled face it looked as chic as a painted one would have looked atop the portrait of Whistler's mother.

She had the quilt done up in a big flat package, and she put her feet on it in the car, as though it might, from sheer naturalness of the roses, ramble out of the sedan window. The pearls in the little box she held tightly in the bag in her hands.

The big car shot out over the graveled roads. Wentworth was at the wheel. Abbie wished John would do the driving. As a matter of fact Wentworth, born to the wheel, with all the younger generation, was the more alert driver, but Abbie could not think so.

"You know, Wentworth, I wish you wouldn't go so fast. Can't we go a little slower and see the country better?"

"You're sort of cracked about the country, aren't you, Grandma?"

"Yes, I guess I am, Wentworth. But if you'd gone over these same roads in a covered wagon, when there wasn't even a trail in the grass, you'd be, too."

At the top of a hill, John said something to his son, and the big car slowed down and stopped. "Take a drink, Mother," John waved his hand to the panorama before them, "but don't get intoxicated."

In the distance the Platte sprawled out lazily in the morning sun, the thick foliage of its tree-borders green against the sky's summer blue. There were acres of yellow wheat stubble where once the buffalo had wallowed, fields of young corn where once the prairie grass had grown, great comfortable homes and barns where once the soddies had stood. There were orchards and pastures and cattle, and a town nestling under the sheltering shade of huge trees. And soft white languorous clouds slipped into the east.

As they looked, there was a humming sound, and like one of the dragon-flies from the old creek bed, an aeroplane came out of the southwest. As direct and as fast as the southwest winds, it shot toward Omaha, back over the road that the Deals' and Lutzes' and the Reinmuellers' plodding oxen had come. From the hilltop near the Platte, Abbie Deal watched the mail plane go back over the road that the plodding oxen had come.

They slipped into Omaha at ten o'clock,—the Omaha that had been the raw frontier town, but was now a city of nearly a quarter million.

Mack, at home from the bank, came out to meet them when they turned into the driveway. The Mackenzie Deal place, a huge brick structure, with its clipped lawn and its sunken garden and its lily pools, was lovely in the morning sunlight. And it belonged to a man who had lived in a soddie until his thirteenth year, and to a woman whose first home on the prairie was hung with burlap to keep out the cold.

"Let me take your bag, Mother."

"Take the package, Mack, but I want to carry this myself." And they all laughed that Mother would trust no one with the pearls. She got slowly out of the car, her limbs a little numb. For a few moments she could not walk steadily, so that Mack put his arm around her and helped her up the wide steps.

In the house, Abbie asked at once for Katherine. The moment had come. It had been sixty-two years coming and now it was here. The winds had blown it by . . . the winds she could not stop. The clock hands had ticked it off . . . the time she could not stay.

Old Abbie Deal, with her snow-white hair, and her eighty years beginning to sit heavily upon her, climbed the mahogany-railed stairway with its imported carpet. A ladder with sapling cross-pieces . . . bare pine steps . . . a mahogany-railed stairway with thick imported carpet.

Katherine was in her room. Abbie knocked and went in, the little bag tightly clutched in her hand.

"Well . . . Granny?" Katherine did not seem flippant to-day. She was gentle, a little tender. She kissed her grandmother with genuine affection and sat down beside her.

"Here they are, dear." Abbie laid the pearls in Katherine's lap, her blue-veined hands trembling.

It was as though they had brought everything to Katherine,—had heaped their all into her lap,—the fruits of their labor, the results of their pioneering. The price of the prairie had been paid. The debt was canceled. For Katherine they had fought the prairie fires, split open the prairie furrows, and planted the corn. For Katherine they had set out the trees and made the roads and built the bridges.

Katherine took the pearls out of the little velvet box.

"Thanks, Granny, dear. They're darling."

There was no great surprise. She had spoken in a matter-of-fact way. "Thanks, Granny, dear. They're darling."

Well, she could not sense it. She was young and had never wanted for a thing in her life. She could not realize all the hardships which had been undergone since Abbie Deal's wedding night,—all the privations which had been endured while the pearls lay in the box for sixty-two years waiting for the time to come when a Mackenzie bride could wear them.

"I want to tell you about them. Could you . . . for just a few minutes, Kathie? I don't want to take your time . . ."

"Sure . . . Granny . . . tell me about them."

"They were Isabelle Anders-Mackenzie's, Kathie. After her death they became my mother's and then she gave them to me in the old log-cabin on my wedding night. They always seemed to me a sort of symbol . . . standing for everything that was fine and artistic and lovely. You probably don't understand, but the work on the land in our early days was so hard that it took all of our time and strength to keep body and soul together. There was neither time nor opportunity for the things that many of us wanted, with all our hearts, to do. But we kept our eyes on a sort of gleam ahead, a hope that our boys and girls could have all the things we could not have. And so the pearls became a symbol to me of those things. I said Margaret could wear them at her wedding, thinking we would have everything to go with them. But you can't always do with life as you wish. Sometimes life does things to you. And so we didn't have much to do with, and Margaret was married without them. Isabelle was married suddenly on the eve of war, and Grace never married . . . and now they're yours, the first granddaughter to marry. They've gone in a sort of circle, from wealth, through hard times, back to prosperity."

"I'll love them, Granny." Katherine kissed her grandmother again. Then she rose and slipped her arm through Abbie's. "Now, Granny, I want you to come in and see the spoils of war."

Out in the upper hall, with Persian rugs hanging over the mahogany-railed balcony, most of the relatives seemed gathering. Margaret and Dr. Baker had just driven in. Isabelle and Harrison Rhodes had arrived the previous evening. Stanley's and young Dr. Fred's wives were both there with their children. One room had been converted into a receiving room for the gifts, and it was into this one that the whole clan gathered. Dainty gifts from exclusive shops were there. Many countries had contributed their loveliest to Katherine Deal. Abbie, wandering among the tables, made little clucking noises of delight. "My, my, Kathie, whatever can you do with them all? How beautiful! And to think that I was happy to get some quilts and plain dishes and an old rooster and six hens!"

Mack came in and wandered aimlessly about. Every one was there in the room, now,—Mack and Emma, Isabelle and Harrison, Margaret and Doctor Baker, Grace, John and Eloise, Laura, Wentworth, Stanley's and Fred Jr.'s wives, Katherine and Jimmie Buchanan—— Suddenly it seemed to Abbie that there was some concerted plan that they should all gather. Two or three were whispering mysteriously.

"Are you ready, Daddy?" It was Katherine. "There's something else we want to show you, Granny. We're too anxious for you to see."

Abbie turned toward Katherine who was holding the cord of a silken drape in her hand. Katherine's head was thrown back. Her eyes were merry. She was excited about something. "All set. Eyes front and guide right, Granny."

She pulled the silken cord and the drape parted. Behind the soft folds there hung a huge painting in a wide dull gold frame,—the painting of a lovely lady in velvet draperies, her reddish-brown hair curling over her shoulder, and a string of pearls at her neck. A hat with a sweeping plume was in one hand,—held by long slender fingers that tapered at the ends.

Katherine waved an airy hand. "Here she is, Granny. Allow me to introduce to you Isabelle Anders-Mackenzie, painted with my pearls on her . . . the little wretch."

Abbie Deal stared. The faint coloring of excitement under her old cheeks slipped away. One hand went up to her wrinkled throat and the other above her pounding heart. She turned to Mack. "You don't . . . not really, Mack? It isn't . . . ?"

"Yes, it is, Mother . . . your grandmother . . . my great-grandmother . . . Kathie's great-great-grandmother. It's the original and it cost like the old Harry, but Katherine has been after me ever since she heard you tell about it. I had the deuce of a time getting it, too. The agent traced it from Aberdeen to London and then to Edinburgh and back to London."

Abbie turned to the picture again.

"Can you beat it, Granny?" Katherine was laughing and calling to her. "All in one fell swoop I get six tons of china, nine carloads of silver, a darling new house, a homely new husband, *and* a snobocratic ancestor and her pearls."

Abbie Deal stood in front of the picture with Katherine's flippant words rippling past her. Old Abbie Deal, with her snow-white hair in its neat little knot at the back of her head, with her dumpy pudding-bag figure and her long, gnarled fingers that tapered at the ends, stood and stared at the picture. And standing there, looking up at the lovely lady, old Abbie Deal began to cry. They are the most painful tears in the world . . . the tears of the aged . . . for they come from dried beds where the emotions have long burned low.

Mack put an arm around his mother and patted her shoulder awkwardly. "Why, Mother, dear! Katherine, we shouldn't have . . . I never thought, Mother . . . only the pleasure . . ."

They all closed around her, making comments. Jimmie Buchanan and Wentworth stood off, a little embarrassed.

The others all explained it volubly to each other.

"It was too much of a surprise . . ."

"Yes, she's too old to have a surprise sprung . . ."

"The trip up here was too much for mother at her age."

"It's those weeks of sewing. I told her that quilt was too much . . ."

"No,—it's the whole excitement together."

Laura Deal came through the little knot. "It isn't *any* of those reasons, is it, Grandma?" she said. "I know what it is . . . but I don't know how to say it."

Abbie dried her eyes. "I'm all right now." She even smiled at them. "My, my, Kathie, tears on your wedding day. Whatever will you think? How selfish of me,—I'm that ashamed! But when I saw . . . when I saw the lovely lady that I used to dream about . . . it just came over me . . . in a sort of wave . . . all the wonderful things I planned to do when I was young . . . and never did."

CHAPTER XXXV

ABBIE was back in her bedroom and dressed, now, for the wedding, in the lavender silk with the lace collar from Vienna. Margaret had dressed her hair and Isabelle had manicured her nails and Grace had powdered her skin,—with Abbie a little uncertain of the outcome as though, in her excitement, Grace might have purchased gunpowder by mistake.

She loved the beauty of everything connected with the affair, but she was tired. It was queer how much more she could stand around home than when she was away. The work in the house, the care of the chickens and flowers,—the whole responsibility of the home place was not so tiring as something unusual and out of the ordinary like this.

It was nearly time to go to the church when there was a little movement outside the door and she heard Katherine's voice, "I want to see grandmother."

The door opened and Katherine stood on the threshold, in the exquisite whiteness of filmy lace, her eyes luminous, her face softened.

"My . . . my!" Abbie Deal raised her hands in admiration, "you take my breath away. You look like *her*, Kathie . . . but you're even lovelier."

With a swift little movement of the short lacy skirt, Katherine was across the floor and down by her grandmother. She caught Abbie Deal's wrinkled old hands in her firm young ones. "Granny . . . I wanted to see you a minute. You've not liked me a lot of times, I know. We've been miles apart most of the time . . . but I wanted to come in and tell you that nothing really counts but Jimmie. Oh, Granny, I'd go with Jimmie . . . just as you did with grandfather. I'd live on pumpkin seeds, you know." She was laughing a little, with moist eyes. "And dig a house in the side of a tree, just as you did . . . you know . . . all those things I've heard you tell about . . . Oh, heavens, I'm going to cry and I'm all made up, but Granny . . . I wanted you to know . . . that, after all, I'm just a lot of things you think I'm not . . . Oh, you won't understand . . ."

Abbie Deal patted the lacy shoulders and with gentle old fingers touched the upturned face. "Why of course, Kathie, . . . of course, dear, . . . Grandma understands, the clock hands go round . . . and Grandma understands . . ."

The wedding was all that the wedding of Mackenzie Deal's daughter would be,—a thing of extravagant simplicity. There were beribboned pews, soft lights, and chaste white tapers in silver candelabra against green palms. There was the organ's mellow voice and the rich contralto one of the bride's aunt, Isabelle Deal Rhodes, the well-known Chicago singer. There was Mackenzie Deal with his bald head and his horn-rimmed glasses and a lump in his throat. There was Mrs. Mackenzie Deal in her orchid and silver lace, a little too concerned over the details of the affair to think of her emotions. There were all the Deal relatives, well-groomed and prosperous-looking. And there was old Abbie Deal, sunk down low in the pew, the lavender silk dress with its lace collar from Vienna over her pudding-bag body, a knot of white hair at the nape of her neck, her tapering, gnarled fingers trembling with age in her lap.

The bride was at the altar now,—lovely Katherine, in her white lace and satin, with the heirloom of pearls around her neck. Old Abbie's thoughts went over the cycle of one hundred and thirty-five years. Satin and pearls in a Scottish mansion,—a peasant dress and a head-shawl in an Irish hut,—a wine-colored hoop-skirted merino in a log cabin,—a navy-blue silk in a cottonwood and pine farmhouse,—white lace and satin and the pearls again in their beautiful modern setting.

"Do you take this man . . . for better . . . for worse . . . death do you part?"

"I do."

The same solemn question, solemnly answered. Would it be as faithfully kept? Abbie wondered.

And now it was all over. Katherine and Jimmie had left for the east. The big house had been quietly put to rights by two soft-footed maids. The whole Deal clan was gathering in the sun-room with its striking green and black and orchid English chintz hangings, and its fountain spraying over cool ferns and rocks.

Emma was bustling about hospitably, seeing that every one was comfortable. "Come on in, Donald. Sit here, Grace."

Standing in the doorway, Abbie heard Margaret coaxing Fred Jr.'s youngest with "Come to Grandma, Baby." It was still hard for Abbie to remember that two of her children were grandparents.

Then they saw her standing in the doorway.

"Come in, Mother."

"Sit here, Mother."

"No,—over here, Mother."

Mack brought a cushion, Isabelle a stool.

"Are you comfortable, Mother?"

How they thought of her bodily comfort,—always her physical needs. Not one ever said, "Are you sad, Mother?" or "How does your mind feel?" or "Does anything hurt your heart?"

Abbie, sitting in the big ivory chair with cushions at her back, found herself slipping away from the group, standing apart from it, looking at the members of it in a detached way. How efficient they all were,—and how smart,—and how easily they did things. They went hither and yon, either for business or pleasure affairs,—into Chicago, down south . . . sometimes abroad. Mack, now, was saying something about going down to New York the last of the week.

"*I* had a chance . . ." For the first time Abbie Deal spoke. Her voice cracked a little because of its age. From the depths of the big chair it cracked in its earnestness. "*I* had a chance to go to New York once."

Grace looked up quickly and then walked over to Isabelle. She spoke very low and turned her head so that her mother might not hear: "See! That's what I've been telling you. I've noticed that in her quite a little lately. Just detached sentences like that with no special meaning. It would just *kill* me if her mind . . . at the last. . . . But she does that quite often, now. 'Well, well, the clock hands go 'round,' she'll say, right out of a clear sky. Or, 'Dear, dear, the winds blew it all away.' And now this one, '*I* had a chance to go to New York, once,' . . . childish, that way."

In the big chair, Abbie Deal was chuckling a little to herself, shaking with silent laughter.

"What's the joke, Mother?" Mack spoke from across the room.

"Nothing much. I was just wondering about all of you . . . now . . . if I had gone."

"See . . . ?" Grace was grave in her anxiety, ". . . like *that*."

Abbie Deal sat looking out at the family gathered there in the beautiful sun-parlor, sat there with half-closed eyes like an old Buddha looking out on the generations. Eighty years of living were behind her,—most of them spent in fighting,—fighting the droughts, the snows, the hot winds, the prairie fires, the blizzards,—fighting for the children's physical and mental and spiritual development, fighting to make a civilization on the raw prairie. Bending her back to the toil, hiding her heart's disappointments, giving her all in service, she was like an old mother partridge who had plucked all the feathers from her breast for the nest of her young.

Old Abbie Deal, so near the borderland now that she held intercourse with both worlds, sat there looking out through half-closed eyes at the children and the grandchildren and the great-grandchildren.

"Well, Will . . . there they all are. What do you think of them? I did the best I could."

You did well, Abbie-girl.

CHAPTER XXXVI

GRACE DEAL, in her roadster, went back to summer school early in the morning. John Deal and his family left about the same time for Cedartown. Isabelle and Harrison Rhodes were remaining in Omaha for a few days' visit at Mack's, before making the rounds of the other homes. Abbie rode back with Margaret and Dr. Baker.

On the way, Margaret asked: "Don't you want to go on up to Lincoln with us for a few days, Mother?"

"No. Oh, no," Abbie said hastily. "I'm tired and I'll be real glad to get home again."

When the big car stopped under the Lombardy poplars near the sitting-room porch of the old farmhouse, Margaret got out with her mother and helped her up the short walk to the house.

"I just can't bear to leave you here alone, Mother. Don't you want me to stay all night with you? Fred could run out and get me to-morrow or I could go in on the morning train."

"No. Oh, no. I'm all right. I'm just tired from the excitement. When you're used to being alone you don't mind it a bit."

"Promise me you would call some one on the phone the first minute you didn't feel well."

"I promise. I would call Christine. She's got a phone in now, but she certainly begrudges the money. Anyway, I won't be alone much more this summer. Isabelle will be here next week, and Grace will be home again soon, and Laura is going to come and stay a few days."

When they had gone, Abbie Deal opened some of the windows to air out the house. She had a whimsical notion that the things seemed glad to have her back,—the table where old Doc Matthews had rolled his pills, the walnut cupboard, Will's corner what-not. There was something human about them as though they shared her thoughts,—as though, having come up through the years with her, they held the same memories.

She fed her chickens, watered the sweet-peas, picked the dried leaves off her geraniums, and went over the whole yard as though to greet every bush and shrub after her absence.

For the next few days she went slowly about her household duties with the same little sense of pleasure she always experienced after she had been to one of the children's homes. How could old women bear to sit around with folded hands? What mattered it that the children all had such nice houses, there would never be any real home for her but the old wing-and-upright set in the cedars and poplars.

By Friday night she had accomplished a lot of extra small tasks, setting an old hen that was foolishly wanting to raise a family out of season, gathering some early poppy-seeds and putting fresh papers on her pantry shelves. At five-thirty she started her supper. As she worked she tried to hum an old tune she had known when she was young, an old song she had not thought of for years and years, until Isabelle had sung it over the radio in the winter:

"Oh . . . the La . . . dy of . . . the Lea,
Fair and . . . young and . . . gay was . . . she"

She had to make long pauses between the syllables to get her breath.

"Beau . . . tiful . . . exceed . . . ingly
The La . . . dy of . . . the Lea."

Her voice cracked and went up or down without her volition, so that even though her mind heard the song, her ear scarcely recognized the melody.

"Many . . . a woo . . . er sought her . . . hand
For she . . . had gold . . . and she . . . had land,
Every . . . thing . . . la la . . . la la"

She had forgotten what the words were right there.

"The La . . . dy of . . . the Lea."

She was completely out of breath, so that she had to sit down a few minutes before starting to put her dishes on the kitchen table. As she sat looking at the old table, she suddenly wished that she could pull it out, put in all the leaves, set the places for the children and then call them in from play,—not the prosperous grown people she had been with so recently in Omaha, but just as they were when they were little. Queer how plainly she could see them in her mind: Mack's merry round face with its sprinkling of freckles, Margaret's long dark pig-tail, her gray eyes and her laughter, Isabelle's reddish-brown curls and her big brown eyes, Grace's square little body with her apronstrings always untied, John's serious face,—a sort of little old man who did not want to be hugged. How real they seemed to her. One could almost imagine that it was they who were playing, "Run, Sheep Run" out there now instead of the neighbor children.

Abbie Deal had never forbidden the north-end children access to her yard, and their high-pitched voices calling "Going-east . . . going west . . ." came to her now from the region of the cottonwood windbreak. Yes, it sounded for all the world like her own children out there.

As she got up and went about her supper, putting a little piece of meat on to cook, her mind slipped to the fact that she had promised to make a short talk on the following week at the sixtieth anniversary of the founding of the city of Lincoln. She must begin to think of what she could say. There was plenty to talk about but she dreaded the speaking. She hoped her voice wouldn't quaver and break. That was the trouble of being old. Your body no longer obeyed you. It did unruly and unreasonable things. An eye suddenly might not see for a moment. Your knees gave out at the wrong time, so that when you thought you were walking north, you might find yourself going a little northwest. Your brain, too, had the same flighty trick. You might be speaking of something and forget it temporarily,—your mind going off at a little to the northwest, too, so to speak.

She glanced up to see what time it was, and discovered that the clock had stopped. Whatever had happened to the faithful old thing? It must be wearing out, for she was sure she had wound it.

She opened the door with the little brown church painted on the glass, and reached for the key. Suddenly,—so suddenly that it was like a flash,—a queer feeling came over Abbie Deal. It was unlike any she had ever experienced,—a tightening of the throat and chest as of cold icy hands upon her. She tried to take her arms down from their stretched position, but it was almost impossible to move them for the pain. In a moment the icy hands released their hold upon her as quickly as they had clutched at her, but they left her so weak and shaken that she started into her bedroom holding onto the backs of the chairs.

She lay down on her bed to get herself in hand. There was a sharp pain now in the back of her head and it seemed a little hard to breathe. For a moment she wondered if it could be that her time to die had come. No, that could not be. She was a little sick, but she had been so many times. "I never *do* die," she said to herself and smiled a little at the humor of it.

The sun's rays slanted along the floor from the west sitting-room windows. The meat was cooking, for the air was filled with the odor of it. Robins were singing outside in the poplars. The neighbors' children ran across the yard with cries of "All's out's in free." They would trample the grass a little, but children were worth more than grass anyway. She must not get sick, for she was planning to go to something in a few days. For a few moments she could not think what it was, and then she remembered. It was the old settlers' meeting in Lincoln. There would be a lot of old folks there and they would tell their reminiscences all day. No doubt she would be bored to distraction. Old people usually bored her. No, that was not right. Something was wrong with that thought. She was not young. She was *old*. She, herself, was one of the old settlers. How strange! Well, she would go. Her mind seemed not quite under control. She tried hard to think whether she was to go in the big shining sedan on the straight graveled roads or in the creaking wagon through the long swaying grass. *Blow . . . wave . . . ripple . . . dip. Blow . . . wave . . . ripple . . . dip.* She felt ill. It was the swaying of the prairie grass that made her ill.

If she were taken sick she had promised to do something,—something with the little brown box at the side of the bed. Suddenly, she remembered . . . call Christine. That was it. Good old Christine! . . . Old friends . . . were best. Maybe she ought to call Christine in the little brown box. Her arm slipped around the rolled silk quilt at the foot of the bed. Such a soft silk quilt . . . and an old patched quilt in front of a sheep-shed for a door. There it was again,—her mind going northwest.

The sun slanted farther across the carpet. Whoever was frying that meat, was letting it burn. The children shouted very close to the house: "Run, sheep, run." It was nice to know the children were all well and out there playing,—Mack and Margaret, John and Isabelle, Grace and the baby. She hoped they were taking good care of the baby,—the baby with a face like a little white rose. She would let them play on until she got to feeling better, and then she would get up and finish supper.

That queer thought of death intruded itself again, but she reasoned, slowly and simply, with it. If death were near she would be frightened. Death was her enemy. All her life she had hated death and feared it. It had taken her mother, and Will and the baby and countless old friends. But Death was not near. The children playing outdoors, the sun slanting over the familiar carpet, the meat frying for supper,—all the old simple things to which she was accustomed, reassured her. A warm feeling of contentment slipped over her to hear the children's happy voices. "All's out's in free," they called. It was almost time for Will to come in to his supper. It was the nicest part of the day—the robins singing in the poplars—the meat cooking—the supper table set—every one coming home—the whole family around the table—all—Will—the children. She must wind the clock before they came in. You—couldn't—stop—Time—

It was hard again to breathe,—the icy pain—in her chest—

Oh . . .

Immediately the children were quiet. The robin had stopped singing. Whoever had been frying meat had removed it from the stove, and some one must have pulled down all the shades. It was strange to have all those things happen at once,—the robin cease singing, the children stop playing, the meat taken from the stove, and the shades pulled down. For a moment it was as though one could neither see nor hear nor smell. At any rate she felt much better. The pressure in her chest and in the back of her head was gone. That was nice. It seemed good to be relieved of that. She breathed easily,—so very easily that she seemed not to be breathing at all. She sat up on the edge of the bed. She felt light, buoyant. "I'll wind the clock and finish supper now and call them in."

Through the semi-darkness of the house there was no sight or sound. But as she looked up, she saw Will standing in the doorway. For a moment she thought he was standing under honey-locust branches in a lane, but saw at once that it was only shadows.

"Well, Will!" She stood up. "I'm so glad you're home. You've been away all day, haven't you? Where were you, Will? Isn't that stupid of me not to remember?" She moved lightly toward him, but suddenly stopped, sensing that for some reason there was a strangeness about his presence. She stood looking at him questioningly, a little confused.

Will was looking intently at her, half-smiling. She would have thought he was joking her—teasing her a little—if his expression had not been too tender for that.

"I don't quite understand, Will. Did you want something of me? . . ." That was a way of Will's,—always so quiet that you almost had to read his mind. There was no answer, but at once she seemed to know that Will was waiting for her.

"Oh, I must tell the children first. They *never* want me to go." She turned to the window. "Listen, children," she called, "I'm going away with Father. If some one would pull up the shades I could see you, but it doesn't really matter. Listen closely . . . I'm only going to be gone a little while. Be good children . . . You'll get along just fine."

She turned to the doorway. "It seems a little dark. You know, Will, I think we will need the lantern. I've always kept the lantern . . ." Her voice trailed off into nothing. For Will was still smiling at her, questioningly, quizzically,—but with something infinitely more tender,—something protecting, enveloping. Slowly it came to her. Hesitatingly she put her hand up to her throat. "Will . . . you don't mean it! . . . Not *that* . . . not *Death* . . . so *easy?* That it's nothing more than *this* . . . ? Why . . . *Will!*"

Abbie Deal moved lightly, quickly, over to her husband, slipped her hand into his and went with him out of the old house, past the Lombardy poplars, through the deepening prairie twilight,—into the shadows.

It was old Christine Reinmueller, who came in and found her.

"*Ach . . . Gott!*" She wrung her hard old hands. "Mine friend . . . de best voman dat efer on de eart' valked."

The children all came hastily in response to the messages. In the old parlor with the what-not and the marble-topped stand and the blue plush album, they said the same things over and over to each other.

"Didn't she seem as well to you last week as ever?"

"Do you suppose she suffered much?"

"Or called for us?"

"Isn't it *dreadful*. Poor mother . . . all alone . . . not one of us here . . . as though we had all forsaken her just when she needed us most . . . and after all she's done for us . . ."

It was then that little twelve-year-old Laura Deal turned away from the window where she had been looking down the long double row of cedars and said in a voice so certain that it was almost exalted:

"*I* don't think it's so dreadful. I think it was kind-of nice. Maybe she didn't miss you. Maybe she didn't miss you *at all*. One time grandma told me she was the very happiest when she was living over all her memories. Maybe . . ." She looked around the circle of her relatives,—and there was a little about her of another twelve-year-old Child who stood in the midst of his elders in a Temple,—"maybe she was doing that . . . then."

THE END

Miss Bishop

CHAPTER I

IN 1846 the prairie town of Oak River existed only in a settler's dream. In 1856 the dream became an incorporated reality. Ten years later a rambling village with a long muddy Main Street and a thousand souls welcomed back its Civil War boys. And by 1876 it was sprawling over a large area with the cocksure air of a new midwestern town fully expecting to become a huge metropolis. If all the high hopes of those pioneer town councilors had been fulfilled, the midwest to-day would be one grand interlocking of city streets. As it is, hundreds of little towns grew to their full size of two or five or ten thousand, paused in their growth, and admitted that none of them by taking Chamber-of-Commerce thought could add one cubit to its stature.

So Oak River, attaining the full strength of its corporeal self some years ago, has now settled down into a town of ten thousand, quite like a big boy who realizes that the days of his physical growth are over, and proceeds to look a bit to the development of his mind and his manners.

The chief source of the big boy's pride is the school,—Midwestern College. It stands at the edge of town in a lovely rolling campus, sweet-smelling in the springtime from its newly cropped blue-grass and white clover, colorful in the autumn from the scarlet and russet and gold of its massive trees,—a dozen or more pompous buildings arranged in stately formation, a campanile lifting its clock faces high to the four winds, a huge stadium proudly gloating over its place in the athletic sun. Concrete driveways and sidewalks curve through the green of elms and maples, and young people walk or drive over them continually,—a part of that great concourse of Youth forever crossing the campuses of the world.

Until last summer, an ancient brick building known as Old Central Hall stood in the very middle of the group of fine modern structures, like a frowzy old woman, wrinkled and gray, surrounded by well-groomed matrons. A few mild-spoken people referred to the building as quaint, the frank ones called it ugly—but whenever there was talk of removing it, a host of sentimental alumni arose *en masse* and exclaimed: "What! Tear down Old Central?" And as the college board consisted one hundred per cent of alumni, Old Central continued to sit complacently on, year after year, in the center of the quadrangle, almost humanly impudent in attitude toward the rest of the buildings.

To several thousand people it was so familiar, so much a vital part of their lives, that when last spring, a regretful board guiltily sounded the death knell, many more alumni than usual arrived on the campus at Commencement time, quite like children called home to see a mother on her deathbed.

Those who had not seen her for several years found her worn and cracked and disgracefully shabby, with her belfry half removed and extra pillars placed in the dismantled auditorium for safety's sake. But, even so, there were two or three present who recalled that like any other aged soul who has outlived her usefulness, she had once been as strong and bright and gay as a bride. That had been in 1876, when Oak River itself was still young.

On the sixth of September of that year, so important to the thirty-two young people entering the new hall for the first time, the building rose like a squatty lighthouse on a freshwater lake, for it stood in the center of forty acres of coarse prairie grass bent to the earth with the moisture of a three-day drenching rain.

It was still raining dismally at eight o'clock on that Wednesday morning—a slow monotonous drizzle that turned the new campus into a sea—a Red Sea, for that matter, as the brick dust around the newly erected building made of the soggy ground a rust-colored mud. Wheelbarrows leaned tipsily against the new walls. Mortar boxes held miniature chalky pools. The approach to the big doors, unpainted as yet, was up an incline with wooden cleats nailed on it, upon which the girls in their flowing ruffled skirts tottered so perilously that their long thin hoops quivered up and down in rhythmic sympathy.

Inside, a few potential students stood about in the hall, which was almost too dark for any one of them to get an enlightening look at his neighbor. The newly plastered walls were scarcely dry, so that the atmosphere here was seemingly as moist as that without.

Chris Jensen, a young Dane, just starting out on his janitor duties, stood solemnly at the doorway with a broom, and after the entrance of each young neophyte, brushed out puddles of muddy water with the air of having swept a part of the River of Sorrows out of the infernal regions.

The first comers all watched him soberly. No one said anything. Everyone was cold, the huge coils of pipes around the rooms having as yet no intimate relation to any heating plant. All was as merry as a burial service.

Then a young girl opened the door and blew in on a gust of rain-filled wind. An expansive smile from a wide cheerful mouth greeted the assembled mourners as she gave one sweeping glance toward them all.

Chris Jensen, with broom poised for her entrance, grinned cheerfully back, his pale eyes lighting with responsive mirth.

"Velcome to school," he said in Danish accent and lowered the threatening weapon. It was the first word he had uttered during the whole moist morning.

With the girl's coming some new element entered the room, as though a bright pigment had suddenly been used on a sepia picture.

She was not pretty. One could scarcely say what it was that set her apart from the others,—humor, vitality, capability, or some unknown characteristic which combined them all. It was as though she said: "Well, here I am. Let's begin."

Removing shining rubbers and a dripping brown cape with a plaid hood at the back, she placed them in the hallway that gave forth a strong rubbery odor, and came up to the other students.

She had on a long plaid dress, brown and red, over narrow hoops, with ruffles curving from the bottom of her skirt up to the back of her waist, and a tight-fitting basque brave with rows of brass buttons marching, soldier-like, four abreast, across the front. Her hair was piled high in the intricate coiffure of the day and drawn back into curls.

She gave one look at the funereal expressions of the assembled embryonic collegians. One girl, highly overdressed in a green velveteen suit, was shedding copious tears into the expensive lace of a large handkerchief.

"What are we waiting for?" the newcomer said with some asperity. "Let's go on in."

Like sheep, the whole group, under the new bellwether's leadership, tagged meekly after her into the assembly room—a room so huge that the wildest optimism of the most progressive of Oak River's citizenry could scarcely conceive a day when it would be filled with youth.

A young instructor sat at a desk just inside the door, two others were consulting by a window. Everything about the young man at the desk was thin. He had a thin body, a high thin forehead, a long thin nose, a thin mustache of recent raising straggling over a thin-lipped mouth. A blank book, very large and very white, was open in front of him over which he held a pen poised for action.

He appeared so timid in the face of the situation that when he managed to emit, "Will some one please start the enrollment?" the girl looked about her inquiringly and then marched sturdily up to the sacrificial altar as it were.

"Your name?"

He looked so embarrassed that the merry eyes of the girl half closed in crinkling humor and she stifled silent laughter.

"Ella Bishop," she said demurely.

He wrote it with great flourishes, his hand making many dizzy elliptical journeys before it settled down to an elaborate "E" with a curving tail as long as some prehistoric baboon's.

When he had finished the lengthy and intricate procedure, he paused and asked shyly:

"Your age?"

"Sixteen."

As this was executed in the less spectacular figures, it did not consume quite so much time.

"Residence?"

"Oak River, now . . ." And in further explanation, "We just moved in from the farm—my mother and I—and settled here."

"I see. On what street, please?"

"Adams Street—half way between Tenth and Eleventh."

He looked up as though at a startling piece of news. "Why . . . why . . . that's right across the street from *me*." And flushed to his thin forehead.

The green velveteen girl, who had been weeping continuously, suddenly tittered, a bit hysterically.

By this time the timid one had been joined by another instructor, evidently for monetary reasons, so that immediately there was a flutter of pockets and bags,—one big-boned German boy extracting gold coin with difficulty from the lining of his homemade coat, while a freckled girl of apparent Scotch lineage turned abruptly to the wall and deftly removed a roll of bills from some unknown source in the region of her left lung.

When the last name had been entered by Professor Samuel Peters' agile pen with much shading of downward strokes and many extra corkscrew appendages, the president called the students to order in the church-pew seats of the huge assembly room, in which immensity the little company seemed lost.

The faculty consisted of four instructors besides President Corcoran. They were Professor Loren Wick, mathematics, brown-whiskered and paunchy, with a vague suggestion of his last lunch somewhere on his vest,—Professor Byron Carter, grammar and literature, small and nervous with gray goatee, eyeglasses and a black cord,—Miss Emmaline Patton, geography and history, a solid appearing woman, both as to physique and mentality,—as though an opinion once formed became a necessary amendment to the laws of the Medes and the Persians,—and the thin, embarrassed Samuel Peters, he of the coquettish pen, who was to teach spelling and the intricacies of the Spencerian method of writing.

These now with President Corcoran, who was to teach a mysterious subject called Mental and Moral Philosophy, filed up on the rostrum and sat down in a solemn row. Evidently the transmission of knowledge was to be a melancholy procedure. The girl, Ella Bishop, felt her heart pounding tumultuously with the formality of the occasion. The green velveteen girl mopped seeping moisture diligently.

A new reed organ with many carved cupids and gingerbread brackets stood at one side of the rostrum. President Corcoran, a short plump man whose kindly face was two-thirds hidden behind a duck-blind of beard, indicating the musical instrument, asked if any one could play, whereupon the green velveteen girl, having foreseen the possibility of this very prominence (and hence the velveteen) dried her eyes and volunteered with some alacrity.

Shortly, the assembled students were singing "Shall We Gather at the River?" and any one glancing out of the high Gothic windows with prairie adaptations, where the rain splashed and ran dismally down, could have answered honestly, "No doubt we shall."

There was prayer, in which the president informed the Lord of the current events of the morning, including the exact number of matriculations, and then, suddenly, abandoning statistics, asked fervently for divine love and light and guidance in the lives of these young people, which latter part of the petition seemed somehow to reach immediately the place for which it was intended.

When he had finished, there was an announcement or two, a reading of many and stringent rules with penalties attached thereto for nonconformity, and another song of such dry characteristics as might counteract the moisture of the first one:

". . . In deserts wild
Thou spreadest a table for thy child."

Then classes,—and Midwestern College was fairly launched.

CHAPTER II

THE girl, Ella Bishop, entered whole-heartedly into this first convocation of the new college,—as indeed she would have entered into anything, an auction sale or an Irish wake.

Morning classes for her followed one another in rather sketchy fashion. With a surreptitious flourish of many cold chicken legs, lunch at noon was consummated in a room politely termed the physical science laboratory, but whose apparatus consisted largely of a wobbly tellurian, a lung-tester, and a homemade air-pump which gave forth human-like sounds of torture. One group sat in the recitation seats, one on the edge of a long table, and a few girls under Ella's efficient management gathered in a friendly arrangement of chairs in a far corner. The instinct to run to cliques settles itself in the breast of every female child at birth.

Afternoon saw Ella in Miss Patton's class reciting a little vaguely concerning the inhabitants of South America, and in Professor Peters' class watching with fascinated wonder as he executed a marvelous blackboard sketch of a fish never known to any sea, with the modest assurance that they too could be in time as proficient as he—although once it did briefly occur to Ella to question what specific importance could be attached to the resultant accomplishment.

The close of day saw her at home in the modest wing-and-ell house "on Adams between Tenth and Eleventh," where her widowed mother was attempting to settle the furnishings.

She removed her wet things and slipped into another dress which strangely enough was made of the same plaid goods as the one she had worn to school. A mystified onlooker could not have known that Ella's father, before his death, had taken over two bolts of cloth from a merchant at Maynard in payment for a horse—and that for several years now

Ella's wardrobe had consisted entirely of red-and-brown plaid trimmed with blue serge, or blue serge trimmed with red-and-brown plaid.

"Shall I wear the pork and beans to-day, Mother, or the beans and pork?" she sometimes asked facetiously.

At which joking her mother's expression would become hurt and she would answer: "Oh, Ella . . . you shouldn't make fun . . . Father . . . the cloth . . . like that. . . ."

Mrs. Bishop seldom finished her sentences. She was so uncertain about everything, so possessed by a sense of helplessness since her husband's death, that at sixteen Ella had assumed management of the household and become the dictator of all plans.

Just now she accomplished more in the first half-hour of her brisk labor in the unsettled home than the mother had done in the whole day. She whisked things into place with marvelous dexterity, chattering all the time of the greatest event of her life,—her first day at the new college.

She could give the names of practically all the other thirty-one students. The big-boned German boy was George Schroeder. He had been a farmhand and could scarcely speak English. The small weazened-face boy who was so sharp at mathematics that Professor Wick had spoken about it was Albert Fonda, a Bohemian boy. He had told Professor Wick he wanted to study astronomy, and that nice Professor Wick had said he and Albert would have a class if there was no one in it but they two. The Scotch girl was Janet McLaughlin and she had made them all laugh by saying that she thought the day would come when cooking and sewing would be taught in schools. Imagine *that*,—things you could learn at home. The girl in the velveteen dress was Irene Van Ness, the banker's daughter, and she had cried because she didn't want to go to this school, but her father was one of the founders of it and had made her go. Irene was half-way engaged to Chester Peters, brother of the penmanship teacher, who went east to school,—the brother, she meant, not The Fish, —though how any one could be *half*-way engaged was more than she could understand.

Indeed, half-way measures were so unknown to Ella Bishop, that carried away by her own entertainment she was now imitating the instructors, describing her fellow students, impersonating Irene playing the organ so vividly that her mother laughed quite heartily before suddenly remembering there had been a bereavement in the family the past year.

The wing-and-ell house into which the two were moving sat behind a brown picket-fence not far back from the street. Two doors at right angles on the small porch opened into a dining-room and a parlor; the porch itself was covered with a rank growth of trumpet-vine. Inside, there were sale carpets tacked firmly over fresh oat straw, the one in the parlor of dark brown liberally sprinkled with the octagon-shaped figures to be found in any complete geometry, the one in the dining-room of red with specks of yellow on it looking like so many little pieces of egg yolk dropped from the table. The parlor contained an organ, a set of horsehair furniture of a perilous slipperiness, a whatnot, and in the exact center of the room a walnut table upon which Ella had arranged a red plush album, a stereoscope with its basket of views, and a plaster cast of the boy who is never quite able to locate the thorn in his foot. A plain house, but striving to be in the mode of the day.

As Ella went now to the parlor door to shake out the crocheted tidies that belonged on the backs of the horsehair pieces, she glimpsed a young man walking slowly past the house in the rain and gazing intently at it. At the noise of the opening door he turned his head away suddenly and started walking faster down the street. "There he goes," she told her mother, "the young man whose pen is mightier than his swordfish." And laughed cheerfully at her own wit.

She watched from the shadow of the doorway and saw him cross the street, turn into the large yard with the two cast-iron deer, and go up the steps of the big red-brick house with the cupola on one corner.

"That's Judge Peters' house," Mrs. Bishop said, "the woman next door . . . was telling . . . The other son . . . She said . . . medicine or law . . . or something. . . ." Poor Mrs. Bishop, slipping through life, always half-informed, never sure of any statement.

"Yes, that's what I told you, Mother. Don't you remember? That fits in with what Irene Van Ness said—that she is half-way engaged to Chester Peters who is away at school and is coming home in a few years to go in his father's law office. This writing teacher's name is Sam, and Irene Van Ness says you never saw two brothers so different."

Ella's first day at school had been one containing many and varied bits of information. Keen, alert, the young girl was interested in every human with whom she came in contact.

On Thursday the rain had ceased, so that the short walk to school was a thing of delight. The college building sat so far back in the prairie pasture that at least half of Ella's journey was through the grass of the potential campus. It lay to the west of Oak River, near a winding prairie road running its muddy length at the south of the pasture and beyond. Oak Creek was to the north, a wandering gypsy of a stream, that after many vagaries of meandering, joined the river.

All of the keen senses of the girl were alive to the loveliness of the day and the joy of living. To her sight came the wide spaces of the prairie whose billowly expanse was broken only by clumps of trees which indicated the farmhouse of some early settler, and by the far horizon where the sky met the prairie like a blue-china bowl turned over a jade-colored plate. To her ears came the drone of Oak River's sawmill, the distant whirring of a prairie grouse, and the soft sad wail of mourning doves. To her nose the pungent odor of prairie grass and prairie loam after their drenching rain, and from the direction of the creek-bed the faint fragrance of matured wild crab-apples and hawthorn.

Plodding along through the lush grass she could see many of the new associates ahead of her wending their way up to this new Delphian oracle—this Greek temple with lightning-rods—the big-boned George Schroeder and the weazened little Albert Fonda and the Scotch Janet McLaughlin. A two-seated open carriage with prancing bays and jangling harness and swaying fly-nets came across the uneven ground and drew up beside her. An old colored man in a high silk hat was driving; Irene Van Ness was in the back seat.

"Come, get in," Irene called pleasantly. And Ella picked up her long ruffled plaid skirt and clutching it with her books, climbed up on the high seat beside her. Irene had on a blue silk dress with white pearl buttons and a flowing cape to match.

As the carriage bounced over the ground they passed a cow grazing near the building and when it snatched a greedy mouthful of the damp luscious prairie grass, Ella said: "That's Professor Wick's cow—and see how much like him she looks."

It set Irene to laughing—the cow gazing placidly at them over a great mouthful of grass, for all the world like Professor Wick looking calmly over his bushy whiskers.

Men were building the new wooden steps today, but placed the board with the cleats over the open framework for the two girls. Chris Jensen stood at the top and caught each one by the hand as she went teetering and giggling up the incline.

The day was something of a repetition of the first, without any of its depressing effects. Professor Wick conducted a class in experiments in which the human-voiced air-pump was the leading character, Professor

Carter made an heroic attempt to initiate the novices into the mysteries of Chaucer, Miss Patton, coolly rearranging the year's outline to suit herself, moved deliberately out of South America into the British Isles, and young Sam Peters added a flourish of fins to his aquatic vertebrate.

And the evening and the morning were the second day.

CHAPTER III

ELLA Bishop, healthy, country-bred, alive to every fresh sensation, enjoyed her studies in the new college immensely, but to say that they were the least of her pleasures, is to admit that it was not that she loved her classes less, but that she loved her classmates more. Peculiarly a lover of human contacts, she brought to every day's work an exuberance of spirits, a zest for living, a natural friendliness toward every one in the little school, from President Corcoran to Chris Jensen.

Toward the new neighbors she felt also the same healthy curiosity and friendly spirit. On Friday morning of that first week Sam Peters caught up with her as she was leaving home and carried her books up the long straggling street and across the coarse prairie grass to school. For his shyness she had only sympathy, and when he confided to her that he was not particularly pleased with teaching but that his father had wanted him to try it, her heart quite ached for the unhappy appearing fellow.

On Saturday for the first time she saw Judge Peters leave the big brick house with the cupola on one corner like a stiff hat over one eye.

And to see Judge Peters leave the house and start down to his law office was almost like seeing an ocean liner leave dock. Swinging a cane without change of beat, he walked with a long slow gait as rhythmic as four-four time in music. He was tall, pompous, solemn. Black side-whiskers formed the frame for his face, a wide black cord connected his glasses with some strategic spot on his coat, black gloves added their share to the ensemble, a bit of red geranium in his buttonhole completed the work of art.

By October, when the Indian summer days had come, the judge and his wife, in the neighborly fashion of an early day, came one evening to call.

Mrs. Bishop had been making apple butter a little messily and inefficiently in the back yard all day. She had stirred the concoction in the iron kettle hanging by a chain over the fire, using a big wooden paddle, until, as she said, she was too tired to think. Having burned the last batch, she had left it in the kettle until Ella could come home to clean up the disagreeable mixture.

So when Judge and Mrs. Peters arrived, she was completely upset at the unexpected coming of so much grandeur. She fluttered about, removing her apron, pushing chairs a few inches from their original positions, picking at imaginary threads on the floor. Even at sixteen Ella was far more poised than her frail mother, undaunted by the pompous entrance of the Judge with his meek little wife in tow. Mrs. Peters wore a Paisley shawl and a black velvet bonnet with pansies outlining the rim and satin ties under her patient looking face.

"We came to pay our respects to the newcomers in our fair city," the Judge announced with pompous formality.

The little wife nodded meek assent—and Ella saw then how like his mother was the shy penmanship teacher.

The entire call was made in the manner for which the judge set the pace. So clothed was he in formal phrases, it seemed to Ella that he said everything the hardest and longest way. To remark that the weather was mild was really all he meant when he said that there had been a noticeable lack of inclemency in the activity of the elements.

Once he turned to Ella with exclusive attention: "You have no doubt made the acquaintance, at least in the capacity of student to instructor, of my elder son, Samuel?"

"Yes," Ella said, "oh yes, sir." Mercy, she thought, he is making me feel frightened, too. No wonder his little wife is cowed.

"You have no doubt heard ere this that I have a younger son, also." And before Ella had a chance to reply, he went on proudly: "A younger son, Chester, studying law at Winside—a bright scholarly lad—I may even go so far as to say brilliant. He will make of the law a thing of truth and beauty and justice."

"That's certainly nice, sir." One was not required to say much in his presence. He needed only an audience for his own bombastic speech.

"Chester and Sam are very different," he stated with no apparent loathness in comparing the two openly. Ella was sure she saw the little wife flush and draw back as though struck. "Chester has none of Sam's backwardness and timidity,—has much that Sam lacks."

And she felt an embarrassment for the mother she could scarcely control when he added: "Sam is his mother,—Chester very like me. I am very proud of Chester. He will make a great lawyer,—yes, indeed,—a brilliant lawyer."

Ella was to remember that proudly reiterated statement years hence.

"I am very happy to hope, also, that Chester will some day bestow his hand and heart upon the daughter of my banker friend, thus uniting the old families of Peters and Van Ness."

So that was it, thought Ella—perhaps Irene's "half-way" engagement to Chester was merely an understanding between the families.

"I wouldn't like that," she thought. "When I'm engaged I want the man to love me for *myself,* and not for any other reason." Then she looked around the simple little parlor with the sale carpet and the cheap curtains, the horsehair furniture and the home-crocheted tidies and laughed to herself, "I guess he'll like me for just myself, all right."

After the call the man's egotism so lingered in her mind and the bald comparison of the two sons made such an impression upon her, that in the weeks to come she found herself forming a dislike of the younger Chester even before she had seen him,—feeling a relative compassion for the shy young instructor so earnestly teaching the swinging arm movements of his Spencerian writing.

A half dozen times that October he walked home from the college with her, so timidly, so self-effacingly, that in spite of laughing silently at his unattractive shyness, she felt a renewal of sympathy for him.

Her mother asked her about it: "This Sam Peters, Ella . . . do you . . . how do you . . . ? You see, he seems . . ."

"My word, Mother," she could always translate her mother's halting thoughts, "you don't think I especially *like* him, do you, just because of walking along the same way home?"

Her mother's eyes filled. "I don't suppose . . . I won't be staying with you . . . long, Ella. I'd like . . . if you could get settled . . ."

Ella ran to the frail little woman and clasped sturdy arms around her. "You're going to stay with me a long time, Mother. And I don't have to get settled yet for years and years."

Mrs. Bishop wiped her filling eyes with the corner of her apron. "Just so . . . you won't . . . an old maid . . . I wouldn't like . . ."

Ella threw back her head and laughed her hearty laughter. "Don't you worry. I won't be an old maid." Suddenly her voice dropped to a husky sweetness. "I have too many dreams for that, Mother. I think sometimes it is as though I am weaving at a loom with a spindle of hopes and dreams.

And no matter, Mother, how lovely the pattern—no matter how many gorgeous colors I use,—always the center of it is . . . you know, . . . just a little house in a garden and red firelight and . . . the man I love . . . and children . . . and happiness. For me, Mother, that's the end of all dreaming."

CHAPTER IV

☙ ALL that fall life in the young college was a never-ending journey of adventure for Ella Bishop. Full of vigor, her keen mind grasping every advantage of her new surroundings, each morning with eager anticipation she donned either the blue-trimmed-with-plaid or the plaid-trimmed-with-blue and ventured forth upon the search for her own particular Holy Grail. But school life to this girl from the country was not only an avenue of approach to knowledge, but to that larger experience,—contacts with her fellow humans. She never lost interest in the most insignificant of her classmates,—held open house for them all in the chambers of her heart. "There isn't one of them but has some likable qualities," she told her mother.

"You're like your father, Ella," Mrs. Bishop would say with moist eyes. "I declare—he seemed . . . his friends . . . he knew every one . . . and then, to think . . ."

"Friends!" Ella always disregarded her mother's depressed attitude. "Do you know, Mother, I'd rather have *friends* than any amount of money."

Her mother managed a wan smile. "I guess . . . your wish, Ella . . . you'll get it . . . with Father gone . . . leastways, there'll never . . . there's no money now . . ."

So with an exuberance of spirits Ella went happily to school each morning through the lovely Indian summer of the midwest's October, with a few wild flowers still colorful in the prairie grass,—through the chilling rains of November when the mud-puddles on the way held white rims of ice,—and through the heavy December snows which sent the young Danish janitor out with a horse to break a path that the girls with their flowing skirts might get through the field.

At Christmas time Chester Peters came home, and Ella admitted with something akin to regret the superiority of the younger brother's charm. There were several social events of the community to which she was invited,—a masquerade party in the town hall, a more select one on New Year's Eve at Irene Van Ness's big home on Main Street, and a bob-sled ride to the town of Maynard, including an oyster supper while there. Chester Peters was Irene Van Ness's escort, although Ella told herself with reluctance that Chester did not appear to be a very ardent lover inasmuch as he paid far more attention to a holiday guest from away than to Irene. It was true that Irene was not pretty,—she was sallow and scrawny, and attempted to cover these discrepancies with a continual change of fine clothes. Poor Irene, with all her nice things she never appeared very attractive. No wonder she was merely "half-engaged" to Chester.

Ella went to the party at Irene's with Samuel Peters. And while he did not attract her in the least, in all honesty bored her, with her usual effervescent spirits she managed to have a grand time in spite of his rather depressing presence.

The big snows of winter melted, huge chunks slipping off the college roof so that every dash up the wide new wooden steps was a gamble with the back of one's neck the object in peril. Spring came on, a gorgeous creature, with the prairie campus turning to lush green as though a lovely new dress had been made for her, with wild roses trimming the green of the gown, with wild hawthorn buds for her hair, wild crab-apple blossoms to perfume her, and prairie larks to sing for her. Chris Jensen set out young elms and maples in two curving lines toward the door of the building, a huge half-ellipse of little switches a few yards apart, around each of which he placed a small barrel for protection. George Schroeder and Albert Fonda worked with him after school hours in order to help pay their tuition. When the three had finished, the tiny trees looked almost ludicrous, mere twigs hidden by a half-hundred pickle-kegs on the broad expanse of the prairie campus.

Spring turned to summer with the meadow-lark's voice stilled in the torrid heat and the prairie grass curing for the hay barn. All vacation Chris Jensen hauled water to the tiny trees, so that President Corcoran said to him: "Chris, when future generations sit under the great branches of towering elms and maples, they ought to think of you."

"Vell, py golly," Chris beamed with the praise, "I'll be den as old as Met'uselah, an' ve'll all be pickin' dill pickles off de trees."

The summer ended and school began.

While life for Ella the first year had been largely one of adjustment to the new conditions and getting acquainted, the second year proved to be one of greater growth with several constructive plans taking shape. For no sooner had a young men's debating society been formed, than Ella was champing at the bit. In her belief, no masculine student could tread paths over which his feminine colleagues might not go, and so largely through Ella's efforts in which she found her Man Friday in one Mary Crombie, the Minerva Society came into being.

They met once a week in the small room on the third floor into which President Corcoran allowed them to move,—and it was not noticeably surprising to any one that Ella was made the first president.

With Ella, six others composed the personnel of the charter membership—Irene Van Ness and Janet McLaughlin, the Scotch girl, homely and lovable, and Mary Crombie, frank and efficient—one Mina Gordon, little and lithe and gypsy-like, Emily Teasdale, the college beauty, and Evelyn Hobbs, soft-spoken and shyly humorous.

For several months the seven charter members composed the society in its entirety, but with the growth of self-assurance in speaking, in perpetrating their essays and original poems upon each other, came a desire for new worlds to conquer, and the exclusive bars were let down to admit six more Daughters of Wisdom.

Lusty debates were indulged in, which settled so far as they were able, the burning questions of Equal Suffrage, national party accomplishments, and the brighter effulgence of Rome or Athens.

On Friday afternoons when the secret business meetings were over and the doors opened to the proletariat, the small room on third which was the rendezvous for Minerva's handmaidens became the mecca for those outside the pale. Other girls arrived to listen to the pearls that dropped from the lips of the chosen few. Sometimes a group of the young men came also and caused much confusion as to the bringing in of extra chairs, and the fluttering of feminine pulses,—feminine pulses being as they were of a far more fluttery type in the late seventies than those of recent years.

Ella Bishop was in her element at these meetings. Whether she had the management of the entire program or the mere duty of slipping one-half of the black calico curtain across the rather shaky rod to meet its other half, she performed her task with deep fervor. Whether in the chair as president, handling with dictatorial power the noisy wooden potato-masher she had brought from home to serve as a gavel, or sitting humbly in the cold outside the door as sentinel, like some little Rhoda at the gate, she put all her energy into the duty. Her rival in managerial capacity was Mary Crombie whose high-powered energies took the form of a deep belligerency toward anything masculine. That woman would one day vote,—that woman would sometime hold office,—would compete with man,—this was her battle cry. The girls agreed with her in most instances, but the Friday afternoon on which she declared with widely sweeping arm gestures that some day a woman would sit in the cabinet at Washington, they all burst out into high girlish laughter at the absurdity.

A library was formed that year, and while it consisted in its entirety of *Pilgrim's Progress*, the plays of one William Shakespeare, *Uncle Tom's Cabin, Swiss Family Robinson, Plutarch's Lives,* Fox's *Book of Martyrs,* and the highly romantic and therefore thoroughly dog-eared *Barriers Burned Away*—it was indeed the nucleus of what eventually became a library of many thousand volumes.

The students were for the most part serious, studious, almost overzealous. President Corcoran threw himself heart and soul into the building of a great college. If at times he became discouraged, if the worn-out apparatus of the laboratories, the half-furnished classrooms, or the small number of students worried him, he did not show it, but placed the whole of his energies with those few students and the people who had so enthusiastically founded the school.

In that second year there descended upon the authorities the terrible knowledge that young men and young women of the college were paying romantic attention to each other. When the worthy board found out this crime of the ages, they straightway made a ruling which was printed and passed out to all forty-six students. The ruling set forth: "While it is expected that the ladies and gentlemen of this institution shall treat each other with the polite and courteous civilities, there is a condition which transcends the proprieties of refined society. Anything like *selection* is strictly forbidden. Private walks and rides at any time are not allowed. Students of the two sexes by special permission of the president can meet privately, for the transaction of business and for that purpose only."

Be it said to President Corcoran's credit, that he labored faithfully with the board for several hours, attempting to explain that world-old human philosophy, that the apple which is strictly forbidden, becomes straightway the one fruit every Adam and Eve desires. But the committee on rules and regulations was adamant, and for two years the ruling stood on the college books, until that most potent of all weapons, ridicule, caused it to become obsolete.

At the end of the second year Sam Peters was dropped from the list of instructors. In spite of his marvelous dexterity with a pen, Sam and his exotic-looking fish and the elaborately constructed hand with its protruding index finger which he could draw so skillfully were not considered of enough importance as aids in mounting the ladder of success to warrant their continuance.

Judge Peters and President Corcoran thereafter avoided each other assiduously, due, it was rumoured, to Judge Peters having turned the full weight of his extensive vocabulary upon the president, using in addition to the words found in his dictionary, a choice selection of those that were not.

Poor Sam's life under the withering criticism of his father was far less comfortable than before. He went to work soon in a grocery store where he kept the books with his fine Spencerian penmanship, somewhat embellished with intricate figures of hands whose long protruding index fingers pointed to the various commodities, but as he had to wait on trade in addition to the bookkeeping, and as trade in the seventies and eighties bought much salted mackerel and kippered herring, he rather lost his desire to do the fish.

At the first increase in his bookkeeping wages, he dressed in his best, crossed the street, and with almost as much formality as his father might have employed, asked Ella to do him the honor to marry him.

"Oh, no, Sam, I couldn't. I couldn't *think* of it."

"There's somebody else you like?" Sam's pale blue eyes blinked at the hurt.

"Yes," said Ella, and added hastily: "Oh, no,—I don't mean that, Sam. I wasn't even thinking of what I was saying when I said 'Yes.' I meant, I hope there will be some one some day that I can care for. I have an ideal in my mind. I can almost see him." She grew so enthusiastic that even Sam, as obtuse as he was, realized there was no hope for him. "I can see how tall he is . . . and broad-shouldered . . . and even though I can never see his face—in my fancy, you know—some way I just feel that I'll know him right away when I first see him."

"Then . . . he doesn't . . ." Sam swallowed with difficulty. "He doesn't look like me?"

"Oh, no." And at the sight of the flush on his thin drawn face she held out her hand to him. "I'm so sorry. You know . . . how it is. If you can't,—you just can't."

"I suppose not."

"But I'll be your friend, Sam . . . for all my life."

"I'm afraid friendship . . . doesn't mean very much, Ella."

"Oh, yes, it does, Sam—truly it does. Friendship is a wonderful thing—a perfectly wonderful thing. Let's make a promise. No matter what girl you marry,—and no matter what man I marry,—let's promise to be friends all our lives. Will you?"

Sam lifted his thin hurt face. "If you say so, Ella."

"I do say so." She spoke happily as though the whole question were settled with satisfaction to them both. "It's a promise. We'll always be friends. When I'm an old lady and you're an old man—isn't that funny to think about, Sam?—we'll be *friends*." It sounded as though she were bestowing an honor upon him,—that a young priestess was anointing him.

It was a persuasive way she had with people, even at eighteen—the art of getting them to see a thing from her viewpoint, to believe it was their own decision.

So Sam went away, stepping almost jauntily—taking Ella's promise of undying friendship. Poor Sam Peters, carrying away a friendship—who had come for love.

CHAPTER V

BY Ella's third year a teachers' course and a music course were launched—and she straightway began studying didactics. To clerk in a store, do housework, or teach school were the only three avenues open for any girl, and her mind's selection was immediate. To teach—well, at least until her Lochinvar came riding by, she admitted to that innermost recess of her heart where dwelt her real self. To have a home of her own—children—nothing could ever take the place of that. But she could not look at the lovely picture hanging there so sacredly in her heart and place therein any young man she knew now. The only one who had ever offered himself was Sam Peters—and Sam was unthinkable.

The college boys were all good young chaps. She admired their energy and their sincerity, but to her fastidious mind there was no one outstanding among them—George Schroeder with his big head of rough hair, his foreign accent and his constant praise of anything Germanic—

little Albert Fonda with his obsession for the study of the moon and the stars—or any of the others.

So the last two years were spent in a frame of mind as fancy-free as were the first two. Those last ones saw the faculty enlarged by the additional courses—Professor Cunningham for the didactics—Miss Susie McAlister for the music—the former friendly and humorous—the latter so devoted to the goddess Euterpe that she lived in a world apart, breathed the atmosphere of the upper strata.

Newcomers entered the young college, knowledge was disseminated, minds expanded, the Minerva Society waxed strong in numbers and oratory, the prairie grass was cut, the elms and maples looked superciliously down on their pickle-kegs from a height of five feet. Growth was in the air.

One might ride in state now to the very door of Central Hall in a public vehicle termed "the hack,"—but always with the precautionary measure of placing a newspaper or one's shawl on the seat so the red of the plush cushions would not identify itself too intimately with one's clothes.

The spring of 1880 came on and the first class was to graduate. Ella sent applications to the Oak River Board, to Maynard, to Maple City, to every place she thought there might be a chance for a teaching position.

Janet McLaughlin was elected at Maynard, Mary Crombie at Maple City. Mina Gordon and Evelyn Hobbs and Emily Teasdale were all to be married. Irene Van Ness was to stay at home in anticipation of Chester Peters' sudden desire to become wholly and completely engaged. And still Ella had not secured a position.

The time for final examinations was in the offing. For harried days and sleepless nights, Ella and the eleven others comprising the first graduating class crammed for the fray. No dates for execution could have contained any greater element of dread than the June third, fourth and fifth marked with warning crosses in twelve almanacs. Ella grew wan-eyed, lost appetite and weight, and always among her worries was the realization that she had not yet been hired for fall work. Her one great wish had been to get a school near enough so that she could live at home with her always-frail mother. Sometimes in the night she awoke in a cold perspiration with the appalling thought that it looked as though she might not get any school at all. She would lie awake with tense nerves and think: "But I must . . . I *have* to get a school. . . . Mother has put me through the college . . . she hasn't enough to live on . . ." All of which was not highly conducive to a healthy physical condition or calm mentality for the figurative Ides of March on which the examinations were to be held.

And then,—the miracle happened. President Corcoran called her to his office and asked her how she would like to teach English Grammar in the college. The school was growing,—they were rearranging classes—

Ella thought she could not believe what she was hearing. She was dreaming,—would waken in her bedroom and laugh at the wild fancy. But no, President Corcoran was saying: "I have watched you for four years, Miss Ella. You have done good work in grammar. You have a keen mind, an open heart, an enviable disposition, and that something which seems to me the very soul of the teaching profession—a keen interest in your fellow man."

No one knighted by a king's touch ever felt so honored.

There was the formality of the written application, the waiting of a few days for the decision already made in board meeting,—and Ella Bishop was to stay on at her youthful Alma Mater and teach. To earn a salary, even though modest, support her mother, live at home,—the whole world took on brilliant roseate lights.

"What have I ever *done* to have so much good luck?" she said over and over to her mother.

"You're like your father, Ella. He . . . there was something . . . he was always . . ." Mrs. Bishop groped, moist-eyed, for the explanation. "You go into things . . . just the way . . ."

The examinations ended with no fatalities. Commencement was a reality, and under the bright glow of the knowledge of the new position, a thing of happiness and joy. Happiness and joy to Ella Bishop is meant, for to the towns-people, friends and relatives of the twelve graduates the merrymaking had its difficult moments. On Sunday, President Corcoran gave a tedious, if earnest, Baccalaureate address,—on Monday, class-day exercises were held. On Tuesday, four of the twelve members of the class delivered orations, each of forty-five minutes' duration,—on Wednesday, four more held the rostrum for another three hours,—on Thursday, the last group spoke for three more hours to a wilted, perspiring, dog-tired audience of the faithful. George Schroeder, not yet over his German accent, gave a glowing tribute to his beloved Goethe. Albert Fonda spoke on "The Course of the Stars." Mary Crombie presented the case of Woman's Rights so forcibly that she half ripped out a sleeve of her navy blue silk dress. Ella gave all she had ever known or would ever know about "Our American Authors." Irene Van Ness, whose father had written her oration, presented a profound dissertation on "The Financial System of Our Country." "Across the Alps Lies Italy," "Heaven Is Not Reached by a Single Bound," and "Black the Heel of Your Boot" were conspicuous by their presence.

The long-drawn-out exercises were in the auditorium. The girls were trailing silk dresses with camel-like humps in the rear over wire bustles. Long gold watch chains entwined their necks, coming to rest somewhere in the region of their padded bosoms. The windows were open to the stifling summer air, the June-bugs, and the sound of stamping horses tied to hitch-racks. The odor that penetrated to the farthermost corner of the huge room was a combination of June roses and livery barn. Palm leaf fans whacked vigorously against buttons and lodge emblems. There were instrumental and vocal numbers,—solos, duets, trios, quartets, and choruses. There were invocations and benedictions, presentations and acceptances. Never did it take so long to go through the birth pangs of graduation.

Twelve tables in the hallway, representing each graduate, were laden with bouquets of home-grown flowers, gold watches, pearl-handled opera glasses, plush albums, and many duplicates of cushioned and padded "Poems of Keats,"—or "Burns" or "Shelley."

Chris Jensen, resplendent in a new suit of purplish hue which gave his red face the appearance of being about to suffer apoplexy, guarded the treasures.

The sixth evening the Alumni banquet was held in the auditorium cleared of a portion of its pews, but luckily for the long-suffering public, the attendance was limited to graduates and faculty wives. The whole procedure had consumed as many days as the fundamentalists' conception of the genesis of the world. Small wonder that the entire community rested the seventh day and called it holy.

At this first Alumni banquet less than two dozen sat down to the tables. President Corcoran referred in his talk to the possible day when two hundred graduates would sup together. It did not seem possible to contemplate.

Ella felt that it was one of the happiest events in her life. Examinations passed, the nightmare moments of her oration behind her—nothing now but the friendly intercourse with those closest to her in school, and the warm glow of the knowledge that she had won the cream of the teaching positions. Life was all before her. She was young,—gloriously young,—only twenty. She could do with her life as she wished.

Happy Ella,—not to know yet for a little while that life is to do as it wishes to you.

CHAPTER VI

ELLA could scarcely wait to begin her work. Sometimes in the summer she would go over to school, tramping through the campus grass to where Chris was mowing, and get the key to the building.

"May I take the key to Central Hall?" she would ask when he had put down his scythe and come swinging across the newly-cut grass to meet her.

"Say . . . vy you always call her *Cendral* Hall," Chris asked once, "ven dey ain't but von anyvay?"

"Don't you see, Chris? Look around. Here, stand over here,—can't you see a lot more buildings there,—one over here and one there,—a calisthenics building there,—and a huge library,—and a science building,—and maybe a teachers' training one?"

But even though Chris, open-mouthed, looked and looked, he could not see a calisthenics building, nor a huge library, nor a teachers' training building,—nothing but a plain three-story one with a few straggling ivy vines clinging desperately to the hot bricks in the prairie sun. Only those who have dreams in their minds and courage in their hearts when they are young see such mirage-like things on familiar horizons.

Her classroom was to be on the second floor at the front, with a tiny inner room opening from it. "My office," she said under her breath many times a day to get the thrill which the words gave her. The potential office was a little room in the tower over which the bell hung. To hear the resounding clang of that brass-throated messenger directly over her was to feel its vibration in every nerve of her being. It was more than the mere ringing of a bell,—it was a call to knowledge,—a summons to life itself. Already pigeons had begun to nest in the tower and when the bell rang, they flew violently out like so many frightened loafers. Sometimes they tapped the swinging thing themselves in their turbulent activity.

There were windows on three sides of the little tower room. From them she could see the town to the east, four thousand people now—that was what the college had done for Oak River—the rolling campus to the south—well, anyway, the short prairie grass sloped down an incline—and farm land to the west as far as the eye could see, some of it cultivated, much of it still rough prairie land with no sign of road or fence, and with horses and cattle, herded in little bunches, grazing on its vast unbroken expanse.

Surprisingly, the September morning on which Chris rang the bell for opening classes was almost a replica of the rainy one on which Ella first entered four years before. Remembering the dismal reception of those half-frightened newcomers, she stationed herself near the big doors and greeted every freshman as though he were an honored guest arriving for a social event. President Corcoran, coming through the hall, smiled behind the ambush of his whiskers. "Whatever that girl does, she *does*," he said to Professor Cunningham in passing.

All fall, Ella Bishop taught grammar classes as though she had invented adjectives and was personally responsible for subordinate clauses. Papers she carted home in sheaves. Notebooks she perused so thoroughly that not an insignificant "for him and I" or an infinitesimal "has came" dared lift its head without fear of her sturdy blue pencil. Still so young, she made no effort to disengage herself from student activities. She was adviser for the now-flourishing Minerva Society. She helped start a tiny college paper called the *Weekly Clarion*. She was secretary of the modest little Faculty Family Club. "She's just about an ideal connection between faculty and students," President Corcoran told his wife. "Young enough to get the students' viewpoints, with a nice older dignity when necessary."

Sometimes a little daring crowd of students would plan to slip away in a hayrack or a bob-sled to Maynard to dance, and hearing it, Ella would try to think of some new entertainment to counteract the scheme.

Altogether life was full for her and very, very interesting, swinging along at a lively tempo for the times. The town was growing. Mr. Van Ness built a three-story bank building, renting out the upper floors to the Masons and the Odd Fellows and the Knights of Pythias. Every day Judge Peters walked pompously down Adams and Main Streets in four-four time, his gold-headed cane swinging out the rhythm. Sam slipped quietly down to the grocery store at daylight. Chester wrote home glowing accounts of his own activities over which Irene hung with tremulous hopes. Mrs. Bishop attempted to keep house, but the results were so confused and messy that Ella put her young shoulder to the wheel and did much of it over when she came at night.

The graduating class,—Class of 1880, the members always reminded their friends, as though there had been a dozen others,— had started a round-robin letter. Ella and Irene Van Ness were the only ones living in Oak River, so the package made trips to ten other localities before its return to the city of its birth. Mina Gordon and Emily Teasdale and Evelyn Hobbs all had new names now and were almost maudlin in their wishes that every one else in the class could be as happy as they. Mary Crombie and Janet McLaughlin were enjoying their teaching, the former having started a little Woman's Suffrage organization which she hoped would expand and sweep the country. George Schroeder was teaching and anticipating saving enough money to go to Heidelberg to school. Albert Fonda's report for the most part read like a treatise on astronomy,—Albert having hitched his wagon to all the stars.

On a Friday night in November, Chris came into Ella's room with a noisy depositing of mops, pail and brooms. She sighed and prepared to gather up her work to leave. That Chris,—he seemed to haunt her this week with his jangling paraphernalia.

He kept eyeing her furtively, she imagined, with a large show of cleaning activity but not much progress. Was it possible that the big bungling fellow had something on his mind?

"Why does every one always pick on me to unload their troubles?" she was saying to herself, half in exasperation, when he began:

"Miss Bis'op, I got news for you." His fat face was red, his pale blue eyes winking nervously.

"Yes, Chris?"

"I be gettin' marriet next veek."

"Well, Chris—congratulations. I didn't know you had a girl here."

"Oh, s'e not nobody here. S'e come by Ellis Island to-day. Next veek s'e get here to Oak Riffer—den ve get marriet. I rent a leetle house across from school over der by Smit's."

"Well, that's fine. I'm sure she's a nice girl, too, Chris."

"Oh, s'e nice all right. I not see her, now, come six year. S'e vait 'til I safe money and send for passage. S'e healt'y and goot vorker. S'e he'p me safe money."

Dear, dear, thought Ella—how unromantic.

"What's her name, Chris?"

"Hannah Christine Maria Jensen."

"Jensen?"

"Yah."

"The same as yours? Is she any relation to you now?"

"No-o." He threw back his head and laughed long and mirthfully. "Denmark, s'e full of Jensens."

Ella was interested, as indeed she always was in her fellow man. She could not quite seem to keep a hand out of the affairs of every one around her.

"Where will you be married?"

"I don' know. By the Lutheran preacher's house, mebbe."

Suddenly, Ella had an inspiration,—one of those enthusiasms with which she was eternally possessed. "Chris, would you like to be married at my mother's house? Wouldn't you like to have your—your Hannah Christine Maria come right to our house from the train . . . and have the ceremony in my mother's parlor . . . and then a little supper with us afterwards?"

The blond giant's eyes shone,—his fat face grew redder with emotion. "Py golly, Miss Bis'op, I like it fine an' I t'ank you."

Now that she was launched on this new interest, she went into it, as always, with heart and soul. Several times she went to the little cottage at Chris's plea for advice. She took over a half-dozen potted geraniums—sent eggs and bread and fried-cakes for the first breakfast—would have taken the dresser scarf or curtains from her own room if neccesary.

When the girl arrived, she proved to be apple-cheeked and buxom—her flesh hard and solid, her pale blue eyes and pale yellow hair contrasting oddly with the flushed red of her face. So in the parlor of Ella's home, Miss Hannah Christine Maria Jensen became Mrs. Hannah Christine Maria Jensen, after which the newlyweds and the Lutheran minister and his wife sat down with Ella and her mother to what the Oak River paper later termed "a bounteous repast."

When they were leaving for the cottage, Chris said, "To my dyin' day I'll nefer forget dis kindness."

He talked to the girl a moment in Danish and turned to Ella: "S'e say s'e tink s'e can mebbe come vork sometime to s'ow you her respeck."

It touched Ella. It was always to touch her a little,—Chris and Hannah Jensen's dog-like faithfulness to her all the years of her life.

It was not an astonishing piece of news to any one to hear in the spring that Ella had been elected for another year at a five-dollar-per-month increase in salary.

"I'm afraid . . . Ella, . . . you'll be an old maid," her mother said plaintively, "that way . . . teaching . . . kind of . . . seems like . . . "

"I can think of lots worse things, Mother," Ella laughed. "Marrying a worthless man, for instance, and having to take in washing or be a dressmaker. I wonder if the day will ever come when a married woman can do anything more than those two things?"

But Ella knew she would not be an old maid. Something told her so—some singing voice down in the innermost recesses of her heart. As well as she liked her teaching,—to have a husband and home and children,—these were better. These were the things for which her healthy young body and warm heart were intended. She knew.

CHAPTER VII

IN that second year of Ella's teaching, Chester Peters, having finished his school work, was at home and in the law office with his father. Judge Peters took occasion to tell any one who would listen what a brilliant chap Chester was and how he would make of the law a thing of truth and beauty. He never said much about Sam, eggs and flour and salt mackerel evidently not conforming to his ideas of either beauty or truth. Irene Van Ness had a new fur coat, sealskin with mink trimming, a long row of dangling tails around the shoulders and hips, and a mink cap to match. People thought surely Chester would marry her now that he was settling down, and Irene fully shared the desire.

Ella felt sorry for her, could not conceive of a half-hearted romance like that,—was soon to know more about one.

It was a cold Friday night in November. It had snowed all day and now the whiteness of the drifts lay over college and campus, town and prairie. There was a concert in the college auditorium given by the new glee club,—the Euterpeans, they modestly called themselves,—the proceeds to go to the library fund. But at the supper hour, Ella had given up going. "To have a sore throat any night is bad enough," she said irritably to her mother, "but to have it on Friday night with a concert on is a disgrace. This is the first thing I've ever missed."

But she would not listen to her mother's timid statement about giving up the concert too. "The Peterses will come for you as they expected, so you go just the same. I'll help you get ready."

Mrs. Bishop was only in her forties, but to have been forty-six in the eighties was to have been an old woman. She wore a heavy black wool dress, a thick black cape with jet-bead passementerie trimming, a black velvet bonnet with a flat crêpe bow on top and wide crêpe ties under her chin.

Judge and Mrs. Peters came for her, the high-stepping blacks tossing their manes and jangling their sleigh-bells vigorously the few moments they were forced to stand at the horse-block.

After they had gone, Ella took some medicine, gargled with salt and water, rubbed goose-grease and turpentine on her throat and pinned a wide piece of red flannel around that offended part of her anatomy.

For a little while she read in her bedroom by the warmth of the sheet-iron drum, then deciding childishly to make some maple candy, she descended to the kitchen. When she had carried the pan of melted maple sugar back upstairs, she opened her bedroom window to get a plate of snow upon which to drop spoonsful of the hot concoction. It was a favorite confection of the times—these hardened balls of maple candy. The cold wind blew in and the carbon street lights flickered. There was no snow within reaching distance and so while Reason told her that she was doing a foolish thing, Desire caused her to throw a crocheted shawl around her shoulders and step out onto the roof.

As she turned to go in, the window slipped down with a noisy crashing sound. She was at the glass in a moment attempting to raise it, but it would not budge.

At first she worked frantically at the sash, and then when she realized the seriousness of the situation, with more dogged deliberation.

The cold was penetrating and she drew the shawl tightly about her and tied it in a knot in order to work with the stubborn window. When it still would not yield, she thought of summoning some near neighbor. But there were no lights at either house.

She walked gingerly to the very edge of the slippery roof and considered jumping. "Yes, and break my ankles," she thought, "and then faint away from the pain and be covered with snow when Mother comes home. She'd think I was the woodpile." She grinned nervously and shivered.

So this was the way they all felt, was it—Babes in the Woods—Princes in the Tower—and she on the kitchen roof?

Something clammy lighted on her nose. It was beginning to snow again. She let out a lusty and prolonged "Hoo-hoo-oo." No answer came from any source on the deserted street but a mocking echo. She began to shiver again and a cough strangled in her throat.

She hurried back to the window and beat with her fists but the glass would not yield. If she had only left on her sturdy shoes instead of wearing the soft woolen homemade slippers, she could have sent one flying through the pane.

But even as she grew desperate with genuine fright she could hear some one coming up the street, crunching along over the snow-packed side-walk. As he passed under the carbon street-lamp she could see that he carried a valise.

"Hoo-hoo," she called loudly, "will you please stop a moment?"

The man slowed immediately, and when she called again, he came across the street and then through the snowdrifts of the yard, stepping along with high striding walk. "What is it?" he asked. "What's wanted?"

Ella could not recognize him in the semidarkness, and decided that he was a visiting stranger, but in her desperation would have accosted President Arthur himself.

"I'm terribly sorry to bother you—and highly ashamed of my predicament—but I'm trapped out here on the roof for doing such a silly thing as stepping out here to get a pan of snow. The window slipped down behind me. I've tried to break the glass—I thought glass was supposed to be fragile—and I'm certainly not a weakling—but I can't even crack it."

The young chap laughed and put down on the steps the valise he had been holding all the time. By the faint glimmer of the street-lamp he looked big and substantial.

"Where can I get a ladder?"

"There's one in the barn, just inside the door on the wall to your right."

He strode off to the barn and Ella could see the flare of a match against the darkness and hear Polly snort and rise to her feet. When he returned, he was holding the ladder balanced across his shoulder. With no word he placed it in a snowdrift by the kitchen wall and held it firmly.

"Come on," he called. "But be careful."

When she was half way down, one of the flimsy cloth slippers dropped.

"See here," he said suddenly, "you can't walk in this deep snow. I'm going to carry you around to that porch."

"Oh, no—thank you. I'll manage." She felt shy, ashamed of her loose, flapping wrapper now that she was part way down and near the strange young man. "Besides, I have goose-grease and turpentine on my throat,—and it's smelly. . . ."

At that he threw back his head and laughed good-naturedly, and for answer picked her off the ladder with no comment and rounded the corner of the kitchen where he set her on her feet in the porch between the cistern-pump and a washtub. For that short distance, she had not been able to see his face distinctly. There had been only time for a fleeting impression of his big cold overcoat and his muscular strength,—and a certain queer sense of liking his personality. She wondered vaguely with swift questioning if it were true—that one radiated personality like that—so that another could tell—even about a stranger—and in the dark—

"Thank you so much for your trouble."

"It was a good thing I happened along or you might have had a sorry time. Even yet, you'd better go take a sweat," he advised solemnly.

"And quinine and white pine and tar and molasses and onions and sulphur." Her voice cracked a little. And they both laughed.

"Now that the rescue is accomplished, can you tell me hurriedly where Judge Peters lives?"

Ella pointed out the big brick house where the iron deer stood on frozen guard in the snowdrifts.

"I see. Chet has been my roommate—and I'm here to go in the law office with him and his father."

"Oh, how nice," Ella said almost before she realized. Nice for whom, Ella? It gave her a warm friendly feeling toward the young man.

"Well," he held out his hand, "Delbert Thompson is the name of the gallant fireman."

"Ella Bishop," she gave him her own cold one, responding cordially: "I teach in the college here—Midwestern."

"You?" He was incredulous. "I thought you were a little girl—with your hair in a thick braid down your back that way."

"No." And she sang slightly:

"The heavenward jog
Of the pedagogue
Is the only life for me."

They both laughed—it seemed very easy to laugh with the pleasant young man—and then he was gone, crunching along the snow paths with his valise. And Ella went into the house quite distinctly aglow with a peculiar new sensation.

When Mrs. Bishop came, Ella told her all about the funny experience, and Mrs. Bishop was terribly upset,—the exposure to the cold and the trusting of her girl to the clutches of an utter stranger that way. But try as she might in her little fluttered and frightened way, she could not seem to arouse her daughter to the enormity of the danger in which she had been. Indeed, when that daughter was dropping to sleep later, all swathed up in a fat pork poultice after a mustard foot bath, she was thinking she wished she could have seen the young man's face. "I could see how tall he was . . . and his broad shoulders," she thought, "but try as I would, I couldn't quite see his face." And then, suddenly, the familiarity of the words were so startling that all drowsiness left her. For a long time she lay staring into the darkness of the night, thinking of the rest of the prophecy she had made to Sam: "But some way I feel sure, Sam, that I will know him right away when I first see him."

When finally she was dropping off, she dreamed of weaving a tapestry on the kitchen roof, but she was so cold that she must weave in the center of the picture a great deal of red firelight—and—a little cottage—and children—

CHAPTER VIII

THERE was now a freshly painted sign over the door of an office next to the new Bank of Oak River which said "Peters, Peters and Thompson." And the strange and wholly informal meeting of Ella and the firm's new young partner had taken upon itself a bright and shining halo of romance. And life had begun to hold new experiences.

Inherently honest, Ella grew cunning and sly with her own self that month,—would not admit that she was dressing for the new young lawyer, —that she was attending every gathering of college and town in the hope of seeing his big broad shoulders and ready smile. She grew sensitive to his entrance into a room, knew through some peculiar psychic information without turning her head that he had arrived. Gradually she grew to feel that he was looking for her, too.

So immediately mutual was this attraction that by the holiday time he was her exclusive escort to all the social events of the community. In January people were teasing her. Even her students could bring the telltale color to her cheeks by an innocently uttered innuendo. Chester Peters seemed to have breathed a bit of the highly charged atmosphere also, for he was more attentive to Irene than he had ever been,—and Irene was glowing these days, her sallow face lighted by the first real hope of the culmination of her long liking for Chester. Chester Peters and Irene Van Ness—Delbert Thompson and Ella Bishop—it was a common sight to see the four tramping laughingly in single-file through paths shoveled in the deep snow or riding in Judge Peters' two-seated sleigh with the jet-colored high-stepping horses that matched the Judge's black side-whiskers. Sam did not figure in the gayety—went quietly to the grocery store where he kept the books in his flowing Spencerian hand, and handled the eggs that the farmers' wives brought in for trade. There seemed no great change in Sam's courteous attitude toward Ella,—except that his eyes now were not only wistful, but tragic. Sensing his shy longing for her, Ella sometimes felt a hearty impatience toward him. Why should the loveliest thing that had ever come into her life have a shadow cast upon it by the moon-calf attitude of Sam Peters?

By February, Ella was formally engaged to Delbert Thompson. It was one of those things she could scarcely believe true. It seemed all too sudden—too beautiful a thing to come to definite words so soon. Just a few months before and she had never seen him, save in her own girlish dreams. She had loved the courting, the imagining the possibility of what might come, the holding to her heart the delicate unfolding flower of romance. And now this February evening Delbert had her in his arms, was lavishing warm kisses on her cool lips, and she was saying, "Delbert—it's too soon. It has all happened too quickly."

At that he was throwing back his head and laughing his boyish ready laugh. "It's not too soon, Ella—nothing's too soon. We'll be married right away this spring."

"Oh, not *this* spring, Delbert. I should teach one more year . . . to get ready . . . and save money . . . and maybe *know* you better," she added, a bit shyly.

"You're a cool little piece, aren't you, Ella?" He held her off and asked anxiously for the dozenth time, "You do love me, don't you?"

"Oh, yes, yes, Delbert. I do love you . . . so much. But . . . wait a little . . . I must be so sure . . . it's such a big thing . . . to understand just what this love *is*."

"It's *this*." Delbert laughed and crushed her to him until she nearly cried out in the strength of the embrace.

But Ella knew better—Ella Bishop knew her love was something more than that—something more deeply beautiful,—something infinitely more delicate.

So in a whirlwind of courtship it was settled. Ella was to resign and they were to be married in June as soon as school was out.

When Irene Van Ness heard it, she cried a little. It did not seem quite understandable to her,—she had gone with Chet Peters ever since their High School days. The whole town knew she was Chet's girl,—no one else paid any attention to her. But he had never once mentioned marriage. She bought goods for two whole new outfits and took them to Mrs. Finch, the best dressmaker in town.

All spring Ella lived in the rarefied atmosphere of her romance. But instead of detracting from her work, it merely accentuated her fidelity to it. Every class brought her nearer to the end of her teaching and so she told herself she must give her best to that teaching while she could. This roseate happiness which was hers bubbled over into thoughtfulness for others, a warm kindness toward her students, an energy which sought to make the most of every opportunity to be helpful.

"I am teaching under the assumption that every young person in my classes has to learn from me *all* the English grammar he will *ever* know," she explained laughingly to Delbert. "By pretending that what I can't teach them now in the few remaining months they will never know, I hustle and make the most of my time."

"You're a bundle of energy," Delbert would say proudly, "so different from most of the girls with their kittenish ways and their silly little talk."

"I thought men were supposed to like that kittenish kind," Ella would suggest a bit jealously,—for the very feminine reason of getting him to disagree.

"Oh, they may be all right to flirt around with,—but for a wife, who wants a coquette?"

Delbert was to move into the Bishop home. It was a feature of the marriage which gave him some chagrin.

"It doesn't seem quite the thing to do, Ella. It ought not be that way," he would sometimes protest.

But Ella, practical as always, would laugh his humiliation away. "We bought the house after Father died and it's all paid for. I'm an only child . . . Mother has to live with us anyway—no matter where we would go. So what difference does it make?"

This last of March she spent her spring vacation doing the work of two women, for her salary, not any too large, had by necessity to stretch over many things. So, up on a sturdy stepladder, she papered the bedrooms with dainty flowered wallpaper. She washed and ironed the curtains, scrubbed and painted and cleaned.

"If it would only stay so until June." She surveyed her handiwork with the guilty acknowledgment that her mother was not much of a housekeeper. "I wish I could afford a hired girl just to stand guard and keep it nice."

April came in, soft and gentle, with the martins coming and the pussywillows over on the campus creek bursting into gray fuzziness—with time flying on such golden wings that Ella must even begin to think of her dresses now. Dresses in the eighties being, as they were, massive architectural works of pleats, flounces, panels, panniers, bustles and trains, she intended to have but two—a white silk one for the ceremony and a navy blue silk. "But no plaid," she grimaced.

"Do you think I should be so extravagant as to have a white silk one made, though, Mother?" She always went through the routine of asking her mother's advice although she knew the decision would have to be her own.

But almost to her amazement, her mother said definitely: "Yes . . . oh, yes. I had . . . the pale blue one, you know. Your father thought . . . He said I was so pretty. . . . It's just one time. . . . When you're old . . . you live it all over."

Each of these days was filled with happy tasks. Students must be helped tirelessly over the rough places, the house kept in order, her mother assisted, some plain sewing done at home, all her plans for the little June wedding perfected. Sometimes Ella stopped a moment to analyze herself. "What is there about me that is so different from other girls?" she would think. "When I stop to think about it, no one ever does anything for me. I always see to everything myself. Wouldn't it be nice sometimes to have some one else,—Mother, for instance,—take some responsibility? Even Delbert . . ." She felt a momentary disloyalty at the unspoken thought—"Oh, well," she laughed it off. "I'm just one of those people who get about and do things myself, I guess."

On the third of April, she started home at five o'clock. The campus grass, now in its sixth spring, was beginning to look almost like a lawn, the old prairie coarseness of the first two or three years having given place after continuous mowing and the sowing of blue-grass and clover to a fairly pleasing green sloping sward. The hard maples and the elms, planted in their curving horse-shoe formation up toward the building, were actually beginning to seem like real trees, although the barrel-staves around their bases for protection from wild rabbits still detracted not a little from their looks.

As she went down the long wooden sidewalk, she could see Chris in the distance burning leaves. Wild geese flew north, robins dipped low in front of her, sap on the sunny side of a soft maple was dripping clammily on the ground. All the signs of springtime had come,—*her* springtime. There was so much to do,—so many places to go, Irene was having a party in a few days, she and Delbert were driving to Maynard soon where he had business for the Judge,—he had said it would be a regular honeymoon trip with Judge Peters' team and shining new buggy. She was going to look at material for the white dress and compare it with the silk she could get here. Life was so full,—so joyous. How could there be unhappiness in the world?

"There just *isn't* any," she said to herself with a gay little laugh.

But there was unhappiness in the world. She found it out the moment she entered the house, and saw her mother sitting idly, a letter in her lap, tears on her cheeks.

"Mother, darling," she was at her side and down on her knees in a moment, "what's wrong?"

"My only brother is gone, Ella." And the tears overflowed again. "My Eddie—my little brother. One more sorrow for me, Ella." Then she added as casually as though it were not of great import, "And his daughter,—his little Amy . . . she wants to come . . . here with us, you know, Ella . . . and live awhile."

With a cold feeling that life had played her a trick at the very time she wanted life to be most gracious to her, Ella picked up the letter.

It was true. Cousin Amy Saunders, eighteen now, wanted to come out from Ohio and stay with her Aunt and Cousin Ella.

I've nowhere to go, and I don't know what to do. Could you let me come a little while, just until I can get over my sorrow for dear Papa? And, Auntie, I haven't a cent. I don't want to be a trouble to any one but . . .

Ella finished in a daze of mind, conscious that she was deeply annoyed at that which seemed like an intrusion just now. Silently she put the little pink note back in its little pink envelope, and almost without volition raised it to her nose. A faint odor clung to it. For a moment she forgot the import of the message in the whimsical desire to place that elusive fragrance, so strangely familiar. Something in the woods. May-apples—that was it—mandrakes—the cloying fragrance of the waxy-white blossoms of the May-apple.

CHAPTER IX

☙ MRS. BISHOP kept wiping her eyes and sighing. When Ella had stared at the little pink and fragrant epistle for a long moment, her mother asked helplessly: "Oh, Ella, what . . . do you . . . what shall we do?"

"Do?" Ella was suddenly all briskness and decision. "There's just one thing to do. Send her some money and tell her to come on."

"Oh, Ella . . . with you going to get married. You're such . . . you're a good girl. First, you have me . . . on your hands . . . your newly married life . . . and now little Amy."

Ella's eyes wavered away from her mother's. "I was just thinking, Mother, now that it's turned out this way—Amy coming—maybe you and she could live here together. Delbert and I could get rooms—down town, in the building above Judge Peter's office. She'd look after you, you know, and I would be so close to come if I were needed."

That old childish look of fright came into her mother's moist eyes. "To leave Mamma, Ella? To leave me behind . . . when . . . I might . . . at best I may have only a year or two more . . ."

It moved Ella as it always did. Impatient she might feel, but one sight of that little delicate figure shrinking into its shroud of fear, and Ella was always on her knees, her strong young arms around it.

"Don't think about it any more, Mother. I'll manage you both somehow."

When she told Delbert about Amy's coming, he was not overly enthusiastic.

"Not that I should be the one to object, Ella dear,—your own house—and I just moving in. I can't quite swallow my pride yet about that. Some day, don't you forget, I'm going to be the one to furnish you with a new home. It will have colored fan-shaped lights over all the doors and windows—and a black marble fireplace and this new walnut grill-work between all the rooms."

It pleased Ella. She loved that ambitious side of him,—those plans he always made for their future. It would be nice to have some one upon whom to lean. In all her twenty-two years she had never known the time when she could shift responsibility,—do anything but stand erect on her own two feet.

He caught her to him now, his flushed face against her own cool one, his kisses hot on her lips. "To think I'm to live with you . . . in the same *house* . . . the same *room* . . ."

"Delbert!" She drew back, a little shy as always. Never yet had she felt entirely responsive to those warm impulsive caresses. Just now he chided her for it. "You're an iceberg, Ella. You don't love me."

"Oh, yes, yes, Delbert,—I *do! How* I love you. You don't *know!* But . . . give me . . . time. Let me. . . ." She could not finish.

How could she tell him that love was such a fine thing, so exquisite, that she wanted to hold it in her heart awhile as one gloats over a pearl—or glories in the beauty of a rose—before wearing it? Sometimes—she wondered vaguely—if Delbert could quite understand that love was something infinitely more lovely, something far more delicate than the mere physical. Then in sheer anger at her disloyalty she would put the thought from her.

There was just time to get the third bedroom upstairs ready for the young cousin before her arrival. Mrs. Bishop's room was on the first floor, and there had never been any reason to furnish the third one upstairs which had been used as a storeroom.

But now Ella went back to the cleaning with only a few nights after school and one Saturday left in which to finish. She put the hat-boxes and her father's army equipment down in the cellar, papered and painted and hung up fresh curtains, and took her own best bedroom chair into the cousin's room.

As she worked, her interest in preparing for the guest overcame her resentment at that which had seemed at first like intrusion. "Poor little thing," she thought,—"left an orphan,—my own little cousin Amy . . . and I not willing to share a roof with her."

Irene's charade party was to be on Friday night, and it was just possible that Amy would get to Oak River in time to attend it, Ella thought, and decided it would be a nice way to initiate her into local society.

It turned out that it happened just that way. Amy was getting in on the four o'clock train from the east on Friday. Ella left school early. Delbert came and hitched up Polly and they were at the station long before the steam whistle sounded down the road. The train was a half-hour late—

there had been cows on the track and the trainmen had been compelled to get out and extricate one from a trestle, the conductor said when he swung down from the coach. He appeared to show quite a solicitous attitude toward the girl as she came down the car steps. Evidently they had become rather good friends on the ride out.

Amy was lovely, Ella admitted that to herself. She was small-boned, softly rounded, the delicate pink of her flesh the texture of a baby's. Her wide eyes, too, were child-like in their blue candor. She wore a little gray dolman trimmed with baby blue, and a little stiff gray hat with blue cornflowers on it. It gave her the appearance of a soft little turtle dove, with a blue ruff. And she was fragrant with the scent of her letter—something that reminded Ella vaguely of the cloying sweetness of waxy-white mayflowers.

Also she was a helpless sort of little thing, Ella could see. She was not sure of anything,—her baggage, her checks, her way about. Delbert looked after everything for her and she thanked him so prettily that he flushed with pleasure.

"She makes me think of a kitten," he told Ella afterward, "a fluffy little kitten."

What was it Delbert had once said about kittens? Oh, yes, she remembered,—they were all right to flirt with— She put the thought quickly from her mind.

After supper, Delbert came for the girls and the three walked through the soft April night to the charade party at Irene Van Ness's home. The big house was bright from top to bottom,—hanging lamps with glass pendants and side lamps in brackets on the walls gave forth their limit of light. The heavy walnut furniture, the dark chenille portières, the thick-flowered Brussels carpet, and the Nottingham lace curtains, all looked rich in the night lights. Silver gleamed on the sideboard, and one caught whiffs of chicken and oysters when the kitchen door swung back. It was rumored that Mr. Van Ness had even ordered Sam Peters to send to Florida for a box of oranges.

Irene had on a new rich plum-colored satin—square cut in the front, from which her neck rose scrawnily, her dull complexion challenged by the purplish shade of the dress.

When Ella came downstairs with Amy, she was plainly aware of the admiring whispers that went around. Amy did look lovely—"bewitching" Chester Peters said before every one, so that Irene flushed a little. She wore pink silk, her plump form squeezed into the hour-glass shape which was the mode of the day, the low-cut front revealing the milky whiteness of her flesh. Her hair was a high mass of yellow curls through which a black ribbon was drawn, the one touch of mourning for her recent loss. Her wide blue eyes stared at the new-found friends with babyish candor. She had the merest suggestion of an impediment in her speech which certain of the young bloods there seemed to find quite entrancing, as they formed a little circle around her almost immediately.

At the end of the evening of charades and singing around the piano, a few dancing games, and the consumption of much rich food, there was no little rivalry over seeing Amy home. Chet Peters high-handedly won her promise, but when he was waiting at the foot of the stairs for her, Delbert tried to put him off with a curt: "No, you don't. I brought her and I'll see to her myself." Chet, however, won his point and carried Amy off into the warm spring moonlight.

When they left, Ella could see that Irene was making an ineffectual attempt to keep back the tears.

In the days that followed, the whole crowd knew that Chet Peters was quite mad about Amy Saunders. It worried Ella to the depths, to a great measure spoiled the days which should have been so happy. Irene was her best friend and was now too hurt to come to see her. It all made an upsetting state of affairs.

"Oh, why did she have to come just now?" Ella sometimes said to her mother.

But her mother was vague, uncertain what to say, could only look to Ella for decisions on the subject.

And Amy? Sometimes she went with him as coolly as any woman of the world and sometimes she clung to Delbert and Ella as though she were a child and afraid of Chet's ardent wooing. Ella could not read the girl clearly. Was she too young and innocent to know her own mind? Did she honestly dislike Chester? Or was she assuming a virtue when she had it not?

"I like him," she said one day to them both, her blue eyes wide and soft and child-like. And added with engaging candor, "But I like Delbert better." And to Ella, with a half-sad little smile: "You're the one I envy."

She said it so prettily that Delbert flushed with pleasure.

Ella scarcely knew what to say. Among all the girls of her acquaintance in her four school years,—among all the girls in the classes of her two teaching years,—she had not known one quite like Amy. She was so sweet, so guileless,—and yet,— This time, instead of vague Mrs. Bishop, it was Ella, herself, who could not finish a sentence.

CHAPTER X

ON the Saturday that Delbert was to drive to Maynard on business and to which Ella had looked forward, Amy remarked with her usual beguiling candor that it was such a lovely day she wished *she* could go too. There seemed nothing to do but to take her. One could scarcely conceive of leaving the young guest behind to sit in the house on such a spring day.

So the trip that was to have been almost a wedding journey became a rather different sort of thing. Ella felt cross as they started, chiding herself for having a beastly disposition, but on the long drive with the Judge's horses keeping up a steady swing, the scent of the spring day in the air, and Amy and Delbert gay and talkative, her unquenchable spirits rose too, and she felt such a magnanimity toward all mankind that her momentary disappointment was forgotten.

When they were ready to make the return trip, Amy placed herself in the middle of the seat. "I'm the littl'st," she said with her faint suggestion of a lisp. "I want to sit between you so I won't fall out."

Ella felt provoked at the absurd childishness, but Delbert laughed.

The horses were not so fresh as in the morning and the drive seemed longer. Amy quieted and fell asleep as they jogged along.

"She's like a baby instead of a young lady, isn't she?" he said to Ella—and with his finger tips touched the creamy whiteness of the curve under her chin. At which Amy sighed and moved in her sleep so that her head fell over against his shoulder.

At home Ella sprang as nimbly to the ground as her long skirts would allow, but Amy, rousing from her nap and yawning, made such hard work of it that Delbert helped her down carefully. As she put her foot on the carriage step, she slipped and would have fallen if he had not caught her. For a long moment she lay smiling in his arms until he set her hurriedly on the horse-block.

The first of May Ella bought the goods for her dresses—twenty yards of lovely silk with nosegays of flowers strewn over its snow whiteness and sixteen yards of wide stiff blue silk and four dozen wooden buttons to be covered with the same material. She opened the packages on the bed in her room and could scarcely take her eyes from the beauty of the white one, the little bouquets of pale pink rosebuds and baby-blue forget-me-nots standing out in silken relief against the shimmering background.

Amy came in to see them, and went into such esctasies over the white silk—her enjoyment of its loveliness so genuine—that Ella told herself she would forever forget all the impatience with her she had ever felt. The girl was merely immature—her joy lay in the material world almost entirely. As for the future, she would let that take care of itself for a time. Amy would not want to stay with them forever,—she would marry,—Chet, perhaps, as he was apparently infatuated with her. At any rate she was the type that married young. Never again would she let the actions of the girl displease her—now that she was assured of their naturalness.

In the late afternoon Ella took the package of silk to the little weather-beaten house where the dressmaker lived.

The woman was quite excited over the news that she could have the honor of making them. "I've heard of you, Miss Bishop, and saw you, and my neighbor girl here next door has went to you, and she says you're the best teacher she ever seen in her life. She says you make them students talk right. Well, gracious, I says to her, it's the Lord that gives you your talkin'—what can a mere teacher do about it? But I guess I got to admit maybe the Lord'n you is in cahoots."

But it did not take Ella long to realize that maltreating the king's English had very little to do with the woman's natural knack for dressmaking. She brought out a lovely pale blue silk,—"for Irene Van Ness,"—glowing with pride at the name of the customer. "She has always went with that Chester Peters 'n while I wouldn't want any girl of mine to tie up with him—I guess there's plenty about him—there's them that must have their own ideas. But they say she's eatin' her heart out over jealousy of some girl here visitin'. The rich has their troubles the same as us dressmakers, I guess."

Ella said she must get right at the planning for it was growing late. So the woman brought out her "Colored Plates of Ladies of Fashion" and was immediately lost to the world of gossip.

In the days that followed, Ella made many trips to the little weather-beaten house in the far end of town. Having a dress made in the eighties was having a monument built.

On a Wednesday afternoon in the last of May she felt almost too tired to stand through the long ordeal of the fitting. School all day, doing her portion of the housework when home, then the fitting,—and still the day was not over, for she and Amy were going up the river with Delbert after supper.

"I wonder if the time will ever come that one can walk into a store and buy a dress all made," she said to the woman down on her knees.

The dressmaker shifted two or three pins with the muscles of her mouth. "Good land, no. The' ain't no two sets o' hips 'n busts 'n shoulders in the world alike. No—that's *one* thing ain't never goin' to be invented by nobody. 'Til the end o' the world folks has got to have dresses made for ev'ry separate one."

When Ella arrived home, Delbert was there, and also there was word awaiting her to come to President Corcoran's office at seven-thirty to a hastily called meeting of the faculty over some Commencement difficulty.

"That settles going up the river," she said.

"Oh, no," Amy pouted, "I want to go."

Ella ignored it and turned to Delbert. "You know, Delbert, I wouldn't want any one to hold a single criticism against my work if I could help it. No one can say that I've not done my duty right up to the last."

"Of course not, Ella. It's right, too."

Amy's big china-blue eyes filled with tears. "I'm so disappointed. This beautiful evening—there's going to be a moon. I've counted all day on going. You see, Ella, you and Delbert are out all day." Her soft lips quivered, "But when I'm just here with Auntie, I look forward to little things like this."

"Where's Chester?" Ella was a little tart in tone.

Delbert answered that Chester was with his father who was having two men in the office for business—farmers who had made the date with him. Then he added: "I could take her, Ella—if she's so disappointed. We could walk over to school with you first and then go back down to the river."

Ella thought of her own self at Amy's age—she was nearly nineteen—remembered her self-reliance and self-discipline, and felt a disgust for her cousin's childishness and an annoyance at Delbert's succumbing to the soft little wiles of the girl.

She shrugged a lithe shoulder. "Oh, of course—she ought to be taken," she admitted dryly, and went for her own wraps.

Amy recovered her spirits then, chattered gayly all the way to Central Hall, left Ella with, "You're not mad are you, Ella?" Tired as she was, it took all of Ella's self-control to maintain her poise.

"How long do you think you'll be in the meeting, Ella?" Delbert was wanting to know.

"I haven't the least idea." To save herself she could not help an acidity creeping into her tones.

"I'll probably be waiting here in the hall for you."

"You needn't bother."

She went in to the office, thoroughly annoyed at her own annoyance. "Sometimes I think I'm my own worst enemy," she said to herself.

The meeting lasted late, involving as it did a necessary change of plans and their attendant preparations for Commencement. During the entire time Ella held herself to the line of duty, schooling herself in the concentration of her part in it.

When she came out, she looked about. But there was no one in the hall.

She walked across the campus with Professor Cunningham and Miss McAlister, scorning the idea that they accompany her on down Adams Street to her home, went into the house where the lamp was still burning for her and on up the enclosed stairway to her own room. There she undressed, got into her long white cambric nightgown with its embroidered yoke, and brushed her thick dark hair. When she was ready for bed, she took her lamp with its red flannel in the kerosene bowl and tiptoed down the length of the hall to Amy's room. Cautiously pushing back the door and holding her hand in front of the light in order not to disturb the sleeping girl, she looked in. Amy was not there.

A cold icy hand clutched Ella's heart and strangled her breathing. The gray deep river—a leaky flat-bottomed boat—or an upset canoe—or a fall from a rocky ledge—or—or—

She felt, rather than saw, her way back into her room, blew out the light to have the sheltering darkness, sat stiffly on the edge of the bed to stare into the enfolding blackness.

After a long time she heard the far sound of the outside door, the closer creak of the stair one, and the softly padded tiptoeing of the girl down the hall.

Ella lay back on her pillow. But for an hour or more she continued to stare into the engulfing darkness.

CHAPTER XI

☙ Morning and sunshine and the sweet May odors from the yard brought to Ella clearer vision and a mind swept of all doubts. Why should humans—decent souls who despised the perfidious—

ever be besieged by disturbing and disloyal questions? It was not worthy of her,—was not trustful of the love which had been given her. As she dressed she made a little prayer to the God of Lovers,—and the humble request was: "Keep us both from unworthy thoughts."

She left the house cheerfully, before Amy had come down. All day long at school she was busy and contented. In the late afternoon at home she found Amy demure and gentle, slipping quietly about the house doing a simple task or two. Some May-apple blossoms drooped limply over the side of a vase,—mute reminder of the river trip.

"That's one flower should stay in its natural woodsy habitat," Ella said gayly. "Never pull a mandrake."

She did not notice that Amy's wide blue eyes looked up, startled and fearful.

Delbert did not come in the evening. Sometimes he had extra work and stayed at the office. Neither was there any word from him, for the telephone was but a new toy being tried out by a handful of people in the east.

Chester drove up in the new buggy with the prancing blacks, but when Amy saw him, she said hurriedly to Mrs. Bishop: "Tell him I have a headache"—and ran up the enclosed stairway.

Friday morning Ella went as usual to school, her active mind placing all the day's tasks in neat pigeon-holes: classes, a test on diagraming, see Professor Wick about Clarence Caldwell, meet with Miss McAlister and Professor Cunningham on a committee, go to Mrs. Finch's for a fitting, ask Irene about some music for the Alumni—the third banquet, now, with thirty-three graduates eligible to attend.

A busy morning—and then in the afternoon just before the one o'clock class was called, Chris Jensen came to Ella's recitation room, tiptoeing with noisy boots—squeak—squeak—all the way down the length of it. He grinned as he handed her a sealed note.

"Iss dis somet'ing you can use?"

"Thank you, Chris."

"Pleased to do t'ings for you, Miss Bis'op."

The note was in Delbert's handwriting so that Ella slipped into her office to open it alone. Sometimes he sent her these little messages by Chris,—about nothing at all.

She tore into the envelope with its *Peters, Peters and Thompson* in one corner.

But *this*,—this was different. Ella's heart pounded strangely at the queer letter and the same icy hand of Wednesday evening clutched at her throat.

DEAR ELLA:

Something has happened. I must see you this evening,—and talk with you.

DELBERT.

What—oh what had happened? Something that night. Why must Delbert talk with her? About something of that night. Why had he sent a note at all? He could come any time he wished. It was preparing her. For what? For something about that night.

Like the tom-toms of the jungle it beat its monotonous refrain: *Something that night.*

The one o'clock bell rang directly over her head with loud clamorous insistence, and the pigeons flew out in noisy response, their wings brushing the windows. The bell! The bell meant service to others. Oh, no, not now,—not this afternoon when something had happened. The bell meant obligations. No, no,—nothing was important but that something had happened,—something vital,—something more serious than classes, —something to do with the things of the heart. The bell meant duty. Duty! One's duty had to be performed, no matter under what stress. Go on in there like a soldier. But something has happened, I tell you. Stop whimpering. *Go!*

Head up, Ella stepped into her classroom.

All afternoon she could hear the pigeons coo and their wings beat against the bell. And then to her tormented mind they were no longer softly cooing pigeons but great black bats that, like her thoughts, would not stay away. They swirled about her head, harassing and torturing her —the bats and the thoughts. They flew about her in all their ugliness, through the work of the three periods.

"The definition, please, for a transitive verb."

Something has happened.

"Name the principal parts . . ."

I must see you this evening.

"What type of clause do we prefer there?"

Something has happened.

CHAPTER XII

☙ ELLA taught all her classes. She walked down to Mrs. Finch's and stood through a tedious and loquacious fitting. She found her mother not feeling well and put cold packs on her head.

When the bell rings, the Ella Bishops of the world answer the summons.

But she could eat no supper. She sat at the table and made futile little stabs at her plate, nibbling a saleratus biscuit, so her mother would not notice and worry.

Amy cast furtive glances at the two occasionally, her long thick lashes sweeping her cheeks whenever she looked away. Mrs. Bishop made plaintive and tedious remarks about the dull pain in her head. It was a tense meal.

"I'll wash the dishes," Amy volunteered with feigned lightness.

"No, I'll do them myself." Ella wanted activity for her body to deaden the constant questioning of her mind.

When she heard Delbert open the picket-gate and come up the board walk, she slipped outside and met him under the rank growth of the trumpet-vine at the edge of the porch. He stood and stared at her with no word. By the rays from the dining-room lamp, she could see that he was haggard, his lips drawn taut.

"What *is* it?" The thing was now frightening her beyond endurance.

"Let's walk, Ella. I have to tell you something. Let's get away . . . from the house." He threw a nervous glance toward the lamplight beyond the screen door against which a June-bug was thumping noisily.

"No." She heard her own voice as though coming from far off and detected the terror in it. "Tell it *now*. Right *here*." She felt that she was choking, so that she put both hands across the beating pulse of her throat.

"It's . . . about Amy." His voice sounded desperate.

She knew it. Something had been trying to tell her so for days. And she had refused to listen. Now in the flash of a split second she knew that she had sensed the thing from the first.

"You love her." She found herself saying it for him. In her whole life to come no one would ever accuse Ella Bishop of sidestepping the truth. Some sturdy element inherited from her pioneer father gave her strength to shoulder the hard part of the interview. Even now, in the crisis of the tense moment, she had a swift understanding of herself, a sudden fleeting premonition that she was always to do that for other people—assume their burdens.

"I . . . I . . . am afraid so." He was breathing hard,—was suffering. "Come over here . . . where we can talk . . ." He put his hand on hers to draw her to a bench in the yard. Ella pulled it back as from a striking reptile.

"Let me explain, Ella." His voice sounded as though he had been running. "When I went up the river with her, I *swear* to you . . ."

"No . . . that's enough."

She turned away.

He called her desperately: "Ella . . . come back."

But she had gone, in one swift flash, back into the house—the screen door clicking sharply behind her. Up the stairs with running feet—up to the darkness of her room—up to face despair—up to the black midnight of—

But in front of her own bedroom door Amy met her, barring the way to that dark haven.

"Oh, Ella, whatever will you say to me?" She tried to put her hand on Ella's arm, but pulled it back at the sight of the older girl's wild face.

Suddenly she began to cry, little, superficial, cowardly tears. "Ella . . . I'm sorry. I never meant to."

Meant to.

Ella stared, white-faced, at the soft pink features contorted into a baby-like expression of fear until Amy cowered before her.

"What are you going to do about it?" the young girl looked out between trembling fingers.

Do! Do!

"Ella, you aren't . . . you don't think you can still marry him, do you?" Genuine fright was in the soft voice.

Ella glared at the human who could conceive the thought. The young girl misinterpreted the long icy silence,—all the unanswered questions,—for suddenly she took her hands from her face and said dryly, with a little jaunty twitch of her shoulder. "Well, you can't. He *can't* marry you now. I'll have you know that."

It was with fascinated horror that Ella gazed now at the girl. What? What? Oh, what?

She wet her moist lips, tried to make the words come. Her knees were water.

"You mean . . . ?"

"Well . . . he has to marry me . . . now."

"You . . . you little . . . *animal*," Ella said. And crumpled to the floor.

CHAPTER XIII

ALL night and a day Ella lay on the bed in her darkened room without removing her dress. All night and a day she crushed her face into the pillow and prayed to die. "Don't let me live. Please don't let me live," was her constant petition.

Her mother tiptoed to the door at intervals,—plead plaintively with her daughter to see her. But there is no sharing Gethsemane with another. When one crosses the brook of Cedron into the Garden, one goes alone.

Toward evening there was a different voice at the door,—Amy's childish one. "I'm going, Ella." And in a moment: "Ella, . . . let me see you a moment before I go, won't you?" And when there was no answer, "Ella, don't be mad. Please don't be mad."

Ella wrapped the pillow about her head and moaned into its feathery depths.

At dusk she heard a buggy drive up. Her ears sharpened by distress conveyed the fact to her that there was more movement in the house than there had been all day. A door slammed twice, there was a sound of a man's low voice—Delbert's—the dragging of a trunk or box, a high childish call of "Good-by, Auntie." And the world had come to an end for Ella Bishop.

Toward morning, she pulled the clothes from her exhausted body and got into her gown. For the first time, she felt that she wanted her mother. Like a little girl, bruised and hurt, she crept down the stairs, felt her way through the darkness of the rooms, into her mother's bedroom, and crawled into bed with her.

"Mamma—comfort me." It was the cry of a wounded thing.

But her mother's heart was pounding so furiously from the shock, and she said her head was splitting so terribly, that in a few minutes Ella got up and dressed again and gave her medicine and wrung out cold compresses for her. So after all, it was Ella who did the comforting.

Sunday passed with tragic nerve-racking slowness. Once she threw out some dead mandrake blossoms and scrubbed the vase vigorously, as though she would cleanse it from all past association with the cloying odor of the waxy flower. Like a haunted thing then her mind would again travel in sickly imaginings up the river where an empty boat was nosed into the wet sand, drag itself up the bank and creep into the nearby woods where the May-apples grew in shady cloistered places—She would moan aloud in the agony of her mental illness and dark despair.

On Monday morning she dragged herself to her classroom. Duty—obligations—service. These await every one who comes out of the Garden.

"Oh, Miss Bishop, have you been sick?" a freshman girl asked.

"Just a Sunday headache," she answered with studied composure.

All day she taught with painstaking thoroughness. Not all the world's heroines are listed in the archives.

"Another use of the participle should be kept in mind."

Where did they go last night?

"Analyze it orally, giving attention to the function of the participle."

She's a cunning little thing—like a kitten.

Not a student could have detected any let-down in the detailed instruction. Ella Bishop's heart-break was her own.

She stayed until five, assisting a pretty young girl with an outline for an essay. The student was only four years younger than the teacher, but to Ella, noting the girl's spontaneous smile, there seemed all the difference between blooming youth and tragic old age.

When the work was finished, she put on her hat and walked down through the June sunshine, redolent with the odors of Commencement, across town to Mrs. Finch's weather-beaten house.

The little dressmaker greeted her with: "Well, well, here comes the bride." And before Ella could respond she added: "The blue one is all finished to the last stitch, but *the* one has to have another fitting, so I'm glad you've came."

Ella held herself together with studied effort. There would be a great deal of this to meet now, and she must face it with composure. "You won't need to finish it, Mrs. Finch. I'm not going to use it."

"Oh—you'll wear the blue instead? But I *wouldn't*, Miss Bishop . . ."

"You don't understand. I'm not getting married at all."

"Oh, Miss *Bishop*. You don't . . . ?" But something formidable in Ella's face made her stop abruptly.

"Sometimes one just changes one's mind," Ella said quietly.

Mrs. Finch was embarrassed. She hardly knew how to proceed. "You'll take the blue one with you then?"

"Yes," said Ella.

"And how . . . about . . . ?"

"The white?" I'll take it too."

"Just the unfinished way . . . with the bottom not hemmed . . . and the sleeves not sewed in?"

"Yes."

She brought it out of an inner room—a shimmering mass of white with little bouquets of pale pink rosebuds and blue forget-me-nots in silken relief against the snowy background—a lovely white monument for the grave of a dead hope, with flowers for remembrance.

With much fumbling of paper and dropping of string the little dressmaker did up the two dresses, the blue one and the white one and the long mousquetaire sleeves of the white which had not been sewed in.

When Ellen took the money out of her purse, the woman said sympathetically: "Just for the blue, Miss Bishop. I wouldn't like to . . . take anything for the other . . . unfinished that way and . . . not to be used just now."

"Thank you—but I pay my obligations," Ella said firmly. And left with the finished blue dress and the unfinished white one which was not to be used just then—or ever.

CHAPTER XIV

AFTER supper Sam came across the street, stepping gingerly around through the young hollyhocks of the back door. When Ella met him at the entrance to the little porch, he stood in embarrassment, his thin throat with its prominent Adam's apple working convulsively.

"I know all about it, Ella."

"Please—Sam—don't talk of it."

"I won't, Ella—now or ever. But I have to tell you one or two things,—it's necessary. I thought if I came right now and got it over, I wouldn't have to bother you any more. Delbert severed his connections with father . . . and left town. You won't . . . won't have to be seeing him. And Chet's gone away."

"Gone . . . where?"

"St. Louis. Father owns a little property there. Chet went to transact some business in connection with it. He just didn't want to stay here longer. He was"—Sam looked up in embarrassment—"quite madly in love with Amy."

"Yes. And Irene?"

"He doesn't care anything for her."

"No—he doesn't. Poor Irene."

For a little while they stood at the back stoop, saying nothing—both in frozen misery.

Sam broke the stony silence then with: "I'd give anything in the world, Ella, to have you happy again."

"I know, Sam. And I'm grateful to you."

"That's one thing I came to say. If ever . . . if you need me, I'll always be there . . . right across the street."

"Thank you, Sam."

"You may seem pretty strong and self-reliant, Ella, but maybe there are times you'd need to . . . sort of lean on some one . . ."

It broke Ella. She, who had held her head high all day, suddenly burst into wild tears. Great wrenching sobs shook her,—and when she was spent with the rocking torture of them, Sam, with untold misery in his eyes, was saying: "That's good for you, Ella—a kind of outlet. God knows, I wish it was the last tear you'd ever have to shed in your life."

So Chester Peters had left town for awhile in the despondency of a weak and hopeless infatuation for Amy. The trail of wreckage left behind her coming was quite complete.

On Tuesday, Ella asked to see President Corcoran after school alone in his office. With no preliminaries she asked if her position had been filled, and when told that it had not been as yet, without evasive excuses she inquired whether or not she could retain it.

President Corcoran's bright black eyes looked at her quizzically through the steel-bowed glasses above the Spanish moss of his beard.

"But your other plans, Miss Ella? I ask only with kindest motives."

"I understand, President Corcoran. I've changed my mind. Am not . . . getting married . . ." If her voice faltered, it was only for a moment. "Probably I never shall."

"I see."

The President sat quietly looking out on the raw new campus with the barrel-staves around the bases of the young elms and maples.

"You are a fine young woman, Miss Ella," he said in a moment. "You would make the young man a splendid wife. If there is any uncertainty . . . yet . . . in your mind?" It was half question, half fatherly advice.

Ella, holding her lips together in a quivering line, shook her head.

"I see."

He waited another moment, thoughtfully, then reached to a pigeon-hole of his desk and withdrew a handful of letters,—apparently a dozen or fifteen,—and dropped them into the cavernous wastebasket at his side.

"Applications," he remarked casually, and held out his hand. "It will be all right with the board, I know."

Ella took the hand which pressed her own in paternal sympathy, but she could not trust herself to speak.

In a moment he asked: "You will devote your fine young energies to the students of this school?"

Something suddenly ran through her body and heart and mind with the thought—some feeling of emotion, which was too deep for analysis.

"It's a wonderful work," the steady voice went on. "It's something like carrying a torch to light the paths for all the boys and girls with whom you come in contact. In dollars and cents it does not pay much—perhaps it never will. For myself—I know I might be able to make more money another way. I have just this spring had that very question to settle. My brother-in-law has wanted me to go into a new manufacturing business with him for which the financial prospects seem extremely good. I have had my struggle with myself and made my decision. I shall teach,—even when the school grows and I need no longer conduct any classes, the contacts will be the same."

When Ella did not speak he went on. "There is no way in the world, Miss Ella, to hold to one's youth. Time passes so quickly. To-day I'm forty. Tomorrow I shall be sixty,—day after tomorrow, eighty. The only way I know to hold on to those fleeting years is to bind myself to youth. If in these swiftly moving years I can pass on a little of that living flame from the torch I carry . . . if I can help light the long steep paths for young people . . . the service I have rendered will be its own reward."

It touched Ella deeply. For days she had prayed for strength to take up her life—asked that something come into her mind and heart to help in blotting out the bitter thing she had experienced. This was it. Quite unexpectedly President Corcoran was helping make it possible to think of something else, to turn from the anguish that held her prisoner day and night.

She, whose life had been clean, seemed to have touched in the last few days the unclean. Some smothering vapor of impurity had blown upon her with heavy sickening May-apple odor, and she wanted to get away from its noxious breath.

This was cleansing. This was purifying. *To pass on the living flame.* That would be her life work. It would take the place of—of this other thing that had besmirched her. She would dedicate her life to it,—throw herself into the work zealously as one might go to a mission field.

Standing there in the plain, half-furnished executive office of the six-year-old struggling college,—with the sincere words of its earnest president still in her ears, Ella Bishop took a vow.

"I will, too," she said solemnly to her inner self. "I, too, will carry on the living flame. I dedicate my life to it—to the students of *this* college. I will stay young with them, help them, serve them. My whole life is theirs. The fleeting years! The torch! The living flame!"

For the first time in agonizing days a faint semblance of calmness enveloped her being—almost a feeling of exaltation uplifted her soul. It was as though, stripped of all earthly longings, she stood before an altar—as though, turning aside from desires of the flesh, she took the veil.

CHAPTER XV

☙ BUT one may not stay on the heights for any length of time. It is not given to humans to breathe the rarefied atmosphere of Olympus continuously. So while Ella Bishop never forgot those moments of priestess-like exaltation, she was to experience them only occasionally, recapture their dignity and glory at rare intervals in her life.

For the most part, the summer was one continuous battle against her constantly rising emotions,—one long period of bitter days and wide-eyed nights. Strangely enough, her greatest comfort was digging in the garden. She who had never cared for the raising of flowers as her mother did, whose love for books had been her hobby, now cared little for the printed word. Books? They were cold—only the ground was warm.

Stories? They were lifeless—only the good earth had vitality. Fiction characters? They were puppets,—only the sturdy blossoms were real. Poems? They were pallid,—only the green grass in the wind knew the rhythm of song.

All that summer she spent every hour which could be spared from the house, working among the flowers. With spade and trowel, seeds and slips, she dug and planted, reset and watered. Prone on the ground with the warm brown earth running through her fingers, she came nearer to respite from the constant aching of her bruised self than at any other time.

"There is something elemental about us all," she thought, "something soothing about contacting our own dust with the life-giving dust of the earth."

Strangely enough, she never spoke of her tragedy to her mother, and her mother, less strong-minded than Ella, took the cue from her daughter's silence and never mentioned it either. But stranger still was the fact that the one person to whom she could speak of it in its bald entirety was Sam Peters.

And then on a warm July morning when Ella was weeding poppies, Sam came across the street. As soon as she saw his pale drawn face and the convulsive working of his thin mouth and chin, she knew he came with trouble.

"Why, Sam, what is it?" She got up from the red-blossomed bed and met him at the edge of the garden.

"It's Chet. He's . . . drowned."

"Drowned?" The dull word sounded like a hollow bell tolled in the distance.

"Yes. He . . . He was on a Mississippi river-boat. The telegram says he just . . . disappeared from the boat. Father's going . . . to St. Louis . . . to find out. I'm to stay with Mother. My God, Ella . . ." The thin little man sank down on the garden seat. "Why couldn't it have been me?"

"Don't say that, Sam."

"But it ought to have . . . what do I amount to? But Chet . . . Chet's brilliant. And Father. . . ." His thin body shook with boyish sobs.

Here was grief again—grief, too, that went back to Amy's coming. For if Chet had not been infatuated with Amy, he would not have gone away —would not have been on a river-boat. Suddenly, with surprising clarity, Ella questioned in her own mind whether the death had been accidental.

It was only a few weeks later—after Judge Peters had returned from his investigation, crushed and bowed, with all the pompous jauntiness out of his walk, that Irene went east to visit relatives. The day before she left, Ella made herself go over to see her, dreading the interview as one dreads any disagreeable task.

But Irene was much calmer than Ella had expected to find her. "I've gone over everything in my mind a thousand times," she said, her thin face wistful. "And I guess there's something about the whole thing that we can't any of us see—something that just had to be for the good of us all—something we may never know—fate maybe—or destiny."

Ella was thankful beyond words when September came,—and work. It is life's most potent medicine for grief. She threw herself into it with mental and physical abandon. And when her heart did not follow, she chided it for sitting on the sidelines and watching her mind and body labor. "Lazy!" she figuratively called to it. "Numbskull" She used some of her ready sarcasm on it. "You think you're crushed and ruined for life, don't you? Well, you're not. Even yet a real man may come riding by. Then you'll be the thing for which you were intended—the heart of a wife and mother."

To ease her pain she tried to picture again some man she might one day love, attempted to conjecture up an attractive new face and features. But all she could see was Delbert smiling down at her with fresh young lips, as he looked before— She would throw herself across her bed and moan aloud in the depths of her unconquered despair.

All winter she held herself with ferocious tenacity to her work. She managed freshman social events, was head of the college young people's inter-church society, was on the Minerva board advisory group, and chairman of the refreshment committee for the Faculty Circle.

"I know a lovely new way to serve potatoes to the Circle members," Professor Cunningham's very domestic wife would say. "First, you mash them . . ."

"The faculty members?" Ella would say languidly.

"Oh, you go on, Ella Bishop," laughingly, "and then you put them on the plate with an ice-cream mold and there they stand up just as cunning, like little pyramids with a clove at the top."

"A clove? Why a clove? Why not a clothes-pin or a prune?" Ella's apparently unquenchable spirits would rise. "I've always wondered if there could be a clove on top of any of the pyramids."

Every one would laugh.

"Thank goodness, I'll always be like that," she would say to herself. And then, as though she had just made a discovery, "I believe on the outside I'll always be gay and lively."

CHAPTER XVI

THE winter was long, cold, snowy. January was one succession of stormy weeks after another with snow heaped over the campus and piled high on the roof of Central Hall. Chris Jensen, shoveling the wooden sidewalk all day, his strong arms throwing out the white drifts, would turn around only to see those paths refilled by the wind-gods.

February was no better. The tips of the young trees on the campus looked thin and black against the opaque sky, with the wind whipping the brittle branches into a rattling fury.

On the third of the month, school was dismissed for a few days on account of a coal shortage. Ella dreaded the enforced intermission, knowing that the very inactivity of it would depress her.

On the afternoon of the first day of the recess a strange man drove up in a bob-sled and hitched his team to the post by the horse-block. Ella, watching him from the window, had a queer feeling that the stranger's coming was portentous. She could not have told why, but she suddenly felt herself grow nervously expectant. He came on up the walk between the drifts, swinging his arms together to bring warmth to them. His long drooping mustache was frozen white, an icy horseshoe above the muffler he wore.

Always afterwards Ella wondered what peculiar phenomenon it was whereby she sensed that he came bearing strange tidings.

Her heart pounding queerly, she opened the door.

"Be you Miss Ella Bishop?"

"Yes."

"If I could come in . . . I got a letter here . . ."

"Oh yes, yes, come in."

Something made her walk over to the kitchen door and protectingly close it upon her mother making mince pies to be frozen for the month's use.

A letter! Letters were strange things. They brought happiness and comfort and companionship, but,—she caught her breath,—sometimes they brought black grief.

The man was having difficulty in producing it, what with two woolen jackets and an overcoat to search.

When he had produced and given it to her, Ella's fingers trembled at the tearing. It was from Delbert Thompson—a pale, sprawling letter of stark appeal.

Ella, I am sick—on my last bed. If you have a heart in you—and oh, Ella, I know you have—come back with the man who brings this. It's the last thing I'll ever ask you . . . for the time is short. Hurry. Please.

Wild thoughts sprang to Ella's mind,—mad thoughts that leaped and chased each other through her hot brain. No. She was through with him,—done forever with him and his little—

If you have a heart in you. That was good, that was! Who but Delbert Thompson knew whether or not she had one?

The man, standing with his arms around the sheet-iron wood-burner, shuffled and stepped about restlessly, soft chunks of snow melting from his high boots.

"Pretty bad, I guess," he volunteered. "Can't last long. Wife poorly, too."

"Where are they living?" Ella heard herself asking in a voice that seemed to come from the far end of the room, like a ventriloquist's.

"Maynard. Next door to me. I run a livery stable. But I come for nothin'. I said I ain't one to charge a dyin' man for an errand I can do."

Ella stood, tense and white, and stared at the man with his thawing horseshoe mustache and his big boots that smelled of his calling.

"I'll be ready in a few minutes," she said.

Her mother was upset. "Oh, Ella . . . a man who . . . who . . ." She had meant to say "jilted you," but something in Ella's stern face kept her from it. She darted about here and there excitedly, her small dainty hands still white from the flour board.

All the time Ella was throwing a few things together, she was saying to herself, "I'm like this. I'll always be like this. People can beat me and lash me, and I'll turn around and lick their hands if they need me. Weak! Emotionally weak as water."

She bundled up in two coats and woolen tights, leggings and four-buckled overshoes, put on ear-laps and tied a woolen fascinator around her hat. Her mother had warmed the soapstone in the oven and wrapped it in a flannel shawl. A fifteen-mile winter ride in an open sleigh on a prairie road in the eighties was a thing with which to reckon.

The ride seemed interminable. Sometimes the two went miles without conversation, for when they opened their mouths to speak, the cold damp air rushed in to fill their lungs, which seemed to collapse like bellows.

On the last part of the trip the cold penetrated the buffalo robes so that Ella's tumbling thoughts even ceased their eternal questioning, her emotions were calm,—the benumbed physical holding complete sway over the turbulent mental.

It was nearly dark when the man drove up to a square house on the outskirts of the town. Ella could see a woman pulling down and lighting a hanging-lamp, a child pressing its face against a window.

"Here we be," he commented, and added, "Thank the Lord. My woman said to bring you into our house first to thaw out. She's been over a lot to the Thompsons'. Guess she's home now, though."

Ella went in, her limbs so stiff with cold that she staggered as she walked. She removed her wraps and sat down by a red-hot sheet-iron wood stove, but the sudden change from the intense cold to the closeness of the room made her feel a little giddy.

The woman flew about noisily, dishing up the supper, chattering, clucking her sympathy: "Poor little thing . . . tsk . . . tsk . . . ," stopping to whisper something to Ella that the child might not hear.

Ella ate a little, without tasting what she consumed. Her body craved sustenance, but under the nervous strain of the ordeal, rebelled at food.

The woman was curious, distressingly loquacious:

"Let's see . . . you're Mis' Thompson's cousin?"

"Yes."

"Let's see, now . . . how long have they been married?"

"I think it was sometime in April or May."

"Tsk . . . tsk . . . the very first thing," whispering a comment.

And when Ella was disappointingly silent: "Did you know Mr. Thompson, too?"

"Yes."

After supper she went over, stepping high through the snowdrifts in her four-buckled overshoes. At the porch of the little shoe-box of a cottage she paused: "Stay with me," she said to some unseen source of strength.

There was a single light in the main room. On hearing the door open Amy came from the dim bedroom. At the sight of Ella she began to cry, weak tears that distorted her pretty, swollen face and shook her misshapen body.

"She's here," she whispered back to the gloom of the bedroom, and apparently with no rancor at Ella's meeting alone with the sick man, crossed over to the far side of the living-room and sat down heavily.

Ella went alone into the chamber of death.

Yes, he was dying. She could see that. This was Delbert dying, she told herself coolly. She would not let herself feel emotion; made of her heart and mind cold and callous things. For a moment she stood by the side of the bed with no word. The dying man only looked at her, searching her face for the answer to some question—perhaps the queer question of why everything came to be as it was.

"Ella!" He touched her hand feebly with a clammy finger.

She drew the member back, shocked at her repulsion to the contact.

"It was all wrong, Ella. Nothing was right . . . but it's too late now . . . God, I've suffered." It was agony for him to talk. "There's no time to waste in going over it."

And when she made no comment, he went on:

"I wanted you to come . . . I had to . . . to look you in the eyes once, Ella . . . your clear, clean eyes . . . and say it was all wrong . . . and tell you . . . I love you . . ." He paused for a renewal of strength, and then went on: "Tell me, Ella . . . will you take her home with you a little while? Just 'til afterward? She's no place to turn. Promise me, Ella. I can't go like this—thinking she's nowhere to go. Poor child! Poor little . . . kitten."

Ella stiffened. "You're asking a hard thing." Her voice, breaking its silence for the first time, sounded as harsh and rasping as a buzz-saw in the still room.

"Yes, I know. It seems terrible . . . but more terrible not to. You can . . . ask strange things . . . when you're dying. Please, Ella . . . just through her hard time. After that, I can't see ahead. Something—God knows what—will solve it . . . maybe. But this very month . . . it's so near. Home to your place—with you and your mother. Just this one thing, Ella. My responsibility to her . . . to the end. It'll make the going less hard . . ."

Ella broke. Like a dammed-up stream from which the bulwark was washed away, all her emotions came surging suddenly. Standing there at the side of the bed she pressed her fingers into the flesh of her face, —into her eye-sockets,—to keep from the wild hysteria of sobbing. Like the rushing of the water through breaking ice on Oak River in the spring of the year, her grief now came surging through her bitterness. For the first time her suffering was for all three,—for Amy crying out her spineless, superficial sorrow—for Delbert going down alone into the strange darkness—for herself, the scorned one, whose agony had been greatest of all.

"Promise, Ella."

"Oh, why is life such a drear stark thing, Delbert? Life was meant to be joyous and lovely."

"You will always have joy and loveliness in you, Ella."

"It should have something besides loneliness and despair."

"You will have neither one, Ella."

"I've suffered so . . ."

"So have I . . . God, how I've . . . suffered."

"How can I go on?"

"Promise you'll . . . look after her . . . through it."

"But what about me? Is my life to be nothing but duty and obligations and service to others?"

"You are so strong . . . and clean. Hold my hand . . . things are . . . are slipping . . . quick,—promise, Ella."

"I promise."

CHAPTER XVII

§ Ella stayed through everything—death, and the many little tasks to do for the dead. Amy had no decision, wanted only to escape the distasteful experience. She wept, and wondered if people thought she looked terrible,—moaned out her sorrow, and was disappointed that her long black veil was not lace-edged.

On the fourth day, the livery-stable owner took them home,—protesting against pay with: "I'm just a neighbor in this case."

The sun was out for the first time since the last heavy snows. Everywhere the drifts were hard, high, and sparkling, but the cold had abated a little.

Arriving at the house, Amy could scarcely move from bodily weariness.

It took the combined efforts of the driver and Ella to assist her from the low seat of the sleigh. In the warm sitting-room, she stood with her back to the door a moment waiting to see what her aunt's greeting would be.

Ella's mother was upset. She scarcely knew what to do with the peculiar situation. The natural warmth of her hospitable nature fought with the cruel circumstances so that she looked to Ella for her cue.

Ella was matter-of-fact. Mrs. Bishop decided that if her daughter was not her natural humorous self, at least she was not uncompromisingly stern. So she immediately became equally matter-of-fact, but without austerity. She shook hands with Amy, but she did not kiss her. She told her she was sorry for her that she had lost her husband, but she said no more about it.

Amy began to cry—weak childish tears, her soft little lips puckered into tremulous sorrow. Ella stalked out of the room and made preparations for supper.

Two days later the enforced vacation was over, and she went back to pick up the loose ends of her work. Sam Peters came over to tell her that if she ever needed him—in the night for errands or anything—he'd be right there across the street. Irene Van Ness came for two reasons—to tell her she was engaged to a Robert Hunt in Ohio, and that she thought Ella was the noblest-souled girl that ever walked on the top of the green earth. And about the first, Ella was sincerely happy. But about the other, she said acridly: "Oh, no, I'm not. I have a special brand of selfishness, all my own. When I give up and do something for some one, the more sacrifice it takes on my part, the more of an exalted feeling of happiness it gives me. I like the abnormal thrill of the self-righteousness. And if you call that nobility of soul, I'll bet the Lord is grinning about it."

"Oh, Ella, you do say the queerest things," Irene had to laugh.

Amy was taken sick on the twenty-fourth of February. There was a wild wind in the night which blew out the street lamps, and Ella, hurrying down the street for Chris' wife, was buffeted about by it. After she had aroused Hannah, she went on to the doctor's, and even though he took her home among the warm buffalo robes of his cutter, she shook with the cold and nervousness.

The wind howled its coyote-like fury around the house. The street lamps went unlighted so that to look out was to look onto the blackness of nothing. Mrs. Bishop could not stand the nervous strain and locked herself in her room. Hannah waited on the doctor and Ella waited on Hannah.

The wind wailed like the crying of a child, and the night wore on.

When the first gray light came into the sullen eastern sky, Hannah carried the baby into the kitchen. It was a girl—plump, healthy, well-formed.

Without a wink of sleep, Ella set out a breakfast for the doctor and was preparing to leave for school. But he said there was no time to eat and he asked her not to go.

As the day wore on, Amy, coming out from a semi-coma, did not appear to be greatly interested in the dark-haired mite Hannah showed her. She slept, roused to tell the doctor she must look a fright, slept, grew weaker, fluttered white lids over glazing china-blue eyes,—died.

For the second time that month, Ella looked at Death as he came for his prey. And for the second time, it was she who had to make all the necessary arrangements, so trivial to the gaunt-eyed specter, so necessary to civilized humans.

The day they buried her was foggy, moist, raw. The pines in the cemetery dripped clammily on the people standing around the pile of yellow clay. The new bronze Civil War soldier on the cenotaph held pools of water in his cap and knapsack. An early bluebird, the color of the dead girl's eyes, fluttered outstretched pointed wings in the hollow bathtub of the bronze cap. Irene Van Ness came over and slipped her arm through Ella's. The minister intoned the service for the dead in a drawling, nasal voice, and then: ". . . we give back to the God who gave her—this lovely young woman—to join her earthly lover in Paradise."

Sam Peters stood a few feet back of Ella, his thin face drawn with sympathy.

When Ella and her mother arrived home from the cemetery, Hannah, walking about with the baby in her arms, said in her broken English she would have to get back now to her own little boy.

The doctor came in to talk with Ella and her mother about the child and give directions for its food. A neighbor handed in a loaf of fresh bread at the back door.

When they had all gone, Ella took the baby in her arms and sat down in a rocking-chair by the western window of the sitting-room where the cold February sun had broken through the fog and was slanting feebly across the floor.

Mother and daughter sat silently for a time and then Mrs. Bishop ventured: "What are we going . . . what to do . . . what about the little thing?"

Ella rocked the soft warm mite pressed to her sturdy body. Under the blanket it stirred and made peeping noises like a chicken.

Oh, why was life so hard, so complicated? Nothing was as it should be. *You will have neither loneliness nor despair.*

"Keep it," she said finally.

"Oh, Ella, the child of a man you had expected to marry?" Some unusual temerity gave Mrs. Bishop the courage to complete her thought in words, swiftly, and with no vagueness.

Ella's lips were pressed together in an aching line. The baby stirred and stretched.

"Maybe I'm starting something new," Ella said grimly, "something biologically new. A youngster with three parents."

CHAPTER XVIII

☙ LIFE does not appear to arrange itself into definite periods at the time one is living those years. It is only when a woman looks back upon it from the hilltop of maturity that she is able to say, "That was the period of my darkest sorrow," or, "Those were the years of my uncertainty."

And though she could not perceive it just then, this was the time that definitely ended Ella Bishop's girlhood and became the period of hei vicarious motherhood.

There had been no relatives of Amy but Mrs. Bishop and Ella. Delbert Thompson's sister wrote that if there was any possibility of another than herself taking the child for awhile, it must be done. Her own three children were still babies and she could not add the newcomer to the group for a year or two at least.

So because there was no other place for it, the baby was to stay for a time. And life became very full for Ella Bishop,—this double life, which was both that of teacher and of mother. And if one thinks as the years went on, she neglected one for the other he does not know the infinite capacity for work and love and understanding in the body and heart and mind of an Ella Bishop.

As for help in caring for the child, the answer came from the Jensens. A sister of Hannah Jensen came from the old country to join them and Ella wanted to know at once about the girl working for her, so Hannah brought her over as soon as she arrived. She wanted to explain something about her sister—tried so hard to make Ella understand, had almost given up to wait for Chris to come and tell it, when Ella suddenly began to comprehend.

"Oh, I see, Hannah. You mean she lost her lover."

"Ya-ya." Hannah glowed at the result of her effort. "S'e luffer . . . s'e los'. . . ." And added with naïve honesty and sadness: "S'e baby . . . s'e los', too."

The girl sat stoically, not understanding. Ella looked at her—healthy, buxom, clean, honest looking. Dear, dear, what a queer thing life was. She hesitated, remembered the child upstairs in her crib. Life was teaching Ella Bishop many things.

"Yes, I'll take her, Hannah, for awhile, until we see how we get along."

So Stena Jensen brought over to Ella's home the various bundles that had come with her in the steerage, expecting to stay a short time—and stayed fifty-one years. Ella gave her the room that had been Amy's, and there Stena unpacked her other two dresses and countless white aprons of deep hardanger work, put her own spread with its wide crocheted trimming on the bed, set up mementos of numerous Jensens left behind in the old country and a pale tintype of a young man, under which she kept for a half-century a pink tissue-paper rosebud, changing it for a fresh one at house-cleaning time from year to year. Sometimes Ella, hearing the girl singing a guttural-sounding Danish song in the kitchen, would stop at the bedroom door and look in at the neatly arranged keepsakes—and gaze for a moment at the photo of the phlegmatic "luffer" with the little artificial rosebud underneath it, placed there no doubt for s'e baby s'e los', too.

Amy's child thrived and grew strong. She was a good little thing after the first part of a year, sleeping usually the whole night through. Ella seemed to have a natural flair for knowing what to do for her. But Stena also assumed much of the care of her and so relieved Mrs. Bishop of any responsibility about the house that Ella sometimes wondered which required the most waiting upon—her mother or the baby.

"Stena spoils you, Mother," Ella would sometimes say jokingly. At which her mother's eyes would fill, and she would say, "Ella, . . . you're not . . . Mamma's sorrow . . . you don't begrudge . . . ?"

Ella would put tender arms around her frail little mother and laugh away her hurt. But she would also say to Stena: "Don't do everything for her, Stena. Just purposely leave her a few tasks. It's better for every one to have something to do."

For months the baby had no name,—then quite suddenly Ella began calling her Hope. For no reason at all, it satisfied something in her—young Ella Bishop, who was not to know the full fruition of any hope.

She had so much to oversee now, her days were so filled with tasks, that she had little time to brood over her troubles. No student ever came to Ella's door to find her too busy to give him attention. If necessary, she stayed at school until shadows fell across the floor of the classroom in Central Hall. If some one needed her, she arrived at her desk soon after the morning dusk had cleared from the sky. She assisted them all,—boys and girls alike. She helped them about participles and finances, adverbial phrases and clothes, split infinitives and bodily ailments, clauses and morals.

Sometimes she scolded about it just to relieve her mind. Ella's tongue could be sharp. She was no soft sentimental teacher. "That Cowan girl," she would say, "thinks conjunctions grow on bushes along Oak River. And she doesn't know a preposition from a thousand-legged worm. I vow I'll never waste another moment with her." But the next morning she would be at her desk an hour earlier than usual to help that Cowan girl.

For a year and a half, then, Ella and Stena looked after little Hope, bathing her, feeding her, exclaiming over her first tooth and watching over her first steps—and one could not have told which was more interested in her development. If they disagreed about her at all it was because Stena thought Ella kept her up too late in the evening—and Ella had to use all her tact to keep Stena from overloading the little dresses with crocheted lace and hardanger trimming.

"Start making lace trimming for her wedding trousseau, Stena," Ella would laugh, "instead of putting so much on her now."

It was the evening of Hope's second birthday, when two of Stena's home-made candles had burned brightly on a huge frosted cake, that the letter came from Delbert's sister. She wrote that she had help now—the youngest child was four, and she thought they could relieve Ella for a time from the care of brother Delbert's child.

As she read, Ella was frightened at the way her heart contracted and her whole body grew cold. If she harbored any idea that her own care of the baby up to this time had been from a sense of duty alone, that letter expelled the last vestige of it. No one could take Hope from her,—no one. If she were served with a law summons even,—she would fight it. Hope was hers. Hope was her baby. She grew almost hysterical in her imaginings—she who was usually so strong and placid,—caught Hope up to her, buried her face in the fat baby neck, drank in the clean sweet-smelling odor of the little body, kissed the palms of the pink hands.

Hope laughed and kicked her little kid shoes together in exuberance that Aunt Ella was so excited over some unknown cause.

Ella wrote the woman a half-dozen letters before she was satisfied with the one she mailed—that the child was well, and as long as she had such good help in a capable Danish girl, she would be glad to absolve the relative from any responsibility for the child. But she could not relax from worry until the answer arrived which plainly signified the woman's relief.

Now she could give her time whole-heartedly to her students, and then hurry down through the campus and past the intervening blocks to the modest home on Adams Street knowing that Hope, her little nose flattened against the pane, would be waiting for "Aunt Ella."

In that summer of 1885 Ella made some changes in the home,—had a new downstairs' bedroom built for her mother and a wide porch across the front and one side of the house after the style of the day. It necessitated digging up the big roots of the trumpet-vine which she always associated with Delbert.

Chris, bringing a spade to do this for her after his working hours at the college, shook a shaggy head over the destruction of the nice shade at the old porch.

"You may have it, Chris, if you can get it reset."

"Py chingo, I take him qvick. But you sure you not voolish to pull him up?"

"No, I don't want it. I just don't care about having it around the place."

So it was with other mementos—Ella carefully removed anything that reminded her of Delbert, as though she would throw open the rooms of her heart to the sunshine and clean that battered and shaken house of all remembrance. She worked faithfully at the task, took out this and that article, hung out all the tender moments to air, shook vigorously all the loved plans, burned every vestige of sentiment. But what did it avail? For every day Hope looked at her with Delbert's eyes and laughed roguishly up at her with Delbert's lips. Even the trumpet-vine, having dropped its seeds, sprang up anew the following spring. You could not destroy that which had so vitally lived. So she gave up the futile task of forgetting and moved all the memories back into the house of her heart.

Because of these, and because Hope grew to look more and more like her father, it came in time to seem to Ella that Hope was her own, and had been born of her love for Delbert before any tragedy entered in. She came to feel that she had given birth to Hope in a travail of physical agony, just as she had borne grief in a travail of mental agony. As time went by, and a measure of surcease came, there grew in the inner court of her heart a little garden of fragrance from which the rank growth of noxious weeds had been miraculously removed. With the child's hand in hers and the child's sweet face upturned to her, by some gracious gift of heaven she was able to walk unmolested in that garden of memories. She confided in no one, could not have put it into words if she had so desired,—but in time she came to know vaguely that to the groveling cry of her prayers had come from Somewhere through the child—a comforting benediction.

CHAPTER XIX

AND now changes came to the young college. For a year or so, Central Hall had taken on a crowded condition. Instructors had been changing rooms at the end of certain periods, in order that some of the growing classes might have places large enough to hold recitations. It had been a common sight to see one of the dignitaries gathering together his paraphernalia in pompous haste and removing himself with reluctance from the room he chose to look upon as his own. Professor Carter with his arms figuratively full of English authors, or Professor Wick clutching a wheel and axle, marching a little grumpily down the hall had been every-day occurrences.

But now all this was changed. A new building had gone up on the campus—a three-story brick with stately white pillars across the front. Administration Hall it was called, and it made Central look a little pale and colorless, although the older building still retained the dignity of possessing the bell which tapped out the periods.

The Minerva Society had rivals—three of them—Greek and Roman goddesses having been named their patron saints, with a fine disregard on the part of their girl followers for the rumored behavior of those early guardians. Two literary societies for the young men also made Saturday night at the college one long period of forensic frenzy.

In 1888, President Corcoran left for another state and President Watts came. Ella dreaded the change. She had gone to school four years while the former was president and taught with him eight more. Twelve years! And he had been a good friend to her. For a few weeks that fall it seemed as though there had been a death on the campus.

President Watts at first acquaintance appeared rather hard and cold. He was an extremely tall man, dark-visaged, as bearded as the men of Biblical times, his hair unruly and his clothes loose fitting. He was only thirty-six and looked much older. Partly because of his height, he gave the impression of being loose jointed—his arms swung awkwardly, his legs seemed more insecurely connected with his body, than other men's legs. Ella grew in time to know his step down the hall outside her door— the quick shuffling gait of those long limbs. President Watts did not teach a class as President Corcoran had done. The school was large enough so that the executive must give his entire time to administrative work.

It was not long before his strong personality began to penetrate every classroom, sweep the campus with ever-growing vitality. Student enrollrent began to increase. New courses were planned. And already there were blueprints on exhibition for a third building. Something about the man was dynamic. Apparently every one responded to the vigor of the new administrative head.

The older professors, who had been connected with the school for all twelve years, might not have shown any outward manifestations of agility. Professor Wick trudged up the board walk of the campus as heavily as ever, the vague suggestion of his last lunch somewhere on his vest. Professor Carter never forsook the dignified calm of his New England upbringing. But even so, they felt a new impetus to work,—the injection of something forceful into the school, and responded loyally. Even Chris Jensen swung his scythe or fed the furnaces with a little more nimbleness.

Classes were rearranged. The hour of convocation was changed. Long-winded senior orations at the chapel hour were dropped, thus rather summarily dispensing with Professor Wick's daily nap. Out of the shuffling of old customs and the side-stepping of an old routine came plans for a larger and more comprehensive educational system.

As much as Ella had thought of President Corcoran, she could see now where his vision for progress had not been so keen as that of President Watts. The former had been an instructor—the latter had the viewpoint of the teacher but also the ability of an executive. The combination was irresistible.

By 1890, music in the college became something besides the spontaneous combustion of youthful voices. The word athletics was rolling glibly off masculine tongues. New teachers were added. A librarian came to sort and list the now-growing collection of books, deftly separating the Emerson *Essays* from the seed catalogues, the popular new *Locksley Hall* from the bundle of Dr. Miles' *Almanacs*.

A Professor O'Neil, representing Messrs. Cæsar, Ovid and Livy, taught for a single year, as his radical views on the origin of the human race, which he so often found occasion to wedge in between the Aquitanians and the Belgæ, proved his undoing and he was summarily dismissed.

Little Albert Fonda, of Ella's class, fresh from post-graduate work abroad, came now as instructor in astronomy, his dark eyes filled with the recent vision of heavenly bodies,—his dark face alight when he spoke intimately of the sun and the moon and the stars.

Nor was Professor Fonda the only member of Ella's class added to the teaching force. In another year came big George Schroeder, back from Heidelberg, for German classes.

Ella met him on the campus just before the first faculty meeting of the new year. They stopped to greet each other under the big elms and maples from which the barrel-staves had long been removed, and in which the purple grackles, having matriculated in their own Midwestern, now gathered to give their harsh college yell of "tchack-tchack."

Although the two had been classmates, Ella called him "Professor Schroeder" when she met him. And he responded with "Miss Bishop." It seemed the better way.

They talked there under the elms of the big new college this was to be. George Schroeder was enthusiastic, filled with a great desire to teach these Midwestern young men and women all he could of the artistic and intellectual life of the universities of the old world. His big voice boomed, his big hands gesticulated, his big shoulders shrugged expressively, as he attempted to convey to Ella all that he hoped to do for the school that had started him toward the goal of his ambitions. Although he spoke perfect English, his voice carried the accent of a fatherland as unmistakable to place as was the throaty "tchack-tchack" of the purple grackles above his head.

Standing there under the elms and maples, he unfolded his plans to Ella, his old classmate,—a desire to make his department at Midwestern in time second to none, to gather about him an excellent corps of instructors, to set a high standard of scholarship, to give courses on Goethe and Schiller that every student of Germanic languages would want to take.

He swung into a fiery German quotation, but Ella laughed and stopped him: "No, no," she admonished, "I can sense the fire and drama of it, but you'll have to give it in my mother tongue if you want me to understand it fully."

"Ach," he gave a shrug of the massive shoulders. "It loses some of its beauty,—my Goethe's *Faust*. I distort the meaning of course when I use it here. And I should not do that. It is disloyal to the master. But I apply it to my new work,—to the buoyancy I feel in the new field.

"A fiery chariot, borne on buoyant pinions,
Sweeps near me now! I soon shall ready be
To pierce the ether's high, unknown dominions,
To reach new spheres of pure activity."

His dark eyes glowed. "I see some day here on the fertile prairie a new Heidelberg, a new University of Leipzig. Can you not see it, too?" His great arm swung out in the direction of the two brick buildings, and Ella, under the influence of his forceful personality, said: "Yes, . . . oh, yes . . . I see it, too."

When she left him, she had contracted his enthusiasm. She, too, saw a great school on the fertile prairie. "If in these swiftly moving years I can pass on a little of that living flame from the torch I carry . . . if I can help light the long steep path for boys and girls . . ."

She walked swiftly to the faculty meeting in a glow of eagerness for the year's work that seemed almost of divine inspiration. She felt a great uplift of the spirit,—a warmth of heart toward all the newcomers. This year she would teach as the Great Teacher taught, with fervor and humility.

CHAPTER XX

☙ QUITE as though her own world were divided also into two hemispheres, Ella's interests these years were in two distinct parts—school and home. As to the former, it was becoming more apparent that the childish days of Midwestern were over, that the school had been but a glorified academy under President Corcoran. Some of the new teachers these days had degrees from eastern schools which Ella imagined they wore like halos. And now came a man named Wittingly—Dr. Wittingly because of a Ph.D.—to be professor of Pedagogy (which was a stylish new title for Professor Cunningham's old classes in Didactics) and whose flag Professor Cunningham was rather forced to kiss.

It grew popular to obtain a leave of absence and go east for a year. And to say that a teacher had just come from Columbia University was to say that he had just held communion with the gods on Olympus. Ella knew she ought to work for another degree sometime if she were to compete with people from the east.

"But after all," she said to President Watts, "a noun is one of the few things that won't change in a century, and a verb, as full of action as it pretends to be, is still a rather stable thing."

President Watts laughed. He had grown to like this frank and energetic Miss Bishop. "But," he added seriously, "I really think you ought to plan to go."

Ella did not see how she could manage. Her salary had to cover all the household expenses. Her mother, little Hope, Stena, the house, all these depended upon her alone. And then to leave for so long,—she had so many responsibilities here.

Hope was growing like a little milkweed. First there had been messy bits of colored papers or crooked little drawings to show Aunt Ella every night, later a wavering seam made with a huge darning-needle, then as time went on, genuine school work, a real number lesson, the word "Hope" written laboriously with plump fingers assisted by the sympathetic wiggling of a pink tongue protruding from pursed lips. For Hope was in school over in the Washington Building of Oak River—the town grown now to over five thousand.

Houses had sprung up around the campus—professors' homes, boarding houses, even a book store and a lunch room. The old narrow board walk had given way to wide black cinder paths and the curving campus drives were had packed too, with cinders. A cow on the campus now would have been too embarrassed to remain.

Besides Didactics giving way to Pedagogy, Mental Philosophy was now flaunting itself as Psychology, Moral Philosophy had become Ethics, and proof was substantiated that the odors of gases in the old Natural Philosophy classroom by the new name of Physics would smell as sweet.

There were more new teachers, a Professor Crooks now was a popular addition to the history department. He talked a great deal about a new freedom of thought and of action, and, though rather permanently married, put his theories into practice by pointed attention to a dashing new Miss Zimmerman of the piano department.

Each year Ella thought the time had come for her break to go east. To study a year at Columbia became almost a necessity toward furthering her teaching career. With President Watt's advice approaching the utterance of a command, she grew more and more sensitive about the delay. But her mother's health was delicate—and she herself was like a mother to Hope. How could she go and leave the child now in these formative years? Under Stena's watchful care, Hope would be clean and well-fed, but also she would be ready to qualify as a citizen of Denmark when the year would be over.

It was 1893 when she went, with Hope ten and Mrs. Bishop at fifty-seven, an old lady, as indeed she had been for a dozen years. Her plan was to stop at the World's Fair in Chicago—which worried her mother almost into an illness, so fearful was she of disaster to her daughter.

"For goodness' sakes, Mother," Ella was moved to one of her infrequent moments of exasperation, "of what are you afraid? I'm thirty-three years old and ought to be capable of looking after myself."

But Mrs. Bishop's anxiety would not allow her to relax until the unknown perils of the Fair and the long journey were over and word had come back that her daughter was safely housed.

The year was a wonderful experience for Ella—with a new viewpoint, a freedom from home responsibilities, a realization that at thirty-three she was still young and full of buoyant spirits in spite of those early tragic events. The whole thing, passed as it had into the shadows of memory, became on that year of freedom a bad dream which was all but forgotten. Only the scar remained—only a sensitive hurt—that made her feel she was not like other young women to whom life gives love and romance.

On her way home she stopped in Ohio to visit Mrs. Robert Hunt—Irene Van Ness. She found Irene happily married, the mother of three little girls, and ready to admit in a moment of confidence a merry disgust of her former mooning over Chet Peters and his indifference to her. They talked of them all freely—the tragic deaths of Delbert and Chester—of Sam's devotion to his parents,—of all the classmates of thirteen years before. Ella went home happily, as though Irene by talking freely of those old days had helped her to bury them. Life was still all before her,—a thing of warmth and light, of friends and family, of work that was pleasant.

She found her mother looking more frail, with a multitude of minor complaints about Stena—she seldom brought tea in hot enough and she changed the sheets too often,—and Stena looking more buxom, with a multitude of minor complaints about Mrs. Bishop—she didn't get out in the yard enough for her own good and she wasn't careful of her eating.

It was at the sight of Hope that her heart warmed. Hope had celebrated her eleventh birthday, and had shot up almost another half-head, it seemed. She was in the sixth grade and her essay on "Why I Would Not Use Narcotics" had won the first place in the contest. She had a new dress that Stena had made her with tucks and crocheted trimming set in the yoke and even in the skirt—and a bead ring that Harry Jensen had given her—

Ella's heart contracted. A bead ring from Chris's son! Boys! It was time she was home. But Hope's sweet face looked honest—her clear gray eyes gazed frankly into Ella's. Ella pulled her close in a swift embrace. "Aunt Ella is home now to stay. We'll have good times. I've lots of plans for you—for one thing, what do you think of this—to start music lessons?"

Hope was to have organ lessons—a piano as soon as Ella could manage —more books of her own—was to go to Midwestern— Everything from now on for Hope. No more dreams for Ella herself. All the air castles for Hope—*hope, which is eternal.*

CHAPTER XXI

IN the spring of 1897 pussy-willows over on Oak Creek had scarcely given place to leaves, until two bombs of gossip burst on the campus with such devastating force that students, meeting, could not decide which piece of news to start discussing first. Usually they gave priority of choice to the Crooks-Zimmerman scandal.

Professor Crooks had carried his freedom-of-thought, freedom-of-soul theory one step too far with the dashing and musical Miss Zimmerman—and now on a Monday morning in April the two were so conspicuous by their absence from their respective classrooms that the ensuing vacuum called for much conversation on the cinder paths under the elms. Wild stories flew about among the students, ranging from the detailed remarks which President Watts allegedly had made to the two in a certain music room, to the detailed actions of Mrs. Crooks upon the facial features of the smug Miss Zimmerman. No one knowing for a certainty just what had happened, there was ample room for the imagination to have full play—and imagination given full play on a campus makes a complete and devastating recreation of it.

Scarcely less exciting to collegians and townspeople alike was the news percolating from the girls' side of the gymnasium that a new game called basket ball had arrived at Midwestern and what was practically unbelievable, that it was to be played outdoors.

For weeks the daring souls who were to launch the new sport sewed on the costumes in which they were to appear, and when the news leaked out that the lower extremity of those costumes were to be *bloomers*, many and sundry were the meetings held behind closed doors by faculty, board, gymnasium instructors, parents, and students, in which the moral and ethical versus the convenient aspects of the garment were discussed.

And for those same weeks practice was conducted in the gymnasium where no prying masculine eye might see. And when the afternoon arrived on which the first outdoor game was to be held, dozens of horses and carriages were hitched at the long rows of posts outside the campus, countless bicycles leaned against the walls of Central and Administration Buildings and more pedestrians wended their way to the ball-grounds than during the previous Commencement.

The girls came out of the gymnasium at the scheduled hour walking sedately enough, eighteen of them, nine for each side, their long hair tied back in horse-tail formation. Their costumes proved to be of sober black flannel augmented by red and blue sashes tied at the side—and the most flagrant critic among the anti-bloomer onlookers could scarcely have found fault with those maligned nether garments, for each pair looked like nothing so much as a skirt, contained six yards of fifty-four-inch flannel, was built solidly below the knees, and when raised at the side would form a high fan-shaped mass of dry-goods to the shoulder with still no sign of parting between the limbs. That potential embarrassment disposed of by the citizenry, there still remained the shock of the partial sight of thirty-six legs, even though a mere one-third of each was exposed,—and when the audience left for home at dusk, after witnessing a long but gently feminine tussle for a ball, they were still as divided in their opinions as the bloomers, whether or not the innovation was right. But the advanced thinkers won, as always, and feminine athletic history was made that day.

Two more new buildings went up that year, Corcoran Hall and Teacher's Training, big brick structures with imposing entrances, and they made Central Hall look like Cinderella in the presence of the haughty sisters. The authorities were planning for the future,—the two new buildings forming the outer corners of a prospective huge quadrangle.

Transportation had gone forward a step. One rode in a jangling street car to the campus entrance now, and the old hack sat among the weeds of an alley in wheelless ignominy, while the little girls of the neighborhood, playing travel, soaked up red stain from the plush seats.

By fall a model training school had opened in one of the buildings with a Miss Sallie Withrow in charge. Miss Withrow was eastern, modern, and as revolutionary in methods as an original colonist. Whereas in Oak River schools, under the eagle eyes of staid midwestern teachers, children were dutifully obeying commands, marching in what approached goose-step formation, reciting when called upon, and raising hands for permission to breathe, Miss Sallie Withrow was allowing children freedom of speech, freedom of action, freedom of study. The bans were off,—and freedom-from-her-mountain-height swooped down upon the children of the model training school.

Ella used to look in upon them sometimes. And fairly often she and Miss Sallie Withrow clashed a little about methods.

"To teach them to look after themselves . . ." Miss Withrow was always explaining.

"Yes, I have a neighbor who does that," Ella would say. "She's just never at home and they always have to look after themselves. So why wouldn't that be the very best instruction of all—not even to be in here?"

They became good friends, but they argued constantly.

"You're just an old-fashioned schoolma'am—the kind that taught Paul Revere," Miss Withrow would say in exasperation.

"But why should children be expected to get through life without discipline—good old discipline outside of self?"

"You don't catch the point at all. They really obey me but they don't realize they're doing it."

"But why shouldn't they realize it? They can't go through life with their civic laws colored over like Easter eggs."

Good-natured banter, but half seriously, shuttled back and forth.

Hope was in High School, dark glossy braids wound round her head, a sweet girl, tractable and appreciative of all that Ella did for her. Sometimes in her imaginings Ella removed the young girl from her life, tried to think how it would have been all these years without her upon which to lavish affection, realized that Hope had given her in return much of the joy of these years. "You will always have joy," a dying man had said.

And now another bomb burst, this time of far more serious import than mere campus gossip.

Peace, which had seemed so unimportant in Oak River because it was ever present, now became a thing of vital importance because it had suddenly flown. Far away the *Maine* had been sunk in Havana's harbor and the wash of the waves caused by its sinking had rippled to a half-hundred homes in Oak River.

The company of guards was leaving for camp—and Harry Jensen, Chris's and Hannah's son, was to go.

Hope went all to pieces emotionally. Ella was amazed, and not quite sure what she should say to her—such a little young thing to be so upset about an older young man.

The two went down to the Armory to see the company leave.

It was a lovely April day in that year of 1898. The grass was beginning to come out, the elms along the streets were showing signs of bursting buds.

Hope was sad, almost hysterical. Ella felt out of patience with her. Just a child! What could she know of the depths of despair? "But I must stay by her," she thought. "She's unduly emotional about it but I must help her all I can."

All was excitement when they arrived. The sidewalks in front of the Armory were jammed with friends and relatives. The Civil War cannon in the park across the street was booming. The G. A. R. band and drum corps stood outside ready to accompany the boys on their way to the train. Ella and Hope could scarcely get near enough to see. Then the crowds were pushed back, the band began to play and the boys were coming,—fifty of them. Ella caught a glimpse of Chris and Hannah Jensen and their two little girls in the crowd. The poor Jensens—with their boy going to—they knew not what.

Near the station the boys were halted and presented with a flag from the Oak River Literary Society. The crowd was so dense that the young captain could scarcely get back to his company after going inside the station for transportation. Children and women were crying. Hope was sobbing wildly at the thought of a young boy. Ella herself wanted to cry aloud—but for *all boys.*

They tried to get closer, but it was not a possible thing. Fathers, mothers, sisters, sweethearts, composed a highly charged emotional mass.

The train came in. By some miracle all the fifty were pushed on board. The train left,— and the boys had gone bravely off to the Spanish-American War.

Ella and Hope walked back home slowly. "He is the nicest young man I shall ever know," Hope said in a tragic voice. But Ella's thoughts were with poor Chris and Hannah and the two young sisters. She glanced at Hope's swollen eyes and soft puckered lips. It was the only time Hope ever reminded her of Amy—when she cried. It was distressingly distasteful to Ella.

CHAPTER XXII

COMMENCEMENT again—eighteen of them now for Ella as a teacher. Summer again—thirty-eight of them now in Ella's life.

Soon after school was out Sam's mother died—slipping away with as little fuss as possible, humbly sorry that she was causing the Judge and Sam any extra trouble. The judge seemed dazed, surprised that she could have done anything so radical without dictation from him. Sometimes that summer he tried to get back into his pompous stride, but his cane had lost its jauntry swing and there was no one to raise red geraniums for his buttonhole. His mother's death meant such deep grief for Sam that Ella tried to show her unspoken sympathy in every way she could.

And by September there was grief for Chris and Hannah, too, for word came that Harry Jensen had died in camp "in the line of duty." When Stena came back from her sister's, Ella hurried to the little white house across the campus.

The two were sitting quietly, their usually busy hands idle. Ella wanted to say something helpful, do something for them in the agony of her sympathy. They appreciated it, they told her with drawn patient faces, but there was nothing to do. The two girls were up in their room and would see no one. The house was clean—in its cleanliness the little white house was always ready for death. Chris said he would sit with Mamma awhile and then he must get back to the sweeping. Their grief was their own. Hannah, staring into the nothingness of space, asked in her broken English what was the use of bringing a child into the world —for this? And no one could answer.

Ella left, her sympathetic heart torn with sorrow for the Jensens and for all who suffer.

At home she found Hope sobbing wildly in her bedroom. "Say it isn't true, Aunt Ella. Say it isn't true." She was inconsolable.

It took of Ella's patience and tact to handle her. Coming from the parents with their deep grief to this superficial sorrow of the young girl, she wanted to shake her, to tell her that she did not know what grief was. "But it's all in the mind," Ella would tell herself. "If one *thinks* he is grief-stricken, why, then he *is*."

Harry Jensen was buried with military honors. The mayor, public officials, veterans of the Civil War, hundreds of citizens in all walks of life participated in paying last honors to the humble janitor's son. Flowers from President Watts and from other members of the faculty, from Banker Van Ness and Judge Peters—a procession of horses and carriages over a mile long—the college glee club singing "He Giveth His Beloved Sleep"—taps over the grave and an echo of taps from the far end of the cemetery. And Chris and Hannah Jensen had paid with their life's blood for a war that need not have been.

It was in the fall of that year also that Professor John Stevens came to Midwestern from the east as an instructor in English literature. He was slender and well set up, with a fine sensitive face. Probably forty, with a touch of gray at his temples, he was the first of the faculty members to be clean shaven. It was almost as though a new type of man had appeared among them, for he possessed more of the appearance of a well-dressed business man than any of the other masculine instructors had theretofore presented. He had a boyish, springy walk, a quick energetic air which set him apart from some of the other rather easy-going dignitaries of the faculty.

He had not been at Midwestern two months until there was a noticeable influence emanating from his well-groomed person to some of the other members. Professor Cunningham startled his classes one day by emerging from behind his fountain-like mustache which to their surprise had hidden a well-shaped mouth. President Watts had his own wild hirsute adornment trimmed down to a mild bun-like appendage on his chin. Professor Carter appeared in a new well-tailored gray suit. Professor Wittingly followed in a dark blue one and a tie that made a genuine effort to blend with the rest of his outfit. Only fat Professor Wick remained impervious to the new influence and presented the same rumpled front with its faint suggestion of his last lunch somewhere on its vast expanse.

Ella found herself admiring the new instructor, his immaculate appearance and his quiet air of deference toward his coworkers. He and his wife took a house on the same block as the Bishop home, so Ella and her mother went over to call soon.

To her disappointment, she found Mrs. Stevens to be an odd little creature, sallow and unattractive, with an almost furtive expression, and so inferior intellectually to her husband that one wondered how she had ever attracted him. Harsh-voiced, querulous, a semi-invalid according to her own diagnosis, she apparently demanded everything and gave nothing. She complained of the change out to the midwest which evidently she held in contempt, and gave the impression that she would make no great effort to fit in with her new associates. Ella went home with the depressed feeling that life had played a shabby trick on that nice Professor Stevens.

The couple came over several times that fall. While Ella and John Stevens talked of books, plays, or school affairs, Mrs. Stevens and Ella's mother discussed medicines, doctors, and a choice assortment of bodily ailments.

It did not take long for Ella and John Stevens to find that they possessed a half-dozen interests in common—James Matthew Barrie with his whimsical writings, Hamlin Garland's new works, and a strikingly original writer by the name of Elbert Hubbard. When Mrs. Stevens, listening in for a moment, remarked that most of what her husband discussed was Greek to her, Ella felt an unbearable embarrassment for him and admired the tact with which he half-smilingly met the statement.

Life took on an added interest now. The days that Professor Stevens walked with her to school were days that started out happily. They talked and found that their ideas on a hundred subjects were interesting to each other. They were silent and found that their silences were pregnant with unspoken thoughts.

He took to dropping into Ella's classroom every day with something humorous to tell her, or pathetic, or instructive. "I thought you'd enjoy this . . ." or "I thought of you right away when I ran across this . . ." would be his greeting.

He formed a little group for reading the new books aloud,—he and his wife, Professor and Mrs. Schroeder, Doctor and Mrs. Wittingly, the Fondas, and Ella.

And when the others found what a splendid reader he was, they gave the unanimous decision that John Stevens should do all the reading. Garland, Kipling, Barrie, the *Little Journeys*—he read them aloud in his expressive way to this small and sympathetic group of listeners.

Ella's admiration for him grew with every contact. It came to be that she was conscious of his entry into a room even as she had been of Delbert in those long-gone days. A door opening behind her and she knew in some psychic way that John Stevens had entered. Always frank with herself, she tried to analyze this new emotion which was filling all her days—knew to an honest certainty that it was the same feeling she had once had for Delbert, augmented now by a maturity of heart, but held in check by a maturity of mind.

Sometimes in the privacy of her own room, with all subterfuge stripped away, she admitted to herself that it was almost as though she loved him. But that was ridiculous,—one of those things that just did not happen to people of her type. However, school herself as she might, the appearance of that tall figure with its springy step coming up the curving walk under the elms was the signal for a sudden acute interest in life. That the regard was mutual was so apparent as to be without question. Straight to her he continued to come with every new article that interested him, knowing that it would interest her, too,—with every plan for his department, knowing that her approval or condemnation was worth considering.

"It's just friendship," Ella told herself repeatedly, "—a platonic friendship." But she said it so often to her *alter ego* that she grew conscious of her own attempt at deception.

It was true that one listening to their daily conversations could have found not the slightest cause for comment, but Ella Bishop knew in all honesty that something physically attractive held them together. "Is this the way people drift into affairs?" she asked herself more than once. Sometimes she thought of Professor Crooks and Miss Zimmerman, dismissed under a cloud of gossip, and shuddered at the memory. But this, this was different. Her liking for John Stevens was so sincere, so thoroughly decent. "Oh, that's what they all say," she broke off wearily, and put him out of her mind, only to find that she was thinking of him again at the earliest opportunity.

Just after the holidays, Sam Peters came across the street one evening to see her. He was nervous, disturbed, experienced a difficult time in getting started on something he wished to tell her.

"It's a little hard to speak about. You've never . . . you've never known me to be gossipy, have you, Ella?"

Suddenly she was frightened. Gossip, how she hated it! Her heart contracted for a moment with the horrible sensation that her very thoughts had broken loose from the cage of her mind and become known. How foolish—no one knew her innermost feelings. Most certaintly she had not worn her admiration on her sleeve.

"It's about . . . Professor and Mrs. Stevens."

She felt the blood mounting to her forehead, stooped to pick up a book to hide the tell-tale fear in her eyes.

"She . . . she takes things from stores," Sam brought it out with painful reluctance. "Kleptomaniac, Ella. Isn't it awful?"

Oh—poor John Stevens! All the sympathy she had half felt for him before this was now doubled.

"Oh, Sam. How terrible!"

"Yes . . . poor Professor Stevens,—I'm sorry for him. Came to Williams and Witwars this afternoon to pay for something she had taken,—told them there was nothing to do but charge anything to him she might pick up. Only he put it a nicer way, said anything his wife might buy and forget to pay for, just charge to him. Went out of the store with his head high, but looking as though he had been hit."

To her secret admiration there was now added this new sympathy.

The reading group was to meet on the first Monday night in March at Ella's home. The day proved to be stormy. The wind blew from the north. The big trees on the campus strained against the force of it but gave up and bent with mad mutterings to the south. It was as though unseen monsters flew by, one behind the other—a long unending procession of madmen. They blew the snow from the roofs of the college buildings, threw down branches, tossed the tops of drifts into the air. They growled and groaned and hissed as they passed by,—all invisible, save their long white hair streaming out behind them.

No one came to the reading circle but John Stevens from a few doors away. When the time was quite past to look for any of the others, the two alone settled down for the reading. Ella asked her mother and Hope to come in, but the former said her head ached and she would rather not, and Hope had to study.

John Stevens had brought *The Little Minister.*

"Long ago . . . a minister of Thrums was to be married, but something happened and he remained a bachelor"—the low throaty voice of John Stevens made the words a melody. *"Then when he was old, he passed in our square the lady who was to have been his wife, and her hair was white but she too was still unmarried. The meeting had only one witness, a weaver, and he said solemnly afterwards, 'They didna speak, but they just gave one another a look, and I saw the love-light in their een.' No more is remembered of these two, no being now living ever saw them, but the poetry that was in the soul of a battered weaver makes them human to us forever."*

The fire burned red in the big coal stove. The mad wind outside whirled down from the north. A deep peace enveloped the two.

"The life of every man is a diary in which he means to write one story and writes another."

Oh, this is what life should be, Ella was thinking. *This* is the way it should be any evening,—any time. He and I . . . he and I . . . ! Mad thoughts,—as mad as the unseen monsters passing by outside,—Tam-o'-shanters of the night,—both.

For a long time the voice went on in rhythmic cadence. " *'I am glad of that,' said the gypsy. 'Mr. Dishart, I do believe you like me all the time. Can a man like a woman against his will?'* "

John Stevens closed the book with a snap. "It's much later than I thought," he said almost brusquely. He left hurriedly,—so hurriedly that Ella knew he too was harboring wild thoughts that passed by like those demons of the storm.

Upstairs in the haven of her room she sat down on the edge of the bed, trembling.

"Now let us look this thing in the face," she said to her reason and to her emotional self,—as though they were two individuals. "It looks to me as though the time had come to let your mind and heart have it out, Ella Bishop. Close the door on the outside world. Speak freely, both of you. No one need ever know. What have you to say, poor thing? Out with it!" She pretended to speak to her heart.

"I want this man for my own. I'd rather be near him than any other human I've ever known. I think he feels the same way about me. I *know* it. I can *feel his* feelings. I'm entitled to happiness. A girl took my lover away once. Why can't I do the same thing? He has no real wife. He's misunderstood, his life half ruined. I could give him everything, love, companionship, happiness. I've only *one* life to live,—why can't it be completely happy?"

"Now, *you!*" She was as impartial as a judge. "What can you say to that?"

"I can say enough." Her clean honest mind took the chair. "In the first place, every one *isn't* entitled to happiness, not at the expense of some one else. Happiness gained that way ceases to *be* happiness. Have ever heard that two wrongs don't make a right? And just why do you drag into this that weak young Amy? You, with your years and your education and your so-called poise and judgment! 'Misunderstood!' Where have you heard that feeble little excuse before?"

"But I want him."

"Perhaps you'd like the moon, too."

"If I gave him the least bit of encouragement . . ."

"You *weakling!*" The judge turned on them both in fury. "You carry a torch, do you? So you're a teacher, are you, carrying a torch to light the way for boys and girls up the long rugged hill they all must climb? That's what you've pretended to be doing all these years, is it? Well, then . . . *carry* it, you *coward!*" She threw herself sobbing across the bed. "You little *fool* . . . *carry* it!"

CHAPTER XXIII

Ella was thankful when Commencement arrived. John Stevens was to leave for the east for the summer months and with his going, she told herself with infinite sarcasm, she presumed she would regain her sanity.

Over and over she said to herself: "This thing has happened to other people, and I've scorned their idiocy, and now it is happening to me." With deepest contempt she used scourging methods on herself, enjoyed with ironic pleasures her own mental flagellations. By autumn time and school she was able to look at the world through crystal-clear eyes, until the day before matriculation when from her office window in the tower of Central she happened to see John Stevens coming up the walk under the elms, stepping along with that boyish springing walk. And then she knew the summer's battle had gone for naught.

She saw him stop to talk with big George Schroeder and in a fever of haste, hurried down to greet him while he was there with the German instructor. The three talked of their respective summers and of plans for the fall. Ella told a humorous anecdote about her vacation, walked down the long cinder path with Professor Schroeder when he started away, and went home highly pleased with the Ella Bishop who was her outer and civilized self.

This was Hope's senior High School year, and Ella made herself simulate such a deep interest in the young girl's dreams that she could have no time or thought for foolish dreams of her own.

In October, she was to go to Maple City, a two hours' ride by train, to address a teachers' meeting. She had no special knowledge of what other members of the faculty had been asked to speak, but assumed that there would be others, for it was a very common custom for several to go each fall.

On the day of the meeting she rose early, dressed with care, and was at the station in time for the eight o'clock train. Miss Sallie Withrow, the primary supervisor, was there,—"primed, I suppose, to expound to all the waiting pedagogues your ideas on complete freedom for the child," Ella joked her.

Just before the train came in, John Stevens arrived. Ella felt that old unwonted happiness surge over her at his presence. As he swung into the station now with his light firm tread, she was thinking again how he was everything any woman could desire,—intellect, manners, appearance,—everything. Far from handsome as to features, that art of dressing well, businesslike air, and general manner set him in appearance far apart from the George Schroeders and the Professor Cunninghams of the faculty.

To-day she felt so pleased that he was to go to the meeting that she set a stern watch upon herself for fear she might put that emotion into her expression. If her feeling for him had progressed beyond the pale of recall, it was at least unknown to any mortal, she told herself, John Stevens included. She was glad that she looked nice, with feminine pride gloried a little in the fact that her new fall outfit was so becoming. She had a blue camel's-hair dress the exact shade of her eyes, with long blue corduroy velvet wrap and velvet toque made from the same material, a gray pointed sea-gull wing on each side fitting over the puffs of her hair and outlining the curve of her face.

If she kept her interest in this man thoroughly concealed, she was not unaware that his face lighted noticeably at the sight of her. Immediately he was merely the courteous fellow-worker of them both, addressing himself rather pointedly to Miss Sallie Withrow.

The three sat together on the train, talking about many things after the manner of those who have much in common. It came out that John Stevens' program was a morning talk and the evening lecture, Miss Sallie Withrow's morning and afternoon talks, Ella's the same. The return trip would have to be made on the evening ten-thirty train.

"But I'm staying over Sunday," Miss Withrow was saying, ". . . a second cousin of my mother's whom I have never seen lives there, and it's my best opportunity to make her a visit."

A silence settled upon the other two. It might have been only a natural one, and it might have been pregnant with thoughts unspoken.

Maple City was several times larger than Oak River, a midwestern city of factories and hotels, schools and churches. Built on a high bluff, it overlooked the river making its lazy way to the sea.

The meetings were held in a rather fine new high-school building. During her morning talk, Ella was all teacher, gave her best to these people of her own chosen vocation, but constantly, and without her volition, through all her professional speech ran a minor pleasurable thought like the far-off sound of a silver bell that she was to be thrown in the company of John Stevens for one whole day by no act of her own. No conscious effort on the part of either had thrown them together. Just fate. Sometimes fate was cruel, and sometimes she was very, very kind.

At the close of the afternoon session, she saw Miss Sallie Withrow leave the high-school building with the cousin, stayed a few minutes longer to answer questions, and went down the long stairway to find John Stevens waiting for her in the hall. The far-off sound of the silver bell became suddenly the chimes of a cathedral.

"Shall we walk?" he said, as casually as though he had asked her to meet him here.

"Yes," Ella said, as though she had told him that she would.

They followed a long wooden walk to the end of a street, then took a path that led along the river road to the top of a bluff. It was then but the beginning of a park which was to be a beauty-spot in later years. Great trees which had clung to the river's bank for a century crowded the hill. Open spaces between the heavier growth showed the burned-out embers of old Indian camp fires. Wooden seats had been placed along the edge of nature's parapet to which an iron fence gave protection from the abrupt fall of the bluff.

Here they sat down and looked over the rich farming valley. October's sunshine slanted through the huge oaks and maples,—October's bright blue sky formed a dome over the scarlet and green and gold of the valley,—and the river ran its lazy way to the sea.

"It's ideal, isn't it?"

"Oh, why can't it always be this lovely?"

They were ordinary words. Any one might have said them,—any one heard them. But they were weighted with much more import. It was as though he said: "Because you are here with me it is ideal," and she, "Oh, why can't we always be together?" But the words remained unspoken, though the two talked of many intimate things.

He told her of his parents, his schooldays, his early engagement to a neighbor girl before he had finished his course, and the struggle to get his extra degrees after this boyish marriage. Down in her heart Ella was glad that at no time did he speak disparagingly of the peculiar woman who must have been a cruel hindrance rather than a helpmate. Only once he said: "When you are young, you go through a forest blindly, seeing nothing clearly. At middle-age you see both ways, forward and back. I suppose Old Age, looking backward, can see and understand it all."

In turn Ella simply and naturally told him of her girlhood. When she came to the part Amy had played in her life, he put his hand over hers, and they sat so until the shadows lengthened.

Everything had been said, everything but the thing they could not say.

It did not seem wrong. Anything so natural and so mutually lovely could not contain evil, Ella was thinking. If she gave any thought now to her early love affair, it was merely to think of it as a song that had been sung and forgotten.

Sitting there in the warmth of the October sunshine she had a feeling that she would carry the memory of this day with her always, for common sense told her it could never be repeated,—that it would be the golden leaf of all the pages in the book.

When the dusk suggested itself they rose and retraced their steps down the river road. They had dinner in an obscure little café where no prying eyes might see them and misinterpret. And then Ella went over to the lecture hall with him, slipping into a rear seat while he went to the front with the committee in charge.

Sitting there in the back seat, hearing the voice of the man with whom she had spent a precious day and with whom she wished out of the entire world she might spend all days, she gave herself wholly to the emotion of his unspoken love for her, let it play about her body as a swimmer revels in the waves. To-morrow she would go back to face the problem of what to do with this friendship which had become something stronger than friendship. Only this evening she would hold it to her heart, would pretend that it was her own, paying no attention to the sober fact that it was but a wistful dream.

The lecture was over. In three-quarters of an hour they would be on the train bound for home. He was speaking to a few people, then hurrying through the crowd to her,—just as it ought always to be. When they had gone out of a side door, and turned to go up the street, there was a far distant flash of lightning and a reverberating roll of thunder. They spoke of the queerness of it so late in the season, but the day had been hot and the storm not unexpected. Another far-away flash and its resultant crash of cymbals!

And now, a few great thudding raindrops hit the sidewalk with noisy clatter so that he drew Ella into a darkened stairway entrance for momentary shelter. Together they stood in the narrow archway while the heavy drops became a pelting shower only a few feet away. Suddenly John Stevens' arms went around Ella and he drew her close.

"Well . . . ?" he asked huskily. "What shall we do with this thing that confronts us? Shall we . . . go home?" His face was bending close to hers. "Or stay?"

Or *stay?* Ella caught her breath in a gasp of understanding. The lights of the dark city were all about them like jewels on an enveloping mantle. Strangers passed back and forth through the summer shower. A dozen hotels sent out their welcoming gleams from a hundred windows. Go home . . . *or stay?* The lovely day had been theirs. And *now?*

A streak of lightning shot across the sky in sprawling fashion, like the rivers of a map.

"Is it . . . is it I, alone, who must make the decision?" Her voice sounded as strange as though it were not her own.

"You are the woman."

You are the woman. She had a wild confused notion that two worlds suddenly stood still in their orbits waiting for that woman's answer,—two worlds, into one of which she must step forever. There could be no half-way measures. She must live either in the one or the other, for entering into one, she must forever turn her back upon the other. Go home! Or *stay!* There were those who broke marriage vows lightly, who shattered the moral code with little compunction. The arms of the man she loved were about her, the face of the man she loved above her, waiting for her in the world of love and desire. In the other waited her mother, Hope, friends, students. . . .

A great flash rent the skies with such blinding light—became for a moment so like a living flame—that it looked to be a flaming torch high above the city streets. A *flaming torch?* Why,—a *flaming torch was meant to light the paths of boys and girls along the rugged way!*

Suddenly she felt sane and strong. Putting the unspoken feeling into words had brought back all her sanity and her strength. There was only one answer. There could never be another.

She put her hands on his shoulders, not in a gesture of love, but rather in one of sadness and pity, that in a world of unhappiness they must forever renounce this exquisite thing.

"Go home," she said.

He drew her close for one disturbing moment as though he could not accept the verdict. Then, "Of course," he said. "You are right."

He slipped her arm into his and they went out of the sheltering stairway onto the moist street and down to the station.

Old Judge Peters was there to take the train. He greeted them affably with long-winded ponderous explanations and the three sat together and talked all the way home.

Sam was at the station with the carriage to meet his father and so took them all up to the Adams Street neighborhood.

"Good night, Judge Peters," Ella said gayly. "Thank you, Sam, and good night." And, as though it were not the end of everything, "Good night, Professor Stevens."

"Good night, Miss Bishop."

CHAPTER XXIV

SCHOOL went on. Classes met and recited. Students passed and flunked. The blackbirds shrilled their "tchack-tchack" in the big trees. The reading circle members came together and listened to John Stevens' attractive interpretations of the modern writers. Ella had her fortieth birthday. Everything was just as it had been, everything but one. Ella Bishop had found a certain peace of soul in the situation.

If John Stevens had been free, she would have given up everything for him. John Stevens was not free. Therefore, she could not continue to think of him in any way but as a friend and coworker. Q.E.D. To Ella Bishop's uncomplicated code of life the problem was as simple as that.

"That's one thing about me," she said to the image in the mirror on that anniversary of her fourth decade. "I can always get the better of my emotions in time. I may fight windmills, but after awhile I have them too scared even to turn in the wind."

She stared for a moment at the face in the glass, admitting with accustomed candor that she did not look the years with her well-kept skin, her dark hair, deep blue eyes with humorous crinkles at their outer edges, red-lipped, generous mouth. For some time she looked at the woman in the mirror who stared unabashedly back. "Forty," she said aloud to herself. "Well," she shrugged her shoulder and grinned to the apparition who grinned cheerfully back, "abandon hope all ye who enter here."

It was noised about on the campus in the spring that Professor Stevens was leaving. Ella heard it first from Miss Hunter of the training school. For a moment the solidity of the trees and bushes and the green sloping lawn seemed wavering in a liquid mist. The college without John Stevens dropping into her classroom, without his springy boyish step down the corridors, without his voice at the reading circle—! All the weeks without John Stevens! Beyond the day of his going lay the bleakness of nothing,—all the to-morrows would be gray. Then she was herself,—calm, poised, unshaken by the news. It was better so. No more watching herself for any betrayal of her feelings. Life would be easier and more simple.

Just before Commencement he came into her office in the tower room to say good-by.

She was bending over a low drawer of supplies when, startled, she grew aware that some one was behind her. She stood up hurriedly and for a long moment they stood facing each other. Then he put out his hand.

"Everything to make you happy and successful," he was making an attempt at gayety.

"Thank you. And to you."

He held her hand a moment, looked at it as though not quite sure of its identity, dropped it and walked out of the office.

The bell overhead tapped and the pigeons with a great whirl of wings brushed past her window.

She was standing just as she had been, when suddenly he stepped back in. His face was drawn and he was biting nervously at his lip.

"It it's ever . . . if it's possible for me to return . . . some day . . ."

"Don't say it," Ella said a little breathlessly. "Don't."

He stood for a moment. Then,—"No," he said, "I won't. Good-by."

He was gone. And all the to-morrows had begun.

Luckily Commencement held double duty for Ella. Hope was finishing her High School course, and the importance of the occasion gave the little home on Adams Street a festive air. There was a fluffy white dress with embroidery ruffles for her made by old Mrs. Finch who was still holding her own with the other dressmakers of the town. It had taken tears and tact to get the sewing out of Stena's hands,—tears on Hope's part and tact on Ella's, for Stena had wanted to make yards of wide crocheted insertion for the gown,—and as Ella said: "Hope, she just doesn't realize that:

"Crochet
Is passé."

Which had the effect of turning Hope's tears to laughter—Aunt Ella was always so funny and understanding.

And so in the excitement of the High School graduating exercises with their attendant festivities, Ella's inner emotional life was set aside like an old worn-out shoe.

"Before I forget all these emotions, I ought to write a book," she said ironically to that other self with whom she always held gay converse. "*The Love Life of an Old Maid*—and wouldn't it contain a gay set of lovers—a man who had married another girl before he met me, and a man who married another girl *after* he met me? And Sam," she added to herself, "don't forget poor old Sam."

And Ella had occasion not to forget Sam that summer.

It was on an evening in August that some one tapped on the screen door and she went downstairs to find Sam standing there, his slim bony face looking white and drawn. He was breathing hard, partly from hurrying and partly from agitation.

"Can you come over to our house, Ella?" he wanted to know. His voice sank to a whisper. Evidently he was laboring under great stress. "I'm in trouble, and I've got to have somebody to talk to. You're always so . . . so . . ." He did not finish.

Hatless, Ella stepped out on the porch and closed the door behind her. "Is it your father, Sam?"

"No, Father's well. He's gone to Maynard to look after his place there and collect the rent. He won't be home until to-morrow."

"What is it, then?" She felt impatient with this mild Sam who could keep her in suspense over a mere trifle.

"Wait until we get over home. You'll come, won't you?" She saw he was trembling.

Ella crossed the street with him to the fussy old house. As they stepped up on the porch it occurred to her that in the two years since his mother's death, she had not been beyond the doorway. She had talked to Sam and his father in the yard, taken neighborly gifts of food across the way many times, but had not gone in.

It was neat inside. She had a swift impression that everything was just as it had always been,—the pink flowered vase on the table, the black crocheted afghan on the couch, the plaster cast of "The Milk Maid." But there was a musty odor as of slack housekeeping.

Sam closed the wide hall door and put his hand heavily on Ella's arm. "I've a sick man here in Father's bedroom. He's very low. The doctor just left, but he's coming back."

He turned and beckoned, and Ella followed him through the old sitting-room with the wide bay-window to the door of the downstairs bedroom. She could hear labored breathing even before Sam held back a faded brown chenille portière and motioned to the humped bulky form of some one under the patch-work quilt.

For only a moment he held it back, then dropped it nervously and came back on tiptoe. He raised miserable eyes to Ella.

"It's Chester," he said simply.

Ella, startled beyond coherent thought, could only stare.

"He wasn't drowned," Sam said quietly. "He came back to-night."

CHAPTER XXV

ELLA, standing there and staring at Sam, could find no word to say.

"It was about seven when he came," Sam said nervously. "Father was over to Wittingly's. Some one came up the side door and tapped. I went to the door and this man . . ." Sam was still having hard work to believe the incredible. "Chet stood there and laughed kind of silly. My first thought was that he had escaped from somewhere. . . . Then he said with that foolish laugh: 'I guess you don't know me. I know you though, Sam. It's Chet.'

"It was horrible. I was terribly frightened. It was like a nightmare. I wanted to call somebody and couldn't speak. I wanted to go and get somebody and I couldn't move."

"Oh, Sam!" Ella's heart went out to the thin little man standing there, locking and unlocking nervous fingers.

"We both stood there, and then he said, 'I guess you thought I got my everlasting by drowning. Well, I didn't. I was mad about . . . Amy . . . and just slipped out to see the world a bit.' Then he stopped and that foolish grin left him and a sober look came over his face, sane, but bitter and terrible, and he said, 'Well, I've seen it, all right.' My God, Ella!" Sam burst forth, "he *has* seen it—the *under* side."

For a few moments the muscles of Sam's thin throat worked convulsively, and then he went on quietly: "Chet stood still there outside the door, and I not moving either. Then he said, 'I meant to come back in a little while . . . after I got over . . . about Amy.'"

Into Ella's numbed mind came a sudden rush of realization, a fleeting thought of all the misery Amy's coming to town had left in its wake. But Sam was still repeating Chet's words:

"'I got passage for Hong Kong on a freighter, and then when I got there . . .' He numbled something about a Chinese girl, and some more that I didn't catch. I hadn't said a word yet. All I could do was stare at him. And then he asked: 'Are Father and Mother . . . ?'

"Then he sort of put both hands out on the door jamb and crumpled down. It was terrible, getting him in. He's huge, a big bloated unhealthy size. I pulled him into the sitting-room and tried to get him up on the couch. I could see he wasn't dead, just unconscious. I kept thinking how Father would come home in a few minutes, over and over in my mind kept going the thought of Father's pride in Chet.

"There wasn't any time left to hesitate. And quick—like that—" Sam gave his thin fingers a snap— "I decided to lie to Father. Lies don't come easy, if you aren't used to them, Ella." He said it as naïvely as a child. "But I knew I'd have to lie or else kill Father. And I owed it to Father. He—Chet—looked pretty near gone. I ran to the telephone and called young Doc Lawrence . . . these new telephones are wonderful, Ella. . . . I thought being a newcomer there was no risk of his recognizing Chet. I figured that I'd say it was just a . . . tramp. If he came to and talked, and Father *had* to know . . . I'd just pretend it was news to me too. But he hasn't been conscious. He's talked some but it's disconnected things—just rambling. Sometimes he thinks he's in Shanghai. Oh, you wouldn't want to hear him, Ella. But sometimes . . ." Sam's voice broke, "sometimes he thinks he's a kid . . . coasting down College Hill."

Ella wondered whether she had ever before felt such deep emotion, known such moving pathos. She wanted to do something for Sam, take over the burden for him. In that one poignant moment she had a fleeting vision of herself living here as Sam had always wanted, helping him. But almost before its inception, she thrust it from her.

Sam fumbled for a minute with the old blue vase on the table and then he spoke again: "I couldn't think of getting him upstairs, so I had to put him in Father's bedroom. Young Doc Lawrence and I got him in there finally. Father came home," his low voice went on. "He was annoyed by it,—scolded some for putting a tramp in his bed. Said I'd have him dead on my hands, and that if I'd had any backbone I'd have called the authorities first thing. I've always been honest with Father and it took all my strength of will to carry the lie through. When he said he'd have gone to Maynard if it hadn't been for the sick man here, I told him to go ahead, that Doc Lawrence and I would look after him. I felt relieved and thankful. When he wavered about going, I could hardly stand it. But he went."

"Oh, Sam." Ella's heart went out to the quiet little man.

"He won't live through the night, Doctor says. It's like having him die twice, you see, to have Father know. I'm praying that he won't regain consciousness. To have him come to and tell! Think how it would kill Father's dream of him—all his old pride in him!"

When Ella could only nod in affirmation, he went on: "When he passes away I've got to carry the thing through. He can't be buried in our lot. Mother would have wanted him by her, but then, there's Father to think about?" He put it as a question but his decision was his own. "No, I've thought it all out. He's got to stay just a stray bum that asked for his supper . . . name unknown . . . until Father passes away. Then if I outlive Father, I could have him moved—and tell folks."

Ella found her voice: "You're doing a big thing, Sam,—a mighty big thing. Your father hasn't always . . ." Then she stopped, annoyed that she had said it.

Keen, sensitive, Sam looked up. "Yes, I know. He hasn't thought I've amounted to anything—handling eggs and sugar and keeping books. Well, I guess I haven't. You'll have to admit yourself, Ella, that Chet would have been . . ." The old familiar phrase died away on his lips, and he changed it apologetically: "If he'd gone straight, Chet would have been a great man."

They stood for a few moments while the labored breathing rattled hoarsely in the room beyond.

Dr. Lawrence came in quietly then. Her heart filled with sympathy for Sam, Ella offered to stay,—to go home and get Stena and come back.

"No," Sam said, "I don't want you to have to be here, Ella. I want to think of you over home, away from it."

"I'm not afraid of death, Sam. I've been . . . I've seen death."

"Yes, I know. But you go on. Come over in the morning if you feel you can."

Stena went over with Ella in the morning. Death had been there and gone. The body had been taken down to the undertaker's when Judge Peters arrived home from his trip.

Sam, pale but steady, met his father at the door. Only his lips trembled. "Father . . . the man . . . the man is dead."

The old Judge was pompous, fussy, a little sorry that he had scolded about Sam bringing the sick man into the house. "Well! Well! We all come to it. The stream of humanity flows ever onward to eternity. Poor wayfarer! Somebody thought a great deal of him once."

Ella's eyes met the hunted eyes of Sam and would have dropped their tears if she had not used all her will power to stay them.

There were formalities to attend to, a law or two to be obeyed, and later a simple burying.

Sam said he thought there ought to be something read at the grave and a song, no matter—no matter who the man might be. He went to the members of one of the church choirs but the tenor was too busy and the soprano had a cold, so there was no music.

Ella and Stena went out with Sam to the short service held on the side of the fence where the sleepers have left no funds for the upkeep of their narrow houses. The tall dry grass rubbed brittle stems together in the wind. Grasshoppers thumped heavily on the plain black box. The minister prayed solemnly for the soul of the dead. But Ella prayed for the living.

By pressing his thin lips together Sam got through the ordeal bravely enough. He held his thin body erect and looked steadily over the nearby field of corn. It was only when they were leaving that he broke for a moment.

When he held the gate open for Ella, he whispered: "My God, Ella, we used to go fishing together down on Oak Creek . . . and we had a menagerie rigged up in the old carriage house. . . ."

Ella held herself rigidly against all emotion until she arrived at the dark haven of her room. Then she threw herself across her bed and cried because life was such a tragic thing.

CHAPTER XXVI

AND now Hope matriculated at Midwestern, the baby who only yesterday had stood with flattened nose against the window waiting for Aunt Ella's return. How the years had slipped silently by. Hope was a freshman and a Minerva sister and a student of primary work in the big new training school.

Miss Sallie Withrow and freedom were gone now, but Miss Hester Jones and bondage were there. And Hope, taking training under the critical, severe, and all-seeing eye of Miss Jones, lived in such a changeable condition of atmospheric pressure, low for criticism and high for commendation, that the little house on Adams Street became the center of all cyclonic disturbances. Ella sometimes thought she had double duty —her own work and Hope's. For Aunt Ella was the port in all storms. One never knew how Hope would arrive at night,—up in the clouds or down in the depths.

"She said,"—to Hope there was only one *She* in the whole college—Miss Jones—"she said I did very nicely with the games," Hope would be all smiles. Or, tearfully, "She said I taught the number-work class as though I didn't understand it myself."

"Well, *who would?*" Ella might be moved to sputter. "The ratio method. Everything ratio—just as though you could go through life settling all problems by comparing a little block with a big block. I'm going to talk to Miss Jones myself."

But if was largely braggadocio, and Ella knew it. For one did not talk critically to Miss Jones. Looking at her large, solid physique, her firm mouth, and her cold gray eyes, one who had come to express himself forcibly merely mentioned that it was a nice day and fled, leaving some one else to render any unfavorable judgment of her department.

And in truth, Ella had enough to oversee in her own department without dipping into another.

For some time the school had been of such size that freshman English was all she taught. But to say that Miss Bishop taught merely freshman English was to utter a half-truth. In reality she taught social science, business administration, morals, manners, religion, literature. Freshman English was but a cloak to hide her interest in humanity, a smoke-screen in front of her general helpfulness. Not that she was weak in her subject. No one could pass on to Sophomore English who did not meet the course's stiff requirments. To timorous and bold students alike she seemed to stand at the end of a long corridor of time, a semester's length away, like some avengingingmangel with up-thrust sword.

And she gave unstintingly of her time and energy. No student ever turned up the gravel path between the rows of evergreen hedge at the little house on Adams Street without confidence that he would see Miss Bishop if she were at home.

"They've seen me in so many and such varying degrees of dress, that I don't know how they can respect me. I've had on cold cream and kitchen dresses—loose house slippers and curl papers. But when a student comes to my house it usually means he has something spontaneous on his mind that, withheld for a while, would gradually curdle, and he would decide not to talk. So I never keep them waiting."

Being human, she often scolded about her tasks outside the schoolroom. "If I were only paid in proportion to what I do," she might sputter. "Look at the people who walk away from their jobs and have some time to themselves. Do I? Never. Papers, plans, picnics, parties. I do everything around that school but help Chris with the mowing and I'd not be surprised to have to take a hand in that some day."

All of which scolding is hard to reconcile with the fact that when the school grew to such size that one or two of the freshman English classes were to be taken over by some one else, she began to make excuses.

"Oh, I can still handle them all, I think. By putting in two extra sections of recitation seats the room will hold twelve more, easily."

And when she was home, scolded furiously about herself. "Now, why did I do that senseless thing—deliberately assume more work than I needed to have done?"

She knew the secret of it was a sort of motherly jealousy for all freshmen. She wanted none to pass her by. "The minute they do that, I shall begin to lose connection with a certain percentage of them—never know them at all."

A queer mortal—Ella Bishop.

Each spring she took a special interest in freshmen students who were not able to go on with their courses, those who had to stop in order to earn money for another year. She would not relinquish her hold on them until she had exacted promises from them to return as soon as they could. She helped many of them get country schools,—often driving her own horse miles to interview directors in their behalf.

Miss Hunter, of the training school, used to say: "I don't see why you do all that. Isn't a written recommendation enough? It seems to me a bit undignified to go charging around the country in behalf of a student."

"Undignified—your foot!" Ella would retort. "The main thing is that *Annie Simpson wants a school.*"

There were more changes on the campus. President Watt's far-seeing eye and executive management had made possible many improvements. From year to year the building progressed. Central Hall was now usually referred to as Old Central,—the ivy vines on its walls were dense mats of green through which the windows peered as from under shaggy eyebrows. Chris was no longer head janitor. There was a supervisor of grounds and buildings, a young man fully trained in architecture. Chris was merely a general repair man, stoker, grass cutter. The supervisor was of Swedish descent, and Chris in the jealousy of his coming confided to Ella that "a Swede ain't not'in, anyway, but a Dane wid his brains knocked out."

The music department had made a reputation for itself, "teaching every known instrument," Ella said, "but bagpipes and the Chinese gong." Sometimes she had to laugh to herself over the jealousies of the voice teachers, particularly those fomenting between Miss Boggs and Miss Honeycutt whose artistic temperaments were of such extreme sensitiveness that a particularly pleasing press notice concerning one usually sent the other to bed with a headache.

Professor George Schroeder's department had grown beyond his dreams. Every day he taught his beloved Goethe and Schiller with all the fire of his own admiration. And every day little Professor Fonda brought to his students some new astronomical knowledge, as though bringing them a bit of the light from his sun and his stars. The faculty was no longer a big family. There were no more faculty picnics or parties. The group was too large. Like a snowball grown too big it had disintegrated socially into small groups.

In 1904 Hope, finishing her intensive training under the all-seeing eye of Miss Jones, modestly felt that she knew all there was to know about primary training.

Sometimes she and Ella had little arguments about it.

"You'll get over some of those theories, Hope. As President Cleveland said, 'It's a condition and not a theory' that confronts you, and all the training in the world won't make a good teacher of you or any one else, just because you or that person had Miss Jones's military sort of training, unless you're a born teacher and can adapt yourself to any situation and still function wisely and well."

"But, Aunt Ella, I can step right into any school now and just *reproduce* Miss Jones's model classwork."

"I'm glad you think so and it will help you immensely to have a high standard before you. But don't forget that you may teach where you will not have model training-school equipment."

"But Miss Jones says we should *demand* the best of materials."

Ella smiled: "You could demand it in some schools until the cows come home and not get it,—and anyway there is much more to teaching than the material aids that surround you."

"Just the same I do think it's *beneath* a graduate of Miss Jones's course even to accept a position in a place where the aids are not up to date."

To which Ella said crisply: "Two of the greatest teachers in the world, Hope, were not equipped with up-to-date material aids—Socrates 'who brought down philosophy from the heavens to earth'—and a Man who wrote with his finger in the sand."

She was as proud of Hope, though, as a mother peacock, and just as at High School graduation, planned to get soft white mull and yards of dainty embroidery for a dress. And when the class play parts were given out and Hope arrived home bearing the rôle of "Rosalind, daughter to the banished duke" for the June presentation of "As You Like it," Ella made no attempt to conceal her delight and straightway began to plan cheesecloth costumes in the Shakespearian mode.

In the late spring, Hope was elected to a good primary position at Maple City, and Ella suddenly realized that her pleasure over it was tempered by the realization that the house without Hope would be almost, in truth, a house without hope.

Commencement, with Hope graduating, took on more of a glamour than any of the twenty-four others had assumed since her own.

Finding almost at the last minute that the auditorium which had been undergoing a siege of redecoration was not to be finished in time, a harassed committee made hasty arrangements for a Chautauqua tent to be pitched on the campus. And so there with the lush campus grass under their feet and the June sun's rays filtering through the rippling canvas, in a forest of Arden composed largely of underbrush from the banks of Oak Creek, trod the duke and Rosalind, Celia, and Orlando and the foolish Touchstone. And when Hope's low vibrant voice came gently, clearly, through the wide spaces of the tent: "*To you I give myself, for I am yours,*" Ella had to wipe away a sentimental tear as surreptitiously as one sitting on the front seat could accomplish.

In July, old Judge Peters died, suddenly, spectacularly, in front of the court-house, his cane dropping from his numbing fingers and his Panama hat rolling into the street.

Sam grieved for him. "Not many had a fine father like mine," he told every one. The Sunday after the burial he went out to the cemetery with flowers. He put some on his father's and mother's graves and then slipped through the barbed-wire and put some on that other one. For a long time he stood there pondering what to do. Responsibility sat heavily upon him.

"I couldn't bring myself to decide," he told Ella. "Mother would want Chet over close to her. But Father—you know how proud he was of Chet, and his pride seems still to live. Seems as though it would still hurt Father to have folks know."

"I'd let things be as they are, Sam," Ella advised. "After all, it doesn't make much difference where one sleeps, does it?"

The summer went away and Hope with it. And the house on Adams Street became a dreary place.

School opened, and more freshmen came—among them a son of Mina Gordon and twin daughters of Emily Teasdale, Ella's old classmates and Minerva sisters. "And if that doesn't make me realize I've passed youth somewhere down the line," she said, "I don't know what would."

But Ella was only forty-four—and looked ten years younger. Professor Schroeder with the prerogative of an old classmate always joked her about it. Meeting her on the campus, if there were no student ears about, he usually greeted her with such approach as: " 'Hail, blooming Youth.' Always you are the same as when we were students."

To-day, with the September sun warm on the campus, and the recently returned students breaking into a hundred fall activities, she saw him and little Professor Fonda coming down the walk together,—the Damon and Pythias of the college in the way of friendship,—David and Goliath in the matter of physique.

Professor Schroeder greeted her with: " 'Hail, blooming Youth!' Fonda, she is like the verse from *Don Juan.*

'Her years
Were ripe, they might make six and twenty springs,
But there are forms which Time to touch forbears,
And turns aside his scythe to vulgar things.' "

Ella laughed and pointed out that if she had passed but twenty-six springs she must, perforce, have graduated at the tender age of two. "And by the way," she told them, "we should plan to celebrate our twenty-fifth anniversary next Commencement."

"Twenty-fifth? Ach—the time!—where does it go? If Fonda here would only stop his solar system awhile,—lock up his Milky Way and take a vacation . . ."

President Watts, bareheaded, was coming down the steps of Administration Hall, and toward them, his long loose-jointed legs moving rapidly. They turned expectantly to him as he came up.

"You remember Professor Stevens of several years ago?" he was asking.

The campus swam in a mist before Ella's eyes and she knew a sudden tenseness of nerves.

"I've just had word of his sudden death," he said. "In one of the new automobiles. They're really very dangerous affairs."

Both of the men were murmuring their surprise and sorrow. Only Ella stood transfixed and unspeaking.

"And perhaps a touch of sadness to our own college is added to the news," President Watts was saying, "by the fact that he was on his way to take the train to come out here."

CHAPTER XXVII

JOHN STEVENS was dead, killed in one of the new automobiles. ". . . On his way to take the train to come out here," President Watts had said.

All the way home in the hot September sun, with the zinnias and petunias still gay in the lingering summer weather, and with people calling out friendly greetings to her, Ella's mind kept repeating monotonously: *If it's possible for me to return some day . . .* Four years had gone by, and he had been returning.

She wanted to get home—to think out this bewildering thing—this new phase of her life—in the haven of her room away from all prying eyes—to remember him, to bring him before her in memory—his kind eyes and strong mouth and the backward sweep of his graying hair. She wanted to forget the bitter news of his death, to pretend for a brief quiet hour that the anticipated trip had been completed, to live in fancy the culmination of that journey. She wanted no one to see her, to talk to her, to mar this hour of memory and the bitter-sweet knowledge of what might have been.

But a student was waiting on the steps for her, and when she had finished with him, and had gone on into the house, Stena met her at the doorway with the information that Mrs. Bishop had one of her headaches and her heart was "acting up again." So Ella took off her hat and put on a big apron, gave her mother medicine and wrung out cold compresses until supper time. After supper there was a committee of Minerva girls coming for advice about celebrating the anniversary of the founding of the Society, so there was not even time to hold wistful memorial services in the secret places of her heart.

In the spring of that year of 1905, she tried to grow enthusiastic about reunion plans, fell to remembering all those first Minerva classmates whom, with the exception of Irene Van Ness, she had not seen for so many years, secured their addresses, wrote voluminously to each girl.

"Girls!" she laughed ironically about the word to Professor Cunningham's wife. "I guess women who have gone to school together continue to speak of each other as 'girls' on through a doddering senility."

She spent long moments thinking of them, calling the roll as it were. Irene Van Ness whom she had seen eleven years before, Mina Gordon, little and lithe and gypsy-like, Mary Crombie, frank and efficient, Janet McLaughlin, big-boned and homely and lovable—

Suddenly with something of a shock, it came to her that she was thinking of them as they had been—not as the years would have made them. With mental reservations she went on with the list: Emily Teasdale would be coming, and if not the lovely dashing beauty of the old days, at least spiritedly handsome in a mature way. Evelyn Hobbs—no, she suddenly remembered. Evelyn would not be there for she was dead.

It was a tender spot in her heart that this first old group held,—something akin to an inner chamber in which incense burned before a shrine of youthful friendship, and even as she received the answers to her invitation, she experienced a vague fear of disillusion and disappointment to see them as mature women. For much water had trickled under the little rustic bridge over Oak Creek since the seven had parted tearfully and with protestations of undying loyalty.

As Commencement drew near, she half regretted her urgent invitations —perhaps the old friends would seem like so many strangers in her home —half wished that she had kept the familiar memories of "the girls." How foolish, she told herself. After all, memory was but a pale moon which the bright sun of flesh-and-blood contact would throw into shadows.

Stena worked hard to get all the rooms in shape for the guests. The house looked nice. Prettily framed prints on the wall and soft rugs on polished floors showed Ella's improved taste. Her mother's first bedroom was now Ella's study, book-lined and containing her writing-desk and two or three fancy baskets concealing the ever-present English papers. The old enclosed stairway was now a wide open one with walnut railing. Some of the old furnishings of the living-room had been relegated to the barn—the stereoscopic views and the plaster boy who was still trying vainly in the dark of a stall to locate the thorn in his foot.

There were endless tasks for Ella, the house, looking after her mother whose frailty now at sixty-nine was marked, planning of the meals while "the girls" would be there, the final examination papers, assistance and advice to the present-day Minerva officers, the reunion dinner. "I wonder why I'm always adding something to my already full days," she said once to her image in the glass. "I just naturally soak up extra work."

At four in the afternoon of the day before Commencement, she drove to the station, holding her horse in steadily once or twice when one of the new automobiles came by. It was a typical Commencement home-coming, June sunshine, students to meet arriving parents, excitement when the train swung into view. There was nothing quite like it to quicken the blood if one were part of the scene, she thought.

When the train had stopped and the passengers crowded down the steps, she saw Irene immediately,—a strange fat woman in her wake. Irene, an old looking girl when she was young, looked scarcely older now than when Ella had last seen her. "Why," Ella thought, "they are not going to seem a bit different." She was elated. The magic of the reunion was beginning.

She and Irene clutched each other with abandon. "Irene," Ella was quite honest, "you don't look any older than . . ."

But Irene was trying to draw Ella's attention to the strange woman—some one to whom she was wanting to introduce her. "And here's Mina," she was saying gayly. And the huge woman was bearing down upon Ella, too. Mina! Mina Gordon, square of body, large spectacles, her face a full moon, two or three chins! Mina, who should have been little and lithe and gypsy-like. Oh, no! The magic was dissolving.

Irene had so many bags that they could scarcely get them in the back of the buggy. Evidently, clothes still played a large part in her life. The three drove up to Ella's home, Mina's share of the buggy seat by no means confined to her rightful one-third interest. There was much to be said. Irene's oldest daughter was married now—her name was Smith and she had a baby boy. Irene was a grandmother. How queer! But Irene laughed and shook her thin sallow face, jangling her earrings merrily. Mina had four boys and two girls. The family had been as poor as Job's turkey, she said, but had always had the *most* fun. Just this year a bachelor uncle's estate had suddenly descended on them like manna and they scarcely knew how to act. Sometimes she even wondered if they'd lost a little of their family fun now that things were so easy.

Just before dinner, Janet McLaughlin surprisingly drove up in the station bus, having come a day sooner than she expected. Janet was well-groomed, her ensemble the last word in modishness, her blue suit tight to the knees with its stylish circular flare. She wore a modish blue hat, close fitting at the back of her head but projecting far to the front with a long brim over the high pompadour of her hair. Janet was a teacher at a distant university, and having taught English history so many years, as Mina puffingly said, by this time she must have been on chummy terms with Mary of the Scots and able to guess every surreptitious thought of Queen Elizabeth's.

In the evening the four walked back to the station to meet Mary Crombie and Emily Teasdale. When the train disgorged the two, the others saw that the years had merely accenuated Mary's early characteristics. Domineering in her girlhood she had turned that quality clubward since clubs had become popular, and in the last few years had been local, county, district, and state Everything in the organization of her choice. A little thinner, a bit more wiry, far more efficient looking, she came elbowing her way briskly through the crowd just as they would have expected her to do. Across her flat chest were gold-mounted glasses on a long chain which she pulled out with a little zipping sound and adjusted in order to look the others over. Immediately Ella could visualize her in the Chair and hear her crisp: "The ayes have it."

Emily was trailing behind her, Emily Teasdale, the lovely spirited belle of their college days. But what had happened? Something or some one had taken all the starch out of Emily. Her dress was nondescript, her hat uninteresting, her face vacuous. She was a little wilted flower, a shadowy woman with no initiative left. Her conversation all the days they were together was one of alibis and excuses. Poor Emily, thought Ella many times, the embodiment of broken ideals, vanished illusions.

So there they all were, all but Evelyn who could not come because she was dead. The years,—what had they done to the six? Irene who had been unhappy over a love affair was now loved and happy. Ella, whose love affair had once been the envy of Irene, had not known the fruition of her hopes. Mary, who had once possessed a great deal of money, had lost it all. Mina, who never had a dollar ahead in her life, had come into a large heritage. Emily, who had been as lovely as a painting, was a faded pansy of a woman. Janet, who had been a homely, raw-boned girl, had developed into a striking woman of self-reliance and poise. All this had a quarter of a century done to a little group of schoolmates.

The four were quite unanimous in their decision that Ella and Janet had changed the least of all. The two seemed, the others said, to be the ones who had kept their youth. It was because teachers had no cares, they assured each other. For Ella and Janet they said there had been no tragedies, no business responsibilities, no hanging over sick beds in the hush of gray mornings, no dark graves. Teaching might be taxing, Mary admitted magnanimously, but it wasn't as though Ella had known the responsibility of trying to get votes for women, and Mina wheezily said that, after all, Janet simply couldn't have been heartbroken over Mary Queen of Scots or felt personally responsible for all of Queen Elizabeth's little escapades.

In the days that followed, the six, with Professors Schroeder and Fonda of their class, attended every activity on a very active campus,—a little group clinging together as though, from sheer result of the connection, they themselves might contact youth.

Emily Teasdale grew almost weepily sentimental over that first meeting with big Professor Schroeder whom she might have married; and Janet McLaughlin spent a large portion of her waking time thanking a kind Providence that she had not let the dashing drum-major in the first old college band hypnotize her into marriage, inasmuch as his career to date consisted largely in being head janitor at the gymnasium.

There were old students of other classes back, too,—successful, unknown, talented, ordinary, those who had accomplished much and those who had not known the fulfillment of any desire. At Commencements, more than on any other occasion, Time, the toll-keeper, says: "Halt. Who goes there? What have you done with the years?"

It was Ella, more than any of them, who bound the past to the present. Active, enthusiastic, apparently knowing all the students, she seemed no less a part of the young generation than of the old. But at best the others were standing at the outskirts of things looking on. Youth not only must be served, but it demands the center of the stage.

And so on the third afternoon they gave up attempting to enter into the Commencement activities and settled down in the study of Ella's home. A lowering sky with an occasional dash of rain and a grate fire added to the coziness of the mellow room where rows of books looked down upon them.

Emily Teasdale and Mary Crombie had brought pieces of needlework, —Emily making an occasional half-hearted attack upon hers, with Mary sitting up stiffly and working as though life depended upon it.

Reminiscences being as they are, the conversation could scarcely have been called enlightening or even interesting to the casual listener. It consisted largely of sentences beginning: "Do you remember . . . ?"

Mary recalled the purloining of grapes from Professor Carter's arbor, Emily a frustrated attempt to paint the brass band's mascot. Mina dragged out of its hiding place a gossipy campus skeleton that probably had not strayed from its closet to jangle its bones for two decades. With an uncanny aptitude for remembering all the foolish and forgetting much of the sensible, Ella and Janet found that they could repeat snatches of countless silly parodies they had once penned for the Minerva society, not one of greater literary value than:

"We were seated in assembly,
Not a soul had room to stir.
'Twas our annual debate day
And a storm was in the air.
And as thus we sat there silent,
Not a maiden there would smile.
'We are lost' the leader whispered
As she staggered down the aisle."

They all came back out of a carefree past,—fatuous episodes, incautious escapades, scraps of verse,—little half-memories. In the semi-gloom of

Ella's study one could almost smell the fragrant pungent odor of rosemary, "for remembrance."

Their farewell dinner was a pleasant meal, with Stena treading heavily in and out, anticipating their every want. Mary and Emily and Janet were going East on the evening train; Mina was taking one to the north in the morning; Irene was staying in town for a week. This, then, was the end of the reunion.

Very soon after dinner they went upstairs while Janet and Mary and Emily packed, all a little sad at the parting. Something had drawn them together again in the three days. The old friendships had been revived, and in addition, there had emerged something more tender, a mature appreciation of each other. Moving in six different orbits now, still the old attraction held them. The twenty-five years had thrown many barriers between them, distance, husbands, homes, children, businesses, social events, a thousand activities. But now that they had renewed the old acquaintance, it seemed as hard to part as on that long-gone time. To be sure, they were not shedding tears and pledging undying friendship, as then, but were promising to get together more often.

And the gathering had done other definite things to them, too: Emily had taken on a little stamina, expressing herself more freely, even wearing her hat with a bit of aplomb, Irene's life had sounded a merry new note. Mary's pronounced tendency to domineer all situations seemed a little less prominent, Janet's self-assured pertness mellowed. Even Mina, jealous of the others' relative slimness, was leaving for home with the solemn declaration that when next they saw her she would be of sylphidine proportions. As for Ella, she had resurrected the old feeling of friendship to such an extent that she felt she would cheerfully cross a continent to see them all.

Reunion! It was a pleasant thing.

CHAPTER XXVIII

☙ MOST of the members of the faculty had been abroad at some time or were planning to go. Miss Hunter and Miss Jones of the training school, Professor and Mrs. Cunningham were going in the summer of 1906. "And I could go, too, if I would ever save my salary," Ella complained of herself. "I don't know what the trouble is. I don't seem to do anything worth while but it just goes."

But if she had taken a complete survey of her activities she would have realized that keeping up a home, paying wages to Stena, supporting a frail mother who often needed the services of a physician, caring for Hope and sending her to school all those years had made inroads on the teacher's modest salary.

The Cunningham group wanted her to join them, and Ella was tempted, but another duty faced her and she had no mind for the trip while the possibility of Hope teaching in the college confronted her. For two years now to the joy of Ella's prideful heart Hope had been very successful in her work at Maple City. And with the position for a primary critic teacher opening in the training school Ella played every possible card that she could to get the place for Hope. Honest and frank as nature itself, for the first time in her life she found herself playing up to people. "That's what mothers will do for their offspring," she thought. "I see now how parents will stoop to almost anything for their own."

She cultivated Miss Jones assiduously although they had not a great deal in common. She was especially solicitous to President Watts. She went out of her way to talk to the board members. "I'm ashamed of myself," she admitted. "But I do so want my girl home that I'm not quite level-headed about it. And it isn't as though she couldn't do the work well. My alibi is that I'm doing the school as well as myself a favor."

Ella's deep desire was granted. Hope was elected and took her place, as modest as it was, on the faculty, catalogued as assistant supervisor, in reality handmaiden to Miss Jones.

"Now this year," Ella thought, "I'll save every penny for the grand tour. The stage is all set. Hope home here with Mother, Stena so faithful. Next spring I shall be with the pilgrims myself." It gave her a warm feeling of joyful anticipation. She read travel books by the dozen, by day figuratively crossed the Bridge of Sighs and at night dreamed of wandering through the Louvre.

But she did not carry out those dreams.

For Fate, that old woman of the loom, stepped into the picture in the spring and directed that the time had now arrived for Hope herself to meet Romance. And like many of the tricks the old woman plays, the meeting took place in a most unlooked-for way and when least expected.

To be specific it happened at ten minutes past two on an April afternoon in Room Twenty-one of the primary training department. To be sure it was also ten minutes past two in other departments of the college;

but in Room Twenty-one of the training school it seemed most specifically ten minutes past two—that lazy, languorous time of day.

The windows were open to the warm breeze. An unsanitary-looking fly buzzed in and out, daring the students to catch him. Out on the campus little new leaves were pushing their way hurriedly through the brown buds of the maples. Chris burned weeds by the tennis court.

Nineteen girls, who were taking the primary course, lined the walls of Room Twenty-one, notebooks in hand. Some of them were majoring in primary training and minoring in other subjects. Some of them were minoring in primary work and majoring in getting engaged. But on this Wednesday afternoon at ten minutes past two, there was no way of dividing the gayly frivolous from the deadly earnest by their appearance. Due to the spring weather, all alike looked sleepy, dull, uninterested. A pudgy girl with thick glasses over protruding eyes made objectless marks on her notebook. A homely blonde, whom no discriminating gentleman would have preferred, was frankly nodding.

Across the room, near one of the open windows, sat Hope.

It would have taken twenty guesses to have picked out Hope as the assistant supervisor, for having attained the mature age of twenty-four, she still looked as sweet and young as a wood sprite. Her warm brown hair was combed back from her calm forehead and rolled into neat buns just back of each ear after the fashion of the moment. She was dressed in leaf green which gave her the appearance of being one with the elms and maples just outside the window.

If one could not have picked her out of the group from point of age or appearance, neither could one have recognized her through any manifestation of unusual interest in the work going on in the center of the room, for she looked as uninterested and bored as any of the students.

The children in the circle were playing games under the direction of a short, olive-skinned student; and no one could have accused the children, themselves, of being bored. With that wide-eyed interest in life in which the mere matter of weather has no part, they were entering into the oft-repeated plays with as much ardor as though participating in them for the first time.

At that particular moment a very immaculate little girl, whom one knew at a glance to be specimen of the perfect female child, spoke: "William is not standing correctly." She said it definitely, didactically and critically.

William immediately straightened his spindling, overall-clad legs, and the perfect child looked about her for further opportunity of correction.

"In years to come," said Hope—of course, to herself—"she will be president of a woman's club or chairman of some reform league."

A health game was now well under way. William, of the temporary slouchy attitude and the permanent overall legs, took the center of the circle.

"Will you have a dish of oatmeal and cream?" he asked, and pointed to one of the expectant group.

"Yes, thank you," said the honored one.

"Will you have some fried potatoes?" He pointed to another.

"No, thank you."

"Will you have a dish of stewed prunes?"

"Yes, please."

Any rank outsider could have sensed the point. It was as apparent as the pointer, himself, or the pointee. There was on in educational circles the first of the great reforms in eating—all the edibles which did not point the way to health were scorned. All the dainty morsels which were over-rich received the "thumbs down" of these little Romans. Their attitude was that if you ate fried potatoes you would be relegated to some region of the lost. If you ate oatmeal you would enter some Valhalla of bliss.

"Will you have a piece of pie?" William's active if soiled index finger veered to the perfect female child.

The p.f.c. shook her yellow curls and assumed a horror-stricken air of dramatic proportions.

"Oh—no, thank you." She threw into the answer a world of repugnance. And then, further realizing her own nobility of soul, she turned to the student teacher: "Miss Anderson . . . my mamma had pie this noon . . . raspberry pie . . . a big piece sat right by my plate . . . and I never touched it."

"Why, you little halfwit!" said Hope. (Oh, certainly to herself.) From which unuttered exclamation one may gather how very far afield had gone her regard for her own teachings this warm afternoon.

Sitting there in the midst of her chosen life work, Hope was admitting to herself a waning interest in it. And simultaneously with her digression she was mentally flaying herself with a bludgeon of self-criticism. As mystified as chagrined at the way her attention was slipping, she realized that for some unknown reason she felt at odds with her profession. She had always been wrapped up in it,—just like Aunt Ella. She wondered what Aunt Ella would say if she knew how this third year of her teaching was beginning to pall.

Too often recently she had been picturing herself down a vista of years in a future of training schools and lectures, dividing the fried potatoes from the oatmeal, the pie from the prunes—and the perspective was not so satisfying as she had once thought. It was something she felt would hurt Aunt Ella deeply to know, and the thought made her disgusted with her own attitude.

In the midst of her self-chastisement, and near the close of the children's health game, the door opened and the Head appeared. Not a head, but *the* Head,—Miss Hester Jones. If one wanted to be facetious, one might say that there was a hat upon the Head, for Miss Jones was hatted and gloved in the correct tailored way that one would expect Miss Jones to be, and being large and imposing, she carried about her person all the dignity and age which Hope, the assistant, failed to possess.

Quite suddenly the atmosphere in Room Twenty-one changed. It was as though, upon opening the door, Miss Jones had inserted the cord of an imaginary electrical charger into an invisible socket. The occupants of the room came to life. The blonde leaned forward with a deep and vital interest in the health game. The fat girl with the thick glasses began writing unimportant words vigorously in her notebook. The fly disappeared into an outer sun-flooded world, as though there were no use trying to fool with a personality like Miss Jones's. Hope, the good lieutenant that she was, almost saluted her superior.

The Head crossed to her now, said a few low words of explanation to her, looked complacently at the keenly interested girls flanking the walls, stopped to say good-by to the participants of the game circle, and vanished into the sun-flooded world herself, although not by way of the window.

The figurative electric cord having been withdrawn from the socket, the occupants of the room slumped into their former state of lethargy. The homely blonde closed her eyes. The fat girl tucked her pencil into her blouse pocket. Hope returned to her own analytical soliloquy.

The circle game was changing now. They were about to perpetrate the classic known as "Chicken Little."

"Heavens!" said Hope (oh, most assuredly to herself). "If I'm ever in a large brick building with bars at the windows it will be from an overdose of Chicken Little."

"The sky is falling," said Chicken Little, in the person of William the conquered. "I will run and tell Henny-Penny." And the orgy of gossiping was on.

In the midst of the wild rumors which seemed to obsess Chicken Little there was a knock on the door of Twenty-one—a loud and vigorous knock, almost immodestly so, for one usually approached the model training school with something of timidity, silence, and veneration.

"I heard it with my ears. I saw it with my eyes. A piece of it fell on my tail," declared the newsmonger in the circle.

The girls all straightened up, cheered with the pleasant anticipation of having the monotony relieved, although it would probably prove to be nothing more exciting than a student or a parent. Hope rose, crossed the room, and opened the door, preparatory to slipping out. But she did not slip. It was not a student. One had grave doubts about its being a parent. A very tall, very well-groomed young man stood on the threshold.

"I beg your pardon," his voice boomed hollowly from the empty hall.

"You'd better," thought Hope critically.

"May I speak to you for a moment?" His voice was still far from weak.

"I will run and tell Turkey-Lurkey," threatened the tattle-tale in the circle.

Hope had time to say acridly (yes, indeed to herself), "All right . . . go on and tell," as she stepped out and closed the door.

The man looked at Hope, standing there, cool and aloof and questioning. "I'm sorry to bother you." He had a most engaging smile. "My name is Jones—Richard Jones—of the firm of Blake, Bartholomew, and Jones of Chicago. And while I'm here between trains, I'm trying to form a rather belated acquaintance with a cousin of mine."

"Oh!" Hope smiled then also. And that made two engaging smiles turned loose in the hall. "You're Miss Jones's cousin." She became gracious and friendly. "Miss Jones is the head of our department. But she's not here. She has just gone . . . starting over to the Maynard High School to give her lecture. She's been gone such a little while—she was here a few minutes ago—that I'm sure you could catch her. She takes the yellow street-car at the northeast corner of the campus."

"Yes?" Miss Hester Jones's cousin looked at the cleft in Hope's chin, and repeated, with certain slight variations, "I see . . . the northeast street-car at the corner of the yellow campus."

"You can take a short-cut," the owner of the chin declivity suggested.

"Yes?" said Mr. Jones vaguely, and added more definitely, "Oh, yes."

"You go down these first steps and turn to the left. Then you follow the walk past the Administration Building . . . Do you know where the Administration Building is?"

"No," said Mr. Jones, almost in despair. "Oh, no."

"It's the first building to the north. Then you take the curved walk and you will find the street-car at the end of it."

And while the consensus of opinion among the other members of the firm was that Mr. Richard Jones was far from dull, he seemed to have acquired a sudden impenetrable density.

In the intensity of her desire to do the gracious thing for the head of the department, Hope further volunteered: "I'll walk out to the steps and point it out to you." Which all goes to prove that stupidity occasionally has its place in the scheme of things.

They went out on the training-school steps, where the elm leaves budded and the bees droned and the April sunshine lay in little golden pools.

"The campus is gorgeous, now, isn't it?" the man said affably.

"Lovely," the girl agreed. "Now, there . . . around that walk . . . over there."

"It's a perfect day, isn't it?"

"Quite perfect. You've only a few minutes."

"Thank you so much. I hope taking you away from your class like this hasn't queered you in any way with your teacher."

"I," said Hope, a little coldly, "*am* the teacher."

"You? Do you mean to stand there and say . . . Well, can you beat . . . ?"

"You'll have to hurry," said the teacher with finality. "Good day." And she went into the building and closed the huge door impressively.

As she stepped back into Twenty-one, her head very high, nineteen girls watched her keenly, thirty-eight adult eyes looked at her curiously.

"They ran into Foxy-Loxy's den and they never came out," accused the gossiper of the circle.

Several girls grinned openly, not to say suspiciously. The homely blonde tittered and nudged the owl-eyed fat girl in her well-cushioned ribs.

"Just for that," said Hope (oh, absolutely to herself), "you will pay . . . and pay . . . and pay . . ." Aloud, and quite distinctly, she said: "Observation class dismissed. You will each hand in on Thursday a well-written nine-hundred-word paper on The Relation of Games to a Child's

Health." And knew, with an unholy glee when something like a dull moan issued from the audience, that she had nipped in the bud more than one canoe ride and stroll on the campus.

At four o'clock, preparing to leave her office, she pushed back the calendar on her desk, weighted down a bunch of lesson plans with a plaster cast of *The Laughing Child*, straightened the sepia copy of *The Gleaners*, and closed the desk. When she turned around Richard Jones of Blake, Bartholomew, and Jones stood in the doorway.

"I missed her," he grinned cheerfully.

"I'm so sorry," said Hope, and added (oh, exclusively to Hope), "Oh, no, you're not so grieved."

"And now I'm stranded here until ten o'clock, and you're the only one in town I know."

Know! The Nerve!

"Well," she suggested pleasantly, "the college library doesn't close until nine."

He was thoughtful. "And I never *have* read Fox's *Book of Martyrs* or *Saint's Rest*," he admitted.

At that, Hope laughed aloud. And Dick Jones laughed too. And the plaster cast laughed hardest of all—diabolically—but behind their backs.

All of which is the long and circuitous sequence of events which led Hope to bring home to her Aunt Ella's a young man of whose existence she had not been aware at nine minutes past two that afternoon,—to bring him home solely from duty and out of courtesy to Miss Jones, she explained so many times to Ella, that this discriminating woman was forced to hide her tell-tale eyes from her foster daughter.

Ella was like a mother hen with a chick who has suddenly shown some new interest in life. It was the first time Hope in her more mature years had seemed to be thrown out of her calm poise at masculinity. And dragging him home as though responsible for him! While she helped Stena add a dainty dish or two to the dinner, she nursed her surprise and a certain sense of worry.

But during the dinner hour, Ella admitted grudgingly to herself that he was thoroughly likable. And it *was* something to know he was Miss Jones' cousin.

When he was leaving, he told Hope that he would stop again on his way back from his trip,—a promise that did not seem to antagonize her, Ella thought.

On Thursday it seemed nothing short of dishonest not to speak about him immediately to Miss Jones but he had asked her not do so for the reason that he wanted to surprise her by dropping in at the college again in a few days. On Monday of the following week, whenever Hope heard a noisy approach in the hall, she grew slightly chilly and showed a tendency toward flushing at the cheek bones. But two days of the week went by, and he had not come back.

On Wednesday afternoon, as she went down the steps of the training school and rounded the building to the north, she nearly collided with him—the returning relative of the Head.

"Oh . . . !" She was genuinely distressed. "Didn't I tell you? I *thought* I did. Miss Jones goes over there every Wednesday afternoon," she explained earnestly.

"Does she?" Mr. Richard Jones was apparently torn between the intensity of his surprise and the depths of his mental pain.

"Every Wednesday," repeated Hope.

"I see . . . persistency . . . perseverance . . . stick-to-itiveness. It's in the blood."

To mitigate Mr. Jones's disappointment over the unintentional misunderstanding, Hope took him home again.

"Well, Stena," Ella said, upon glancing out of a window, "here comes our nice young man again. It isn't going to be every Wednesday, is it?"

CHAPTER XXIX

☙ April flung one more lovely week over the campus. On Wednesday afternoon Hope stood before her desk calendar and absent-mindedly drew two distinct circles around the two previous Wednesday dates. Then, with sudden alarm, she rubbed them out so vigorously that there were only smudgy holes left where the figures had been. When she looked up from the calendar, she saw Mr. Richard Jones standing in the doorway.

"My cousin . . . ?" He was beaming cheerfully. "Is she here?"

"You know she isn't," said Hope coldly.

"But you told me she went Wednesdays."

"*This* is Wednesday." There were icicles on the statement. "You know it is."

"Is it?" He walked over to the calendar and ran an investigating finger up the columns. "Why, so it is," he admitted amiably, and then asked curiously, "What made those two holes in your calendar?"

"Days that were wasted," said Hope evenly, "so wasted that I cut them out."

Quite suddenly, Richard Jones was not flippant. "They were not wasted." He was all seriousness. "They were delightful . . . so lovely that I came back to have more of them before we have to take my cousin with us." And then, as quickly, he returned to his former lightness. "The year's at the spring . . . the horse at the curb . . . my face is all clean . . . your hair is all curled . . . God's in heaven . . . all's right with the world."

Hope had to laugh at that, and knew there was not a particle of use in trying to trace the various processes by which her mental equipment was assuring her that it was her duty to entertain him once more for the sake of Miss Jones, in spite of his flagrant fabrications.

So eliminating all analysis, and looking only at results, one might have seen the two, fifteen minutes later, driving through a woodsy road where the sun flecked the rubber-tire tracks through dancing shadows. The drive ended at the one college café, the Mellow Moon—the first of the many eating places which a generation later were to be found on every corner.

It was while they were dining that they heard a shrilly triumphant, "Miss Thompson . . . oh, Miss Thompson!"

"Somewhere a voice is calling," said Richard Jones, "tender and true."

The voice was the voice of the perfect female child, and with its insistent decision and two forceful hands, she was dragging her parents to the table nearest the beloved teacher.

Hope spoke to the obedient parents, made a pedagogical-sounding remark to her adoring pupil, and then turned to discuss the critical question of dessert with Richard Jones.

"I'd love a piece of pie," she said wistfully, "but I can't have it."

"Can't? Why the 'can't'?"

"Because this energetic creature across from me"—she spoke very low—"watching my every movement, is the personification of all my work. She is the symbol of my career. I teach her to scorn fried potatoes and laud oatmeal . . . to eschew pie and chew prunes. I know that's an awfully low type of humor, but I couldn't help it. I ask you, then, could I sit here, under her eagle eye, and order pie . . . and let her see all my theories come tumbling down?"

Richard Jones grinned his interest.

"But if I ever leave . . ." she threatened.

Mr. Jones sat forward. "Yes? When you leave? You mean when you marry?"

"Every woman teacher who marries must leave the faculty," said Hope definitely. "There is a ruling to that effect. But it does not necessarily follow that, inversely, every one who leaves, has married. As I was saying . . . " She was a little confused. "Oh, yes . . . if I ever leave, I shall do just that . . . recklessly, before them all . . . the student teachers . . . your cousin, the Head . . . the perfect female child . . . all of them. I shall order the richest pie I can get . . . and eat it in their presence. It would be symbolic. It would be a gesture of freedom. It would be signing an emancipation proclamation. It would be snapping my fingers in the faces of the gods."

The little student waitress came up for the order.

"Prunes," said Hope to her resignedly, "stewed prunes."

It was when Richard Jones was leaving Ella Bishop's home in the evening that he quite brazenly came out with the declaration that he wanted to dine with Hope again the following Wednesday. And Hope, with one fleeting assurance to herself that there was no more comforting bit of philosophy than that one might as well be hung for a sheep as a lamb, said she would expect him.

On Monday, May took the nice spring weather by the hand, and the two fled precipitately, leaving behind them cold, rainy, disagreeable weather.

And then on Tuesday, the Head came into Hope's office. "This terrible rain!" she began in her ponderous way. "I'm glad I'm all through with the Maynard lectures."

Hope's heart missed a beat. So Miss Jones was through with her Wednesday trips. The perfect tête-à-têtes would cease. So she might as well speak of him now.

"A young man cousin of yours . . ." she had to busy herself among her papers to hide the agitation of her face, "was here looking for you."

"My cousin? Well . . . I haven't seen him since he was in his teens. How time does fly. And to think he's going to be married,—to a girl named Daphne Dunham. Isn't that euphonious?"

Hope's heart crashed head-on against the stone wall of the news. But her mind was saying stanchly: "People have more than one cousin. No doubt she has a dozen."

But Miss Jones was going placidly on. "He is the only cousin I have, and I do hope he is getting a lovely girl. He's a dear boy . . . but something of a philanderer, they tell me. Now that he's to be married, though, I'm sure he'll settle down."

Hope's heart seemed scarcely able to move in the midst of its wreckage. All that it could think was that to-morrow was Wednesday,—the day that Richard Jones was to come again.

Then her mind began to take charge of the situation.

"You've been taking your dinners at the Mellow Moon, haven't you, Miss Jones?"

"Yes, excepting of course those evenings I've been at Maynard. Why?"

"Oh, I just wondered. I'm dining there to-morrow night with a guest. I thought perhaps you'd join us."

Miss Jones thanked her, said not to wait if she was not there by six-thirty. And the day's work had begun.

All the rest of the day and Wednesday morning it rained. And all Wednesday Hope went doggedly about her work.

In the late afternoon, swathed in a brown raincoat, with her dark hair tucked under a cap, she was splashing through the damp, dripping campus toward home.

With the swishing sound of a water-soaked raincoat, some one was coming rapidly behind her. She stepped aside, but a masculine hand closed over her own hand that held the umbrella.

"My cousin . . . ?" He had the nerve to laugh at that—this modern Claudius who could smile and smile and be the villain still.

"Your cousin . . ." She forced herself to laugh too. "Your cousin has gone to the county commissioners to report your weakening mentality."

There was a blazing fire in the grate at Aunt Ella's when they arrived. Hope left the villain standing in front of it, looking after her, when she mounted the stairs to dress. She wished he hadn't looked like that—clean-cut and attractive—standing there so easily in front of the fire.

In her room she put on a brown dress, decided she looked ghastly, and changed it for a crimson one. When she came down, the two made their way under the dripping elms, over the slippery walks to the Mellow Moon. Two students, the homely blonde and the fat girl with glasses, smelling romance, left their seats in the far end of the room and came to take places at the next table.

"Miss Thompson . . . oh, Miss Thompson," broke forth an adoring sound.

"Ha!" said Richard Jones. "There's the voice that breathed o'er Eden."

"Why don't they ever eat at home?" commented the object of the adoration, irritably, as the perfect female child pulled her pliant parents to the other adjoining table.

The vacant chair turned against their own table seemed to eye Hope like a silent accuser. Miss Jones had said not to wait if she had not arrived at six-thirty. So the two ordered, ate and conversed—the last activity being somewhat handicapped by the close proximity of many ears. Hope was more nervous than she had ever been in her life.

And then she saw Miss Jones come in.

"Look, Mr. Jones," she said in a small voice that sounded flat and unnatural.

"At the what?"

"Don't you see her?"

"Which 'her'?"

"Your cousin . . . over there by the door."

"Oh, is my cousin over there? I thought you said she went every Wednesday."

"She did . . . but she's finished."

"Then so am I. Listen, Hope Thompson. There's something I want to explain to you before she comes."

"Oh, don't try to explain." She was looking at the heavy figure of the Head, who had stopped to speak to Professor Cunningham. "I know all about it."

"I should have told you." He was all seriousness. "I've just let things drift carelessly along . . . and happily . . . from week to week. But you won't let it make any difference with us, will you?"

Any difference! Hope smiled. She was thinking that Napoleon might have asked it of Josephine when he divorced her.

When Richard Jones saw the tremulous smile that was meant to be cheerful, he said quite savagely: "I'm all kinds of a cad to let you hear it from some one else. Who told you?"

"Miss Jones. . . your cousin. She said Miss Dunham was a lovely girl." Miss Jones was now talking to the football coach and his wife, halfway down the room. "And I congratulate you."

"What for? Who's lovely?"

"Miss Daphne Dunham . . . your fiancée."

"My what?"

"Fiancée." And then, quite didactically, she explained: "The girl you're engaged to."

"Good lord." He was gazing in deep amazement toward the chatting group. "I'm not engaged to anybody . . . Daffy-down-dilly, or any one else . . . not for a few minutes yet anyway. I don't know where you got that, but it's immaterial just now. Listen, Hope, listen closely." He leaned nearer to her across the college café table. "I'm not the Head's cousin . . . nor her uncle . . . nor her grandfather. I never saw her before and I don't care a tinker's dam if I never see her again. I never heard of her before the day you first talked to me. I'm terribly sorry to tell you this here . . . and now. Can you hear me? These two human phonographs over here are recording it all."

The blonde girl and the fat one with glasses scarcely moved a spoon, so anxious were they to catch the conversation.

"You mean you haven't been her cousin?"

"Not any of the time . . . not even Wednesdays." He grinned.

"But you said you were."

"Oh, no, I didn't. You came out in the hall looking as sweet as a peach and as cold as a peach ice. I said: 'My name is Jones and I'm looking up my cousin.' And you said, 'Oh, you're Miss Jones's cousin'; and thawed out and acted cordial. My cousin is a little freshman. Her name is Bartholomew—Mary Bartholomew. But when you insisted that Miss Jones was my cousin . . . even though the woods are full of Joneses . . . and looked at me like that . . ."

"Don't be talking about it. She's coming this way."

"Yes . . . I'm going to talk about it. I'm going to be talking about it after she gets here, if you won't listen now. Would you have gone out to dinner with me if you had known I wasn't the Head's cousin?"

"Most certainly not."

"Don't you see . . . I had to? There was nothing else to do. The minute I saw you I knew you were the girl for me."

The girl-for-him gasped.

"I love you . . . and I want you to marry me and leave school. You'd have to, you know. You said there was a ruling."

Miss Jones came up. There were introductions.

The little student waitress came up too.

"Go right on and order," said the Head in her supervising way, "while I look over the dinner card."

"Prunes and cream, Miss Thompson?" asked the little waitress familiarly.

Like needles to two magnets, Hope's eyes turned to the eyes of Richard Jones. The eyes of Richard Jones were twinkling . . . and then the twinkling changed to something less mischievous.

"Or pie, Hope?" He asked it gently—so gently that, instead of a prosaic item on the menu, it sounded like the first few lines of an old love poem.

Hope looked across the table china at the impostor. Over at the next table the homely blonde and the owl-eyed fat girl strained their aural organs to catch every word. Across the other aisle the perfect female child bent worshiping eyes upon her adored teacher.

Then—quite deliberately Hope made the gesture. Quite definitely she signed the proclamation. Quite distinctly she snapped her fingers in the face of the gods. For even as she spoke to the little waitress she was smiling across the china toward the junior member of Blake, Bartholomew, and Jones.

"Pie . . ." she ordered recklessly, "the chocolate pie with the whipped cream and marshmallow icing." And, instead of a prosaic item on the menu, it sounded like the rest of the lines of the old love poem.

CHAPTER XXX

☙ So Hope was to be married, and Ella knew the joy of witnessing another's happiness. Europe? She had no thought for it now—the Bridge of Sighs was but a plank across a stream, the Louvre might have been filled with circus posters, for all she cared.

She began buying things for Hope,—cloth for sheets one day, bath towels another. Good sense told her that she was spending more money than she should have done. "No, you keep your own money, Hope. It will come in handy. Don't forget this is probably the last thing of the kind I shall ever do for you."

So they shopped together, and Ella knew she was having as much excitement out of the expeditions as Hope. "I'm not so generous," she told herself honestly. "I'm really rather selfish, getting as I do such joy out of buying the pretty things."

There was a blue serge suit to be made by the local tailor,—a long skirt stiffened with buckram and a short stiff jacket with large banjo-shaped sleeves. There were fourteen yards of soft green crêpe de Chine to be purchased and ten yards of taffeta for the underdress. Then the wedding dress itself of soft white with dozens of yards of narrow lace to be used on the skirt which was ruffled to the waist. All summer Ella forgot pedagogy in her vicarious motherhood. All summer she purchased and planned and sewed. Her mother tried to help, but she muddled the patterns, sewed in the wrong sleeve, and Ella or Hope or Stena had to rip out and do it all over.

And sometimes in the summer as Ella worked, she thought of the dress upstairs in a chest,—the shimmering white dress with the pink rosebuds and the blue forget-me-nots in silken relief,—which had no hem, and into which the sleeves had never been sewed. But more often she thought only of Hope and the happiness that was hers.

Dick came twice during the summer and Ella, living the romance of the two young people, felt romantic too.

The wedding was in October—at the home. Ella wanted a church wedding with bridesmaids and the new pipe-organ playing and ushers from Hope's college classmates, but in that particular thing Hope seemed to be more sensible than Ella. "Oh, Aunt Ella,—*no*. Think of the expense and the fuss,—and the sort of—oh, I don't know, the *straining*."

Ella gave in. "I suppose you're right. But it's only once in a lifetime." In her heart she knew that she was wanting a wedding so lovely that it would take the place of two,—Hope's own and the wedding that had never been.

So it was planned to be small and in the home. At that it turned out that Ella could not draw the line for guests. Over and over she sat with a paper and pencil and tried to eliminate all her friends to some semblance of a crowd of medium size. Faculty members, townspeople, janitors, students who had been in Hope's classes— In despair she gave up, and Hope took the responsibility of choosing a few of the ones closest to her.

"But, Hope—they're all my friends."

Old lady Bishop nodded over her quilt-block. "Yes . . . Ella . . . her friends . . . she was always friendly . . . like Pa . . . I don't know . . ." Her voice trailed off uncertainly.

So Richard Jones came for his bride and they were married on an October day with the campus trees green and gold and scarlet, with the haze of the Indian summer clinging to far horizons like the ghostly white smoke of long-dead campfires. Professor Wick, who had been an ordained minister, performed the ceremony, his new suit surprisingly immaculate and his bushy whiskers trimmed to an almost immodest closeness. President and Mrs. Watts were there, and Professor and Mrs. Cunningham and the Schroeders and the Fondas and the Wittinglys. Miss Jones was there taking all the credit for the match, and Miss Boggs, singing "Oh, Promise Me" with a bit of a smirk for having been chosen over Miss Honeycutt, and Chris and Hannah Jensen, a little stiff in their new clothes. Stena in a hardanger apron bossed the Minerva society sisters who served the refreshments, and old Mrs. Bishop came outside her bedroom door for the ceremony but vanished afterward like a little old frightened doe.

And then the young people were gone in a merry shower of rice and good wishes, and the guests had departed, and Ella and Stena and old Mrs. Bishop were alone. Life seemed suddenly to slump for Ella, and to have no meaning.

All winter only the thought of her postponed trip abroad gave her any renewal of keen interest. With the expense of the wedding over, she was saving every cent for the coming summer's outing.

Her one worry was her mother. She seemed more frail and gentle, and what worried Ella more than her apparent weakness, she possessed a vague dreaminess, at times a fairly definite unconcern over what went on about her. So seldom now did she inquire for college news, spoke more and more often of the past. Once or twice she seemed a little sly to Ella about her small activities of the day. All Ella could ever get from her in answer to the question of how she felt, was that she was tired, and maybe her head hurt a little.

If Ella could have known the mental wanderings of the gentle old soul, she would have been filled with an agonizing sympathy. For many afternoons when Ella was in school and Stena upstairs in her room, old Mrs. Bishop stole into her bedroom, closed the door and lived in a little world of her own.

With trembling old hands she would take from its wrappings in her closet the light blue silk dress of her girlhood, slip it over her head and pat it into place lovingly. Then she would open her lowest bureau drawer and bring forth a white lace scarf of dainty weave. This she would drape laboriously around her shoulders with stiffened arms and fasten with a hair brooch.

To the onlooker the effect would have been ludicrous: the incongruity of the thin old neck and wrinkled face rising above the low-cut lustrous silk gown that had been made to enfold a winsome maiden. But to old Mrs. Bishop the picture must have seemed eminently satisfying. She would gather the gleaming folds in her little knotted blue-veined hands and walk about the room with slow mincing steps.

Then she would sit by the window in her dainty old dress and try to remember. It gave her a feeling of stability, a connection with life which she did not always seem to have. She could not explain to her daughter. Ella would not know what she meant, for no one could understand. But sitting there alone in the soft old dress she seemed to be able to leave her body. For a little while she would wait, and then the strange thing would happen. She would rise out of her physical self and join her young husband and the friends of her youth. All the magic of health she could feel,—all the joy of living. She could look back at herself sitting there so old and tired in the chair and laugh at herself. She could talk with the one she loved, and move about in a world peopled with all her friends of the early days. It was a lovely experience. She waited each day for the time to come—that witching hour—grew to long impatiently for it, was childishly cross when Saturday and Sunday, with people about, kept her from her rendezvous.

Some uncanny sense of time gave her the cue to return to normalcy. "It's time to come back," some unseen thing would tell her. Then she would return to meet her tired body, become merged with that feeble old person who was herself. She wanted no one to know about it, was stealthily careful to move about quietly as she put the loved things away.

Then she would emerge from her bedroom, fatigued in mind and body.

"Did you have a goot rest?" Stena would ask.

"Very nice," old lady Bishop would answer with averted eyes.

By spring, when her mother seemed no worse, Ella began making definite arrangements for the trip which was to mean so much to her. Sometimes looking at the gentle little woman whose life was so confined, her heart smote her. "If it were not for you, Stena, I wouldn't think of going," she would say. "Are you sure she will be all right?"

"S'e vill be no better an' no vorse dan if you are here. I'll vash her an' iron her an' cook her an' s'e vill be no different. You go an' forget dat mamma."

The last of March the others who were to go had settled definitely on the tour. Professor and Mrs. Schroeder, Professor and Mrs. Wittingly and Miss Hunter comprised the group. It was a congenial crowd and in the decision of joining them that Friday Ella felt a thrill of pleasure permeate her whole being. All afternoon her thoughts had wings as active as those of the pigeons in the tower.

It was rather late when she left her classroom. The March wind blew her long skirts about her all the way home. Fine particles of dust seemed permeating her eyes and nose. A snow fence across one corner of the campus had stopped a low brown pile of loam and sand and subsoil,—spring's dust blizzard with dirt for drifts.

When she went into the house Stena was setting the table. The dining-room looked cozy and inviting after the encounter with the distasteful elements.

"Where's Mother?" she asked.

"S'e hasn't come out of her room," Stena said. "Not since her nap."

Ella felt a vague uncomfortableness even then; so much so that without removing her things she went at once to her mother's room.

Over in the big chair by the window she sat,—dressed in the blue silk dress she had saved from her bridal things. She was laughing softly and speaking to some one. Ella looked about hastily. Her mother was talking to some one not there.

"Mother!" Ella's heart contracted in a spasm of deep dread, fear of some unknown terror, the thing she had vaguely suspected the last few weeks.

But old lady Bishop only laughed vacantly into the shadows. She had forgotten how to come back.

CHAPTER XXXI

❧ This was a new trouble—a real one—one of those that swoop down with dark smothering wings and engulf one in the blackness of despair. Ella had their own physician in, then a mental specialist out from Chicago. There was, of course, nothing to do but to care for the frail little body left behind when the mind went on its long journey into the land of shadows.

She was gentle, sweet, docile,—wanted only to move about her room with its familiar objects. Ella tried taking her out into the other rooms with the thought that the change might brighten the mental outlook.

But at the doorway of her bedroom, she clung with her bird-like little hands to the casing, whimpered like a child, and looking up at Ella, shook her head with a pitifully frightened, "No, no."

When Ella, scarcely seeing for the tears, led her back to the haven of her room, the old lady sat happily down in her chair by the window and began rocking and humming a cracked and weird little air that had no melody.

Ella gave up her trip. To Stena's scolding she said, "No, I can't, Stena—not now."

"But s'e doesn't care. S'e wouldn't *know*,—and I take shust the same care as if you vas here."

"Yes, I know that, Stena. That part would be perfectly all right. I'd trust you every minute. It's just that I have to be here, too. She might . . . Stena, she *might* suddenly get all right. What if I wouldn't be here? What if she got all right for just a little while,—and then . . . wasn't again? Don't you see,—I *must* be here."

"Vell, I suppose so. But you plan and safe your money . . . and den a big disappointment . . . it seem not right."

Ella turned away. "I'm not a child. I've had disappointments before."

Eventually she settled down to her work with renewed energy. Her mother's condition would never be changed, the doctors told her, so there was no use to forego any of the many activities outside her classroom work. Her mother's little body was well cared for by the faithful Stena who kept her clothed in immaculate aprons and white lace caps for which she crocheted endless trimmings. Other than that the old lady was no care, had no desire but to sit and rock and sort her colored quilt-blocks and hum her weird and cracked little song that had no melody.

Ella was in her late forties now, but so gradually that she could not have told how it came about, she found herself active socially with girls many years younger. Going to the same social functions, belonging to the same organizations whose personnel from year to year remained women of about the same age, she gradually slipped back at intervals to younger groups. No one ever gave her age a thought. Wit and humor and lively spirits are of no age,—and a woman who holds them all with no conscious effort is ageless. The Minerva literary society, and an English club,—the P.E.O. sisterhood, Altrusa and D.A.R. all were her fields of activity.

Hope came to visit one summer in 1909, sweet and matronly and rather more modish than in her teaching days. Two years later in the early spring she came home again, and Ella had a new concern—the coming of Hope's child. Sam Peters came over one March evening just at dusk to tell Ella if she ever needed help—in the night or any time—not to hesitate to call him.

It was the last of March when Hope was taken sick. There was a wild wind in the night. How queer, thought Ella, dressing hurriedly. A wild wind in the night! It tore around the house with malignant fury. Wild winds and birth,—they seemed always to go together. With amazing clarity the night of Hope's birth came back. She even remembered the street lamps going out and the blackness of the night, so that involuntarily she hurried over to the window and looked out. Electric lights at the intersections of the streets swung crazily on their long wires but held their glow. And now there was a telephone with which to summon aid—no need for Hannah either, with the trained nurse ready to come at the call.

Like a soldier on duty, she summoned the nurse and the doctor, comforted Hope, called Stena to make a fire in the kitchen range, went into her mother's room to see that she was covered and sleeping. The old lady slept like a child, unaware that a new life was coming, equally unaware that an old life was ebbing,—slept and dreamed little queer dreams and smiled in her sleep.

Ella thought she could not stand the strain of the long night and the day that followed. With sympathetic nerve tension, she lived the hours with Hope. That other time it had not touched her deeply. Great bitterness had so mingled with whatever sympathy she might have possessed that the one counteracted the other. But this was Hope,—like her own flesh and blood.

Dick arrived soon after the noon hour,—in a noisy new automobile, with chain drive and carbon lights.

Ella did not go to her classes. It was one of the few times in her life in which she put anything ahead of her school work. The nurse moved quietly up and down stairs. The doctor came, went away, came again. Stena went about her homely duties on exaggerated tiptoe and with guttural whisperings. Dick would not come down to eat. Ella sat by the kitchen range, all her heart upstairs with her foster daughter, and thought of many things. Old Mrs. Bishop, combed and immaculately clean in her white apron and lace cap, rocked in her room and hummed a cracked and weird little song with no meaning.

It was not until late afternoon that a high shrill wail came from above.

It rang out so suddenly in the hushed atmosphere which had just preceded it that it brought Ella from her chair to her feet.

"There!" shouted Stena, and sat down limply with her gingham apron thrown over her head and burst into tears.

The baby was a girl, plump, healthy, well-formed. Ella moved in a daze as one thinking he is living over something that has happened precisely the same way before. All her thought was for Hope. Crazily, she kept feeling a superstitious fear that the whole thing would repeat itself,—that Hope would come out from a coma, flutter the lids over her blue eyes,—die. She stood transfixed with the thought, could not move for the paralyzing fear.

"Is she . . . ? How . . . ?" She could not say the words for the dryness of her throat.

"She's going to be all right." The nurse was cheerful. In the clutches of her paroxysm of fear, Ella imagined too cheerful.

But Hope was to be all right. Life to Ella swung back then to a normal thing of gratitude, work and interest in her fellowman.

Dick left in a few days, to come again as soon as possible. Ella went back to school. The house took on a routine which revolved about the newcomer. Once Ella took the little thing in its dainty blankets in to her mother's room.

"See, Mother." She held the blue and white covering back from the round red face.

The old lady stopped rocking and bent forward to look inquiringly at the wee mite. "A little baby!" She spoke so naturally that the tears sprang to Ella's eyes.

Why, she seemed all right! *Oh, Mother, hold on to it,—hold on to your undestanding.*

"Yes, Mother. Isn't she cunning?"

"*I* had a baby once," she said proudly.

Oh, yes, Mother, try to remember that I am your baby.

Then, less sure, she stared at Ella. "Did I. . . didn't . . . I have a baby . . . once?"

And while Ella, tear-dimmed, could only nod, she started rocking and humming a cracked and weird little song that had no melody.

At the end of the month, Dick came for Hope, a pretty matronly Hope, all anxiety for the welfare of the bundle she would let no one else carry. Gretchen, she called the baby. "Gretchen Jones. I like the quaintness of it," she explained.

"Well, Aunt Ella,—once more I have to thank you for seeing me through." She was saying good-by, now. "Do you suppose I'll ever, ever be able to repay you for all your kindnesses to me all my life?"

"Oh, that's all right, dearie." Ella was too tender at the parting to talk.

"I know,—when you're an old, old lady you can come and live with us. Can't she, Dick?"

"Sure, she can. That *will* be a way to repay her. Sure."

"You're nice children, and I thank you," said Ella Bishop. But she knew that not when she was an old lady, or ever, must she thrust herself into the privacy of this little family.

CHAPTER XXXII

FOR nine years, old Mrs. Bishop rocked in her room, sorted her colored quilt-blocks and sang the cracked and weird little song that had no melody.

There were those who said Ella's devotion was Quixotic, that a long desired trip abroad would have harmed no one, the old lady least of all, that Stena's attachment to the invalid was so strong as to be marked, and under those circumstances Ella was free to go any summer that she wished. But she refused to go. "She might get sick . . . and there's just a possibility she could get all right for a little while—she almost did, once—and want me. If I were on the other side of the ocean I coudn't get here."

But she continued her many activities in the community. Mrs. Bishop did not miss her, and more than ever Ella was the mainspring of the machinery of a half-dozen organizations,—some professional, others merely social. The college itself was mother to a host of organizations,—each department fostering its kind, while some of general character were broader in scope. Among the popular ones was the *Schillerverein* sponsored by Professor Schroeder. He who entered its portals must forget the English language, express himself only in German, no matter in what depths of unintelligible jargon he might laughingly flounder. German songs, German speech, German refreshments,—the members of *Schillerverein* steeped themselves in a Germanic atmosphere.

In these educational circles with which she was so closely identified all these years, Ella had seen many new ideas and methods come to light, some to stay definitely, some to disappear like the dew of the morning. She had seen the rise and fall of the Pollard method and the Speer method and a dozen others. Vocational instruction now was emphasized everywhere. For a time it looked as though it was to be everything. "They're swinging the pendulum too far the other way," she scolded. "To make a wobbly horse-radish grater is now considered of far more importance than the king's English."

School and home—home and school—she moved energetically between the two, never forgetting one for the other.

In those nine years Hope made three or four visits home, bringing her little daughter,—a lovely dark-eyed child with creamy-satin skin of almost Spanish-like beauty. She came when the child was two and four and six. Life was pleasant for Hope with a devoted husband, her beautiful child, and a good income. And then life was no longer pleasant. The war hounds were unleashed, and their far-off frightful barking heard in the tiniest village of every state.

This threatening clamor sounded even more harsh in its contrast to the hitherto peaceful life of the college. War clouds hanging above the campus became of far more consequence than the fluffy masses of haze floating across the blue which Professor Fonda had always thought so important.

Attendance at *Schillerverein* fell off from forty to twenty,—to a half dozen. Few wanted to be associated with so Germanic a club. On a certain Friday night, Professor Schroeder waited an hour for a possible attendant, took the basket of *kaffee-kuchen* which Mrs. Schroeder had sent, turned out the lights, and walked slowly down through the campus, —like an old man.

Hope came home the next year, a frightened tearful Hope, with little seven-year-old Gretchen who could not understand why it was anything but grand for Daddy to have a uniform and high leather puttees and to get a long ride on a big ship.

One after another the college boys left. The draft was on. Recitation rooms thinned out, took on a feminine appearance. When Professor James of the English department left, Ella took over his classes. She plunged into Red Cross work, collected food, clothing and funds. She taught conscientiously all day, remembering always that Hope would be waiting to see her at the Red Cross headquarters to tell her the latest news. And so, Ella Bishop, with no husband of her own to follow in tortured imaginings, must then be as torn in her emotions as the others.

Professor Schroeder's classes fell away to almost a negligible attendance. There had grown up on the campus a vague spirit of hostility toward him,—a tendency to refer to him as the Hun. The courses on Faust and Schiller were dropped.

Sometimes Ella ran into him on the campus, walking along under the elms that reminded him of his linden trees. Unless with Professor Fonda, he walked a great deal by himself these days, his huge shoulders drooping, his former long stride slackened to a slower pace. No longer did he greet her with his jovial "Hail, blooming youth." Always he stopped almost timidly to see whether he was to be received warmly or with the cool nodding of an averted head. His deep-set eyes looked hurt, tragic.

To Ella he presented a pitiful result of a foolish and unreasoning hostility. Sensing her sympathetic understanding he sometimes sought her out as though he wanted to talk to one with less animosity than the others. Miss Bishop seemed always a mother confessor to the people with whom she came in contact. In her presence they dispensed with all subterfuges, became themselves.

"How can I deny loving my fatherland?" he would break out. "Cannot they believe that I love my America more?" And sometimes shaking his leonine mane sadly: "Music and literature—they have no nationality. Wagner . . . Goethe . . . Schiller . . . what have they to do with it?"

Watching him go down the campus walk, Ella felt a sisterly tenderness toward him, realized that a patriotism which knew no reasoning at the moment was crucifying good old George Schroeder.

Dick came back from the wars wounded, and it seemed for a time after his release, so long was it before he felt strong, that instead of Ella making her home with the young people as they had suggested, they would be living at the old house on Adams Street.

But the physical wound cleared, if not the memory of the experience, and Dick and Hope and little Gretchen, nine now, were back in their own home.

The Red Cross shop was closed. Restrictions on food were lifted. A memorial was built on the campus to the boys who never came back,—a campanile with its clock faces looking toward the four winds of the world and its chimes playing every hour. Professor Schroeder's department was consolidated with the department of Romance Languages. The war was over,—all but the hideous after-effects which could never be called "over" while the generation lived.

Life went on in the old home much as before. Stena washed and ironed and cooked and cleaned, put a fresh tissue-paper flower under the picture of the pale young man every spring, and took care of the little old lady who was like a fragile China doll.

Ella took the supper tray into her mother every evening and stayed to see that she was happy and comfortable. On an evening now in May, with the tulip buds showing a gleam of color through green slits, and the spirea bushes bursting into white foam, she took the tray to her mother's bedroom, placing it on the walnut bureau until she could arrange the little table for her.

Old Mrs. Bishop sat in her chair by the window, her head on a stand in the crook of her arm like a child, sound asleep. Ella pulled up the teatable and then bent to waken her, raising her head gently so as not to startle her.

But old Mrs. Bishop would not waken.

Ella stared for a moment at the dainty face, waxen-white under its snowy lace cap.

She was gone, smiling faintly, gone to seek her lost mind in the shadows.

Ella stooped and picked up the fragile little body in her own strong arms and sat down in the old rocking chair for a few moments before she called Stena. And as she rocked, she wept wildly, deep sobs shook her, and some of the tears were for all the sorrows that she had been compelled to bear in her life, and some were for the long years in which she had not known a real mother, but some of them were merely for the loss of the cracked and weird little song that had no melody.

CHAPTER XXXIII

☙ After her mother's death, Ella thought she ought not to keep Stena. But Stena was as frightened over being turned out as old Mrs. Bishop had ever been.

"I'm sisty-two," she said, "and dat's too old to fin' a new place. I safe my money—vy can't I keep my room and shust stay vidout vages?"

It touched Ella that Stena did not want to leave. And sometimes she had been so impatient about her. But Ella Bishop always paid her obligations, so they settled on a new scale of wages and Stena stayed on.

The longed-for European trip could not be taken for awhile after the war, and when conditions had cleared and groups of the faculty were turning their faces toward the old world once more, Ella had the one severe illness of her otherwise healthy life, which made such inroads into her savings, that she put aside the dream as unfeasible until she had caught up with her finances.

In coming back from her illness, she lived through that experience which comes only to humans who have gone into the Valley a little way and returned to the sunlight. With the memory of the shadows still fresh within her, the world took on new coloring, sweeter sounds, more fragrant odors. Never had she known tulips so brilliant, robins' songs so lovely, lilacs so sweet-scented. It was as though the misty shadows which for a day or two hung about her, in lifting, had cleansed eyes and ears and nostrils until they functioned with renewed acuteness.

The school was a huge unwieldy thing now. Ella sometimes laughed to herself to think of those old days when the faculty was a big family, holding reading circle meetings, or having a picnic together, with a half-dozen baskets containing the refreshments. A faculty family picnic now, for sheer size would have looked like the county fair, a faculty reading circle in its circumference would have encircled the athletic field. She missed the old familiar camaraderie at times, clung a little to the Wattses and the Wittinglys, the Fondas and the Schroeders. New people came in almost every year and occasionally an old familiar face dropped out. Professor Wick and Professor Carter died,—not long afterward, Professor Cunningham. Sometimes Ella thought of sandy-haired Professor O'Neil dismissed for his monkey talk and his daring statements about a new social order and wondered whether he would now be considered even slightly radical.

Old Central was now carrying out its name in truth, for it was almost in the exact center of the great sweep of buildings which rose on all sides. It looked worn and shriveled, and, covered with heavy ivy vines as it was, gave the appearance of a shrunken old woman peering out from under her green shawl. Ella had moved from her old classroom into Corcoran Hall. It had given her a queer feeling to leave the inner office in the tower room and the pigeons with their eternal "coo coo," "although when you stop to think of it," she had admitted, "these present ones are about forty generations removed from their ancestors I first knew."

Surveying the school as one disinterested, she could see a hundred changes. "For better or for worse?" she asked herself. "More often better," she acknowledged, "sometimes not so good."

Before the turn of the century a new element had crept into the college,—a national sorority. Nine girls, by some secret process of selection, having been given a charter, had become Kappa Kappa Gammas, rented the old Banker Van Ness home and proceeded to establish themselves as Midwestern's social *élite*. Another had followed and another,—and others. Kites, keys, crescents, anchors, arrows, all jewel-set, sparkled now above the hearts of Midwestern's fair ladies,—and triangles, shields, scimitars, serpents, and swords, all flashed now on the lapels of Midwestern's brave men. Dinner dresses and tuxedos, evening gowns and spike-tails had followed in their wake until now there was not a corn-fed lass who did not have a dress which was held on by a mere shoulder strap,—not a corn-fed boy but knew, if he did not own a full-dress, where one could be most cheaply rented.

"Poor old Minerva society," Ella would say, "once 'the four hundred' of the campus!" and would add with a dry bit of sarcarsm, "Just to think that we were merely studious and funloving and literary—no Minerva sweethearts or queens chosen for their shapely legs or general kissableness!"

Dancing, instead of being the misdemeanor it once had been, was now a part of the social fabric of the school. Student pressure and changing public opinion had removed the bar. Where it had once been a reproach to mention the pastime, now faculty members took their turn as patrons and patronesses of the classes and fraternities sponsoring it. Where it had once been thought the height of daring to slip away to Maynard and dance, now it was an unheard-of procedure. Once a sin, now a social virtue. "O the tempora of the times. O the modes of the customs," Ella sometimes flippantly juggled the words.

Miss Bishop was a favorite chaperon. "The first hundred years I enjoyed it," she confided to Sam Peters. "But the same music, flowers, young people, the second hundred it gets to be something of a nuisance. I've been the fifth one so many times . . . have read the item so repeatedly: '. . . chaperoned by Professor and Mrs. Hess, Professor and Mrs. Alderslot and Miss Ella Bishop,' that when prizes are given for the campus's best running fifth wheel, I'll get it."

In truth, there was no faculty member so called upon for a thousand things by the student body as Ella,—to chaperon, advise about decorations and refreshments, making over dresses and having tonsils removed—to aid in writing theses and wording applications for jobs—a confidante for those financially embarrassed and to lovelorn swains.

And now every year a student or two found shelter under her own roof. Every year she gave a little financial aid to some one of them who otherwise could not have finished.

She had a sly way of finding out things she wanted to know. "You will hand in a five-hundred-word article on 'My Ambitions.'" Or "For Monday, a brief paper on 'Characteristics I Admire.'" All these she perused herself. No hired reader of human type articles for Miss Bishop.

Although particular about the mechanics, she admitted to herself that she really cared more for the contents than the commas, gave far more thought to the spirit than the spacing. More than one young chap revealing in an assignment his tendencies to a display of temper quite surprisingly found himself in Miss Bishop's office freely discussing self-control with her. Many a young girl admitting in an English paper envy of her better-dressed classmates found herself later in that room laughing with Miss Bishop over the story of the prolonged life of the old Scotch plaid dresses and emerging with a clarified outlook on the subject of clothes.

President Watts was now seventy-seven, his long shambling legs moving a little more slowly, but his active mind as keen as ever. Ella wondered sometimes whether it would be possible for other figures so picturesque to come after these: Wick, Carter, Cunningham, Wittingly, Schroeder, Fonda,—the ones from the old days. It never occurred to her to add another picturesque figure: Miss Bishop.

And then Professor Fonda died, as though having looked long upon the heavens he had suddenly become one with the moon and the clouds and the Milky Way. After his death, Ella's heart went out to old Professor Schroeder who seemed more lost than ever without his comrade. Once at Commencement time, now 1929, he stopped to talk to her under the elms grown old along with these two. When he shook his big head sadly, it was as though a hoary old lion tossed his mane.

"Fonda's gone on and my work has gone. The labor of nearly a half-century swept away," he said mournfully, but with no bitterness. "Where are they all now—those students I taught and loved?

"Sie horen nicht die folgenden Gesange,
Die Seelen, denen ich die ersten sang?"

"You'll have to translate, Professor Schroeder, I never studied it, you know."

"That's right,—you did not know my Goethe in the language in which he is loveliest. You have missed much. It is:

"They do not hear my later measures,
The souls to whom the first I sang."

He stopped and looked out over the campus,— the wide rolling green and the great buildings, the hoary old trees and the campanile erected to the memory of the World War boys who had gone from his Midwestern to meet in combat the boys from his Heidelberg. Then he said quietly as though she were not there:

"I thrill and tremble, tear on tear swift follows;
My stoic heart grows wild and soft,
What I possess as things remote I see,
What I have lost becomes the real to me."

He stood for a few moments, deep in thought, and then saluting her in courtly old-world fashion, turned and walked slowly down the green sloping campus.

CHAPTER XXXIV

☙§ It was that very afternoon when the letter about Gretchen came from Hope. Gretchen had just graduated from High School—eighteen now, it simply couldn't be possible—and once more Hope was turning to Aunt Ella in time of trouble. "And to whom else could I go, Aunt Ella, but my port in all storms?"

Dick was having trouble again, a result of the old wound,—she was going to Hot Springs with him, and would it be at all possible for Gretchen to come to Aunt Ella's and go to school? They had always planned to send her east but finances were just too low, with Dick's hard luck about his health—

Already, even before finishing the long letter, Ella had mentally refurnished the south bedroom in ivory and yellow to go with Gretchen's Spanish-like beauty. Already she felt younger, gayer, to think of the lovely girl there in her home. It would be like having Hope all over again.

Life took on a new lease for Miss Bishop that summer. And when Hope wrote that her daughter would be there in time for the rushing parties, and she wished Aunt Ella would see that everything went off as well as it could, Miss Bishop began mentally looking over the sororities with appraising eye.

Driving to the station in her coupé, she felt a genuine thrill of excitement over the coming of the young girl. It had been three years since she had seen her and some periods of three years are much more important than others—from fifteen to eighteen for instance.

When Gretchen came down the steps of the Pullman, Ella drew in her breath at sight of the sheer loveliness of the slim thing who wore her clothes like a manikin. Tall, olive-skinned, with geranium-colored lips, Gretchen was the possessor of a cool little air of detachment which might have passed for hauteur if she had not been so friendly.

Dear, dear, Ella thought, picturing to herself in a swift mental flight, her own entrance to school and that of Hope:—her own sturdy body in its plaid ruffled dress and brass buttons, its heavy square-toed shoes, laced up to the calves of her legs, the mop of hair piled high on her head in its intricate criss-cross braidings,—Hope's shirtwaist and long pleated skirt, and ugly stiff sailor hat. "Clothes have improved, if nothing else," she admitted to herself.

Gretchen settled comfortably in her pretty room and if Ella chanced to be a bit disappointed over the nonchalance with which the girl took in the new artistic furnishings, she put the thought aside.

Gretchen's attractive looks and her connection with Miss Bishop proved to be a ticket of admission to almost any social organization with which she cared to affiliate. Ella did her best to subdue an overwhelming pride in the striking appearance of her charge and the admiration which followed in her wake.

"I love to look at a pretty girl, and not having been irresistibly beautiful myself, I appreciate it all the more," she said to Sam Peters, who protested immediately against the disparagement of herself.

Gretchen was indeed lovely, "a perfect model for the girl on the magazine cover," Ella thought to herself. She introduced her to a few young people, and no more labor on her part was necessary, for the modern lovely girl quite capably looks after herself.

Gretchen became, then, one of the most rushed of the rushees, and when the breakfasts, luncheons, teas, dinners, and evening parties of that hectic week were over and the fraternity shouting and the sorority tumult had died, she was returned to Ella's home on Adams Street by a victorious group of Kappa Alpha Thetas in a sixteen-cylinder car. Ella was still up in her room and called to Gretchen to come on in and tell her all about it, wondering idly as she did so whether she would ever get too old to care about such things.

The girl came in, slim and lovely and poised. Evidently all the rushing had not moved her to abandon that cool little air of detachment. As she related the events of the evening, Ella was thinking: "I know the kind. She's the type for whom people fall over themselves. She demands much without even realizing it. And she gets it.

"This is the way of it the wide world over—
One is beloved and one is the lover;
One gives and the other receives.

Gretchen will be the beloved,—the one who receives. As far removed from Amy in method as can be,—but nevertheless a modern sophisticated version of her."

Gretchen wore her Theta pledge pin. It was apparently characteristic of her that at no time had she let her emotions run away with her mental processes. She had thought it all out carefully, she told Aunt Ella,—chosen wisely, she thought, and well. "I was not going to let any of them sweep me off my feet. Perhaps I really had the best time at the Pi Phi house,—the girls were awfully attractive,—and the Delta Gammas were thoroughbreds, but some way I felt that Kappa Alpha Theta would land me in the end where I want to go."

"And where do you want to go, Gretchen?" Ella was amazed at the freshman's viewpoint, was remembering her own green, country enthusiasm when she entered the new school, Hope's naïve, bashful girlishness. "Yet I don't know why I should be surprised," she thought. "This isn't the first modern-day freshman I've known."

"Oh, well," Gretchen laughed lightly, "maybe I can tell better where I *don't* want to go, and that's into a schoolroom to teach."

No, she wouldn't. The Gretchens do not usually choose the teaching profession.

"I've thought this all out, that since Father had his illness, he can't begin to do the things for me that he would have. Mother is sweet and anxious for me, but worried over Father and rather helpless. So it's up to me to make the most of my opportunities and push my way along,—meet the right people, make the friends who will be of most advantage. . . ."

Ella found herself blinking a little as at a flashing light. "Friends . . . of most advantage," from the mouths of babes. She had never thought of friends that way,—almost laughed aloud to think of some of her oldest friends,—old Sam Peters, Chris and Hannah and Stena. Dear, dear,—friends of most advantage!

So Gretchen, slim and lovely and cool, went her freshman way, more wordly wise than Ella.

CHAPTER XXXV

§ As time went on Ella realized how nice it was to have Gretchen there. It brought the sorority young people to the house,—made life flow on about her in a gay bright stream. Even though she was tired and went to her room, it was not unpleasant to hear the rise and fall of the merry chatter below. Yes, it kept her young in soul and mind,—was a magic cord that bound her still to youth. And she herself had never quite relinquished that youth, never quite outgrown being one of the crowd, was not above swinging into the rhythm of the life of Gretchen's friends. As the time she found the three kinds of fudge sitting about her kitchen cooling on platters, and left the hastily scribbled note in Vachel Lindsay style propped up against a kettle:

Do you remember ages ago
The time
The kitchen
Was filled
With cocoa?
There was brown fudge on a purple platter
And pink fudge and white fudge
And pale tan fudge on a whitish platter.
Years on years I but half remember
Man is a glutton for sweets they say
Through May and June and then dead December.
Who shall end my dream's confusion?
Life is a pink and brown and white illusion.
I remember, I remember
There were sugar and chocolate and nuts and eggs
There were kettles down from all the pegs
Bending one to another
From north and south
They infinitely echo in the red caves of my mouth.

This half-way meeting of flippant youth kept her, too, a part of that youth, made the fleeting years find her not dimmed in eye, dulled in mentality nor cold in heart. Only the body turned traitor, only from the physical was toll demanded by the years.

Her hair was snow-white now, and she kept it beautifully groomed. Her carriage always erect, her head always held high, one saw little by which to count her years. It was only in the privacy of her room that she admitted to fatigue. She grew more and more fastidious about her person, her skin, her nails, her clothes. "You can get away with careless grooming when you are young, but not at my age," she would think. She wore a great deal of navy blue and white, navy blue school dresses offset by immaculate white collars and cuffs,—frilled ones that melted into the white of her hair and softened her aging face and hands. For evenings she chose white, a lace with which her hair vied for snow whiteness. And she was not above deepening the pink of her cheeks. She looked modern, smart, aristocratic, she who had been but a plain girl, with only nice eyes and a cheerful smile for her assets.

During the winter, she realized that as well as she thought she had understood her freshman girls before Gretchen came, she was having a better opportunity now to see them at close range through the girl. Not that they could all be classified like so much animal life under observation in the laboratories, but the viewpoint of many, naturally was the viewpoint of Gretchen.

And to study her and the changes that had taken place in all young femininity, Ella sometimes called up pictures of herself and of Mina Gordon, Emily Teasdale, Janet McLaughlin, and of the others who had constituted the feminine population of the college in that long-gone day. Individuals would always differ as long as the world lasted, but just wherein lay the general difference? She thought of Evelyn Hobbs gently fainting away one evening when a strange man opened the door of her room at the boarding house. She could visualize Gretchen's hauteur under like circumstance and her possible: "Just what's on your mind? Whatever it is, kindly step out and take it with you." She remembered the silly titterings and heart palpitations with which the Minerva girls always greeted the masculine contingent at those long-gone Friday afternoon programs, the customary vehement denials from a girl of that day that she so much as liked a young man until her wedding invitations practically were issued. Physical courage, honesty, figuratively looking life straight in the eye,—these attributes were the modern girl's.

And just as she had decided entirely for that modern girl, Gretchen might breeze in and so casually observe that Papa Rigdon (all professors were papas to her) "must hold the theory, Aunt Ella, that every unmarried woman like you should mingle socially a great deal with men to receive a missing stimulus," Ella would grow pink behind the ears and vote mentally for the old femininity which surrounded itself at least with a semblance of reticence.

The end of Gretchen's freshman year was the fiftieth anniversary of Ella's old class. But no one made any move to celebrate it. Professor Schroeder's health had broken—he was at home behind closed blinds, waiting for—he knew not what—perhaps "to pierce the ether's high, unknown dominion—to reach new spheres of pure activity." Janet McLaughlin and Emily Teasdale were dead. Professor Fonda was sleeping out in Forest Hill, above him a simple stone with the carving:

We have loved the stars too deeply
To be fearful of the night.

"We'll just let the fiftieth reunion go," Ella thought a bit morbidly for her usual gay self, "and plan to have a reunion . . . Sometime . . . Somewhere."

Gretchen went home, but only for the summer. The plan now was for her to take all four years at Midwestern. Ella would not accept anything for the girl's board. Hope and Dick were having his illness to combat and she insisted that she could help them to the extent of keeping their daughter.

Gretchen's sophomore year saw her back at the old home on Adams Street, cool and unperturbed over a rush of dates, and intensely interested in dramatics. Tolstoy and Shaw and Oscar Wilde were her daily diet and she openly discussed delicate points of attack which made even Ella, used to modern youth, feel a bit embarrassed. It made her smile, too, to think of "dramatics" at Midwestern in her own student days, a scene from "Merchant of Venice" in Minerva Hall with the old calico curtain pulled aside by two perspiring supers signaling frantically to each other, and a plump Portia in a wild costume composed of President Corcoran's wife's black silk dolman and Irene Van Ness's little brother's velvet pants. Now a play was the last word in attention to detail, a perfection of scenery, props, and costumes.

It was toward the last of her sophomore year that Gretchen was cast as Lady Teazle, and, as always, on this Saturday morning she was living her part at home, discussing details of hairdress, costume and jewelry of the times.

Ella was vaguely aware that the prospective Lady Teazle had been rummaging about upstairs half the morning but it was not until she heard her give a squeal of delight and call, "Oh, Aunt Ella, I look like a million dollars," that it came to her just what the girl had been doing.

When Ella came to the foot of the stairs she looked up to see Gretchen, slim, graceful, her brown eyes glowing, starting slowly downward dressed in Ella's wedding dress.

The new-old thing with its bunches of flowers on the white of the silk, turned now to a deep ivory, looked surprisingly not old-fashioned on the girl. Queer as it was with its panniers and its countless yards of pleating, it had merely the appearance of a lovely quaint party dress. Her prettily molded arms were bare, and in her hand she held the long sleeves.

Ella watched her slow descent, fascinated, as one looks at a natural phenomenon over which he has no control, a transfixion of gaze at the oncoming of a storm. Her mind seemed numb, unable to function. She wanted to call out, to warn her, to tell her to go back out of her sight so that she would not have to witness the painfully embarrassing scene of seeing her aunt in distress. She wanted to cry for the desecration. And then she wanted to laugh for the deference. For the girl was saying: "Where did the *darling* thing come from?" and, "Oh, *could* I wear it? I'll be the perfect Lady Teazle."

One graceful hand slipping along on the banister, she made the slow descent.

"Am I not *perfect?* Isn't it the answer to a maiden's prayer? May I wear it? What does the sweet old auntie say?"

Pictures tumbled about crazily in Ella's head, the bald-headed man who sold her the material wishing her much joy, the standing for hours while Mrs. Finch pinned the uncut goods about her,—the first overwhelming sight of herself in the dressmaker's glass. Emotions came surging over her that she had thought long dead,—the crushing sensations of wild despair, of hurt pride, of righteous anger. For a brief moment she felt them all with poignant reality. How queer life was. Only yesterday she had been trying on the lovely thing at the dressmaker's. And to-day, with snow-white hair and slowing step, she was watching another young girl, looking like a Gainsborough, come down the stairs in the shimmering gown.

"You're stunned speechless at my gorgeousness, aren't you?"

Delbert was long dead. Amy was long dead. And yet here was the dress. Things lasted longer than people. She, too, would die and the dress would still lie in the trunk, all the bouquets of flowers crumbling to dust,—all the little pink rosebuds and the blue forget-me-nots falling into nothing.

"What's the answer, sweet pumpkin?"

"Why, yes—you may wear it."

Gretchen held out the sleeves,—long and narrow, gathered in mousquetaire fashion into their seams.

"Look—how funny! They were never sewed in,—and the hem is only basted. It almost looks as though it had never been finished."

Old Miss Bishop stood looking at the lovely freshness of Delbert Thompson's granddaughter in the old-ivory silk with the bouquets of raised flowers.

"No," she said simply, "it was never finished."

CHAPTER XXXVI

ELLA's trip abroad became one of those mirage-like visions that appear on the horizon but vanish as one draws near. "I do hate to think of going in a wheeled-chair," she said to Stena, "but if I wait much longer, it will lie between that and being carried on a stretcher."

Stena scolded. "You do too many t'ings for odders. One t'ing one year for somebody . . . one t'ing anodder. Now look—dis year! Dis house wasn't goot enough for G'etchen." Stena could never get her tongue around that combination of "gr."

"Oh, yes, it was, Stena. It was just natural for her to want to live at the sorority house a year. I would, too, if I were young. And next summer for sure I take my trip. Miss Hunter is going again and Professor and Mrs. Alderslot, and believe me, so am I."

Stena grumbled. "I vait 'til I see you on de boat."

For Gretchen was at the Theta house in her junior year. She had lived happily at Ella's for two years but after coming back in the fall of her third year, she had gone straight to the point. She wished she could stay at the sorority house the rest of the college course. She knew it was quite impossible, that it would be more expensive, realized there was no use crying for the moon, but did not believe in beating around either bushes or truth, and that was that.

Ella had thought the matter over for a few days, had come to the conclusion that there was argument on Gretchen's side, and decided, Ella-like, to see that the girl had her chance. "I'm supplying the extra money," she wrote to Hope, "so I believe you will agree that it can be done. You know there is something about living in the midst of things on the campus that beats staying with an old Aunt Ella over on Adams Street."

Gretchen was too honest to protest. "I think you're a luscious old peach. I suppose I ought to be noble and say I couldn't think of accepting the offer, but I'm crazy to do it, and will take you at your word that you really want me to."

So Gretchen moved out, but came dutifully back at intervals to report. Ella enjoyed her cool appraisal of the girls, their dates, the house mother, wondered as always at the methodical way in which she went about cultivating people who would be most helpful to her. Stanch in her loyalty to modern youth, she would not admit that they were deteriorating in any sense. "They're brighter,—maybe not quite so stodgily thorough as they used to be,—but keener. When I look back on the first students here of which I was one, standing bashfully around, waiting to be pushed into something, I'm ashamed of all of us. My modern students,—they do 'go places and do things' as they say."

Gretchen had accepted many and sundry dates from the moment she arrived on the campus, but they had always been fraternity boys, and so in the winter of their junior year when she appeared at Ella's with a tall red-haired young man from away whom she introduced as Mr. Jack Burdick, Ella was moved to later inquiry.

He was living in Chicago now—was a salesman—she had known him when she was in high school—he came from a wonderful family—he was in town on business and just dropped in to call.

"He looks older than to have been in high school with you," Ella suggested.

"Oh, he wasn't in school *with* me. That wasn't what I said. I knew him when *I* was in high school."

Something struck Ella, as peculiar intuitions will do,—a fleeting thought of a bit of evasiveness on Gretchen's part, so that when old Stena came in later to say she had just seen Gretchen with her redhead again in a "svell car," Ella was vaguely troubled.

And when Gretchen failed to speak of the visit, although mentioning less important trivialities, all of Ella's accumulation of knowledge of young people told her that something was not quite right. She wanted to inquire from Hope, but Hope was at the Springs again with Dick and she would not trouble her. "Besides, she's my girl temporarily and it's my problem. I'll see it through myself."

Ella, herself, saw them two weeks later, slipping through a winding drive of the campus in the big roadster, and when later Gretchen failed to mention him, she felt that she must act. She pondered a long time on the procedure. With Hope it would have been so different,—Hope was like her own, brought up in her way, with her own ideals. There was something of Amy in Gretchen,—she must be looked after,—but how to go about it with this lovely, slim young girl who was modern, cool, detached. There seemed no element of childishness about her.

She approached it with lightness as though it were of no consequence. "I saw you with your Mr. Burdick, Gretchen, but you passed up your decrepit old aunt with hauteur." That was the best way, you could not preach at these young moderns.

"Oh—so! Spying, Aunt Ella?" She laughed, certainly not spontaneously.

"A-huh! Hiding behind trees on the campus just to see you pass by."

There was a long pause, as though she pondered. And then the girl said: "I'm afraid I've got it bad, Aunt Ella, the old malady, love."

"Why, Gretchen, really?"

"Really."

"Of course, it was to be expected,—but you're young . . . and just your junior year this way. You've no . . . plans, yet, have you?"

The girl gave a short dry laugh and shrugged a lithe shoulder. "Scarcely, not as long as . . . well, I would say 'as long as Jack has one perfectly good wife,' but she's neither good nor perfect." Coolly and a bit defiantly she looked unflinchingly at the older woman.

Ella thought she must take hold of something to steady herself. Oh, why was life so hard? Life was meant to be happy without deep problems to solve. This past year had seemed singularly free of complexities and here was one of the utmost seriousness staring her in the face.

"Oh, Gretchen—no." It was a wail of distress, so deeply did she feel it.

"Yes, Aunt Ella—yes!" It was a cry of challenge to an older generation. Then suddenly Gretchen broke, cried a little wildly. All her coolness was gone, her poise shaken. The little tale she related was so old, that Ella, herself, could have told it instead of listening patiently, sympathetically to every broken word. Jack had been in town first on business,—that part was true,—he had called because he had known her,—they had driven around, he had come again and again,—now it was the real thing. His wife didn't understand him, she didn't care for him, was a card shark, gone all the time, but he was afraid he'd have difficulty in divorcing her, his business being wrapped up with his father-in-law's.

Such a sordid little tale from the lips of the lovely young thing! Ella's heart bled for her, for Hope who would be distressed, for Dick whose pride Gretchen was, for all young things who have to face life as it is.

The problem took all of her thought. She did not know just what to do. A hundred girls she had talked out of foolish ventures, a thousand times she had assisted with advice or material aid. This was different. Gretchen was so close to her, so nearly her own flesh and blood, so coolly independent, so modern. Oh, why had this come up just now? Life had been uneventful the past few months, which meant entirely peaceful. She wasn't so young as she once was,—why should she have such problems confront her at her age?

It was two weeks later upon coming home from acting as chaperon at the Sigma Nu spring party that she found Gretchen and Jack Burdick alone in her home, Stena's hour for retiring coinciding exactly with the time the parties usually began.

She talked pleasantly with them for a time, handling young people wisely these days including as it did the condition of mind in which one approached them.

When the young man was helping Gretchen slip on her short fur jacket to leave, Ella said carelessly: "Why don't you stay here to-night, Gretchen? Won't you be too late for the house?"

"Yes, I think I will be; it's not hard to get out of," she grinned cheerfully at Jack Burdick, "but not so easy to break into. I may, Aunt Ella, I may come back, but I may not."

Ella had a sudden uprising of wrath toward the girl. Augmented no doubt by her physical weariness, a great anger seized her that this slim young thing could have the audacity to defy the conventions, could be standing coolly there with a young married man of her acquaintance, saying, "I may do this" or "I may not." She wanted to shake her, to spank her, to put her in her place with sudden vehement force. For a moment she had a violent antipathy toward all modern young people with their cool way of appraising every one and everything. She had a wild foolish brainstorm of wanting to do something about it, of forcibly bringing back the old days when young people were ruled with an iron hand by parents, by teachers, by society. Standing there in her spring party dress, sleepy, weary in body and soul, old Miss Bishop staged a mental revolution that, could it have been let loose upon an unsuspecting world of young people, would have found them all locked behind heavy doors, subsisting on bread and milk until they might come to their senses.

Then the king of reason as suddenly called a halt on the stick-and-stone throwers of her mind, all the violent revolutionists dropped their missiles, and she was herself,—a modern teacher, handling modern young people wisely and well.

"I think I *must* know, though, whether or not you are coming, Gretchen," she said soberly.

The girl dropped her eyes from the serious ones of the woman. "I'll be back in less than a half-hour."

Ella paced her room. Something must be done. To-night. This could not go on. She was responsible for this impossible situation. When the girl came upstairs Ella called her at once into the bedroom and went directly to the point.

"Gretchen, I think you'll agree with me that this can't go on. It's dangerous, not only dangerous to you both but a cause of anxiety to your father and mother and to me. It will end in your sorority pin being taken from you. It will interfere with your work, put a cloud on your reputation, and *never*, as long as you live, bring you one moment of genuine happiness."

"Happiness?" the girl broke out. "That's what I'm looking for! That's what Jack Burdick is looking for! That's what we *all* want, isn't it? If Jack Burdick can give me my happiness . . . if I can give Jack Burdick some happiness . . . having none in his home . . ."

"Happiness," Ella said grimly, "gained at the expense of some one else ceases to be happiness. I know that if I know no other thing."

"Just *how* do you know, Aunt Ella?"

How? What was the girl saying? Was she thinking her Aunt Ella did not know these things?

"Forgive me, Aunt Ella, if I hurt you." The cool velvety voice went on. "I don't mean to, in any way, you understand that. But I'm frank, you know, and so won't attempt to camouflage my meaning. Tell me, Aunt Ella, honestly how can *you* know anything about it—how *can* you,—an old maid school teacher tucked away with your books here at Midwestern—how have you ever been able to understand *life?*"

Ella Bishop looked at the lovely slim girl standing there at the doorway in the arrogance of her youth.

A dozen answers rose to her lips, a thousand thoughts flew to her brain. They beat with throbbing rhythm against the chambers of her mind as the pigeons beat their wings against the windows of the tower in Old Central.

She felt angry, insulted, robbed of some gift. Why, she would tell this disdainful girl—this modern young woman who thought the present generation had a monopoly on all the emotions—she would tell her that she, too, had been red-blooded, warm, vital,—that all her emotions had known life. That she, too, had known love and desire, and been violently swayed by them both. Love and desire, they had both been her own. But love had gone its lonely way. And desire. . . .

Suddenly all her anger left her and she felt very old.

. . . and desire shall fade, and man goeth to his long home.

With all the self-control at her command, she stilled her trembling lips, and laughed, a little ruefully, but it passed for laughter.

"Oh, I don't know about that, Gretchen," she said with studied calmness. "Life to an unmarried school teacher hasn't necessarily been all participles and subordinate clauses and term papers."

CHAPTER XXXVII

IT was time now to make preparations for the trip if she intended going. Ella wondered why she kept thinking of that insidious "if she intended going." Of course she was going. But having Gretchen so constantly on her mind, she seemed to have lost interest in making plans. Sometimes she thought she would tell Gretchen about her love for John Stevens,—it might have an effect on this apparent infatuation of hers for the young married man. But to what effect? Modern young girls were not Elsie Dinsmores upon whom the telling of a story with a moral would have the slightest result.

In fact she could visualize her merriment, in fancy hear her flippant remarks: "What, you, too, Bruty! Why you sly old vamp, whoever would have thought it of you,"—and more of that sort, with specific references to Cleopatra or Helen of Troy or more probably Greta Garbo.

No, her pitiful little secret was not to be the mark of Gretchen's gay shafts.

Something more must be done, something to get her away—something to take the place of this youthful infatuation—

And so Ella faced the truth of that subtle suggestion which her heart had been trying to tell her mind. If Gretchen could go abroad with the other five sorority sisters who were going,—spend that wonderful summer in London and Paris and Rome—

"Oh, no," her mind was protesting. "I couldn't do that much for her, —not *that*. I've always wanted to go. Time after time I've given it up. I owe it to myself. My life doesn't have to be one of entire self-denial. I've given up things all my life."

She seemed to plead with some one not to consent to her doing this absurd thing. But just as surely as she had satisfied herself that it was all Quixotic, all a foolish sense of altruism, just as surely would she find herself insisting that she must do it.

"She's not even my own flesh and blood," she would protest to this argumentative conscience of hers.

"She's your Hope's little girl, and she's in danger."

"But I can't go about saving people from their own foolish sins. If she would slip into a silly love for this man here and now, she would do a similar thing any time and anywhere."

"It's a crucial age. She's young. If you can get her through this time . . ."

"No, I'm going to give myself this trip. I've planned it for years. It's a reward of merit for . . . for everything."

"You're old,—with your work all behind you. You would merely sight-see and soak up some information. She's young,—and has all her life . . . perhaps a career before her."

"But *I* came through such an affair . . . by myself." Back she would go in the dual character she was playing. "*I* couldn't run away. No one helped me . . . or sent me abroad. *I* had to fight the thing out here."

"Maybe you were stronger in character . . . in fact, you certainly were. Isn't that why you should help—now—some one younger and less strong?"

After dinner she phoned for Gretchen. She felt an overwhelming joy, was consumed by that exhilarating sensation she always experienced when about to give happiness to another.

"I'm really not unselfish at all," she told herself when she put down the receiver. "I like to do things like this so well that I enjoy giving myself the thrill of it. In reality it's one type of selfishness."

Gretchen came, her graceful figure with its gliding walk crossing the lawn to the side porch where Ella sat in the fresh spring evening.

"Did you want something special, Aunt Ella?"

"Yes."

"I rather gathered so."

"How would you like to go with your sorority sisters on the European trip, Gretchen, with Madame Volk and her music students?"

"How would I like to crash the pearly gates and purloin Gabriel's horn? But what *is* this—an examination in fiction plotting?"

"Something on that order. I'm rather thinking, Gretchen, that you can go."

"Using what for money?"

"American dollars."

"Whose?"

"Mine."

The color slipped away from the girl's face. "Aunt Ella, you . . . you don't mean that."

"Yes, I do, Gretchen."

"For me to go with you?"

"No . . . I'm not going."

"Oh . . . I see. I thought there was a catch somewhere." She stood up, her slim figure graceful against the new green of the rose vine. "And you not go." Her throaty voice was the embodiment of sarcasm.

"But if I choose to send you in my place?"

The girl laughed shortly and shook her lovely head: "I see through you like cellophane. In fact, Aunt Ella, I shall now tell you the entire workings of your mind. You're worried about me and Jack Burdick. You think if you'd get me away . . . abroad . . . it would wear off . . . 'it' meaning love to me—infatuation to you. To that end, you're willing to give up your trip. You're an old smoothy,—in fact you're probably the noblest soul that ever trod over campus dandelions,—but I just couldn't let you be *that* noble . . . not to-day, Miss Bishop."

There were always forces to be met in Gretchen which had never been Hope's. Hope had been entirely feminine, pliant and lovable,—easily molded. Gretchen's mind was that of a frank boy's, going directly to a point.

It pleased Ella that the girl showed so little tendency to be grasping; she had accepted much in the past without demonstration, but evidently she felt this was carrying it too far, and with no further controversy expected to close the subject.

But in the days that followed, Ella, with much argument and explanation had her way, and Gretchen left with the girls after Commencement week. Stena was in such a state of disgust that she would scarcely talk to her mistress whom she characterized as "too voolish to be vidout a guardeen."

"After all, Stena," Ella said, "it's awfully nice to know you can sit on your porch all summer . . . no summer school . . . no tramping around Europe . . . just relax and rest."

And when long interesting letters came from Gretchen with the tang of the salt sea in them and the breath of Scotland moors, Ella insisted that the girl was seeing more with her young eyes than she herself could have done,—which elicited only a portentous snort from Stena.

When Gretchen came back from the trip for her senior year, she kissed Ella warmly. "Never as long as I live can I forget what you did for me. What can I ever do for you in return?" She stood, slim and lovely and glowing, some inner light lending warmth to her usual aloofness.

"It's payment enough to see you so happy, Gretchen. It is much better than having gone."

"Would it recompense you, just partly, say the first down payment if I told you your little scheme that I saw through all the time worked to perfection—that I'm cured . . . and not a little disgusted at the Gretchen of last spring?"

"It finishes the payment." Ella, too, glowed with happiness. "Account settled in full."

"But don't be hasty and give to much credit to the mere separation, Aunt Ella. I could have gone over foolishly thinking I loved him, and have come back foolishly dittoing. But it's because of a new man—the grandest old thing you ever knew. First I met him going over . . . then he was in Paris with . . ."

"Oh, Gretchen," Ella was laughing. "Out of the frying pan into . . ."

"But *what* a fire! His name is Smith, . . . not so hot maybe to think of that Jones-Smith headline when the announcement comes out, . . . but wait until you see him, . . . Ronald Smith. And is he good looking? He's tall and broad and 'andsome and well-to-do and *not married*." She gave an exaggerated little squeal of rapture and kissed Ella again.

Old Ella Bishop was very happy. So much so that she hated to say the thing that was on her mind, that owing to the cut in salaries which every one was having to take she thought perhaps Gretchen would have to give up living at the Theta house and come home.

"Oh, *that!*" The girl waved it aside as a mere triviality. "I intended to. Since I've lived there I've stalked my prey—so it's home again, home again for me. And I suppose it would never occur to you, you clever old virgin . . . well, anyway you're a virgin . . . that I'd rather have my grand Ronald . . . Mr. Smith to you . . . come to see me here this year in the privacy of this little living-room than in the middle of the arena at the K.A.T. house?"

Ella was almost ready to turn out her light that night when Gretchen came to the bedroom door in her gaudy pajamas. Looking up from her book, she was struck anew with the charm of the girl's loveliness.

"Aunt Ella, I almost forgot to tell you something awfully odd. After we got back home, in one of his letters Ronnie said he had found out that his grandmother was an old schoolmate of yours."

"She was? I wonder who?"

"Her maiden name was Van Ness, Irene Van Ness."

"Irene . . . was . . . your . . . Ronald's grandmother?" It sounded forced from her, like a thing unbelievable.

"Oke. She went to school here when you did, he says."

A whirl of thoughts went about in Ella Bishop's head with dizzying effect after Gretchen had gone. "Ronald Smith is Irene's grandson." She said it over to herself with bewildered patience.

When Amy Saunders came to town and left grief and trouble in her wake—when she married Delbert who should have married Ella herself,—Gretchen, here, was to be born of that line later. When Chester Peters went away because of a mad infatuation for Amy, Irene who loved him, married another—this Ronald Smith was to be born of that line later. Was it possible, then, that all the suffering and humiliation of that early day *had* to be, in order that Gretchen and Ronald might have this very beautiful love for each other? Oh, no, that was a foolish thing. One could scarcely put it that way. Fate never went to that degree. And yet—it would not quite leave old Ella—the thought that out of all that misery and suffering of a long-gone day, two generations later had grown a lovely romance,—like the white lilies that cover stagnant pools in the tropics.

CHAPTER XXXVIII

AND then very suddenly old President Watts died—one Friday night, with all his engagements marked on his desk calendar for the following week.

The blow came with unforeseen force to the old faculty members who had worked with him for years upon years.

"It's one of the most peculiar relationships in the world," Ella thought, "that relation of the superintendent of a public school to his teachers, or the president of a college to the women faculty members. He is like a husband or father in every sense but the family life. I knew President Watts almost as well as his wife knew him,—every mood, everything that irritated him, everything that gave him happiness, his ideas on practically anything one could mention. I could read his mind, detect his reactions to various incidents. I went to him for sympathy and advice and criticism. I could console him and scold him and encourage him.

"I think there are no finer friendships in the world than these, utterly devoid of sentiment, but completely abounding in understanding. I could feel not much worse at his loss if he *had* been my husband."

She dreaded thoroughly the advent of a new president, watched the papers, questioned any one who might have information. Two or three local men were suggested, heads of departments, but when the news was announced, he proved to be from a college in another state,—Melvin Bevans Crowder.

When he came, it was noticeable that he was extremely young, efficient, progressive. Tactful, too, for that matter, as he made no changes to speak of that first year. But with capability and diplomacy he was molding the school to suit his plans, instituting innovations and gradual changes.

When Ella drew her salary now with its twenty per cent cut, she looked a little ruefuly at the check with its diminished figures. "Reduced pay," she said, "in some jobs would call for reduced effort on the part of the jobber. But I don't know how any teacher can have the heart to take it out on her students when they are so entirely without blame for conditions. The next generation has the big task of pulling the country back to normal times,—so I suppose the least we teachers can do is to inspire our young people to as high ideals as we can. In other words, I guess the teacher is the last one to let outside conditions affect her work."

Ronald Smith, the magnificent, came from Ohio several times during the year to see Gretchen. It gave Ella a warm sense of pleasure to witness their happiness. "All my life I've been looking on at these things instead of participating in them and I can't see but that it gives me about as much joy," old Miss Bishop said.

Ella Bishop had lived past many inauguration days in her three score and ten years, but never one before that had for its immediate and personal effect the closing of her bank and leaving her with no pocket money. She made light of it along with most other patriotic citizens until the day for the bank's opening came, when Sam Peters came over to see her. Sam was showing his age more than ever this spring,—looked the old man he really was, with his thin parchment-like face and slim trembling body.

He had heard bad news and as usual had come across the street to tell it to Ella himself—to try to protect her against the storms, as he wished he might always have protected her.

He sat down in her pretty living-room, his cane between his bony hands.

"Did you have money in the Bank of Oak River, Ella?"

"Why, yes, Sam. Almost all I had. Why?"

"I hate to tell you, Ella, but they say uptown it's to open only on a restricted basis, virtually liquidated."

Cold hands were clutching at Ella's heart and throat. Money—she had not given enough thought to it in years gone by. Now, what was Sam saying?

"How do you mean, Sam?"

"You'll be asked to sign what is called a waiver,—give up a certain per cent of your deposit,—fifteen, twenty, thirty, whatever seems necessary. Then they will open up and you will be allowed to draw probably one per cent per month of the rest."

"One per cent, Sam? Twelve per cent a year only."

"Yes."

"But, Sam, that would take . . . years to get it?"

"Yes." He twisted his cane nervously between mummy-like fingers.

"But, Sam,—I'm not as young as I used to be." It was the first time she had allowed herself to admit old age to any one. "I thought . . . I hadn't expected to work much longer."

"It's hard luck, Ella. I'm more sorry than I can tell you."

She got up and walked around the room, straightening a pillow, touching book-ends. "I suppose I haven't thought enough about . . . old age,

Sam. It always seemed so far away,—and the present so full of important duties."

"You're not old, Ella. Except for your white hair you don't look a day older than . . . almost when you started to teach." Love is not blind—it merely sees that which another can not.

She stopped in front of the little old man. "Do you know, Sam, I'll tell you what I had told no one, not a soul. I had expected next year to be my last. Just this spring I made up my mind that I'd teach only one more year. But now,—one per cent per month . . . for years." She sat down a little heavily like a tired old woman. "That will squelch *that* plan right now." Then,—"I know what I'll do, Sam." She was suddenly alert, the old Ella. "I'll teach three or four years more and give a thought to nothing *but* money. I'll just reverse my attitude. It will come first. Gretchen is graduating. I'll cut out entertaining students from this day on, every bit of help to any one, and think only of myself. You just *have* to be selfish in this world sometimes, don't you, Sam?"

She talked on rapidly, enthusiastically, while little old Sam Peters sat and twirled his cane.

"Three years more, Sam, instead of one. That's my deadline. I'll save every cent but the smallest sum for actual living. Then I won't have to worry. I've been too easy, I know,—too ready to think there was no end to salaries. I can think of a dozen things I've done that I shouldn't. But you'll see from now on, Sam. I've had my lesson."

Old Sam Peters stood up. He looked out of the window at the pale March sunshine on the dirty snow of the hedge.

"As a . . . what you might call, last resort, Ella . . . there's always my . . . house and name . . . and anything I have."

A mist sprang to her eyes and she put out her hand. "You're so good to me, Sam. I wish . . . I wish it *could* have been."

Old Sam Peters pressed her hand. "That's all right, Ella. You couldn't help it."

"And we've been good friends, Sam."

"Yes . . . we've been good friends."

He went a little shakily down the steps, through the hedge, and across the street to the yard with the rusty old deer.

CHAPTER XXXIX

☙ IN spite of the short distance to the college Ella drove it every day this spring. With jealous care, Chris Jensen always fought for her rights. No one could run over Miss Bishop while Chris was around if the correction lay within his power. As when, in parking the car as near the entrance to Corcoran Hall as was possible, she happened to mention to him that she usually found the car of a student or of another instructor in her chosen place, old Chris immediately set out to right the great injustice to his favorite. Getting no satisfaction from the superintendent of grounds or the new president Crowder that any special privileges could be shown, Chris stubbornly painted a small sign: "Miss Bishop. Do not park here." And slyly planted the sign half under a bridal-wreath bush near Corcoran Hall. When called to his attention by an irate assistant, the superintendent of grounds passed it off with: "Oh, let the old codger leave it there if he gets any satisfaction out of it."

"The only annoying feature about it," Ella said to Gretchen with the humorous twinkle of her old eyes, "is that I ran into it and split the 'e' off, so it now reads 'Miss Bishop. Do not park her.' "

It was only two weeks later that Ella received the note. Chris brought it to her, clumping along in his heavy work shoes up the walk between the hedges. When she saw him coming it occurred to her that she had not noticed how he had aged the last year. One grew used to another through the years, and seeing him that way every day, she had not been able to notice the change. Why, he was old, Chris was,—an old man, his broad shoulders stooped, his arms swinging limply at his sides, his massive head drooping forward so that his iron gray hair hung over his forehead. His step, too, was slow and not quite steady.

She went at once to the door to meet him. "Are you hanging me a May-basket, Chris?" She spoke lightly, gayly, as she often did. It was one thing that had endeared her to those who did manual labor about the campus. "That Miss Bishop,—she's nice to everybody, ain't she?" one workman might say to another.

"Not like that Miss Rogers who acts as though she was smellin' something," might be the answer.

But to-night old Chris would not joke. He delivered the note with dignity and left with no word, clumping along down the walk with shuffling gait and loose swinging arms.

Still standing outside the door as Chris had left her, Ella read the note.

It was from President Crowder—brief, gracious, explanatory. There were to be several changes in the faculty and he thought it much better that she know about the change in her own department before the board met. Delicately veiled, with the kindest of motives, it suggested that she might prefer to get in her resignation prior to the board's action.

Stunned, she could only stand and peer through her eyeglasses at the words of the surprising message. Not quite able to absorb the enormity of the thing that had just descended upon her, her mind darted away from the paper in her hand to the thought that it was Chris who always brought her bad messages. "He's like Eris whom the Greek gods used to send with messages of discord," she thought whimsically. "Just change the 'Ch' to 'E' . . . his name ought to be Eris Jensen . . . instead of Chris."

Then her mind came back to the full import of the note,—and she groped for a porch chair.

For a long time she sat there on the porch in the deepening twilight, —the letter in her lap. Anger toward President Crowder shook her body so that it trembled uncontrollably. In a moment the anger gave way to wounded feeling. A deep sense of hurt pride enveloped her whole being. She had been *asked* to leave,—subtly, delicately,—but what mattered the method? In another year or so she had intended going of her own volition. It made no difference now what she had intended,—she had been *told* to leave.

And then the hurt quite suddenly gave way to fear,—a cold and unreasoning fright. She had not made enough provision for the future. In the years that were gone there had always seemed so many who needed her help. Life had sped along so quickly. Yesterday she had been young with all the years of life unlived. To-day she was old with not much to show for those years of service to the college and community. Service was such a vague immaterial thing,—you could not handle it nor show it to your friends nor exchange it in the market place.

Because this was true she had gone her blithe way, putting from her the thoughts of old age. And suddenly here it was. Would it be a still harsher thing, dependent old age? That pitiful little one per cent which would be meted out to her! Would the small savings be ample to cover all?

By a system of arithmetic as old as the science itself she worked her problems. Her small income made the dividend,—the possible number of years she might live became the rather pathetic divisor,—the quotient resulted in a pitiably small sum which must henceforth cover all expenses. The meagerness of it frightened her. Old age seemed to have developed horns and cloven hoofs, to have taken on a demon-like leer. For the first time she felt genuine panic,—for the first time seemed thinking of herself. Hitherto she had brushed away all her troubles with humor and sane philosophy,—but all her bravery could not hide the Thing that confronted her to-night. The tissues of her courage seemed as weakened as the tissues of her body.

"On a pinch, I could go to the old people's home," she said to her frightened self. At the thought a cold hand seemed clutching her heart. She had visited that home once. It had been pleasant and comfortable, almost luxurious because of various bequests. But the old ladies who had been there sitting on the big porch aimlessly watching the world go by, alien souls, women from whom the glow of living had died,—old ladies with knitting and palsied heads and loose artificial teeth. Quite hastily she put her hand to her mouth and smiled at the inadvertent gesture. At least if she found it necessary to go there eventually she would see plenty of things to amuse her. Pathetic rôles were not meant for her.

Over and over in the deepening dusk she worked on the problem of what to do with the remainder of her life. That potential trip abroad was a huge joke now. Why had she not saved more for herself? Why had she seemed always to have others on her hands?

If worse came to worst she could take a pay roomer or two, do private tutoring. Again and again she tried with courage to work out her problem, so much harder than algebra.

"Let X equal the unknown quantity," she said to herself.

But there was no answer, not in the back of the book or anywhere. Not until God closed the book would old Ella Bishop find what X equaled.

CHAPTER XL

ON Monday morning she drove over to school, turning in at the north gate just in time to see Chris wave an assistant librarian's car away from his chosen spot for herself.

"Little upstart," he was muttering, "hasn't been here but eight or ten years. Thinks she can pick out her . . ."

"Chris . . ." Ella said suddenly when she was out of the car. Why not tell Chris first of all,—wasn't he the only one left with her from the old days? "Chris, I'm through teaching. I'm resigning to-night."

"Vell . . . dat's funny, Miss Bis'op. You and me bot'. I'm quittin', too. Only I ain't got to resign like you on paper. Just tell old Long-legs I'm t'ru,—and dat's all dere be to it,—just *t'ru*."

Ella looked at the old man bent over there by the snow-white blossoms of the bridal wreath, no whiter than the locks of hair straggling down on his forehead.

Then he straightened and for the fraction of a moment old Ella Bishop's bright blue eyes caught the watery blue ones of the old janitor. For the fraction of a moment they saw eye to eye and heart to heart. Suddenly, with no words, each knew the other had been let out.

"Aw, I ain't carin', Miss Bis'op," the old man broke the embarrassment of silence. "Don't you care, neider."

"No, I'm not either." She spoke lightly. "Not at all."

"Neider am I," old Chris repeated stoutly. "Not a bit. Not a mite."

If Miss Bishop secretly entertained thoughts to the effect that both the gentleman and the lady did protest too much, she kept them to herself.

Suddenly he burst out: "Maybe I *am* old, but I don't feel so. I'm strong," he spoke belligerently as though Miss Bishop had indicated otherwise. "Strong as an ox. See dat." He rolled back a blue denim sleeve and displayed flabby old muscles. "Anyways," he added a little ruefully at the sight, "it don't take no great shakes of strengt' to clap erasers 'n dust 'n chase de trainin'-school kids out o' Old Central."

He turned his head away. Miss Bishop understood. English department or janitor work. What difference did it make?

It was the next night that she picked up the *Daily Clarion* and walked over to her favorite chair under a bridge lamp. It was a lovely evening. She could hear all the Maytime sounds of the college town,—cars slipping by, the chimes from the campanile ringing out the hour with rhythmic announcement, a group of fraternity boys shouting unmelodiously: "The Girl in The Little Green Hat." She could smell all the Maytime odors that so associated themselves with preparation for Commencement, fresh paint next door, lawns after the late spring rains, honeysuckles outside the window.

For a moment she held the paper idly, remembering her own part in starting the crude little sheet a half-century before. Then she recalled that this was the issue which would announce the changes. It startled her to see it in black and white: *Miss Bishop Resigns.* She felt a justifiable pleasure in the paragraph referring to her long career, a genuine gratitude toward President Crowder for handling the situation so adroitly. He had saved her pride if nothing else.

She read on down: ". . . Among other changes for this year, the student body will say good-by to Old Central. Those who return next fall will find it listed among the missing. Razing of the old building will begin the morning after the Alumni banquet which will be held this year for sentiment's sake in the old auditorium."

It moved her unaccountably. She and Old Central—both would be listed among the missing. And old Chris—she must not forget him. He, too, had been associated with Old Central since its beginning.

And if Ella Bishop sat idly for a long time with the paper in her lap, let no one enter into the hushed inner chamber of her thoughts.

After a time she arose and took a light wrap from the hall closet, calling to Stena that she was going out for a walk by herself. Once outside, she turned up the street toward the Jensen's little house across from the campus. When she tapped at the door, there was a muffled tread in the hall and old Chris himself came, shading his weak eyes with his hand.

"Good evening, Chris."

"Vell . . . Miss Bis'op." He took a sooty old pipe out of his mouth and gave an apologetic glance at his blue and white socks quite free from inhibiting shoes. That was the way Miss Bishop had affected him for several decades.

"Chris, they tell me Old Central is to come down at last." To her surprise, she had to make an effort to keep her voice steady. She had not realized that it was meaning so much to her.

"Yes, dey do say so." At the risk of a conflagration old Chris was pocketing his pipe. "Come on in, Miss Bis'op."

"No, no thanks. You still have a key I suppose, Chris?"

Old Chris nodded. "Yes, ma'am," he added.

"I wonder if you will let me take it. It's so nice to-night, I'd just like to go over the old building for the last time in a sort of 'We who are about to die, salute you' attitude."

Old Chris had never head of the *Morituri Salutamus* but he recognized fully the emotion in Miss Bishop's voice.

"You will laugh at me for being so sentimental," she said apologetically.

"No, I von't," old Chris shook his heavy gray head. "I von't laugh at you. It's got me a-feelin' blue, too. I know every crack in de plaster 'n every knot in de woodwork."

He shuffled back into the dark interior of the cottage and brought back the key,—a huge affair, like a key to some ancient castle.

"Good night, Chris, and thank you. If you see some one prowling around Old Central, don't shoot or send for the campus policeman."

Ella Bishop walked up through the campus under the elms. The moon was full and there was the heavy scent of syringas in the air, snatches of music came from Fraternity Row, and laughter from the steps of Alice Wayland Hall. It had the smell and feel of all the long-gone Commencements.

In front of the Old Central she paused and looked at it with appraising eye. In the moonlight all discrepancies in the old building were hidden. One could not see the cracks in the brick under the ivy nor the settling window-frames nor the slight sagging of the steps. It looked sturdy, unyielding. It seemed holding up its head proudly. Like Miss Bishop.

She turned the huge key and pushed the iron latch which had clicked to three generations. Softly she stepped into the shadows of the hall. It was stuffy and chalk-scented,—but friendly, as though it welcomed her home. She had a swift feeling that the old building wanted her to know it held no grudge about her leaving, and smiled at the foolishness of the thought.

She crossed the hall and mounted the stairs, her hand slipping along the bannister which was as smooth as old ivory from the polishing of countless human palms.

Straight to her old classroom she passed, a large room with its rows of recitation seats, half in the moonlight, half in the shadow. She was not just sure what it was used for now, but had a faint impression of manual training projects on a bench by the window.

Toward the front of the room where the instructor's desk stood, Ella Bishop walked softly as people do in the presence of the dead. A composite picture of all the classes she had ever taught seemed before her. Personalities looked at her from every recitation seat but she did not realize that in point of time they were sometimes fifty years apart.

There was Frank Farnsworth, indolent, mischievous, even stupid in English courses because he did not care for them, wanting only instruction in business administration. Why did she remember him? There was Anna Freybruger. She was a missionary, some one had told her. Over there sat Clarence Davis, a congressman now. Here laughing Esther

Reese, a happy wife and mother. She summoned them back out of the shadows, not mature nor successful, but young freshmen, needing her guidance.

Slowly she circled the room, recalling a dozen events of the olden days. Queer how easily they came back to-night.

Then she turned toward the tower room, opened the door and stepped in. Once it had been her Gethsemane. On a day she had come in here full of happiness and the joy of living. When she went out, some of her had died. The part that had lived she had dedicated to young people, warming her cold heart at the fire of their youth, putting into her work all the love and interest she would have given to a husband, home, and children. Here she had said good-by to John Stevens, her love and admiration for him unbesmirched.

She crossed the little room, opened one of the windows and sat down by it. The May breeze, sweet with the smell of Commencements, came in and touched the soft tendrils of her white hair.

Memory went back on the road of the years. She tried to sum up the results of the journey. Nothing,—but age and near poverty. Foolishly, she had thought the teaching itself would compensate her for all of her devotion to the task. A deep bitterness assailed her. It was not right nor just, to give all and receive nothing. She had been a fool to think that if you gave your heart the service rendered would be its own reward.

Across the boulevard the sorority houses were lighted to the last window. Cars were at the curbing. Young people came and went. How unnecessary she was now to this newer college life. Once she had seemed indispensable. Slow tears came, the more painful because hitherto she had met life gallantly with high hopes, deep courage, boundless faith.

Ella Bishop raised her face to the May sky as though to hold intimate conversation with some one. How foolish she had been to think that by binding herself to youth she could retain her own light spirits. That early dedication of hers to the lives of her students was all Quixotic. That old idea of carrying a torch ahead to show them the way to unrevealed truths had been all wasted effort. Every waking thought she had given to them, watched her every act and decision that she might be a worthy example.

There were instructors who heard recitations and left their responsibilities hanging like raincoats in their lockers. She had not been able to do that. She had given the best that was in her, not only that her students' minds would further unfold, but whenever they needed assistance for those other sides of their lives, the physical and the moral. A suggestion of eye-strain in a student and she had not rested until the matter was rectified. A knowledge of recurring headaches and she had not known peace until the source was traced. And then that other thing which she had noticed among the newcomers, that elusive thing which was neither all physical nor all mental nor all moral, that subtle thing which crept into the lives of youth. How she had pondered over it, questioned and advised. Many a mother, less motherly than herself, had not known the danger, or having known, had lifted no hand to guide. All this she had done for her students,—and what was her reward? Old age and poverty. And perhaps later,—loneliness. For youth not only must be served, but after that it forgets. Tears came again. And some were for lost youth and some were for advancing age, but some were for a faith that was shattered.

There was nothing now to look forward to—but death. Death! How little thought she had given to it! So full of living,—her hands so filled with duties,—she had existed only from day to day, doing the hour's tasks as well as she could.

She pictured herself lying dead—out in Forest Hill by her mother—under the leaves—

Suddenly a pigeon flew against the bell overhead and it tapped, so that in a great whirl of beating wings all the pigeons flew from the bell tower, their bodies almost brushing the windows. Startled, she jumped up and looked furtively behind her. She had that queer suffocating feeling that one has when he is conscious of a frightened sensation. Usually placid, she realized her heart was pounding wildly. All at once the familiar old building was cold and forbidding. It was as though there were soft footfalls, phantom whisperings. The ghosts of all her yesterdays seemed haunting the place. Was her brain addled? Had she played too long with her memories? Was she slipping mentally like her mother? All her poise was gone. She wanted to fly as from a tomb.

It seemed almost a physical impossibility for her to return through that shadow-laden classroom.

She gathered herself together and crossed the office to the classroom door. Eerie rustlings, low murmurs, faint mocking laughter played tricks with her imagination. The bell tapped faintly. The pigeons swirled past the window again.

In a perspiration of nervousness, she crossed the moonlighted floor of her old classroom, passed through the upper hall, down the long stairway with its bannister polished by a thousand hands, and hurried out into the clear air of the night.

She crossed the campus and went home, tired in every portion of her body, every bone aching, every nerve tingling with fatigue. At home she went straight to her room with an intense longing to get quickly into the cool depths of her bed. She took off each garment wearily, stopping once or twice to cast longing eyes toward the haven of her couch with a half-formed decision to drop onto it as she was. With extra effort at control she finished the task and slipped into the welcome comfort of that familiar port of rest.

Getting under the quilts was like crawling under leaves, she thought vaguely. Either one meant rest. Rest for a tired teacher. What difference did it make—quilts or leaves? There was peace under either. To let your tired mind and body sink into the blessed comfort of them,—quilts or leaves,—to let them cling softly and gently to you, easing the ache and the long, long weariness.

What difference did it make? Leaves . . . or quilts . . . ? Quilts . . . or leaves . . . ?

CHAPTER XLI

"You know, Gretchen, I think I'm not going to the Alumni banquet this year." Ella Bishop was sitting in front of her dressing-table and speaking over her shoulder to the girl in the hall. She had tried to make her voice casual, matter-of-fact, but she had a feeling that it quivered and cracked "like the old woman I suppose I might as well admit I am," she thought.

"Not going? Why?" Gretchen, attractive as always in a white sport outfit, came to the door.

"Oh, I just thought I wouldn't this year—leaving as I am. . . ." She said it so lightly that she was highly pleased with herself. "And as long as Old Central is to come down—you know it just wouldn't be good taste to consume food in your own mausoleum."

"Oh, Aunt Ella, what a terrible thought."

"And anyway I've been to a thousand. My word, Gretchen, some time I'm going to sit down and figure the hours I've spent at them, and the words I've heard going to waste in the ponderous speeches that have been made. Now, for instance . . . let's see . . . I began going in 1880 . . . this year would make fifty-three times . . . no, fifty-two . . . I escaped one, anyway, the year I was East. Fifty-two Commencements

. . . say three hours each allowed for sitting at the tables,—one hundred and fifty-six hours . . . that's . . . wait a minute . . . over nineteen working days of eight hours each." She was enjoying her bit of irony.

> *"The hours I've spent at them, dear heart,*
> *Are but so many words to me,*
> *I count them over, every one apart,*
> *Their ora-tor-ee! Their ora-tor-ee!"*

She laughed at her own light humor,—had complete control of herself now. "For nineteen full working days have I listened to flowery rhapsodies or ponderous advice. As for the energy expended, it has been immeasurable."

"Oh, but you *must* go." Gretchen was earnest in her vehemence. "The very fact that you *are* leaving, Aunt Ella, is the biggest reason for being there."

"I suppose you're right. Who am I to shirk?" she answered in the same light vein she had been employing. "Twenty full days would end the whole thing with a flourish, make it an even number, and one can always go into a sort of coma and think of other things if the oratory proves too powerful an anesthetic. And, anyway, I'll have perfect peace and freedom for they haven't asked me to talk this year."

It was rather an important Commencement, what with its being Ella's last while a faculty member, and Gretchen graduating. Hope and Dick came in time for the festivities, Dick never quite rugged since the war and so never quite the success he might have been, Hope heavy and sweet-faced, and both wrapped up in pride for their lovely daughter. And Ronald Smith came, driving through with his grandmother, old Mrs. Irene Van Ness Hunt, wrinkled and sallow, and looking so much older than Ella that one could not imagine they had been girls together. But she had a whole rumble seat full of bags containing gay lace dresses and high-heeled pumps, and every time she shook her sprightly old head, a different pair of long earrings jangled against her magenta-colored cheeks.

Ella housed them all but Ronald who stayed at the Phi Psi chapter house.

The night of the banquet they were all going together over to Old Central, which, lighted from top to bottom, was making merry on the eve of its own private Waterloo.

Every one was ready quite on time but Gretchen who seemed slower than usual with her dressing. Ella was groomed and ready long before the young girl, a full half-hour before Ronald came to join the group. Always punctual, she could not tolerate the careless way in which the young people seemed to regard time.

"At least, let's be there when the fruit cocktail is eaten," she called up the stairs, and added more for her own pleasure than the waiting group: "I can visualize the whole thing from that well-known cocktail to lights out. I could even stay at home and hear in my head every word that will be spoken."

Old Miss Bishop looked nice. She had on her white lace dress and black velvet evening wrap. Her snow white hair was beautifully groomed and even the inevitable black velvet band at her throat which she wore this last year served not only its pitiful little duty of covering those telltale shrunken neck tissues but of accentuating the loveliness of her hair and the pose of her head.

There were so many cars parked around the campus when they arrived that Ella said: "An unusually large attendance, it looks . . . that will be on account of sentiment for Old Central. We really shouldn't have been late."

She hastened the pace of the group a little, but Ronald and Gretchen, strolling exasperatingly up the curving walk and around the Administration Building toward Old Central, called to them not to be in such a hurry. Ella was thinking sentimentally that the lights of the old building looked familiar and friendly sending out their message for all to come to the festivities with no thought that to-morrow night and other nights they would not beckon.

One of the big busses that had replaced the old jangling street car disgorged a few people who slipped in ahead of the little group of six. Otherwise, the campus was deserted.

"We're the *very* last," Ella complained. As though Ronald and Gretchen had not used skillful maneuvering to see that this was so.

Old Chris stood in the lobby, almost unrecognizable in his best suit and large shining shoes. His massive gray head was held a bit stiffly above his low loose collar, and his wide bony shoulders drooped heavily under the weight of their years.

As these last comers entered he pulled on the rope dangling through his big gnarled hand. High above them in the old belfry the bell rang, and with a great whirl of wings the pigeons flew out.

"Pretty nigh de last time," he said to Ella as she passed. "Don't it sort o' get you?"

She nodded wordlessly.

Just inside the door of the old auditorium they paused. Something was unusual, Ella was thinking. Not for years had there been such an enormous turn-out. She caught a fleeting vision of rows upon rows of tables, a multitude of people seated at them, flowers, class banners, white-coated waiters, overflow tables in adjoining rooms.

The bell might have been a signal, for the orchestra broke into "Pomp and Circumstance." Something was happening. The diners were rising as one man. All faces were turned toward the group at the door. President Crowder and the chairman of the board were coming toward them. They were offering Ella their arms, one on her left, one on her right. Ronald was slipping off her velvet wrap. Gretchen was whispering: "All for you, sweet pumpkin."

Applause broke, wild and unrestrained. In a daze Ella took the arms of the two men and together they walked the full length of the huge room.

Together the president and the board member opened a double gateway of ferns and escorted her to a chair at the head of the long sweep of tables. The chair was rose covered, and when they pulled it out and seated her in the sweet-smelling bower, Miss Bishop looked like a white rose herself. The president and the board chairman seated themselves at each side and the great audience sat down. There was an orchid corsage at Ella's plate,—and quite trivially it came to her that she had never worn an orchid in her life.

It was all very hard to comprehend. Her mind felt numb, callous, incapable of concentrated thought. A drowning person must feel so. "It isn't true," she kept thinking. "I'm moving about only in dreams. This thing hasn't happened for me. I'm an old woman, worn out, poverty stricken, shelved, with nothing to show for my life."

Conversation broke on all sides with a humming noise of pleasure. All of the people closest were leaning toward her speaking to her. But she seemed without emotion, as though the years had wrung her out, hard and dry, like an old dishcloth. She spoke and smiled mechanically and made futile stabs at her fruit cocktail. What had she said once about a fruit cocktail—something sarcastic? It must have been years ago.

In that same numb and callous way, she finished the courses with the others, not quite understanding, never quite comprehending the thing that was happening.

The dining over, the toasts began. They were all for Miss Bishop "who has given a lifetime of service to the upbuilding of this school," or "who perhaps more than any other faculty member of the half century has had a deep and lasting influence upon all students."

Presently she seemed to come out of her stupor. In a great sweep of understanding, the thing that was happening suddenly did seem true. She was being honored. This was for her. All her old students appeared to have returned. Never had there been such a huge reunion,—not in the whole history of the college. They had come back to honor Old Central—and her.

They toasted her, told jokes on her, teased her, praised her. A United States senator admitted that if it hadn't been for Miss Bishop he might still be saying "have saw." A prominent minister said that next to his parents, Miss Bishop had influenced his life more than any other human. A millionaire merchant, who had arrived in his own plane, told the audience that when mothers were lauded, not to forget one of the very best of them all, Miss Bishop, *mother of students.* A mechanical engineer said he had done a little figuring and found that if Miss Bishop's influence for good upon her hundreds of students could be computed and turned into—

There were cries of "Technocracy" and good-natured banter.

It was the new president who said that in the brief time he had been here he had come to realize that Miss Bishop was one of the chief representatives of the real spirit of the school, courageous, progressive, high-minded, *human.*

The last of the speakers was the chairman of the board who said it had been one of the happiest tasks of his life to journey two hundred miles in order to present his old instructor, Miss Bishop, with the highest degree that had ever been given by the college,—a D.M.H.S.,—Doctor of Mind, Heart and Soul.

Through it all Ella Bishop sat quietly, poised, head up, facing the great throng whose eyes were all upon her. And the wine of new life flowed through her veins.

Sitting there while the speeches went on, sweeping around her, like waves about some little island of her own, her mind was a swiftly changing kaleidoscope of thoughts. They darted hither and yon, those thoughts, like white-hot bits of steel flying from the anvil of her mind, struck by the hand of God. She seemed endowed suddenly with some great power hitherto unknown to her, a prophetic vision to see life as a whole. Little pieces of her life swept together, small incidents tumbled into shape, so that a completed pattern visioned itself before her in one compact unit.

The whole mosaic of her life spread out in front of her. For a few moments it hung before her mind as a tapestry might have been displayed before her mortal eyes.

Once in her youth she had started to weave a tapestry at the loom of life with a spindle of hope and dreams,—and the center of the fabric was to have been a little house in a garden and red firelight and the man she loved and children. But the threads had been broken and the spindle lost, and she had woven another. And now for these brief minutes everything was understandable. Every decision she had made was thread of the loom, every incident in her life was a silver or scarlet or jet-black cord woven into the warp and woof of the fabric. And surprisingly the black threads were necessary to throw into relief the figures of the weaving.

For a few moments she had a complete vision of things as they are. An occult power was her own for that brief time. Some unknown force seemed saying: "Here is the work of your life. Take one swift look. It is not given to many to see the completed whole. This is what you have woven from the threads God gave you."

Ella Bishop dropped the lids over her eyes for a moment in abject humility before the loveliness of the scarlet and blue and gold of the weaving.

Never before had such understanding been given her; vaguely she sensed that never would it be again. All rancor concerning the forced resignation was swept away in a flood of understanding. She was closing her work before her faculties dimmed, singing her swan song on a high clear note. To-morrow she would be an old woman. To-night she was ageless. Yesterday she had merely mumbled the words that life was eternal. To-night she knew it. She feared nothing now . . . poverty or old age or death. None of them existed. There was no end to the soul of her . . . to the real Ella Bishop . . . here or anywhere . . . not while all these people lived . . . or their children . . . or their children's children. The remembrance of her in men's hearts would not be for anything she possessed,—but for what she had done.

Something was tapping at her memory,—some long forgotten dream of her youth. Suddenly she remembered,—that early dedication of her life. Why, she must have . . . almost without realization . . . by doing her simple duty from day to day . . . she must have given some of the living flame that glows more brightly as the ages pass.

She had nothing to fear,—here or beyond. Out where Professor Fonda lay sleeping the stone said:

We have loved the stars too deeply
To be fearful of the night.

The stars had been Albert Fonda's deepest love. Her own love was the students to whom she had given her life. This, then, could be her own confidence and faith at the end of the journey:

We have loved humanity too deeply
To be fearful of the dead.

The last speech was over. The great assembly was calling for her. She must say something. This was her last opportunity. She must stand and tell them what she had just discerned,—that every thread of life's weaving must be strong, every fiber firm. True to the dedication of her life she must tell them of this knowledge she had just acquired.

Old Miss Bishop rose. The applause was deafening. Before she passed from their lives she must teach them one thing more . . . these men and women she loved. But how could she approach it? What could she say? She looked over the vast sea of faces. No, it was too late. You cannot teach a great truth like that in the space of a few moments. You may only accomplish it, little by little, day by day, over a long period of time. If she had not done so by example and precept in a half-century's teaching, she could not do so now. And perhaps she had. God knew.

She stretched out her arms to them all, with superhuman effort stilled the trembling of her lips. "The book is closed," said old Miss Bishop. "Hail and farewell."

And the affair was over.

They crowded around her, congratulating her, pressing her hand, giving her merry messages. When they left, group by group, she had a dozen dinner dates and out-of-town week-end invitations. Not that old indefinite "Come to see me, sometime, Miss Bishop," but "to-morrow night at seven" and "next Friday on our silver wedding anniversary."

Every group which left put the same question: "Are you ready to go now? We'll walk over to your car with you." And as many times she answered: "Thank you. I'm not quite ready."

Even when Ronald and Gretchen and the rest of the party came for her it was the same. It was Gretchen who intuitively sensed it. "Come on," she whispered to them all. "I believe she *wants* to be the last one."

Just inside the hallway with its cracks in the scarred walls, old Ella Bishop stood, erect and smiling, and bade the great throng of students good-night. Like a mother she watched the last child break the tie which bound it to home.

For a few moments then she stood alone watching the shadowy figures move across the campus under the giant trees,—north—south—east—west —down the four roads of the world.

Then she walked firmly over the worn threshold and closed the doors that had swung to a thousand youthful hands.

The bell tapped and the pigeons with a great rush of beating wings flew out of the tower.

Old Chris turned out the lights.

THE END

The Day of Retaliation

ANNA BRUNEMEIER dressed a chicken at the sink of the farmhouse kitchen. The strong raw odor of the scalded feathers made her head ache. The unpleasant sight of the entrails sickened her. Her feet pained. She felt unusually tired. But then, she was always tired these days. She arose mornings unrefreshed, dragged through long working hours, and fell into bed heavily soon after supper. She felt burdened, oppressed and clumsy. It is the price of coming motherhood.

It was April, and raining. Not the usual soft, bud-unfolding, misty rain of April, but a fierce, pommeling downpour. Just outside the screened porch door the water rushed out of a tin spout into the rain barrel, filled it, and dropped sloppily over the sides.

Gus, her husband, came to that door now, stepped inside the porch, shook himself like a spaniel and slipped out of his boots. As he came on into the kitchen there was an odor about Gus, too, that sickened Anna—his wet, steaming clothes and the rubber of his yellow slicker.

"Pretty damp," he remarked amiably.

Anna acknowledged it with a dull "Yes."

Gus hunted around on the clock shelf for his jackknife and, finding it, started back to the porch. As he passed the sink he paused.

"Elsa didn't ever cut the leg off the thigh joint," he volunteered, and pointed a wet, stubby forefinger at the designated piece. "She left the second joint on the leg bone. It made a bigger helping."

He was not cross. He was not dictatorial. His mild voice held no definite disapproval. He had merely given forth a simple statement, casual and informative.

But a hot wave of anger flooded Anna's body, a tingling, uprolling tide of resentment that swept over her and settled in dull red puddles of blood on her cheek bones.

Elsa! Elsa! Always Elsa!

Having deposited his unpremeditated information, Gus got into his muddy boots and went out again into the rain.

Elsa! All the dislike that Anna possessed for the dead Elsa wrapped her now like a garment. All the jealousy that she felt for Gus's first wife concentrated in a dull pain of hatred. If only she could remove the memory of the girl that Gus had loved—still loved—she could be happy. But Elsa was a thorn that could never be plucked from her flesh, an ulcer that grew on the very vitals of her being. If only the dead Elsa would let her alone, allow her to be Gus's wife with no interference. But she seemed to come to Anna—Elsa did—and stand beside her. Soft-eyed and dark-haired and gentle she came. It was as if she said: "Just a year ago these things were mine. At this time last year I went about these rooms. Just so I did my housework. But Gus came and took my hand and spoke tender words. *I* was loved, Anna."

It was an unbearable thought—that Elsa had been the loved one.

The chicken finished, Anna went about other tasks, paring potatoes, chopping cabbage, cooking beans. All the rest of the day at her work she was bothered by the unseen presence of the dead Elsa.

All that day, and the other days of that week, Gus himself brought Elsa many times into the house. Once it was with, "Elsa she culled out her chickens about now and sold the irregulars." Again it was with, "Elsa she baked her bread on Fridays." And one day it was, "Elsa she made *kaffee-kuchen* every little while."

Not cross, not unkind, just casually informative, it wore on Anna's mind like the dripping of water from the eaves. For it rained all week. The creek was high. The world seemed a soggy thing over which there would never again be sunlight.

Anna was never idle. She sewed and baked and swept. She cleaned the cupboards and the downstairs closet, brushing Elsa's coat and sweater which were now rightfully hers, but which nothing could have persuaded her to wear. She hated every one of the garments. And looking at Gus, sitting smoking by the stove on the rainy evenings, she half hated him too.

It did not seem possible that one person could be both so loved and so hated. Every fiber of her being loved him—his big strength and his good looks—and yet it seemed, at times, that every fiber of her being also hated him, loathed him for still loving Elsa. For she felt it was of Elsa he was thinking, sitting so quietly by the range on the rainy evenings. She wished that she could shake him out of his silence, bring him back to her, have him for her very own.

On Saturday it stopped raining and the sun came out in a blaze of warmth that fairly pulled the green from the trees, turning the farmyard into a place of steaming humidity. Gus came to the door in the late afternoon and tossed his heavy raincoat into the porch.

"Anna, I got to help Emil Schlappe with a sick horse," he called. "You feel like you could go after the cows?"

"I can go." There was something stolid in Anna, a trace of blood in her that had not changed with two generations of living in a country where women are not stolid.

She finished cleaning a window and washed her hands. Then she took a shawl down from a nail and drew it around her, not for need of warmth in the moist spring air, but because there were times when a woman should wear a wrap. She put on heavy rubbers and started out, picking her way between pools in the lane road. As she walked she was thinking that it was just such a late afternoon and on just such an errand that Elsa had been drowned.

There had been hard rains earlier in the season the year before and the creek had been on this same sort of rampage, rolling sluggishly over the rye land. Elsa had gone for the cows, just as she herself was going now. No one ever knew how the accident happened. There might have been a cow at the edge of the creek and Elsa might have waded into the water to drive her out. She might have tried to get a switch off an overhanging willow tree. Or she might have fainted on the high bank at the far end of the pasture. The whole countryside had discussed the possible cause and had come to no conclusion. The body had been found floating gruesomely against the wire fence down on the Emil Schlappe place. The entire community had sorrowed.

Anna, herself, had been contentedly at home with her parents five miles away when the word came over the phone that Elsa Brunemeier was drowned. It had meant nothing to her then but the excitement of the news, the loss of a none-too-well-known church acquaintance, a general sort of sympathy for Gus.

And then, so strange is fate, last fall she herself had taken Elsa's place.

She had reached the end of the lane now, and stopped to pick up a cottonwood stick with which to whack old Spotty if she proved lazy. The sun shone warm across the spongy pasture. The ground was sticky, the new wild herbage steaming. The cows were at the far end of the pasture still nibbling the juicy grass. Anna picked her way across to them, her feet denting the soft ground. She could see the high creek now. It flowed darkly through the willows like a pleasant old friend turned sullenly unrecognizable. And Elsa had in some way been a victim of that treachery, a sacrifice to that unfaithfulness.

It made Anna stop and look at the picture, fascinated by the ugly danger concealed there under the willows. She paused to imagine the unpleasant details—finding Elsa, bringing her home, Gus's grief. She, herself, had sat in the Lutheran church through the two long sermons of the service. Brother Roerheimer and Brother Schulte had reviewed the beautiful life of the dead woman. Gus had kept his head bowed in his pew. Had hung over the casket when they were leaving the church. Had called "Elsa, come back," so that every one heard him. Had almost fainted as they finally pulled him away. Even then, she had wondered vaguely how it would seem to be so deeply loved by a nice man like Gus.

And then a few months later, as unbelievable as it seemed, Gus had come over to her father's house in his car to call on her. On his third trip he had asked her to marry him. There was no time to make any special preparation for the marriage. Husking was on and Gus needed her immediately. He had said there was plenty of bedding and linen in the house—all of Elsa's things—no use to wait. So she had come. There had been nothing romantic about it. Just a ceremony at the minister's—and then cooking dinner for corn-huskers.

No, she was not particularly loved. She sensed it. She was a housekeeper, a drudge, a convenient helper. Gus was not unkind. Nor especially kind. Just matter-of-fact and very quiet. And he still loved Elsa. That was what hurt. She would not have minded the work, or the quiet, unsmiling way of the man, or the ill feelings with which her body was now racked. But to live with—and work for—and bear a child for a man who did not love you. . . . It did not seem right.

She was leaning now against a wet post of the pasture fence whose rotting bark sloughed off on her dress. It was not like Anna to be idle, but her thoughts seemed of more importance to-day than her duties. She clung to the distasteful idea: Bearing Gus a child and he loving Elsa all the time. She wondered if she, too, were to drown in the little stream like Elsa, whether he would care a great deal.

Standing by the fence, idly whacking her cottonwood stick at the bushes, she let her mind dwell on the picture of her own death, imagined the people gathering in the church and sitting solemnly waiting for the mourners to come. She visioned Gus hanging over her dead body—heard him call her as he had called Elsa, "Anna, come back"—saw them pull

Gus away from her coffin. It gave her an abnormal desire to hurt him by her own death, to drown herself in the dark waters in order to shake him out of his moody quiet, and make him give his mind wholly to her.

The cows had come slowly and lumberingly across the pasture now, snatching greedily at a few last choice morsels of lush grass. Reminded of duty, Anna relinquished her dark thoughts of drowning, turned and plodded behind the cattle.

Gus was not at home when she arrived at the house. She put potatoes in the oven, sliced ham in readiness for frying, and set the table for supper. Then she climbed the narrow stairs to her bedroom.

As one throwing fuel on the fire of her jealousy, she opened the top drawer of the shining pine dresser where Elsa's things still lay. In orderly precision they stared back at her—the collars and cuffs and the folded aprons. They affected her strangely, these intimate things of the woman she hated. For half a year she had seen them there in the drawer just as Elsa had left them, and not once had she ever touched them. All her own things were across the room in a highboy she had brought with her from home.

Now she reached forth a cautious hand and picked up a lace collar. The thought of Elsa's white neck rising from it maddened her even as it fascinated her. She laid the collar down and picked up other things one by one. She wanted to crush them, to tear them, in a symbolic crushing and tearing of the love Gus held for their owner. One fragile undergarment she wrung between her strong hands until it lay crumpled and torn in her lap. The act gave her an unholy pleasure. Replacing the rumpled garment, she reached for a green plush handkerchief box at the back of the drawer and drew it out. The lid lifted to her trembling, jealous fingers and disclosed a tumbled array of handkerchiefs.

Vaguely she wondered then at the confusion of the contents, in marked contrast to the neatness of the rest of the drawer.

With an inborn sense of orderliness she began straightening the squares of cotton and linen. Her hand, slipping under them, touched paper.

For only a moment Anna hesitated, and then she drew the paper out. The two folded sides of a thin sheet separated themselves in her hand almost without her volition.

"April nineteenth. My dearest Fred," said the letter.

Anna stared. *My dearest Fred!* Some intuitive thing deep within her consciousness knew the contents even then. Fred was the name of the young fellow with whom Elsa had kept company before marrying Gus. Her heart stopped with chilliness for a moment, and then raced hotly on. One long ink-stained blur across the page blotted out the words so that part of the closely written letter was illegible. A corresponding long ink stain ran across the soft whiteness of a handkerchief.

April nineteenth! The date on which Elsa had met her tragic death in the high waters of the treacherous creek. Wide-eyed, Anna was taking in the words that remained unblotted, the broken sentences left to carry their startling revelation.

"——can't go on longer with Gus . . . loving you all the time . . . living a lie . . . stand it longer . . . when we were students in the Lutheran college . . . awful mistake . . . always wanted to marry you . . . crazy this way . . . about out of my head . . . since you were here . . . couldn't sleep . . . come to my decision . . . write you definite plans . . . must burn this . . . no one ever find it . . . always your own Elsa."

Anna stood and stared wildly at the blurred streak, sweeping across the page like the hand of God blotting out part of the confession—stared at the ugly black ink stain on the soft whiteness of the handkerchief like the ugly black sin on the soul of Elsa.

Again and again she read the shocking message beginning with "My dearest Fred," and ending with "must burn this . . . no one ever find it. . . ."

And no one *had* found it—not then. And no one at all but the very one who most needed to find it. As though the sky had opened and dropped its message of peace to Anna! As though Fate had taken care of the secret for a year, saving it in the cheap plush handkerchief box until Anna should come for it!

More calmly now she tried to think out everything. More carefully she set together the little bits of evidence. The burning love-letter had been written before Elsa went for the cows on that fatal day. And what of the ink blur besmirching the page? And of the corresponding blot on the handkerchief? Might not the writer have been frightened at some one coming unexpectedly into the house? Did Elsa in her fear of detection snatch up the letter, hurriedly run to the handkerchief box and cram its inky paper into the hidden pocket? Did Death, then, lurking in the dark waters of the old creek immediately afterward take its toll of the wife who was not true?

Anna lifted her eyes from the amazing thing in her hand and looked out of the window toward the sullen creek. Elsa, the good, had sinned.

Elsa, the worshiped, had deceived. Elsa, the loved, had not loved. Why, she, Anna, was the good one of the two. *She* was the true one. *She* would be the loved one when Gus found this out. *When Gus found this out.* The words poured into her heart like a softly flowing ointment, miraculously soothing and healing the raw, smarting wound that had hurt her so long.

She heard a sound downstairs—the closing of a screen door—so that she hastily shut the drawer and placed the paper in the bosom of her dress. She walked hurriedly down the narrow stairs, her hand at her breast where the letter lay like a weapon ready for use.

Gus was coming in the door with a little pail of cookies from Mrs. Schlappe. With a soothing calm flooding her whole body, Anna greeted him cheerfully. Instinct told her that the time for the amazing revelation was not ripe. After supper, when Gus would sit smoking and silent, thinking of Elsa, she would tell.

In that new tranquil manner she prepared supper. After the meal she washed the dishes, set her bread, and took up some sewing by the kitchen table. With the rise and fall of her breathing, the letter against her breast rose and fell too. She felt a security in its faintly crackling presence, a sense of holding the upper hand over Gus. For a long time they sat so—Anna, sewing, feeling the fluttering nearness of her child and the fluttering nearness of the letter; Gus, idly smoking, staring at the shining blackness of the range.

After a time Gus rose to wind the clock and lock the doors. And Anna had not told. When she went up the narrow, built-in stairway to bed she hurriedly took out the amazing letter, opened the green plush handkerchief box and slipped the paper into it. Then she locked it and placed the tiny key in another drawer. Tomorrow, if even once he mentioned the name of Elsa, she would turn on him and tell.

It was toward noon the next day that Gus, coming up to the house, said to her: "Elsa she used a different broom for the porches." It was not cross, not dictatorial, just casually informative. And surprisingly, it did not seem to hurt Anna to-day. She smiled to herself as he said it. Yesterday at this time it would have been almost unbearable. To-day it had lost its sting. Yesterday she would have known nothing to reply to him. To-day she might have answered if she had chosen. But she did not choose. She would wait until he said something more biting, something that she could not stand, something that cried out for an answer.

And the answer would be waiting upstairs in the green plush handkerchief box.

A week slipped away. Several times Gus brought unknowingly the presence of Elsa, the loved, into the house with him. Once it was with "Elsa she churned oftener," so that Anna, tired from much pushing up and down of the old-fashioned dasher, almost turned on him with the weapon of her news. But she held herself, and waited for something more crucial.

The week slipped into a month and the month into August. And Anna had not yet told. Always she was waiting for that more bitter thing—that critical thing which she could not endure.

Heat descended on the community now, the torrid, corn-growing heat of the midwest. Anna, in her clumsiness, picked up apples and dried them.

"Elsa she sometimes made fresh apple-cake," Gus volunteered, not cross, not dictatorial, merely informative.

But the time had not yet come. Some day he would say a more biting thing and she would turn on him. It was as though she waited for all the references to Elsa to accumulate at some special time—as though she wanted the dramatic touch to come as a great crisis to the humiliation of her love for Gus.

When Gus was out working, Anna sometimes took the letter out of the box and gloated over the blotted, revealing lines, the written evidence which would smite his love for Elsa. She held imaginary conversation with him. The day when she would be goaded into telling, Gus would look at her in amazement, breaking his stony silence with: "I don't believe it."

"Oh, you don't?" she would retort with scorn. "Wait, and I'll show you."

By September, with the corn safely maturing, there was no rain. So dry was the grass that it made a rustling, crackling sound when the chickens walked in it. Anna canned grapes. The heat from the sun and the heat from the range seemed to burn her like fire from two giant caldrons. Gus, coming into the kitchen, passed the range. Then he paused and turned back. "Elsa she dipped out some of the juice first and made jelly of it before she canned the rest," he volunteered.

A fly buzzed aggravatingly around Anna's perspiring forehead. A bit of hot juice splashed across her hand. Suddenly the thread in her brain snapped—the slender, cautious thread that held her secret. At last Gus had cut the fragile thing with the knife of his criticism.

Anna whirled to him, her face livid with the heat and something else. Her gray eyes flashed wild. She flung out her hand.

"Oh, Elsa! Elsa! Elsa!" Her voice rose in a crescendo of madness. All day it had been coming and now it had come. "Elsa!" she shrieked. "Always Elsa. Some day I'll tell you. . . ." She threw back her head and laughed, high, mirthless laughter. "When I tell you . . . one of these days about Elsa. . . ."

She looked at Gus, standing there speechless, his mouth dropped open in amazement. She wanted to hurt him, shame him out of his calm, compel him to love her. "I'll tell you *now*," she shrilled suddenly. Anger and jealousy were boiling up in her like the thick, purple sauce in the kettle. "Right *now*. I'll go get it . . ." She dropped the long-handled dipper on the table, and the sweet grape juice dripped stickily onto the floor.

She ran clumsily from the room to the foot of the built-in stairway. She, who for weeks had walked ploddingly at her tasks, now ran frantically, her foot hitting and overturning a chair. Gus followed her stupidly. The color had slipped away from under his summer-burned skin so that it gave him a peculiar mask-like expression of fright. "Now . . . right now," she called back, her voice high, strident. "Then you'll talk some more again of your nice Elsa!"

Up the stairs she ran, lifting the cumbersome weight of herself violently. At the head of the stairs she flung herself across the hall into her bedroom and ran to the dresser. With hands fumbling madly for the key to the handkerchief box, she suddenly sank to the floor.

"Gus!" she called. "Send for help, quick!"

In a daze she could hear disconnected sentences from Gus at the phone: "No . . . don't wait . . . right away. Get off the line, you curious coyotes!" He was calling the Schlappes. "Tell Emil to bring your mother, quick!" Gus's voice was no longer mild.

People came. They moved about Anna strangely—sometimes dimly and far away, sometimes coming close like huge, distorted giants with false faces. She was conscious that she was saying foolish, meaningless things, but they were quite beyond her volition. Gus's face came and went with the others, white and staring. Once she made an effort to speak to him: "The grapes, Gus! I got to get up and finish the grapes. Elsa she always finished. . . ." But she was swept away on a black wave which her struggling senses thought was the swollen water of a sullen creek.

A long time later—whether a day or a year or an eternity she did not know—she floated back to rest on the shore. Her first sensation was the lightness of her body that for weary weeks had been so cumbersome. Through the window she could see starlight shining. Queer, but it made her think of the rays of some star of which she had heard—a star that stopped once—somewhere.

Vaguely she sensed a rustling, pecking noise over in the basket near her bed. And quite suddenly her mind cleared and she knew. It was her baby, A deep feeling of peace enveloped her.

And then she saw that it was not starlight at all, but the first faint rays of the sun shining slantwise through her bedroom window.

Out in the hall on the couch she could see old Mrs. Schlappe nodding sleepily. Anna called her weakly. Mrs. Schlappe jumped and sat up straight.

"My baby—which is it?"

"Oh, ya. . . ." The old woman got up laboriously and hobbled over to the bed. "A fine girl."

"Where's Gus?"

"Gus?" The old woman could scarcely get herself awake. "Gus . . . oh, him? Vy, Gus has vent up to Omaha to get a nurse . . . a *trained* nurse. Between you 'n me 'n de gate post, you don't need a *trained* nurse any more'n I do. I've took care of t'irty-t'ree voman. I been countin' 'em up. Like as not I've missed some, too. It's t'irty-t'ree anyway, and out o' all dat number only four of 'em died and seven or eight babies. But you couldn't stop Gus, I tell you."

The old woman's voice went querulously on: "I say to him, 'All right, if you vant to pay forty-two dollar a veek . . . it's all right mit *me*.' 'N' he say . . . de softy . . . 'I'll pay forty-two dollar a *day* if it'll save my Anna.' So doc televoned. He say a goot one is shust registered. Ain't dat folderol? Like a hotel. So Gus has vent. It's a vonder he t'ought I was goot enough to lay here by you. He acted *gans närrisch* over you. Valked de floor 'n talked about you till doc make him go outdoor. . . . I guess you got him scare talkin' about a note you hide."

Anna was fully roused now, all her faculties clear.

"What did I say?" She raised her body weakly on an elbow. "Tell me quick. What did I say?"

The old woman pushed her back. "Here, none o' dat. You lay down. I'll bring you de baby. Don't you vant to see your baby?"

Anna's voice was authoritative. "Tell me what I said."

"You say foolishness a-plenty all right, about a note dat you hid avay and locked under de water of de creek bed already yet. You say Gus couldn't find it for de key is in de kettle of grape sauce. But most of 'em do like dat. I know a voman vonce who say ven she get up she is goin' to poison de neighbor takin' care of her . . . and dem goot friends."

The old woman brought the sleeping baby and placed it in the crook of Anna's arm. Fascinated, Anna watched it stretch its arms in little sleepy, objectless motions and then open its eyes. Gus's eyes—large and blue. Gus's hair—dark and wavy. Gus's mouth—full-lipped and generous. For a long time Anna lay without taking her rapt eyes from the face of the child.

Subdued noises downstairs roused her from her long reverie and then, clumsily tiptoeing, his hat in his hand, Gus came into the room and up to the bed.

Anna looked up to the man hanging wonderingly over her. "Gus, you're disappointed?"

"Not on your life. I'm glad it's a girl."

"Ain't she nice . . . her round little head and her funny little hands?"

Anna's plain face was glorified. Gus laid his big hand gently on her hair as though a clumsy touch might brush aside some magic light he was seeing there.

"Gus. . . ." Anna looked up at the man bent protectingly over the bed. "I been thinking . . . poor Elsa . . . she never knew what I know now . . . the feel of a baby in the crook of your arm. It made me sorry for her . . . and I been thinking it would be kind of nice . . . if we call the baby Elsa."

Gus's face turned red, a brick red that ran below the tan of his skin. "I got no wish to quarrel with you, Anna." He twisted his hat on nervous fingers. "But I told quite a few folks already yet about the baby . . . and when I was drivin' past the newspaper office . . . the editor was standin' out in front . . . 'n I guess I felt kind of important about it. . . . Anyway, I drove up by the curb and told him, too, and the paper was just goin' to press. Maybe you'll give me Hail Columbia for this . . . but already yet I told the editor to put in the paper that her name was little *Anna.*

"Gee, Anna——" He broke off suddenly and dropped on his knees by the side of the bed. "I'm glad I got you safe. You had me crazy. I thought I was goin' to lose you. Anna, if I'd lost you I'd a-gone too. You was out o' your head from the start, I guess. Anna, do you remember runnin' up the stairs talkin' about Elsa, how you had something you was goin' to tell me about her? You must have been out o' your head, wasn't you?"

Anna nodded. She slipped cool fingers through Gus's hair. "Sure I was, Gus. Don't pay any attention to it. I must have been plumb daffy!"

And then Gus rose hastily, edging away with a lingering look at Anna, because the new nurse was coming in. The nurse was tall, cool-looking, calm-eyed. She came over to the bed and took Anna's hand in her own capable one. Anna clutched at the hand in her eagerness.

"Listen," she said quickly, very low. "Before any more times goes by I want you to do something for me." Her voice shook in the intensity of her earnestness. "There's a blurred-looking letter in a—in my handkerchief box, over there in the right drawer of the dresser. The box is locked and the key is in the left drawer behind some aprons. I want you to get the letter out and take it downstairs to the cook stove. Don't let Gus—my husband—see what you're doing, and don't let that old Mrs. Schlappe even catch a glimpse of what you've got. You burn it in the range. Stay there right by it till there ain't a scrap left. Promise me that, and then I'll rest or do anything you say."

"You're not asking me to do something you'll be sorry for when you get up?"

"No—oh, no! I'll never be sorry. I can't rest with it there!"

With hawk's eyes Anna watched the nurse take out the letter. With straining ears she listened to the departing tap of her slippers on the wooden stairs. With taut nerves she waited until the white-uniformed woman came back. Then she raised herself a little so that her hot, searching eyes could read the calm ones of the other. "Did you burn it?"

"Yes."

"All to ashes?"

The nurse nodded and smiled. "*All to ashes!*"

Anna Brunemeier dropped contentedly back on her pillow, and lifted the baby's little pink, clutching hands to her cheek.

Will the Romance be the Same?

ON AN afternoon in the merry month of May, Mrs. Mary Wakely, forty-seven, clothed in a kitchen dress with a towel bound round her graying hair, sat on the floor of the attic in her home, sorting pieces of cloth from an old scrap-bag, and was not so merry.

There are those who will scent at once the battle of spring house-cleaning in the air.

Mary Wakely was the capable wife of Sam Wakely, the active mother of six hilarious Wakelys, the energetic overseer of a big house, and consequently the holder of that undistinguished position which the world at large in jocular vein lists as "no occupation."

The Wakely house sat in the middle of a grassy yard in the middle of a small town in the middle of one of the middle western states. And as the United States is the most important nation in the world (save in the prejudiced eyes of the inhabitants of a few other countries) it follows without controversy that the Wakely home was quite the center of the universe. And so it was, just as all the homes of the Browns and the Smiths and the Joneses are the center of the universe, to the Browns and the Smiths and the Joneses.

The whole place had a lived-in look, which is a polite way of saying that it was not quite as neat as it ought to be. Because the Wakely family was large, and expenditures waxed equally large in that bold proportion which bills bear to the size of families, not everything was in repair at one and the same time. When the lattice under the porch was in perfect condition, the screens would begin to have a faded, peeled look. When the screens were finally repainted, the porch boards would show signs of warping.

Every spring the dandelions slipped up brazenly in the clover and bluegrass. And every spring, with exasperated repetition, Mary Wakely made a noble gesture toward eradicating the pests, but with indifferent success. Always in the middle of the task, neighbor boys came for Tod or Ken or Bo to go fishing, and neighbor girls dropped in to hold giggling converse with Gwen or Louise. When Mary Wakely saw her family melt away, one by one, she invariably remarked apologetically to the butcher knives and bushel-baskets: "Oh, well, let them go. It's the very happiest time of their lives." Which was quite the key to Mary Wakely's character, a little too lenient maybe, a bit too sentimental perhaps.

To give the roster of the Wakely family sounds like calling the roll in a classroom. Mary Wakely (née Bohanan) had been the town belle twenty-five years before when she married Sam Wakely. Sam was a bookkeeper then in the Oakville State Bank, but a kindly providence removing one man above him, and a wrathy board of directors removing another, he had been cashier now for many years. The husky and noisy results of the Wakely-Bohanan nuptials were: Hal Wakely, aged twenty-four, Louise, aged twenty-one, Gwen and Ken, who arrived together seventeen years before, Thaddeus, who had almost forgotten that dignified appellation in the "Tod" under which he had moved and had his very lively being for fifteen years, and Paul Bohanan Wakely, called "Bo" by Oakville friends and enemies, who trailed along seven years behind Tod.

It seems almost a matter for abject apology that, added to this number, there were also Aunt Dell Wakely and Hettie Hess, both of whom the family had inherited along with the old Wakely estate. Aunt Dell was Sam's aunt, a fleshy, florid, fatuous woman who believed that she had been marked for apoplexy for years. But the stubbornness with which she met all minor issues bidding fair to thwart her, had so far refused to yield to the various "rushes of blood" so frequently and eloquently described in detail to the family. Hettie Hess, of problematical age, who often remarked acridly that she wished to the land she had some meat on her bones, might have passed in more sophisticated circles for a maid, but not in Oakville. To be sure she worked for her bed, board, and a stipend; but on days when her "rheumatiz" sent her to lie on a bony, twinging shoulder, or days when she felt an additional grievance toward life in general and the Wakely youngsters in particular, she simply sent word that she was not coming downstairs. No, one could scarcely insist that Hettie Hess was the typical modern maid.

On this specific day in merry spring, Mary Wakely and Hettie Hess were cleaning house. And Mary Wakely in a kitchen dress with a towel bound round her graying hair, sat on the attic floor sorting an old scrap-bag's contents, and was not so merry. For there were so many things stored away on the third floor that the task looked stupendous. All of the old Wakely things left from another generation were there, and some of the Bohanan ones which Mary had brought over home when her mother died, old Wakely and Bohanan dresses, bonnets, cushions, pictures, curtains, quilt scraps, patterns. Every year Mary Wakely put forth strenuous, if subtle, efforts to get rid of them, but Aunt Dell would puffingly climb the narrow built-in attic stairs, settle herself in an old arm chair, and watch the sorting process with an ancient but alert eye.

Surreptitiously, Mary would attempt to throw out some of the flotsam left upon the shore of time, impersonated by the floor of the attic, but the covert act could never be consummated without Aunt Dell seeing it. A few moments before this, Mary had attempted to rid the figurative beach of some of its wreckage in the form of an old bird-cage, to be met with Aunt Dell's, "Dear, dear, that's Dicky's little house. I can remember so well how he always chirped when we put seeds in this very same little dish. I couldn't bear to see that thrown out, Mary. I believe I'd hear his little chirp in my sleep." So Mary, with superb resignation, had replaced the battered home of the departed Dicky, lest such dire consequences as a phantom cheep cross Aunt Dell's heavy slumber.

And now, as Aunt Dell appeared to be engrossed in an old photograph album, Mary slipped away from the piece-bag and casually edged a wire dress-form toward the top of the stairs. But Aunt Dell was on the job instantly.

"You ar'n't intending to throw *that* away, are you, Mary?" Her voice held volumes of reproach.

"Why, yes, I was, Aunt Dell. What good will it ever be to us?"

"Oh, I wouldn't think of it, Mary. Why, you might want to fit something on it some day for one of the girls when they are away to school."

To be sure the form was as foreign to present-day maidenly figures as though it were of some prehistoric female. Wide-shouldered, padded, wasp-waisted, it looked like a wire skeleton of Queen Elizabeth. But back to the cluttered shore of time Mary Wakely rolled it, with a fleeting wicked thought of the language the fastidious Louise and the artistic-minded Gwen would use when she told them.

Hettie Hess was dusting a pile of old things in another corner. "A mess, I call it," she was grumbling. But that was scarcely an innovation. She always grumbled. The family thought no more of Hettie's constant mumbling than of a continuously leaky faucet. It might be annoying if one stopped to think about it, but if it could not be repaired, why stop to think about it? She mumbled and grumbled her way through the day's work, her mind a little at loose ends, going off on tangents; her sentences never finished, trailing off into nothing.

Just now she brought a pile of dog-eared books and dumped them aggrievedly down by Mary Wakely. "Them old scrap-books . . . that there corner . . . I declare, Mis' Wakely . . . leaves tore out . . . I suz . . . every year . . . pick up 'n pick up. . . ."

Mary Wakely opened the top scrap-book. Originally it had been a book of her father's, recording the uprisings and the downsittings of the members of a lodge known as "The Knights and Ladies of King Arthur's Round Table," although just how the ladies happened to be sitting in at that particular round table she had never known.

Over the erstwhile memoranda of the lodge knights and their ladies, verses were pasted. Mary herself had pasted them in when all the world was young and joyous and romantic, when Sam Wakely and Matt Dorring and George Hines had all wanted to go with her. How had she ever found time to paste poems in the old secretary book? Her days were so rushed, now, so filled with countless necessary activities, that it did not seem possible she had ever had leisure to cut out poetry, to say nothing of pasting it back in a book. She turned the pages of the long-forgotten record of flamboyant ceremonies. There was Kipling's *Vampire*, Riley's *Old Sweetheart Of Mine*, a bit of *Khayyam*. There were verses from Meredith's *Lucille*. Several pages ran to Ella Wheeler Wilcox—*Love's Window, Love's Task, Love's Rainbow*.

Aunt Dell sat heavily in the rocker and sorted pieces of calicos, returning them all jealously to their boxes. Hettie's voice grumbled its far-away accompaniment: "I declare . . . same old things . . . dust 'em 'n dust 'em . . . I suz . . . every year . . . such a mess . . ."

Where had they gone, those old thrills, that old romantic feeling she and Sam had felt for each other? How golden and dream-filled and illusioned life had been! Mary Wakely, forty-seven, maturely heavy, in a kitchen dress, with a towel bound round her graying hair, sat and turned Time's pages.

> Was his love then, the love of the river? And she—
> Had she taken that love for the love of the sea?

She could hear Sam's deep mellow voice as he read the smooth, singing verses aloud. She could see him, too, in his white flannels, sitting in the hammock on the old Bohanan lawn. How much in love they had been! How romantically, deeply, terribly so! Not all the masculine movie stars were more ardent in their lovemaking than Sam had been. Where had they gone, those old romantic moments they had planned to keep alive? Where were they now, those old thrills which they had said could never die? They had not kept them alive any more than all the other long-married, staid old couples. Their conversation now consisted for the most part of the annoying fact that Bo's teeth needed straightening, of the big expenses incurred by Hal and Louise away at school, of paving taxes and a leaky kitchen roof. Oh, *why* did romance fly out of the window when children came?

"Dear, dear!" As one hears faint far-away wind in the poplars, Mary could hear Aunt Dell's comments: "Every one of these blocks must be saved to be pieced some day," and Hettie's "Dusted 'n dusted . . . put 'em here . . . what in time . . . this corner . . . I suz . . ."

She turned the stiff, mucilage-crusted page. Alone on the page and in a bracket of purple ink, as though set aside for special honor, was a little poem, evidently cut from a magazine. There were several verses, but they all ended with:

After years I'll come to meet you—
Will the romance be the same?

Above the purple-inked framework a bunch of little dried violets was crushed into the soft pulpy paper. Under the violets, in Sam's writing, were the words: "To be read together on our silver anniversary."

It might have been written the day before, so clearly did the picture come to her, the resurrection of a little dormant memory which had been lying away under a shroud of crumbling violets. They had read the verses together, pressed the flowers together, and then Sam had taken his fountain pen and written the words. They had laughed at the mere thought of any change, at the absurdity that romance would ever die. It had been one of those certainties of life not even debatable. As for the thought of a silver wedding, that had been too far in the future to contemplate, a huge joke, that in the then glamorous present they should have spoken of a date so far removed. It had seemed centuries away. And now their silver anniversary was one week from the next Saturday.

It did not seem possible. Where had the time gone? Out from the little purple frame stared the statement: "After years I'll come to meet you." And the statement was true, true by twenty-five long years. From under the little crumbling violets stared the question: "Will the romance be the same?" And the question must be answered one week from the next Saturday.

Mary Wakely sat on the attic floor and thought of Sam, young, ardent, lithesome, wooing her under the trees of the old Bohanan home; and Sam, now, heavy, wide-girthed, bespectacled, gray patches above his ears, talking of paving taxes and dental bills and a leaky kitchen roof. That, then, would be the answer. Romance was never the same. But this was the queer part, when she stopped to analyze it, she herself was still romantic. She still cared for sentiment. That seemed always the way—one kept the romance and one ceased to remember. Suddenly she realized that the idea was almost identical with one of the Ella Wheeler Wilcox poems she had just passed in the book, and over which she had thrilled and wept in her youth. She searched until she found it and read it avidly:

> This is the way of it the wide world over
> One is beloved and one is the lover.

Yes, that was for all the world the way it had turned out. And the humbling thing about it, the pride-eating thing, was that Sam, whose soul had once been aflame with a god-like passion, was soon the beloved, and that she who had been so ardently wooed, proved in the long run to be the lover.

She turned back to the pages of the violets. "To be read together at our silver anniversary." Neither one had remembered the verses. Only by chance had she run across them. Already preparations were under way to celebrate the occasion. Very well, they *would* read the poem together. The evening of the anniversary, after the guests had gone, she and Sam would read the verses. And perhaps, no, certainly, Sam would tell her that he had never forgotten those moments of exquisite romance. Possibly, no, assuredly, it would take only the sight of the verses and the violets to have Sam reveal the fact that he had never ceased to remember those glamorous hours of young love.

All that week they worked hard at the cleaning of the big rambling house, Mary and Hettie Hess. To be sure they had some help from the other members of the household. When school was out, Ken managed to carry a few papers to the alley and burn them, and Tod, with much elaborate preparation in the way of oiling, screwing, and petting his second-hand motor-cycle so that it would navigate, in four days' time made three successful journeys to the junk pile with a few tin cans in the side-car. Gwen took so much time to change from her school things into a work dress which she thought sufficiently *chic*, rearranging a satin band around her head, that it was dinner time before she had accomplished anything. Bo, attempting to wash screens with the garden hose, was almost immediately the center of centripetal force for all the neighborhood youngsters, whereupon the screen washing deteriorated rapidly into a series of imported Indian monsoons. Aunt Dell sat heavily in the most comfortable chair in each room as it was under process of being cleaned, and held grimly on to all the old Wakely things and some of the Bohanan ones.

"She has seen the things from my side of the house around here so long that she thinks they belong to her," Mary told Sam. "I've always suspected she made up some of the reminiscences she tells me, and now I know. She had my mother's box of sea-shells in her lap this morning and was telling Bo how she picked them up, and, Sam, she *has never been anywhere near the sea.*"

Mary and Hettie Hess worked under extreme pressure in order to get through before the anniversary. "Like horses . . ." Hettie mumbled. "I suz . . . this closet . . . looky here, Mis' Wakely . . . never stays put . . . same things . . . pick up 'n pick up . . ." A raven of a woman croaking her "nevermore."

On Wednesday of the following week, the cleaning was practically finished. By Thursday there was a tumbled slant again on all of the first rooms cleaned. "What is the *matter* with this family?" Mary would say in exasperation. "The Downings and the McIntyres can clean and it will *stay* clean. Tod, take that bird's nest out of this room immediately, and, Bo, there *are* better places for a bicycle tire than on the davenport."

On Friday, Louise arrived home from the University, gay and lovely and full of sorority gossip. Something always seemed to happen to the household when Louise blew in. It took on a foolish gaiety which it had not previously possessed. Louise had on a fetching new green and white sport suit. "I hope you don't mind, Mother. I got it at Garwin's and charged it. We hadn't planned it but when I found they were wearing sports to the Beta party instead of the printed chiffons we first thought, there wasn't time to write. I got new white pumps . . . and

I picked up this green costume jewelry for a *sparrow's* song . . ."

More bills! How they crowded always in a sort of unending nightmare. But how fresh and glowing and deliciously pretty Louise looked in the gay outfit. Only one more year and she would be through.

Louise did not appear to be what one could call vitally interested in the house-cleaning. She seemed to have something vaguely important on her mind. At the first moment in which she could catch her mother alone it came out with geyser-like burst. "Mother, I've been dying to tell you . . . but with every one around . . . the kids all under foot . . . Hettie all ears . . . and Aunt Dell calling from the far end of the house: 'What's that you're sayin', Louise-y?' I haven't had a chance. Mother, next week I'm having company . . . here at home. Listen—Rod Robinson, *himself*. Can you feature it?" Hands on her mother's plump shoulders, she gazed into her mother's blue eyes with rapt expectancy.

"And who," said Mary Wakely, "is Rod Robinson—himself?"

"Oh, Mother," Louise's voice held deepest reproach, "please don't show such ignorance—such *abysmal* ignorance. Rod Robinson," she lowered her voice to a reverent whisper, "made the winning touchdown in the game with the Aggies."

Mary dropped her eyes that they might not show their tell-tale twinkle. When she looked up her heart missed a beat, for she saw something in her daughter's own brown eyes that she could not ignore.

"Why, Louise," there was a little catch in her throat. "You—you like him?"

Louise's head dropped to her mother's shoulder. "I'm just *nuts* about him. I think of him in the daytime—" Louise's muffled voice went on, "and dream of him at night. The very glimpse of him gives me high blood pressure."

"And he—?" Mary asked. "Is he—" she dropped into Louise's vernacular, "nuts about you?"

"I don't know," Louise said forlornly. "Sometimes I think he is—but more times I think he isn't. It just keeps me palpitating between subnormal and high fever."

Dear, dear! How different girls were than they used to be. How frank! Why she herself had not even acknowledged to her mother that she loved Sam until after his proposal.

Louise was speaking again huskily. "That's why I'm so crazy about his stopping here. A week from tomorrow he's going through Oakville and he asked me if he could stop off. I just went *deeleerious*. I want everything just ideal, Mother. His family is a regular up-to-the-minute one. Things just *have* to be nice here. You and Dad will be all right—but the kids—I wish they'd be *half* civilized for once. And I want Hettie to keep her place, and her mouth shut—and it wouldn't make me sore if Aunt Dell would have that stroke she's always talking about."

"*Louise!*" There were limits to which Mary would allow her modern children's talk to go.

"I didn't mean that, but you'll see that she fades gently somewhere into the scenery, won't you?"

Mary was reassuring. "Don't worry. We'll have everything nice, dear. The house will be all clean, and the children, models. When did you say he was coming?"

"A week from Saturday night."

"Why, Louise, the anniversary night!"

"Oh, no, Mother," Louise was the embodiment of despair. "It's the only night he can stop. We wouldn't want the whole town coming."

"But the invitations are all out."

"Imagine—that gang being here! If he has to meet all the natives! You know yourself, Mother, that a big bunch of Oakville people look like the villagers in *Carmen*."

"They are our friends, Louise," Mary was a little stiff. "And though they may not be as sophisticated, they are assuredly as fine people as the young man's friends."

"And there's no way out?"

"Absolutely, there's no way out. You'll just have to entertain him some way at the party." Mary's voice held the last expression in finality.

On Monday morning Louise went back to school. All that day and the following days, Mary and Hettie Hess worked under extreme pressure in order to get through before Saturday.

But to Mary Wakely, all through the heavy work, all through the rug-beating and varnishing and turning of curtains, shone a little gleam ahead like a light in the forest. She had kept the incense burning before the shrine of romance, and perhaps Sam had kept it also. Steeped in business, hustling day after day to make a living for the big family, no doubt Sam, too, still cherished the memory of those glamorous days, would recall them with fervor on their anniversary night.

Saturday, itself, dawned bright and lovely with the scent of peonies and syringa on the sweet May air. The household was early astir, Mary and Hettie Hess beginning the baking of cakes and nut wafers immediately after a sketchy breakfast.

Louise blew in just before noon when preparations for the event were well under way. But all the activity for the party was to Louise but an accompanying chorus to herald the approach of the star performer, Mr. Robinson himself. "You're positive everybody will be up on his toes for a good impression, Mother?" she repeatedly asked.

By six, the House of Wakely was as near perfection as it could ever hope to attain. Only once in a blue moon did it ever have that highly polished, finished appearance, Sundays, perhaps, for a few fleeting moments, the late afternoon before a holiday, an hour or so before an expected guest would arrive, was everything in place and every one well-groomed.

When Mary Wakely was dressing in the soft new silk, a little rose-colored thread of fancy wove its gay way through her heart as definitely as the rose-colored thread shimmered in the white of the new gown. When the guests would have gone, she was to meet Sam, and they would read the verses together, not as Mary Wakely, the mother of six, and Sam Wakely, the middle-aged, bespectacled bank cashier, but as young Mary Bohanan with stars for eyes, and young Sam Wakely, lithe and handsome. Sam could not have forgotten that moment of high rapture when they had read the verses in the old Bohanan hammock, could not have forgotten that pledge to romance any more than she.

To be sure there were some moments before the guests arrived which one could scarcely call of a romantic nature. Sam's waist-line having added a cubit to his latitudinal stature since last it had been encased in the suit he was to wear, necessitated setting over the buttons. He stood and waited impatiently while Mary made the change. There was one mad search by half the family for little Bo's best necktie, in which drawers were whisked out and the contents madly turned over, until some one happily remembered that Bo had taken it off Sunday afternoon and stretched it around a young plum tree. Gwen and Louise, possessing a velvet jacket in common, each chose this particular occasion upon which to claim individual ownership. They argued pleasantly, but definitely and continuously, with a certain stiff politeness.

"Pardon me, Louise, but you certainly heard me say that I was wearing it with the blue silk crepe."

"Pardon *me*, Gwen, but with Rod Robinson coming, most assuredly I ought to have first choice."

When Tod had dressed—oh, much too hastily—he took occasion to work a little more on his decrepit motor-cycle, which called forth from the more polished Ken, weighted down with his seventeen years, "Tod, get up from there. And don't start that darned greasy old egg-beater to-night." To which advice, Tod made swift, brief and decisive answer: "Go kiss a dill pickle." Immediately thereafter, confused but pronounced sounds issued from the side porch, as of subjective disturbances caused by two bodies of equal solidity coming in close contact.

Aunt Dell, dressed in an ancient magenta-colored watered silk, which made her anticipated stroke seem imminent, and with her entire cameo set—brooch, earrings, bracelet and watch chain—ornamenting her person, sat heavily in the biggest chair and waited for the guests.

Hettie mumbled her way around the rooms, her mind going off on tangents: "Them ice-cream dishes . . . I suz . . . somebody's left 'em . . . tea-towels . . . I declare . . . pick up 'n pick up. . . ."

When Mary was dressed, she took a fleeting survey of herself in the glass. She saw there a blue-eyed woman in her late forties with too much weight, her blond hair sprinkled with gray, small lines about her eyes, deeper ones in her forehead and a duplex chin.

Turning away from the glass, she took the old scrap-book under her arm and started downstairs. As she passed the bathroom she saw Hettie in her too-long brown silk, holding dripping towels at arm's length, heard her muttered: "Soppin' wet . . . I suz . . . seems to me . . . them boys. . . ." Coming to Tod's and Ken's bedroom, she gave one fleeting glance therein, and as a too-ardent optimist attempts to shut out the unpleasant things of life, closed the door gently upon the special type of interior decorating visible to any passer-by.

Down the stairs she went, the old book under her arm. To an onlooker it was only a dog-eared scrap-book. To Mary Wakely it was the altar to Romance—the odor of dead violets the incense—the rhythm of the verses a prayer.

They all made comments about her: "Gee, Mom, you look ritzy," and "A Follies girl has nothing on you."

When for a moment there was no one around, she slipped the scrap-book back of a reading lamp on a table in the big hall. It was open at the verses, and the words in their purple framing and the violets pressing their little blue faces against the poem gazed back at her with assurance. Across the border of Time they called to her:

After years I'll come to meet you—
Will the romance be the same?

And then the first of the guests arrived. Incongruously, they were Dick Edwards and his wife, and Sue McIntyre and her husband. Dick had been Sam's best man, and Sue had been Mary's bridesmaid twenty-five years before. Also they had been engaged. They both mentioned it, even laughed about it. To Mary Wakely, obsessed with her idea of resurrecting Romance, it seemed almost sacrilegious. How could they mention it? How could they laugh? After years they had come to meet, and the romance was not the same.

The rooms were soon filled with the gay, friendly folk of the small-town crowd who knew each other so well. Their voices floated high with talk and laughter. Sometime during the early evening, the hero of many a football war arrived and was introduced, after which Mary Wakely was vaguely conscious of the fact that he and Louise had slipped out to the swing on the side porch.

And then there was a little program. Grace Ivorson sang just as she had sung at the wedding. Perhaps not "just as she had sung," for Grace's voice at fifty was not what it had been at twenty-five. The minister made a talk, and Dick Edwards of the Oakville Bon Ton Grocers, on behalf of the guests, presented Sam and Mary with some very nice silver. Sam made a neat little speech in which he confided the fact that they had had the six children for the express purpose of being able to use the eight-piece set.

And all through the happy, informal, small-town party there sang a little silver song in the heart of Mary Wakely.

And then the affair was over. The last of the guests were going down the steps into the moon-filled, sweet-scented night. The last gay words floated back: "Good-night, Sam—good-night, Mary. Lovely time—coming again to the golden wedding."

Sam and Mary turned into the big hall. *The time had come.*

Sam was standing there only a few feet away from the table where the book stood open at the verses, where Romance waited to be recognized and welcomed. In their little purple bracketing the verses waited for Mary's lover.

"Nice party, Mother." Sam was not noticing the scrap-book. But one could not expect him to do so with it standing against the wall, surrounded by a half dozen other things, a vase of flowers, a reading lamp, two or three magazines, a framed photo of Louise, a dish of nut wafers.

"Sam," Mary's voice quivered in its earnestness. "There's something over there on the table I've been saving for you."

Sam sauntered over to the table. The years turned back for Mary Wakely. What was a quarter of a century to a gay, gallant knight who had picked violets and promised that after years the romance would be the same? Starry-eyed, she watched her lover approach the little altar which together they had once erected to Romance.

The moment in its deep importance, fraught with the sincerity of its meaning, should have been very quiet. It was scarcely that. The radio, tuned to a high-powered station, was emitting "Face the Music and Dance." Ken was adding to the gaiety of the nations by accompanying the ensemble with his banjo and shouting the words. That both his voice and his banjo were off-key seemed not to worry him to any extent.

From outside the dining-room window where the syringas flung their fragrant breath, came the deafening roar of the motor-cycle engine. "Whatever is that boy doing," Aunt Dell wanted to know, "after *midnight?*"

Gwen came hurriedly to the dining-room door with Bo making excited but futile attempts to hold her back. "Mother," she called, "whatever do you *imagine?* Bo's been eating ice-cream out of a dish that some one left . . . I *saw* him . . . one on the sideboard. I even think it was old Mr. Jarvis's. *Ugh!* For crying out loud . . . think of old Mr. Jarvis and his *whiskers* . . ."

With one part of her brain Mary Wakely heard all the turbulent family noises. The other was turned toward the Great Moment, as Joan of Arc may have paid no attention to annoying trivialities, but kept her eyes turned to the Light. Sam was looking in the direction of the verses, now, the verses with their fragrance of by-gone Junes. His hand was on the book. He picked it up—looked at it in a puzzled way. And then he spoke. "I'm glad you saved me some. They're cracking good." *And he set the book aside and reached for the wafers.*

The light in Mary Wakely's eyes slowly flickered out. It gave place to a baffled expression, half chagrin, half incredulity. She looked at Sam Wakely, heavy, wide-girthed, bespectacled, with gray patches above his ears. Under his very nose the faint old fragrance of the violets pled with him, and he thought she had meant the wafers. Before his very eyes the rapture of the little poem called to him, and he thought she had saved him something to eat.

He took a handful of the brittle cakes and began munching them. He swung his jaw vigorously, the crisp wafers crackling a little.

Hettie Hess came through the hall, her best brown silk crackling with the wafers. Over on the table the sweet fragrance of the dead little violets and the sweet rhythm of the forgotten little verses looked out from the old scrap-book. Hettie's ferret eyes landed on them. "Looky there, Mis' Wakely . . . good suz . . . one of them old scrap-books . . . my land . . . got down from the attic . . . such a mess . . . beats all . . . shall I take it back up?"

"No, leave it there," said Mary Wakely. She used the same tone that one might use in saying "No, leave the flowers on the grave."

Hettie trudged out of the room, mumbling mild execrations.

Sam Wakely, big, substantial, wide-girthed, stood and munched the nut cookies with keen enjoyment. "Well, Mother?" He was slipping his arm through Mary's and starting with her toward the dining-room. "They tell me the first twenty-five years are the hardest," he said blithely, "but think of the next twenty-five—with our slippers and the radio and books and magazines and a lot of grandchildren—won't they be comfortable though?"

Psychologists say that two emotions can not occupy the mind at the same time. The king, Romance, has no humor. And the king's fool, Humor, knows no romance. Quite suddenly, in the throne-room of Mary Wakely's mind, Humor, the fool, slipped up behind Romance, the king, sent him sprawling and threw him out. At the sight she let forth a laugh, a chuckling, rippling, body-shaking laugh.

Hal was still tap-tapping on the bare varnished floor. Ken was adding to the general confusion with the sixteenth interpretation of "Face the music and dance . . ." The backfiring of Tod's motor-cycle came from the rear of the house. Gwen and Bo, giving no intimation of an armistice were deep in "I did *not*," and "You might *catch* something. . . . *Imagine!* Old Mr. Jarvis and his *whiskers!*"

Mary Wakely laughed as she looked up at Sam Wakely, heavy, wide-girthed, unlithesome, munching nut wafers in the midst of all this familiar hilarity. "Comfortable?" she repeated, her too, too solid flesh shaking with vigorous laughter. "I'll say they will."

And then, suddenly, simultaneously, they stopped by the double windows. Outside in the cool, dark porch stood slim young figures in such close proximity that, while it was only surmise that their two minds held but a single thought, there was direct evidence that their two hearts beat as one. For the arms that had so effectively enfolded the slippery pigskin on the field of honor, now appeared to be repeating the process with a daintier, lovelier burden.

Overwhelmed at the import of the words they heard, the parents seemed too near a state of partial paralysis to move on out of range of the low, earnest voices:

"And you'll love me all your life, Louise?"

"Oh, Rod—all my life—and forever."

Sam and Mary Wakely turned to each other, gropingly, clingingly, in the surprise of those bewildered emotions which parents inevitably experience at the first startling realization of such news. Sam's arms went around Mary and he drew her close. "Golly, Mother," he whispered, cheek to hers, "romance is always the same, isn't it?"

"Always!" Mary whispered back.

And they tiptoed away, stealthily, guiltily.

Star Across the Tracks

❧ MR. HARM KURTZ sat in the kitchen with his feet in the oven and discussed the world; that is to say, his own small world. His audience, shifting back and forth between the pantry and the kitchen sink, caused the orator's voice to rise and fall with its coming and going.

The audience was mamma. She was the bell upon which the clapper of his verbal output always struck. As she never stopped moving about at her housework during these nightly discourses, one might have said facetiously that she was his Roaming Forum.

Pa Kurtz was slight and wiry, all muscle and bounce. His wife had avoirdupois to spare and her leisurely walk was what is known in common parlance as a waddle. She wore her hair combed high, brushed tightly up at the back and sides, where it ended in a hard knot on top of her head. When movie stars and café society took it up mamma said she had beat them to it by thirty-five years.

The Kurtzes lived in a little brown house on Mill Street, which meandered its unpaved way along a creek bed. The town, having been laid out by the founding fathers on this once-flowing but now long-dried creek, was called River City.

For three days of his working week pa's narrow world held sundry tasks: plowing gardens, cutting alfalfa, hauling lumber from the mill. For the other three days he was engaged permanently as a handyman by the families of Scott, Dillingham and Porter, who lived on High View Drive, far away from Mill Street, geographically, economically, socially. And what mamma hadn't learned about the Scott, Dillingham and Porter domestic establishments in the last few years wasn't worth knowing.

Early in his labors for the three families, pa had summed them up to mamma in one sweeping statement: "The Scotts . . . him I like and her I don't like. The Dillinghams . . . her I like and him I don't. The Porters . . . both I don't like."

The Porters' house was brick colonial. The Scotts' was a rambling stone of the ranch type. The Dillinghams' had no classification, but was both brick and stone, to say nothing of stained shingles, lumber, tile, glass bricks and stucco.

The Porters had four children of school age. Also they had long curving rows of evergreens in which the grackles settled with raucous glee as though to outvie the family's noise. The grackles—and for all pa knew, maybe the young folks also—drove Mrs. Porter wild, but pa rather liked the birds. They sounded so countrylike, and he had never grown away from the farm.

Mr. Porter was a lawyer and a councilman. Mrs. Porter was a member of the Garden Club and knew practically all there was to know about flora and fauna. She went in for formal beds of flowers, rectangles and half-moons, containing tulips and daffodils in the spring and dahlias and asters later. She ruled pa with iron efficiency. With a wave of her hand she might say: "Mr. Kurtz, I think I'll have the beds farther apart this year."

And pa, telling mamma about it at night, would sneer: "Just like they was the springs-and-mattress kind you can shove around on casters."

Mrs. Scott went to the other extreme. She knew the least about vegetation of anyone who had ever come under pa's scrutiny. Assuredly he was his own boss there. Each spring she tossed him several dozen packages of seeds as though she dared him to do his worst. Once he had found rutabaga and spinach among the packages of zinnias and nasturtiums. But pa couldn't be too hard on her, for she had a little cripple son who took most of her time. And he liked the fresh-colored packages every year and the feel of the warm moist earth when he put in the seeds. The head of the house was a doctor and if he happened to drive in while pa was there, he stopped and joked a bit.

The Dillinghams' yard was pa's favorite. The back of it was not only informal, it was woodsy. Mrs. Dillingham told pa she had been raised on a farm and that the end of the yard reminded her of the grove back of her old home. She had no children and often she came out to stand around talking to pa or brought her gloves and worked with him.

"Poor thing! Lonesome," mamma said when he was telling her.

Mrs. Dillingham had pa set out wild crab apple and ferns and plum trees, little crooked ones, so it would "look natural." Several times she had driven him out to the country and they had brought back shooting stars and swamp candle, Dutchman's-breeches and wood violets. Pa's hand with the little wild flowers was as tender as the hand of God.

When Mr. Dillingham came home from his big department store, he was loud and officious, sometimes critical of what had been done.

In winter, the work for the High View homes was just as hard and far less interesting. Storm windows, snow on long driveways, basements to be cleaned. It was always good to get home and sit with his tired, wet feet in the oven and tell the day's experiences to mamma. There was something very comforting about mamma, her consoling "Oh, think nothing of it," or her sympathetic clucking of "Tsk . . . tsk . . . them women, with their cars and their clubs!"

Tonight there was more than usual to tell, for there had been great goings on up in High View. Tomorrow night was Christmas Eve and in preparation for the annual prizes given by the federated civic clubs, his three families had gone in for elaborate outdoor decorations.

There was unspoken rivalry among the three houses too. Pa could sense it. Mrs. Porter had asked him offhandedly, as though it were a matter of extreme unconcern, what the two other families were planning to do. And Mr. Dillingham had asked the same thing, but bluntly. You couldn't catch pa that way, though, he reminded mamma with great glee. "Slippery as a eel!" Had just answered that the others seemed to be hitchin' up a lot of wiring.

But pa had known all along what each one was doing. And tomorrow night everybody would know. The Porters had long strings of blue lights which they were carrying out into the evergreens, as though bluebirds, instead of black ones, were settling there to stay through Christmas.

The Dillinghams had gone in for reindeer. They had ordered them made from plyboard at the mill, and tonight the eight deer, with artificial snow all over them, were prancing up the porch steps, while a searchlight on the ground threw the group into relief.

The Scotts, whose house was not so high as the others, had a fat Santa on the roof with one foot in the chimney. In a near-by dormer window there was a phonograph which would play Jingle Bells, so that the song seemingly came from the old fellow himself. It had made the little cripple boy laugh and clap his hands when they wheeled him outside to see the finished scene.

All this and much more pa was telling mamma while she ambled about, getting supper on the table.

Lillie came home. Lillie was the youngest of their three children and she worked for the Dillinghams, too, but in the department store. Lillie was a whiz with a needle, and a humble helper in the remodeling room. She made her own dresses at home and tried them on Maisie, the manikin. That was one of the store's moronic-looking models which had lost an arm and sundry other features, and Lillie had asked for it when she found they were going to discard it. Ernie, her brother, had brought it home in his car and repaired it. Now she hung her own skirts on Maisie to get their length. That was about all the good the manikin did her, for Lillie's circumference was fully three times that of the model.

The three of them sat down to eat, as Ernie would not arrive for a long time and mamma would warm things over for him. As usual, the table talk came largely from pa. He had to tell it all over to Lillie: the blue lights, the reindeer, the Santa-with-one-foot-in-the-chimney.

Lillie, who was a bit fed up with pasteboard reindeer and synthetic Santas at the store, thought she still would like to see them. So pa said tomorrow night after Carrie got here they would all drive to High View, that he himself would like to see them once from the paved street instead of with his head caught in an evergreen branch or getting a crick in his neck under a reindeer's belly.

They discussed the coming of the older daughter and her husband, Bert, and the two little boys, who were driving here from their home in another county and planning to stay two whole nights. A big event was Christmas this year in the Mill Street Kurtz house.

After supper when Lillie started the dishes, pa went out to see to the team and mamma followed to pick out two of her fat hens for the Christmas dinner.

In the dusk of the unusually mild December evening, mamma stood looking about her as with the eye of a stranger. Then she said she wished things had been in better shape before Carrie and Bert got here, that not one thing had been done around the place to fix it up since the last time.

"That rickety old shed, pa," she said mildly. "I remember as well as I'm standin' here you tellin' Carrie you was goin' to have that good new lumber on by the next time she come."

It was as match to pine shavings. It made pa good and mad. With him working his head off, day and night! He blew up. In anyone under twelve it would have been called a tantrum. He rushed over to the tool house and got his hammer and started to yank off a rotten board.

"I'll get this done before Carrie comes," he shouted, "if it's the last thing I do."

A psychoanalyst, after much probing, might have discovered what caused pa's sudden anger. But mamma, who knew less than nothing about psychoanalysis, having only good common sense, also knew what caused it.

Pa's own regrets over his big mistake made him irritable at times. He was one of those farmers who had turned their backs on old home places during the protracted drought. Mamma had wanted to stick it out another year, but he had said no, they would move to town where everybody earned good money. So they had sold the farm and bought this little place on Mill Street, the only section of town where one could keep a cow and chickens. The very next year crops were good again and now the man who had bought the old place for so little came to River City in a car as fine as the Dillinghams'. Yes, any casual criticism of the Mill Street place always touched him in a vital spot of his being. So he yanked and swore and jawed, more mad than ever that mamma had walked away and was not hearing him.

It was not hard to get the old boards off. Soon they lay on the ground in a scattered heap of rotting timbers. Bird and Bell, from their exposed position across the manger, snatched at the alfalfa hay, quivered their nostrils and looked disdainfully at proceedings. The cow chewed her cud in the loose-jawed way of cows and stared disinterestedly into space.

Looking at the animals of which he was so fond, pa admitted to himself he needn't have ripped the boards off until morning, but balmy weather was predicted all through Christmas. And mamma had made him pretty mad. Suddenly the fire of his anger went out, for he was remembering something Ernie had said and it tickled his fancy. The last time Carrie brought her little boys home, Ernie told them it was bubble gum the cow was chewing and the kids had hung over the half door an hour or more waiting for the big bubble to blow out. Tomorrow night the little kids would be here and the thought of it righted the world again.

Mamma came toward him with two hens under her arms as though she wanted him to make up with her. But he fussed around among the boards, not wanting to seem pleasant too suddenly.

His flashlight lay on the ground, highlighting the open shed, and the street light, too, shone in. An old hen flew squawking out of the hay and the pigeons swooped down from the roof.

Mamma stood looking at it for quite a while, then all at once she chucked the hens under a box and hurried into the house. When she came out, she held Maisie, the manikin, in front of her and Lillie was close behind with her arms full of sheets.

"What you think you're up to?" pa asked.

"You let me be," mamma said pointedly. "I know what I'm doin'."

She set up the manikin and with deft touches Lillie draped the sheets over its body and head and arranged it so it was leaning over the manger. Then mamma put pa's flashlight down in the manger itself and a faint light shone through the cracks of the old boards.

"There!" said mamma, stepping back. "Don't that look for all the world like the Bible story?"

"Seems like it's makin' light of it," pa said critically. "The Scotts and the Dillinghams didn't do nothin' like that. They just used Santy Clauses."

"I ain't doin' it for show, like them," mamma retorted. "I'm doin' it for Carrie's little boys. Somethin' they can see for themselves when they drive in. Somethin' they'll never forget, like's not, as long as they live."

Mamma and Lillie went out to the fence to survey their handiwork from that point. They were standing there when Ernie drove into the yard. Ernie worked for the River City Body and Fender Wreck Company, and one viewing the car and hearing its noisy approach would have questioned whether he ever patronized his own company.

They were anxious to know what Ernie thought. There were the horses nuzzling the alfalfa, the cow chewing away placidly, and the pigeons on the ridgepole. And there was the white-robed figure bending over the faint glow in the manger.

Ernie stood without words. Then he said "For gosh sakes! What in time?" The words were crude, but the tone was reverent.

"Mamma did it for the kids," Lillie said. "She wants to fix a star up over the stable. Mrs. Dillingham gave an old one to pa."

Ernie had been a fixer ever since he was a little boy. Not for his looks had the River City Body and Fender Wreck Company hired Ernie Kurtz. So after his warmed-over supper he got his tools and a coil of wire and fixed the yellow bauble high over the stable, the wire and the slim rod almost invisible, so that it seemed a star hung there by itself.

All the next day pa worked up on High View Drive and all day mamma cleaned the house, made doughnuts and cookies with green sugar on them, and dressed the fat hens, stuffing them to the bursting point with onion dressing.

Almost before they knew it, Christmas Eve had arrived, and Carrie and Bert and the two little boys were driving into the yard with everyone hurrying out to greet them.

"Why, mamma," Carrie said. "That old shed . . . it just gave me a turn when we drove in."

But mamma was a bit disappointed over the little boys. The older one comprehended what it meant and was duly awe-struck, but the younger one ran over to the manger and said: "When's she goin' to blow out her bubble gum?"

After they had taken in the wrapped presents and the mince pies Carrie had baked, pa told them how they were all going to drive up to High View and see the expensive decorations, stressing his own part in their preparation so much that mamma said, "Don't brag. A few others had somethin' to do with it, you know." And Ernie sent them all into laughter when he called it High Brow Drive.

Then he went after his girl, Annie Hansen, and when they came back, surprisingly her brother was with them, which sent Lillie into a state of fluttering excitement.

So they all started out in two cars. Ernie and his girl and Lillie in Ernie's one seat, with the brother in the back, his long legs dangling out. Carrie and Bert took their little boys and mamma and pa. Not knowing the streets leading to the winding High View section, Bert stayed close behind Ernie's car, which chugged its way ahead of them like a noisy tugboat.

Everyone was hilariously happy. As for pa, his anger about mamma's chidings was long forgotten. All three of his children home and the two little kids. The Dillinghams didn't have any children at all for Christmas fun. We *never lost a child, he was thinking, and the Porters lost that little girl. Our grandkids tough as tripe, and the Scotts got that cripple boy*. It gave him a light-hearted feeling of freedom from disaster. Now this nice sight-seeing trip in Bert's good car. Home to coffee and doughnuts, with the kids hanging up their stockings. Tomorrow the presents and a chicken dinner. For fleeting moments Pa Kurtz had a warm little-boy feeling of his own toward Christmas.

Mamma, too, said she hadn't had such a good time since Tige was a pup. And when one of the little boys said he wanted to see Tige when they got back, everyone laughed immoderately.

They passed decorated houses and countless trees brightly lighted in windows. Then around the curving streets of the High View district, following Ernie's noisy lead so closely that Carrie said they were just like Mary's little lamb. Across the street from the Porters' colonial house, Ernie stopped, and they stopped too.

The evergreens with their sparkling blue lights seemed a part of an enchanted forest. Carrie said she never saw anything so pretty in her life and waxed so enthusiastic that pa reminded her again of his big part in it.

When Ernie yelled back to ask if they'd seen enough, pa waved him on. And around the curve they went to the Dillinghams'.

There were other cars in front of the houses. Pa said like as not the judges themselves were right now deciding the prizes, and by the tone of his voice one would have thought the fate of the nation hung on the decision.

At the Dillinghams', the little boys waxed more excited over the reindeer, lighted by the searchlight which threw them into snow-white relief. Yes, pa said, it was worth all the work they'd put on them.

Then to Doctor Scott's, and here the little boys practically turned inside out. For Santa himself was up on the roof as plain as day; and more, he was singing "Jingle bells . . . jingle bells." When he stopped, they clapped their hands and yelled up at him: "Hi, Santy! Sing more." And the adults all clapped too.

Then Ernie signaled and the little procession swung down out of High View and circled into the part of town where the blocks were prosaically rectangular and everything became smaller; yards, houses, Christmas trees.

"Look!" mamma said happily. "Ain't it nice? There ain't no patent on it. Everyone can make merry. Every little house can have its own fun and tree, just the same as the big ones."

Over the railroad tracks they went and into Mill Street, where Ernie adroitly picked his way around the mushy spots in the unpaved road, with Bert following his zigzag lead. And the trip was over.

There were Bird and Bell and the cow. There were the pigeons huddled together on the stable roof. There were the white Mary and the light in the manger, and the star. The laughter died down. Everyone got out quietly. Carrie ran her arm through her mother's. "I like yours, too, mamma," she said.

Inside, they grew merry again. Over the coffee and the doughnuts and sandwiches there was a lot of talk. They argued noisily about the prize places for the decorated houses, betting one another which ones would win. Carrie and Lillie both thought the lights in the trees were by far the most artistic. Ma and Ernie's girl were for the reindeer at Dillinghams'. But Lillie's potential beau and Ernie and Bert and the little boys were all for the Scotts' Santa Claus. Pa, as one who had been the creator of them all, stayed benignly neutral.

After a while Ernie took his girl home. Her brother stood around on the porch awhile with Lillie and then left. The little boys hung up their stockings, with the grown folks teasing them, saying Santy could never find his way from the Scotts' down those winding streets.

Mamma and pa kept their own bedroom. Lillie took Carrie in with her. Bert went up to the attic with Ernie. Mamma made the little boys a bed on the old couch, with three chairs in front to keep them from falling out. She had no sheets left for them, but plenty of clean patchwork quilts.

In the morning there were the sketchy breakfast and the presents, including a dishpan for mamma, who had never had a new one since her wedding day; the bit and braces pa had wished for so long; a flowered comb-and-brush set for Lillie; and fully one-third of the things for which the little boys had wished.

The children could play with their new toys and the men pitch horseshoes, but mamma and the girls had to hop right into the big dinner, for everyone would be starved. Ernie's girl and her brother were invited, too, and when they came, said they could smell that good dressing clear out in the yard. The hens practically popped open in the pans and mamma's mashed potatoes and chicken gravy melted in the mouth. Oh, never did anyone have a nicer Christmas than the Kurtzes down on Mill Street.

It was when they were finishing Carrie's thick mince pies that the radio news came on, and the announcement of the prizes. So they pulled back their chairs to listen, with the girls cautioning the menfolks, "Now stick to what your bet was last night and don't nobody cheat by changing."

The announcer introduced the committee head, who gave a too wordy talk about civic pride. Then the prizes:

"The third prize of ten dollars to Doctor Amos R. Scott, 1821 High View Drive." That was Santa-in-the-chimney. And while Ernie and his group groaned their disappointment that it was only third, the others laughed at them for their poor bet.

"The second . . . twenty-five dollars . . . Mr. Ramsey E. Porter, 1484 High View Drive." The blue lights! With Carrie and Lillie wanting to know what the judges were thinking of, for Pete's sake, to give it only second, and mamma and Ernie's girl calling out jubilantly that it left only their own choice, the reindeer.

Then a strange thing happened.

"Listen, everybody."

"Sh! What's he saying?"

"The first prize . . . for its simplicity . . . for using materials at hand without expense . . . for its sacred note and the fact that it is the personification of the real Christmas story of which we sometimes lose sight . . . the first prize of fifty dollars is unanimously awarded to Mr. Harm Kurtz at 623 Mill Street."

A bomb would have torn fissures in the yard and made an unmendable shambles of the house, but it could not have been more devastating.

For a long moment they sat stunned, mouths open, but without speech coming forth, and only the little boys saying: "He said you, grandpa; he said you."

Then the hypnotic spell broke and Ernie let out a yell: "Fifty bucks, pa! Fifty bucks!"

And mamma, still dazed, kept repeating like some mournful raven, "But I just did it for the little boys."

Several got up and dashed over to the window to see again this first-prize paragon. But all they could see was Bird and Bell and the cow out in their little yard, an old dilapidated shed, and high up over it a piece of yellow glass.

In the midst of the excitement pa practically turned pale. For it had come to him suddenly there was more to this than met the eye. What would the Scotts and the Porters and the Dillinghams say? Especially Mr. Dillingham, whose expensive reindeer had won no prize at all. He was embarrassed and worried. The joy had gone out of winning the prize. The joy had gone out of the day.

The girls had scarcely finished the dishes before the Mill Street neighbors started coming to have a share in the big news. The Danish

Hansens came and the Russian family from the next block, all three of the Czech families down the street, and the Negro children who lived near the mill. They were all alike to mamma. "Just folks." She made coffee and gave everyone a doughnut. In fact, they ate so many, that late in the afternoon she whipped up another batch. Also, out of honor to the great occasion, she combed her hair again in that high skinned-up way and put on a second clean apron. Two clean aprons in one day constituted the height of something or other.

"Somebody might come by," she said by way of apology.

"They'll get stuck in the mud if they do," said Ernie. "I'm the only one that knows them holes like a map."

Mamma was right. Somebody came by. All River City came by.

Soon after dusk, with the star lighted and Bird and Bell back in the shed, the cars began to drive past in unending parade. Traffic was as thick as it had ever been up on Main and Washington. You could hear talk and laughter and maybe strong words about the mud holes. Then in front of the yard, both the talk and the laughter would die down, and there would be only lowspoken words or silence. Bird and Bell pulling at the hay. The cow gazing moodily into space. The pigeons on the ridgepole in a long feathery group. White Mary bending over a faint glow in the manger. And overhead the star.

In silence the cars would drive away and more come to take their places.

Three of them did not drive away. They swung in closer to the fence and all the people got out and came into the yard. Of all things!

"Mamma, there come the Scotts and the Porters and the Dillinghams." Pa was too excited for words and hardly knew what he was doing.

But mamma was cool and went out to meet them. "Sh! They're just folks too."

The Scotts were lifting the wheeled chair out of the car, which had been custom built for it. Doctor Scott wheeled the little boy up closer so he could see the animals. Carrie's little boys ran to him and with the tactlessness of children showed him how they could turn cartwheels all around his chair.

"Why, Mr. Kurtz," Mrs. Porter was saying, "you're the sly one. Helping us all the time and then copping out the prize yourself."

Pa let it go. They would just have to believe it was all his doings, but for a fleeting moment he saw himself yanking madly at the shed boards.

Mrs. Her-I-don't-like Scott said, "It's the sweetest thing I ever saw. It made me feel like crying when I saw it."

Mrs. Dillingham said it made their decorations all look cheap and shoddy by the side of the manger scene. Even Mr. Dillingham, who had won no prize, said, "Kurtz, you certainly deserve it."

Pa knew he couldn't take any more praise. At least, not with mamma standing right there. So he said, "I guess it was mamma's idea. She's always gettin' ideas."

Right then mamma had another one. "Will you all please to step inside and have a cup of coffee and a doughnut?"

The women demurred, but all the men said they certainly would.

So they crowded into the kitchen, mink coats and all, and stood about with coffee and doughnuts. And Lillie got up her courage and said to Mr. Dillingham, "I don't suppose you know me, but I work for you."

"Oh, yes, sure; sure I do," he said heartily, but Lillie knew he was only being polite.

"And this is a friend of mine," she added with coy bravado, "Mr. Hansen."

Mr. Dillingham said, "How do you do, Mr. Hansen. Don't tell me you work for me too."

"Yes, sir, I do," said Lillie's new beau. "Packing."

And High View and Mill Street both laughed over it.

Mrs. Scott said, "Did you ever taste anything so good as these doughnuts? You couldn't find time to make me a batch once a week, could you?" So that Mrs. Dillingham and Mrs. Porter both said quickly, "Not unless she makes me one too."

And mamma, pleased as Punch, but playing hard to catch, said maybe she could.

Mr. Porter was saying to Ernie, "You folks ought to have some gravel down here on Mill Street."

And Ernie, who wasn't afraid of anyone, not even a councilman, said with infinite sarcasm, "You're telling me?"

The big cars all drove away. Three or four others straggled by. Then no more. And pa turned off the light of the star.

The house was still again except for the adenoidal breathing of one of the little boys. Even Ernie, coming in late, stopped tromping about upstairs. Everyone had to get up early to see Bert and Carrie off and get back to work. It made pa worry over his inability to get to sleep. This had been the most exciting day in years.

Mamma was lying quietly, her heavy body sagging down her side of the bed. It took all pa's self-control to pretend sleep. Twice he heard the old kitchen clock strike another hour. He would try it.

"Mamma," he called softly.

"What?" she said instantly.

"Can't get to sleep."

"Wha's the matter?"

"Keep thinkin' of everything. All that money comin' to us. Company. Attention from so many folks. Children all home. Folks I work for all here and not a bit mad. You'd think I'd feel good. But I don't. Somethin' hangs over me. Like they'd been somebody real out there in the shed all this time; like we'd been leavin' 'em stay out when we ought to had 'em come on in. Fool notion—but keeps botherin' me."

And then mamma gave her answer. Comforting, too, just as he knew it would be. "I got the same feelin'. I guess people's been like that ever since it happened. Their conscience always hurtin' 'em a little because there wa'n't *no room for Him in the inn*."

In time, because of the sticking of the old organ's keys and the threatened collapse of a lung, when even Jed's muscular right arm could no longer coax wind into its asthmatic interior, it was put aside and a modest pipe organ installed.

With no questioning of church authorities and without benefit of appointment, at the first practice for dedication, Jed Miller with greased hair and in a new too-blue suit, arrived to disappear importantly behind a wing of the new organ and begin another decade of pumping.

When the organist took her seat and the Gloria rolled forth, a member of the choir who could see Jed from where she sat said that his face shone with the apparent joy of being an accessory to these melodious notes. Perhaps it did something to Jed. It may be that in his simplicity of thought he gave the woman at the keys very little credit for the music, felt that it was he alone who caused the notes to pour forth on wings of song—for from that time he voluntarily added much of the care of the organ and the entire church to his services.

All this constituted the whole life of the quiet little man—a mere uninteresting existence of one who knew neither deep sorrow nor tumultuous joy, who would never experience either the ice or the fire of living.

If once a week, for a time, he felt real happiness, it was a mere ripple of pleasure by the side of a great tidal wave of excitement that overwhelmed him once a year. This was the high point of Jed's existence. Toward this hour was all else pointed. For this one exultant moment did he live. Christmas Eve at the church!

In those years of the eighties and nineties Santa Claus was a single entity—an individual upon whom one could count specifically in regard to time and place. You heard his bells and he arrived through the side door of the church onto the pulpit, frostladen and breathless. He bade you farewell and disappeared through the same door. You heard his bells die away in the distance and knew he was gone for an interminable year. He did not walk the streets advertising toothpaste or barbecued sandwiches or basket-ball-games-in-the-Coliseum-several-good-seats-left-at-thirty-five-cents.

There was one and only one Santa. In that town he was Old Jed Miller, but of course you did not know that for many years. You went to the church on that night of nights clothed in several layers of flannels, a dress, coat, muffler, knitted hood, mittens and overshoes. Wedged between equally well-equipped adults, you rode with them in the cutter, your short feet not quite reaching the warm soapstone, your mouth and nose filled with snow-laden air and buffalo hairs.

Even as you turned the corner near the church you saw the lights shining through the colored-glass windows out over the snow and in a sickening sensation of fear wondered if you had missed one moment of the rapture. Although practically nothing could have tempted the fat old mare to budge from the spot, you had to wait while she was tethered to the rail between the hitching posts.

When, at last, over crunching snow you went up the steps, your muscles twitching, your mouth dry—almost were you ill in the pit of the stomach. At the doorway you gazed upon Paradise, with a swooning of senses at the sight. Resuscitated after that first shock, they became as acute as a bird dog's.

For the eyes there was a great Norway pine sparkling against the white of the wall, packages on and under it, the shining pipes of the new organ beside it reaching up into heaven. . . . For the ears, the rustling of papers or angels' wings, it was hard to tell which, and the voices of the congregation singing "Joy to the World" . . . For the nose, odors of cinnamon and peppermint, fresh popcorn and cooked molasses, crushed balsam and burning wax.

In due time there followed a program to which you did or did not personally contribute, depending largely on the timely question of whether you were in a state of health or had just passed (or were in due process of acquiring) mumps, measles, chicken-pox, whooping-cough, or the shingles. But whether or not you donated your services, the pieces spoken were practically all known to you, being largely a repetition of those that had been perpetrated the year before and many years before that. There was the perennial Notta-creatcher-wa-stir-ring-not-teven-a-mouse, and one which had been handed down from year to year but which you had never satisfactorily translated, sounding as it did like "Lattuce in they clabbered, lattuce in they say."

The program happily over, you saw Old Jed Miller go behind the pipe organ again, heard the music of an old hymn which all would sing, sensed on the verge of a nervous breakdown that after its seven verses it was finally dying away into silence. And then . . .

A stillness vast and limitless save for a hysterical giggle or two! This was the moment supreme—this the one toward which all the other moments of all the hours of the year were directed—so vital that the illness came again in the pit of your stomach, and your arms and legs twitched in an ecstasy of emotion.

There were bells tinkling faintly and far away, then closer, bringing every tingling hair root to life. Fascinated, you could not take your eyes from the side door, so that when it shook a little, you shook too. He never missed. How could he time himself so definitely to the program's end?

The bells jangled now with mad, breath-taking closeness. The door opened. He bounced in merrily, short and rotund, with a round little—*you know*, the word you ought not say out loud—that shook like a bowlful of jelly. The children roared their welcome—all but you. You hid your face for a moment because of the world-shaking event that was taking place.

He called "Merry Christmas, children!" many times and said that Pikeville was one of the places he liked best of all to come. He told what a hard time he had getting here and how the reindeer were stamping outside, impatient for him to hurry. Then he sauntered over to the tree and said well, well, he guessed he'd better begin to call the names on the packages. Thereupon he handed them out with such intimate comments that it was unbelievable how he could know so much town gossip.

When you went up for yours he said something so personal that you realized anew how uncanny was his knowledge of your everyday life. Sometimes he called the boys by family nicknames which you would scarcely have expected him to know: "Tweet," or "Tubby" or "Babe," so that everyone in the audience laughed.

Yes, he knew every one. "Here's somethin' fer Tommie Graham. Hi, Tommie, what's this I hear tell ag'in' ye—hitchin' on to the back of Schmidt's grocery cart? Hev you been?"

"Y-yes, sir."

"Ye won't no more?"

"No, sir."

The audience roared, and, red-eared, Tommie received his gift.

He knew all, heard all, saw all—this Santa who stopped here en route to other towns.

Sometimes, when the exercises were nearly over, a swaggering older youth whispered across to you: "Ho, ho! You think that's a real Santa Claus, don't you? Well, it ain't. It's Old Jed Miller dressed up thataway."

But questioned, your parents had the retort supreme for you. "Didn't you see Old Jed Miller go behind the organ to pump and never come out?"

It was true. You admitted the fact of seeing old man Miller disappear into the cavernous depths behind the organ, and because you were unaware that a panel in the sturdy oak wall slipped out of place if one knew where to locate its sensitive spot, you admitted readily enough that Santa Claus came in while old man Miller was still behind there. Sometimes they added still another proof: "Wasn't Santa Claus fat? And isn't old man Miller thin as a willow whistle?"

It silenced you, so that you were convinced for another year, and no hulking boy with bragging tongue could shake your faith.

The thing that gave you the most confidence in the fabulous wealth and generosity of the little man in red was the fact that when the gifts had all been handed out, he called the boys and girls to the platform—that is, all those who had not reached their tenth birthday. Unbelievably he gave each one money. Thirty, forty, fifty, even sixty boys and girls—he gave them all a shining quarter. He had done so for years.

He had one ruling. Every child must walk up to the tree by himself. No babies in arms and no holding parents' hands.

There were those who thought that Pikeville babies learned to walk earlier on account of the Santa Claus quarter.

It was traditional. All the presents given out, Santa walked to the edge of the platform and held up his hand for silence. . . . The older people in the audience laughed and nudged one another. "It's his big moment," and, "Just lives for it," you might hear, but not understand.

"Now I want all the boys 'n' girls who kin walk up here by theirselves—'n' is under ten—every one to come up ag'in." He patted the big pockets of his scarlet coat and called out in his commanding voice: "I've got a little somethin' else for each one of you."

The rush to the Klondike then began.

Santa Claus held up his hand for silence. "I've watched all the children of this here town 'n' I sez to myself, sez I, they're pretty good younguns; I guess I'll give every one some money."

There was lusty shouting, so that he held up his hand again. If you were very close you saw how worn and calloused it was, like a hand that worked in gardens, and you wondered why.

"Before I go back to my home——"

("Where you live?" a bold boy perennially asked. "Oh, up ayont Iceland er Greenland—som'ers in *the Artics*.")

"——there's three things I want ye should always remember. Live upright lives. Do some good in the world with this here money I give ye. And always keep the Christmas spirit in yer hearts, and when ye git older, bring all the happiness ye kin to other little children at Christmas time. Do ye promise?"

"Oh, yes, sir."

"All right, then—here goes!"

Shining quarters—one for each child. Again he knew about all the children. "Johnnie Quinn, you got yer last one a year agone. You was ten in July." Oh, my goodness, think of him knowing that!

You clutched your quarter tightly and went back to the pew where your parents sat grinning. "Look, he gave me money."

"Well! Well!"

You clutched it all the way home—this different money that came from Iceland or Greenland or *the Artics*, but was strangely the same kind of silver money your parents possessed on rare occasions. If you dropped it in the snow you bawled to the moon and held up the whole congregation on the steps until it was retrieved.

Santa had told you to do good with your money. Sometimes you gave it the very next Sunday to the Sunday school, so that you might rid yourself of all further responsibility in the ethics of its disposal. Sometimes, after due meditation in which you were torn between moral rectitude and the fleshpots, you sent it to the missionaries via the Ladies' Society with the righteous satisfaction of having converted countless heathens. Sometimes, human nature having been quite the same in the not-always-so-gay nineties, you bought huge white gum hearts and licorice with it, waiting conscience-smitten for bad luck to follow, immeasurably relieved when it failed to appear.

Always the little man ended with that same pronouncement which he gave like the benediction. "Remember! Live upright lives. Do something good with yer money. Always keep the Christmas spirit in yer hearts and try to make other children happy."

Ah, well, you were not always upright. You did not always do good with your money. But, perhaps mellowed a little by that benediction of long ago, you did resurrect the Christmas spirit each year.

Then suddenly you were ten and had passed the traditional quarter-gift age—too soon knew the disillusioning truth. Santa Claus was old man Miller. It was disappointing, but after the shock of the discovery was over, you joined the conspirators. Because you had so loved the great moment, you, too, kept silent and saw the other little children of the town walk up excitedly for their money.

Then after a time, when you were much older, you saw something else: the drama and the pathos that were old man Miller. You saw how all year old Jed Miller lived for this one hour of giving. It seemed foolish, saving from his small wages to give it away in one reckless hour of abandon. Don Quixote mowing lawns! Pikeville called it plain dumb.

And then the old man grew feeble and rather forgetful but still he gave much of his time to the church, although it must have been harder for him. He annoyed some of the people, particularly the Reverend Julius Parkinson who had come from a larger place, for before the services Old Jed would squeak-squeak about the church, fussily passing out hymn-books, getting down on his knees to hunt for a child's lost penny.

The membership was changing. There were more important people in it now—Mrs. Adelbert Tobin, for instance, who was both a pillar and a power. She and the Reverend Parkinson agreed between them that the services would possess more dignity without the preliminary squeakings of Old Jed.

"He's an institution," a few old-timers protested.

"He's a nuisance," Mrs. Tobin retorted.

So a new and younger man was asked to care for the church and surprisingly given a small wage for doing so.

You may tell an old family dog that he is no longer a member of the family but it means practically nothing to him. With this same pleasant scope of vision, Old Jed chose to look upon the newcomer as a mere assistant and went about his faithful, if squeaking, way.

And then, Christmas was coming. Mrs. Tobin was to have charge of the exercises and she explained to Jed that they were dispensing with his services behind the organ and simultaneously with his Santa Claus impersonation.

"I won't have him spoiling my program with his crude ways and illiterate speech," she announced. "The time has come to tell him so in plain words."

There could be no mistaking the plainness of Mrs. Tobin's words. She told Jed they were to have a pageant this year—a beautiful, moving artistic pageant. There would be Joseph and Mary and the Christ Child, shepherds and wise men and angels. Children would represent Hope and Courage, Fear and Selfishness, Truth and Service, Love and Faith.

In fact, every perfection and every frailty attendant upon humans was to be represented in Mrs. Tobin's artistic pageant; everything in short, except a fat Santa Claus in a disreputable old red suit and dirty white whiskers. She told the other ladies that she thought for once Old Jed had got it through his head.

And she was quite right. Old Jed got it through his head. All the life went out of him. He disappeared from church and from his old haunts. When it occurred to some one that he had not been seen around much, Doctor Waters went down to the unpainted house at the end of Maple Street. He found Old Jed in bed, told questioners uptown that he guessed the old man was about done for. He left him medicine, told him to keep quiet and promised to drop in again.

Christmas Eve came with the lights from the church streaming out on the snow and the Norway pine green and sparkling against the white wall.

Every one had to give Mrs. Tobin credit for her pageant. It was more artistic than the old "pieces" spoken in hodge-podge order. There was a nice dignity about the whole program with its aura of spiritual significance, as Mrs. Tobin had so aptly predicted. The wise men and the shepherds, Truth and Service, Hope and Love were letter-perfect. The angels sang their final song and the pageant was over, when bells sounded loudly at the side door. Mrs. Tobin looked startled, and every child drew in an excited breath.

The door opened and into the midst of the artistry and the spiritual significance bounced a little old Santa Claus in a disreputable red suit and dirty white whiskers. Every child let out its breath in one wild shout. Every parent said, "Of all things!" or, "Thought he was sick."

Doctor Waters half rose from his seat and sat down again. Mrs. Tobin gave a very good imitation of a lady smiling when eating a lemon.

"Bet ye thought I might not git here, but here I be." He might have swayed a little.

The dignified pageant turned to a riot, noisy and hilarious. Santa gave out the presents, calling names with gusto and adding personal comments to every excited child who came for them.

" 'N' now I got somepin fer everybody here under ten." He slapped his heavy pockets. "I be'n watchin' the children o' this here town 'n' I sez they's pretty good. So I looks all around my house. . . ."

"Where is it?" called the perennially bold one.

"Oh, I ain't tellin'. Som'ers up ayont Iceland er Greenland—er *the Artics*."

There was a quarter for each one, as there had been for over thirty years. It was just as the silver shower ended that it happened.

A little flame suddenly darted up from a dipping candle on the tree, curled its yellow-red tongue around the branch, leaped to the next one.

Women screamed. Men jumped to their feet. Children stood fascinated with horror, watching the little red tongues crackle toward the upper branches.

And then the little old Santa sprang to it, grasped the flaming thing in both arms, wrenched it from its sand-filled keg, and kicking open the side door, went out with his torchlike burden.

Doctor Walters hurried after the old man; a dozen adults followed.

They brought him in from the snow to the side room of the church. Doctor Walters said it was not the burns: that the old man should never have left his bed. "Must have been mighty hard for him to get dressed and come up here."

There was scarcely a dry eye there in the little room filled with grown people. It was not just that Old Jed was dying. It was the memory of those Christmas Eves when they had been little, so that it seemed Youth and Childish Happiness were going out with him now.

"The's three things." He roused himself, thinking they were children there around him. "Live upright lives. Do good with this here money. Always keep the Christmas spirit . . . 'n' make . . . other children happy. Do ye promise?"

"We promise."

Outside, people were grouped around the door. Children, clutching quarters, pestered their parents with questions. "What happened to Santa? Did he get hurt?"

"No, nothing can happen to Santa."

"Well, who's that in there, then?"

"That's Old Jed Miller."

"Well, what's happened to *him?*"

"He's going away."

"Where?"

"Oh, up—maybe up beyond *the Artics*."

Afterward, recalling how little work he had been able to do that year, every one realized how he must have skimped himself to save for that last Christmas.

Telling it after many years, the whole thing sounds too sentimental for this practical age. Such an outmoded tale about Old Jed Miller giving away his hard-earned money to the children—as old-fashioned as that one about the men who long ago brought Another Child gifts of gold and frankincense and myrrh.

I Remember

☙ THIS is not a story nor a journey into Christmas only, but something of the writer's own background and childhood, a group of memories not necessarily related to each other. I shall recall them as one picks apples out of a basket, this one—and this one—and this—

Many incidents in our childhood we can remember clearly. Some we cannot recall in their entirety. The ending is lost out of memory or the beginning has faded from mind and only a remnant of the happening stands out in clarity. Why has the beginning faded or the ending grown dim? We do not know.

The earliest half-memory that I retain is the picture of a porch at the end of a long grassy path with low bushes on each side. There are flowers by the high steps and vines over a lattice. I seem to have been hunting for the place and am running up the path breathlessly, frightened and tired. My mother comes toward me, and while no words of conversation remain in my mind, the memory of relief and safety, after having been lost, is very strong.

The picture is so plain and yet so disconnected with definite time or place that, during my mother's lifetime, I asked her if she could help me decipher the puzzle, for I had a desire to associate the memory with its actual locality. Once or twice we discussed it as gravely as though it had been of vital importance. Was it at Grandmother Anderson's? No, because the path at Grandmother's curved around the house and this was straight. Was it up at Aunt Kit's? It couldn't have been, because she had an open stretch of grass and this had bushes beside the path. Was it over at Uncle Tom's? No, because he had no porch with high steps and a lattice, only a stoop. Perhaps it was a dream. Decidedly no. Dreams are shadows beside this clear picture. And so it remains—a little half memory, with no beginning and no end.

I was born to middle-aged parents at the tag end of their big family. Because they had seven grown and nearly grown children—the three oldest in their twenties when I arrived in their midst—I probably held the world's record for the number of bosses over me. Certain rare advantages attend such an administration. With impunity one can always tell some inquisitive adult member of the family that certain other adult members have given their permission to do thus and so. It usually stops all further annoying questions and is a method which was frequently employed by me. So I lived my childhood among a host of older people, playing, reading, fancifying, singularly free from responsibility.

Our home in Cedar Falls, Iowa, was plain and comfortable. It had started out to be a white-painted, green-shuttered type of eastern wing-and-ell house, but in my time additional bedrooms had been built onto it and atop it, so that its design was no longer catalogued in any architectural book, its painting a practical gray and the bedrooms numbering seven.

It had tall glowing coal stoves and many glass lamps, china wash bowls and pitchers, center tables and high bureaus, and an organ, until that most wonderful of birthdays when draymen backed up and unloaded a piano, leaving me stunned with surprise.

The walnut furniture was sturdy and unmatched. But through the cushioned depths of its big worn chairs I have sunk into the apple orchard of the March sisters in *Little Women* and into Caddam Wood with Babbie and the Little Minister, so far away that it seemed nothing could call me back. Once my mother took away a half-read book, one of the few things she ever did which seem not sensible, for I mentally constructed the rest of the story with far more disastrous results by the change of authors.

On the floor of our home were flowered carpets which had to be taken up twice a year, laid out on the grass and beaten into limp subjection, then put down again over a layer of papers and fresh oat straw. Part of the family crawled along one side of the room and pulled and tacked, while others smoothed down the straw so the results would not be hilly in spots.

Out in the carriage shed there were a high-topped buggy and a cutter, and in the barn a fat lazy mare named Nancy, which my father thought too rambunctious for the womenfolks to drive.

The front yard and narrow side ones belonged to my green-fingered mother. In them she could revel in flowers to her heart's content. During the long summers, columbine, roses, peonies, bleeding hearts, snowballs, flowering almond crowded each other in jealous profusion, while the porch was smothered in her specialty: fuchsias. Neighbors brought sickly fuchsias to her, as one takes an ailing animal to the veterinarian. She kept the plant a few weeks, returning it to the owner in a state of convalescence, her diagnosis: "It just needed a little loving."

But the back yard was my father's domain. No town lot ever knew more intensive farming. If he were alive today and could look out of my study window to a back yard of grassy lawn, flowers, lilac hedge and juniper, none of which is edible, he would join the pessimists who think the country is going to the dogs. For in his back yard every inch of space was utilized by eatables which served the family from the first lettuce leaf until the last turnip was dug. Incidentally, no modern child with his out-of-season vegetables can know the pleasure of nibbling those first baby lettuce leaves in the spring, like a starved rabbit, or wryly tackling an acrid pieplant stalk, after a winter of fats and proteins.

It seems unbelievable that so much could be contained neatly in one backyard: the garden, a barn, a carriage house, chickens and their yard, a shed for wood (cut to its even stove lengths), a coal shed, sidewalks, a cherry tree, a little plum thicket, gooseberry and currant bushes, a grape arbor and hammock, with long rows of white and purple grapevines following the two high board fences. There was even a playhouse which my father had built for me. It had a real window which went up and down, providing the weather was not too dry for it to stay up, or too damp for it to go up at all. Its *pièce de résistance* was a discarded sewing machine upon which one could pedal furiously, pretending long journeys over land and sea and air, as though some god of Mechanics were whispering of such trips to come in the adult future.

It was my world. The woodshed was a medieval castle on whose steep-pitched roof one could cling precariously while looking over far-flung possessions. On occasion, whole paper doll families lived in the currant bushes. The plum thicket and dark spaces under the grapevines were grottoes to be explored. The paths between the vegetables were streets inhabited on both sides by temperamental ladies whose gowns were beet red or onion green; and when one of my big sisters returned from a trip to New York, the widest lane suddenly became Fifth Avenue. A wish today for my little granddaughter would not be for more outside entertainment or material gifts from family and friends, but imagination and a stout and merry heart.

There were a great many relatives constantly coming and going, in and from our home: big brothers and their wives, big sisters and their husbands, uncles, aunts, cousins, second cousins, cousins by marriage, and those always welcome, if vaguely known, people designated by our parents as "early settlers we used to know." Constantly another plate was to be put on the table, an extra can of fruit brought from the cellar, more potatoes pared.

There was usually a good Danish girl to help, too, for a whole colony of Danes had come to town, fine people whose thrifty boys were to become merchants and bankers, and whose young girls were not then averse to working in kitchens. Our Hannah and our Lizetta stayed with us until their respective marriages. Once we had a Danish dentist, a smartly professional young woman, who wanted to "work out" while she learned good English, with everyone in the family joking about her choice of households, where the conversation was a bit careless, if sprightly.

Our parents had come into Iowa as pioneer settlers before their marriage, Mother at eighteen with her family, Father two years earlier with his own people, a cavalcade of wagons traveling out from Illinois, crossing the Mississippi on the ferry when there was not a railroad west of the river.

Mother drove one of her family's teams all the way out, and she used to tell about her wagon tipping over as she went up the steep bank of a creek bed, and how the eight precious sacks of flour tumbled into the water, and the goose feather pillows started floating down stream as though the geese had come alive, with all the young sisters hurrying along the bank after them and laughing so hard they could scarcely run.

Mother taught school for a time in a log building. Then she and Father were married on a New Year's Day in a log cabin from which the furniture had been moved to make room for the guests, a feasible procedure because the day was as balmy as spring. When the time for the ceremony arrived, Mother came down a ladder from the loft, but as though to offset his discrepancy, even if somewhat incongruous for her surroundings, she had a rather elaborate trousseau: a white wedding dress, a pink flowered silk, a gray silk plaid, and a long fringed white silk shawl and matching bonnet, purchased with her school money in Chicago and hauled out from Dubuque by team. That merchandise wagon, driven by my father, also brought her an iron-weight Seth Thomas clock and a high black walnut cupboard. The clock stands today in a niche expressly built for it in my own hall; and the cupboard is in my daughter's dining room, looking, for all its ninety-four years, a bit smug over the satiny hand polishing it recently received, and no doubt trying to forget that its dark doors were once my blackboard upon which many a "cat hat mat" have been chalk scribbled.

Father and Mother lived for years across the road from my Grandfather Streeter's farm. He died before I was born, but his personality had lived on, and I heard much about him on all sides. He was "the honorable Zimri Streeter," a member of the first Iowa legislature after the capitol was moved from Iowa City to the new Des Moines. He was known as "Old Blackhawk," representing as he did the county of that name, and also, because of his Yankee wit, "the Wag of the House." He had come into the young state in 1852, no boy pioneering in the virility of youth, but in his fifties, and with a big family: his little wiry wife, three sons—of whom my father was one—and seven daughters. They were a sturdy long-lived people. One of those daughters, when she was ninety-two, was telling about the death of a sister. "Her doctor wasn't any good," she confided. "She might have lived years yet. Why, she was only eighty-six."

Because of the June freshets, the marshy land, and the crossing of the swollen Wapsipinicon, it took the wagons three weeks to travel that last hundred miles from Dubuque on the Mississippi to a point between the two clusters of cabins on the Cedar River which became the cities of Cedar Falls and Waterloo. There had not been a house on the way excepting the log tavern at Independence.

On dollar-and-a-quarter-per-acre government land, they built their first cabin, and when the report came that the Indians were on the warpath all the settlers came hurrying to it because the cabin was the largest, and because my grandfather had the leadership which some men naturally possess. Old Zimri would tell them what to do.

The scare went into nothing, as most of those early Iowa scares did. A few were tragic, as the one near Lake Okoboji when all the white settlers were killed but the little Gardner girl, who saw her father shot, her mother and the other children clubbed to death, and whose daughter in time became my schoolmate.

Old Zimri was full of his jokes, and those seven daughters were as lively as jumping beans. I knew them only as middle-aged or old ladies, but because of their sprightliness then, can well believe how they overflowed the cabin with their merriment. They made their own clothes and their own fun, laughing their heads off at everything, with special hilarity for the tricks perpetrated on the young men courageous enough to come courting. So when, as a young girl, I read my first midwestern pioneer novel, I knew the author was not altogether right for picturing pioneer women as drab creatures forever standing forlornly at the doors of soddies or log cabins and quietly going mad. If my father's seven lively sisters had ever gone mad, at least it would not have been quietly.

Soon they began marrying the more hardy of the candidates who had borne up under the teasing. Mary took "the Justice"; Cornelia, the new doctor; Lavina, Lucinda and Julia, promising farmers. Lucy and Sarah married brothers. If you married one of the seven Streeter girls, you acquired a combustible sort of creature and an excellent cook. It would be noisy and argumentative in your home, but never monotonous. My father was their quiet brother. He had a mild drollery about him but was not very talkative. Those garrulous girls must have taken it out of him.

Both Grandfather's and Grandmother's roots reached deep into the New England of pre-Revolutionary days: back to Dr. John Streeter and a Stephan Streeter who married Ursula Adams, to Captain Remember Baker, one of the Green Mountain boys and a cousin of Ethan Allen, who was shot by an Indian, his head cut off, and buried by a British officer (a particularly gory and hair-raising episode to my childish ears).

Grandfather was one of the Iowa signers for the new Republican party when it split from the Whigs, and he may have been the first of the reactionaries, for there is an old letter from him, while the legislature was in session, in which he tells the family that he "probably did more setting on unwise measures than anyone in the House."

To say that he was politically minded is to put it far too mildly, for the story went that he would drop everything at the slightest provocation and go to town, there to argue over politics in the stores, on the street corners, or from the back of his disillusioned horse. Grandmother was serious and energetic, a worried little soul who wore a black lace cap in her older years. She had her own opinion of all this constant political harangue, and as he left for town was apt to call out to her liege lord: "Don't even *speak* to a Democrat today or you'll never get home."

Finally the Dubuque and Sioux City Railroad, later becoming the Illinois Central, came creeping across Grandfather's farm like a giant mole run, and the first train crossed his fields on April Fool's Day, 1861. But there the roadbed stopped, not to go on for four years. For a war was on.

Every life has it big moments, and Grandfather's came during the second Lincoln campaign. Governor Kirkwood appointed him to go down into Georgia, contact General Logan's Fifteenth Army Corps, and bring back the soldiers' votes. No, there wasn't any V-mail in 1864. He left with his flowered knapsack and arrived in Atlanta just as it fell. All communications to the North were cut and he was bottled up with the army and had to march with Sherman to the sea. Sixty-five years old then, he had to endure all the hardships of the march, subsisting at times on corn from the fields. But his only complaint when he got back was that he had lost his hat.

He idolized Lincoln, and on the day the news of the assassination came, in his grieving he went out alone into the timber and cut the initials A L in a tree, where they remained a half-century, the rough bark growing in and filling the scars long before those other scars made by the fighting were healed.

Although he lived a long time after his great adventure, life must have been anticlimactic. Once he said to my mother: "Ever stop to think you can't do away with anything? Chop that maple down, burn the wood, and Ma'll up and leach the ashes for lye. Scatter the leaves and they'll make mulching. Seeds that have shook off will come up. No, sir, if you can't kill that old maple, you can't kill me. I'll be in something around here, even if it's the prairie grass or the wind in the timber."

He is in "something around here." A book. My *Song of Years*. And now the land he preempted a century ago is incorporated into a seventeen-hundred-acre airport. Planes drop down from the sky where only the wild geese flew, and land on runways built over the spot where his oxen and horses completed their five weeks journey out from Illinois.

It was several years before my birth that our parents had moved from the farm into that wing-and-ell house in Cedar Falls, one of Iowa's prettiest towns, set in the woods by the Cedar River.

A wandering Frenchman, one Gervais Paul Somaneaux, had found the lovely spot and built a cabin, then gone his light-footed way. A trapper lived around the stream for a time, but for eight years after his leaving no one trod its banks but red men. Then came two white settlers from Michigan and each built a cabin, to be followed by a group of brothers who bought their claims and water power. They built a sawmill and a gristmill, started a ferry and platted a village. In this manner were the Midwestern towns, planted on the prairie grass or carved out of the forests.

Although our town was a half century old in my childhood, there were still a few blocks of native verdure into which little girls ventured for only a few yards and scuttled back to the safety of fences. But it had a homey, substantial appearance and an educational atmosphere. Public schools were among the best in the state. There was an expanding normal school which soon became a full-fledged college. There were churches galore. Lodges and clubs were in full swing. Hundreds of substantial homes, some with many bay windows and gingerbread trimming, iron fences and hitching posts, clustered along the maple-lined streets. There were local band concerts and important lectures by famous names, and the big event of college Commencement, which lasted three days and to which whole families took lunch baskets and ate on the green sloping campus. My first taste of Shakespeare was the Commencement plays given in a huge tent, and no Evans or Barrymore or Olivier has thrilled me more than some lanky college boy—attired in the velvet jacket of a professor's wife—under a slightly wilted Forest of Arden, giving forth in Midwestern twang: "*If there be truth in sight, you are my Rosalind.*"

There was bobsledding down Odell's Hill, and there was the annual pilgrimage for wild plums, red haws and thorn apples, although one such journey culminated in painful lectures for a small playmate and me because we came home laden with fruits and flowers which looked strangely domesticated to parental eyes. As my fellow criminal became an English professor in a state university, she must have shed any bad effects of her one juvenile delinquency.

In our town there was camaraderie among all the children. Danish Lutheran, German Evangelical, Irish Catholic, two Jewesses—they were all friends. The word "class" meant only what grade you were in at school. "Our Town!" A nice place in which to have spent one's childhood.

At least once each summer my parents took me on a long and exciting trip. As the great day approached, I lived in such a daze of anticipation that I was like the old woman in the nursery rhyme: "Lauk a-mercy on me, this can't be I." For we were going up to Mount Vernon township to see my mother's people, and it was *nine miles away*. And what length of time do you think the trip would take us, jogging along behind old Nancy? Just half as long as it recently took a jet-propelled fighter plane to cross the continent. Lauk a-mercy on me, this *can't* be I.

With all those adults in the family, I was prepared for the journey by an assembly plant, belt line system: scrubbed by one big sister, combed by another, and buttoned by a third.

This sisterly triad saw us off in the high-topped buggy: my bewhiskered father, my gentle mother and excitable me. I had to sit on a stool between the two and so close to Nancy's hind quarters that every little while she would slap her coarse old tail across my face with all the effect of a hundred sharp fiddlestrings.

As we drove down the shady street, the town suddenly took on a different aspect than it held on ordinary days. By some legerdemain we had become sightseers, looking upon familiar scenes with the eyes of tourists. With the buggy whip Father would point out local historical spots as though I had never seen them before. "Soldiers getting ready to fight long ago, drilled there in the park with brooms and sticks over their shoulders." Or, "In the early days there used to be tree stumps right here in the middle of Main Street. Anybody got drunk, the town council would set them to grubbing out the stumps. Folks said lots of mornings you could hear the axes going."

Above Nancy's clumping across the river bridge, he might call out: "See down there? About there's where we used to ford the river when we first came to Ioway. Remember, Mother?" And in fatherly explanation to me: "Wasn't even any bridge across the Mississippi in 1852, let alone one here on the Cedar." Small wonder that his youthful passenger grew up to write Midwestern pioneer stories, when they were served practically with her food and drink.

Over "the dump" we went and out on the country road, narrow and grass-grown then, wide and paved now. At a certain point there were two ways to go, over the open road or the one at the edge of the woods. The treat was mine to choose, but instead of a treat, it became a torment, so fearful was I of missing something on the discarded one. I have since made the choice between going to New York or Hollywood with far less mental disturbance.

When the decision could be put off no longer: "Well . . . then . . . I guess . . . the woodsy way."

And soon there would be the woods road where the huge trees were so close together the sun scarcely penetrated, and the great shadows beyond concealed *no telling what*.

The ground was eternally damp with soggy leaves and uncountable timber flowers. There would be violets, Dutchmen's breeches, waxen Mayflowers, or the loveliest of them all, the bluebells. And at the side of the road itself, queer orange-colored lilies, wild sweet Williams, ox-eye daisies and thousands of shaggy, dusty-pink bouncing Bets. There were red-winged blackbirds, bobolinks, yellow-throated warblers, an occasional killdeer. Woodpeckers kept up their insistent knocking on tree doors which never opened to them. Brown thrashers whirled up from the grass. Meadow larks sang their hearts out on rail fences. Oh, many things one never sees from a speeding auto or cloud-topping plane.

Sometimes we happy three became so engrossed in the sights that Nancy would stop and snatch at the lush growth, and Father would let her nibble for a few moments as though she, too, must share in the pleasure of the day.

Finally we were turning into the farmyard where the big white house stood among the tall butternut trees. I remember it filled me with awe to think there had been another one just like it which burned down a few nights before the family was to move into it. I would close my eyes to picture the leaping flames and the black smoke, then open them hastily to the relief of seeing the sturdy house intact.

Butternuts dropped their dark green bombshells onto the dust of the driveway. Brown beehives followed the line of the picket fence toward the side door. The slanting cellar doors, covered with sunning milk crocks, were immaculate from sand scrubbing.

Father took old Nancy to the stable to be unhitched. When one made a call in the eighties and nineties, it lasted all day and included two full meals with a snack between. Uncle Jim, my mother's oldest brother, came up from the barn. He was short and heavy, with a broad, kind face and stubby beard. Aunt Sarah, whom he had married when he was an old bachelor of forty, came out, too. She was small and spry and wore her crow-black hair parted in stiff precision, combed down tightly over her ears like my china dolls.

Mother's easygoing relatives thought Aunt Sarah carried her neatness too far. She kept rag rugs over the carpets to protect them, and newspapers over the rag rugs to protect *them*. She welcomed us hospitably, but before we went in sent a sharp glance toward my stubby shoes to see if they passed the acid test.

They tell us that memory is more related to the sense of smell than to any of the others. It must be true, for although the exact appearance of the kitchen remains one of those half memories, I can still smell it—that combination of homemade soap, freshly baked bread, cinnamon rolls and the damp milky odor of the adjoining buttery.

And now Aunt Sarah was saying: "Go right on in. She's there in her room."

We went into the sunny east room. *And there she was.*

My Grandmother Anderson sat in a big chair with a hickory staff at her side and her full skirts forming a gray calico pool around her. She was in her eighties, short and dumpy, shaped like the pictures of Queen Victoria. She wore a white netting cap with wide strings tied under her fat chin, and unlike Grandmother Streeter's wrinkled and worried countenance beneath its black cap, her face was placid and seemingly without lines. She had no teeth and her soft lips puckered into a little pink circle.

The first of the interview was always embarrassing to me and I seem to have required a bit of maternal pushing. She would then put her hands on top of my head, run stubby fingers into my hair, slip them down my face. "My . . . my!" she would say. "Hoo muckle hae ye grown." For my grandmother was Scotch and she was blind.

Because Mother always deferred to my grandmother's opinion, taught me by inference that she was someone practically perfect, she seemed the personification of Wisdom. She could tell about happenings in Scotland three-quarters of a century before. She could repeat whole psalms which she had memorized before the darkness overtook her. She knew who married whom in the Bible and their "begats." But more important to my expanding emotional side, she was Romance. I had heard the story many times.

As the young girl, Margaret, she had lived with her parents in their humble cottage on the Scottish moors. When she was sixteen a young man rode up one day and asked for water for his horse. He was from the gentry and had become separated from the rest of the hunting party. The two talked for a time and when he left, it was with the promise that he would come back to see her. This he did, many times, with the neighbors wagging their heads and saying no good would come of it. But young

Basil loved the pretty Margaret, married her and took her to live with his mother in the large ancestral home. Grandmother would tell complacently that the first Sunday they went to church she refused to leave her parents to sit with the pew-paying gentry, so Basil went up to the loft with her.

Apparently Basil's mother was not too pleased with the little peasant daughter-in-law, but took her dutifully in hand to make a lady of her, dressing her differently and teaching her the duties of her new station in life. But when the girl grew too homesick, she would discard her finery and with her shawl over her head slip out to the stable for a saddle horse and ride across the moors to see her people.

In time Basil's mother died and Grandmother was sole mistress of the big house. Uncle Jim, Aunt Jane, Aunt Margaret and Aunt Isabelle were all born there. Aunt Jane especially remembered it well, for she was a girl of ten when they left it.

Basil took a trip to America to see what the new country was like, was gone for months, and there was a report that the vessel had been lost at sea. Previously he had signed notes for a friend, and when the creditors heard the ship was lost, they closed in on the estate to confiscate it. *Roup* signs were posted that the house and contents were to be sold. Because the horses could not be removed from the stable under the *roup* sign, Grandmother with two of the children walked over the moors to get her parents to come and bid on some of her personal belongings.

But the boat had not gone down. Grandfather arrived back in Liverpool, heard about his losses, and sent for the family to meet him there. They came, laden with as many possessions as had been saved from the sale, Grandmother carrying a basket containing her lovely Chelseaware china.

The journey to America was wild and perilous in the little sailing vessel, which was six weeks on the way. They went up the St. Lawrence, and at Quebec, two weeks later, my mother was born.

When they moved to the farming lands of Illinois, Grandmother's peasant blood asserted itself. Assisted by her oldest son, the dependable Uncle Jim, she became the real manager of the family, while Grandfather, fitted for no work, remained the white-shirted gentleman to the end, and died there. It was then that the family came on into Iowa by team and wagons, camping by the trail for the many weeks which the two-hundred-mile trip took.

All this story with its endless details fascinated me, and my grandmother became many things to my childish mind. She was Wisdom. She was Romance. She was Adventure. And through her, too, came a dawning realization of change. Before that mental expanding, life to me had been only today or at most the faraway time of next week or month. Now I sensed a longer period of slipping time, a remote past and a distant future. Grandmother had been slim and sparkling, pretty and sixteen. Here she sat, fat and toothless, blind and eighty-four. It was almost impossible to reconcile the two pictures. So came my first conception of life moving continuously on and with the moving, great changes taking place. It was very sad. At least it would have been, excepting for the fact that these summer reunions held no time for sadness.

Other relatives would arrive: Aunt Jane, Aunt Kit, Aunt Margaret and their husbands, Uncle Rob and his wife, a miscellaneous assortment of cousins. There was a loaded table out under the butternut trees, with several chickens pecking about sociably near it in callous disregard of their fried friends on platters. Some of the cousins wielded long paper brushes over the table to frighten away the flies, a proceeding which seemed merely to annoy them slightly for they returned merrily to the feast.

Uncle Jim helped Grandmother out to the table and she came stepping along hesitantly, her staff tapping the ground. She lived on soft foods and while we were gorging on the chicken and sweet corn, she ate an egg upstanding in its wooden cup. I can even remember the way she tapped neatly around the top of the shell to remove it.

After dinner there was visiting under the trees and Uncle Rob tipped his chair against a tree, and in a clear voice sang "Mary of The Wild Moor" and "Bonnie Charlie's Now Awa'." Mother's family could sit and visit pleasantly over inconsequentials longer than any group I have ever known. There was something about them which was very close knit. They were gentle and affectionate with each other, a bit too emotional maybe, and quite in contrast to my father's energetic, bantering people who were opinionated and spunky, covering their deepest emotions with flippant talk and joking feebly on their deathbeds.

But I know now that which no child understands at the time: *that there is something eminently satisfying and stabilizing in childhood to be surrounded by many relatives whose roots lie deep in a single community.* And should I not know? For I had sixteen sets of uncles and aunts who settled in and replenished that section of Iowa.

We had to leave early on account of the long trip home. It seems incredible that nine miles was ever thought such a journey. Grandmother took her hickory staff and followed us down the length of the picket fence, waving in our direction, as though she could see us drive away.

Back to our home on Franklin Street was back to another world far removed from the farm in Mount Vernon township, and brought with it a feeling of nothing to live for now that the big day was over, a depression of spirit, happily never lasting beyond the first "yoo hoo" from one of the neighborhood playmates.

And then, on a hot August day, we journeyed back to Grandmother's house. Whether or not we drove by the woods or over the prairie road seemed immaterial on account of the strange thing they had told me. And although we chose the woodsy way again, everything was diflerent. The bouncing Bets were wilted and pale. There was a noticeable lack of bird songs. Only the timber phoebe was calling plaintively, and the mourning dove.

At the farm the bees were buzzing, the crocks sunning on the cellar door, and the chickens pecking about unconcernedly. But a solemn hush was in the air and even the sunlight looked wan and queer. Horses and buggies were at the hitching posts and all the way down the fence. I had never seen a big black box like that before. It was out under the butternut trees in the very same place where she had sat so recently. Change again! *Things always change.*

The minister talked, and while I did not then comprehend his words I read them many years later in an old scrap book, and he had said: "Her life was filled with labors, *but was uneventful.*" Uneventful? To go from a peasant home to an aristocratic one, only to lose it later and go back to the soil for a living? To take the perilous six weeks voyage across the sea and to pioneer in the new Midwest? To make the trek by team to a still newer state, through prairie grass and creek bed and timberland? Something of that "uneventful life" is in *A Lantern In Her Hand.*

On that August afternoon the country choir sang, but not "Mary Of The Wild Moor" nor "Bonnie Charlie's Now Awa'," which I thought a grave error as they were her favorite songs.

We rode in a plodding line up the hill to the burying ground which Aunt Kit's husband had once given to the country community from his farm lands. Often we had to stop, and Nancy would try to snatch a morsel of greens, but Father jerked her up chidingly, as though today she must not do so pleasant a thing.

I remember the dusty grass and the 'hoppers getting up under my dress and leaving their tobacco stains on its whiteness, and the headstone of an aunt near by which said ISABELLE BELOVED WIFE. But most of all I remember my mother's tears, for she was not a crying woman. Standing by her side, my hand in hers, I had a sudden realization that the dead woman meant as much to my mother as my mother meant to me; that my mother's distress was as deep as mine would have been had she been lost to me. For the first time I knew what it was to feel more sorry for someone else than for myself. For the first time *I knew sympathy*.

We went back to the farm for a late afternoon meal under the trees. There was a feeling of relief in the air, with the usual good food and the relatives all visiting quietly together in their amiable way. Why, everything was going on as though nothing had happened! In childish self-questioning I could not understand it; with no philosophy to aid me, could not then accept the fact that life always closes over the vacancy and goes on.

They are memories of a vanished clan and an outmoded era, but for a time my grandmother was the center of both. As I write of them in my study, I can see in a corner cupboard beyond the fireplace, an ivory-colored cup and saucer with lavender blue flowers, the only one left from the Chelseaware set she carried so carefully on the journey from Scotland one hundred and thirteen years ago.

There are countless other memories of childhood:

Sunday school, with the circle of red painted chairs, and my singing lustily "Jesus Loves Even Me," but thinking for a long time it was Eve and me, that Adam's copartner and I were of special distinction.

The Easter egg hunt in my Sunday school teacher's home when I broke the blue vase and cried frightened tears, only to have her put an arm around me and say that no vase was worth a little girl's grief, for which I gave her a lifetime of admiration.

The day one of the numerous long-distance cousins came and her eagle eye lighting on me effacing myself under the table, dragging me forth with a sprightly "So this is the little cousin I've never seen" and sat down, pressing me close to her ample bosom and apparently forgetting me. To this day I can feel her smothering arms, see her plump hands clasped in front of my supine person and hear her voice going on above me while she married off or buried all the relatives. The misery in my eyes must have been lost on a mother and three big sisters, for they only assisted in the marrying and burying. That I didn't have the gumption to get myself out of the human trap is symbolic of the difference in the generations, for no modern child would stand it. My legs went to sleep and my brain atrophied. I used to think I sat there a month, but know now it couldn't have been more than a week.

Then there was public school, and the first visiting day for parents, with my mother coming and looking so nice in her dark black silk wrap and bonnet. But oh, the embarrassment of it! And I must never let her know how terrible she made me feel *because she came in the wrong door.*

And there was the matter of the paste. The teacher told us we were going to make scrap books, the very thought of it giving an added zest for living. Two girls were assigned to make flour paste at home and bring it for the whole room to use. I told my assembled family about the coming event, and one of the big sisters, sensing and sharing my happiness, said she would make me a jar of paste, too. When I bore it proudly to the teacher, as one contributing her share to society's welfare, she said shortly: "Well . . . who told *you* to bring paste?" Crestfallen, I took it to my desk, but Fate worked hand in hand with Retribution, for the two girls forgot theirs, and the teacher had to come down to my desk and ask for mine. A psychoanalyst would say it made its definite imprint, for more that once in adult life, when about to proffer some unasked favor, I have hesitated momentarily, wondering whether or not the "paste" would be well-received.

And in a higher grade there was the first experience in debating. The procedure was explained, including the new words "affirmative" and "negative." The question to be debated was: Resolved, that winter is better than summer. I was affirmative. And what's more, the *leader* of the affirmative. Came the great day and I went to the front of the room. "Ladies and gentlemen," I began, at which there was a faint titter proving that my appellation had been chosen unwisely. But I was firm with them. "Ladies and gentlemen," I repeated. "You can always get yourself warm on a cold winter day, but you *can't never* get yourself cool on a hot summer day." Maybe my earnest glibness caused the outburst, or maybe it was their pent-up emotion, but everyone broke into laughter. And the teacher said: "Sit down. This wasn't meant to be funny. If you can't think of good reasons, don't give any." I sat down. Funny? I had no more intention of being funny than Douglas did when he debated with Lincoln. Through all the years—at least until air conditioning became known—I have never changed my mind that you could always get yourself warm on a cold winter day but could never get yourself cool on a hot summer day.

The climax to childhood's long year was Christmas. In the summer it seemed too remote to visualize plainly or to feel its spirit deeply. It was a word, not an emotion. In the fall it began to take upon itself form and subtsance, like a light seen afar off. After Thanksgiving it was a steady glow toward which you walked with unwavering faith. A little later real preparations began: Packages were smuggled into the house. Absent members of the family came home. The table grew longer. The seven bedrooms filled up. Pies were made—cakes baked—cookies—candles—oysters—a tree—chickens—dressing—odors—mysteries— The radiance enveloped that child who was I like a mantle.

On Christmas Eve there was always an oyster supper, with dishes of crackers at strategic spots down the length of the table and bouquets of celery standing upright in their glass containers. After supper there was the trip to the church where the tree reached the rafters and you shared its brilliance with friends and neighbors. But even that was a mere forerunner of the excitement awaiting at home.

Everyone, from Father down, hung up his stocking. (Mine was no bobby-sox affair, but a long home-knitted one, as thick as a board and practically as stiff.) The scurrying about with the packages, long-hoarded, took until bedtime. Then the interval in which sleep would not come, and when it did arrive seemed surprisingly to have lasted only a few minutes before you were aroused by the shouting of the first "Merry Christmas" and realized that this was IT.

Dressing in the semidark with teeth chattering from excitement as much as from cold. Going downstairs to find a big breakfast of pancakes and sausages which you could scarcely eat because this was The Day. The table finally cleared of its cloth and everyone standing around its old walnut length. The waiting for some late comer, gone to bring the clothes baskets in which to throw the papers. Someone else saying to save the string. There was good stout cord on all those packages.

"All here, now?" No, someone was assembling the scissors.

"All ready now?"

"Yes . . . *now*." And life stood still, for its moment supreme had arrived.

With everyone watching, you went to your stocking under the old clock mantel and returned to the table with it. You were deliciously embarrassed with all those eyes upon you. On all sides people were making remarks which caused laughter. In all probability they did not remotely approach wit, but laughter comes easily to a child and you were happy. There was so much fun going on that in a sudden sweep of emotion you felt sorry for the people all over town, all over the country, who could not live there in that rambling old house set high in its snowy yard.

That house has long been torn down and no one remembers what became of the old table. But younger families assemble around other tables, and sparks of the Christmas spirit from the old house rekindle the fires each year in homes from Long Island to Los Angeles.

There are countless other small childhood memories:

The constant runaways. To hear that thud . . . thud . . . thud . . . coming nearer, with sound of splintering wood, and your heart pounding as loudly as the horse's hoofs while you ran up on a porch, "anybody's porch," as your parents had cautioned you to do.

Riding in a milk wagon one day with a 'teenage brother while he stopped in front of houses and clanged his bell and the women came out with bowls into which he turned the milk from a quart measure, while germs— of which you had never heard—no doubt perched about on the bowls' brims.

Picnics at Rounds Bluffs, built up now with surburban homes, but deep timber then on a high bluff, below which ran the river, down to which the little boys always ran pell-mell immediately upon arriving, panting back again up the long steep incline. The eternal male forever showing off his prowess before the female of the species.

Many memories! Some clear and in their entirety. Others only half remembered, with the beginning lost or the ending forgotten. Someday, surprisingly, we may be able to remember. For shall I not—on a day —go up a grassy path, afraid and tired, having been lost for a time? May not my mother come toward me, so that I experience a deep feeling of relief and safety? And quite suddenly I shall know the end of the story.

The name of Bess Streeter Aldrich has come to stand for two qualities among members of the American reading public. The first is the ability to tell a good story — a story full of the movement, the ever-present interplay of character and event, of life itself. The second is a particular realization of the courage and achievements of the men and women who settled the American Midwest. Mrs. Aldrich's work reflects a thorough understanding of the heartbreaks and hardships which these early settlers had to undergo, but it conveys equally well the robust and romantic view of life which frequently illuminated their existence and transcended its harsh material conditions.

With these qualities, Mrs. Aldrich's books have become among the most popular of the twentieth century, giving pleasure to literally millions of readers. This colorf TREASURY contains two of her finest and most successful novels. Of the novels, A LANTERN IN HER HAND — perhaps her greatest book — tells a story of the settle-